RADLEY'S APOCALYPSE FOR HORNY MONSTERS

HORNY MONSTERS
BOOK FIVE

ANNABELLE HAWTHORNE

WET LEAF PRESS

ISBN: 978-1-949654-34-9 (ebook)

ISBN: 978-1-949654-35-6 (paperback)

ISBN: 978-1-949654-36-3 (hardcover)

Written by Annabelle Hawthorne

Published by Wet Leaf Press

www.wetleafpress.com

Cover Design by R. F. Kenney

Interior Design by Wet Leaf Press

*This book is for those who have survived
the end of the world
and somehow got back up again*

CONTENTS

SPRINGTIME

Mike Radley yawned, then stretched his arms, causing his left shoulder to pop egregiously. Opening his eyes, he realized he had drifted off to sleep. It had been a long night chasing a swarm of scarab beetles out of his house, and he had apparently drifted off sometime after breakfast.

The scarabs themselves were the result of an empty tomb that had been discovered on the other side of his otherwise empty basement. Since it was originally thought to be a crack in the foundation, everyone had been surprised to find that the fissure in the otherwise smooth concrete led somewhere else. Once Tink the goblin had declared the wall to be non-load-bearing, Abella had been brought in to knock it down with a single punch. The gargoyle had been happy to help, but not so much when a colony of scarabs fled the room and crawled across her stony flesh. Despite being impervious to their clicking jaws, Abella had squealed and nearly taken everyone out with her wings in her hurry to brush them off.

"How long was I out?" he asked. His head was currently in the lap of the home's resident banshee, Cecilia. Her pupils were white like pearls, and though she was blind to the visible spectrum as he understood it, she was capable of seeing souls and spiritual energy. Able to see the souls of the scarabs, she had been a huge asset tracking them down. Each time the colony attempted to set up a new nest, Tink would punch a hole in the wall with a hammer while everyone pitched in to catch them in some cloth sacks that Tink had once used to make her clothes out of.

1

"Perhaps an hour." Cecilia's voice had a soft Irish lilt to it, and her white hair floated about her as if she was suspended underwater. Like her eyes, her hair was a startling white color, save for a thick lock of red just over her right eye. "You needed it."

"I suppose." He sat up and groaned, his back tensing up. He had only meant to sit for a few minutes, and his body protested being prone on the bench for so long. He yawned again, then gave the banshee a peck on the lips. A chill ran through his body. "I didn't miss it, did I?"

Cecilia smiled. "You wouldn't hear the end of it if you did. There's plenty of time. Sofia is getting lunch ready if you want to help."

"I'll see what I can do." When he stood from the swing, she floated up to join him. Caressing his cheeks with her hands, she winked and then vanished from sight. With the banshee gone, he felt a bit warmer already.

Out in the front yard, a small cluster of centaurs moved about, trimming away the last branches of winter. It was the middle of March, and they were getting ready for the spring equinox celebration, which Naia had promised him would be a sight to behold.

When he had first moved into the home nearly nine months earlier, the front yard had been just a small sidewalk that traversed what couldn't have been more than thirty feet of grass. Now, though, it was home to an illustrious garden maze, at the center of which stood a magnificent sundial that had been recently polished. The giant bushes of the home had been trimmed into topiary figures by the centaurs, and already this month, he had chased away a few randoms who had wandered into his yard to take pictures.

The Radley estate hadn't always been so popular, but magical homes had a way of gathering attention, both good and bad. Chasing off people who wanted to take pictures of the bushes was far preferable to the literal battles he had fought in the yard with monsters and witches alike. It had been almost six months since the last incident—which was the current record.

A pale figure wandered out from the maze and held up a hand in greeting. It was Sulyvahn the dullahan, who was also Cecilia's twin.

"Yer lookin' well rested, milord." Sulyvahn was holding a small bucket full of clipped flowers that had yet to bloom in one hand and a pair of shears in the other. While the centaurs maintained the rest of the gardens, the dullahan had somehow become in charge of the flowers themselves.

Mike nodded. "You didn't see any of those beetles out here, did you?"

"That I haven't." Sulyvahn pulled one of the flowers from his bucket and eyed it with suspicion, then gave it a shake. A tiny green light fell out of it and bounced off the ground. It looked like a tiny devil, and it stood up and chittered at Sulyvahn angrily.

"What is it?" asked Mike.

"Just a pest." Sulyvahn gave the creature a hard flick with his finger, and it vanished in a puff of smoke. "Now that spring is almost here, we be seein' a bit more o' them. They're creatures from my world, no idea at all why they be showin' up."

"Hmm." Mike made a mental note to bring it up next time he saw Titania, the Queen of the Fae. He had only seen her twice since November, and both times had been brief. The queen never came to the real world but visited his mind while sleeping. It was a strange arrangement, but it allowed her a short respite from the fairy court. "Should we be worried?"

"Nah. Little buggers are like locusts. They'll just start eatin' everythin'. I'll get the centaurs to spray some o' that silvered water to get them out."

"You do that." Mike waved in parting and walked inside the house.

The smell of freshly baked goods tickled his nose, and he walked across his living room and into the dining hall. It was the biggest room in the house, currently, able to sit everyone comfortably. Tink had custom-made chairs for everyone to accommodate their unique body shapes. At the moment, the doll Jenny was sitting on a small wooden chair across from a large rat that wore a crown on his head and plastic glasses that looked like they had been taken off of a Mr. Potato Head.

Jenny's face was the placid smile of a thrift shop horror, but Reggie, the Rat King, wore an expression of doubt. Mike paused to see what they were looking at, and realized that the two of them were playing Battleship.

"Problem?" he asked.

"I am fairly certain she is cheating," Reggie said. The empty plates on the table rattled threateningly, but Reggie had long ago stopped letting the haunted doll intimidate him. The rat king and Jenny, once enemies, had apparently worked past many of their differences, and it said quite a lot about their relationship that Jenny didn't actually attempt to hurt him. "I have yet to figure out how."

"Hmm." From where he stood, Mike had a great view of Jenny's board. She had snapped the boats into pieces and scattered them about. As far as he knew, the rules didn't explicitly state that was forbidden, which would probably be argued about later. It wouldn't be the first banned game in the house as a result of rule breaking. "Well, good luck."

"Thank you," Reggie said, and Mike continued into the kitchen.

The smell of baked goods reached him well in advance, and he entered in time to see a feminine figure with a very shapely ass bent over in front of the oven. He paused to admire the view, then kept moving when Sofia stood holding a muffin pan.

"Corn bread?" he asked. He saw that the counters had been covered in different baked goods, such as pies and cakes. "Seems a little basic."

The cyclops turned to regard him with a long stare. She stood well over a foot taller than him, but he feared her tongue more than her physical presence. Though she could be sweet when the two of them were alone, she typically chose to berate him over little things. It didn't bother him anymore because he knew for a fact that it just played into her kink.

"I *thought* it would be nice to offer something that wasn't so sweet." She lifted the door of the oven with her foot, which caused it to slam with a metallic bang. The kitchen itself had expanded toward the end of February, but nobody knew why. This had allowed Mike to purchase a much larger fridge and redecorate the place so that it looked almost like a kitchen in a high-end restaurant. Sofia had appreciated the extra room to cook and had spent a good chunk of the winter prepping meals that tasted like they had been cooked by professional chefs.

"Sounds like a great idea," he offered. "I love corn bread."

She huffed at him, then moved the pan over to cool. "Aren't you supposed to be helping somewhere?"

"Yep." This was an outright lie, but it would get him out of the kitchen without further discussion. He snapped up a small pastry from the edge of the counter on his way out, then dashed out of the kitchen when she opened her mouth to yell.

When he passed the dining room table, Reggie's arms were crossed in anger, his whiskers twitching. A pair of forks hovered threateningly over his head.

"The rule book does not have to explicitly state that you can't break the pieces," he declared in anger. A small rat squad Mike hadn't noticed before huddled nearby, clearly fearful for their king. Reggie squinted beady eyes at Jenny, who stood defiantly with her hands on her hips. "In the instructions, it clearly states that you were to place your ships fully on the board. By breaking your pieces, they are no longer ships, and that means you are unable to even start the game!"

A heavy pitcher lifted in the air, but Mike grabbed it as he walked by. "He's got you there, Jenny." He set the pitcher down at the other end of the table. "Jenny, if you mess up the table settings, you'll piss off Sofia."

The forks immediately dropped out of the air and clattered on the table. Though lacking a mouth, Jenny was able to blow a loud raspberry before hopping down from the table and running into the living room. Reggie just shook his head as he put the forks back where they belonged.

"Thank you," he said. "I was afraid we were about to have another Clue incident."

Mike shivered, then shook his head vehemently. "We don't talk about the Clue incident," he reminded the rat king.

Reggie snorted, and Mike left. Not having a destination, he decided to head out back to see how preparations were progressing for the equinox.

His backyard was so large that it rivaled the front and was now easily half the total land his home sat on. A large fountain sat in the middle of the garden, and the massive oak tree behind it dominated the view. Just past the tree was a gentle slope that terminated at a stone wall with a large wrought-iron gate. Beyond the gate, the occasional howl of a demon could be heard, but as long as it remained locked up tight, Mike wasn't worried about another invasion from the Underworld.

That, and Cerberus was always watching. The three-headed demon dog was loyal to Mike now, and she sat on the other side, always watching for trouble. Tethered to the Underworld by dimensional chains, she couldn't come more than a hundred feet into the backyard before reaching the end of her tether. He felt bad that Cerberus could never properly join the household, but it was probably for the best.

A few centaurs milled around a device that looked like a cross between a snail shell and a water tower. Tink had built the thing over the last two weeks and was inspecting a large cistern she had attached to the base, which consisted of long lengths of pipe that went beneath the ground and around the home to the front yard.

"How's it going?" Mike asked when he walked up. He took a bite of the pastry and almost groaned in delight when the buttery texture traveled through his entire mouth. There was a hint of some kind of berry, but he couldn't quite tell what. It was somewhere between raspberry and blueberry, which made him wonder if it wasn't both.

"Tink find small problem, fix with hammer." The goblin indicated a broken pipe made of PVC that sat off to the side. Mike's best guess was that she had smashed it with the hammer and replaced it.

"So you think it will work?" He had thought the idea of a sprinkler system was a good one, but implementing it was a bit of a problem. The water in the home was fed to it by a spring buried deep beneath, which meant there was no easy way to hook anything up without potentially disrupting the spring itself.

"Husband look here." Tink pointed near the bottom of the cistern, and when Mike bent down for a closer look, she snatched the rest of the pastry from his hand and stuffed it in her mouth.

"Hey, that was mine!" He crouched so he was at eye level with the goblin. She wore a work apron and had dirt smudged all along the green skin of her arms and legs. Her reddish hair had been pulled back into a ponytail, revealing the short yellow horns on her forehead. When he had first met the goblin, she had stolen his tools. A fight had ensued, which turned into sex, which now meant they were married—according to goblin law, anyway.

He wouldn't trade her for anything in the world.

"Husband pay for doubting Tink," she informed him with a condescending pat on the cheek. Her mouth was still full of pastry as she spoke.

"She's got you there, lover." The water in the fountain swirled into a frenzy, and the nymph Naia appeared. A statuesque beauty, she had blue-and-green hair that rippled behind her as if she stood in a breeze. Her feet were translucent, her body made of the very water she stood in. "But yes, we tested it this morning. It should work."

"I guess that leaves the star of the show." Mike looked past Naia at the oak tree. "Where is Amymone?"

Naia pointed upward with her finger and rolled her eyes.

"Again?" He looked up into the thick branches of the tree and was just able to make out a figure through the mostly bare branches. The dryad was huddled up against the trunk on one of the higher branches, a book clutched tightly in her hands.

"Apparently this one is a good read," Naia explained. "We were making too much noise, so she went up there for some peace and quiet."

He nodded. Once she was properly hooked by a story, it was nearly impossible to get the dryad's attention. He could climb the tree and try to convince her to come down, but nobody seemed to be in a hurry to start the festivities.

Tink spent the next thirty minutes showing him the sprinkler system she had built. The way it worked was that Naia would summon a giant surge of water from her spring and force it into the cistern, which would activate the sprinkler system properly. Apparently whatever Amymone had planned for the equinox was going to require a lot of water.

Up on the rooftop, he saw a dark figure wave to get his attention. He squinted to see who it was and managed to make out the large stony wings of Abella the gargoyle. She was pointing at the front yard, but because she was backlit by the sun, he couldn't make anything else out.

He left Tink behind and went through the house. Jenny and Reggie had their faces pressed against the glass. Behind them, Death stood with a hot cup of tea in one hand and a small saucer in the other.

"What's going on?" he asked the grim reaper.

"I am not sure, Mike Radley." Death took a sip of his tea, the hot liquid vanishing in the darkness. Mike was grateful that it went somewhere other than his floor, but he had no idea where that would be. "This man has been standing there for several minutes now. Perhaps he is lost? If so, he is free to use one of my maps if needed, but I must insist he return it."

Frowning, Mike opened the door and stepped outside. Standing at the edge of his yard was an older man in a white sweater vest holding a newspaper under his arms. He wore silver spectacles, and his mouth was hanging open as he gazed up at the house.

Mike looked around the yard and saw that the centaurs were still working, but a couple of them had grabbed their bows. Over by the far wall, a large creature that vaguely resembled a dragon lifted its head and snorted. The Jabberwock had been rebuilt after the incident with the shadow on Halloween but was now trained to obey voice commands from Mike. It was hard to say what the stranger might be seeing, because the geas had a way of keeping anyone from seeing the fantastical creatures in his front yard. The effect used to only apply to creatures inside the home, but as the home grew, so did the geas.

"Can I help you?" Mike kept his distance.

The man hadn't stepped into his yard yet, which meant the geas would protect him from a magical assault. Even if the stranger walked in and tried to cast a spell, the lion statues that stood above them would drop down and crush him to a pulp. Really, his main concern was any sort of physical assault, and Mike's danger sense (courtesy of Naia) would warn him of impending harm.

"The end is near," the visitor said with a raspy voice, then lowered his gaze. His eyes were cloudy, like partially cooked egg whites, and his hanging mouth barely moved. The voice Mike heard was ethereal in nature, like someone speaking through a large tube. "Prepare yourself for judgment, child of—"

As if he was suddenly disconnected, the man lurched forward and his pupils appeared. When his jaw shut, his teeth clacked together, causing him to wince and rub at his cheek. His dark-brown eyes focused on Mike, and a scowl formed.

"Are you the new homeowner?" he asked. It was as if the past few seconds hadn't occurred. Mike scanned the street, convinced the threat was still out there, that this stranger was little more than a decoy.

"Excuse me!" The man stepped onto Mike's property but still maintained his distance. Though the ominous voice was gone, his body language was now aggressive. If not for the fact that he looked like a disgruntled professor who most likely battled heartburn on a full-time basis, Mike would have felt more intimidated. "Are you the new homeowner?"

"I am." Mike had learned long ago that the less he said, the faster conversations would end. It had been a survival skill for years, due to his social anxiety, but now he had better things to do than piss around with some lame-ass Mr. Rogers knockoff.

"My name is Murray. I live next door." Murray stuck his thumb out to the right, looking briefly like a hitchhiker. "I don't want to be that guy, but you and I have a problem."

"We do?" Still worried that a threat was imminent, Mike crossed his arms and begrudgingly gave Murray his full attention.

"Yes, we do, Mr....?"

"Radley. Mike Radley." Mike didn't bother offering his hand.

"Michael. While I appreciate all the work you've done to improve the grounds, I'm afraid I must insist on expressing my outrage over all the noise you keep making." Murray's cheeks were now red, and his hands had balled into fists. It was clear he was working himself up.

"What noise?"

"Ever since you've moved in, I've had to call the cops multiple times because of the noise at your house. Like last night's party, for example."

"Um…" He thought back to when Tink had knocked holes in the walls and when everyone had shrieked when the scarabs had flooded the upstairs hallway. The women of the house had reacted in different ways, which was why the third-floor hall had frosted over, and there was one broken window on the second floor where the fairy girls had started their own bug rodeo. Though the home had leaked noise on more than one occasion, it had only been during far greater battles than home extermination, and those had been outside.

"Don't pretend you don't know what I'm talking about." Murray pulled a piece of paper out of his pocket and handed it over. "I've spoken with my attorney. On his recommendation, I am letting you know that I intend to sue if you keep it up. I am losing valuable sleep, and it is affecting my job performance. I also don't appreciate all the extra foot traffic you've brought to the neighborhood. This is supposed to be a nice place."

Mike took the paper. It looked like Murray had taken a picture of a computer screen displaying the local noise ordinance with his phone, then printed that image out with the remnants of a fossilized ink cartridge.

"Well?" Murray asked, looking quite satisfied with himself. "Do you agree now that we have a problem?"

Mike folded the paper and stuck it in his back pocket. He had once stabbed a demon in the head before collapsing a pocket universe on it. There was also the time he had fought witches in the front yard, and even the incident with Titania, Queen of the Fae. While Murray posed very little threat to him in pretty much every way, he definitely wanted the man off his lawn. The last thing he needed was a nosy neighbor. "Thanks for letting me know. I'll try to keep it down."

Murray, looking very satisfied with himself, straightened his sweater and left.

Mike watched him go, then pulled the paper out of his pocket. He would have Beth look at it later. While he didn't necessarily feel like dealing with a court battle, she would know exactly how to handle it.

And what of Murray's strange behavior? His King Théoden impression clearly hadn't been an act, which warranted a proper investigation. Next time he spotted Lily, he would see if he could convince her to spy on him. If nothing else, the succubus could hop into Murray's dreams tonight and take a peek around to see if anything was amiss.

"It's always something," he muttered, then stuck the paper back into his pocket. Despite the incident with the scarabs, it really had been too quiet lately. Taking a deep breath, he looked at the gathering of people in his yard and crossed his fingers.

Hopefully it wouldn't get too crazy.

The Labyrinth beneath Mike's home had seen better days. Enough progress had been made with the repairs over the last six months that Beth was finally able to traverse it on her own without a sturdy pair of hiking shoes, but it was still treacherous to walk in some areas. The shadow, a nameless menace with magical powers, had used a magical text called the grimoire to take a shortcut to the middle of the Labyrinth, where he had encountered the naga Ratu.

The battle had not ended well for the naga.

Upon arriving at the naga's lair, Beth saw Ratu sitting on a large, soft chaise lounge beneath a modified sunlamp. Though Ratu had survived the attack, her recovery had been agonizingly slow. Currently, her upper torso was that of a human, and her lower body was the long, slender form of a cobra. Her snake skin was shedding, and she had apparently convinced the fairies to help her out by scraping it away with stones that looked like pumice.

"Ah, you're early." Ratu put down the magical text she had been reading.

The book shimmered momentarily before the cover expanded and sealed it shut. "I wasn't expecting you until later."

Beth felt the heat rise in her cheeks. Originally, she had planned to arrive early and perhaps mess around a bit with the Minotaur Asterion. He was a couple hundred pounds of muscle wrapped around a gentle soul. He also had an enormous cock of which Beth had become quite fond.

Sneaking away to a hidden part of the Labyrinth for a quick fuck was definitely Beth's idea of a fun time, but no amount of lube or foreplay would be able to help her with an issue that had developed earlier in the week.

"I ended up with some extra time on my hands," she offered. "It's looking better down here."

"The rats have been a big help." Ratu let out a sigh. "Can I get you some tea or something?"

"No, please. Stay where you are." Beth sat on a nearby chair and appraised the naga. The scale patterns that shimmered across Ratu's skin had finally returned, and her fangs were a normal size now. Still, she looked paler than normal, and whenever the naga shifted, she winced. "Guess you and the Labyrinth are going to need more time."

Ratu nodded. "The magic I used to survive was not a spell to be taken lightly. I essentially became one with the earth as much as possible without losing myself. My recovery is speeding up, however, and I expect to be in good health in the next few months. Maybe then I can tackle the secrets of the grimoire."

The grimoire was a book of magic bound in leather with an apple on the cover. The house had been attacked on multiple occasions based only on rumors of the book's existence. During the most devastating attack, Beth had managed to take it back from the shadow just prior to his untimely demise. For now, the grimoire was being held in a safe place where nobody could get to it —inside the belly of a friendly mimic.

A centaur wandered over with a silver platter that contained a pitcher and some cups. The centaurs were amazing healers, but Ratu had demanded that she herself oversee the repairs to her home. At the moment, a small team of them occupied the naga's lair and did their best to help.

"So what's new with you? It's been a couple of weeks since I've wandered down here."

"Not much, I'm afraid. Much of my research was destroyed. What little I have left is either a complete mystery or merely parts of a larger puzzle. Some of the artifacts I had in storage were also destroyed, so now there's wild magic down here." The naga frowned, then shook her head. "It's a little bit like the scarabs from last night. Magic is bouncing around everywhere, just looking for a new home. I've had the rats bring me plenty of replacement items, so if you see random objects lying around, that's what those are for, and you should definitely not touch them."

"It's not…something I should be worried about, is it?" Beth suddenly felt like she had exposed herself to danger by coming here.

"It's very rare for enchantments to be able to cross from objects to living tissue. Based on my research, you shouldn't see any harmful effects." Ratu frowned. "However, one of the destroyed objects was something Dana brought me to reverse her curse. It was a terrible loss."

"Oh." Beth wasn't sure how to respond to that. Ratu and Dana had been working together to find a way to undo her curse. Dana had been killed by a necromancer, who had then fused her soul to her body. As she was unable to ever truly die, her eternal destiny was locked to her new zombie form, which presented some serious ramifications if the spell could never be undone. Dana had gone on a long trip to hunt down some magical items that could reverse the spell, but the trip was a mixed success when she couldn't find them all.

Beth was certain the news would be devastating. "Does she know yet?"

Ratu shook her head. "She doesn't. My hope is that the enchantment from the flask will eventually find a new home and it won't be an issue. Even if I still had the flask, I'm in no condition to pursue a cure for Dana's plight. I haven't been in a state like this since—"

The naga paused, then frowned. "Never mind. Anyway, now that you're here, I have a favor to ask." She reached into the pocket of her sleeve and withdrew a crystalline vial. Inside, a black liquid sloshed around.

Beth recognized it immediately. Some time ago, a demon had imprinted a part of his soul onto hers as a way to control her. After Mike had destroyed the demon, the demon's soul fragment tried to take over her body. Ratu had built a device to filter it out and then bottled up the resulting ooze.

"What do you want me to do with that?"

Ratu held up the vial and gave it a shake. It was like staring into the void, for light didn't reflect off of its contents properly. "I've been racking my brain to try to figure out why the shadow tried to take this from me. I can think of several reasons, and none of them are good. After much deliberation, I've decided I would like it stored away in the Vault. I'm in no condition to destroy it, and need it kept safe."

Beth nodded and took the vial. "Out of curiosity, why didn't you stick it in the Vault sooner?"

Ratu groaned in disgust. "My own stupid ego. I've been holding on to it ever since I could move around again, thinking I was the best person to keep it. However, last night, some of that wild magic attached itself to a robe I was wearing, and the fabric itself tried to strangle me. In a better state, I could easily manage an aura of protection, or detect the presence of magic. But... I'm not in a better state. If I can't even protect myself from an angry robe, then I definitely can't handle anyone who would come looking for that."

"I'll take care of it." Beth slid the vial into her pocket. She could feel an ominous chill where it rested, and wondered if it was a psychosomatic reaction or something more sinister.

They spent the rest of their visit discussing various things but primarily Beth's spiritual health. Ever since the incident with the demon, Ratu had done frequent checkups to ensure that there were no lingering issues with Beth or her soul. Beth helped Ratu rearrange some of the magical artifacts she still had stored. This was usually a job for Asterion, but these objects had been damaged and required a more delicate touch than the Minotaur could provide.

Once she had finished her visit, Beth left the Labyrinth and was led by a rat to a shortcut that took her directly to the house. The rats had chewed a portal in a small alcove that led her to the servants' quarters on the second floor. The servants' quarters had been hidden behind a false wall and could only be opened by the rats on the inside. While this was a perfectly good shortcut to the Labyrinth, Beth preferred taking the magical door in her closet. It was the atmosphere of mystery that she craved, watching that long stone corridor appear where there should be wooden walls, feeling the cold breeze on her face from the caverns below. Seeing the ceiling disappear in darkness above as the Labyrinth was revealed by the glittering lights on the stalactites.

That, and Asterion could meet her at the entrance to the Labyrinth. As he was a typically surly character, watching his eyes light up when he saw her always made her day. She frowned at the thought of what had happened earlier. It was a problem that had occurred in the past, typically after some rather intense rounds of self-pleasure with her larger dildos. A quick medical search online revealed that it was either simple bruising, vaginitis, or cancer. There didn't seem to be anything in between.

Truthfully, it was most likely her current sex life. While she absolutely adored the time she spent with either Asterion or Suly, both of them had abnormally shaped cocks that pushed her physical limits. No amount of lubrication would rectify the resulting problems concerning bruised inner tissue.

It reminded her of the time one of her bigger dildos had slipped free of its mount during a rigorous session. Upon popping free, it had remained inside her when she had tried to sit up to see what had happened, forcing the toy even deeper. The resulting pain had been horrendous, and it had been several days until she had felt comfortable doing anything again.

She made her way down the stairs and then to the kitchen. Just past the pantry was an unassuming door with a concrete set of stairs that went down to the basement. Sofia was busy making more pastries but paused when she saw Beth by the stairs.

"What are you doing?" she asked.

"Putting something in the Vault for Ratu," Beth replied. "Can you come with?"

It was a general rule that nobody should go in the Vault alone, and she had known that Sofia had been baking since early this morning.

Sofia nodded.

The basement was cold. Up until last night, the only thing down there had been an enormous freezer in which Sofia kept prime cuts of meat. Now, though, there was a large opening across from the freezer. Beth pulled a piece of chalk from beneath the freezer and drew a door on the wall, then knocked on the concrete. Shimmering lights appeared and formed straight lines, revealing a magical door that opened with a creak.

The air of the Vault was supernaturally cold, and Beth chased the shadows away by flipping the light switch. The room was large and looked very much like a thrift store, except the objects contained within its walls could potentially kill.

She was careful not to touch anything as she made her way to the back. There was a glass display case where Jenny used to be stored. It was a perfect home for the vial.

Once the vial was in place, Beth turned around and paused at the sight of a painting that had been wrapped in paper. It sounded like someone was whispering from the other side, and she shook her head in an attempt to dislodge the sound. The room suddenly felt like it was closing in, and she took a few steps toward the door before losing her train of thought and wandering elsewhere.

It wasn't until she had crossed the room and was about to put her hand on the painting that she received a powerful smack from a long wooden spoon on the back of her hand. Yelping, she yanked her hand away and saw that Sofia had hunched over to step inside the Vault.

"That one's really nasty," she said, then helped guide Beth out of the room. "Painted by a man who had gone insane and killed some people. Anyone who sees the painting becomes haunted by dark figures until they die."

"Wow, seriously?" Beth rubbed her hand, then pulled the Vault shut. As the seals engaged, the chalk vanished.

Sofia nodded. "A very unpleasant mess. It was actually in the Library's restricted section for a bit. I gave it to a previous Caretaker for safekeeping.

Despite being miles away from the information desk, I could hear the damn thing whispering from time to time."

"That's seriously creepy. So what haunts it? Ghosts? Demons?"

"*Demons* would be the best word." Sofia started up the stairs. "At least, as far as you know them. Demon is kind of a blanket term, like alcohol. Can apply to many different things that share similar properties."

"I thought all demons were the same?" Beth stopped to peek in the room where the scarabs had come from. The middle of the room had an empty pedestal, and the ground had been swept clean of the pottery shards they had found. The working theory was that the scarabs had been trapped inside something that had broken. Of course, this could have been something that had broken yesterday or a decade ago; it was impossible to tell.

But when Beth looked at the smooth walls, she caught just a hint of color smeared around the room. She wondered if there hadn't been something painted there that had been worn down over time by scuttling legs.

Sofia laughed behind her. "Yes and no. There are plenty of things that call themselves demons but aren't. Biblical demons are the ones everyone is most familiar with. Ones like Lily and Oliver. These are angels that have fallen from heaven itself. But many religions have demons of their own with different origins."

"I see." The answer itself made sense but opened the floor to a lot of questions. Beth turned away from the room and started up the stairs behind the cyclops. "So it's really just a matter of nomenclature. Something nasty and from a dark place must be a demon?"

Sofia nodded, closing the door behind them. Back in the kitchen, she turned on the sink to wash her hands. "That's one way of looking at it. Categorizing demons is a tricky business because one of the defining qualities usually involves devouring a human soul."

"Not a lot of those just lying around, right?" Beth pointed to a pastry. "May I have one?"

"You may." Sofia had pulled some dough out of a large bowl and was kneading it. "And thank you for asking."

"I'm not a child." Beth picked up the flaky pastry and bit into it. There was a type of jam inside that made her think of strawberries. "This is really good."

"Thank you." The cyclops smiled.

"So a follow-up question. If demons can exist from different religions, doesn't that mean multiple religions are valid?"

Sofia laughed. "Ah, the eternal question. Which religion has it right? Well, in a way, all of them."

"But how is that possible?" Beth asked.

"Simple." Sofia set the dough down and put her hands on her hips. "Don't trust everything you read. Each religion has its own agenda, for better or for worse. And when you rely on a human, of all things, to remain unbiased while passing the information along, you're bound to get a few mistakes, some personal interpretations, maybe even a few exaggerations, opinions, etc."

That explanation made sense. Beth and Mike had done a ton of research into the afterlife and the Underworld in an attempt to traverse it and get Cecilia back from the fairy realm earlier the previous year. Notes had been made about multiple gateways that could be found there, and the destinations were often unpleasant.

"Is there a text that has it right?" Beth asked. "One that only contains the truth?"

Sofia grinned. "If there is, I certainly haven't seen it. As readers, it's our job to question what we are reading, to learn how to read behind the lines. Just because it's been put in print doesn't make it trustworthy, no matter how hard we want to believe." She picked the dough back up. "You have to remember I was raised when the Greek gods were still kicking about. I've lived in a society where people could commune directly with the gods themselves."

"Whatever happened to the gods?"

Sofia shrugged. "Great question. It's interesting how some gods simply disappear, isn't it? Best as I can tell, they all just kind of vanished one day. Were they hunted? Did they just leave? Or did they rely on belief to continue existing? I really don't know. Maybe we were never meant to know."

Beth watched Sofia with the dough, and a giant grin crossed her lips. "Would you like some help with this?" she asked. "I would love to talk about this stuff some more. What were the gods like?"

"Most of them were major assholes," Sofia said. "Wash up and I'll tell you."

MIKE COUNTED ALMOST THIRTY CENTAURS IN THE FRONT YARD. THOUGH THE moon tribe lived in a magical greenhouse behind his home, they used a shortcut the rat king had built to come directly to Mike's front yard from the middle of their village. Though he didn't know all their names, he recognized them as the men and women who took care of his yard. It was something he had never asked them to do, but he was aware it was a thank-you for rescuing them from persecution in their former land.

He was disappointed to see that their chieftain, Zel, was not among them.

He rarely saw her anymore but understood why. The centaurs had spent most of the winter mapping out the vast jungle where they lived, and had been working on an expansion plan, which required Zel's full attention. The topography of the area allowed for some phenomenal agricultural opportunities, but they needed a central location for that. Over the winter, Mike had managed to bring in some livestock for the centaurs to raise, and what had once been a small collection of yurts and hay had become a full-fledged village. The tribe was flourishing, and though he missed his friend, he couldn't be happier for her.

Besides, they had an agreement to meet every once in a while and just chat. He found himself looking forward to those days, if only because he felt like they were miniature vacations from the day-to-day happenings in the house.

The centaurs milled about his yard with the other members of the household. A retinue of rats kept close to Reggie as he used the railing of the home to watch the proceedings, and Cecilia sat on her swing next to Suly. Down in the yard, a space had been cleared, and the centaurs had rolled out a pair of large drums. Not ones to dillydally, they had apparently decided it was time to start a party of their own. A group of centaurs appeared wearing feathered anklets on their legs, along with bells, beads, and anything else that would flair out dramatically.

Looking down at Kisa, Mike said, "Looks like they're going to start dancing." Standing at around four feet tall, Kisa had once been human, but a cursed object had transformed her most of the way into a feline. She wore an emerald dress that matched her eyes, the same dress she had worn for Zel's chieftain ceremony so many months ago. "You going to join?"

He didn't even have to ask that question. Ever since the night he had mated with her, not only had they bonded, but she was now his familiar. The magic inside his body was now somehow mirrored in her own, and when she was next to him, he could sometimes feel her emotions. Right now, her heart was racing in excitement at the idea of dancing with the centaurs, and he couldn't help but smile.

"It's more like they're going to join me," she uttered with a grin, then vaulted over the railing. After landing without a sound, she jogged out toward the drums and was greeted with an enthusiastic cheer.

"She seems happy." When he heard Beth's voice, he tensed up a little. Turning around, he saw that she had changed into a peasant blouse with a red skirt that went to her ankles. In each hand was a glass of wine, and she handed one to Mike. "Are you going to dance too?"

He chuckled, then took the wine. "Nobody wants to see the electric slide."

"I don't know. I bet you could get the centaurs to do it with you. Would probably be interesting to watch." She sipped her wine with a grin.

"Knowing my luck, they'd like it so much that they'd start doing that instead of what they currently do." He had seen the centaurs dance on a few occasions, and each time had been exciting. There was one centaur in the tribe that could actually do a backflip, which was apparently a sight to behold. "I promise traditional centaur dance is far more impressive than what a bunch of drunk people in a bar can manage."

"Not a fan of line dancing?" Beth smirked.

"I'd rather eat my own hand," he grumbled, his mind going briefly back to middle-school gym class. To this day, he had no idea why an entire month had been dedicated to country dancing. He couldn't hear "Achy Breaky Heart" without having flashbacks to the school gym.

"But you do dance. I've seen you."

His cheeks burned for a moment. Kisa loved to dance, and on more than one occasion, she had enticed him to join. She would literally dance circles around him while he tried to keep up, but at least he could sway to a basic beat without feeling awkward. The idea that Beth had been watching made him nervous. It was a throwback to before he had moved into the home, to before he had fallen into a life of magic, mayhem, and intimacy with the many women in his home.

"When the mood strikes me, yes, I do."

Beth looked at her drink, then slammed it. She took a deep breath, as if steeling her nerves, then stuck her hand toward him. "Come. Dance with me."

He swallowed the lump in his throat, then raised his hand to take hers. Though he and Beth had lived in the same house for several months, it seemed like their schedules never allowed them to properly connect. She was the day to his night, the two of them often pulled in opposite directions.

But at last, maybe for a few minutes, they could finally be on the same schedule.

A yellow light descended from above, flashing erratically, and then Daisy appeared on his hand. She stood a few inches tall and had a body that was a cross between a human and a bumble bee. Though she was deaf, she could hear through the vibrations in her wings, and she was signing frantically.

"What's she saying? I can't follow." Beth frowned at Mike.

"Apparently there's a problem out back. They need my help." Though Mike couldn't sign at all, he was able to understand Daisy through the magical bond they shared. It was as if the words appeared in his mind, which was extremely useful in times like these. "Guess my dance card is full. I'm really sorry."

Beth smiled, but it didn't quite reach her eyes. "Please look me up when you get back?"

"Of course." He set his glass down on a small table by the porch swing and then went inside the house. It was the only way to get from the front yard to the back without scaling the sides of the home, which he had done on occasion.

Once out back, he found Naia in her fountain with a concerned look on her face. Amymone was on her knees at the base of her tree, her hands placed against its thick bark. Her face was screwed up in both concentration and frustration.

"Everything okay?" he asked.

"No." Amymone groaned and stood. "Apparently there's a problem."

"With what?"

"I thought I had saved up enough energy over the winter to help the plants bloom." Amymone's job at the home was to maintain the ecosystem around the house. Connected to all the vegetation around the house through the roots of her tree, she was able to subconsciously manipulate not just the plants of the home but the microclimate that existed inside the geas. On a conscious level, she could command all the plants to emerge from hibernation and bloom, which was what today's party was supposed to be about.

"What's the problem?" he asked.

"I suppose being dead for several years." In a fit of madness, Amymone's tree had been cut down by the previous Caretaker, Emily. Luckily, the dryad had managed to hide her heart wood away prior to the attack so that the tree could be reborn. However, this had resulted in her soul being stuck in the Underworld until her tree had been replanted. "For a good chunk of the winter, I was asleep, just like my tree. But I didn't spend all fall stockpiling reserves for this moment, which means I'm running on empty now." She picked up a rock and threw it in frustration, then smoothed out her dress. "Fuck."

Naia snorted, a sound that was somehow almost musical coming from the nymph. "Sounds like you already know what the solution is, sister."

"Beg pardon?" Amymone looked over her shoulder at Naia.

"You need to fuck. Him." Naia jerked her thumb at Mike. "C'mon, you know you wanna. You've mentioned it before."

"Naia!" Amymone hid her face with her hands, and her bark-like skin turned a deep shade of brown that was almost black. "The whole point of talking about personal stuff like that is for you to keep your fucking mouth shut!"

Mike laughed. Though the two weren't actual sisters, they certainly acted like it.

"Seriously, though, fuck him." Naia pointed at Amymone's tree. Small buds were struggling to emerge from its branches. "I know you've been dying to, and now that you're not bald anymore—"

"*Naia!*" The dryad stomped her foot, and one of the tree's massive roots hurled a chunk of dirt into the nymph's fountain, causing the water to turn brown. Naia frowned, then crossed her arms as the water beneath her swirled violently, then blasted the debris back out of her fountain and onto the lawn.

Over the winter, Amymone had lost all her hair and curled up at the base of her tree to rest. Her long, green locks had returned in the last couple of weeks, locks that would undoubtedly turn a golden brown with the fall.

Mike put himself between the women, his hands held up in surrender.

"Naia, if Amymone isn't interested, then we need to respect that. Amymone, we won't do anything you don't want to do. Now, if you'd like to watch me spank your sister for being a snitch, I think we could arrange something." Though his relationship with many of the others had become carnal over time, he had always made clear that sex wasn't a prerequisite for staying in the home. "Is there some other way we can help you out?"

Amymone turned away from Mike, her hair covering her face.

"Don't pout," Naia told her. "You were the one who got everyone excited for the equinox. You didn't even have to do it this way."

"Oh?" This was news to Mike, and he turned toward Naia. "What do you mean?"

"Amymone doesn't have to wait for the equinox to do anything. She kind of wanted to make a big fuss this year because you actually seem to care about the little things and she was trying to impress you. Previous Caretakers would generally just bring her reading material and leave her be, but she remembers how you came out during the winter and put a blanket over her when it snowed."

He nodded, remembering how he had fussed over Amymone. She had been recently revived before winter had come and had worried more than once about her tree suddenly dying again. Unable to hire a local company to care for his magical tree, he had made sure to clear snow around the base of the tree and had watched the weather in case temperature fluctuations were too rapid.

Once she had come out of hibernation, he had kept her in books. As she was able to easily read five or six a day, he had tried to convince her to use a Kindle. She had stubbornly insisted on paperback only, which he found a bit morbid on account of paper being made from wood. Regardless, he had to agree that the new book smell couldn't be beat, and the two of them would often pick a book to read together over a week and then talk about it.

Amymone groaned, then crouched. "If I had been doing it a little bit at a time, then it would be fine. I just can't make everything happen all at once, not this year."

"I'm sure everyone will understand," he explained. "It's okay to have ambitions, but it's also okay to fail. It's how we all learn."

"You sound like an after-school special," she muttered.

"But he's right," Naia added.

The dryad groaned again, then stood. "You do realize this is not at all how I expected our first time to be, right? I was thinking maybe closer to summer, way after my awkward winter phase had ended. I could lure you up into my tree, maybe there's just enough moonlight to see each other. The wind would rustle through the leaves, the crickets would be singing, we would look into each other's eyes for a good, long while…"

"That would be her romantic streak," whispered Naia, though Mike was certain Amymone could hear. "She gets it from all the romance books she reads."

"Oh, fuck off," Amymone retorted. "I'm allowed to want what I want. That's my prerogative. You only get one first time after all."

"Surely it isn't your first time…," Mike muttered.

"First time with you." Amymone winked. "But I guess I'll have to settle. I did kind of build this event up in everybody's mind, so what's done is done."

"But your magic will give her the boost she needs," Naia added. "Since she's connected to her tree, she can take that energy and use it to help the plants and flowers bloom on time."

Mike nodded, a crooked grin on his face. While it wasn't uncommon to solve his problems with sex, he did find it amusing that he was officially going to start spring with a bang.

"I guess we're probably in a hurry." Amymone approached her tree and bent over, her hands pressed against the bark of the tree. "In a way, maybe this is kind of exciting too. We can be strangers passing in the night, or perhaps —AYE!"

Mike had snuck up on the dryad and given her ass a playful smack. She had wide hips that were complemented by a slender waist and very thick thighs, all of which had become exposed when her short dress made of leaves had ridden up. When she looked over her shoulder at him, he gave her another playful smack.

"That's for making things unnecessarily hard on yourself," he informed her.

"Oh, do you want to do some role-play?" she asked, wiggling her butt for him. "I'll be that pesky rhododendron that just can't get enough water, and you can be a beefy firehose."

"Um, what?"

"Oh, I know! Maybe I'm a bonsai tree, and you're here to tuck my branches in. Use those fingers to push my branches in place, tie me up a little. Oh, I know! You can be the dirty gardener, and I'm just a bush waiting to get trimmed."

Mike looked to Naia for help. The nymph was laughing.

"She's just fucking with you," she told him. "I think."

He turned his attention back to the mischievous dryad. She was chattering on now, something about his bark being worse than his bite. Using one hand to pull her gown up to give him access, he summoned his magic from deep within. It was wild magic, a cross between the abilities of a nymph that Naia had given him when he had become Caretaker and the fae magic from Cecilia.

Sparks of electricity formed along his torso and then ran down his arm until they gathered along his hand. The idea of controlling this magic had been impossible six months ago, but after so many opportunities to practice, he had learned a few new tricks.

With the gown pulled to the side, he noticed that Amymone shared a feature with Naia. Neither the nymph nor the dryad had a butthole, but Amymone did have the largest labia Mike had ever seen. They were dark brown with a swirling pattern that reminded him of the grain on his new office desk.

"Are you stumped?" Amymone looked over her shoulder at him, mirth on her face. It was clear she was still running with the dirty gardener gag. "I promise it works like the others you've seen. I am really hoping you have a green thumb."

He didn't reply. Instead, he allowed his fingers to just barely graze her labia and watched in immense satisfaction as the sparks leaped from his fingertips to her body.

"Oh shit!" Amymone's body went rigid, and her legs shook. He touched her again, sending an additional wave of energy through her body, and she leaned forward into her tree. Her forehead now rested on the bark, and he could see tiny, little lights migrating up the trunk.

Interesting. He used his fingers to explore her, marveling at how soft her skin felt despite how rough it looked. After pushing her gown farther up her body, he rubbed the small of her back while he fingered her with the other hand.

Amymone's spine made wavelike motions as she gasped and grunted against her tree. He was already hard, a benefit of the nymph magic flowing through his body, and he paused long enough to take off his pants. His cock sprang free, despite the slight chill in the air.

"Ooh, give it to her, lover." Naia was sitting on the edge of the fountain, her legs crossed beneath her. Miniature cyclones danced across the water's surface, and the fountain was jetting water almost twenty feet into the air.

"Yes, please," Amymone begged. "Fertilize me!"

Ugh. Fairly certain that her plant puns were a deliberate attempt to screw with him, he kept his attention on the curves of her body. As he stood behind her, she was just short enough that his cock rested on the top of her ass. He looked down at her feet to see that little tendrils had sprouted and sunk into the ground. With a tentative push, he realized she wasn't budging, no matter how hard he pressed.

A smile crossed his face, and he leaned back far enough that he could push his cock into place.

"Ooh, are you about to plant some*thing*!" Amymone let out a shriek as he buried himself inside her, allowing his magic to flow directly out of his cock and into her body. He could feel them connect on a magical level, and the tree was now glowing as if infested by fireflies just beneath its bark.

The dryad cried out in pleasure, and Mike leaned forward until he was resting on her ass. He moved his hands along her belly and up to her breasts, and he gave them a squeeze. Her skin felt soft, but her breasts were where he could really feel how firm her flesh was. It took a powerful grip just to give them a squeeze, which emboldened him to be as rough as he wanted.

Inside, his magic was now flickering back and forth between her and him, driving their arousal to greater heights. He fucked her hard from behind, varying the tempo in tune with her reactions. At their feet, little flowers sprouted all along the ground, and he had to move his toes to keep them from getting tangled in the new growth.

"Naia…" Amymone looked at her sister. "I…need…water."

The nymph gave a salute, and the swirling water in the fountain blasted into the cistern. Tink's design allowed for the water to be pumped directly to the roots of the plants; otherwise, the partygoers would all be enjoying a very cold shower.

"More," Amymone begged, then looked at Mike. "You, not her," she clarified.

Happy to oblige, he pounded her harder from behind. He moved his hands along her body, then slid them around to the front to squeeze her breasts some more. When he went to play with her nipples, he realized they felt pointed, bringing to mind the tip of an acorn.

The tree creaked, and the bark split in a few places. Light glowed from within, and Mike briefly worried that something bad was about to happen. However, it was Amymone's tree, and no matter how hard he was fucking her, he didn't think she would allow it to come to any harm.

He dropped his hand along her waist and summoned a handful of magic, then sought out her clit. Unlike the fleshy nub to be found on a human woman, hers was quite hard and most likely made of wood like the rest of her.

Amymone swore, then gripped the tree tightly as her hair bloomed. Tiny leaves appeared all along her body on the ends of twigs barely thicker than the average nail.

When she finally came, the tree shook, dropping leaves and branches all around them. The roots shifted about, tearing up the yard, but the ground under their feet remained steady. Birds that had been nesting took flight, and more than a few dropped down to Naia's fountain to complain to the nymph about their harsh treatment.

Mike clamped down on the tough skin of Amymone's hips and let out a deep groan that transformed into a growl. His magic expanded inside his body, then pumped itself into Amymone. The tiny sparks of magic flowed through the dryad's body and into her tree, and he watched in amazement as they circled the trunk and then split apart, some going up and most going down.

Naia's fountain turned into a rush of water as she pumped hundreds of gallons of liquid into the cistern Tink had built. Below his feet, he could actually feel his magic migrating away from them and traveling beneath the house.

A collective cheer rose from the front yard. Though he couldn't see what was happening there, he was certain it was similar to what he saw in the back. Amymone's tree creaked as all its leaves opened at once, showering them in tiny lights that looked like butterflies. The flowers in the back all bloomed at once, each one emanating its own unique musical note. More lights emerged from the foliage and faded away on the breeze as the land came to life.

"More," Amymone cried, but this time, it was at Naia. "More water!"

As Naia pumped more water into the cistern, Mike pumped himself into Amymone once again. She let out a low moan, and the roots of her tree shifted about. Though he had no desire to pursue another orgasm, it felt good just to be inside her, to cling to her sturdy frame and just enjoy the feel of her body against his.

"You weren't kidding," Amymone muttered, then looked over at her sister. "I'm all tapped out. That was definitely not the short end of the stick. Holy shit!"

"More tree jokes? Seriously?" When Mike pulled out of Amymone, he was surprised he didn't see any of his cum follow. He assumed she had absorbed it all, which didn't surprise him.

"Oh, please." Amymone pushed herself to a standing position, then turned to face him while adjusting her gown. Her nipples were, in fact, shaped like tiny acorns. She grabbed his cock and gave it a playful squeeze. "You're not one to talk. After all, you're the one who brought all the wood."

Mike groaned. "Please, no more," he begged.

"You're saying you want me to leaf it—" She never finished her statement, because Naia had summoned a jet of water to hose her down. Both of them laughed, and Mike couldn't help but join in as he put his pants back on.

MIKE CHECKED THE TIME ON HIS PHONE AND SMILED. THE PARTY FOR THE equinox was apparently going to roll well into the night, and he couldn't be happier. The setting sun cast long shadows that had draped themselves over the garden, but many of the magical flowers had started glowing. It was like looking at a field of stars in his own lawn, truly a sight to behold. They had already chased off a couple of people who had wandered in while everyone gathered. Mike had mentioned to Tink that it was time to put a locked gate in the front yard.

Beth was currently dancing with Sulyvahn. Mike wasn't sure if she had seen him when he came back, but she was clearly having a good time with the dullahan, and he was very reluctant to butt in.

The centaurs milled about with food and drink, and it looked as though anyone able to come was there. Even Dana had come out to visit—after finishing up a project for the centaurs in January, she had turned her attention to the giant mechanism on the third floor. Last year, the shadow had unlocked a mysterious door on the third floor to reveal an observatory with a dilapidated telescope inside.

Mike hated that room. The few windows it had were boarded up from the outside, but when they had tried to open the large sliding wall that allowed a telescope to see the sky, it had been to a place of absolute darkness, though it was still the middle of the day. The observatory was meant to view a place that wasn't here on Earth, and it frightened him to think about what might be looking back when they finally fixed it up.

Still, it gave Dana something to do, and though he hated the room, he never felt like he was in danger while in it. The door had to be removed, because nobody was certain what the password was to get in, and it didn't seem like it could be opened from the inside. Now it just sat on the floor of the room, and Tink could often be found studying its inner mechanisms to try to figure out its secrets.

There was movement down by the lions, and Mike headed to intercept the newcomer. He assumed it was another jogger, or someone out for a walk that wanted a closer look, but paused when he saw a man in brown pulling a dolly laden with a sizable wooden box on it. The party cooled rapidly as the man walked past everyone, all of them holding still as if not to be seen.

The delivery man looked confused for a few seconds as his eyes slid over everyone, then finally landed on Mike. "Mr. Radley?"

"That's me."

"Great. Would you like me to bring this inside, or…?"

"No, you can just leave it right there, please." Mike wasn't expecting a package and was immediately suspicious.

"I mean, I can, but…" The delivery man looked around again. "Isn't this a wedding reception?"

"It's just a rehearsal dinner." Lily slid up beside Mike, her arm going around his waist. The succubus gave him a tight squeeze. "For two people who are very much in love, isn't that right, Mikey-bear?"

She pinched his cheek hard enough that he winced.

"Yeah, well, I might be having second thoughts." He moved toward the delivery man, who set the crate down. "Sent away for a new wife; this must be her. Hope she has enough air in there."

Lily laughed obnoxiously, and the delivery man just shrugged and held out his tablet for a signature. After getting one, he took his dolly and left, leaving Mike and Lily standing over the box. The party livened up again, but the random interloper had definitely put a damper on the mood.

"What did you buy me?" Lily asked, then ran her fingers over the wood. "I'm guessing it was expensive."

"I haven't bought anything. Tink or Beth must have ordered it." He made eye contact with Beth, who stood nearby with Sulyvahn.

"Wasn't me," she told him.

"Must have been Tink, then?" He looked at the packing label, but it didn't have a return address. "At least, I hope it was her." His luck with random packages on his doorstep wasn't great.

"Should we open it?" Lily asked, her tail appearing over her shoulder. It looked like she was going to wedge it into a gap in the wood when the crate shifted on its own. The party came to an abrupt stop as all eyes now rested on the mysterious delivery.

"I think we should definitely open it," Mike said, taking a step back. "But not inside. And definitely not without backup. Everyone, stand back." He held up his hands and walked in a circle. "I don't want anyone getting caught up in this. Yuki, where are you?"

"Here." The kitsune had been sitting up on the porch. She already had a pair of shimmering spheres of ice in her hand that were swirling around and forming into a pair of icy spikes.

"Abella, I need some—" The gargoyle landed behind him with a solid thump. "Muscle," he finished.

"I'm on it," she said, then grabbed the lid. Tink appeared with Kisa in tow, both of them looking very concerned.

"No time like the present," Mike muttered, then knocked on the crate. "You can come out with your hands up, or we can just set this thing on fire. Your choice."

Whatever was inside the crate thumped on it loudly. It sounded like Morse code for an SOS, so Mike nodded at Abella, who then sank her fingers into the wood and pulled.

A diaphanous white substance made a thick ripping sound as Abella lifted the lid, and her features went from confused to horrified. She immediately tried to force the lid back on, but whatever was inside was now fighting her, and the crate was bouncing around on the sidewalk.

"Kill it!" Abella cried, her eyes falling on Mike. "We have to kill it!"

Shrieks of panic went up from the partygoers. The centaurs, now expecting battle, rushed for whatever weapons they could find. The temperature in the air dropped as a large icicle formed over the crate, ready to drop at a moment's notice. Tink and Kisa grabbed Mike by the hands and pulled him away, but Lily was now at Abella's side as she was trying to force the lid shut again.

"Wait, what? Wait!" Lily's face went from serious to concerned as she suddenly fought against Abella, wedging her tail into the box. "Abella, stop!"

Abella shook her head vehemently, then used her wings to shove Lily to the side. Lily looked to Mike for help, her eyes pleading.

Mike ran up to the crate and put his hands on the other side. Whatever was rustling around inside was becoming frantic, and the wood creaked as Abella used her thumbs to press nails back into the wood.

"Mike?" This was from Yuki, who was waiting to drop the icicle. "What do you want me to do?"

"You don't understand," Abella growled. "The thing in this box, it is dangerous, more dangerous than you can ever know. We had these in France; they killed thousands of people."

Mike wanted to trust Abella, to let Yuki drop the icicle, but the look of panic on Lily's face gave him pause. He looked from Abella to Yuki, then back to Lily.

"This one is different," Lily promised. "You have to trust me."

Abella snorted, and Mike paused. He hadn't come as far as he had by making assumptions, and clearly whatever was in this box needed to get out. Abella wanted to kill it, Lily wanted to let it out, but the choice needed to be his.

He decided to follow his gut. Placing his fingers on the edge of the lid, he looked at Abella and shook his head.

"Help me open it," he told her. His words seemed to stun her, for her hands slipped off the lid, and it burst open from inside. A humanoid figure leaned over the edge of the side and coughed, then took a deep breath. It was a woman with dark, black hair that hung over her head, and she looked up to see everyone standing around her.

"Did I make it?" she asked in a tiny voice.

"You sure know how to make an entrance," Lily said from her spot on the ground. "Probably would have been better if you had called first."

Mike tried to step around to get a better look at her, but his hands were stuck to the lid by the sticky, silken material. When he pulled them away, he realized that the same material he had seen earlier now clung to his fingers, and his heart slammed in his chest once he realized what it was.

"If you'll make some room," said the newcomer, and she pulled herself out of the box. Her pale torso came easy, but where her butt should have been was a large, shiny black surface that kept coming out of the box. Mike felt his heart racing now as several legs appeared and stretched out, allowing the newcomer to stand and look around.

Cries of alarm came from multiple directions, and the stranger suddenly looked uncertain. Mike took a few steps back, fighting the panic that had taken root inside him. It was an old and common phobia, one that took him back to his own traumatic childhood that included weeks on end sleeping in the unfinished basements of distant relatives and old family friends.

"Eulalie?" Dana pushed her way through the centaurs, her eyes wide in astonishment. "Is that really you?"

"Uh…yeah." Eulalie drew herself up to her full height, now standing over Mike. "This was very…last minute, and…um…"

Dana ran up to Eulalie and embraced her tightly. "It's so good to see you!"

Mike took several deep breaths in an attempt to calm himself. His mind was struggling to reconcile what he was seeing, but somehow, Lily and Dana seemed to know who she was.

Dana released the newcomer, who now turned her attention back to the crowd.

"Hi. My name is Eulalie." She smiled nervously and gave everyone a wave. "Emily said I should come here if I ever got in trouble, so…here I am." From the waist up, Eulalie looked like she was in her midtwenties, with raven hair that covered most of her face and hung past her shoulders. Her dark eyes were like pools, and Mike was drowning in them already.

From the waist down, she had the glossy black body of a spider.

A CASE OF THE SHIVERS

T he group walked to the front door with Mike in the lead. The porch creaked under their collective weight as they gathered, and a gentle breeze caressed the nearby pillars. He reached for the front door, ready to allow Eulalie inside.

When his fingers touched the knob, he hesitated.

It wasn't because of his magic. One of his many gifts from Naia on inheriting the house was the ability to not only sense danger but also to somehow know when someone was a good fit for the house. He felt neither of these things right now but still couldn't put his hand on the knob and officially invite her inside.

Instead, his mind focused on the shiny chitin of her lower body, the rustling movement of her many legs, and the strange, rounded pads at the bottom that made soft scratching sounds when she walked. Spiders clearly didn't have needle-thin feet at the ends of their legs, but that was a fact he'd never expected to confront in such a wild manner.

Eulalie's body reminded him of the Andersons' basement. They had been friends of his father, and their basement had been far more comfortable than the back seat of his mother's station wagon long after he had died.

The Andersons never spent much time in their basement, which had worked out in his favor for a couple of weeks. However, it was thick with cobwebs his mother had dismissed, and not all the webs had been empty. In the middle of the night, he had wandered through a particularly thick web on the way to the bathroom. What he had thought was just a few sticky strands of web stuck to his face was revealed in the dim light of the bathroom to be a burst egg sac of baby spiders that scurried frantically all over his mouth and nose.

His screams had woken the whole house, causing his mother to berate him in front of their hosts for being such a pussy. He was only nine at the time, and when the Andersons kicked them out a week later, his mother had blamed him for it.

Standing at the door of the house, his skin was once more covered in those imaginary spiders. The others noticed his apprehension, most likely wondering if he had sensed something dangerous about their visitor. The moment was officially awkward, which was now compounding the situation.

Eulalie didn't seem to notice. She moved past him and opened the door herself. Once inside, she looked around and then turned to Mike with a grimace on her face. "Sorry to be pushy, but where's the bathroom?" She bit her lip and flexed her legs, doing a pathetic little dance in his front hallway. "I've been in that box a really long time, and even I have limits."

Dumbfounded, Mike pointed toward the hallway by the stairs. She shouldn't be able to come inside without his invitation. Had Emily invited her in at some point? "It's near the back door, you can't miss it." He didn't bother asking how she was going to fit on the toilet.

"Thanks!" She ran down the hallway, startling a cluster of rats who had been watching from the safety of the stairs. He heard the door slam, then turned to face Lily and Dana.

"Give me the very brief version," he spat at them. It wasn't so much that he was mad that they had withheld the information, but the shock of seeing a half-spider woman had thrown him off entirely. Now that Eulalie was out of sight, his heart felt like it was working properly again.

"Eulalie and her sister, Velvet, live out in Oregon," Dana said.

"With Bigfoot," Lily added. "And their father."

"Excuse me, did you say Bigfoot?" This was from Beth, who stood behind everyone with Sulyvahn. "Seriously? How tall is he? What about his, uh, hands?"

Sulyvahn laughed. Abella, who stood in the back, let out a grunt of disgust and jumped into the air with flapping wings. The yard was nearly empty now, save for a few centaurs who were moving about and cleaning up the celebration of spring.

"They're good people," Dana said. "Their father asked us not to tell you they were living there."

"Why?" Mike asked. "It's not like I was going to kick them out or anything."

"It isn't like they would know that," Lily told him. "And besides, there's another reason."

Dana tilted her head in curiosity, but Mike held up his hand for silence.

"Look, I get you thought you were doing the right thing," he said. "But what would have happened to her if neither one of you had been here? Abella would have killed her, and I wouldn't have known better."

Lily and Dana exchanged a look. He could see that Lily wanted to argue but knew that he was right. Dana, as always, was inscrutable.

"Well, good thing we were here, then," Lily responded. "So get over it." She pushed her way past him into the house. The others followed, but Tink paused before stepping through the door.

"Husband want Tink get club?" she asked. "Just in case?"

He ran his hand through her hair, then rubbed his thumb along one of her horns. She purred in delight and leaned into his thigh.

"It should be fine," he told her with a smile, his hands automatically supporting her. "But maybe keep the swearing down until she gets to know you."

"Fucking bug eater," Tink grumbled, then walked inside. "Tink no care what spider girl thinks."

Everyone had spread out in the living room. Tink joined Kisa on the couch with Jenny sitting between them, and Quetzalli held a food platter with one hand while using the other to stuff her face with pigs in a blanket. Cecilia hovered by the window, a look of concern on her face.

Realizing that everyone had decided to stay and watch him question the newcomer, he shooed them off while waving his hands. Tink grumbled as she stormed up the stairs with Kisa, and Cecilia simply vanished. Sofia grabbed Quetzalli's tray with a promise of more if she came to the kitchen, and the dragon followed her.

He didn't want Eulalie to feel like she was being put on trial, and was grateful when nobody complained. He did ask Beth and Dana to stay. Lily stood in the corner of the room because he knew better than to try to shoo her off, and he saw Jenny had tucked herself in a corner to watch. That, too, was also not a battle he was going to win, so he let her stay.

When the toilet flushed, Mike wondered how Eulalie had managed to go to the bathroom. Did she have a human butt? Or maybe she peed like people did? These were stupid questions to wonder about his guest, but his mind was much happier pondering these things until she stepped back into the hallway.

It was the legs. Each one was black and glossy, and they rustled when she moved. He wondered if she could walk along the wall or even the ceiling and if the plaster could sustain her weight. A cold chill went up his spine as she came out of the hallway. Once back in the living room, her whole body moved upward a foot now that she wasn't about to hit her head on the ceiling.

"That's so much better," Eulalie said, then looked at everyone. "I'm so sorry for showing up unannounced. I didn't have a choice."

"You should have called," Dana told her. "Or sent an email."

"I would have if I could." While Eulalie spoke, one of her legs lifted and stretched out. When it eventually settled back to the ground, another one lifted and went through the same routine. "But that was no longer an option."

"Apparently," Lily grumbled from her corner. "You fucking FedExed your-self across the country."

"It wasn't technically FedEx," she said, then assumed a weird squat that made it look like she was sitting. This put her at eye level with Mike, which gave him something to focus on other than her body. "But yes, I did cram myself in a box and mail myself here. An overachiever at the post office decided to be nice and put extra nails in the box, which meant I couldn't get out."

"What brings you here?" Mike asked, his voice squeaking a little.

"I don't know," Eulalie said, turning her focus on him. He could see his reflection in all the extra eyes on her forehead. "Wait, sorry, that came out wrong. I have good reasons for coming but am unsure of the root cause. My sister and I disagree on the severity of the situation. I believe that as Caretaker, you may hold the key to solving our dilemma."

"That's my job." His voice was steady this time. "Tell me everything."

"Thank you." She crossed her hands across her belly. "To begin with, my father, Darren, passed away over the winter."

Lily let out a noise like a squeak and left the room. Mike found this to be an odd reaction but kept his attention on Eulalie. Trying to figure out what was going on inside Lily's brain was a madman's game.

"I'm sorry to hear that," he said. "Was he, uh, like you?" He looked at her legs again.

"No, he was human," she said with a wistful smile. "And he was wonderful. The only reason I bring it up is because it relates to why I am here. Everything I'm about to tell you started shortly after his death. When he died, it was like a change had come over the forest. It seemed circumstantial at first, but a pattern started to emerge. My sister refused to see it, but my whole life is patterns, and she's just being stubborn."

"What do you mean by patterns?" asked Dana.

"There's a barrier around our home, much like your own," Eulalie said. "The former Caretaker Emily gave my mother permission to live there, where she would be safe from people hunting her. The magic that protects the place distracts and confuses anyone from entering who doesn't belong."

"We could use some of that here," Beth grumbled. "Maybe people would quit loitering in our yard."

"The magic isn't foolproof. Anyone determined can breach the barrier, or even just someone who gets really lost. My father used to patrol the boundary almost every day. He would occasionally find a lost hiker, or even a hunter who had tracked game into the area. Nothing too problematic."

"But after he died, no more patrols?" Mike asked.

Eulalie nodded. "For a time. My sister took them up, along with Uncle Foot. Sorry, Bigfoot."

"The *actual* Bigfoot?" Beth's eyes were shining with curiosity. "The real deal?"

"The one and only," Eulalie replied. "He also goes by Sasquatch, but don't call him a Yeti if you meet him. He's been living with my family since before I was born. It's why his sightings have been less frequent lately. Usually he would only leave to have meetings with other cryptids, or maybe he would get in a fight with my dad and leave to cool off."

"What the hell? What would your dad want to fight with Bigfoot about?" Beth was leaning forward so far that it looked like she may fall off her seat.

Eulalie chuckled. "One time, Bigfoot drank all my dad's whiskey. It was a special reserve he had managed to pick up on one of his trips, but Uncle Foot felt like getting tanked and drained the entire bottle in less than an hour. While Uncle Foot was passed out drunk, my dad got pissed and shaved a reverse mohawk from his forehead down his back. When he woke him, Dad told him if he was going to be a giant, hairy ass then he should look like one."

Beth let out a squeal of mirth, then waved her hand apologetically. "I'm sorry, I'm just excited is all."

Eulalie looked at Mike. "Bigfoot fan?"

Big something fan, he thought to himself. "What was happening on these patrols?" he asked, hoping to get back to the subject at hand. "And tell me about the patterns."

Eulalie's eyes narrowed. "At first glance, the patrols were fine. Nothing ever happened. But then a pattern of nothingness emerged. Even on patrol, you're bound to see some form of game. Like a bear or a deer. Or maybe you don't see the animal, but you do see signs that it was there. But there were no signs at all, as if something was chasing our prey away.

"Anyway, once I realized Velvet and Uncle Foot were coming back with less food than ever, I did something I haven't done in a while. I set some traps of my own. I don't usually bother myself with hunting, but a girl's gotta eat."

"With…" He gestured at her waist, the word now stuck in his mouth.

"Webs? Yes." She reached under her skirt with one hand and pulled out a white glob of fluid that balanced perfectly on her middle finger. With a few deft movements, she created a cat's cradle, then shifted it around again so that the ensuing web looked like a butterfly. "Unlike my sister, my strengths lie in web building." She looked around, then awkwardly crumpled the web and shoved it in her mouth.

"Thorry," she muttered. "Not thpothed ta wipe it on clothes."

Mike just stared at her, his mouth hanging open.

"What did you catch in the traps?" asked Dana.

"Some small game," Eulalie replied. "Not enough for a proper meal, but arachne can go without for some time if we have to. Now, a lack of game is one thing, but it was too perfect. What really caught my attention was when I discovered that something had taken down my bigger traps. It isn't all just webs, mind you. I incorporate the environment into them. Some of my traps had been sprung, but it looked like the animals had been removed. Other times, I discovered that the trap had been taken down entirely, which doesn't make any sense. Not only are they difficult to spot, but some of these were high up in the trees. Someone would have to climb fifteen feet just to take them down.

"Therefore, this pattern of nothingness isn't natural. Something is chasing away our food, but for what purpose?"

"Interesting." Mike pondered this information and stared at the floor. "There's nothing else in the forest with you guys?"

"Not anymore," she replied. "We had a huge goblin problem some years back—"

"Goblins?" His head snapped up. "You had goblins?"

"Yes. They took up residence in one of the cave systems, kept breaking into our barn and causing problems." She waved a hand dismissively. "That is a problem we took care of years ago. Even if they had somehow survived this long, they would be too stupid to evade my traps."

Mike nodded. Tink was a genius in many ways, but he had been assured by Naia that her intelligence was off the goblin species chart entirely. "So something is taking down your traps and chasing off your food."

"I see it like a chess match. Our pieces were being eliminated before we even knew the game had started. I'm here to get some new pieces to come and help us."

At the mention of chess, Mike couldn't help but throw a dirty look at Jenny. Checkers was one of the few games he would still play with her. The doll gave him a little wave and pushed herself farther into her corner.

"And Velvet disagreed?" Dana asked. "Doesn't seem like her."

Eulalie nodded solemnly. "She's really struggled with everything since Dad died. When I brought it up, I got lectured on being self-sufficient and how we didn't deserve to live if we couldn't do things for ourselves, blah, blah, blah. And Uncle Foot took her side because he promised Dad he would take care of us."

"So why didn't you just call?" Dana shook her head. "Or email, text, whatever. It's not like you're cut off from civilization."

"Oh?" Mike asked. He wondered what sort of technology the cabin in Oregon had. If anything, he bet it had a rotary phone.

"By the time I thought about contacting you, we actually had been cut off. Completely." Eulalie sighed. "The very same day I realized my traps were tampered with, I came home to discover that the fiber line we had run to our home had been severed and carried off. And cell service has always been spotty at best, but now it just doesn't exist out there anymore, almost like it's being blocked. Whatever is out there was watching me and making moves of its own. Velvet and I got in a huge fight over it, and I told her I was leaving to get help."

"Why didn't Bigfoot bring you?" he asked. He knew Bigfoot could move between trees using magic portals, but wasn't entirely certain of the mechanism.

"This house was cut off years ago, but we had no idea why. Having Bigfoot and a giant spider wandering the neighborhood trying to find this place would be a terrible idea. There isn't anywhere nearby we could just jump to. He needs certain trees when he travels." Eulalie chuckled. "So he helped box me up and dropped me off at a shipping office in Kentucky. There are still plenty of trees there for him to sneak around in."

"Seems like he could have come a lot closer," Beth said with a frown. "If it's trees he needs, anyway."

"Oh, he hates coming out east," Eulalie said. "And don't bother asking me why. Anytime I ask him about it, he furrows his head up and looks like a gorilla trying to force a monster shit out." Her cheeks flushed, and she covered her mouth. "Oh, I'm so sorry!"

"Don't worry about it," Mike reassured her. "Our swear jar is full anyway; it's how we fund this place. It's a goblin problem of our own."

"Thank you, I—" Eulalie froze as Death entered the room carrying a teapot in one hand and a View-Master toy held to his face. His bony fingers were long enough that he could casually flick the lever that changed the image inside. He did this as he walked past, the View-Master letting out a hushed click as he chortled in glee.

"Can you see what he has?" Mike asked Beth.

"On it." She stood and followed Death into the dining room.

"Was that a ghost?" asked Eulalie in awe. "That teacup was just hovering. It was so wild!"

"That's…complicated." He heard Death protesting loudly, and Beth came out of the dining room with the slide reel in her hand. She handed the slide to Mike, who held it up to the light.

"I will have you know, Mike Radley, that I paid mistress Tink the sum of twenty dollars for that slide," Death announced as he walked back into the room. "By the laws of state and local commerce, that item rightfully belongs to me."

He focused his eyes on one image at a time and let out a laugh. The pictures were all of Tink in various states of undress, though a few of the pictures were just downright goofy. In one of them, she was wearing a pair of Mike's boxers on her head with her nose sticking out of the fly.

"Mistress Tink?" he asked. "Since when do you call her mistress?"

"Transference of titles is another valid form of currency, Mike Radley." Death held out his hand expectantly. "Now please return my property."

"Yeah, sure." He extended his hand out, but Beth snatched it away from him.

"Where did you get twenty dollars?" Beth asked.

"Who are you guys talking to?" Eulalie asked in a whisper.

"Just a sec," Mike replied, curious to hear Death's answer.

"I found it," Death replied in an indignant tone.

"Where?" Beth asked.

The grim reaper scowled at her, the tiny flames in his eyes brightening. "In your bedroom," he replied. "On the floor. Unattended."

"That was my twenty dollars," Beth informed him with a scowl. "I keep cash in my purse for emergencies. It must have fallen out. Though I'm not sure how, because I never go anywhere."

"Aha!" He held up a bony finger. "Per the rules of finders keepers, that money belongs to anyone who finds it when nobody else is nearby."

Beth squinted at him. "Finders keepers isn't a valid law. But if it were, it certainly does not apply while inside a domicile. Otherwise, I could go into the office and claim your maps or your teacups whenever I wanted as long as you weren't around."

Death raised a hand to make a counterpoint but faltered. "Hmm. Perhaps I misunderstood the full tenets of finders keepers, and I see that I have made an egregious mistake," he admitted. "In effect, those pictures now belong to you. Please accept my apologies. I would be happy to loan you my View-Master should you wish to view them."

"Ugh, no thanks. Here." Beth handed the disc over. "You can have it back. But no more taking money from my room."

Death took the disc from her and deftly slid it into place as he rushed out of the room toward the kitchen.

"And I want my own title!" Beth shouted after him. "Make it something good!"

"Are you guys arguing with a poltergeist?" Eulalie asked.

"That's just Death," Dana replied. "Try not to let him walk through you. It feels awful."

"Wow," she whispered with shimmering eyes. "I always wondered what it would be like here but never imagined it would be this busy! Emily invited Velvet and me when we were little and told us about some of the people who lived here, but I kind of forgot about them until I saw them out front. The banshee is pretty, can't believe I forgot about her."

Beth nodded. "That would be the geas," she said. "It alters memories when the old Caretaker dies."

Eulalie sighed, then looked at Mike. Her eyes glittered under the lights of the living room. "This is so interesting, and I wish I were here under different circumstances, I really do. I often dreamed of coming here and getting to know all these different people, and maybe even being allowed to stay. But we need help. This is a lot to ask, but would you come to Oregon and see if you can help us? We just want somewhere to live in peace, I promise."

Mike nodded. The land was his, and therefore, so was the responsibility. "We can head out in the morning," he told her. "We don't have a Bigfoot, but we do have some tricks of our own. You lead me to the cabin and I'll see what I can do."

"Thank you so much, I—" She opened her mouth to say something else, but her stomach growled. Wincing, she put her hands on it. "It's been a while, sorry."

"C'mon," Beth said, then took Eulalie by the hand. "Let's see if we have anything for you to eat, then we can figure out what to do next."

Mike watched them go, then let out a breath he didn't know he had been holding. Once he was certain Eulalie couldn't see him, he shuddered. Even though Eulalie seemed nice, he couldn't look at her legs without feeling baby spiders all over his face. He felt bad and promised himself he would do his best to get over it.

UP ON THE ROOF, ABELLA GAZED BALEFULLY ACROSS THE YARD. THE PARTY HAD long since wrapped up, and though she was watching for signs of movement, it was the conversation inside the house that she was listening to.

She could hear it in his voice. A slight hitch here and there, or a quick clearing of the throat. Mike was nervous about this Eulalie character, and for good reason. The arachne were dangerous, and if she had her way, she would have held that crate shut until someone set the damn thing on fire.

Footsteps on the roof alerted Abella that someone had joined her. It was Kisa; she recognized her soft footfalls. The cat girl sat next to Abella and pulled her knees up to her chin.

"You never sit with me," Abella noted. The roof of the home was big enough that they rarely even saw each other. In fact, if Kisa held still for long enough, Abella couldn't even hear her breathing or see where she was. It was some type of magical invisibility that made people forget she was there.

Kisa's ears flattened, and she let out a low growl. "Sorry," she mumbled. "That one kind of slipped out because I'm all worked up. Can I tell you something?"

"I suppose."

"That thing down there gives me the shivers." Illustrating her point, Kisa's spine stiffened, and she shook her head. "Like, holy shit. I've never seen a spider up close before, but her whole body is just…damn."

Abella nodded. "Have you ever wondered why humans have such a reaction to spiders?"

Kisa shifted forward, her tail moving around erratically.

"Can't say I have," she muttered. "Don't really stare at spooky shit and wonder why it's so spooky."

"It's primal. You fear things that are different, but it goes even deeper with arachnids. It's not just that they have eight legs and too many mouth parts. Your ancestors were hunted by them relentlessly. They could wipe out entire villages overnight if they wanted to, and only those who had a healthy dose of fear survived to pass the tales along. It's no different from your fear of the dark."

"You're saying that people are afraid of spiders because of the arachne?"

Abella nodded. "Think about the things humans are afraid of. Some are logical, like falling. Public speaking is bad. But why are spiders so high up on the list? Most of them are harmless."

"Hmm." Kisa surveyed the yard while toying with a bracelet on her wrist. It was a pretty yellow band that matched a similar one Tink sometimes wore. "It's kind of weird, but I'm half a cat because I wore a cursed collar to fix my shattered legs. I'm not really in a position to argue."

"Do you know what hunts man?"

"Tigers. Sharks. Taxes." Kisa smirked at her own joke.

"Do you know what hunts the arachne?"

"Really big fly swatters?"

Abella snorted in disgust. "The answer is nothing. No being in their right mind willingly hunts them for food. If this is just silly for you, I'd prefer you go someplace else to sulk."

"You really hate them, don't you?" Kisa looked at Abella expectantly.

Abella pursed her lips and nodded. "More than anything."

She spread her wings and leaped from the roof, soaring over the yard and then circling higher when she reached the edge of the geas. Down below, the yard had come to life with fairies, insects, and lightning bugs. Their chorus reached Abella's ears but brought her no joy as she attempted to reach the clouds.

How could Mike trust Eulalie so quickly? Despite Lily's assurance that the arachne was safe, what if she tried to mate with him? It was instant death to mate with the arachne, and Abella would die before allowing Eulalie to make a move on Mike.

She wanted to punch something or someone, but her options here were limited. To correct the issue, she flew outside the geas. The magic was like a leash once she passed its boundary. It compelled her to return, but she could resist for a while. The sky had taken on the azure hue of twilight, and she wasn't worried about being spotted.

While soaring over a nearby park, she caught sight of a group of teens down by the edge of the lake. They were laughing while throwing rocks at a pair of ducks that were out on the water. About fifty feet behind them was a large stone monument dedicated to the park, where they had leaned their bicycles.

With a grin, she landed nearby on the soft ground and wrapped her arms around the monument. She used her tail and talons to keep from sinking too far into the ground while she carefully lifted the conical monument into the air. As long as she didn't tilt it from side to side, it should remain structurally sound.

Once it was free of the soil, she wiggled her fingers down its cool sides until she could get her hands beneath the bottom and then lifted. The monument went into the air high enough that the bikes fell into the gap it had left. With a smirk, she set the monument down on top of them.

The bikes creaked as they bent and became pinned. Only their mangled wheels remained visible. Should they ever be removed, the bikes would be completely unusable.

With a chuckle, she used her tail to wipe away her footprints and then lifted into the sky. Other than the laughing teens, the park was abandoned, and she wasn't too worried about being spotted. She wished she could see their faces. Dishing out petty justice hadn't made her feel much better, but it was a start.

She flew toward downtown and found one of her favorite perches on a local church. After folding her wings about herself like a cloak, she pressed herself against the stone facade and shifted the color of her skin to match. From here, she could watch people moving about the city without fear of being seen.

The pull of the house was growing stronger, but her anger made it easy to stay away. At some point, the compulsion would be too much, and she would have to take to the sky to protect the home once again.

No, that wasn't correct. She would fly home to protect *him*.

She could still picture the day she had met Mike, how she had listened in panic to his screams for help. The Mandragora hadn't been fed in forever, and it had been trying to consume him. Her limbs had been stiff, and she had fought to wake up and rescue him.

He had seemed so helpless in that moment but had accepted her without any fear. It had been that way with all the Caretakers, an immediate kinship they felt with the monsters of the house. But Mike had been different. He had been just as enamored with her as she had been with him, and she couldn't wait to feel his soft flesh against her fingertips.

She imagined humans felt the same way about plush dolls as she did about them. They were so fragile and cute she simply couldn't help it. This was a feeling the others of her clan had never shared, which was the main reason she was even here.

Pierre was the other.

Moving along the edge of the church steeple, she paused when she saw the gargoyle that had been built on the corner. It was like a devil, with large horns and fangs. The stone was new, maybe only a decade old.

Had it really been so long since she was here last? Time was an interesting construct for her. Her kind were capable of being still for months or even years if they wanted. It was like hibernation, and they would only awaken if threatened. The last time she had come here was after a fight with Emily, but she couldn't remember what the argument had been about. The protective geas had no problem altering someone's memories and always did so when Caretakers changed.

At the time, she had been contemplating leaving the house because of something Emily had done. Still angry after arguing with her, Abella had come here to blow off some steam, ultimately deciding the house was still her safest bet for survival.

She crouched along the edge, her eyes and ears on the people down below. A pair of women walked along the sidewalk, laughing at each other while they held hands. When she closed her eyes, the images came unbidden.

The French city of Marseille was sprawled out beneath her. The faint light of distant torches twinkled like fireflies, but her attention was squarely focused on the couple walking on the path beneath her.

They had met earlier, a nobleman and a young woman who lived down near the docks. If not for the class disparity, she wouldn't have paid them much attention, but the way he had spoken to her was far too familiar.

The man left after a brief discussion about the baked goods being sold in a nearby cart, but the woman took her sweet time picking out bread before leaving. Abella had waited and been amply rewarded when the commoner met the noble in an alley next to a cobbler's shop. The two had embraced like lost lovers, only to be chased away by a stumbling drunk.

It had been easy to follow them. The night was dark, and there weren't many people out. Abella had moved along the building tops, making sure to keep the couple in view. The man led the woman to an isolated garden where they found a stone bench to sit on.

Abella gripped the edge of the roof she was on in anticipation, her fingers crushing the brick into powder that scattered on the breeze. The man sat on the edge of the bench and the woman on his lap with her back to him. He playfully grabbed her breasts through the thick fabric of her dress while licking her neck.

"C'mon, c'mon," Abella muttered, then licked her lips. It was very rare to get the opportunity to watch humans fuck, and it was usually through a window, or with the view blocked by awnings. The woman was grinding her ass on the man's lap, and Abella could hear both their hearts thumping from where she sat.

The man ran his fingers through the woman's hair. Abella mimicked the move with her own hands, wondering how it felt to him. Her hair, being made of stone, was stiff and fairly unyielding. She had touched human hair before but only on corpses. Humans were very squishy by nature, but their hair fascinated her most of all. What would it feel like to run her fingers through the thick locks of a woman? Or even a man?

As she shivered in delight, her tail moved of its own accord and thumped on the stone of the building. Down below, the woman paused for a moment, her wide eyes scanning the area.

"Did you hear something?" she asked in French.

"I only have ears for you," he replied, then spun her around in his lap. He undid the laces of her dress to free her breasts and nibbled the pale flesh around her nipples. "Let me taste you," he muttered.

She acquiesced, her head tilting back. This gave Abella a phenomenal view, and she brought her tail around to put her foot on the tip. The last thing she wanted was to get so excited that she scared them off.

The woman was making noises that reminded Abella of a cat. They were gasps of joy and pleasure. Abella squeezed her own breasts out of curiosity, then frowned. It definitely didn't feel as good for her as it did the woman below.

The man was now fumbling with his belt, and the woman was doing something beneath her skirt. Clothing fascinated Abella, and she watched as the two of them shifted about for a moment before coming to a halt. They both let out moans of pleasure.

"Holy shit," she muttered. He was definitely inside her now, and the woman had arched her back. This wasn't just some chance meeting for either of them. Was she a servant of his? Or perhaps a secret mistress? Abella could see the ring on the man's finger. Marriage customs among humans were very quaint but not always honored.

So a forbidden romance, then? Maybe he was forced to marry for land or wealth, and the woman was a childhood love of his. Perhaps they had been in love this entire time, their whole relationship forced into seclusion. That would make this tryst even more precious, more passionate.

Abella gasped at the sudden sensation in her pelvis. Her hand had moved on its own down to her groin, and she stroked her stiff labia with the knuckles of her fingers.

The woman dismounted, then moved so that she was bent over the bench. The man moved to penetrate her from behind, and as he pressed forward, they both let out cries that sounded like startled birds.

Groaning, Abella bit down onto the wall to keep from making any noise. Her teeth ground against the fine stone, and she let out a grunt as she worked one of her fingers into her triangular vagina. Designed for laying eggs, it was easily stretched, which meant a single finger wouldn't do.

She was up to four fingers when the man pulled himself out of the woman. His cock was hard to see in the darkness, but she could make out glistening fluid on the head of it that reflected the distant lights. The lovers shifted about so that the woman could take his cock down her throat, and Abella could hear her groan and swallow as the man came.

Abella was close to an orgasm of her own and was strongly contemplating using the thick tip of her tail as a cock substitute when she heard the ominous creak of stone wings up above her. She groaned in disgust as another creature landed on the building behind her, then licked her fingers clean before turning around.

"Peeping on the humans again, I see." Her brother Pierre smirked at her. "Aren't you supposed to be scouting right now, runt?"

She snorted at him. "You know I would have finished my task before indulging my fancies."

Pierre shrugged, a movement that sent a ripple through the massive muscles of his chest. Out of all her siblings, he was by far the largest. Only a couple of men in the clan were larger than him: their leader, Torsten, and Seneca, their shaman.

"I would expect no less of you," he said with a grin that showed all his fangs. The large

horns on his head curled downward like a ram's, and he moved to join her on the edge of the building. "Don't these fleshlings know there's a plague?"

"It's about passion, Pierre. They're in love." She spoke to her brother in whispers that couldn't be heard by humans from ten feet away, much less the top of a building. "Look at how he pines for her."

Pierre grunted. "If he pines for her, then why does he leave her before she finishes adjusting her dress?"

Abella watched in dismay as the nobleman threw some coin down for the woman and wandered off into the night. The woman tucked the money in the folds of her skirt and spent a couple of minutes rearranging her clothes before she left the garden. Gone was the illusion of love and passion, and the whole interaction now felt tainted.

"Hmmf." Pierre snorted in disgust. "They can't even breed properly. He has given her money for what? Access to her loins? Disgusting."

"They breed for fun," she explained, then stood to her full height. She was a whole head shorter than him. "And it is the oldest profession in the world for a reason. Do you think she deserves shame if she earned some coin to feed her family?"

"Breeding creates more of them," he grunted. "She may have earned some coin, but what now? Will that coin feed the child that is born next summer? The humans are foolish, and I wish your fascination with them would wither like a flower in the fall."

Abella said nothing. Any argument she had with him here would only continue once they were back, and some of her other siblings would likely join in.

"That's what I thought," he muttered. "Come home, Abella." He opened his wings and leaped into the sky. She watched him ascend and then looked back down at the gardens below.

"Fuck," she muttered, then opened her wings to follow. Pierre was dozens of feet above her as she flapped her wings, and she was almost fifty feet above the garden when she heard the clattering of metal followed by a scream that was cut off.

Curious, she widened her ascent and looked down onto the cobblestone road below. Near the edge of the alleyway, she could hear the ringing of metal as a solitary coin rolled across the street and struck a stone before coming to a halt.

Instead of ascending, she hovered up above, moving her head back and forth in the hopes of catching another sound. The streets below were silent.

As she turned her head to look away, she spotted movement out of the corner of her eye along one of the nearby rooftops. The dark figure scurried across the roof with the woman slung over its shoulder, then leaped a thirty-foot gap onto another roof.

"Pierre?" She looked up at her brother, who was watching her. He had a look of confusion on his face.

She followed the mysterious creature. It rustled when it moved, and there wasn't enough light to see what it was. Perhaps a vampire? It had been a while since Abella had even heard of one actively hunting. There had been a clan in Eastern Europe that had gone head-to-head with one, and only a couple of them had lived to tell the tale. Usually if a creature like that was discovered, the clan would initiate contact to avoid a potential misunderstanding. There was plenty of room for everyone as long as the humans didn't cause trouble.

And if they did, the clan would see fit to set things right. She dreaded the day she would be commanded to kill a human, but she would do it to protect her family from destruction.

The figure jumped off a nearby roof and landed in the street, its body momentarily illuminated by a lantern that hung over the road.

Abella nearly fell out of the sky, and Pierre swore under his breath. The creature below had the legs and abdomen of an arachnid.

"Pierre?" she asked, her eyes wide. When she looked over at her brother, his face had become a mask of anger.

"We need to follow it," he said, his tone serious. "If it's passing through, then we'll let it go. But if it's part of a nest…"

He didn't have to finish. An arachne nest could wipe out a city in a matter of months, which would bring the men in white. Monster hunting would begin anew, and her kind would see their heads mounted on buildings once more.

Down below, a man sneezed. The sound brought Abella back to the present, and she lowered her gaze to follow his movements. He was an older man in a white trench coat, and his footsteps were nearly silent. Though he was just some late-night churchgoer, she couldn't help but be reminded of the men who had hunted her kind through the centuries.

"Baiseurs," she muttered. If the Order found out that the house was harboring an arachne, they would waste no time laying siege to the place. The society had been bad enough, but a worldwide organization devoted to maintaining order and hunting monsters was an entirely different problem.

She turned to look at the gargoyle next to her. It loomed over the ground below, its expression haughty. In truth, it was much closer to a generic demon in appearance than one of her own kind, but it was merely a poor derivation of real events that had occurred centuries ago. A clan had gone rogue and started hunting humans for sport. As a result, the Order had arrived and slain them all.

And now? The true name and purpose of the gargoyles had been lost to history. Now they were nothing more than a silly fairy tale that carried no weight, a creature to be placed on buildings for birds to shit on. They had become the garden gnomes of buildings.

With a glance, Abella confirmed that nobody was down below. Snarling, she gave the statue a shove, which ripped it free of the building. With little effort, she cast it over the edge and then moved along the side of the building so she wouldn't be spotted. The sound of the statue shattering brought a smile to her face. She had broken the last one nearly fifteen years ago. Maybe the church would spend its hard-earned money on feeding the poor instead of stupid decorations this time.

If not, she'd be back eventually. From her new vantage point, she watched the police arrive. A small crowd formed, including the man in the white coat she had seen earlier. His face was pockmarked in scars, and he stood with his hands casually in his pockets. Maybe he was a wealthy patron of the church, now worried that his donation would go to renovations instead of actually helping people.

But that was rarely the way of things. Most humans would rather buy their way into heaven than earn it. For the first time in her life, Abella wished that Lily were nearby. The two of them would have a good chuckle over this.

She fought the pull of the house for a couple more hours. It was now late at night, and the crowd had dispersed. Other than a couple of people who crossed the police tape to grab souvenirs, she hadn't seen anyone in almost an hour.

Once back in the sky, the house attracted her like a beacon. What could have been a leisurely glide became a frantic push. Her gut filled with terror, and her mind was flooded with anxiety. What if something had happened while she was gone? What if the society had returned? Maybe Eulalie had attacked Mike! Her wings pumped hard and fast, and the feelings vanished immediately upon crossing the boundary of the geas.

From up above, the house was quiet. A couple of lights were on, and she landed on the roof in a crouch, her gaze once more on the street. A couple of centaurs milled about in the darkness. She realized they were carrying spears, but they seemed to be relaxed. Basic guard duty.

Inside the house, Mike was talking to someone. She leaned over the edge to hear him better, then let out a groan.

"Oh, Mike," she muttered in dismay. What was she going to do with him?

MIKE STOOD OVER HIS DESK WITH A MAP OF OREGON LAID OUT. A RED outline had been drawn on it, and Reggie stood near the edge with his paws splayed out.

"I believe we can get you to here," he told Mike while tapping on the map with a claw. "My intel says there are some abandoned cabins we can chew our way to, but we need to verify before we make you a big enough portal to go through."

"Hmm." He leaned over the map and let out a sigh. "I guess get us as close to the boundary as you can. Nobody should be waiting for us, but if they're watching, they will come."

Lily, who sat across from him, shook her head. "I don't see why you have to go," she told him with no small amount of anger in her voice. "Literally anyone else can go. Amir is still out there, and it bothers me that we haven't heard from him. If he's put any sort of force together, he is watching for you to leave the house."

"I know. But even if he is, he won't be able to force his way through. Based on Eulalie's explanation, only people who become seriously lost ever slipped through. Never anyone with a purpose. What do you think?" He addressed his question to a crystal ball on the desk. Inside the ball, he could see Ratu reclining on an ornamental chair.

"I agree with this assessment," she declared. "The geas here lets people onto the land, but they can't see the truth of things. I attempted to scry the location earlier, and it is practically unreadable. In fact, that map of the boundaries you have is insufficient. Much like the greenhouse, the land itself is bigger on the inside. Even if Amir could track you to Oregon, he couldn't track you directly."

The succubus scowled. "But what about here? Once he knows you're gone, what's to stop him from dropping by and storming the place?"

Mike looked at Ratu, then back at Lily. "We actually have options, but that's going to depend largely on you. Ratu, do you want to explain?"

"No." The naga lifted a cup of tea to her lips. "She needs to hear it from you, not me."

He frowned, then looked at Lily. "This is actually something Ratu and I have been working on for a while. Ever since the whole Underworld incident, we've been working on different ways to keep the society guessing, and we think we have a solution."

With a natural pause, he hoped Ratu would take over. She did not.

"So," he continued, "Ratu got the idea from a magic bag of marbles. I'm...not even qualified to try to explain the theory behind them. Apparently, she has found a way to make it look like I'm in two places at once."

"And that involves me." Kisa spoke up from the corner of the room, which caused Lily to jump.

"Fucking sneaky-ass kitty cat," the succubus swore, placing a hand over her heart. "I forgot you were there."

Kisa stuck out her tongue in response.

"Kisa is my familiar," Mike explained. "We aren't entirely certain what that entails—"

"Other than constant fucking," Lily added.

"Once you go cat, all others fall flat," muttered Kisa, her tail twitching.

"But what it means," Mike interrupted with a raised voice, "is that Kisa now has a soul signature similar to my own. That's actually a by-product of the, um…"

"Constant fucking." This came from Reggie, who nodded sagely. "A beneficial side effect of maintaining your harem."

"They're not my harem. Please, everyone, stop interrupting." Mike noticed Ratu was laughing into her sleeve. "And you're not helping."

"I'm not buying it. A similar signature doesn't mean shit." The succubus crossed her arms. "You aren't selling me on this idea."

"Similar won't do the trick, but this will." He opened the top drawer of his desk and pulled out a silver band. "Ratu has enchanted this bracelet to amplify the signature. We tested it a few times, and it seems to work."

"It almost works," Ratu added. "Amir cannot scry within the geas. At best, he will be able to see that Mike is in two places at once as long as he is on his own property."

"Which means he will need visual confirmation," Lily said, realization dawning on her face. "So if he comes around…"

"Then we need someone who can look like me," Mike finished. "What do you say? Wanna play dress-up for a bit? You can even boss everyone around and put on a good show."

"There's still a hole in this," Lily told him. "If they're watching the house, then they'll notice the sundial isn't being turned."

"Tink is already on it. She is making a replica of the dial top that rotates. You will have to go out every day at a certain time and spin it."

"And a simple, nonviolent scanning spell will reveal I'm not you."

"Unless I'm with you." Kisa now stood in front of Lily. "Which they might not notice. Going unnoticed is my thing."

Lily looked down at Kisa, then up at Mike. "You really thought this through, didn't you?"

He laughed. "It's not like I've just been sitting around doing nothing. Especially with Sarah roaming about. Protecting this place is my number one job."

The soul of Sarah the witch had been trapped inside a necklace after she had died trying to kill him in the greenhouse. During last year's siege, it had been recovered by Sarah's mother, Elizabeth. Nobody had any clue what happened afterward. It was possible that Sarah had learned her lesson and would be content being a proper cunt somewhere else entirely, but even he doubted that.

"So then why go?" Lily asked. "If protecting this place is your number one job, why not send someone else?"

Mike looked at the others, then wandered over to the window. Out in the yard, he could see the fairy lights sparkling in the garden. Centaurs moved around the perimeter, making sure to give the Jabberwock a wide berth.

"Two reasons. The first is that I've noticed the geas here isn't working properly either." He thought about all the people who had wandered into his yard recently, but that wasn't what bothered him. "Yesterday, someone tagged this place on Instagram. The Radley estate, they called it. Cecilia was in the picture. She looked like a regular person, but that's just it. People used to come here and not see any of you at all. You were invisible. But now? It isn't the case. The neighbors could hear us last night, and that was hardly the noisiest we've ever been. I need to know why it isn't working properly, and the fact that a similar effect is happening in Oregon may be a clue. As the Caretaker, this is my problem to fix."

Lily let out a grunt. "I guess that's valid. But maybe the problem is here and leaving is the wrong thing to do."

"That brings me to the second point." He turned to face the room. "It's a feeling. I actually feel something drawing me to Oregon. I hadn't thought about it really until Eulalie brought it up. That time I went to the fae realm, we went through Ireland, remember? I could feel the property I own out there calling to me but forgot about it. What if there's something I'm supposed to do? We've all just assumed that I take over caring for this place, but what if there's something else? Kind of like the sundial. Maybe the geas itself needs to be reset? I don't know."

"What did Naia say?"

"She didn't have an answer. In fact, she went blank when I asked, and we know what that means."

Lily nodded. "The geas is protecting the answer."

"You got it. So this is what needs to be done. Tomorrow, I'm planning on going to Oregon, but this all hinges on your willingness to stay here and pretend to be me."

"You aren't going to just tell me to do it?" She flipped her hair defiantly. "I may just tell you no."

He smiled at her, then walked around the desk until they were only a couple inches apart. The smirk on her face melted when he touched her cheek.

"And that would be okay," he said. "We would figure something else out."

Her lips parted as she stared into his eyes. It looked like she was going to say something, so he waited.

Lily grinned, and she reached out and pinched his nipple through his shirt.

"Ow, fuck!" He swatted her hand away and covered his chest.

"I'll do it," she told him. "But I plan to be a huge fucking diva about it. And you'll owe me. Big."

"I expect nothing less," he said with a laugh. "King Reggie? Have your people make the necessary plans. With any luck, Bigfoot can help us set up a portal of our own to come back, so we won't have to risk the safety of your crew."

"It shall be done." The rat king gave Mike a salute, which caused his crown to fall off his head. He picked it up in his teeth and leaped down from the table. As he left the room, Beth walked in with a concerned look on her face.

"Mike? I need you to come with me."

"What's wrong?"

"It's Eulalie." Beth's brow was furrowed, and her voice contained a hint of panic. "There's something wrong with her."

Concerned, he followed Beth out to the garage. Dana had invited Eulalie to stay in her room beneath the garage, which had been an old oil pit that had been turned into a room. Dana stood in the middle of the room, her focus on Eulalie, who sat in the corner. A small web had been built as a supportive hammock, and Eulalie had gone limp inside it.

"Eulalie?" He moved close to the web but stayed back. Her eyes fluttered open at her name, and she let out an exasperated sigh.

"I'm sorry, Mike, but I won't be able to lead you to the cabin." She sat forward, her arms resting on the webs.

"Are you sick?" he asked.

"Worse," she replied. "I'm getting ready to molt."

He shuddered in revulsion. There was no hiding his reaction this time.

"Can we wait a day or two?" Beth asked. "Until you're done?"

"It's going to take way longer than that," Eulalie replied. "Nearly a month."

"A month?" Mike was incredulous.

Eulalie nodded. "A month of discomfort and feeling bloated, followed by my exoskeleton cracking and falling apart as the tissue beneath expands. It isn't a pleasant process to watch, and I will be extremely vulnerable to injury that whole time and become a liability. I thought I had more time, but packing myself up in a box and being sedentary may have triggered it."

"It's okay." Dana moved toward Eulalie and took her hand. "We'll figure something out."

Eulalie looked at Mike, her eyes imploring. "None of this worked out like I thought it would, and now I'm a huge imposition. This fucking sucks…sorry."

"The jar is full already," he reminded her.

"I just…will you please go help my sister? I'll do anything."

"Eulalie." He kept his eyes up as he approached, trying to avoid looking below her waist. When he held out his hand, she took it. At once, he realized that her skin was covered in extremely fine hairs he hadn't noticed before. Marveling at how soft her fingertips were, he gave her a confident smile. "Don't worry. We'll take care of everything. And you are welcome here as long as you like."

"Thank you," she said, then leaned forward and hugged him. Her arms were surprisingly strong.

Velvet was crouched up in the tree, her legs splayed out among the branches. She was careful not to jostle them, afraid that she would knock free some of the ice that had accumulated there.

A young buck had wandered into the glade and was almost beneath her tree. It had been a little while since her last proper meal, and her stomach felt tight with hunger. She had been extra hungry recently and had no idea why.

Probably a perk of getting old, she thought to herself. Nobody knew how arachne morphology worked anymore, and she wondered how many molts she had left until she became old over a matter of weeks, just like her mother had.

At least it would happen to Eulalie first. Then the two of them could figure out if they got aches and pains like people did. True, one of her leg joints squished when it was cold out, but that was because she had injured it a couple years back and it hadn't healed straight. It would be right as rain eventually, but it was still annoying.

When the buck was beneath her, she dropped down out of the tree and tackled it to the ground. It let out a cry of alarm, but she snapped its neck with her powerful arms before it could fight back. She bit its neck in a few places, her digestive enzymes and venom now being pumped through its circulatory system. The venom would help the creature relax in its final moments, and the enzymes would soften it up for consumption later.

She slung the buck over her shoulders and waited for Emery to fly over from his secret perch. The imp landed on the animal's head and rested on its stubby antlers.

It was a few miles through dense forest, but she traversed it with ease. The woods were eerily silent, which wasn't abnormal whenever she was out for a hunt. They could sense the predator moving among them, but it was more than just animals hiding.

The forest itself felt afraid. It was a stupid idea to have, but even when she hunted, she could still hear the river, or feel the wind currents as they blew through the trees. Everything had gone absolutely still, the whole world silent except for the soft padding of her feet on snow.

"I don't like this," Emery muttered from his perch. "I feel like something is wrong."

She nodded her agreement. "I'm moving as fast as I can. Seems like game is getting harder to come by. At least this one wasn't all the way by the barrier."

"There was something off about that bear," Emery added. "I wish you hadn't eaten him."

"Well, it didn't kill me, so your wish is wasted. Besides, I—"

Near-microscopic air currents moved across the sensitive hairs of her body, and she froze in place. They were the result of something circling around her behind the trees, and she scanned the perimeter. Her eyesight was extremely good, particularly when it came to movement, but whatever was out there remained hidden.

She kept walking as if nothing was wrong, then frowned when she detected more movement from up ahead. There were two of them now, and they were moving parallel with her.

She was being hunted. It had been over a decade since something had bothered to tangle with her, and even longer since she herself had become prey. Whatever it was, it was either stupid or crazy.

And now there were three of them.

"Emery, move onto my shoulder, please."

"I am quite comfortable—"

"Not a request, Emery." She threw the imp a warning look. His features softened into understanding, and he hopped onto her shoulders, his feet grabbing tight to her jacket. The material was thick and warm, but she wore it mostly because it had been her father's.

She debated abandoning her kill and watching from the trees up above, but her hunger kept her from doing so. The winter had been a long one, and she had spent far too much time mourning her father's death and not enough hunting. Poor Eulalie couldn't even help, because it was hard to spin webs when the world was frosted over.

A branch snapped, and something dark leaped out of the shadows, moving so fast that it was a blur. It let out a screech of rage, but Velvet used the buck as a makeshift club and smashed it into the creature before leaping into the trees above. She didn't get a good look at her attacker, because she dropped out of the tree to avoid a rock the size of a suitcase being launched at her head.

Emery screamed as she tumbled, but she landed on her feet and bolted. The pine needles rustled around her as her attackers gave chase, and she cursed the meal she was being forced to leave behind.

Chirps and hoots could be heard now as the hunters chased her down, but she was no ordinary prey. She danced among the treetops and scrambled over boulder fields so fast that she nearly lost them on multiple occasions, but the damned things were fast.

What were they? It wasn't the first time they had been attacked, but it had been so many years since another cryptid had appeared in the forest.

"Damn you, Emily," she swore under her breath. The prevailing theory was that the former owner of the land had given blanket invites to many creatures in the hopes of creating a sanctuary for them. This alone would allow them to breach the barrier, but there was no way of knowing if that was still true because Emily had died.

The hooting stopped, and Velvet dropped out of the tree when she sensed something big moving her way. It was a log that had been sharpened and strapped to the branches overhead, and it narrowly missed her.

They had been herding her. Down on the forest floor, she backed herself up against a stone slab and watched as they emerged from the shadows. They stood between three and four feet tall, and their skin was a mottled gray. They were humanoid with vicious teeth and comical potbellies. A couple of them drew bows and nocked arrows.

"Not today," she muttered, and drew the pistol from its holster. It was a SIG P220, also her father's. He had carried it for years in case of a bear attack. She had never had any use for the firearm and had only brought it along because it felt like he was still by her side.

One of the humanoids fired its bow, and she scuttled to the side, the arrow shattering on the rock. The other took longer to aim, and the SIG barked twice. The first shot went wide, but the second caught the creature in the chest, sending it back with a loud oomph.

They rushed her, and she got off two more shots before they were on her. She lashed out with her legs, then grabbed one and smashed its skull into the rocks. The creature didn't die, but the others fell on it almost immediately to tear it apart.

"Fuck this," she muttered, then snatched up Emery, who had gotten knocked off. She leaped over the slab of rock and tumbled head over feet down the other side before dashing off into the woods again. Behind her, the sounds of pursuit became louder.

She knew the woods around her like the back of her hand, and she dashed off toward a deep ravine to the west. Once there, she jumped, crashing through dense pine-covered branches before landing nearly thirty feet below.

"That should—" she began, but two of the creatures landed in front of her. She fired the SIG two more times, dropping them both. Up above, the trees had become loud with the sound of crashing bodies, and Velvet dashed away. When she looked over her shoulder, there were maybe ten of them in hot pursuit.

Up ahead, she spotted more movement in the trees, but it was something far larger than the squat humanoids. She ran past a thick ponderosa pine and was relieved when the figure stepped into view.

Standing almost nine feet tall and covered in thick fur, Bigfoot let out a roar that startled birds out of hiding, then grabbed one of the creatures before it could stop and smashed it into a tree so hard that the trunk splintered. The others were undeterred by this new development and moved to attack him.

Bigfoot slammed a massive fist into one of the creatures, launching him through the trees and out of sight. Another got kicked hard enough that its head was on backward by the time it landed, its eyes already rolling up in its head.

"We need to go," he growled, then wrapped his arms around Velvet and pulled her behind a tree. They were instantly out of the ravine and over half a mile away, teleported by his magical ability to walk between the trees. They could hear the creatures hooting in the distance. In just a few steps, Velvet and Bigfoot were another mile away.

"What the hell were those things, Uncle?" She looked back over her shoulder.

Bigfoot's face scrunched up, which was impressive to behold, as very few things rattled him. "They went by many names once upon a time. Teihiihan. Others called them Nirumbi. They were a blight on the land. Murderous little cannibals nasty enough to unite the human tribes. I thought they had been wiped out."

Velvet smirked. "I bet people think that about all sorts of cryptids."

"Yeah, well, these ones were an odd lot." They traveled another hundred yards and were now ten miles away. "Even if they were still around, this isn't where they normally live."

"Did they migrate?"

He shook his head. "I don't know. But we need to get you home first and make a plan. They will be looking for you and will have the advantage at night."

Velvet sighed. "Wish I still had my sword."

He chuckled. "I'll sharpen a stick for you."

The clearing around their home appeared almost as if by magic, and relief filled her body once she saw the log cabin and the nearby barn. They walked along the overgrown path that no longer saw any use from her father's jeep.

"I'm glad you found me," she said.

"I came running as soon as I heard the gunshots." He stopped next to the barn and raised a massive arm to lean on it. "I don't know what I would do if something happened to you."

She smiled. "You would do what you always do—keep being Bigfoot."

He squinted at her, then laughed. "Because that's what Bigfoot does." It was an old joke he had told her as a child. He and her father had gotten in a disagreement that involved alcohol, and her dad had told Bigfoot to get a job. This had caused Velvet to pester him endlessly about what sort of job he was going to get.

"C'mon, let's head inside and see if there's anything to eat." She knew there wasn't, but there was always the hope that her sister had stashed a raccoon or a pair of squirrels somewhere.

When she opened the front door of the cabin, she realized Bigfoot was still out in the yard, his face concerned.

"Uncle Foot?"

"Velvet, I—" Bigfoot stumbled, and his pupils dilated. He let out a groan and tipped over as if in slow motion, his heavy limbs thumping on the ground.

"Uncle Foot!" She was at his side in an instant. When she rolled him over, she noticed an arrow sticking out of his shoulder. It came free easily and had only barely penetrated his fur. The wound wasn't deep enough to hurt him, which could only mean one thing.

"Poison," Bigfoot muttered as she dragged him toward the cabin. He was heavy, and it took several minutes before she even had him up the stairs.

Just as she got him inside and closed the door, the nearby forest came to life with the sounds of chirps and hoots.

OREGON TRAIL

It was almost noon when a small retinue of rats tracked Mike down at the bench by the back gate with Cerberus. Cerberus, in human form with a spectral chain around her neck, bared her teeth at the rats. She stopped when Mike patted the center head. He had discovered a few months ago that the center head was like the alpha of the pack. The only reason Cerberus was grumpy was because she knew Mike was leaving.

"You be good while I'm gone," he told the hellhound as he stood. "No barking at the fairies. No growling at Tink. Lily is fair game though."

This last one got a sheepish grin from the center head. Though Cerberus considered Mike her boss, Lily was definitely second-in-command due to her demonic nature. There was no way Cerberus would ever consider doing anything to the demon.

"Master come home soon?" she asked. The heads took turns with each word, the speech slightly stilted as a result.

"I will come home when my business is done." He gave Cerberus a hug, then kissed each forehead. "I'm counting on you to protect the house."

Cerberus backed away, her features solemn as she nodded. The large chain fastened around her neck retracted into the Underworld as she walked through the iron gate. Once she was on the other side, the spectral chain vanished and Cerberus reverted to her true form in a flash of crimson flames. She let out a howl and ran into the mist of the Underworld as Mike closed the gate and locked it.

When he made it to the top of the yard, Dana was waiting for him next to Naia's fountain.

"How is she this morning?" he asked.

Dana frowned. "She's fine, but…it isn't pretty."

"You look like you're ready for an adventure," he said. With Eulalie unable to go, Dana had been the first to volunteer to guide him. Ever since she'd died, her memory was perfect, which would help them find the cabin in the woods. "Is that…Ticktock?" He was referring to the backpack she wore.

"No, Ticktock is staying here," she explained. "As long as he has the you-know-what stored away, it makes more sense to keep him here."

Dana was referring to the grimoire of Morgan le Fey. The magical text was full of powerful spells, and its rumored existence alone had caused multiple attempts to break into his home. The mimic had been instructed to swallow the damned thing if anyone tried to take it. He had been tempted on a few occasions to just ask Ticktock to do it, but he wanted Ratu to search its pages before he did. If it really was one of the most powerful magical texts ever, it might hold the secret to bringing Dana back to life.

"That's really smart. I'm glad you thought of it. So…what are you bringing?" Mike asked.

"Spare change of clothes. For myself and—"

"Me." Quetzalli stepped out of the garage, her purple hair nearly iridescent in the sun. A silver horn sat in the middle of her forehead, and beneath it was a streak of either dust or cobwebs. "If Dana is coming, then I am too."

"There may be a fight," he warned her.

"I'm no stranger to a fight." She winked at him. A dragon stuck in human form, she was able to manipulate electricity and could speak about storms for hours. "My horn has grown half an inch in the last three months, so my control is getting better."

To elaborate her point, she held her hands apart, and he watched tiny streamers flow back and forth between her palms. He opened his mouth to say something, but Dana put her hand over his lips.

"I know what you're going to do," she told him. "And if you make an electricity joke, I will punch you."

He held up his hands and tried to wipe the smirk off his face. "Okay, that's fair. I'll keep it to myself."

"Now, that's actually shocking," Amymone quipped from up in her tree.

"Could you zap her?" Dana asked.

Quetzalli frowned. "No. Wood is a poor conductor."

"Go, go," Naia told them before leaning out of her fountain to give Mike a hug. "You'll only encourage her if you pay her any attention."

Up in the tree, Amymone laughed, then looked down at Mike. "She's not wrong. Make sure you come home, okay?"

He nodded, and they all followed the rat to the front of the house. Out front, Tink had constructed a small shed off to the side of the house. A pair of centaurs stood next to it, and one of them held out a scroll and a small bag for Mike.

"From Zel?" he asked. They nodded, and he took the bag and put it over his shoulder. It rattled with potions inside, which brought a smile to his face. Last time Zel had sent him off with potions, things had become very interesting.

"Tell her thank you for me." He debated having them tell her he missed her but figured it might be inappropriate for them to pass that to their chieftain. Zel was constantly busy, but he was no different. As a change from taking care of the house and its occupants, this little excursion was already beginning to feel like a small vacation.

Reggie stepped out of the shed and put his crown on. "We just finished. You will need to crawl through the hole. The cabin is abandoned, but the only place we could manage a portal was in the cellar. The building is a bit unstable."

"It's not gonna fall on me, is it?" Mike picked up the backpack he had stuck there early that very morning. Inside it was a spare change of his own clothes and some food that Sofia had prepped for him. There was also a compass, a multi-tool, and other supplies he had packed for emergencies.

Reggie shook his head. "It shouldn't, but I doubt it makes it another winter."

"Good to know." Mike picked up the coat he had set next to his bag and put it on. He saw Quetzalli do the same thing, then looked at Dana.

"No coat?" he asked.

"Why bother?"

"Fair point. I guess we're just waiting for Yuki."

The front door opened, and the kitsune stepped outside. She wore a white fur coat that went down to her knees and a pair of fur-lined boots. Once off the porch, she crossed the yard and stood next to Mike. Yuki placed her hands on her waist and grinned. Her canines looked as if they had been recently polished.

"Excited?" he asked.

"Very." She placed an arm around his shoulders and smiled. "Been a while since I've seen somewhere new."

"That makes both of us." He looked around at everyone that had gathered. Cecilia waved to him dreamily from the front porch while Tink scowled at him nearby. The little goblin wasn't happy to be left behind, but he felt like he was in good enough hands with Yuki. The snow-covered forests of Oregon would give her a huge advantage.

"Oh, don't worry, little goblin." Lily stepped out of the house but had already shape-shifted into Mike. "You can always snuggle with me at night."

"Fucking horny bitch," Tink muttered, then ran up and hugged Mike around the waist. "Husband come home safe or Tink be really mad. Bite husband real good this time."

"Oh, I know you will." During an intimate moment earlier that morning, she had bitten him on the neck hard enough to leave a mark. When he let her go, she moved over to stand with Kisa, who was sitting on the stairs. Next to her was Lily, a mirror image of himself. "As for you, try to behave."

"Of course I will," Lily told him in his own voice. "'Cause I'm a sexy Boy Scout. Be prepared, right? Now where are my bitches at? We're gonna be fucking for days!"

"That's not what I sound like," he muttered.

"C'mon, bro, it's all good." Lily threw her arms around Mike and gave him a good squeeze. She lowered her voice to a whisper. "I'm going to knock everybody up while you're gone, just you watch. I've got enough of your baby juice packed away to make mommas out of all of them."

"What?" His mouth was suddenly dryer than it had ever been.

"Gotta go!" Lily stuck out her tongue and walked back up to the front door. "I've got a date with a kitty cat." When she looked down at Kisa, the cat girl nodded and slid the silver bracelet onto her wrist.

Mike groaned as they went inside. He knew he could trust Lily, but she wasn't making it easy for him.

"Mike?" Beth walked up from the garden with Sulyvahn in tow. "Are you leaving now?"

"I am." He gave her an awkward wave. "Hopefully this goes better than last time."

She grimaced.

If the roof was still attached when he came home, he would consider it a win.

"I guess that's that," he said, then opened the door to the shed. A cold blast of air came through it. "So let's—"

Abella landed with a thud in front of him, causing him to jump.

"I'm going too," she said, her dark eyes glittering.

Mike blinked in astonishment. "I thought you couldn't leave the house."

"I cannot," she told him. "Unless the Caretaker is in danger. I believe you are walking into danger right now; therefore, I am going with you."

"Abella, I—" He looked over at Beth, hoping she would interject. Without Abella, the home's strongest defenders would be away.

"I know what you're thinking," Abella said. "The home will be fine without me. It can be rebuilt. You cannot."

Famous last words, he thought.

"They have the centaurs and the lizard," she added while gesturing at the Jabberwock. "And Lily is almost as strong as I am. In fact, this place is more well-guarded than when you first moved in. And if someone should actually breach the house, I'm sure Ratu and Asterion would show up to help as well."

He thought about arguing with her but to what end? She had already made up her mind, and he wasn't sure he could convince her otherwise.

"We'll need to be careful," he informed her. "Apparently, the cabin is a bit unstable."

"I'll go last," she said. "You've made a wise decision."

He looked over at Yuki, then back at Abella. The two of them alone had been enough to fight off a possessed Jabberwock; he couldn't imagine an obstacle they couldn't handle.

"I guess it's time, then." He looked at the house, then at Beth. "Call me if there's trouble."

She nodded knowingly. "You do the same."

Once he was through the portal, the plan was to have the rats close it. If something drastic occurred, the shed could be destroyed, which would accomplish the same thing.

When he tried to go first, Yuki shoved him out of the way. Her tails swished behind her as she crouched to go through the hole that had been chewed into the wood of the shed. On her way through, she summoned a ball of light in her hand, then cast it into the dark room ahead. It illuminated a dirt cellar decorated with wooden shelves that were covered in a thick layer of dust.

"Me next." Dana pushed her way past him, followed by Quetzalli. He received a nasty shock from her in passing. Shaking it off, he crouched down to go through the opening and felt the temperature drop.

Now in the cellar, he turned on his phone's light and looked around. Yuki had already found the stairs and had opened the hatch up above them, which let in some light. She and the others were on their way up when Abella squeezed through the portal.

The gargoyle grunted, then popped through. The wall vibrated, and the portal shimmered for a second, but it held. When Abella stood, her wings wrapped around her body like a cloak.

"And?" he asked, expecting her to retreat through the opening. He didn't know if the house would simply call her back or demand she return.

"And you should go first," she said. "In case the stairs collapse." Her brow was furrowed as if in concentration.

He nodded, then headed up. The cabin was drafty, and he saw that it was also empty. The others had apparently gone outside. The front door was missing, which accounted for the chill. Behind him, the sound of creaking wood filled the air, so he made haste to get outside as well.

The others were waiting, their eyes on the forest. He assumed by their relaxed postures that they were away from prying eyes. Behind him, the cabin groaned in protest as Abella crossed the living room and stood in the frame of the door.

"So which way from here?" Yuki asked him as Abella stepped out of the cabin.

"That way," both he and Abella said, pointing to the northwest. For him, it was like a lure, an attraction that told him exactly where he needed to go. "You feel it too?"

Abella nodded. "It is like the house. I have an urge to fly there right now."

"You can go ahead if you want," he told her.

"My place is by your side." She moved next to him, then bowed her head. "Not that you had a choice, but thanks for letting me come."

He said nothing. His feelings about her presence were mixed, and he was afraid that he would put his foot straight in his mouth. Though grateful that she was by his side, he was well aware that she was the home's bouncer, and hoped that nobody came around looking for trouble.

So he smiled at her. Maybe her decisions weren't what he would have picked, but he wanted to make sure she knew that he was still on her side. The air was much colder here, so he slipped on a pair of gloves and tightened the straps on his bag. Once finished, he took Abella by the hand. Her grip was strong and welcoming.

"Let's go for a hike," he said, then led them into the forest.

THE RATS TOOK ABOUT AN HOUR TO CLOSE THE PORTAL, BUT BETH STAYED TO watch until they were done. The structure would remain until Mike was back. The last thing they needed was an emergency, and portals could only be chewed into enclosed spaces. It had something to do with how reality folded, but when Reggie had described the process to her, the details had mostly gone over her head.

She checked her phone, then looked out at the yard. Last time Mike had left, they had been attacked by vengeful spirits. The sunny weather did little to cheer her, as she was painfully aware that Mike had taken the home's heavy hitters with him. If something happened that required brute force, she felt ill-equipped.

"Lass?" Sulyvahn came around the side of the house, a bucket in one hand and a trowel in the other. "Ye look a bit wired to the moon. 'Twas wonderin' if I were able to ease things a bit for yerself?"

"That obvious?" She was suddenly aware of the heavy tension that had settled into her neck. It was stress, and her usual coping mechanism of wine and orgasms wasn't an option.

"Aye." Sulyvahn reached into the bucket and pulled out a rose. "This one reminded me of yer own self, it did. Beauty and thorns, all rolled in one."

"Thank you." She took the flower and inhaled its aroma. The yard smelled like a floral boutique ever since the equinox ceremony. She had watched in awe as the entire yard came to life at once, the flowers blooming and the various flora expanding in size. It had been like watching a time-lapse video.

"Maybe it be nerves." Sulyvahn set the bucket down. "I know ye fear for the home."

Cecilia manifested up on the porch. The banshee was sitting on her swing, and her white skin was almost blinding in the bright light of day.

"The home will be fine," Cecilia told her. "He won't be gone long. I'm always watching. I'll raise the alarm if I see something amiss."

Beth smirked. "I know you will. If you two will excuse me, I have some work I should be doing."

Suly gave her a dramatic bow as she left.

Once inside, she walked into the office and sat down with a groan. While it was true that she could find something to do, she wasn't in a position to concentrate on any task.

The room connected to the office was a sitting room full of Egyptian arti-facts. Death walked out of it, holding a cup of tea in one hand and a chil-dren's book about pyramids in the other. Upon noticing Beth, he set the book down on her desk.

"Would you like some tea?" he asked.

"Yes, please." She looked up at him. "Even you can tell how stressed I am?"

"Hmm?" Death studied her for a moment. "I was offering for the sake of etiquette, but you do look troubled. I'm thinking maybe a lavender blend."

"Sure, thanks." She watched him go back into the study, then looked down at the book he had left. It claimed to have a reading level perfect for third graders, and when she opened it, she noticed that Death had been scribbling in the margins.

"Pyramid." She tapped the word Death had circled. A line connected the word to a triangle he had drawn on the side. Flipping through the book, she saw that he had made notes, particularly in the chapter about death rituals. Clearly, something had caught his interest, which was a far cry better than booty pics of Tink.

It suddenly occurred to her that someone had taken those pictures.

"Hey there, hot stuff!" Lily-Mike walked into the room, her legs far apart as she waddled. "Sure is hard walking around with these massive fucking balls in here, am I right?" To emphasize her point, she unzipped her pants and pulled out a set of testicles that would have been perfectly at home on a trailer hitch.

Beth laughed. Lily gave the testicles a poke, which caused them to make a sloshing sound.

"What the fuck are you doing?" Beth asked, trying hard not to blush. Even though she knew it was just Lily screwing around, she was still looking at a weird version of Mike's ball sack.

"Told Mike I was gonna knock everybody up. Can I borrow your phone?"

Dubious, Beth handed over her cell phone while Lily rested her giant nut sack on the desk. Her tail appeared and took the phone, holding it away from them so that Lily could snap a few pictures.

"Try to look impressed or something. We should send these to Romeo later and try to squeeze a laugh out of him."

"You're incorrigible," Beth told her but made her best surprised face with one hand just over her mouth.

"I'll look that word up later," Lily told her, then snapped a few. Death walked in as the pictures were being taken, only to do an immediate U-turn out of the office.

Beth and Lily laughed. Mike's features melted away so that Lily looked like herself. "You looked like you could use a laugh."

"I did. Nerves, I guess."

"Nah, it's not just that." Lily leaned back in her chair. "You're the head honcho now, the man of the house. You've got responsibilities to meet, and you're hoping to avoid what happened last time. Which, by the way, totally not your fault."

Beth shook her head. "This isn't a confidence thing. The house just feels surprisingly empty is all. If something goes down, are there enough people to help?"

"Hmm. The way I see it, the king has left the castle." Lily leaned forward in her chair with a smirk on her face. "But remember that the queen is the one with all the moves. It's been quiet for months, and if anyone is watching, we just have to confuse them until he gets back."

"I guess." Beth leaned back in her own chair as Death reappeared in the door.

"My apologies for the earlier intrusion," he said, then set a cup of tea in front of Beth. "You seemed to be rather busy."

"We're just setting up a prank for Mike," Lily explained.

At the word *prank*, the fire in Death's sockets blazed.

"Oh, I do enjoy a good prank! Please let me know if there's anything I may do to assist you!" He put his bony hands together and tapped his fingertips excitedly.

"Er, yeah, no problem." Beth took the tea and sipped it. "Thank you."

However, when no discussion about a prank was immediately forthcoming, Death excused himself, leaving Beth alone with Lily.

"So are you gonna ask?" Lily said after a few minutes of silence.

"About?" Beth had zoned out, her thoughts on the others. She now wondered if Lily had been talking.

"Your woman problems."

Beth felt heat flood her face, and she tried to hide behind her teacup but only succeeded in spilling some of it on herself.

"Don't try to deny it. You look like a woman who spent all day on horseback." Lily leaned back in her chair far enough to hump the air for emphasis. "Big difference between well fucked and fucked up."

"How could you tell?" Beth asked, her voice barely above a whisper.

"It's in the way you sit."

"I see." She really hoped Lily was far more observant than the others. It was an embarrassing topic of conversation in the best of times, and she didn't want the whole house knowing about her issue. She went to sip some of her tea, wondering how much to tell the succubus.

"If I had to wager a guess, it's that our resident size queen has finally stretched herself too thin."

The comment had been deliberately timed, and Beth spit her tea out and coughed.

Lily laughed, a satisfied look plastered on her face. "Ah, that was worth it. I'm right though, aren't I? You're all fucked out."

Beth wiped the tea off her chin and frowned. "Lily. Keep your voice down," she muttered.

The succubus shrugged. "I mean, if you don't wanna talk about it and continue to be a party to sexual repression—"

"*Lily*." Beth mimed a lock and key over her mouth. "I'll talk, but shut the fuck up."

A literal tiny padlock appeared through Lily's lips, holding her lips together like a macabre piercing.

"Your theatrics aside, yes, I'm having some trouble downstairs." She detailed her gynecological issues with the succubus, not expecting her to be of any real help. It was at least nice to have someone to confide in.

Once Beth was finished, Lily pulled a key out from between her breasts and unlocked the padlock.

"Sounds rough," she said. "Can't say I have the same issue, for obvious reasons. I'm surprised you haven't talked about this with the nymph yet."

"Frankly, I didn't want to talk about it with anybody."

"Naia isn't just a water fountain with benefits. I bet she could give you all sorts of tips and tricks, but that's beside the point. She's also a natural healer. She was practically the only thing holding Romeo together for the first month or so."

"But how do you heal…" It suddenly occurred to her that it didn't matter, and she felt dumb for not thinking about it before. With Mike gone, she could use Naia's tub in private.

"Go ahead," Lily said, waving toward the door. "Don't sit on a sore cooch just to keep me company."

"Thanks." Beth was almost to the door when she noticed Kisa sitting in the corner.

Oh God. "How long have you been there?"

"Long enough to tell Lily that incorrigible means she'll never improve her behavior." The grin on Kisa's face made Beth think of the Cheshire cat. "I'm supposed to stick by her side, remember?"

Lily laughed. "This little black cat is starting to grow on me."

Mortified, Beth ran up the stairs to Mike's bedroom. Once the door was closed, she walked into his bathroom. The tub inside was several feet across and could easily fit a few people.

"Naia?" she asked.

"Beth." The faucet turned on, and the tub filled a few inches. Naia's head emerged from the water, though "emerged" wasn't quite right. The nymph herself was made of water, so it created the illusion that the tub was magically five feet deeper. "Do you need something?"

After a brief explanation from Beth, Naia filled the tub up with steaming hot water. Beth took off her clothes and climbed into the bath, sighing as the warmth seeped into her skin.

"This already feels good," she said. "I've only got a shower in the bath I share with Yuki."

"You should ask Tink to put in a tub," Naia told her. "Though it wouldn't have the same perks or be as large as this one."

"Why not?" Beth ran her hands along the cool surface of the rim. "Wouldn't it just be some additional pipes?"

"A bit more than that. Here, lean back." Gentle hands appeared from beneath the water and pulled Beth against the side. Naia manifested beneath the surface, creating a nymph body pillow beneath Beth's torso.

Beth closed her eyes as Naia gave her a scalp massage.

"The pipes that connect my bath to the spring aren't just regular pipes," Naia explained. "They are made from a special kind of material brought in for this exact purpose. Nymphs are bound to their springs, unable to leave their boundaries. Therefore, the pipes were made special from bits of my spring and other materials."

"Like some type of magical compound?" Beth asked. The fingers in her hair soothed her, and her whole body was tingling. In fact, she could feel the aches and pains in her pelvis leaving her.

"Not a bad way to think of it. Powerful fae magic plus some metal I've never heard of, and then some minerals from as far down as my essence goes." An extra set of hands now worked the kinks in Beth's neck. "Feeling any better yet?"

Beth explored her vulva with her fingers. Some of the tenderness had already disappeared. "I am, thank you."

"You know, there *is* a way we could fix this problem for you permanently." A third set of hands now rubbed her shoulders while a fourth set began working her feet. "So that you wouldn't have to worry again."

"I'm all ears."

"I could give you the gift," Naia whispered, her voice like velvet. "Bless you like I blessed Mike."

Beth's eyes opened. "Like a soul exchange?"

"Yes. You are already the next Caretaker in line, and you are right for this house. I feel safe enough offering it to you."

She mulled it over. By going through the process with Naia, she would be inexorably linked to the nymph forever and, therefore, the house. "Would I have magic like Mike?"

Naia laughed. "Nobody has magic as he does. But yes, you would have some magic of your own. For one thing, your body would be able to keep up with your sexual adventures. No more soreness. In fact, you would always be as wet as you want to be. That isn't really a trick Mike can use."

"I guess not." Did she really want to be like the others? It felt weird so casually deciding to part with a little bit of her humanity in exchange for the magic Naia offered. However, the possibilities being presented would also put her on a more level playing field with everyone else. As of right now, she was the only true human in the house.

The moment that thought crossed her mind, she felt all the threads of her insecurities knit together. It wasn't so much that Mike was gone and had taken the others. It was the fact that she felt inadequate, that she was still an outsider. Even something as simple as the banshee scream was a trick in Mike's arsenal. All Beth really had was a monster kink and a law degree. Neither of these was very useful in a fight.

"Are you sure?" Beth asked.

"The fact that you hesitate to even accept such a gift tells me I'm right about you." Another set of hands were massaging her calves now. "And I can also promise you that the process is quite enjoyable."

Beth chuckled. "I'm sure it is. But I guess what I really want to ask is whether I will still be me? Afterward, will I be a different person?" She thought of how the magic had eventually corrupted Emily. It wasn't a path she wanted to walk on.

"In a way," Naia replied. "It will be no different from the first time you had sex. You will still be the same person, but what *will* happen is that certain doors will be open to you. It will be your choices that define how you walk through them, and that is when you may become someone else. It will be your choice."

Beth closed her eyes. She knew she could trust Naia, but this was a big moment.

"I accept," she whispered in excitement.

More hands touched her now. They massaged her breasts and her hips and even teased her labia. She let out a tiny moan as the warm water encased her body. Though her upper half was above the tub, the water climbed her skin until it was just below her chin.

The hands pulled her down beneath the water, and she opened her eyes in time to see Naia's face in front of hers. The nymph's blue eyes were ablaze with light as she put her hands on Beth's cheeks.

"And now we shall become one," Naia told her and pulled her in for a kiss.

The water surrounded Beth completely, and she realized she was now breathing through Naia's mouth. Each breath made her mouth tingle in a way that reminded her of inhaling cold air after sucking on a mint. The invisible hands had pushed her legs apart, and unseen digits toyed with both her openings.

She moaned into Naia's mouth, their tongues now twisting around each other. Beth's body felt like it was on fire, trying desperately to mix with the cool water that surrounded her. This created a buzzing sensation that resonated through her entire body.

Breathe me in.

Naia's voice came from inside Beth's head.

She took the deepest breath she could. Her lungs tingled, the sensation spreading through her entire chest and upper arms. The fingers toying with her labia were now vibrating against her clit, and she spread her legs wide at the sensation of pressure against her vagina.

Take me in.

The swirling water around them glowed green and blue, and a pair of thick water tendrils pressed against Beth's crotch. She opened her legs and let them push inside her. Pressure was building on her asshole, so she reached back and pulled her butt cheeks apart to give Naia better access.

Once the amorphous water was inside her, it began to expand. Beth gasped and let out a low moan, but Naia's tongue had become water as well and moved down her throat.

There was a moment of panic when Beth realized there wasn't any air to inhale. The water penetrated her now in all three openings, and she started to fight as her vision went dark around the edges. Her whole body tensed as an immense orgasm built, but the fear of drowning was taking over.

Trust, Naia told her. *Trust me.*

Having little choice, Beth inhaled.

The water filled her lungs, but it was as if she was breathing cold air. Her eyelids fluttered as a sense of peace came over her, and then it no longer felt like she was breathing at all.

It's like I'm drowning, she thought.

The water filled her body, rushing inside her. Naia's laughter filled Beth's ears as her whole body thrummed with sexual energy. She was on the brink of coming, but something held her back.

Open yourself to me.

Naia's voice came from everywhere at once, and the room filled with blinding light. When it receded, Beth realized she was no longer in the bathroom.

She was hovering in a field of stars. Her hair drifted around in front of her face, and when she went to tuck it back, she saw that her arm was translucent.

"Where am I?" she asked.

"With me." Naia appeared in the void, her body made entirely of water. The runes on her body were glowing bright, the light too intense to look at directly. "I'm surprised your consciousness is in here. Do you recognize this place?"

Beth nodded. When her soul was being filtered to rid it of Oliver's influence, she had been in a similar place. "Am I just a soul right now?"

"You are," Naia answered. "And you're about to become so much more."

When Naia pressed herself against Beth, she could feel the two of them merge together. For a moment, she felt like she was in two places at once, touching herself and being touched.

"The human body is roughly two-thirds water," Naia whispered to Beth as their souls continued merging. In the back of her mind, Beth was dimly aware of her body being stretched and distorted by the water as it forced its way inside her. "And in a moment, it will all be replaced with me."

The humming in Beth's body reached a crescendo, and she came. One of the distant stars exploded, sending pink-and-purple light out into the universe.

"It isn't just a spiritual swap," Naia explained as her soul encased Beth's and continued sinking in. "I can change you from the inside. Take what's already there and improve it. I am the magic, and the magic is me."

The light from the exploding star reached them, and Beth came again. This set off another supernova nearby.

"For a moment, we will be one." Naia had vanished, her voice now coming from Beth's lips. "And as I fill you with my light, so shall you fill me with yours."

"*Naia!*" Beth gasped, and another star exploded. The wave of energy stretched her out, but before she could regain her shape, she came again. Another blast wave twisted her about, and she groaned as yet another one twisted her up.

We are mixing, Naia told her. *We are the water. Together, we flow.*

Beth cried out Naia's name again as the two of them swirled together. She was now without shape or form as she let the magical waves wash through her. Her consciousness expanded as they mixed and became one.

I can see who you are, Naia told her. *I can relive your life.*

Memories rushed through Beth's mind, ranging from her childhood to now. She was a teen, holding her breath beneath the ocean. She was an adult, walking across the stage at graduation. It was her first night in her apartment, and her fingers hovered over the latch of a briefcase carrying her secret stash.

Yes! Naia's voice was filled with excitement. *Let me see it! Let me feel it!*

Hours upon hours of memories of Beth finding different ways to pleasure herself swirled around them. Dildos of different shapes and sizes, each one stranger and more monstrous than the last. The time Beth had mounted one to a pillow and come so hard she ruined the case. The tentacle-shaped dildo she'd tried to fuck in the bath. The time she'd caused a dildo to fold and it broke in half.

Oh, that sweet frustration, you seek its release! Beth was now experiencing the memories as if she was there again, only the sensations were overlapping each other. Her first time with the Delightful Dragon was overlapped with her first time fucking Asterion. Now she was with Suly as he bent her over the sundial and fucked her hard from behind. Now it was the time two weeks ago when she had fingered Asterion's ass while blowing him, hoping to tease some extra cum out of his cock.

"More!" Beth cried. "I want to feel more! I want to feel it all!"

The memories became like water and spun around them. The stars in the sky were exploding so fast now that Beth and Naia were condensed into a sphere of sex, energy, and light.

Let us become one!

Naia's voice was full of exultation, and Beth could see the nymph's past unfold. She was now there for all the times Naia had had sex with Mike, then backward to Emily, and then the next Caretaker before. Every sexual encounter overlapped with one another as pleasure pounded through her very core.

One last memory caught her attention. Naia was standing in the woods by a burbling spring when a figure stepped from behind a nearby tree. It was Amymone's tree, and the dryad stood by the figure, a look of excitement painted onto her face.

"I accept," Naia said.

"I'm glad." The voice was soft, and Beth couldn't tell if it was a man or a woman. Their features had been blurred away, as if someone had rubbed a thumb over paint before it could dry. When they held a hand out for Naia, the nymph took it. Power rushed through her body, and she let out a cry as the nearby ground erupted and the house pushed its way up through the soil. Amymone cheered in excitement as the ground swelled and pushed nearby trees away.

The memories disappeared, and it was just Beth and Naia now. The two of them had become one, a swirling mass of magic that sat alone in the dark. There was a single moment of silence, and Beth realized she could no longer tell where she ended and the nymph began.

At that moment, they had become perfectly balanced. Then, with a single pulse of magic, Beth's ears were filled with the sound of roaring as it all came apart. The sensation stole her breath and forced heat through her body. Naia moaned Beth's name over and over again as the energy built between them.

With one final scream, they came. The universe was nothing but light, and then the two of them separated.

Back in her body, Beth realized she was in the air. She was in a reclined position and surrounded by a watery sphere. Her belly was distended, and she screamed as the orgasm from the soul exchange caused her to tense up and spray water out of her body. This water gradually coalesced into Naia, who proceeded to press herself against Beth.

"That's right, come for me!" Naia demanded as her magic raced through Beth.

Beth obeyed, and the watery orb sprayed outward in every direction, soaking the walls and floor of the bathroom. She fell but was caught by jets of water that laid her gently down in the tub. Her whole body shook as she tried to grab something, to brace herself as one last orgasm pushed itself free.

Her hands found Naia's, and their fingers locked together as Naia pressed her lips to Beth's. She was surrounded once more, the water of the tub rushing around her to form a giant bubble. Her body was hot and cold at the same time, and steam had fogged up the mirror and windows. Closing her eyes, she whispered Naia's name like a prayer.

When Beth finally opened her eyes, she was above the water. The light that came in through the windows seemed brighter and more vibrant. It was like someone had adjusted the color and saturation levels of the whole world. Birds sang in the distance, their song calling to her. She longed to be outside, to feel the open sky above her and the breeze on her face.

"How do you feel?" asked Naia. "I'm very curious. I've never experienced such a strong bonding before."

"Amazing." Beth's whole body felt relaxed, as if her muscles had been stretched and put back into place. "Am I…different now?"

"Go look." Naia gestured to the mirror. Beth stood, her legs wobbling beneath her. From the bath, she gasped at her own reflection.

It was undeniably her, but there were subtle differences. Her hair was now curled perfectly, despite being wet only minutes ago. Her lips had an extra splash of color that complemented her complexion perfectly. And her eyes. They glowed as if she was staring into a bright light.

Naia rose from the water and wrapped her arms around Beth's waist. She settled her head in the crook of Beth's neck and smiled at their reflection.

"Welcome to the sisterhood," she said, then planted a kiss on Beth's neck. "You've been deeper inside me than any other man or woman, by the way. I don't just say that to anybody."

Beth snorted hard, then laughed. "I can easily say the same," she said between her own tears. "Oh my goodness, I feel so light! Like I can do anything."

"You'll find there are lots of things you can do now," Naia told her. "A touch of precognition, a dash of charisma, and my personal favorite…" One of her hands slid down and cradled Beth's upper pubis. "No more tenderness. You'll be able to handle anything you put your mind to, within reason. That Delightful Dragon of yours should still be handled with caution. Personal lubricant won't ever be an issue again, so that should help."

"Thank you." Beth leaned her head over so that it was on top of Naia's. "This gift you've given me is…I mean…thank you."

"You're very welcome, lover." Naia helped Beth out of the tub. "I'm afraid we made a bit of a mess, so be really careful—"

Beth felt an icy pain stab her through the stomach. The sensation distracted her, causing her to slip on a wet patch. Her legs shot out from under her, but there was nothing to grab onto and she fell. Instead of her head hitting the floor, the water on the floor rushed together beneath her, creating a thick bubble of fluid that acted as an airbag. It sprayed outward in every direction on impact, turning a nasty fall into a soft bump.

"Oh shit, that was scary." Beth sat up, now covered in water. "I'm okay though. Thanks for the save."

Naia said nothing. Instead, she stared at Beth from her place inside the bathtub, a look of shock on her face.

"That…that wasn't me," she said in a hushed tone, breaking the silence. "I tried to manipulate the water, but it was already being moved with magic. Your magic."

"You gave me water magic?" Beth looked around the bathroom. It was a wet disaster, and even the towels were soaked. She reached out mentally, wondering if she could make it move. All it did was drip off the walls.

Naia shook her head. "That's just it. That's not even something I can do." She bit her lip nervously. "We need to talk to Ratu, right away."

THE COLD AIR OF OREGON BIT AT MIKE THROUGH HIS JACKET. THE SNOW ON the ground was only a couple of inches thick but crunched loudly when they walked.

Dana and Quetzalli were in the lead, while Yuki brought up the rear. Mike saw that she was swishing her tail over the snow where they walked, and their footprints were vanishing as if wiped from a dry-erase board.

Up ahead, the trees parted. There was a hanging fog in the air that shifted away from them as they approached. When they stepped through it, a tingle ran through his whole body.

"We're inside," he said. The magic felt similar to the geas but not quite the same.

"How do you feel?" asked Dana.

"Kinda hungry," he answered, then pulled a granola bar out of his pocket. When he went to open it, he noticed the wrapper had been opened already. Curious, he pulled the bar out and laughed. A third of it was gone, and he knew it had to have been Tink.

"May I have some of that?" Quetzalli asked, clutching her stomach. They had been walking for over an hour now, and she was probably just as hungry.

"Here, you can have your own. This one has goblin cooties." He pulled a couple more out of his backpack, then handed over his water bottle. They took turns drinking out of it while Abella and Dana kept watch.

"Is this like being at the house?" he asked Abella. "It's not the geas, but it feels familiar to me."

She nodded, then looked up. "It's been so long since I've seen the forest. Ever since Europe, actually."

"Were you brought over through a portal?" he asked.

"Freighter," she responded. "Was a long journey. I had to sit inside a box."

"Kind of like Eulalie did." The mention of the arachne's name caused Abella to scowl. "You don't like her, do you?"

Abella's cheeks darkened. "No, I do not."

"She seems nice."

"That doesn't impress me. Don't think I didn't notice how she suddenly couldn't bring us on this trip. There's one in the house and one waiting for us at our destination. Nobody builds a trap as the arachne do."

"My magic tells me she is safe." He patted his gut. "Besides, why go through all this trouble to get me if they could just leave the cabin and snack on some hikers?"

"I haven't figured that part out yet," she admitted.

"They're different." This came from Dana, who slowed down to walk with them. "The arachne are killers, but their mother wasn't. Every time she laid eggs, she crushed them all because she could tell they would never be able to coexist with humans. Velvet and Eulalie were the only two out of hundreds of eggs that she allowed to hatch because she could tell they were different."

Abella snorted, then walked away from them to join Yuki.

"She really doesn't like them," Dana observed.

"There's always more to the story than we think," Mike said. "I'll admit, the whole spider thing freaks me out. I had a bad experience with them as a kid, and they are kind of being shoved in my face right now."

"I thought you'd enjoy it," she said.

"How do you figure?"

"Always took you for a leg man." She winked at him.

When he laughed, it was almost like a bark. "Okay, you've got me there," he admitted. "Though it's more the whole package, I guess." He thought about the different women in the house. There really wasn't a pattern among them other than not being human.

"For me, it is the hips. Sounds strange, right? But there's something to it. A girl with hips has got some curves to begin with. And don't even get me started on leggings."

"Oh?" Mike snuck a glance over at Quetzalli. The dragon's human form had very voluptuous curves. For the first month she was a human, it had been almost comical to hear her bitch about how parts of her anatomy would keep moving even after she had stopped. "I feel like leggings are one of God's final gifts to mankind," he continued. "A proper pair of leggings can make a house-wife look like a goddess."

Dana smirked. "Maybe we could have Tink make us a pair of leggings with eight legs. It would be like immersion therapy or something."

"That would be—" A cold feeling filled his gut, and he paused.

"What's up?" Dana asked him.

"Something bad is about to happen." His eyes were drawn up into the trees where he saw movement. He had barely raised his hand to point it out when Abella wrapped her wings around him, blotting out the light.

Someone yelled, and he heard multiple projectiles shatter against Abella's body. When she unwrapped her wings, the tree had been engulfed by a mass of ice. Three squat figures fell out of the tree and landed in the packed snow beneath.

"What was that?" he asked. When he looked over at Dana, he saw that she had arrows sticking out of her chest and shoulders.

"Arrows, apparently. Bad ones." Dana pulled one out and sniffed it, then made a face. "They've been dipped in something nasty."

"Was it just these three?" he asked.

"If so, they were firing them pretty fast," Quetzalli said as she came over. "I would surmise that—"

The cold feeling hit him again, and he tackled Quetzalli to the ground as another volley launched over them. A barrier of ice formed in front of them, and Yuki shouted in anger.

Through the clear ice of the barrier, he watched Dana pull a dagger from her pants and flick her wrist. The blade extended to reveal a sword that looked almost like a katana and was very similar to the one Sofia carried. The zombie charged into the fray, the sword hissing through the air as she swung it.

"Where the hell did she get that?" he asked, then looked down at Quetzalli. "Are you okay? You didn't get hit, did you?"

The dragon grinned, her cheeks crimson from the cold. He was on top of her and suddenly aware that his hands had been planted along her ribs. Her breasts were large enough that when they had flattened, they now pressed against his wrists.

"I'm okay," she told him, then gave him a little kiss on the nose. The resulting shock made him bite the tip of his tongue. "My hero."

All around them, the forest came to life with the sounds of chirps and hooting, as if a thousand horny owls were vying for his attention. He moved off Quetzalli and chanced a glance over the top of the barrier. Yuki was summoning four-foot long spears of frost that flew up into the trees once formed. Dana and Abella were protecting the kitsune from projectiles. With every passing moment, Dana looked more like a porcupine than a woman.

The cold feeling returned, and he looked back in the direction they had come. A group of the stout little men emerged from the forest, their teeth bared.

"Abella," he called out as he covered Quetzalli's ears with his hands. "Ears!"

The gargoyle shoved her fingers in her ears as he took a deep breath and then let out a piercing cry. It was the banshee magic he let loose from within, a hair-raising sound he had practiced for hours with Cecilia's tutelage. What had once been a loud shriek now sounded like a dissonant blast of more than one voice. Not only was it painful for others to hear, but it was also downright terrifying.

The little men panicked and turned to run. A couple of them hesitated, the scream not enough to frighten them off.

Quetzalli raised her hands and summoned lightning from her fingertips. When it struck the pair, they let out a howl of agony and fell to the ground, their bodies twitching even after she stopped.

In a moment of respite, Mike reached into his pockets and pulled out a small baggie of earplugs.

"Time to kick some ass," he told Quetzalli as he handed her a pair. "It's gonna get loud, so put them in."

She grinned, then stuffed the plugs in her ears.

"You may be making a lot of noise," she shouted with an arched eyebrow. Electricity crackled all along the length of her horn as the air around her crackled with energy. "But I want you to remember that lightning does all the work."

Above them, thunder rumbled in the clouds. Laughing, they both ran to join the others.

VELVET YAWNED, HER JAW CLICKING AS SHE DID SO. THE FRONT DOOR OF THE house had been barred and the windows shuttered. Between some of the fierce winter storms and the goblin attacks so long ago, the cabin was perfectly capable of being turned into a defensive fortress for a little bit.

Unfortunately, it wasn't meant to be manned by only one person. Emery helped out where he could, flying around the house and constantly checking windows for movement.

Bigfoot was out cold on the couch. She had feared the poison was lethal, but Bigfoot wasn't most creatures. He had started rambling around midnight in an ancient language that made the air feel thick and heavy. Around two in the morning, he had gotten into an imaginary argument with her father about cheating at poker. Mostly, what he said was nonsense.

At five in the morning, Bigfoot had ripped a gnarly fart that made her eyes water but had finally settled. Other than the occasional groan, it seemed like the worst had passed.

During this period of time, Velvet had watched as the little people had come out of the woods to inspect her home. They were aware she was in the cabin and stayed back but had ransacked the barn. She watched in dismay as they lost a large chunk of their supplies to the invaders and had actually cracked the door to take a couple of shots when the opportunity arose.

It was strange that the little people weren't trying to break in. If they knew she was there, why not press the attack while Bigfoot was down?

Something wasn't right, and she thought back to her argument with Eulalie. Her sister had been convinced that some intelligent force was conspiring against them, but Velvet had refused to see it. These people outside her home seemed smart enough to survive, but based on their behavior, they weren't the ones in charge.

So who could it be?

"Velvet?" Emery landed on the frame of the door, his tiny limbs clinging to the wood. "You need to eat something. It's almost dinnertime."

"I suppose." She peered through the window once more. There wasn't any sign of the little people now. Still, she hated to look away.

"I'll keep watch. Take five minutes, go eat and drink. It'll be okay." He shooed her off, and she walked into the kitchen to see what he had brought her. It was a raccoon Eulalie had trapped a couple of weeks ago, tidily wrapped in a web. She opened her mouth wide for her fangs to descend, sank them into the tenderized flesh, and drank.

The cocoon in her hands shriveled up like a giant Capri Sun as she drank the meal inside. When she was done, she got herself a glass of water from the sink and was grateful when liquid flowed from the faucet. Now that the cabin itself was under attack, Eulalie's concerns seemed well-founded. Hopefully, the little people wouldn't find out how to ruin their water supply.

"Something is happening out there." Emery frowned, which was almost comical. His long, pointed nose hung down over his lips, making him look like a sad little troll.

"What?" she asked.

He didn't have to answer, because she heard it. It was faint at first, but someone was tapping on the walls of the cabin. The sound amplified as others joined in. She peered through the shutters to see that one of the little men was using his spear to poke at the siding.

"Can they get in?" she asked.

"I don't know," Emery answered. "But we need to get them to stop."

"Damn." She looked over at Bigfoot, who was still asleep. Even if she wanted to run, where could she go? Her uncle still needed time to recover, which was a scary thought as well. Whatever poison was in his system must be potent indeed to have dropped him as fast as it had, which meant it would probably kill her outright.

She went into the kitchen and picked out an old cleaver from the knife drawer. After grabbing the broom from next to the fridge, she met Emery at the front door. "I'm going to need you to make a little noise while I go out through the roof."

Emery made a face like he was going to argue, but the tapping intensified. One of the creatures was now trying to wedge his spear into one of the shutters. She threw the imp a knowing glance, then reached down toward her spinnerets to withdraw some webbing. Though she was unable to create the intricate webs that her sister could make, it was still strong enough to cocoon a creature.

She used it to attach the cleaver to the broom handle, then gave it a practice swing.

The imp nodded. "How long should I wait?" he asked.

"Count to thirty." Velvet flexed her legs and leaped up into the loft. From here, she was able to let herself into the attic of the cabin. It was mostly full of boxes from their childhood, things her parents couldn't bear to part with.

There were also several boxes of canned soup for her father in case of emergencies.

She stopped to touch the corner of one of the boxes. It suddenly occurred to her that the last time the box was opened, her father had been alive. Tears forced their way into her eyes as she tried to sniff them back.

"I am *not* crying over fucking soup," she muttered, then moved to the hatch that had been bolted shut from the inside. Her father had installed it for their mother and them when they were little so they wouldn't wake him up if they went out at night. She put her hand fondly on the bolted passage, took a deep breath, then slid the bolt out of the way and pushed it open.

It moved with nary a sound, and she was out on the roof. The afternoon air was chilled, and her breath was coming in tiny clouds that vanished on the breeze. Down below, she heard Emery let out a shriek of alarm and start banging on one of the windows.

Her sense picked up one of the little men directly beneath her. Near the back of the cabin, she cast a wary gaze toward the tree line. Seeing there was nobody coming, she chanced a look over the edge. The cannibal carrying the spear was moving toward the corner of the house. His back was to her.

She dropped down from above, then swung her makeshift halberd in a wide arc. When she struck the creature in the head, the blade stuck in its thick skull. It fell with a grunt.

"Plus two to damage, bitch." She yanked the cleaver out of its skull and used the reflective blade to peek around the corner. Two of them were moving toward the racket that Emery was making, but a third was using its spear to try to force open the shutter that went to her father's room.

Seeing red, she charged around the corner and sprinted toward the Nirumbi forcing open the window. It let out a screech of rage when it saw her, but she sank her fangs into its neck before it could do anything else.

The Nirumbi farthest from her cried out and threw its spear. She used the Nirumbi she held as a shield to block it, then drew the SIG and fired. Her shot hit the Nirumbi that had thrown the spear in the chest, and it went down. The third raised its own spear, but Velvet swung her makeshift weapon hard enough that it cleaved through the little man's arm.

The broom handle broke. She pulled the spear out of the Nirumbi in her mouth and threw him at his friend. They both fell down, and Velvet used the spear to pin them together at the belly.

"Nirumbi kabob," she muttered with a grin, then leaped onto the roof. A second later, three Nirumbi came around the corner to investigate, but Velvet was on her way to the other side of the house. She found two more Nirumbi nervously circling the house.

She dropped down from above and fired the SIG. It took four shots this time, but she killed them both and took their spears before fleeing to the roof. By now, the air was filled with hooting as they tried to track her down. A group of them had emerged from the barn, but Velvet kept to the back of the cabin. She snuck back inside and latched the hatch shut.

Down below, Emery was shrieking his little head off, but the tapping had already stopped.

"I bought us some time," she told him, then picked up her father's rifle from the dining room table. "I'm thinking we can pick a few more off from the roof."

Emery nodded, then pressed his face to the gap in the window. "Should I make another distraction?"

"Nope." She moved past him and pulled open the front door. The Nirumbi were so busy scanning the roof that she was able to squeeze off two shots before they fled. Her aim with the rifle was far better, and she slammed the door shut and bolted it.

"Disgusting," Emery remarked as he watched through the window gap.

"Death is never pretty but sometimes necessary," she told him.

That was a fact that her father had drilled into her since she was little, ever since she could hunt. She had cried the first time she had caught a rabbit on her own. The poor thing had looked terrified when she snapped its neck as her mother had taught her.

"They're eating their own dead." Emery moved away from the window so that Velvet could look. Sure enough, the two she had shot were getting carved up by their brethren as if they were worried the meat would suddenly go bad.

She debated taking another shot at them, but a small group had formed a semicircle around the front door. They were holding bows, and she knew better than to mess with poisonous arrows. Maybe if she went up top, she could snipe a couple? Over near the barn, a group of them appeared from out of the forest.

"Shit," she muttered, then moved over to Bigfoot. "Uncle Foot? Hey!" She tried slapping him into consciousness. "I really need you to wake up right now!"

"Velvet!" Emery's wings flapped frantically as he backed away from the door. "They're lighting torches!"

She moved to the window and yanked it open. The nearest Nirumbi let out a squawk of alarm as she looked down her sights at a trio of Nirumbi who were trying to build a fire out of hay from the loft. Smoke was already climbing from the stack when she fired, taking out one of them before slamming the window shut.

"Uncle Foot!" She screamed as she ran to the kitchen window. When she opened it, she could sense the arrow coming at her and dodged. It passed harmlessly through her hair and stuck in the fridge. Ducking down, she pulled the window shut as two more arrows came in.

"What do we do?" Emery's eyes were wide as he hovered before her. "Velvet, we need to run!"

"I'm not leaving without him," she said, looking over at Bigfoot.

"But you can't leave with him." The imp screwed up his features. "Maybe if you open a window, I can lead them away?"

"They're not stupid; they know we're still in here." Frowning, she looked through the gap in the window again. Torches were being lit. The idea of leaving Bigfoot behind made her sick to her stomach, but her feelings wouldn't matter once the flames made it through the wooden walls.

Could the cabin even be set on fire? It was magical in nature and was bigger on the inside. It was something they had never tested for obvious reasons. She said a little prayer as the cheering Nirumbi came toward her, their torches held high.

This was her home. It was the only place she had ever known, and now she was going to die inside it.

From the forest, there came a piercing cry that made the hair on her legs stand on end. The sound permeated the house, and Bigfoot shifted uncomfortably on the couch in response.

"What the hell was that?" she asked. It was apparent that the Nirumbi didn't know either, because they turned to look outward, the cabin now forgotten.

The cry came again. This time, it sounded like a pair of voices screaming counterpoint to each other, causing her veins to fill with ice. What dreadful creature could conjure such a sound?

The nearest Nirumbi carrying a torch turned toward the cabin and came at them. Its beady eyes glistened in the light of the flames as it drew close.

A dark shape crashed into the creature from above. It was a beast with dark skin and powerful wings that flapped mightily. When the newcomer turned to face the cabin, Velvet realized she was looking at a woman with flattened features and pointed ears. Her skin was made of stone, and her lips curled up to reveal a pair of fangs. It was a gargoyle, as beautiful as she was deadly.

The gargoyle trampled the Nirumbi into the ground with large talons, then paused when a spear shattered on the back of her neck. She turned her dreadful gaze on a nearby cluster of Nirumbi and scowled.

"Wha—" Aghast, Velvet could only watch as the gargoyle barreled into the Nirumbi. They scattered like leaves, but the gargoyle snagged a pair of them and flew into the sky. Tiny shrieks filled the air when she dropped them a few seconds later.

Fat snowflakes began to drift across the yard, followed by a thunderclap. The weather had rapidly turned, and the air felt electrified. Velvet realized she was holding her breath.

The Nirumbi nocked arrows and held them up, clearly tracking the gargoyle. Velvet debated moving to the roof for a better view, but thoughts of this were dashed when icy spears rained down from above. A pair of women emerged from the forest, causing the Nirumbi to panic and switch to their spears.

One of the women had fox ears with a trio of tails whirling behind and wearing a thick white coat. She held a shield made of branches that had been tightly woven together. There were a few arrows protruding from it.

The other was Dana. There were easily twenty arrows sticking out of her, and she collected a couple more plus a spear as she charged into the little men, swinging her sword and cutting them apart.

The Nirumbi had enough. They let out shrill cries as they broke and ran for the forest. Velvet half expected her rescuers to let them go, but the fox summoned a volley of ice that caused a momentary whiteout. That shrill cry came again, followed by several thunderclaps. Frost covered the windows, preventing her from seeing anymore, and she backed away from the door.

The storm outside raged for several minutes, then came absolute silence. She nearly jumped out of her skin when someone knocked.

"Velvet?" It was Dana. "Are you in there?"

Velvet ran to the door and threw it open. Impossibly, her friend had come for her. She would have hugged the zombie if not for all the arrows sticking out of her.

Dana flicked the sword a few times to knock the blood off it, then folded it up and handed it over.

"I probably should have brought this back sooner," she confessed.

"Yes. You should have." Velvet smiled, then looked over Dana's shoulder. The yard was covered in a thin blanket of snow, and all around were several Nirumbi-sized lumps beneath it. The air smelled of blood and ozone, and she walked outside with Emery right behind her.

The fox woman knelt over one of the lumps, her nostrils flared as she sniffed the air. Nearby, the gargoyle thudded into the ground and rose, her features twisted in disdain, then indifference.

"Thank you," Velvet said. "You guys saved us. Please, you have to help me. Bigfoot is hurt."

"Poison?" asked the fox. "I can smell it. I may be able to do something to help that." She made it to the door and gave a little bow. "My name is Yuki, by the way."

"Thank you, Yuki." Velvet watched her walk inside and kneel next to the couch. She turned her attention back to Dana. "How did you get here?"

"Magic rat portal. Will explain later. This is Abella, by the way." Dana gestured at the gargoyle.

"I will stand watch," Abella informed them, then lifted into the sky and disappeared.

"You have no idea how glad I am to see you," Velvet said. "Those weird little guys came out of nowhere, and I—"

Movement from around the barn caught her eye, and she turned her head, her heart coming to a stop. One of the figures was a woman with a large horn coming from her head, but all Velvet could focus on was the man next to her.

He wore a brown coat and jeans and was talking with the horned woman. The wind was catching in his hair, causing it to billow ever so slightly backward. Dark-brown eyes that reminded her of earth sat just above a smile that made her entire body hot and smooshy at the same time. In her gut, she felt the heat shift from her belly, immediately down to her groin. She suddenly felt heavy, as if the ground was about to swallow her up.

"You must be Velvet." When he spoke, it was as if his voice wrapped around her like a warm blanket. "My name is Mike. I'm the new Caretaker."

"Caretaker?" Emery shook in anticipation.

"And you must be Emery. I have something for you." Mike reached into his pocket and pulled out a shiny coin. "I got this a while ago, in case I made it out this way. It's a real silver dollar, and—"

"*Shiny!*" Emery snatched the coin from Mike, then landed on his shoulder as he gave the coin a bite with his teeth. "It's real silver, Vee, real silver!"

"Uh, yeah." Velvet's brain wasn't forming any words, and she just stared at Mike. It was as if she couldn't get enough of the very sight of him, and she felt her groin tighten beneath her.

"Not to be that person, but can we head inside?" Dana pulled one of the arrows out of her leg. "Pincushion isn't my favorite look."

"Yes, please, come in." Velvet's mouth was dry, and her hands shook as she led them into the house. When she followed Mike inside, all she could think about was what it would be like to run her hands through his hair, to touch his skin, to feel him up against her body.

But most of all, what their children would look like.

CONFLICTED

T he snow crunched beneath Mike's feet as he walked through the
forests of Oregon. In front of him, Yuki walked on top of the snow,
carrying her shield, leaving no trace of her passage. Up above,
Abella circled.

The Nirumbi, in their haste, had made no effort to hide their tracks. The
ones who had survived the slaughter at the cabin had gathered into a larger
group and headed north. Though his tracking skills were only slightly better
than the average person, the thirty-foot-wide path made of tiny footprints and
discarded spears made his job easy.

"Anything up ahead?" he asked, then looked up. Abella held up both fists,
which was the signal for no. He adjusted the strap on the rifle Velvet had
loaned him.

"Then we keep going," Yuki said. They had spent the night in the cabin
and were now trying to track the Nirumbi. The plan was to find where they
were hiding in the woods, then figure out what to do with them. The internet
had been no help—in fact, his phone had been unable to acquire any kind of
signal since their arrival.

With Bigfoot still sleeping off his poison, they would have to wait for him
to wake up before they could leave. Quetzalli and Dana had stayed behind
with Velvet in case of another attack. Not only could Quetzalli shock any
attackers, but the away team would hear the resulting thunder and be able to
send Abella back to assist.

"Here's another one," Yuki declared as she knelt in the snow. Mike joined her and frowned.

The Nirumbi had been quick to carve up their own at the cabin before being forced to run. While fleeing, some had obviously fallen due to injuries and had received similar treatments. This one had been hastily hacked apart and was missing both legs and an arm.

"Why the fuck do they do this?" Mike asked.

"Don't know," Yuki replied. "Quetzalli had some ideas, but her information is rumors from hundreds of years ago. Her best guess was that it was a way to honor the dead or the act has some kind of religious implications."

"Thou shalt eat thy dead?" He looked away from the little man on the ground. "Would hate to see the other nine commandments."

"It's not really for us to judge," Yuki said as she summoned a blanket of snow to cover the body. "To them, the act of eating their own is no different from you brushing your teeth after meals."

"That serves an actual purpose though," he objected.

"And you think this doesn't? At a bare minimum, their bodies become food for others. You only find it detestable because you were raised with the idea that you don't eat Grandma when she dies."

"Maybe that started because grandma is too chewy," he said. "Not a lot of great meat on an elderly woman."

Yuki snorted. "Maybe humans don't eat Grandma for the same reason that Nirumbi eat one another—as a sign of respect."

Mike nodded. Though cannibalism didn't make complete sense to him, his own lifestyle could be seen as immoral and confusing to others.

They continued onward for a few more minutes before the path narrowed, leading them down into a small ravine surrounded by majestic trees and thick bushes blanketed in snow. If not for the footprints, they would have missed the narrow path that ran beneath a trio of very large pine trees.

Yuki crouched and went ahead of him. He knelt to follow but paused when he heard Abella thump into the ground behind him.

"Nowhere to land inside," she told him. "It's completely surrounded by trees."

"Great," he muttered, then followed Yuki in. When he emerged from under the tree, he stared in awe at the large stone overhang above them. They were surrounded by trees on every side, and the overhang itself formed the entrance to a large cave.

"Wow," he muttered, then snapped a few pics with his phone. "Do you think this is one of the goblin caves?"

"Maybe." Yuki inspected the mouth of the cave. It was only a few feet tall, and Mike would need to crawl to properly fit inside. "From what I can tell, they all went in here."

"So what's the plan?" he asked. "Find a way to follow them in, maybe flush them out?"

"Hold up." Abella moved to the mouth of the cave and inspected the rim. She traced the edges with her hands, then moved away from it with a frown. "This is a recent opening."

"How can you tell?" he asked.

"It would be hard for you to notice, but you can see where the edges look clean." She pointed at a few areas. "Moss grew along here, but there's a thin line where there used to be stone. This cave was blocked off at some point, but it's been recently opened."

"Hmm." Yuki swished her tail, and the snow around their feet turned into frosty cyclones as the snow shifted about. What would have taken hours to find with shovels became only a couple of minutes when a pile of rubble was revealed away from the mouth.

"Aha!" Abella picked up a small boulder and hefted it up to the opening. She rolled it back and forth, then pinned it against part of the wall. "This piece came from here," she noted.

"So the Nirumbi dug their way free?" he asked.

"When you dig, the dirt goes behind you," Abella told him, then dropped the boulder. She inspected the rim of the cave again. "There are scratch marks on the outside. Big ones."

"Bear?" he asked.

"You wish." Abella opened her hand and put it against the stone. "Some of these gouges are deep enough for even *my* fingers to fit inside."

"Something dug them out?" He moved to where Abella was standing. "Who and why?"

"All questions we may not like the answers to." Yuki looked down at the rubble. "If we can fit this back inside, I can help seal the entrance."

Mike stood back as Abella pushed and rolled boulders back into the opening. Yuki created a ramp made of ice, which caused the boulders to roll farther down into the cave. He kept expecting the Nirumbi to arrive and fight back but assumed that maybe they had had enough.

Yuki blasted the cave with ice magic, creating a thick wall of ice that sealed the rocks in. They backed out of the small clearing, and Yuki stayed behind long enough to use one of her tarot cards to break apart the overhang. It collapsed, creating an even bigger pile of rubble outside the cave system.

"Even if they can dig their way out of that, it will take them weeks," she said. "And once the ice starts melting, this part of the cave will flood."

"I guess that means mission accomplished?" He tried to sound nonchalant about it, but his thoughts were on the large claw marks. Who had found the Nirumbi and let them out?

"The sooner we get home, the better," Abella declared. She took off, leaving Yuki and Mike alone in the forest.

The two of them exchanged a look. He wanted to ask the kitsune if she knew why Abella seemed so tense, but knew that Abella would hear them. His few attempts this morning to start a conversation with the gargoyle had gone nowhere.

"I guess we just need to get Bigfoot back on his feet," he said. "He can help us get home."

"That could still be a couple of days," Yuki replied. "Whatever they dosed him with would have killed a lesser creature. His magical nature meant it wasn't fatal but just barely."

"I guess the question is whether the attack was intentional. Were the Nirumbi sent by someone, or did Velvet happen to wander into their territory?"

"No idea. But their territory is inside that shitty cave, and they're welcome to it." They were following the tracks in reverse now, and she was walking beside him. "Did you know that Emily used to talk about this place? I always wanted to come check it out, but she kept telling me there was nothing to see. Naturally, now I know why."

"The arachne?"

"Mm-hmm. Some say gunpowder was invented by the Chinese just to scare them off. Their bodies are covered in fine hairs, gives them amazing sensory abilities. However, melt those hairs off and they're like a bunch of drunks in a bar."

"Have you ever run across one before now?"

"I hadn't. I'm still young for my kind, and the arachne had largely migrated to Europe. Between the big cities clustered together and a population unfamiliar with them, they were better able to thrive." Yuki paused, then looked back. Her ears twitched. "You feel that?"

He stopped and looked where she was looking. The forest was silent, other than the occasional thud of falling snow. "I'm not picking up on anything dangerous, if that's what you're asking."

Yuki frowned. Her tarot cards appeared in her left hand, and she fanned them out. "I feel like we're being watched."

"Maybe some of the Nirumbi got locked out?" He readied the rifle, his finger resting on the trigger guard. While not a sharpshooter by any means, he had been able to earn the marksmanship merit badge when he was a scout. If anything came out of the woods, he was confident he could at least hit it.

"Not Nirumbi," she said.

They stood this way for long enough that Abella joined them. The gargoyle tilted her head from side to side, then shrugged.

"I don't hear anything," she said. "If something's out there, it isn't even breathing."

"That's ominous as fuck," Mike said. "Let's head back and hope whatever it is will be just as scared of us as we are of it."

"I was never scared," Abella muttered, then took back to the sky. Mike watched her circle overhead and then let out a sigh. Hopefully whatever was bothering her would resolve itself.

Beth sat on the edge of Naia's fountain with Ratu's crystal ball in her lap. Naia was lying in the water, her features barely visible above the surface.

"And?" asked Ratu. It looked like she was in bed, her dark hair fanned out around her head.

"Nothing out of the ordinary here," replied Zel. When Beth had sent word to the centaurs that she needed a checkup, she had been surprised when Zel herself had arrived. "Vital signs are normal, and I'm not seeing anything in her bloodwork."

"That's all you have to say?" asked Beth.

"I love what you're doing with your hair," Zel added. "But that's to be expected, right?" She looked over at Naia.

"Indeed. Beauty without peer, and minimal effort too." Naia smirked.

"Hmm." Ratu's voice barely came through the crystal ball. She picked up the cup of tea on her nightstand and sipped it. "That certainly rules out a few theories of my own."

"Such as?" Beth asked.

"Hybridization. I wondered if perhaps you had become part nymph, beyond the soul swap, that is. I also worried that perhaps a recent breeding had caused some overlap. Your dalliance with the dullahan could have had unexpected consequences, much like Mike did with Cecilia."

Beth blushed.

"As far as I can tell, she's still human." Zel packed away the small apothecary she carried with her. "I'm afraid I can't be of much help."

"Your assistance was very valuable." Ratu bowed her head. "Now that we have ruled out the obvious, we must step into the realm of hypotheticals."

Beth frowned. She didn't like the idea that what was happening with her was hypothetical. In fact, nothing strange had happened after the tub incident, and she was already content to leave the issue alone. However, Naia had insisted on Ratu's input.

"Have you spoken with Mike yet?" Ratu asked.

Beth checked her phone. The picture Lily had sent Mike was still on *delivered*, which meant Mike hadn't seen it yet. This troubled her, but there wasn't much she could do about it. "I haven't," she told them.

"That man gets himself into the best kind of trouble." The naga chuckled, then refilled her cup. "I am ready to posit a theory."

"Lay it on me."

"According to Naia, your mind was actually inside the soul swap with her. This is not a normal occurrence and proof that something exceptional has happened. I believe your soul may have a special susceptibility to change."

"How so?"

"Let's look at the evidence. Your soul has left your body on more than one occasion, allowing your body to give host to a tormented soul."

"She prefers that we call her Jenny," Naia added.

"Regardless, Beth's soul has been displaced on more than one occasion. In a separate instance, a powerful entity, the demon Oliver, was able to graft a piece of his essence onto your soul. This required that we run your soul through a magical filter, which *almost* didn't work, I might remind you. You were purified, in a manner of speaking."

"So how is this all related?" Beth asked.

"Souls aren't liquid in nature. Think of them like a slow-moving fluid. You dip your finger in a pond, it will look the same after you pull your finger out. Poke your finger in pudding, not only will some stick to your finger, but it will take some time for the hole to close."

"But I control the process," Naia said, sitting up in the fountain. "She shouldn't have been able to take more than I offered."

"And I don't think she did." Ratu paused and leaned away from the orb. When she came back, she was holding a small sandwich. "Think back on the finger analogy. If Beth was the finger and your magic the pond, it wasn't just a quick dip—it was a soak. Her soul, while mixed with yours, had a giant open wound. You can't soak an open wound in water and expect nothing to happen."

"I'm infected with magic?" Beth asked, barely able to contain her excitement.

"I prefer the term *blessed*. But yes. Over the course of her years, Emily was able to nurture and grow her own talents in the realm of magic. It required hard work and dedication, but it did start with the nymph's blessing. For you, I suspect your soul may have attuned itself to Naia's, thus fast-tracking the process. Think of it like a transfusion. You've been steeped in powerful magic, or maybe 'calibrated' is a better word? Aligned? No matter." Ratu waved her hand dismissively.

"Beth can do magic now?" Zel had pulled out a notebook and was scribbling notes. "Water magic specifically, or…?"

"My guess is simply a natural talent for it. Water manipulation was a coincidence. Rather, she was about to cave her own head in and her magic protected her."

"So does that make me a witch?" Beth asked. "Or a wizard?"

"When you can do magic, you can call yourself whatever the fuck you want." Ratu sighed. "But this also comes with a burden of its own. She needs to learn some basics, if for no other reason than to avoid injury. Based on what I've heard, she has more power than she can handle."

"But my magic protected me," Beth said. "How would it hurt me?"

Ratu cleared her throat. "When it comes to magic, your imagination is the limit. Your bones could have become rubber, or you could have shrunk to the size of an insect. There's no telling what you're capable of in your current state. You also need to remember that magic always comes with a price. Sometimes, the cost isn't worth paying." The naga leaned off orb again and came back with a quill and a piece of paper. "I am writing down some basic texts for you to read from the Library. I'll send this to Sofia, and she'll make sure you get them. You have to study, if only to avoid blowing off your own face."

Beth nodded, doing her best to contain the ball of excitement that had formed in her belly. The idea that she now had her very own kind of magic felt much like winning the lottery. What would her magic be like? Would it feel cold, racing through her veins like ice? Or perhaps it would be like fire, eager to erupt from her fingertips.

"After I look at these books, should I study under someone?" She moved close to the ball. "Would you be able to teach me?"

Ratu smiled, then shook her head. "I am in no condition to help you right now. Besides, my understanding of magic is focused on enchantments and objects. My own abilities are of a divine nature, so I'm not sure how much help I would be. In fact, I would recommend Yuki for the job, if she'll accept."

"I can help a little bit." Amymone appeared from her tree, hanging upside down by her legs. She folded the page she was on in her book and then closed it. "And Naia too. Our magic is nature-based and very niche, but we can explain some of the basics. We taught Emily, when she first came here."

Naia smiled, but her grin faded. She turned to Beth, a somber look on her face. "We all know the shadow drove her ambition, and a similar thing can still happen to you. You have to be careful."

"I will," Beth promised. She looked up at Amymone. "When can we start?"

"After you get those books from Sofia." The dryad swung back and forth, her skirt held in place by a few convenient vines. "I would focus on meditative practices. Being able to touch your magic is a great start."

Naia nodded. "Mike figured that one out pretty fast. But his magic is…well…"

Beth laughed. "Somehow more useful than you'd expect," she finished.

"His magic is something else completely," Ratu added. "Neither divine nor inherent. It doesn't have a label. When he advances enough, he may choose to pursue spellcraft. By then, you will likely be a suitable instructor for him."

"Divine…versus…inherent…" Zel was scribbling furiously. "So it's different being born with magic versus acquiring it? What about the rules of heredity? Is magic passed along genetic lines?"

"Depends on the magic." Ratu opened her mouth extra wide, shoved the whole sandwich in, and swallowed it in one bite. "Sorry, I'm hungry and can't wait any longer. Typically, inheritance is usually only a factor if the creature itself is magical. Dragons are a great example, as well as my own kind."

"What about half-breeds?" Zel looked up. "For example, what if your mother was a naga and your father was a human?"

The naga laughed. "*If* they could actually conceive a child, it's possible. It's been a long time since any crossbreeding has occurred, and you can thank the Greek and Roman gods for that. Caused nothing but problems, and it actually became a huge taboo to breed with humans because of it."

"Fascinating." Zel closed her book. "Let me know if you need anything from the herd. It was nice to see everyone."

The centaur bowed low, then headed off toward the door of the greenhouse.

"You'd think she'd want to take the shortcut home," Beth noted.

"She probably wants some time to herself," Naia said. "When you're the one in charge, you don't often get opportunities to be alone. Besides, she has a lot to think about."

"Like what?"

Naia shrugged and flashed a smile. "That isn't my burden to share," she said, then turned her attention to the garage. The door opened, and Eulalie stepped out. She was wearing a dark tank top with a matching black skirt with white stripes down the side.

"Am I interrupting something?" she asked.

"Not really." Beth noticed that Eulalie's lower half didn't look as glossy as it had the day before. "Do you need something?"

"Just spreading my legs. Slept like the dead, and I didn't mean to be out for so long." She walked over to join them, her legs moving in a rhythmic fashion. Beth had felt uncomfortable yesterday being so close to Eulalie, a reaction she felt guilty about.

Today was different. Her fear had been replaced with curiosity, and she couldn't help but notice thin gray cracks had appeared along Eulalie's legs.

"Did you hurt yourself?" Beth gestured at the lines.

"No. This is normal." Eulalie looked at Naia. "Am I allowed to soak in the fountain?"

"Everyone is welcome. Unless you pee in the water. Then I might drown you." Naia winked.

Beth watched Eulalie as she stretched out in the water and sighed. The fountain was big enough for the arachne to properly spread her legs, and she floated around like an ominous lily pad. As tempted as Beth was to stick around and get to know Eulalie a bit more, there was something else on her agenda.

"I've got some things I need to take care of," she announced. "See you all later tonight."

"Have fun." Naia gave Beth a knowing look.

With a skip in her step, Beth headed for her room and let herself into the magic cave in her closet. It didn't take her long to reach the Labyrinth. As she approached, she saw the fairy trio chasing one another around the mirror pool, trying to push one another in.

"Can one of you find Asterion for me?" she asked. For the first time, she realized the fairies shimmered when she looked at them. Each one was surrounded in a colorful field composed of their unique color. They left spectral trails behind them as they whizzed about her.

"Ooh, you seem different today," said Cerulea. She was blue and had beetle-like features.

"I think she's extra pretty." This was from Carmina. Shaped like a dragonfly, she zipped about, inspecting Beth's face up close with compound eyes. "And she smells good too."

Olivia, using her long grasshopper legs, bounced up and down next to Beth. "I think it may be feeding time," she announced with glee, then the

RADLEY'S APOCALYPSE FOR HORNY MONSTERS

three of them flew into the Labyrinth, leaving a trail of glitter in the air that slowly descended.

Beth laughed, then straightened out her dress and waited. It took a bit, but the doors of the Labyrinth finally creaked open. Ever since getting knocked off their hinges by the shadow, they didn't fit quite right. They made the entrance look even more ominous.

Asterion stood between the doors, his ax casually held over his shoulder. He took a few steps forward and snorted. The dark fur of his body made it look like he was covered in soot, and he had grown a small patch of fur between his horns that looked suspiciously like a mohawk.

"My friend." He greeted her with a voice that rumbled like an old Harley Davidson. "Have you come to walk the Labyrinth with me?"

"I have." She moved to his side. He held out an arm, and she wrapped her arms around it and clung to him while they walked. "Take a girl somewhere quiet?"

"Hmmm." A smile crossed his face. Though he was generally slow to process information, this was a task he was well versed in. Asterion led her through the maze, careful to step around the traps. The fairies, sensing an easy meal, circled them while giggling.

"You seem extra...pretty today," he told her.

"Thank you." She stroked his bicep. It was like trying to squeeze a piece of metal wrapped in leather. "Has Ratu been keeping you busy?"

"Indeed." He took her through a few turns she didn't recognize, and then they stepped into a room with a pond in the middle. A small island with soft grass had been built in the middle.

"This is new," she told him.

"The lady built it for me," he said, then scooped her up with one arm and walked through the water. It came up to his waist as he crossed. When he set her down on the island, she kicked off her shoes and savored the sensation of the soft blades beneath her toes.

"What do you need an island for?"

"To make you...more comfortable." Asterion smirked. "The ground is soft, like a human bed."

"You had this built for me?"

"Indeed." He set the ax down on the grass. "It will be more comfortable than the rocks."

"Let's find out." She moved into his arms, tilting her head to kiss him.

Asterion obliged, letting out a grunt of approval when she squeezed the head of his cock through his loincloth. She explored his lips with hers, smiling at the feel of his stiff fur against her face. When he put his hand on her breast, she placed her hand over his own.

"Feel free to be rough with me," she told him, her whole body tingling as if full of starlight.

"Hmmm…I do not wish to hurt you," he replied.

"Don't worry. You won't." She squeezed his cock hard, then gave it a couple of pumps. "And I'll tell you if you do, so don't worry about it."

He looked doubtful but nodded his acceptance. When he squeezed her breast, she moaned, then pushed him onto the ground. Surprised, he toppled over, his loincloth flapping to one side to reveal his massive member.

She felt a surge of energy and confidence. When she knelt to take his massive member in her mouth, she could hear Naia's voice in her ear.

Use your tongue on the frenulum. Slow strokes up and down, fast ones side to side. Beth could almost picture the nymph's smile as she gave instructions. Not one to disobey, Beth followed them.

The noise Asterion made was somewhere between a grunt and a bellow. He lifted his head to see what Beth was doing, then placed his hand on the back of her head.

"I can be rough?" he asked.

"Only if I can." Beth smirked at him, then opened her mouth wide.

The Minotaur forced her head down onto his long shaft. What ordinarily took her several minutes of concentration and slobber was accomplished in seconds. His massive glans pushed against the back of her throat. Her gag reflex was nonexistent, and she inhaled him. She tried to take him all the way, but he pulled on her hair, stalling her progress.

Breathe through your nose. There's plenty of room. The nymph's encouraging words helped Beth relax. *Your body is ready for this. You just have to trust me.*

Naia guided Beth through the deepest blow job of her life. When Asterion came, she couldn't swallow fast enough. Sperm shot out her nose and pooled on his belly. Her sinuses didn't even respond, and she took a deep breath through her nose to swallow what she could. Each gulp filled her with energy, and she felt a fire inside that needed to be quenched. The fairy girls dropped out of the sky, greedily stuffing their faces with what Beth had missed. They were like Mother Nature's horny cleanup crew.

"It's my turn," Beth told him, then squeezed the base of his cock. He grunted, a big grin on his face. Asterion could easily go twice; it was something about his genetic makeup. The fairies let out a cheer and moved away as Beth positioned herself over his waist, her legs spread wide.

When she lowered herself, she deliberately missed his cock, letting it slide up her belly instead. While grinding her pussy on the base of his shaft, she gave his cock a good rub, marveling at how it slapped her above her belly button. It was both wide and long, and she couldn't wait to feel it stretch her out, to test her new limitations.

Asterion groaned. Beth looked down to see that Carmina had latched her mouth onto the edge of his urethra and was sucking.

"I've got a better use for you," she declared, then wiped some of the semen off Asterion's gut and pulled down her top to reveal her breasts. She swiped some of the cum on her nipples, then pulled the fairy off Asterion's dick and moved her to her breast.

Carmina, without missing a beat, latched on like a magic nipple clamp. It made Beth's skin tingle pleasantly, so she snatched Cerulea out of the air and repeated the process with her other breast. Both fairies were hungrily nibbling on sensitive flesh, which sent tingles up and down Beth's spine.

"Time to test her out," she muttered, then slid up Asterion's shaft while pressing it flat against his belly. She was practically sitting on his chest once she could switch directions and move back down. His huge glans pressed against her swollen labia, creating a tremendous amount of pressure as his shaft bent before forcing her vaginal lips apart.

Beth groaned, then stopped for a moment to acclimate. She was soaking wet, and it was almost like the core of her body was now liquid metal. There was just enough friction that she could feel every glorious inch as it slid inside her, but the experience was not like anything she had previously felt. It was almost as if she had grown millions of nerve endings all along the interior of her vagina, and she could tell exactly where the head of his penis touched her inside.

She cried out, her eyes filling with tears. It was almost like every previous sexual encounter had been but a shadow of what could be. Her lower body felt so full as she slowly approached the base of Asterion's shaft, and the sensation of being stretched apart was perfectly balanced between pleasure and pain.

The fairies were now biting the edges of her nipples, and when she grabbed her own breasts, they flattened beneath her hands to remain in place. Olivia landed on Asterion's forehead and looked at Beth expectantly.

She snatched up the green fairy and placed her at the base of Asterion's cock. All the fairy girls were stretchy like elastic, and she knew they wouldn't get hurt, even if squished. Beth lifted her hips long enough for Olivia to wrap her long legs around Asterion's girthy shaft, then slid back down. A tiny mouth licked her all around her clitoris, sending delightful tremors through her body.

"Beth." Asterion was looking at her in awe as she started with a slow grind. She usually rode on top of him but had to stop every so often to take a breather. His thick glans kept pushing up against her womb, an act that usually hurt.

Not anymore though. The rigid tissue of her cervix no longer had any complaints as she shoved herself onto him. She laughed in delight as her lower belly distended along the path of his cock. Maybe her magic would make her stretchy like the fairies? Was that a choice she could make? If her body could be made to stretch, how big of a cock could she physically take?

A chill ran up her spine, and she groaned. Movement off to the side caught her attention, and she saw that the pool of water was moving now, circling the small island like an eddy.

Oh God. She discovered that the water was reacting to her movements. When she shifted from her slow grind to a steady motion that slammed Asterion's hips into her thighs, she felt the heat inside her body build as the water splashed and spilled onto the nearby banks. Was her arousal triggering the water's movement?

"Beth, I…" Asterion's eyes were bugging out in his head, and he placed his hands on her hips. "I am getting close."

She leaned forward and put her hands on his horns. This caused her ass to lift off the ground, and she gave the Minotaur a kiss on the nose.

"Fuck me like you mean it," she growled.

Asterion snorted, then slammed himself into her.

The shock wave of pleasure went straight to her skull, then scattered through her limbs as he repeated the act. He paused to regard her with those puppy-dog eyes of his, and she responded by putting her hands on his chest.

"Is that the best you can do?" she demanded.

He slammed into her again, then let out a grunt that sounded like a train coming to a stop. Beth put her hands on his neck and squeezed.

"Yes!" she cried as she slammed her full weight down onto his cock. The water around the island was climbing into the air, creating ribbons that crossed over one another. When he came inside her, she could feel liquid heat suffuse her whole body.

She slammed herself onto Asterion hard enough that Olivia shot out like a rubber ball, bouncing off a pair of rocks before tumbling onto the grass. The fairy girl let out a belch and went limp.

"More, more!" Beth could feel her orgasm building and watched in awe as the streamers climbed higher. Asterion groaned, his eyes rolling up in his head as his massive cock twitched inside her. She felt like she was plugged into him, able to move her body in a perfect rhythm that kept him from coming down from his own orgasmic high.

She was gasping now, and her body felt like a giant rubber band, stretched to the limit. When she finally snapped, she let out a shriek of delight as the water around them exploded, showering the small island in a miniature rainstorm. Desperate to ride the waves of pleasure coursing through her, she was able to tease out a second, smaller orgasm that accomplished the same effect. The ground was drenched, and she could barely see now that her hair was in her face. Carmina had fallen off one of her breasts, and she tried to hold Cerulea in place as a third orgasm built. Down below, Asterion was moaning, his fingers digging into the damp soil.

The water sloshed along the banks as the ribbons began to climb into the air again. For just a moment, Beth felt a connection with the small lake, her heart and mind expanding to fill the chamber.

The connection faded when a loud buzz filled the air. A yellow light fell from above like a shooting star, then stopped to hover in front of Beth, weaving about to get her attention. It was the fourth fairy sister, Daisy. She was signing frantically, and Beth had to fight a groan of disappointment as she squinted in an attempt to focus.

"Someone's causing trouble in the front yard?" It was her best guess, and Daisy, though deaf, could hear vibrations through her wings. Beth's stomach dropped as the call of duty tempered her lust.

Daisy nodded, then shot off for the center of the Labyrinth.

"Guess we'll have to finish our fun some other time," she said as she pulled herself off Asterion. The Minotaur groaned, sat up to help her stand, then flopped back as if relieved.

Beth hastily threw on her clothes and then jogged to the mirror pool. The path they had taken in hadn't been complicated, and it was easy enough to find her way out. Once past the gate, she stood on the edge of the water and looked at her reflection. Even though she had been soaking wet only minutes ago, her hair was starting to curl itself back into how she had styled it that morning.

With a grin, she took a deep breath and hopped in. The water was cool to the touch as the Labyrinth disappeared and she was rushed to the house.

BACK AT THE CABIN, MIKE HUNG HIS COAT ON A HOOK BY THE DOOR AND THEN sat down in a comfy armchair by the fire. The warmth of the crackling heat was complemented by the pleasant smell of burning pine that permeated the cabin. He let out a sigh and kicked off his shoes, then put his feet up on the ottoman so that the heat would reach his toes.

"Master." Emery flew up, carrying a thermos. "Some coffee to warm you."

"Please just call me Mike." He smiled at the imp, then took the thermos. "And thank you. Is there a full pot? The others might want some."

"But of course, Mas—Mike." Emery beamed and then shot across the cabin to the kitchen. The little imp was surprisingly strong and easily manipulated the coffee pot despite it being almost as big as he was.

Mike closed his eyes and enjoyed the warmth of the fire. Quetzalli came out of Darren's room, wearing a thick sweater and leggings.

"Where did you get those?" he asked.

"Dana bought them for me." Quetzalli grabbed the hem of her sweater and lifted it above her belly. "I like how it holds everything in place. I feel far less wobbly this way."

God bless you, Dana, he thought to himself. The dark leggings left little to the imagination, and Quetzalli forgot to lower her sweater when she turned her attention to the loft, giving him a great view of her ass. Up above, Dana had appeared at the top of the stairs, carrying a box.

"Velvet said there's some food in here," she announced. "Que, fix your sweater."

Quetzalli straightened out her sweater. Mike looked at Dana, who winked at him.

"Where's Velvet?" he asked.

"She was checking out the barn. Wanted to see how much damage was done."

"What about him?" Mike looked over at Bigfoot. He was sprawled out across the couch now, and he grunted every couple of minutes in his sleep.

"No improvement. Speaking of which…" Dana set the box on the counter and walked over to squat next to Mike. "The arrows were poisonous, but we don't know what it was. I pulled a bunch of them out of myself and am kind of worried what might happen next time I feed."

"How so?" He leaned forward in his chair.

"The air here is cold, so I packed snacks for myself in a small cooler, which are now in the fridge. But what I mean is that when I eat, my blood will flow for a little bit. That will circulate the poison, and I have no idea what that means in terms of my zombieness."

"Oh." He frowned. Would the poison damage her after feeding? The idea that her regeneration would stall out like a car on a cold morning worried him. "You're wondering if you might go through your supply really fast."

"Correct." She patted him on the leg. "Not that I think you'll mind, but I might have to come to the source."

He nodded knowingly. Dana wasn't physically attracted to him, but right after a feeding, she became insatiably horny and would fuck anything she could get her hands on. It was a situation he made sure to never take advantage of.

"Well, it's a good thing we've got Quetzalli to help," he added. "Whatever makes you happiest."

"You're a good guy," she told him, then patted his knee. She went back to the kitchen and opened the box to pull out some cans of soup. "I'll heat some up for you, since I'm not doing anything else. Do you wanna go out and check on Velvet?"

"Yeah, no problem." He put his shoes and coat back on before going outside. Yuki was busy inspecting the perimeter she had built. Small fortress walls of ice stood around the cabin, with nasty spikes made of ice waiting for anybody who may climb them.

"Everything good?" he asked.

"Kind of." She stopped what she was doing and looked at him. Her green eyes were blazing with light. "Still concerned about what I sensed in the woods. I'm not taking any chances with your life."

"Neither am I." He gave her a wave as he headed for the barn. It looked like it had been in pretty good condition before the Nirumbi had gotten hold of it. The large door on the front had been torn down, which was where he walked in. He found Velvet right away, standing in the back next to an old jeep. Its windows had been broken out, and the interior had been gutted.

"Velvet?"

The arachne turned to look away from him, her fingers swiping at her face. "Sorry," she said with a sniffle. "It's just…this was my dad's car. Back when I was small, he would take Lala and me for rides around the forest. He would spend hours out here keeping it in working order. It was how he got supplies from town."

"It's hard seeing it like this, isn't it?" Mike moved to the side of the vehicle and put his hands on the cool metal. "When I was a kid, my mom and I bounced from home to home a lot. The only constant we had in our lives was our station wagon. I'm surprised the damn thing even ran. It was totaled in an accident, caught on fire and burned to the ground. The picture made it into the paper. I felt like I was looking at the murder scene of a friend." He didn't mention to her that he had been inside, and so had his mother. The fire had claimed his mother's life and freed him from her abuse, but not before leaving a mass of scars along the side of his body.

"My dad last drove this in October. Snuck out between storms to get a few things for the house, then came back." Velvet turned to face Mike and held out a car key. "The last time this key was used, he was alive."

Mike simply nodded, hoping she would say more.

"This whole place was always just us, you know? When Mom died, Eulalie took it the hardest. There were times I thought she was being ridiculous about it. I even told her to move on and caused a few fights. I feel bad about that now. I can't even look at this car without feeling like I'm going to fall to pieces any second."

"And that's okay." He stepped around one of her legs so he was facing her. From this close, he could see the individual hairs on her legs. Where Eulalie's body had been glossy and sinister, Velvet's looked soft like a child's teddy bear. "We all grieve differently. Just tell me what you need."

She looked up at him, her dark-brown eyes shimmering. The other eyes along her forehead glistened like tiny jewels, and he reached out to take her hand.

His magic ignited, catching him off guard, and the two of them froze in place when he shocked her. For just a second, his senses were overwhelmed as they magnified the world around him. The air in the barn was shifting back and forth in microcurrents around his legs, and he could hear the subtle shifting of wings up above. Strands of Velvet's hair stood on end, lifting away from her face as his magic crept along her skin.

"Mike…" Velvet looked at him in awe.

"Are you two okay in here?" Abella's talons crunched the fallen wood of the door as she walked into the barn. The gargoyle looked around the structure and shook her head. "What a shame. You can tell this place has some good bones. I'm sure it can be rebuilt."

Velvet yanked her hand away from Mike and tucked the strands behind her ears. The odd sensation of the air moving around him vanished. "It'll take some time, but we'll get it fixed up. We use this place for food storage, though I guess we could use Dad's old room or something." At the mention of her father's room, her voice hitched slightly.

"Well, that's one possibility," Mike said. "You're always welcome to come stay with us at the house. We have plenty of room. In fact, we have an entire forest inside a magic greenhouse in the backyard. We're even stocking it with game. I'm sure you could work something out with the centaurs."

Velvet looked at him in contemplation for several seconds, then tilted her head. "You would let me come live with you?"

"Only if that's what you want." He looked down at his feet, wondering how much to say. He could tell her about the society, the shadow, or pretty much every attempt on his life. But that wouldn't exactly sell her on the safety of the home. When he looked up at her, he saw that she had tilted her head to one side as if studying him. "I'm not going to lie. Sometimes living with me is dangerous. It's definitely complicated at times. But it wouldn't be lonely."

Abella scowled. Her tail thudded against the ground as she crossed her arms and turned away.

"That's…" Velvet frowned. "I'm not sure how I feel. Don't take it personally."

He nodded. "Let me know if that changes."

Velvet looked at him, then over his shoulder at Abella. It looked like Velvet wanted to say something as she rested her hands on her belly. She tapped her front foot a few times before stepping past him.

"If you'll excuse me," she said, then scurried out of the barn. Abella watched her go, then turned to face Mike.

"You can't be serious," Abella hissed. "One of them is a terrible idea, but both of them?"

"Ah." So this was her problem. He walked over to the jeep and placed his hands on the cool metal. Prior to the Nirumbi's treatment, he could tell it had been well cared for. The man who had maintained this vehicle had raised two daughters out in the wilderness, all while showering them with love. In his opinion, such a person was to be admired.

He turned to lean against the car. "Tell me what you're thinking."

"They're dangerous." Abella pointed in the direction Velvet had gone. "Fast. Strong. Ruthless. If you let them into the house, I cannot protect you there. And the others, they look to you for guidance. They would accept the arachne as one of us, and all it would take is a little bit of planning." She drew her finger across her throat. "In your sleep, one by one."

"I see." He was surprised to hear her speak so candidly about Velvet and Eulalie in such a manner. "What would you have me do?"

"Leave them here. Send Eulalie back." It was clear she had another solution in mind, but he knew she wouldn't say it out loud.

"They are dangerous, aren't they?" He moved away from the jeep and walked toward the gargoyle. "Could easily snap my neck and drag me out into the woods. But so could you, if you wanted. Or Sofia. Lily and Yuki both almost killed me, yet I got away even if it was by the skin of my teeth. Hell, Jenny almost smashed my face in with a table."

"Mike." Her voice was pleading. "I don't know how to convince you."

"I know." He was in front of her now. She was shorter than he was, and he put his hand on her cheek. "You're just trying to protect me. Because that's what you do."

She nodded. Her dark eyes were like pools of ink.

"Do you remember when we first met? How you saved me from the Mandragora?"

"How could I forget?" Her voice was almost a whisper.

"In those first moments, you were so amazing." She had broken through glass windows and grabbed him before he could become Sweet Pea's next meal. "Yet you were frightening. This stone woman with wings and talons. A magnificent tail that swished behind you as you tore me free and saved my life. I was so grateful to be alive that it never occurred to me that you were there to hurt me."

"You looked so pathetic," she muttered, then laughed. "How could I not rescue you?"

"I'm surrounded by amazing women," he said. "Every day, I feel like I see something new that astounds me. But what I've realized is that every woman in that house is different in her own way. Even from her own kind."

Abella looked up at him, her eyes narrowing. "You still want to trust them, don't you?"

"It's not like everyone gets a chance to save my life to prove their worth." He moved his hand around her waist and pulled her close. Her lips parted as he did so. "Please. Give them a chance. For me."

He didn't know what to expect, but Abella pushed him away. She stomped out of the barn and took to the sky in such a manner that he could tell she was angry.

"Well...damn." He sighed, then headed back for the cabin. This was going to take more effort than expected. He pulled his phone out of his pocket and frowned. There was still no signal. Frustrated, he stuck it back. Tomorrow he would try to find somewhere to receive a signal. He could text home to check in and maybe get some advice from Beth or Naia.

Headed back to the cabin, he felt a cold spot in his stomach. It was subtle enough that he almost didn't notice, but when he stopped to scan the trees, he felt it intensify when he lifted his gaze toward the top of a distant pine. Hoping to catch a glimpse of whatever threatened him, he stared defiantly.

The chill flared briefly, then vanished. Whatever danger that had lingered had passed.

Wiping sweat off the back of his neck, he did his best not to run back into the cabin.

It didn't take Abella long to find a rocky outcropping suitable to land on. She was far enough from the cabin that nobody would casually find her but close enough that she could get back if something happened.

"Damn it, Mike." She slammed her fist into the rock, smashing the top layer into dust. Why did he have to be so trusting? She smashed a few layers of rock under her fist before pulling her legs in and wrapping her arms around them.

The sun was on her back, and she closed her eyes and let out a sigh. The warmth was slowly working through her body. Her kind didn't need to eat—in fact, they could absorb energy from just about everywhere. Sunlight was always best, but even a good downpour of rain could make a decent snack.

She feasted on the sunlight, her body huddled in a meditative pose. There was plenty right now to think on, and those thoughts made her feel like she was tumbling out of the sky.

Mike clearly accepted the arachne, but she could sense hesitation on his part. Something was triggering a fear response in him, and she wished he would listen to it. Instead, he was so focused on playing monster philanthropist that he was ignoring his basic instincts.

It also didn't help that the arachne were attractive from the waist up. Her lip twitched, and she dreaded to even acknowledge the effect this would inevitably have on Mike. Thousands of years of evolution had designed them to be appealing, for it was in their nature to hunt, to kill.

And regrettably, to breed.

Abella struggled to keep up with Pierre as he followed the arachne through the streets and buildings of the Panier. They were staying high enough to avoid detection, for even she had heard of the arachne's legendary ability to sense movement. The creature was moving stealthily, and Abella was unable to hear her footfalls. She did hear the occasional grunt from the prostitute and was surprised that she was still alive.

When the Vieille Charité came into view, the Arachne slowed down and approached the building cautiously. She scaled the outer walls of the almshouse and then jumped down into the main courtyard.

As Abella and Pierre descended, the Arachne laid the prostitute on the ground by the chapel. With a nervous glance at the surrounding buildings, she backed away and vanished into the shadows.

Abella and Pierre circled overhead for several minutes, watching. It was too dark to see anything other than the huddled figure on the ground.

"Did she just leave her there?" Abella asked.

"I don't know. The arachne are a strange breed."

"Maybe…maybe she had a change of heart."

Pierre scoffed. "I doubt it. Why would you even suggest such a thing?"

"Because…well, they are half-human, aren't they?" Abella was circling lower now. "Perhaps she decided against eating her and left her where someone would find her."

"You give humanity too much credit to—Abella!" Pierre cried out to her as she descended.

The shadows stretched away from Abella as she landed as quietly as possible next to the prostitute. The woman's eyes were open, and her pupils were dilated. She was drooling when Abella knelt next to her.

"It is okay," she whispered. "I am here to—"

"Abella!" Pierre slammed into the ground behind her and grabbed her by the wing tips. "Look!"

Angry at her brother, she whipped around to face him. His eyes were scanning the pillars that surrounded the chapel, and she saw dark shapes moving among them. From the darkness, they came, their legs silent on the walls and ground of Vieille Charité. Although the largest stood no more than four feet tall, there were dozens of them.

They were Arachne children. With a hunger in their eyes, they approached. Their pale skin and black legs made them look like ghosts floating through the darkness.

"We must flee!" Pierre's wings flared wide as Abella took to the sky. Being smaller than her brother, she was able to get airborne much faster than he could. As she climbed into the sky, she saw dark shapes leaping across the sky above them. Gossamer strands stronger than steel plucked at her wings as she passed through the trap that had been set by the adults, and she was able to make it to safety.

Down below, Pierre growled as he got caught up in their webs. He dodged from side to side but not before an arachne hurled herself from the roof and grabbed onto him. His wings flapped hard as a second, then third arachne scrambled onto him, and he fell to the ground below.

"Abella!" Pierre screamed in rage. "Get to the clan!"

"Pierre, I—" She watched in horror as he battled the arachne. Their fangs and poison were useless on him. He managed to kill an adult and a few of the children before they swarmed. The sheer number overwhelmed him as they tangled him up in their webs. They carried his struggling form up the wall of the chapel. Once at the top, the arachne threw him off.

The first time he fell, nothing happened. But the arachne repeated the process over and over. Abella could only watch in horror as one of Pierre's wings snapped off at the shoulder, could only listen to his howls of pain. The arachne were methodical, and when her brother eventually shattered on the cold hard ground of Vieille Charité, she let out a wail of desolation. His glowing red heart cooled in the night, filling the air with steam as it glowed like an ember until it slowly turned black.

The arachne watched her from below, but she was almost a hundred feet in the air. Her brother's fragments were pushed to the side of the building like ordinary rubble, and the children carried away their human meal as the grown-ups cleaned the grounds. Within minutes, the courtyard was silent. Abella raced back to the clan to tell them what had happened.

The hurt of centuries past was still fresh in her mind as she remembered what had happened next. The clan had held her responsible for Pierre's death, and she had become an outcast among her own family. The arachne had been using the plague as cover for their hunts, and once the clan had made the hard decision to yield ground and leave, Abella had not been invited to follow.

The centuries had been lonely. She had a vague recollection of meeting the Architect. She had been invited to become part of a family once again. Even though the memories had been sealed away, there was an emotional warmth when she considered them.

What could she do about her current arachne problem? For so many years, she had been the muscle, the silent guardian ready to lay down some hurt on whoever threatened the house. To be fair, Mike had gotten into far more trouble already than the other Caretakers combined—*that*, at least, was something she could remember. And right now, he was getting into the kind of trouble she couldn't prevent.

"Hi, Mom. Hi, Dad." Velvet's voice carried over the breeze, causing Abella to cock her head. When she closed her eyes, she could picture exactly where Velvet was. Somewhere about fifteen feet down and fifty feet back from where she currently sat. Careful to rotate without making a sound, Abella tracked the voice to an otherwise unremarkable spot overlooking the valley floor. Tucked in between a pair of pines stood Velvet. She was kneeling on the ground, addressing a pair of seemingly unmarked stones.

She listened as Velvet recounted the last few days at the cabin, including Mike's arrival and invitation to the house. The arachne's voice wavered more than once, and Abella was surprised to see her wipe away tears.

"Dad, I don't know what to do," Velvet confessed. "This has been our home all my life. I feel like if I leave, I'm letting you down. Even worse, I would be leaving you behind. I can still smell you here. Did you know that? It's like your breath clings to every tree. All those patrols, the hikes that we took. This forest is like a book of memories, and I get to open it every time I step outside.

"But I'm also lonely. I still have Lala and Uncle Foot. And always Emery. But that's it. My whole world can be counted on one hand. Mike showed up with four other people, and that's not even all of them! Do you remember when Dana and Lily came? It was all we could talk about, even after you died. What if every day could be like that… Hmmm?" Velvet looked over at a nearby bush. "No, there aren't any birds nearby. Yes, I'll keep watch while you fix your web."

Is she talking to a spider? Fascinated, Abella continued to watch.

"And Mom? I know you and I didn't always see eye to eye, but I could really use your advice on something. I've been having these strange urges ever since Mike came, and I'm worried that it's…well, you know."

No. Abella felt every alarm in her body going off. It didn't take much to realize exactly what kind of urges Velvet was having.

"Lala isn't even here," Velvet continued. "So I can't ask her if she feels the same. She's always been nonchalant about it, but we've never been around a man other than Dad, so…what do I do? What can I do? What if I can't control myself around him, like you did with Dad? What if I lose myself?" Her voice rose an octave. "There are too many things, too many emotions, it's like I can't breathe. I don't know what to do."

Oh, I know what I want to do. Abella briefly wondered if it would be possible for Velvet to suffer an accident. Maybe fall off the side of the cliff or get smashed by a boulder. The others would never suspect Abella.

But she would know. And it wouldn't surprise her if Yuki could do magic to find out what had happened. She didn't dare imagine the look of betrayal on Mike's face; the very idea of it broke her stone heart a little.

"Merde," she whispered. The only solution would be constant vigilance.

Velvet finished her conversation with the dead and left.

Abella waited a bit and then flew down to the memorial. The two stones were made of marble. One had a spider carved into it and the other a human, and they both overlooked the valley floor. The cabin was visible through the branches of the pines, making it a perfect resting spot.

She looked over toward a nearby bush and saw a spider frantically repairing its web. The impulse to crush it was strong, but that would make her no better than an arachne. Besides, the last thing she needed was for the spiders of the forest to tattle on her. If Velvet could talk to arachnids, then Abella needed to assume that nothing she did was private.

She stretched her wings and waited for a bit longer. When the spider was finished, it scurried back into the safety of the bush, leaving the web out for its next meal. Satisfied that the spider was safe now from birds, Abella threw herself off the side of the cliff and let the air currents carry her across the valley.

"I'll be watching," she muttered under her breath.

And when the time came, she would be ready.

Beth burst out of the closet, water soaking her clothes and seeping into the floorboards. Over the winter, Tink had built a special drain beneath the floor of the closet so that it wouldn't make such a mess. A process that used to feel like rushing down a Slip 'N Slide was now more akin to having a bucket of water dumped over her head.

A small crowd had formed in the front room. Beth shut the door and reopened it. The magical portal was one-way, so now she was greeted by coats, a stack of towels, and a hula hoop with glowing runes embedded along the outer rim.

"Strange man outside house!" Tink ran up to Beth, a hammer clutched in her diminutive hands. "Been looking in the windows!"

Beth held the hoop over her head and let go. The runes flared as their magic forced the water off her and onto the floor. It had been a gift from Ratu, but it could only be used a couple of times a day. When the hoop clattered on the ground, she picked it up and stuck it back in the closet. "Where's Lily?"

"Oh, I'm around." The succubus was standing up on the third-floor landing, leaning over the edge. She tumbled forward and into the air, then landed gracefully on the hardwood below. "Time to be the man of the house?" she asked.

"Maybe not yet. Let's see what we have." When Beth looked outside, she saw a man in glasses standing just off the porch. He was clearly trying to see into the windows of the home and was pacing.

Beth opened the door and stepped outside. "Can I help you with something?"

The man was wearing a brown sweater vest and a long-sleeved button-down beneath it. His glasses were perched on the edge of his nose like a squat bird, ready to fall off at any moment.

"Where's Mike?" he demanded.

"May I ask who's calling?" Beth had a pretty good idea.

"Tell him his neighbor is here to talk to him again about the noise." Murray finally seemed to notice Beth, and his cheeks flushed. He promptly adjusted the hem of his vest and pushed his glasses farther up his nose. His fingers went through his thinning hair like a comb.

"What noise?"

"It was a woman screaming. Around lunchtime." Murray's face became smug as he held up his phone. He tapped the screen a few times, and Beth heard shrieks come from the speaker that she immediately recognized as her own. She fought the burning sensation in her cheeks, hoping to hold a poker face.

"Oh. That." Lily-Mike stepped out of the door and walked slowly down the steps. She wore a crimson doublet and bright white pants. The outfit was outlandish, and Beth couldn't help but notice that it included a giant codpiece. "What do you think it was, Murray?"

"I think it's trouble for you," Murray said, his resolve wavering. "You agreed to keep it down."

"Did I?" Lily shook her head. "Last time I checked, there weren't any laws about making noise in the middle of the day."

"Listen here, weirdo, there may not be laws about noise during the day, but this woman is clearly in distress. Now, I don't know what you all are doing over here, but I'm sure the police would be very interested to hear about it."

"I'm willing to bet you have already contacted them." Lily grinned devilishly, which looked especially ominous with Mike's features. "And they didn't give a flying fuck. Am I right?"

"Mike," Beth cautioned and put a hand on Lily's arm.

"And if you must know, the noise was from this one right here." Lily slapped Beth on the ass, causing her to jump. "She was getting fucked so hard she saw stars. It doesn't surprise me that you've never heard the sounds of a woman being pleasured—"

Murray's face turned bright red, and he pointed at them. "Enough! You may think you're funny, Mr. Radley, but I'll have you know that you don't know who you're dealing with!"

"I know exactly who I'm dealing with," Lily replied. "You're the kind of man who sits in silent rage as he tries to fall asleep. Fantasizing about how the world has yet to recognize your greatness. You work hard for someone who takes advantage of you, then come home and pound your meat to VHS porn because you're afraid the government is watching your internet, am I right?"

Murray's mouth was opening and closing like a fish's, and he had gone white. It was like the oxygen had been sucked out of him. His left eyelid fluttered.

"And that's not all," Lily continued. "Because you fall asleep and dream about them, don't you? All those young women, straight out of college, looking for internships and—"

Beth pinched Lily's arm. "That's quite enough, *Mike.*"

Murray looked like he was going to be sick.

"Maybe Murray here should worry less about what we do in the safety and comfort of our own home and worry more about that suitcase full of women's lingerie in his closet." Lily sneered. "It's totally fine to wear what makes you happy, you insipid little shit, but if you think you're gonna come over here and threaten us with the cops in anything less than your best body stocking—"

"*Mike!*" Beth clamped her hand over Lily's mouth as Murray's glasses fell off his face and clattered to the ground. The man's eyes had rolled up into his head, leaving only the whites of them.

In the silence that followed, Beth realized that the yard had gone still. The few centaurs who were out working the yard had paused to watch.

"Murray?" Beth didn't dare touch the man. His breathing had become ragged, and every few breaths, he let out a high-pitched whine.

"Stay back," Lily said as she stepped in front of Beth. "If this fucker blows his load, I'm going to—"

Murray opened his mouth, and a sound like high-pitched static came out of him. It was disorienting, causing Beth to topple over backward and land on her butt.

Lily punched Murray in the face. At the moment of contact, a cylinder of white light surrounded him and blasted her backward onto the porch. The centaurs threw their spears, but they just shattered on the wall of light. The Jabberwock moved to attack but let out a cry of frustration when it was pushed away.

"Shit, shit, shit," Beth muttered but still couldn't stand. Waves of nausea rolled through her body, and she covered her mouth with one hand when she felt her gorge rising.

A mist rose from the ground and drifted out into the street. The centaurs were now grouping up and launching a volley of arrows, but these did no good either. A few of the centaurs toppled over and were helped to their feet as they fled through the doorway to their village.

Kisa and Cecilia were suddenly there. They grabbed Beth by the hands and dragged her up the stairs. The eerie sound followed them into the house but vanished as soon as the door was shut.

A few seconds later, the door opened again, and Lily stumbled in, now in her regular form. Beth was horrified to see that all the flesh on Lily's arm had been burned away.

"What in the unholy fuck is that?" Lily demanded as she plopped down and inspected her arm. When she moved her fingers, Beth could see the exposed muscle slide over itself. "Ow, shit! This really fucking hurts!"

Eulalie stumbled in from the backyard, her hands over her ears. She was dragging long lines of webbing behind her, as if it was leaking from her body. Panic was written on her face as she slumped onto the floor.

Sofia stood by the front window, her sword in hand. She scowled at Murray as he continued to shriek.

"At least that sound can't get in here," she said, then looked around. "Is everyone okay?"

"Naia came inside," Eulalie muttered. "Amymone is hiding underground. I feel like I'm going to be sick."

"Tink have idea." The goblin had her face pressed to the glass. "Maybe start fire?"

"No fires." Sofia looked at Beth. "Who is this man?"

"He's the neighbor. He came to complain about the noise." She remembered what Mike had told her about him the other day. "He was acting weird a couple of days ago. Mike said he seemed possessed. We figured it was the society."

"What the hell is happening out there?" Kisa had joined Tink at the window. "Where are the lions?"

Beth rushed to the window and saw that the front yard had been gobbled up by fog. The outer walls of the property had gone missing. Were they just hard to see because of the fog? "He isn't actually attacking anybody, so maybe the lions don't see him as a threat?"

"I can't...make this..." Lily was focused intently on her wounded arm, her face scrunched up. Smoke rose from the edges of her ruined skin. "It isn't healing!"

"What does that mean?" Beth asked.

Sofia frowned and looked outside. "I don't know," she said.

The front door banged open, and Sulyvahn stumbled inside, his head cradled in his arms. He tripped and fell, spilling black smoke from his neck all over the floor.

"Suly!" Beth went to his side as Sofia closed the door.

"Blasted wretch and all his shoutin'," Suly mumbled. "Wasn't in my right mind, couldna hardly move."

Beth helped him to the couch and then returned to the window. Murray was frozen in place still, his mouth wide open as he shouted. The cylinder was visible now, sending a beacon of light into the sky.

What sort of trouble were they in now? It didn't seem society related, so what could it be? Beth paced in front of the window, pausing only to watch Eulalie use her webs to bandage Lily's arm. The arachne moved quickly, her fingers deftly winding gossamer strands around Lily's ruined flesh. The finished product was an elbow-length glove that shimmered in the light as Lily tilted her arm from side to side.

"I'm afraid that's the best I can do," Eulalie said.

"At least it doesn't hurt, thank you." Lily squeezed her fingers experimentally. "I sure hope the boys down at the docks like their handies with some glove action."

"Oh, however will they manage?" Eulalie offered with a smile. "But at least we're safe inside, right?"

The power fluttered, then went out. The dim light of day through the front window was the sole illumination as Murray continued to scream in the front yard.

VISITORS

An early dinner had come and gone, and Beth sat in the living room, her eyes fixed on the man in her front yard. Murray was still out there, and every few minutes, someone would crack a window to see if he continued to scream.

Not only was the sound disorienting, but an ominous fact had been revealed later. While the house was closed up, his scream couldn't be heard, but the outside world still could. A disoriented bird had bumped into the glass, and Tink had braved the outside world to go rescue it. A strong breeze could be heard rustling the bushes, but the noise from Murray only penetrated the home when the door or a window was open.

Ratu, through her crystal ball, theorized that the sound's disorienting effect couldn't penetrate the home's exterior due to the geas. The sound didn't carry through the crystal ball either, even when Beth took it outside for a minute with ear plugs in. Without being able to hear it, the naga had little to offer in terms of advice.

With no ideas, the household was busy making preparations for whatever siege was coming their way. Sulyvahn had gone through the greenhouse to coordinate with the centaurs, and Sofia had retreated to the Library in hopes of finding information. Eulalie had gone with her, ecstatic to see such a place.

Cecilia hovered by the window, her hands held over her chest. On occasion, she would flicker and vanish, only to reappear minutes later.

The front door opened, and Lily came in. She was wearing Mike's face and carrying Kisa on her back. When she set the cat girl down, Kisa made a retching noise. "If you cough up a hair ball, you'd better clean it up yourself," Lily warned.

"Eat dicks," Kisa hissed, then wandered off toward the kitchen.

"Success?" Beth asked.

"Yeah, we totally pretended to turn our magic sundial, which apparently doesn't give two shits about what's happening out there." Lily flopped down on the couch, her body reverting to normal. Her arm was still wrapped in spider silk, the wound reeking of sulfur. "You know, he's giving our resident screamer a run for her money."

Cecilia chuckled but said nothing.

"Any word from Romeo yet?" Lily shifted uncomfortably on the couch, trying to find somewhere to rest her arm.

Beth picked up her phone and turned it on. "He still hasn't read any of the texts I sent him," she said. She gave it a moment, then turned it off. With no way to charge it, she was only checking every half hour.

"We might need to find a different way to do it," Lily said, then looked over at Cecilia. "How about you, dream girl? I know you were popping in and out of his head while you were in fairyland."

"'Tis true," Cecilia admitted. "But it often took me a long time to connect. I am happy to try though."

"Get on it, then." Lily flopped back on the couch, then looked at Beth. "While I was out there, I tried to get a good look at the edge of the yard."

"And?"

"Nothing. No people, no traffic. It was almost as if—" Lily turned her head toward the office as Death stepped out of it.

"I say," he announced while rubbing the top of his skull. His hood had been pulled down, and he was wearing a giant pair of earmuffs. "That racket is even louder here than it was in the Library."

"Excuse me?" Beth stood. "You can hear that?"

"Of course I can." Death fiddled with his earmuffs. "I was in one of the deeper sections of the Library when I discovered this amazing book about a man named Waldo. It was demanded of me that I find him, so I got caught up in his many adventures when I heard that ghastly sound."

"And you didn't think to investigate?" Lily's voice had an edge to it.

"Oh, I did. I wandered through the Library for hours but couldn't pinpoint its source." Death approached the window and placed his fingers on the glass. "Ah, I see. So there's our culprit."

"His name is Murray," Beth explained. "He started doing that, and we don't know why."

"Well, perhaps I can persuade him to stop." Death stuck a hand in his robe and withdrew a long staff that unfolded into his scythe. The edge gleamed wickedly as he gave it a test swing.

"You're going to kill him?" Beth asked incredulously.

"Certainly not! I cannot go around harming mortals; it's poor manners." He took off his earmuffs and pulled up his hood. "I merely intend to displace his soul for a moment. It won't cause permanent damage, but he will likely lose consciousness."

"Be careful," Lily warned while holding up her arm. "We don't know what we're up against."

"What do you think will happen?" He placed his hand on the knob of the door. "Do you suppose I will arrive to collect myself?"

He stood there, waiting for a reaction. When none came, he chattered his teeth comically, opened the door, and went outside. Death went halfway across the yard before he stopped and stuck the butt of his scythe into the ground. His eyes blazed with light as he waved a hand around, his mouth moving. Beth, watching through the window, could only pick up bits of what he was saying.

Lily had pressed her ear to the glass of the window. Her face was scrunched up in concentration.

"What's he saying?" whispered Beth.

"Hard to tell. Something about consent...wait..." Lily held up a finger. "He's giving him till the count of ten to leave."

"Oh dear." Beth watched as Death dramatically held up a finger, followed by two fingers. Murray seemed oblivious, and when Death got past five, he switched the hand holding the scythe and continued counting on his other hand.

"C'mon, get on with it," muttered Lily.

Death casually spun the scythe around and placed it so that the curve of the blade was behind Murray's spine. With a tug, he yanked the blade through Murray's chest. It passed through the man's flesh harmlessly, and Murray continued to scream.

"That was anticlimactic," noted Lily.

Beth felt her heart fall in her chest.

Death swung his scythe again, then repeated the process. When nothing happened, he used the tip of his blade and poked it into Murray's skull. He even tried forcing the man's jaw closed, but nothing happened. Death marched back up to the house, then tucked his scythe away as he came inside.

"Well?" asked Beth.

"That man has no soul." Death put his earmuffs back on and walked toward the kitchen.

"Excuse me?" Beth followed him and watched as he nonchalantly started prepping a pot of water.

"It is rare, but you see it from time to time. Souls are a precious commodity, after all. Why do you think the universe is so keen on recycling them?" Death turned on one of the stove's burners and set the pot down. "It's a fascinating subject, really. When your soul passes on, there's an excess that gets left behind. I'm not entirely certain who's in charge of that, but—"

"Why wouldn't he have a soul?"

"Oh, I have no idea. That really isn't my area of expertise, but there can be any number of reasons. For instance, it could simply be an error. Humans born without souls often find themselves with a poor moral compass. Some of them have become quite famous for their capacity for murder." Death pulled down a box of tea bags. "I always found it fascinating that I would get to meet them so many times yet never personally collect them. Oblivion is such a strange concept to me."

Stunned, Beth leaned against the counter. "Are you talking about serial killers?"

"Ah, yes. I had forgotten the term." Death picked through his tea collection. He had over a dozen tins of loose-leaf tea. "But they are on the extreme side of things. No, I suspect the mortal in your yard is simply being used as a vessel. His soul has been temporarily misplaced while some other entity uses his body."

"Like what?" Beth moved around the counter so that she stood next to him. He looked up from his tea bags, revealing the tiny blue fires that sat in the back of his eye sockets. Despite being lit from within, the inside of his skull was darker than night. There was no bone to reflect the tiny lights that he used as eyes. "What kind of entity, Death?"

"A loud one." Satisfied, Death picked out one of the tins and set it on the counter. "Would you like some?"

"No."

"Shame. It's going to get quite busy around here. You really should take the time to drink something."

Beth grabbed Death by the front of his robes, her hand immediately going numb. "What do you mean, it's going to get busy?" She was practically shouting now.

"Are you still upset with me over your money? I did apologize." Somehow, he was able to frown, the bones of his face shifting.

She sighed, then let go of his robes. "No, I'm sorry. I'm just freaked out by whatever he's doing out there, and I feel like you're not telling me what you know."

"Oh. I see." Death looked down at his feet for a moment. "I must apologize. I was under the impression that you had figured it out already."

Beth put her numb hand on the counter, her fingers tapping impatiently.

"Figured out what?" she asked when he didn't continue.

"If that man out there is making so much noise that I can hear it from a dimension away, then clearly he is calling out to someone." Death picked out a teacup and then loaded his diffuser. "Or something. The reason he's still screaming is that whatever is coming has to come from really far away."

"Oh shit," she whispered in horror. She'd figured Murray was part of a society plot but never that he was acting as a beacon. What sort of being took most of a day to travel across the world? And why did they need a beacon to lead them?

Death smiled smugly, then pulled an extra teacup out of the cupboard. "I'll make you a nice chamomile. It'll help warm up your hand. Now would you like sugar or do you prefer honey?"

THE DOOR OF THE CABIN CREAKED WHEN VELVET PUSHED IT OPEN. INSIDE, SHE saw Quetzalli sitting on the couch with Bigfoot, who was sitting up.

"Uncle Foot!" She ran to his side and crouched so he could see her better. "I didn't know you were awake!"

"Hey there, fluffy girl." Bigfoot smiled weakly and put his hand on her cheek. "Sorry I worried you."

"If I had known you were up, I would have come sooner." It was late, the hour nearing midnight. She had spent all day checking the woods for any further hint of the Nirumbi. Dana had gone with her, allowing the two of them to catch up. It was amazing to hear just how much had happened to Dana in such a short time, and it reminded her more than once of the tabletop games she played with Bigfoot and her sister.

"I haven't been up long," he confessed. "Whatever was on those arrows was nasty. The good news is that they won't affect me the same should it happen again."

"We've had a great time catching up." Quetzalli had pulled her legs beneath an oversize sweater and held a large cup of hot cocoa. "Did you know that we met before?"

"What? When?"

"Over a thousand years ago."

Bigfoot stretched his arms and winced. "She was a lot bigger then. She's a storm dragon trapped in a human body."

Velvet's jaw dropped. When Dana had said Quetzalli was a dragon, Velvet had assumed she was a hybrid. Bigfoot had spoken often about the elemental dragons that used to control the American continent. The story about the one under Yellowstone fascinated her the most, but he rarely went into details about it.

"It was brief. I stumbled onto one of his meetings and was invited to join them." Quetzalli sipped at her cocoa. "That was before I started working for the fairy queen."

"Wow." Velvet could only stare. "Did you have wings?"

"Big ones. I would ride among the clouds all day, summoning lightning and bringing rain. Do you want to hear about how storm clouds are formed?"

From the corner of her many eyes, Velvet saw Bigfoot shake his head ever so slightly.

"No, but thanks. I'm probably going back out soon, anyway." From where she stood, she could smell Mike's scent. She assumed he was in her dad's bedroom, and wanted to stay away if she could. "I just wanted to check in. Can I get you anything before I leave?"

"I wouldn't mind a beer." Bigfoot raised his eyebrows hopefully. "And some cheese, if we have any."

"On it." She walked to the fridge and opened it up. Her uncle's beer selection was running low, so she grabbed him an IPA. In the process of retrieving it, her eyes settled on a small cooler toward the back of the fridge. The hairs on her arm stood on end as a sweet scent tickled her nostrils.

With trembling fingers, she slid the cooler forward and opened it. The scent from within was overwhelming. It reminded her of earth, rainstorms, and something slightly floral. There were about ten capped shot glasses, each one filled to the brim with a milky white fluid.

"You okay?" This came from Bigfoot. He was watching her from the couch.

"Yeah, just trying to decide which beer pairs with recently poisoned."

He chuckled, then turned his attention back to Quetzalli. While he spoke with her, Velvet grabbed a few of the shot glasses and tucked them in her pockets. She was a couple steps away from the fridge when she realized she had forgotten the beer so went back.

She stood behind the couch, afraid Quetzalli or Bigfoot would know what she had done. When she handed over the beer, Bigfoot gave her a huge smile.

"Be careful out there, bug." He popped the cap off with his thumbnail, then sucked down half the bottle. "Oh, I needed that." Bigfoot furrowed his brow and let out a rumbling belch.

"I will." She scuttled away and then out the front door, her heart pounding in her chest. Outside, she saw that Yuki was over by the barn, so she wandered around the side of the house, toward the back. Her fingers had closed on the glass in her front pocket when she nearly ran into Mike.

He was leaning against the back wall of the cabin, his eyes on the woods. It looked like he had been concentrating on something but relaxed when he saw her.

"Good evening," he said.

"Oh. Hi. I didn't think you were up."

"For just a little bit longer." He gestured at the night sky. Even through the dim lights of the cabin, the Milky Way blazed in all its glory. "I don't often get to see the night sky like this. It's beautiful, isn't it?"

"It is." She took a deep breath and turned her attention toward the sky. A streak of light crossed, and she closed her eyes.

"Making a wish?" he asked.

Her eyes popped open. "If I tell you, it won't come true."

"I was just checking. I didn't want to wish on the same one and steal yours away." He winked at her, and her heart skipped a beat.

"What would you wish for?" she asked. "Since you aren't wishing, it should be fine."

He laughed. "I honestly don't know. This will sound weird, but I'm pretty happy these days. Can't think of anything I really want, nothing big, anyway."

"What's it like? Living at the house?"

"Hmm." He screwed up his face in concentration. "I'm trying to think of a good analogy for you. I guess it would be like if you had twenty sisters, but you were all different types of spiders. I'm kind of making an assumption, since you look different than your sister does."

"It's a fair assumption," she replied. "Our body type gets determined by where we were conceived and the rest of the colony. The idea is that it allows us to adapt to our environment. My spider body is complementary to my sister's, and it makes more sense out here. It's far harder to hide a web from human prey in the forest. People don't generally wander off trail. Hence why I have a hunter's body."

"Human prey?" His voice rose an octave.

"If I hunted humans," she corrected. "I may be different from my ancestors, but that doesn't change where I came from."

"We all come from darkness. It's our job to rise above it." The wind caught Mike's hair and blew it in front of his eyes. His scent permeated the area, which caused Velvet to drool so much that she had to swallow. "So yes, the many sisters theory. Imagine having that. All the women in the house are different. We also have magic rats and centaurs. It's always busy, but then something like your goblin war will pop up, and it usually ends with house repairs. Granted, I know nothing about your goblin war and would love to hear more."

Velvet relaxed. "There isn't a whole lot to tell. We discovered a cave system in the distant hills, teeming with goblins. They started prowling around the area and even attacked my dad's jeep one day when he was coming home. My mom tried to contact Aunt Emily, but she never came. Emery said she had sealed them away but didn't know how.

"My dad decided he and my mom were going to set traps and try to take them out. They were kind of like the Nirumbi, only a bit bigger. The one thing they had that the Nirumbi didn't was sheer numbers. My parents killed almost a hundred of them in a week, yet they just kept coming. The yard was riddled with spears and flint-knap weapons. Goblins are notoriously difficult to kill."

"I'm aware," Mike replied. "The one I live with, Tink, has had a bunch of close calls. Almost eaten by a Jabberwock once."

"A Jabberwock? Like from Wonderland?"

"That's a long story of my own, but yes." Mike grinned.

"My dad shot a goblin in the head once. Almost point-blank." She tapped her forehead. "It broke the skin, but that was it. It tried to bite him, so he put the gun in its mouth and pulled the trigger. That finally did the trick. Guns didn't work very well, but my sword and the traps did. Log traps, boulder traps, you name it. Well, that, and my mom was strong enough to snap their necks if she could get her hands on one. My parents finally got desperate enough that they tried poison. They started with rat poison and worked their way up to something my dad learned about in the military. Uncle Foot was gone almost a week trying to find us a barrel of the stuff. Guess what we learned?"

"Tell me." There was excitement in his eyes.

"Goblins are immune to poison. There's actually a part of the forest we aren't supposed to go to anymore because my parents found a way to aerosolize the stuff in the barrel. Killed a bunch of vegetation." She smiled, thinking of her parents working together. The two of them had been an amazing team, but their ruthlessness when it came to their daughters' safety had been on another level.

"So how did they do it? End the goblin wars?"

"I'm not entirely sure." Bigfoot had taken her and Eulalie to a cave hidden deep in the woods, with instructions to remain inside until he or their parents returned. "I do know that they found a way to drive the goblins back into their cave, but that's it. My parents would never tell me what happened, and we knew better than to ask. They did tell me that the goblins were gone for good, so I can only assume they killed them."

Mike frowned. "Seems a bit extreme, but the only goblin I've met is Tink. She's nothing short of amazing."

To hear him refer to a creature like a goblin as anything other than disgusting awakened all sorts of feelings inside Velvet. Would he ever see her as something other than an eight-legged freak? She was perfectly aware that he had a touch of arachnophobia; she could smell his fear when they had first met. That scent had already disappeared, and she wondered if it had to do with the other night when he had touched her.

She thought about the strange moment they had shared. A sexual current had run through her whole body, and it had taken everything in her power to keep her hands off him. If she hadn't heard the gargoyle's arrival, she didn't know what would have happened.

"The house sounds interesting. Dana told me about your spat with the fairy queen. And did you really tame Cerberus? How did you manage that?"

His cheeks turned red. "Quite by accident. Yuki cast the wrong spell on Cerberus and…" He waved his hands around as if trying to come up with more words but failed. A yawn escaped his lips, and he rubbed his eyes. "Sorry, I promise you aren't boring. Just need sleep. I'm only a weak human, after all."

I don't think that, she thought. "Have a good night, then."

"You too." He gave her a little wave and then disappeared around the corner. She waited a minute for him to come back, but it wasn't meant to be.

The tree line was almost a hundred feet from the cabin, but she reached it in moments. Hidden in the darkness of the pines, she pulled out the shot glass in her front pocket and examined it.

It was Mike's semen. Preserved for Dana as a means of keeping her sane, it contained his viable sperm. Spittle had formed in the corners of her mouth as she pried the cap off, her brain no longer in control of her limbs. She inhaled its scent, and her human eyes rolled up into her head.

Synapses that had never fired before lit up her brain, and she saw flashes of children. They were all daughters but had Mike's hair and his goofy grin. She saw dozens of them, each one a possibility if she were to mate with him. Some were lifting giant stones, while others built intricate webs. It was like standing in the middle of a storm, but each blast of lightning was illuminating the future.

"Oh gods," she muttered, then held the cup to her mouth and sucked down the contents. The cool liquid warmed her belly, and the flashes intensified. Some offspring moved with lethal grace; others struck from the shadows. His children would be powerful, their combined biology a perfect match.

Her mind focused on a little girl who looked different from the rest. Her hair was willowy and twisted about in the wind. She looked up at Velvet with deep-brown eyes that were a mirror image of her own father's.

She gasped, the shot glass forgotten as it fell and landed in the snow. The image was gone, and she had to see this girl again. Would her child have her father's humanity, or her mother's ruthlessness? Without hesitation, she removed the lid of the next shot glass and slammed its contents.

The images came anew, but now she saw the girl standing over a fresh kill. It was a brown bear, and she was sinking her fangs into it. Now the girl was climbing a tree without making a sound. Now she was—

Gone. Blinking rapidly, Velvet hurried to drink the next one. Several minutes passed as she contemplated this mystery child, an ethereal being that reminded her of both Mike and her father. Her heart swelled with pride to see her standing defiantly above a giant chasm with a meticulous web built beneath her.

When she ate the last of Mike's semen, she had one final vision. It was her daughter, standing inside of a large building filled with books. She was an adult now, and she was standing on the ceiling with her hair hanging below her and a book in her hand. The arachne looked up, and their eyes locked. Startled, Velvet's daughter dropped her book.

The book fell almost twenty feet before the arachne reached out with glowing fingers to summon it back to her.

"What is this?" She was back in the forest now, and she knelt to examine the shot glasses, hoping for just a little more juice. This new arachne had been using magic! Was such a thing even possible?

She had to know more, to see her offspring again. Was this how her mother had experienced it? Had she seen her daughters so perfectly in her mind's eye?

What, then, of the others she had seen? For decades, they had spoken about how it would be up to Velvet and Eulalie to decide whether the arachne went extinct. She was aware that her mother had willingly smashed hundreds of her own eggs to ensure children able to resist the instinct to hunt humans for food. Would she have to do the same?

Her belly churned as she stumbled around the side of the house. She felt drunk, a sensation she tried to avoid at all costs. Alcohol never mixed well with her spider biology, and she felt more sick than relaxed. Only, it wasn't booze that had her all messed up.

It was him. She could smell his scent, sense his presence through the walls of the building. Standing outside her father's bedroom window, she could see Mike in bed, his face buried in a pillow. The door had been closed, and it was dark in the room. If she opened the window, she could get inside.

Something shifted at the foot of the bed. She shook her head in surprise, wondering how she could have missed the three-tailed fox curled up there. She had no idea that Yuki could change shapes like that, though she had wondered. Wouldn't it be nice if she could become human and walk among them as an equal rather than an abomination?

She was panting, and her heart hurt. Tears formed in her eyes as she watched him shift beneath the blankets. Something inside her had snapped in the last couple of days, and her entire world now swirled around this man that had walked into her life.

Her mother had warned her multiple times about the drive to mate. It would be an overwhelming urge that would eat her away from the inside as she lost control. However, it wasn't only Mike that she was fixated on, but the girl from her vision. This unborn child could be her father's legacy, and she refused to let that die.

If she bit Yuki while she was a fox, would it be enough to knock her out? Maybe she could mate with him, then run away after. If Quetzalli and Bigfoot didn't catch on…

Uncle Foot. He would know, and he would come looking for her. Eulalie could be made to understand, but her uncle never would.

She let go of the window and ran. It didn't matter where she went; she just needed distance. The air was cold, and she held her jacket tight against her body as she sprinted through the woods. The long branches of the pines hungrily grabbed for her flesh, but she twisted through the gaps in their foliage with ease.

When she was almost a mile from the house, the trees in front of her exploded as Abella dropped through them from above. The gargoyle's face was twisted up in anger as she opened her wings wide, blocking Velvet's path.

Velvet came to a stop, her feet sliding in the snow.

"I saw what you did," Abella said. She held up an empty shot glass accusingly. "Tell me why I shouldn't crush you."

Instead of answering, Velvet bared her fangs and bull-rushed the gargoyle. Abella looked surprised but held her ground. When they collided, the two of them crashed through the trees and tumbled down a hill.

"Leave me alone!" Velvet didn't bother striking Abella. There was nothing her fists could do against Abella's stony hide. Instead, Velvet twisted around the gargoyle and pinned her wings together with a pair of her legs while covering Abella's eyes. Abella stumbled around, her swishing tail pounding through the nearby bushes. Once the gargoyle was off-balance, Velvet swung forward and down, executing a throw that tossed Abella into a nearby tree.

On impact, the snow in its branches fell, burying Abella. Velvet scrambled to get away, but the gargoyle burst free and tackled her from behind. Stony fingers closed around Velvet's neck and squeezed.

"You were ready to fuck him, weren't you?" Abella's breath was hot against Velvet's ear. "And when you were done, you were going to eat him!"

Velvet pulled out her sword. In its collapsed state, she drove it down into Abella's thigh. Sparks flew when the sword slid across stony flesh, and Abella howled in pain. Velvet twisted around to put the blade between them.

"I was not going to eat him!" she yelled, the blade held to Abella's throat. "Please, just let me go!"

"No!" Abella's eyes flicked to the blade. The magical blade was capable of injuring her, and she was wary of it.

"If you think you can choke me out before I use this on you, you're sorely mistaken." Velvet's whole body was tingling now, fire burning in her limbs.

"I'm not worried about a little scratch." As if to emphasize her point, Abella tilted her face to reveal the large crack that went over her eye. It glittered in the moonlight, as if filled with dark crystals.

Velvet pointed the blade at herself and unfolded it. They were close enough to the ground that the point of the blade buried itself in the snow. The sword tried to unfold, but the handle got caught in Abella's open mouth and pushed her off the ground.

When Abella let go, Velvet slid behind her and grabbed the sword. She pinned Abella to the ground and placed the tip of the blade at the base of her skull.

"If you try to get up, all I have to do is press." To emphasize her point, she leaned on the blade. "It's called leverage."

Abella went still, her wings relaxing.

"All I want is to leave," she said. "To get some fresh air, some perspective. You don't know me, but I'm guessing you know my kind. Well, guess what? I don't even know my kind. My mother made sure of that, bless her hearts."

Abella growled down in the snow.

"And you know what else? My mother would want me to kill you. Because despite her enlightenment, she was still a killer because *it's what she needed to be.*" More tears now, hot in her eyes and cold on her cheek as they froze. "And so was my father. He was a killer too. Never wanted to talk about it, but it's true. Both of them did it, and they would do it again to keep us safe.

"But you know what? Because they had to kill, they spent their whole lives teaching me to be better than them. To live a life where I didn't have to make that decision. And right now, I am so confused everything is spinning. Yes, you're right. I do want to fuck him, I can't help it. But kill him? Take his life just to eat? He called a goblin amazing. Have you ever seen one? Of course you have, you live with one. Right now, all I can think about is mating with him and letting him fill my belly with his seed, and that's fine, it's whatever. But do you know what I want even more than that?"

Abella tilted her head, as if to hear better.

"I want him to think I'm amazing too." She lifted the blade and stepped off Abella's back. Before the gargoyle could say anything or move, Velvet folded up the sword and ran.

MIKE OPENED HIS EYES AND LET OUT A SIGH. HE ALMOST DIDN'T WANT TO know what time it was. Once he knew, he would start that mental countdown about how many hours he could still sleep and feel rested. He wanted an early start because he planned to hike to the edge of the boundary and try to get some cell reception. It wasn't unexpected for him to be gone this long, but he definitely needed to check in.

When he picked up his phone, he squinted when it lit up.

"Ugh." He set it back down. It was almost one in the morning, and he was no closer to sleep than he had been an hour before.

Part of the problem was his current bedmate. While Yuki was able to collapse herself into a cute little fox, Quetzalli was an absolute bed hog. The cabin only had one queen-size bed. With Bigfoot on the couch, he'd offered to sleep on the floor, but Quetzalli had insisted they share.

He held still for a minute, listening. There was a slight breeze outside, and he occasionally heard the creaking of floorboards. His best guess was that Dana was pacing. He felt bad that the poor girl could no longer sleep, and wondered what he would do if saddled with so many extra hours.

Quetzalli shifted in bed and said something in her sleep. Though the words were unintelligible, he felt the hairs on the back of his neck rise just before he got zapped. Suddenly wide awake, he slid out of bed and put on his pants and shoes.

Yuki opened her eyes and sat up. She tilted her head out of curiosity.

"Can't sleep," he explained. "But don't worry, I won't go far."

She yawned, then set her head back down and watched him with one eye as he walked out of the room.

Out in the living room, he saw that Bigfoot was asleep on the couch. Several empty beer cans had been stacked in a pyramid on the nearby table, and an old VCR had been hooked up to the TV. *Harry and the Hendersons* was playing on mute.

"He thinks it's hilarious." Dana stood in the kitchen, an e-reader in her hands. "Trouble sleeping?"

"A bit. Quetzalli keeps taking the blankets."

She nodded, then set her reader down. "I'm not surprised. I've seen her sleep. She tosses and turns a lot. I think she dreams about flying around and chasing storms. She's totally into you, by the way."

"I kind of figured." He smiled and sat down next to her.

"If you know, then why haven't you fucked her?" Dana raised an eyebrow.

Taken aback by the boldness of the question, Mike felt his cheeks begin to burn. "I kind of thought you two were a thing and didn't want to cross any lines."

"I appreciate that. But we're not officially anything. My heart belongs to Alex." She sighed and shook her head. "I sometimes wonder if I'll ever fall in love with someone else. Coming to grips with my situation was difficult enough, but I find myself wondering if romantic emotions are frozen in time like the rest of me."

Mike frowned, old feelings of guilt regarding Dana bubbling up to the surface. "I wish I could help," he told her.

"You help plenty. It can be weird sometimes, but I know your heart's in the right place. As for me and Quetzalli, that's just for fun. Lily helped me fill that void for a while, but Quetzalli likes to cuddle after." She leaned forward and lowered her voice. "This will sound silly, but when I'm holding her after sex, I like to pretend I'm feeling the same things she does. Practicing for when I have those feelings again."

"I don't think that sounds odd at all. You're doing the best you can in a shit situation. It's all you can hope for."

"I guess." She looked over at Bigfoot. "I figure a couple more days will see him on his feet. Then we can figure out who is going and who is staying. As far as the Nirumbi are concerned, they seem like a done deal."

"Maybe." Mike thought back to that intense feeling he had experienced outside. He had his doubts but had no evidence.

"If you rub her back, it will help her relax," Dana offered. "She's really into getting rubbed, in case you were wondering."

He laughed. "I feel like you're trying to sell me on having sex with her."

"Have you ever seen those movies where a teen girl talks about her crush all the time and it's super annoying? I've been living in that movie, but all the talk is about sex with you. I could use some peace and quiet."

"And you'd be fine with that?"

"Would I have brought this up if I wasn't? Seriously, Mike. Please fuck her. I'm tired of answering questions about heterosexual sex. Oh, but a warning. She gets extra zappy when she comes."

So do I, he thought.

"So other than a dragon-sized bed hog, what's the real reason you're still awake?"

"I don't know what you mean," he replied.

"I know your scent. You've smelled differently all day, and I'm getting a whiff of something else right now. It smells a lot like pepperoni burps, but I think it's anxiety."

"Oh," he replied. Dana was right; there was something else keeping him up. Ever since that moment in the barn with Velvet, he had been unable to get her out of his mind. In fact, he had walked away from their conversation about goblins only to get some distance. He hardly knew her, and the intense attraction was a little frightening.

"Oof, there it is. Whatever the problem is, you're thinking about it right now." Dana waved a hand in front of her nose and scrunched up her face. "Is it something I can help with?"

"I'm not sure." He pictured the way Velvet looked when she had been standing next to him outside. She had absent-mindedly twirled her hair in one finger while they talked. When she looked at him, he felt like he was getting lost in her eyes. She was his perfect tomboy fantasy. A woman who had lived her life in the forest, with beautiful auburn hair and a sweet smile that made his knees feel weak.

From the waist down…he didn't even mind so much. He supposed part of that was due to the fact that she was covered in soft hair. Her sister's sleek, shiny body was far more intimidating to him.

And what about when he had touched her and his entire body had become ultrasensitive? His magic had never done that before. In the last few months, he had experimented with his own abilities, but it was definitely limited.

He called the abilities and traits he had gained from the others his extrahuman abilities. The banshee scream was the most obvious, and the endurance he had received from Zel had been a godsend on their hike. He attributed his strength in the Dreamscape to Lily, and the fact that his cum practically sparkled now was definitely the fairies.

But there had to be other traits hidden away, ones he hadn't discovered yet. Having no fear of heights was something he had received from Abella, but he would never have known about it if he hadn't taken a ride on the Jabberwock. Was this weird sensitivity related to one of those? Perhaps one of his gifts was reacting to Velvet's presence? It was impossible to know.

"Where does Velvet sleep?" he asked. They had been given a tour of the downstairs, but he hadn't bothered going upstairs yet.

"That's...not the question I expected. The arachne sleep upstairs." Dana pointed at the loft. "It's weird up there, kind of like the house. That whole bigger-on-the-inside thing. When you go up there, stay out of Eulalie's room. She'll get pissed if she finds out you messed with her computers."

"Is she some kind of—"

Dana practically leaped across the table to push her finger against his lips, preventing him from saying webmaster.

"Just don't. It's too obvious," she warned.

He snorted and stood. Dana watched him ascend the spiral staircase to the loft. Somehow, even though he'd climbed the stairs, the ceiling didn't seem any closer. In fact, the space in the rafters looked large enough for several arachne to move about. He wondered if Eulalie and Velvet had used the area as a playroom, able to move about without disturbing the earthbound residents below.

From where he stood, he could see into the first floor. Bigfoot was snoring now, and Dana had put on headphones. He walked along the railing, trying to picture what it was like to grow up in such a place. In a dark nook along the far wall, he saw Emery tucked away in something that looked like a nest. The little imp was asleep, the silver dollar Mike had given him clutched in his tiny claws.

An entire life had been lived here by the arachne family, and he wondered what the next step for the daughters would be. If the Nirumbi had been dealt with, they could return to their normal lives. He suspected Eulalie was interested in the house, but Velvet had too many emotional ties to this place. It wouldn't be hard to connect the two by portal, but that was a discussion for another time.

The rooms were at the end of the hall, laid out side by side. As he approached, he realized he didn't know what he was going to do or say. Waking Velvet up to tell her he couldn't stop thinking about her was not the most tactful way to approach the situation. Confessing it was somehow magic related was also a terrible idea.

"What am I doing?" he muttered to himself, then turned to leave.

When he came back down the stairs, he saw that Dana was pacing while reading her book. She looked up at him briefly as he walked back to his room.

Once inside, he slid his feet out of his shoes and took off his pants. In just his shirt and boxers, he lifted the blankets and tried to slide in without making too much ruckus. The light of the moon was amplified by the reflective snow, which provided the room plenty of illumination. The room seemed colder than usual, and he swore he saw frost forming along the edges of the glass.

Now in bed, he tried to pull the blankets around his head and shoulders in an attempt to snuggle down and get warm. When they wouldn't move, he lifted them and rolled over to see what they were caught on. Expecting to discover them pinched between Quetzalli's arms, he was instead greeted by the sight of the blanket being tightly clutched in her hands.

Her purple eyes sparkled from within as electricity crackled along her eyelids. Once they were looking at each other, she let go of the blanket. The tension on the fabric caused the blanket to pop up, and a cascade of static shocks along her body illuminated the dark space.

She was completely naked.

"What's a girl gotta do to get your attention?" she asked in a quiet voice.

"Quetzalli, I—" He caught just a glimpse of her bountiful breasts before the blanket settled back down, and he suddenly couldn't process his own thoughts. The events of the day had become a yawning void, filled with thoughts of the beautiful woman before him.

Beneath the covers, a warm hand grabbed his cock through his boxers.

"What about Yuki?" he whispered.

Yuki, in fox form, let out a laugh, then jumped off the bed. He saw her move across the room, leaving a frost trail in her wake. Once at the door, she got up on her hind legs to pull it open, then strolled out and shut it behind her.

"Even dragons need a wing fox sometimes." Quetzalli's eyes lit up as she lifted the blankets and pressed herself against him. "I've been practicing with my electricity. So I don't shock you."

"You've already shocked me," he told her, then moved his hand onto her hip and slid it behind her to squeeze her ass. He felt a subtle surge of electrical energy as she sighed.

"You touch me differently than Dana does," Quetzalli said. "There's a certain…roughness that I like."

"Do you like it rough?" he asked her, his nose almost touching hers.

"I'm not sure yet," she replied. "Maybe you should show me?"

He slid his hand beneath her jaw, which allowed him to cradle her head. When he pulled her in for a kiss, the resulting spark lit up the dark space beneath the blankets. It was bright enough that he saw it through closed eyelids, but the pain was brief.

When they parted, he licked his lips. "I have a similar trick," he told her, then allowed his magic to manifest along the hand on her ass. The steady blue glow illuminated them both, and her eyes widened as his magic sank into her body.

"It feels so warm," she whispered. "I can feel your lightning traveling through my veins."

He pulled her thigh forward so that her leg wrapped around his hip. Once she was positioned correctly, he kissed her again. This time, he moved his hand around the thick curve of her ass and teased her puffy pussy lips with the tips of his fingers. More sparks popped between them when Quetzalli stuck her hand down the front of his boxers and he received a zap at the head of his dick. The shock was barely noticeable, and he let out a sigh of relief.

"Told you I've been practicing," she explained, then pressed her body against his. They were pressed together just right that she could still stroke the upper half of his erect cock while he teased her.

He slid his hand from her neck to her breasts. They were supple, and he ran his magic along the edge of her nipple until it was rock-hard. Whenever she moaned or gasped, her eyes lit up with electricity.

"I never understood why they do that," she muttered just before he moved his head and sucked her nipple into his mouth. He teased her areola with his tongue and bit her playfully as she continued to stroke him beneath the blankets.

Quetzalli groaned and shifted, trapping his thigh between her legs. She was partially on top of him now and was rubbing her crotch along the length of his thigh. She left behind a trail slick with her fluids as she touched his chest with her free hand.

The first zap he received startled him but only because she teased him with it first. It was strange feeling all the hairs on his body react just before the spark leaped between them, and she managed to hit him with it right on his own nipple. The second zap let him know it was deliberate, and he let out a gasp, her nipple popping free of his mouth.

"Oh, it's cold out there!" she cried, then tried to adjust the blankets as he sucked her back into his mouth. The fabric kept catching on the edge of her horn, and he nearly laughed when he imagined sticking a cork on it for safety reasons.

Her horn was actually glowing with an eerie purple aura. She continued to hump his leg, her little moans becoming more desperate as she pressed into him. He loved the feel of her skin beneath his hands, the feel of her weight on top of him. Her body was covered in random patches of scales that were smooth to the touch and hummed with energy of their own.

"I want to feel it," she told him. "Your cock. I need it inside me before I burst."

"Before you burst?" he asked around the edge of her other breast. He had spent enough time on the first one that he worried the second one was feeling neglected.

"It's a full feeling, deep in my belly," she explained. "Like a cloud full of rain, but it just keeps building, the moisture piling higher..."

More than happy to move forward while avoiding cloud metaphors, he grabbed her hips and pulled her up his body. Her thighs spread wide to slide out and around his own legs, and he now felt her wet labia rubbing along his shaft. Though he hadn't penetrated her yet, he could feel the hum of magic being established as her magic mixed with his own.

"Are you vibrating?" she asked him in a hushed tone.

He held still to process her question. Between the steady sparks leaving her body and his own magic, his dick was actually vibrating while pressed between them.

"Apparently I am," he said. "This is new territory for us both."

"Maybe we should play the wizard and the dragon." She smiled mischievously. "I'll threaten to eat you, and you can slay me with your mighty wand."

He stared at her in amazement. "Is that...something you actually want?"

"No." Quetzalli grabbed the base of his dick and held it in place as she moved her body to take him inside. "But Amymone said you would make a funny face. She was totally right."

"That little——" The words were conscripted to the void as he entered her. The vibrations in his body intensified, and his magic was now openly streaming inside her. At the same time, her horn was beginning to shoot sparks, and he shifted the blankets away from her head before she could burn something.

"Oh! Gods!" Her voice was a quiet hiss as she snaked her legs beneath his ass and pinned herself in place. "You feel soooo good inside me!"

His cock was pressed up against the far wall of her vagina, but his whole crotch was tingling with pleasure. His own magic seemed to be mixing with hers, and the intensity of the exchange was building between them.

"I never thought it would feel so hot," she muttered. The air was crackling with electrical streamers that came off her horn and fingers. Mike's magic was manifesting all along his belly and thighs as sparks that rose into the air and hovered between them.

"You feel wonderful yourself." He loved the sheer weight of her pressing down on his hips, the feel of her thick thighs beneath his fingers. His magic was now caught up between their magical fields, the room taking on the appearance of a snow globe made of electricity.

"Oh!" Quetzalli adjusted her hips. "When I move like this, I can feel you pressing against my clitoris!" She grunted as she rolled her hips against him, grinding her pelvis hard against his. Sparks jumped between them now, each one lighting up the room.

He closed his eyes and moaned. Whenever she was sliding off his shaft, he could feel the head of his dick vibrate inside her. As she sank onto him again, she was tight enough that her vaginal walls held him still. The sensation of his cock vibrating off and on was sending massive surges of pleasure up his spine.

"I thought you said you were gonna be rough with me," Quetzalli told him, her eyes dazzling in the darkness.

Mike's eyes snapped open, and he lifted his hips into the air. She groaned and put her hands against his chest. The connection between them intensified, and he managed to sit up and pull her torso against his face. Her breasts were big enough that his face was properly buried between them. There was a brief moment when he realized he couldn't actually breathe.

I wonder what Cecilia would think if she had to collect me like this, he wondered. *Or Death. He would probably make me answer a bunch of questions.*

He snaked his hand up along her back until he got a handful of her hair. He twisted it around his hand and yanked, forcing her head back.

"Gah!" Quetzalli had to put her hands behind her to prevent from falling over, but now her breasts were defenseless. Mike licked and bit his way along them while she gasped, her hips shifting about above him. The more he bit, the more he wondered if it was a habit he had picked up from Tink.

Quetzalli was letting out sexy little cries every time he bit a nipple. There was a delicate art to inflicting just the right amount of pain, and his magic let him walk that line perfectly. His magic surged, and the streamers along Quetzalli's body turned a deep crimson.

This is new. Unconcerned, he used his free hand to anchor her shoulder and pull her down, allowing him to penetrate her more deeply.

"Oh gods!" she cried. The singular light in the room had a fluorescent bulb in it, which was now lighting up on its own. It flickered in time with the steady hiss that emanated from the streamers on Quetzalli's horn. "This feels so much different than it does with a woman!"

Encouraged by her words, he fucked her. He kept his hand in her hair but placed the other one on the small of her back, allowing him to hold her in place as he thrust his cock into her. Whenever they were pressed together, he could feel a tremendous amount of magical energy shift and build up while every hair on his body stood on end. Quetzalli's hair was now sticking out in every direction, the air filled with the sound of steady crackling.

It was so easy to let the world around him fall away, to let this beautiful woman become his entire reason for being. He grabbed a handful of her ass and pulled as hard as he could. His dick was now pulsating inside her, and he could feel a steady stream of precum leaking from his body.

She was calling his name. Bits of his magic had stuck to her, but others were now floating around the two of them, creating a spherical grid that rotated around them like a globe. Each one acted like a node, sending streamers to its closest neighbors.

"Uh…" Even though he was buried balls-deep in a dragon, it suddenly occurred to him that they were in the middle of a massive electrical charge. Was his magic technically even electricity? It wasn't like he had ever bothered to fuck someone with a lightbulb in his mouth.

"Oh yes!" Quetzalli's eyes were now shimmering purple orbs, and she grabbed onto his shoulders. "Fuck me, Mike Radley! Fuck me!"

She yanked on his hair, which pulled his head back. This allowed her to kiss him. When their tongues met, the direction of the orb changed, and he felt his magic surge back into his body. His cock was so hard it almost hurt, and he felt that pressure building deep inside his balls as they pulled into his body harder than ever before.

When he came, the magic shifted and he poured massive amounts of semen into Quetzalli. Upon splashing her insides, the sphere shrank down onto her body, bringing all those nodes into contact with her skin. As if electrified, she tensed up so hard that he let go of her hair and put up a hand to keep her from falling over.

Quite by accident, his hand slid across her forehead and hooked onto her horn.

The field exploded outward, spiraled, then came back in. It pulsated in time with Quetzalli's ragged breaths, and she opened her mouth wide and let out a high-pitched hiss. He could feel her pussy tighten up on his cock, but then his whole body jerked as the field manifested again and settled on him.

What was usually a diminishing back-and-forth had somehow intensified. His orgasm was almost immediate as he blew his load once more. Quetzalli tensed up, squeezing his previous deposit out and all over him as the magic swung back to focus on her.

He tried to let go of her horn, but his next orgasm came before he could act. Quetzalli shifted her weight back, causing more semen to squirt all along his belly. In between orgasms, he managed to regain control of his hand long enough to let go, but it was too late.

The electrical field was large enough now that it crawled along the walls of the room as if trying to escape. The whole room was ablaze in blue-and-purple light, and the tiny desk light was dwarfed by how bright it was. Quetzalli's eyes had become molten stars as she screamed silently above him, continuing to ride him like she was going for a world record. The edges of his vision were going black as she continued to drain his body of cum.

He needed to break the connection before he passed out. Each load he put in her was strengthening the feedback loop rather than weakening it, and she was leaking so heavily now that all he had to do was give her shoulders a push. She tipped over backward and fell to one side, causing her to twist and pop off of his cock.

The storm broke, and the field exploded along the walls of the room. Electrical energy crackled as it crept around the room and eventually vanished into the floor. Quetzalli's hands were clenched tight as she twitched on the bed next to him, and he came one last time, covering his belly in spooge.

They lay there silently, their frantic breaths the only sounds that could be heard.

"Do you…think they…heard us?" Quetzalli asked.

"If not, they definitely…saw the…light show."

Once he caught his breath, he took off his shirt and used it to mop up the mess on his belly. There was so much cum all over both of them that there was no way either of them would avoid the wet spot tonight.

Quetzalli didn't seem very mobile, so he helped her beneath the blankets once again. When he slid into bed with her, he spooned her from behind. His arm fit perfectly over her waist, and he rested his hand on her belly, his fingers tracing circles just beneath her belly button. His semihard cock rested between her butt cheeks, which she pressed playfully against him.

"That was wonderful," she whispered. "I was sure sex with a man was interesting, but sex with you? Pure magic."

She said nothing else. Other than the occasional contented purr, she made no further sounds as she fell asleep in his arms.

Exhausted, he closed his eyes and felt consciousness slip away. When the dreams came, he found himself slipping through the clouds on silvered wings as he herded them together to make a proper storm.

The weak, fog-filtered light of morning illuminated the living room of the Radley house, and Beth let out a sigh of relief. A small fire crackled in the fireplace—Tink had spent part of her evening getting leftover timber from rebuilding the Labyrinth in an attempt to keep the house warm.

Beth had spent most of her evening sitting on the couch. Determined not to take her eyes off Murray, she had taken a few catnaps while Cecilia and Lily watched. It wasn't that she didn't trust them to wake her if something happened. It was more that she was afraid she wouldn't be ready to spring into action.

Not that she knew what that would be. Sofia had dropped by in the middle of the night to announce that they hadn't found anything of note. Even with the information that Murray was acting as a beacon, their search had turned up too much material to go through in such a short time. The problem with legends was that it was usually hard to tell if they were real until they were staring you in the face.

Kisa and Tink were curled up together on the love seat. Tink was out cold, her goggles sliding down over her nose. Kisa was lying across the goblin's lap, her arm hanging off the side and touching the floor. Tucked between them was Jenny, the little doll's eerie features staring out the window.

Lily stood at the window with her arms crossed. Her tail swished from side to side in annoyance.

"Oh, good. Now we get to see his ugly face again, even better." She looked over her shoulder at Beth. "Is it time to check your phone again?"

Beth turned it on and frowned. "Still nothing. Literally." There was no signal, and her battery life had drained substantially overnight. She wondered if she forgot to turn it off. "This reminds me of snowstorms when I was a kid. Stuck in the house all day, and—"

"I don't wanna hear about it." Lily turned to face her. "This isn't a snow day, and it certainly isn't something I can relate to."

Undeterred, Beth turned her phone back off and picked up her teacup. With nothing better to do, she stood and headed for the kitchen.

As she walked into the kitchen, she saw Reggie standing on the counters. His nose was twitching, and a group of rats had clustered on the floor beneath him.

"Everything okay?" she asked.

"It is not, Lady Beth." Reggie bowed in greeting. "I have just received word that we've lost track of the colony."

"Excuse me, what? You mean, like…"

"The rest of us, yes." Reggie moved to the edge of the counter. "Sometime in the night, all our portals slammed shut. I've been out here monitoring the situation with this man, and when it was time to change the guard, they never came."

"Reggie, that's terrible!" She set the cup down and took his paw in her hand. "What can we do? Are they okay?"

"I do not know, but I fear the worst. The colony has been living in the space between worlds for centuries. We are survivors. But I don't know who could have cut them off so suddenly." Down below, one of the rats chittered at him. "I agree but don't think that's what happened."

"What did he think? Or she?" Beth frowned when she looked at the rats.

"She said that it could have been an insurrection and we were closed off on purpose. I doubt this only because there have been no rumors of displeasure with the current status quo. My kind have rather enjoyed being official members of this home." He shook his head. "Between the man in your yard and my missing colony, I am at a loss right now. Please excuse me."

With that, Reggie hopped off the counter, and his retinue followed him as he disappeared. Troubled, Beth navigated the kitchen in the dim light and set her cup in the sink. When she turned on the water, it came out at a bare trickle.

"Shit!" She smacked the faucet, then realized it would be better to have Tink look at it. On her way back into the front room, a dreadful thought occurred to her. The electricity was out, and the water was no longer running. Now Reggie's portals had closed.

Were they being cut off?

"Where's the crystal ball?" she asked when she entered the front room. It sat on one of the end tables on a small golden ring that cradled it. She picked it up and blew her hot breath on it.

"Ratu? I need to speak with you right away." Every time she had used the ball until now, the naga had appeared in a matter of minutes. There would be a swirl of purple smoke as the crystal connected to the other side, and then she would appear.

"What's wrong?" Lily asked. Beth held a finger to her lips.

"Ratu? Can you hear me?" She gave the ball a shake. For just a moment, there was a wisp of smoke, followed by the sound of a distant voice. Then nothing.

"Lily, we're being cut off," she said, then set the ball down. "Whatever that thing is out there, it isn't just calling for help. It's isolating us!"

"Fuck!" Lily's shout startled Kisa awake. As she rolled off the couch and onto the floor, Tink was also startled awake. The goblin tumbled to the floor and landed gracefully on her face.

"We need to check on the others." Beth pointed at Lily. "I need you to see if you can get to the greenhouse. Kisa, check the Library. I'll see if I can open the Labyrinth."

She shot up the stairs before anyone could object, her heart pounding. Once in her room, she felt the first hot tear roll down her cheek as she grabbed the knob of the closet and entered the secret combination that would activate the magic and allow her to enter the cave.

When she opened the door, it was still just a closet.

"No," she whispered, taking a step back. Frozen in terror, she heard Kisa yell from down below.

"It's not opening," she cried up the stairs. "When I pull out the book, nothing happens."

No, no, no, no, no. Beth practically threw herself down the stairs and slid across the floor as she entered the office. Kisa was pulling down books frantically as Tink stood by, her features twisted up in horror.

"Magic book is broken," she whispered, then handed it over to Beth.

"How? How is this even possible?"

"How is what possible?" Death strolled out of the sitting room, his face buried in a *Highlights* magazine from the late nineties. He set it down on the desk, then looked at the books Kisa had thrown on the floor. "Did you know that they have hidden pictures in these? I find them quite enjoyable."

"We're closed off!" Kisa stood on a nearby chair so that she was at eye level with Death. "Something happened to the house, and the Library is closed. Do you know what that means?"

Death paused for a moment, then looked at the magazine he had set down. "It means I must ration my reading materials," he said, then picked up the magazine once again.

"Death?" Beth looked at the grim reaper with suspicion. "Why aren't you wearing your earmuffs?"

"Because that dreadful man out front has stopped shouting." Death lifted the magazine to look in it, but Kisa ripped it out of his hands.

"You can be so infuriating sometimes!" She ripped the book in half and threw it to the ground. "We. Are. All. In. Danger!"

"Oh." He scratched the top of his skull, which caused a scraping sound that reminded Beth of fingernails on a chalkboard. "I see. Perhaps we should check on our gentleman caller? I shall accompany you."

Beth nodded, then looked at the others. Tink made a face as if she remembered something, then she bolted out of the room.

"Let's go, then," she muttered, then led Death to the front door and opened it.

Murray was hovering above the ground, his face stretched out in a soundless scream. She and Death moved down the stairs together as he unfolded his scythe. Cecilia appeared, hovering just off to the side as they walked toward Murray.

Off in the corner of the yard, the Jabberwock let out a hiss. The beast had been sitting there ever since it had gotten knocked away, and its attention was now upward. The fog was impenetrable, hiding away the sky.

"Murray?" She called out to him from a distance, but there was still no recognition. When she looked back over her shoulder, she half expected the house to be gone. "Murray, can you hear me?"

"He is not present." Death poked the man in the shoulder with his scythe.

Cecilia put a cold hand on Beth's arm. "Who are they?" she asked, then pointed out into the fog.

Beth felt like she was going to be sick. She didn't see anybody, which meant that Cecilia was seeing spirits of some sort through the mist.

"What do you see?" she asked.

"There are three of them," Cecilia answered. "They're so bright it almost hurts to look at them. And it looks like they're riding—"

"COME!" Murray's voice was like a blast of thunder, sending a shock wave out through the fog. Beth cried out and covered her ears as her dress billowed out behind her.

"That was rather rude, don't you think?" Death closed his scythe and smacked Murray on the head with his staff. "You could at least give us a warning."

A dark shadow appeared in the fog, standing nearly ten feet tall. Beth's heart raced as it came toward them with the sound of clopping hooves. The fog parted to reveal a large horse with fiery eyes, but her attention was caught by the rider. The figure looked to be wearing a high-tech space suit with a mirrored gold visor. When the horse came to a stop, the figure reached over its shoulder and drew a bow. A black cloud circled the figure, then dispersed when it lowered its bow.

"Death," she muttered, taking a step back. There were a lot of things she was mentally prepared to deal with, but a horse-riding spaceman hadn't been one of them.

"Now this is a surprise!" Death put away his staff. "I didn't expect—"

"COME!" Murray's eyes were blazing with light, and Beth let out a shriek of alarm. Glowing eyes appeared in the mist, and a red horse emerged. Its mane and tail were made of fire, and a large man sat on the back, carrying the thickest blade Beth had ever seen. The horse snorted, sending flames along the ground. When they stopped, the man held the enormous blade in one hand, blade down, and dropped it. The sword slammed into the ground and stuck, like a giant stake.

"Oh my God," she muttered, then covered her ears just as Murray shouted again. This time, a black horse came from the fog, and its rider was carrying a pair of scales. His features were gaunt, and when he smiled, Beth could see far too many of his teeth. The horse was carrying assorted goods that emanated a dark aura.

"This is such a surprise!" Death looked at the riders in excitement. "I never expected to see my siblings so soon! What are you doing here?"

As one, they raised their hands and pointed at Death.

"What the actual fuck is going on out here?" Lily's voice was incredulous, startling Beth. The succubus stood at the bottom of the steps, her hand still on the railing. "Who invited the sexy cowboys?"

Cecilia, who was looking skyward, let out a gasp. She shot across the yard like an arrow and tackled Lily hard enough that the succubus crashed into the front door with a loud protest.

The air around Beth was suddenly heavy, and a shadow formed over the group like a giant cloud. When she looked up, she saw a swirling mass of wings, eyes, and gears descend from the sky. The being was larger than the house, and no matter where she looked, her brain struggled to make sense of what she was seeing. What initially looked like an eye became a wing, then a gear, then a mouth.

"DO NOT BE AFRAID!" The voice sent a blast of pressure that forced Beth onto her knees, her hair swirling around her face. She let out a gasp as all the air was forced from her lungs, and she collapsed onto the ground. The house shuddered as if caught in a windstorm, and when she looked up at it, she saw Lily push through Cecilia and throw herself into the house. Her skin was smoldering.

"Oh. Oh my." Death knelt and offered Beth a hand. Her legs wobbled beneath her. "I'm afraid we have a problem here."

Once she was on her feet, she cast a wary glance at the being up above. "This isn't a social visit, is it?"

"No. No, it is not." Death pulled his cowl over his face, then turned to look at her with fiery eyes. "It would seem that the Apocalypse is upon us."

The swirling mass of wings up above roared. Murray tipped his head back and opened his mouth, and a beam of light briefly connected him with the angel. Bands of golden light appeared, each one blazing with runes as the creature sent beams of energy into Murray's body. He shuddered as they brightened, and Beth wondered if he would explode.

When the bands dispersed, they sent a shock wave out that chased away the nearby fog, revealing the stone walls of the yard. Murray stood on his tiptoes, a quartet of blazing wings made of fire spread wide behind him.

When he tipped his head forward, his pupils were widely dilated and one eye was stuck looking to the right, while the other looked at Beth.

"That, my dear grim reaper, remains to be seen." When Murray spoke, his voice was deep and booming, but his lips didn't move. Instead, his mouth was frozen in a macabre grin that showed all his teeth and his tongue. "But yes, dear child, this is no social visit. For I am Mehkhkahrel, and I have gathered us here today to determine if the end is nigh."

IN HOT WATER

E ulalie yawned. Her jaw opened wider than her fist before popping, causing her venomous fangs to slide free from their hiding place. Blinking away the sleep, she saw a terrified rat holding a long broom. It was staring up at her from the floor below. She could smell the hot breath of other rodents watching her from the shadows of the Library.

"Did you wake me up?" she asked while cradled in a small web she had built in an abandoned supply closet on the first floor of the Library. Sofia had given her the space as temporary accommodations while they had tried to do research on the weirdo in the front yard.

The rat bolted through the door. Several other rats followed, leaving the stink of fear behind them. At the foot of the door, a tiny blue figure leaned into the opening.

"Sofia said to get you up," Cerulea squeaked. "She needs you right away."

"I'll be there in a minute." Eulalie yawned again and tumbled casually out of her web. She landed in a crouch, her legs splaying wide for support. Stepping out of the closet, she smiled at the sight of the enormous stacks of books that stretched impossibly into the sky. Cerulea was nowhere to be seen, but her glitter trail was still falling from the sky.

Eulalie's mother would have loved this place. It had every book known to man, and then some. The wide-open spaces were also perfect for climbing, and Eulalie was eager to explore every inch of it once she got the chance.

Outside her room was a giant stack of books she had gone through last night. They had all been dead ends with nothing of value to offer her.

Wondering what could be so urgent, she walked toward the main lobby of the Library. The giant globe that hovered in place was an absolute marvel to behold, held in position by magic. Beneath it, Sofia stood over a small contingent of rats. She looked up at Eulalie, a look of concern on her face.

"The house is missing." Sofia's voice was steady, but Eulalie detected several trembling undertones. There was fear, sadness, and more than a little bit of concern. Each emotion was its own musical chord, and she could hear them all.

"How do you lose a house?"

"The magical book we use to get there is still here, but it no longer opens a doorway to the house, and all the rat portals that go there have been closed."

Eulalie looked at the small crowd of rats, then back at Sofia. "All the portals are closed? We have no way back?"

Sofia shook her head. "Not that I'm aware of. The rats are capable of opening portals, but only on the orders of the rat king himself."

"I see." Eulalie walked up to the small group and watched as the rats backed away from her. Each of them had its own scent, and they all smelled delicious. She narrowed her eyes as she studied them. "Where is this king?"

"I assume back at the house. He is the only one who speaks our language, so even if we wanted them to help us, we have no way to communicate with them." Sofia looked calm and collected, but Eulalie could hear even more emotions in her voice. Shock. Despair. The cyclops was so caught up in her own feelings that she likely wasn't processing information properly.

"Let's not be short-sighted." Eulalie pulled out her phone and frowned. "We don't have internet here, do we?"

"None of the companies will give us a good quote." Sarcasm from Sofia sounded an awful lot like a squeaky violin to Eulalie.

"If he's the only one who can talk to them, then how did you get them to wake me up?"

Sofia lifted her eyebrow. "I didn't ask them. I asked Cerulea."

Eulalie spotted the fairy fluttering overhead. "Can you talk to them?" she asked.

"No," she replied. "I was trying to use the broom to wake you, and they decided to help me out."

"I can work with that. We need a sequence to follow." Eulalie pulled a band of webbing from her spinnerets and began weaving. The rats didn't understand English, but solutions came easy to those who looked for them. "Establish communication with rats. Communicate desire for portal home. If no portal home, then portal somewhere safe, investigate current situation. What does their king look like?"

"You probably saw him. Crown with glasses." Sofia walked toward her. "What are you doing?"

"Bypassing the language barrier to accomplish our first task. If they can understand situational context, it should be possible to convey our needs." Weaving a rat with a crown was child's play, especially done in a chibi art style. When she held up her final product, it was an image of their king in the middle of a tapestry of silken strands.

The rats chittered excitedly for a moment, then went silent as she wove another image. When she held it up, their fear stink faded even further. This image was a picture of her surrounded by food and cartoon hearts. She was certain Sofia probably had pen and paper somewhere, but her web art was far more precise than anything she could do by hand.

That, and she had a bad habit of nibbling on crayons. It was a childhood habit she just couldn't break, and she hated having to pick wax out of her teeth.

"What are you doing?" Sofia asked.

"Establishing that I'm not a threat." Her next image showed her and the king holding hands. The rats looked at one another, but it seemed they were grasping the situation. "Do we have any idea how they figure out where they're going?"

Sofia shook her head. "If you want somewhere specific, I'm sure they have a method. But it's something Reggie delegates."

"Well, we can't have them taking us just anywhere, can we?" It took her almost an hour, but by the time she was done, the rats were busy gnawing a hole on an open portion of the wall. It didn't take them long, because she only needed a hole big enough for her hand.

"Well?" Sofia had left and come back with food for everyone. "Any luck?"

"Let's find out." Eulalie pulled her phone out of her pocket and stuck it through the hole. On the other side of the hole, she could hear the distant bustle of humans talking to one another.

"That was pretty clever," Sofia said, looking over her shoulder. "Getting them to gnaw you a hole to a Starbucks."

"It doesn't even matter which one; they're on every corner." Eulalie connected to the wireless network, as her phone's reception wasn't great.

She tapped with purpose, using one of her government accounts to run a search for property records. It didn't take long to discover a man named Murray who lived right next to Mike.

"Do you suppose he lives alone?" Eulalie asked.

"I have no idea. Wouldn't someone have come looking if he didn't?"

"My thoughts exactly." She pulled up Murray's address and then searched for a street view. Once she had a picture, she pulled her hand back out and started weaving again. The delicious smell of roasted coffee beans reminded her of her father.

She smiled, caught up in the memory of how he would hold his mug first thing in the morning. He enjoyed how the heat seeped into his fingers, relaxing him.

Once finished with her web, she held up her phone for the rats to see. After they looked at Murray's house, she showed them a drawing of her and the rats standing inside it.

As one unit, the rats nodded and found a different spot to chew. A pair of rats worked on closing the hole they had opened.

"We'll have them scout out Murray's house," she informed Sofia. "If it's empty, we can go through and reestablish contact with the house."

"And if not, we can observe from a safe distance." Sofia let out a sigh of relief. "I'm glad you were able to come up with a solution so fast. I'll admit, I got caught up in the idea that the house had been destroyed. Usually, when a location disconnects from here, that's the case."

"There were other places connected here?" Eulalie rubbed her stomach and winced. She was retaining a ton of water as her new carapace expanded. The thin cracks along her legs were the arachne version of a peeling sunburn, and the edges were beginning to lift away.

"Many. The house is the last one, to my knowledge. It got stuck in my head that something could have happened to everyone and that I may be here all alone." Sofia frowned. "I've been alone before. It…was hard."

"You're not alone. You have me. And the rats." She smirked to show Sofia she was kidding. "We'll get it figured out, don't you worry."

She watched the rats as they chewed. It was a fascinating process to observe, because their teeth did sink into the surface of the wall, but it didn't seem like the material was being consumed. Instead, a glittery golden substance was left behind on the edges of the wall as it became a tiny hole and then expanded.

A living room appeared. The hole had opened beneath an end table, and a few rats ran in to scope the place out. They came back and chittered excitedly at the others, and they continued widening the hole.

Once it was about two feet across, Eulalie squeezed through. Now inside of Murray's home, she closed her eyes and listened to her body. The house had a certain stillness to it revealing that nobody had passed through in almost a day. She also could tell that the HVAC system was ancient, resulting in poor air circulation and a dead mouse in one of the vents.

Eulalie moved through the house, examining the furniture. It was old and most likely inherited. A quick trip upstairs revealed a dusty guest room and a master bedroom that looked immaculately kept. She tapped on her phone the whole time, accessing her online shopping account.

By the time the portal was big enough for Sofia to step through, Eulalie had scoped out the whole house.

"Place is empty. Murray lives alone, though there was a lot of women's lingerie in his closet." Eulalie double-checked the address on her phone and put in her order. "Lots of lace. Very little leather."

"Can we see the house from here?" Sofia moved to the front window and pushed the curtain back.

"No. The best shot is from the guest room upstairs, and you can only see part of the yard."

"Wait for night, then?"

"Nope." Eulalie held up her phone. "I've ordered some things from Prime delivery. We're in a two-hour delivery window, can you believe it? We used to have to send Dad into town to pick up stuff from a locker, a four-hour trip after waiting several days just for a delivery!"

"I'm glad you have something to be excited abou—what are you doing?"

"Hmm?" Eulalie had picked up Murray's router. It was an older model, and she flipped it over. "I'm resetting this router. The password is written on the bottom. When my new laptop gets here, I can do some digital reconnaissance of my own, but I need internet access."

Sofia sat down on Murray's couch. She took up a large portion of it, making it look more like a love seat. "I'm afraid I can offer no help in that area."

"That's okay." Eulalie grinned, revealing all her teeth. "Because I'm already the best there is."

WHEN BETH WALKED INTO THE HOUSE, SHE FELT A PRESSURE CHANGE, AND HER ears popped when the door closed behind her. Tink, Kisa, and Cecilia were watching her from their spot at the window. Jenny was nowhere to be seen.

"What the hell is going on?" Kisa's eyes were unnaturally wide.

"Um…" Beth shook her head. Now that she was out of the angel's presence, it was like walking from sunlight into a dim room, but instead of her eyes needing time to adjust, it was her mind. "So…uh…shit. Hold on a second."

She walked past the others, went into the kitchen, and opened the fridge. The food inside was already warming to room temperature, and she pulled out one of the beers Mike had hidden in the back. After popping the tab, she walked back into the living room while drinking it.

By the time she made it back, the beer was nearly gone, and she felt as though she could at least put events in order. Outside, Death was waving his arms dramatically for the three horsemen and Mehkhkahrel. Up above, the swirling mass of eyes and wings watched them.

"Our neighbor Murray is apparently acting as a vessel for the angel Meka…Mekaka…" She finished her beer. "Mehkhkahrel. I think that's what he said. It's his job to do the talking for that thing up there." She pointed at the winged monstrosity.

"That's an angel?" Kisa asked in awe.

"It is," Cecilia responded. "Though I've never seen one so powerful."

"Speaking of, is Lily okay?"

"She went upstairs," Cecilia said.

"Okay, I'll go check on her soon. So yeah, that whirling frisbee of what-the-fuck is acting as the judge. Apparently, Death isn't supposed to fully manifest on this plane of existence unless the Apocalypse has started. So right now, they're all arguing about whether his being here qualifies as the opening of some seal that means we are fucked. Like, on every level kind of fucked." She was shaking now, and she dropped the can when she tried to set it down. A tiny bit of beer spilled on the carpet. "This isn't even about the house anymore. This is about the whole world."

"Oh." Kisa looked at Tink, then back out the window. "Then it shouldn't be a big deal, right? Death didn't come here; he got trapped. That should be simple enough to explain."

"I hope so." Beth took comfort in Kisa's words. "That fog out there? There's nothing beyond it. The whole time Murray was screaming, he wasn't just summoning everyone. We're apparently in a pocket dimension. If the three horsemen had just shown up on our doorstep, then all four of them would be walking the earth and trigger the end of the world. They've been trying to find Death for a couple of months now and have been breaking down magical barriers across the world in an attempt to find him."

"Stupid horse fuckers can't have funny bone man," Tink grumbled. "Maybe Tink shoot down ugly bird."

"Tink? Don't." Beth pointed at the goblin. "I get the feeling you would get vaporized or set on fire or something. You are not to get yourself killed. It would break Mike's heart."

Tink grumbled but nodded. "Tink be good," she muttered. "But not be happy about it."

"So this wasn't an attack?" Kisa almost sounded relieved.

"No. It was never about us at all." She looked out the window and saw that Death was pantomiming using a View-Master. "And I hope it stays that way. I'm going to go check on Lily."

She walked up the stairs, wondering where the succubus could have gone. While there were plenty of rooms to choose from, she had one idea that made more sense than the others.

The door to Mike's room was closed, but she opened it anyway and walked inside.

"Lily?" Even though she got no response, she walked into the bathroom to make sure. Lying in the middle of the empty tub was a small child with black-and-red hair. Her arm was bandaged up in silk, and her skin was smoldering. "Are you okay?"

"I was almost vaporized out there," she responded, her voice tiny. "I came up here hoping to cool off my skin and talk to Naia. She's not here anymore. I don't know where she is."

"Back on Earth is my best guess." Beth explained that they had been put inside a pocket dimension. "Her spring is underground, so she is still there."

"Do you think it's just a huge crater now?" Lily asked. "The neighbors must be freaking out."

"I don't know," Beth replied. She got into the tub and cocked her head. "Why the little kid act?"

"There's less of me to hurt," Lily whispered. "I felt like I was on fire. That's not a sensation I've felt since…" She waved her hand dismissively. "Everything hurts, and I can't leave."

"Of course not. We're sealed in a pocket dimension."

"It's not that. A succubus can always go to her master." Lily's lower lip trembled. "I tried to go to him, to warn him away. It's not just that I can't go to him. I can't feel him! I don't know if he's alive or dead, and I can't feel Naia either!" Her voice rose in pitch as fat tears welled in her cheeks. "I'm afraid, Beth! That thing that's out there could destroy me with a thought if it turned its attention on the house! We are not even ants to it; we're like those things that shit on your eyelids while you just go about your day!"

"Hey, now. Shhh." Beth moved next to Lily and slid an arm around her. The succubus sobbed and rolled toward her. It was just like comforting a child, minus the excessive swearing. "It's going to be okay. Death is explaining things to them now."

"We are so fucked," Lily muttered. "Do you know what the difference between an angel and a demon is? Daddy issues and membership to an exclusive club. That's it. Angels can have agendas just like demons do. If that thing out there came all this way in order to find out if it's time for the world to end, then it will stack the deck in its favor."

"What do you mean? Wouldn't that be against…Sky Daddy's will?" She decided to go with a term Lily would find acceptable.

"Logic and reason don't apply to the divine. They are beings that live outside of time and space. They don't see things the way you do. Why do you think I can take shortcuts through Hell? It overlaps everything, just like Purgatory. I even overlap with myself. How do you think I change shape? I'm not made of flesh and bone but something else entirely. It's like that black shit they pulled out of you; it's pure potential with no direction. Do you know why the universe keeps expanding?" Lily's voice had calmed a little. "Scientists think it's some leftover energy, or whatever. It's because this plane is finite, while others are not. The universe is trying to play catch-up to its big brothers and sisters and will eventually tear itself apart to do so."

"I so enjoy these chats," Beth noted sarcastically. "Very uplifting."

"That thing out there is just a demon who hasn't pissed off Daddy yet. Does that put anything into perspective for you? If it can smash you into powder while coloring inside the lines, it will do so in a heartbeat. The asshole won't even be angry while crushing you. It'll be in such a rush to satisfy Daddy that it'll take the shortcut."

"You have a very dim view of angels."

"Religious politics aside, I can't help you with this one. Just its arrival almost killed me, and if not for our resident screamer, I'd be gone already. If I step outside the house, it will probably kill me on sight. Not send me to Hell—oblivion. Gone, poof! You won't even have dust to put in a jar for Romeo to cry over."

"Beth?" It was Kisa. She came into the bathroom, a frown on her face. Lily shifted out of Beth's arms before they could be seen. "Death needs to talk to you."

"And so it begins." Lily waved Beth off with a tiny hand. "If you need me, I'll be in this tub. I'm the new maiden of the bath, here to dispense orgasms and advice."

"Not looking like that, you won't." Beth pulled the towel off the hook and threw it over Lily's head. "Here's a blankie so you don't get cold."

"Thanks, Mom," Lily mumbled through the towel as she flipped Beth off.

Beth followed Kisa down to the living room. Death stood in the door, his cowl pulled back. The flames in his eye sockets had grown tiny, and he was fidgeting with his fingers.

"You need me?" she asked.

"Yes, I believe I do." Death stared down at his feet. He did a little shuffle, like he was trying to kick a piece of dust off the floor. "It seems I am in need of your legal services, Judge Bethany."

"Okay, three things. Only my grandmother calls me that, and—"

"She's dead, yes." Death smiled sheepishly.

"I'm not a judge, I'm a lawyer," Beth added.

"I apologize. You wanted your own title, and I thought you would enjoy that one, as it is related to the law."

"Oh." She remembered shouting after him the other day for a title. "I appreciate the thought, but I don't want to be called judge anything."

"Princess? Queen? Barrister?" Death paused to gaze at the ceiling in contemplation. "Supreme court justice?"

"Three. Why do you need a lawyer?" she asked.

"Ah. Well, I thought I would impress upon my siblings and the Honorable Angel Mehkhkahrel the things I've learned since arriving at this. My presence here was quite by accident and never intended to set off the Apocalypse itself. I thought that by showing them how I have indulged in your culture that they would realize I came to Earth without any malice toward mankind."

"Okay." Beth waited for him to go on.

"It would seem we have a dilemma. You see, the angel is under the belief that the Apocalypse is at hand and has stated that my continued presence is proof of such a thing. My siblings, who are very eager to walk the earth and destroy it, have sided with him."

"But you were summoned here for a different reason though."

"Yes, but they didn't seem to care. A more brutal version of myself would have been summoned for something as special as the end of the world. The point of the matter is that the angel has ordered that either I leave this plane right away or allow them to formally open the Seven Seals so they can rain judgment on Earth."

"Oh. Oh!" Beth's jaw dropped open. "You can't leave, can you?"

"I cannot." Death shook his head sadly. "Until I have collected the soul of the one known as Amir, I am bound to this world."

"Shit. So where do I come in?"

"Well, the angel was about to pass judgment when I reminded him that it was the law of the land that I get access to an attorney. I also told him I had the right to remain silent."

"And he listened?" She looked out the window. The quartet of chaos was standing there, staring at the house.

"This is an angel of judgment. Of course he didn't." Death wandered over to the window. "But he had promised to consider all angles. I informed them that my attorney would have a unique perspective relevant to my case and then held him to that promise."

Her stomach cramped, and she felt light-headed. What would Mike do in a situation like this? She observed each of the horsemen, watching them as they remained motionless. "Your brothers wouldn't happen to be susceptible to flirting, would they?"

"No. They have no interest in sex. And neither does Pestilence."

"Pestilence is a girl?" She looked at the rider in the spacesuit and realized it was a high-tech hazmat suit.

"No. They're complicated and still figuring things out." Death led her to the door. "Their identity has been in flux for millennia. In fact, Pestilence is their new name. I think they like it, but it's hard to tell now that I can't see their face. When I'm standing really close, I can hear what sounds like thousands of bees buzzing inside. Can you imagine that?"

"Guess I won't have to." She put her hand on the knob and pulled. If Death's siblings couldn't be seduced, then half of Mike's typical strategy was already out the window. "Let's see if we can get lucky."

THE CABIN SMELLED LIKE HOT BUTTER AND CINNAMON. WHEN MIKE STEPPED out of his bedroom, the smell intensified, and he saw Yuki standing in the kitchen. She was ladling oatmeal into a bowl and winked when she saw him.

"Morning." She smiled knowingly before taking a bite. "There's plenty left. You should have some to replenish that energy of yours."

Mike blushed. "I'm guessing everyone heard?"

"Not only that, but you fucked up Bigfoot's VHS collection. His tapes are all messed up. They have these wavy lines all over them."

"Oh shit, really?"

"Yes!" Bigfoot shoved open the bathroom door and limped to the couch. "I had to switch to DVD, and I hate it!"

"Why do you hate DVD?" If Bigfoot were not moving like a geriatric patient with arthritis, Mike would have felt threatened by the angry Sasquatch.

"My fingers are too fucking big for the remote." Bigfoot sat down with a grunt and held up a black piece of plastic that was dwarfed in his palm. It was clear to Mike that each button would be very difficult for the cryptid to press.

"Where's Quetzalli?" he asked.

"Using up what's left of the hot water." Yuki tapped her spoon on the table. "Your bedroom smells like a fuck pit, and you're no better."

"Oh." He couldn't even argue. His stomach was still covered in dry spunk. "I guess I could always take a cold shower."

"You'll freeze your balls off." Bigfoot glanced over his shoulder. The television was displaying the DVD player's loading screen. "Our water comes from a well. Darren put in a heater, but it's old. About twenty years ago, you could get a couple of showers out of it. But now?" He shivered. "If you're in a hurry, you could drop by the hot springs. It isn't a far walk."

"Hot springs?" Mike's mind immediately went to Naia. He wondered how she was doing.

"Yeah, there're a few. Big enough to swim in. Just don't try diving to the bottom; they're deeper than they look. The water gets much hotter, and you might pass out." Bigfoot uncapped a beer that had been down by his feet. "This one time, I was at Yellowstone and saw a guy go swimming in one that was near boiling. Cooked him like a brat. He split open along the sides toward the end."

"Gross." Yuki frowned at her oatmeal. "I saw something like that once in Japan. Very unpleasant."

The front door opened, and Dana walked in. Her nose wrinkled, and she looked at Mike.

"Oh, wow, that's strong." She covered her nose and gave him a wide berth as she moved to sit next to Bigfoot.

A door shut in the cabin, and Quetzalli appeared with a towel around her body and another towel wrapped around her head. She gave Mike a wink and disappeared into their bedroom.

"Maybe I'll hit those springs." He stood and moved to the front door. "Where are they?"

"I'll take you." Dana stood and moved toward the door. "I don't want you getting lost."

Mike grabbed his coat, and they walked outside together. He shivered in the cool air, wondering if the hot spring would be warm enough to counter the chill. Up above, Abella circled for a landing.

"Are we going home today?" She looked unusually grumpy.

"Not yet. Once Bigfoot is up and about, we'll plan for going home." He pulled out his phone and frowned. "I'm also thinking I should head for the boundary. See if I can't get a signal on this thing."

Abella rolled her eyes and held out a hand.

"Give it here. It will take you all day to walk there and back. I can do it in a quarter of the time."

"Thank you." He handed over his phone. "Let them know we're safe. I think our Nirumbi issue is solved." *If that was our main issue*, he thought to himself. Whatever had been watching him didn't seem to be around now. Hopefully it had gone with the Nirumbi.

"I'll be back." Abella launched herself skyward in a motion that scattered a flurry of snowflakes in every direction, blasting Mike with icy shards. He brushed himself off and watched as the gargoyle disappeared over the trees.

"She's in a foul mood," Dana muttered under her breath.

Mike sighed but kept his thoughts to himself.

They walked into the forest, exchanging chitchat. Dana was working her way through a ton of science fiction novels on her phone and was learning conversational Russian as well. She also told him about her progress on the telescope and how she thought it may be operable in the months ahead. The observatory was a room he hadn't spent much time in. It unnerved him how it looked out on an unfamiliar sky. Sometimes if he stared for long enough, it felt like the sky was looking back.

As they climbed higher, trees thinned and were replaced by rocks. The smooth, snowy contours of the forest floor were disrupted by stone outcroppings that looked as if they were fighting their way free of the ice, hoping for just a glimmer of the sun's warmth. The air was thicker somehow, and he picked up the vague smell of sulfur and other minerals.

This made him think of Lily. He was surprised he hadn't heard from her yet, or at least heard about her. She had promised to make trouble, and he was sure someone would have called to complain about her by now.

They stepped through a thin gap in the stones, and he found himself standing on a ledge overlooking a pool of steaming water. He was about to say something when the steam parted and revealed Velvet. She was floating on her back with her eyes closed, her legs spread out around her like a star.

"Ah, shit," Dana muttered as Velvet's eyes popped open. "I'm sorry, Vee. I didn't know you were up here."

Velvet's eyes went to Mike, then back to Dana. He expected panic that he had seen her naked, but was modesty even an arachne trait?

"It's fine," she replied. "I was just taking a dip myself. Had a long night."

"Yeah, you got in pretty late." Dana pointed along the sides of the rocks. "There's a path you can take down to the edge. If you don't mind, I think I'll leave you here."

"Don't want to be our chaperone?" he asked, only half-joking.

"I'm hungry is all." She grinned. "Hungry enough to eat a dragon."

"I like this side of you. Leave a sock on the door until you're done."

Dana rolled her eyes. "Any sense of privacy died when you fried Bigfoot's VHS collection. I wasn't going to say this in front of him, but he teared up when he saw his *Northern Exposure* collection was toast. All recordings of the original broadcasts, something about music rights."

Mike made a face. He really hoped Bigfoot didn't hold a grudge. "Guess I'll see you in a bit."

"Give me a twenty-minute head start." She winked at him and left.

Mike followed the ledge to the base of the spring. From down here, he saw that the ledge they had been on would be a perfect location for jumping into the spring. Velvet was floating in the water, just the top of her head and her spider body visible through the steam.

"May I join you?" he asked.

A hungry look crossed Velvet's face, but he didn't get any sense of danger. The seconds ticked by as she seemed to consider his request.

"Apparently, I stink," he continued. "And Quetzalli used all the hot water."

"Oh, I can tell," she replied. "That you stink, I mean. I also sort of saw what you were doing."

"You were watching us?" He wasn't even going to pretend to be offended. People walking in on him at home was a weekly occurrence.

"No. I was sulking in the barn and saw the light show." She smiled. "Care to explain that to me?"

"It's my magic," he said. "And I would be happy to share more, but I'm getting cold out here."

"Don't let me stop you." She didn't turn around or otherwise indicate that she was going to give him any privacy.

Challenge accepted. Mike didn't turn either. He tossed his jacket to the side and then unbuttoned his shirt. When he pulled down his pants, he could hear the arachne gasp as his cock sprang free. He got in the spring, taking his time to navigate the rocky sides. The water was a great temperature, and he sighed in relief.

"We've been coming here since we were old enough to walk," Velvet told him. "Much easier than trying to fit in a shower. We did that too but only when we were little."

"Not bad. Hot all year round?"

She nodded. "Sometimes it's too hot. It's not like there's a thermostat."

"Of course not." He moved a bit closer to her, his feet feeling along the bottom. It didn't take long before he found a drop-off, and he stood on the edge of it. The water was up to his chest, so he crouched until it came to his chin. "So yes, my magic. It's got some quirks."

"Can you move stuff with your mind?" she asked, her eyes lighting up in excitement. "Or cast spells? Make a fireball?"

"Nothing like that...I don't think." He laughed. "I'm still figuring it out, but it's the reason I can do that screaming thing."

"Awesome," she whispered.

"So why were you sulking?" he asked.

"Ugh." Velvet sank until only her eyes were visible. After a few seconds, she bobbed back up. "It was nothing, just going through some things. I've been thinking about what you said, about the house."

"Don't feel like it's a one-way trip," he said. "Once we can get contact re-established, I bet we can get a rat portal set up. You could stay here and still be part of the household. It isn't a big deal."

"Hmm." She floated closer to him. "I don't know if everyone would be as accepting of that decision."

He waved his hand. "If you're thinking about Abella, I wouldn't worry too much. I don't know the full story about what's going on with her, but she's a wonderful person. Just very protective of me and the house."

"I see." She narrowed her eyes and sank her mouth below the water but not before he saw the grin that had appeared.

What was she up to?

"To be honest, if there really is a problem between you and Abella, you two should talk about it. Clear the air, or whatever you wanna call it."

Velvet shrugged, sending ripples through the spring.

"You don't have to be friends," he added. "But there should be some level of respect. The house is a haven from the dangers of the real world. Despite their differences, everyone knows how to come together and have each other's back."

"Now I find that interesting," she said as she popped above the water so fast that the tops of her breasts appeared. When his eyes twitched to look at them, Velvet grinned and left them on display.

"I'm sorry, find what interesting?" he asked.

"That you all work together. When Dana and Lily showed up last fall, it was surprising to see a succubus helping anybody."

"Lily has her edges," he admitted. "But she's come a long way."

"You can't help yourself, can you?" Velvet was close enough now that he could touch her if he wanted. "Do you always see the best in people?"

"I didn't used to," he admitted. "But then I met a bunch of them that seemed like me. Different, maybe even a little damaged. I think we see it in each other. It's kind of a mutual respect thing and—"

Velvet had bobbed even closer. He sank into the water until they were at eye level with each other, all while struggling to keep his eyes off her breasts.

"And what?" she asked, her voice quiet.

"I think we recognize each other as survivors." It wasn't what he had been about to say, but in his efforts to avoid staring at her boobs, he had totally forgotten what he was going to say.

"Hmm." She looked pensive for a moment, but he realized she was staring at his chest. When he looked down, he saw that part of the scar tissue on his side was visible.

"Car crash," he explained. "It caught on fire before they pulled me out."

She shuddered, then lifted a hand from the water. "I'm terrified of fire," she admitted to him. "Our skin is covered in very fine hairs that we use to perceive the world. Getting them wet isn't too bad, but fire melts them quickly."

When she put her hand on his flesh, he felt his own senses heighten. It wasn't as bad as before, but it was still overwhelming.

"What are you doing?" he asked in a whisper. "When you touch me, I can feel all these extra things. It's like my nerves are being rewired."

"I feel things too," she responded. "But I very much doubt they are the same things you feel."

With that said, she moved her hand down his scars until her arm was underwater. As her fingers slid across his hip, his cock stirred to life, bobbing beneath the water like a lure. They both gasped when her hand settled on his cock.

"We might be feeling the same things after all," he muttered. Velvet's lips were inches from his own, and her eyes had a predatory glint to them that made his throat go dry.

"I…" She looked down as if suddenly realizing where her hand was. "I've never done this before."

The air was thick with steam, and he inhaled it through his nostrils. It mixed nicely with the energy that was already coursing through him. He slid his hand along her cheek, then pushed a few stray hairs behind her ears.

"There's a first time for everything," he replied.

"Yeah, but…" She paused to lick her lips. He could see that she was drooling. "My mother said that this was dangerous. That I may lose control."

She was stroking him now, her thumb teasing the opening of his cock. If this really was her first time, it seemed like she had some natural instinct.

He thought back to what he knew about the arachne. Was he nothing more than prey, caught up in a web of deception? He knew Abella would say that he was.

However, with Velvet so close to him, he felt no danger at all. If she was planning to seduce and hurt him, wouldn't he feel something? Right now, she was just another beautiful woman who was coming on to him very strongly.

His cock twitched, officially registering its vote.

"We can take it slow," he said. "If you think you're about to become dangerous or lose control or whatever, just tell me."

Her eyes had taken on that vacant stare again, and she was stroking him even harder. He responded by lowering his hand to her breasts and playing with her nipples. He reached out his other hand to stroke her waist, but she grabbed him by the wrist.

"That...I..." Her cheeks turned bright red. "If you go much farther, you'll feel the parts of me that aren't...humanoid."

"Is that bad?" he asked. "If you don't want me to touch you there, that's fine."

"It isn't that." She scrunched up her face, then let out a sigh. "I'm just worried it might ruin the moment. You know, if you remember what the rest of me looks like."

"Oh." He ran his hand down her thigh and paused. Somewhere around midthigh, her smooth skin gave way to thick fur.

"See what I mean?" There was a squeak to her voice, a crack in her bold facade. "It would be better if you didn't."

"Didn't what?" His magic was swirling through him now, and he hooked his fingers in the thick hair of her legs and dragged them through like a comb. Even beneath the water, the hair felt light and moved easily through his fingers. He wondered if it was repelling the water. "I don't mind a little hair."

"Mike..." Her voice was pleading now, and she had stopped stroking him. "I don't think I could handle it if you...found me disgusting."

He pulled on her waist, bringing her lips within a breath's distance. When he moved his hand back up her leg, he circled it around her waist and onto one of her other legs. When he squeezed it, she let out a gasp.

"I don't care that you didn't shave your legs for me."

Velvet's eyes lit up, and she laughed. She pushed him back with a playful splash, but he hooked his arm around her waist and pulled her in for a kiss, his lips gentle on hers. Surprised at first, Velvet immediately melted into him with a groan.

He tried squeezing her spider leg again, but she grabbed his wrist and moved his hand back onto her front leg.

"That part of me doesn't feel pleasure," she explained after breaking the kiss. "All my nerves for that are kind of in front of the biggest ass you've ever seen."

"Well, then let's test them out." He had been holding his magic back, but when they kissed, he released it. She moaned into his mouth, and her front legs circled his waist, pulling him in. His cock rubbed against her belly as she continued to jack him off beneath the water.

His magic sank into the spring, then bubbled up from beneath them, causing Velvet's back end to pop above the surface. Swirling around them, his magic caressed her body, and it was almost as if he could feel her with his mind.

He moved a hand between her legs and was surprised when he felt something grab him. Startled, he pulled his hand away.

"That's normal," Velvet told him. "I'm...different down there."

His curiosity was piqued. He went exploring again, running his fingers through her thick pubic hair. Once he found her clit, he realized that what he thought was an extremely puffy set of labia was actually a set of fleshy protuberances that gripped him when he tried to penetrate her. It was as if they were clenched fingers, eager to trap him in place.

"I don't mind different," he told her, then slid a finger inside. He felt her vagina clamp down on his finger, then force it back out.

"Sorry," she muttered, her face red again. "It's...it knows when it's not..."

"Hey, don't worry about it." He moved his hands across her pubic mound. Her labia tried to shoo his hand away by flicking out at him. "Are those meant to hold me inside?"

Velvet said nothing but managed to achieve a new shade of crimson in response.

He chuckled. "It's nothing to be embarrassed by. Communication is actually the key to—"

She forced herself onto him, her body lifting in the water. Her hand had moved off his cock, and he felt those fleshy nubs shift apart as his glans pushed into her.

Velvet moaned, then stared into his eyes. He could see his own magic reflected inside, as well as something else. "I'm sorry, it's...instincts."

He grabbed onto her hips and pulled her down onto him. Her insides squeezed him in stages, allowing him to sink in an inch at a time. She clutched him against her and started breathing heavily.

"I feel so full," she moaned. "And you feel so hot inside me. Does it always feel this good?"

"It's different every time." His magic was surging through his body, and when the protuberances gripped him at the base of his cock, he jumped. This caused them to float out into the middle of the spring, buoyed by the bubbles from down below. An eddy caused them to float in a spiral, his body pressed tightly against hers.

"Mike." When she whispered his name, chills went up and down his spine. "I barely know you, but…this feels so right."

He paused to reflect on that. His life had become a series of strange sexual events, so he had given up on trying to rationalize his encounters. However, something was clearly different with Velvet. He was drawn to her by desires he didn't fully understand, and he hadn't thought twice about pursuing them.

Now, with his cock buried deep inside her, he felt an even stronger connection, a thread that he was desperate to tug at. He was well aware that he was no longer entirely human. His magic was largely sexual in nature.

But what he felt now was longing. Was it his own? Or was it related to the strange feelings he experienced when he touched her?

"It feels right for me too." He closed his eyes and pressed himself into her. It was hard to maneuver while floating, and this was all he could manage. "And maybe, while it feels right for both of us, we should just go with it."

She stared at him for several seconds, as if contemplating a huge decision. He wished he could know what she was thinking.

Velvet's legs surfaced and kicked, propelling them toward the shoreline. His toes touched the rocks below as they maneuvered to the edge of the spring. She rose from the water, her front legs wrapped around Mike's waist. He found his own legs dangling beneath him as she carried him over to a nearby rock and pressed him up against it. Her fingers dug into the cold stone, causing it to crumble beneath her touch, and her hot mouth found his again.

His tongue danced around in her mouth as he was careful to avoid the sharp fangs he discovered along the side. He didn't think she would bite him on purpose, not at this point, but accidents happened. Without a way to use his feet on the stone for leverage, he used his arms. Velvet moaned, her cries reverberating through his body as magic arced between her legs and across the ground.

When she pulled away from him, a line of drool connected their mouths. He wiped it away as she arched her back, giving him access to her breasts. They were soft, but he could feel the thick muscle hidden beneath as he buried his face between them and took in her scent. She had a dusky scent that reminded him of long nights around a campfire beneath the starry sky. When Mike pulled his face out of her breasts and gazed into her eyes, he somehow saw those stars reflected in them.

Down below, he could feel fleshy pincers surrounding the base of his shaft. Whenever he sank into her, they would squeeze tight once he was buried inside. As he withdrew, they massaged his cock and then clamped down the moment before he could completely pull out.

There was also a series of bony ridges inside that felt absolutely delightful. He could feel them moving along the top of his glans as he fucked her.

"Oh, oh yes!" Velvet's human eyes locked on his. "Mike, I'm so sorry, but I promise this won't hurt!"

She opened her mouth wide to reveal her fangs and then bit him on the neck. He felt her fangs slide into his flesh, and fire raced through him, focusing almost entirely on his balls. His danger sense never warned him and still wasn't going off.

He moaned as a pulsing sensation built inside his balls, then he wrapped his arm around Velvet's head to trap her in place. His magic created a band of energy that swirled around them, locking them in position. It seeped into his pores and crept along Velvet's body, vanishing beneath the soft fur of her legs.

When he came, it wasn't his typical eruption. Instead, the orgasm was strung out as he pumped a steady stream of cum inside her. He groaned as her fleshy protuberances milked him. His balls no longer felt heavy, but the pressure inside was already building again.

The swirling band exploded with light, sending a cascade of energy into Velvet's body. Her legs spasmed and went straight, causing her to lie flat on the ground. She closed her eyes and let out a shrill cry that startled nearby forest birds, causing them to fly away in panic.

The pressure in his balls was already intense, and Mike shouted as he pumped her full of cum again. The energy in Velvet was now seeping back into him as the feedback loop strengthened his arousal. Whatever venom ran through his veins was already wearing off, but he continued to flood her womb with cum. So much semen had leaked from her vagina that the air was filled with the sound of sticky smacking.

"Mike, I—" Velvet's human eyes rolled up and her spider eyes closed as she let out another cry of ecstasy. Dozens of field mice appeared from nearby rocks and ran for the safety of the forest.

With one last moan, Mike blasted her womb again, then concentrated on the field of energy that surrounded them. It was reluctant to return, but he pulled it back into his body before the two of them spent all afternoon fucking. His muscles were still sore from last night, and he suspected Velvet could easily outpace him.

Pulling himself free from Velvet's embrace, he stumbled backward and fell on a flat rock, nearly blacking out. His body was flooded with a fiery heat that moved through him and then vanished, and it was almost like he had been punched in the chest.

Mike gasped for air as the world came back into focus. His gaze was fixed on the clouds above, and the chill of the earth seeped into his bones from beneath. The whole world was alive with sounds he had never heard before. It was sensory overload, and he shut his eyes, hoping it would fade like a bad bout of tinnitus.

"Mike?" Velvet's voice was filled with concern.

"I'm fine," he whispered, his own voice bouncing around inside his skull. The sounds had faded, but now he was hearing something else. It was tiny voices, but they weren't speaking words. It was more like concepts, and he could feel all of them.

Hungry.

Danger.

Build.

Food.

"What am I…" He put his hand on his belly, feeling a twinge. His breakfast had been far too small, and he was suddenly starving. "I'm hallucinating. Hearing things, kind of."

"What kind of things?" Velvet's voice was closer now, and she leaned over him with a nervous look on her face, her breasts dangling over his body.

He closed his eyes and concentrated. The voices were coming from different directions. "They're talking about…food. And hunting. I don't understand."

Velvet's eyes widened. "You can hear them?"

"Hear who?" He managed to sit up. His legs were starting to get cold, and he pushed himself along the rock until he could slide back into the spring. The warmth spread through him rapidly, and he sighed and closed his eyes. Strangely, he almost felt like he was drawing magic from the spring, his aches and pains vanishing nearly immediately.

"The spiders."

His eyes popped open, and he looked at Velvet. "Spiders can talk?"

"They can communicate, yes." She moved along the edge of the spring and dipped one of her feet in. The motion was similar to watching a cat paw at its water dish. "They're my friends. They talk all the time. It can get quite noisy once winter is over."

He put his hands to his ears and groaned. "They're loud enough already."

Velvet slid back into the water and bobbed over to him. She had a sheepish look on her face as she pulled his hands from his ears. He was suddenly aware that he was no longer tired and once again full of energy.

"You can tune them out," she explained. "You just have to focus on other things. Treat them as background noise."

"I'm not sure how to even begin." His eyes met hers just as her hand found his cock once more. The air suddenly had a texture to it, and he could feel the water vapor clinging to the hairs of his arms.

"Then allow me to help." With a smile, Velvet took a deep breath and disappeared beneath the water. When she sucked him into her mouth, he let out a long, full-throated moan as her tongue slid along the length of his cock.

He no longer cared what the spiders had to say.

WHEN BETH WALKED OUTSIDE, SHE WAS SURPRISED AT HOW STILL THIS WORLD around her felt. The fog around them billowed as if blown by an external source, but there was no wind.

She was also surprised to see Mehkhkahrel sitting on a raised judge's bench. His clothing was the same, and he tilted his head so that one of his eyes could see her. Up above, the angel hovered. Looking at it for more than a second made her feel dizzy.

"Death has requested that we follow the laws of your land and allow him to have legal representation." Mehkhkahrel's mouth was stretched wide, his tongue hanging out as the words boomed from him like a loudspeaker. "As a being of justice, I have seen fit to grant this request."

"Thank you." Beth looked over at the three horsemen. "If you are the judge, then who is the jury?"

Mehkhkahrel pointed up at the swirling mass with a crooked finger. "I am merely the subconscious of the entity above, an extension of its will. As such, we are not bound by any ethical obligations, for our judgment is free of bias."

Warning sign number one. Beth thought about what Lily had told her. If angels and demons were cut from the same cloth, did that mean the angel was incapable of lying? Technically speaking, if the divine being believed it was free of bias, it would be speaking the truth. Either way, a situation where the judge and jury were effectively the same being was a bad sign.

The angel was just a demon without daddy issues, after all.

"And them?"

"We are the prosecution." Famine's voice had a Southern drawl to it. His skin was dark and shiny, as if he had been dipped in oil. "And it is our firm belief that our day has come that we may walk among mortals and take what is owed to us."

"I see." Beth looked over at Death, then back at the others. "So catch me up to speed. If you all are the prosecution, then what crime has been committed?"

"We demand what is ours!" War was a large man with mottled, sunburned skin and a greatsword to match. He was bald but had a beard made of fire. "To walk among the world and bring it to its knees!"

"Haven't you done enough walking on our world already? In fact, I would argue that all of you exist as a consistent state of things. So why fight to be allowed to start the Apocalypse?"

"Allow me to answer, dear child." Mehkhkahrel now held a gavel in both hands, and black robes had appeared on him. "As I am but an extension of the glorious being up above, so too is the state of the world. People may fight wars, but they are not War himself. What you have experienced in your world is but a pittance compared to the legacy that is rightfully theirs."

"And I see it as a temper tantrum." Beth narrowed her eyes at War. "Nice sword. Isn't that a bit dated?"

War laughed heartily. "Haven't you heard that all is fair in love and war? I care not by what means the battle is won. But since you asked…" He casually picked up the sword, which dislodged a massive chunk of dirt, and rested it on his shoulders. "Though a gun may take a life, I long to feel the hot blood of my enemies rain down upon my skin. I carry this that I may cleave a man in half and watch the light fade from his eyes as my brother collects him."

Beth gasped when she realized that what she had mistaken for his skin tone was actually the stain of fresh blood.

Famine licked his lips hungrily. "And I would see their hope extinguished as the food they feel entitled to cannot reach their bellies. As they mourn the physical things they can no longer afford. To see their bones against their skin as they waste away before my brother collects them."

"Shouldn't you be thinner?" she asked. Famine had a thick gut.

"I bring hunger," he explained. "But that does not mean I should suffer from it."

Behind them, Pestilence raised their hands and waved them about as if speaking. Instead of a voice, it was the sound of thousands of beating wings flapping past, and when Pestilence finished, War let out a bark of laughter.

"Well said!" he exclaimed.

"So it sounds like Death is key to all this." Beth crossed her arms and looked at Mehkhkahrel. "Though these three could walk the land, as long as Death himself isn't physically present, the Apocalypse cannot take place."

"So it is written," Mehkhkahrel responded. "In the bible, which is the word of the being you know as God."

"Does the Apocalypse actually have to happen though?" It was time to try a new angle. "It seems like there's a lot in the bible that hasn't or didn't actually happen."

This caused the angel to tilt his head, which made his tongue flop from one side of his mouth to the other. "This world will end one day as all worlds must. And when it comes, there will be war, there will be illness, there will be starvation, and all shall die. It is the natural order of things."

"But technically, these guys don't have to show up, right?" Beth looked at the horsemen. "From what I understand of the bible, it's meant to be interpretive. So though it says all things will end, it doesn't necessarily mean it has to end this way. For instance, I remember something about a lake of fire. Couldn't that be interpreted as the sun expanding and gobbling up the earth?"

Mehkhkahrel paused for a long time, as if considering his answer.

She continued. "I was under the impression that it was impossible to put into mortal words the will of a divine being who exists outside of time and space. Much like describing the color red to a blind person. I suspect that by having a divine being try to convey these thoughts and ideas, we suffer from mistranslation due to qualia. The terms and conditions of the Apocalypse itself may have been ineffable, meaning that the scribe did their best but couldn't convey the full meaning of God's word.

"In fact, the bible I have seen is not written in its original language. So how do I know the events of the Apocalypse as I understand them don't contain translation errors? Or perhaps the scribe held an implicit bias and wrote their own take on things." Beth pointed at Pestilence. "I doubt hazmat suits existed when the bible was written. If we were to open one now and read the passages out loud, we would discover that this extraplanar being does not match the description of one of the four horsemen. So either the bible is wrong, in which case you have no precedent, or these aren't the horsemen. Either way, any claim they may have to the Apocalypse is null and void, as their coming has not been properly foretold."

"Um, Mistress Bethany." Death tapped her on the shoulder. "I would be happy to verify the identity of—"

She clamped her hand across Death's mouth, the feel of his teeth against her palm causing her whole arm to go numb.

"I don't like that title." Her eyes went to Mehkhkahrel, who now seemed to be seriously studying her. "As your legal counsel, I recommend that you speak only when I grant you permission."

Death mumbled his agreement.

"I move that this case be dismissed on the grounds that I cannot verify either the identities of the horsemen or the grounds by which the Apocalypse is allowed to occur."

War's jaw dropped open, and he looked at Famine. Famine scowled and stepped forward.

"Now, see here," he said a little too loudly. "We can verify that this individual is in fact one of the horsemen of the Apocalypse. And I have a feeling our brother would agree. If three of the horsemen agree that Pestilence is the fourth, then that should be good enough for the court."

"But how do I know that you all are the four horsemen?" Beth gestured at Death. "My client may be the physical manifestation of Death, but he was not brought here for the Apocalypse. A failed spell has trapped him here until he can fulfill his goal. Therefore, even if he is indeed one of the four horsemen, we can prove that the means of his arrival are not of biblical portent. In fact, I would like to know how you all even found out he was here on Earth."

"It was reported to us." Mehkhkahrel's lips curled away from his teeth. "This is a matter that would have been resolved long ago if not for the protection of your home against his discovery."

"But if you couldn't see him, then how did somebody——" She could almost hear her thoughts click into place. Someone wanted Death out of the picture, and it was a very short list. If the options were making Death go home or global annihilation, the choice would have been a simple one.

"Should the four ever walk as one on the soil of the earth, then the Apocalypse shall commence." Mehkhkahrel's voice had a tone to it that Beth didn't like. "It is why we went to so much trouble to bring you here, to this extra-dimensional space, before gathering. There are certain rules."

"See? So it's settled, then?" War's eyes were now glowing in excitement.

"No. This child speaks with wisdom in regard to the book that was written. It is not a true telling of what is to come." Mehkhkahrel looked over at War. "And though I have summoned you from the void, it was not to start the Apocalypse. It was for this proceeding. It is not written that an angelic being shall casually open the Seven Seals of their own whim."

"Fuck!" War slammed his sword into the ground. "But we are all here; that should have to count for something! We have utilized avatars, have walked the land in mortal form, but never have we been so pure! The world is ready for us, ripe for the taking, and you would deny us?"

"You agreed to abide by the laws of this land, as did I." Mehkhkahrel rolled his head so that he was looking at Beth. "And this child has made her case that Death's presence alone is not enough to qualify."

"*Fuck!*" War yanked his sword out of the ground and hurled it into the fog.

"As such, I am ready to pass down judgment." Mehkhkahrel looked at Death. "It's time for you to return to the void."

"Objection!" Beth moved in front of Death. "You said yourself that his being here was an accident. Now you intend to penalize my client for committing no crime!"

"But I believe I established that either Death must participate in the Apocalypse or he must be dismissed." Mehkhkahrel tried to cross his arms over his chest, but they stuck out straight instead and made an X.

"But you also agreed to abide by the laws of this land. He's the defendant, and if he is proven innocent, you don't get to punish him for it."

"Your Honor." Famine wore a shit-eating grin. "This young lady argues that her client be allowed to remain, as he was summoned against his will. Is that correct?"

"It is." Mehkhkahrel's eyebrow lifted in interest.

"Well, since we were also summoned against our will, I argue that we be allowed to remain as well. It's only fair, per the laws of this land." Famine turned his gaze on Beth. "In fact, you can go ahead and send us all back to Earth right now."

"No." Beth's voice barely broke a whisper. Mehkhkahrel himself had said that all four of them on Earth together was the qualifying event.

Famine chuckled. "I'm sorry, little lady, do you have an objection? You see, we aren't eager to go back to the void. We have things we've just been dying to do out here. So what do you say, Your Honor? After all, it's only fair."

"Ob...objection!" Beth held up her hand. "Dismissal of the case by the prosecution with current terms would put undue hardship on my client."

"On what grounds?" Famine sneered at her. "You ain't gonna win this."

"If these four should walk the earth together, then the Apocalypse starts. Death would be forced against his will to join in, which could be seen as a form of indentured servitude, forced labor, or even slavery. All of which is forbidden by the laws of my land." She glared at Famine, then turned to Mehkhkahrel. "You said so yourself that you would agree to our laws, but it seems like every choice made leads to the destruction of my whole planet. That would indicate a premeditated bias on your part, and you said you were free of such a thing."

Mehkhkahrel regarded all of them in silence for several seconds. War tried to say something, but Pestilence put a hand over his mouth.

"I have much to ponder," Mehkhkahrel finally revealed. "Both sides have shown much logic this day, and I see that this child is right. To dismiss this case would be to unfairly punish the defense."

Beth let out a sigh of relief.

"But the prosecution has rights as well. So it would seem we are at an impasse." Mehkhkahrel looked at the horsemen. "I think it would behoove both sides to think of what they want the outcome to look like. In forty-eight hours' time, we shall reconvene. At that time, we shall determine Death's fate, as well as the world's." He lifted his gavel and slammed it down. A shock wave rippled out, causing him and the horsemen to vanish in its wake.

Beth sank to her knees, her heart pounding and her mouth dry. She had come so close!

"Countess Bethany, I know this may be a bad time, but someone is trying to get your attention." Death pointed at the house. When she looked over her shoulder, she saw Cecilia frantically waving her arms.

"Of course they are. And I don't like that title either. Too stuffy." Beth rose and straightened her skirt. She was almost to the porch when Cecilia grabbed her by the hand and pulled her through the open door. Inside, Tink was on the couch in the living room, her eyes closed and her breathing shallow.

Kisa stood over the goblin with tears in her eyes. "I found her in the basement," she said. "Just outside the Vault. She won't wake up."

"Tink? Tink!" Beth knelt on the couch and gave her a shake. She put her head on Tink's chest and heard the dim thumping of her heart. "What was she doing outside the Vault?"

"I don't know." Kisa stood. "But it's open. I tried to shut it, but the door won't close. I could hear something inside whispering to me. It wanted me to come in. It's some kind of spirit, so it didn't really have any effect on me."

"Okay, let's move her to my room. Our visitors outside are gone for now, so let's get everyone accounted for. Cecilia, please go find Reggie and Jenny." She stood at the bottom of the stairs and raised her voice. "Lily! I need you right now!"

The door of Mike's room opened, and the succubus came out, still in child form.

"What's happening?" she asked.

"The usual. World is ending, evil entity in the basement. Sound like fun?"

Lily hopped over the railing and fell three stories, her body expanding as she became an adult again. She landed in a crouch, her tail whipping out behind her.

"I could kick a little ass." Lily grinned. "Let's go see what's haunting the basement, shall we?"

"Okay, looks like we're ready." Eulalie had a mass of equipment spread out on Murray's dining room table, and she snapped the casing of the small drone she had purchased shut.

Sofia stood nearby, her face in awe.

"How did you afford all this?" she asked.

Eulalie had purchased a trio of laptops, some headsets, two phones, and a drone. It had been a couple of years since she had played with one. She used to have a racing drone that she'd lost to an accident with a barn owl and just hadn't had the heart to build a new one after.

Besides, testing military drones was far more fun.

"My entire life, I've lived in a house with no bills. My father used to make spare money selling wood carvings so he could afford some luxuries. It isn't like we didn't have plenty of time." Eulalie had finished setting up the third laptop. Though they weren't top-of-the-line models, they were very capable of downloading and installing a modified hard drive backup she had stored in the cloud for just such an occasion. "After I finished school and started doing government work, all I had to do was make some key investments based on rumor, speculation, and maybe a little market manipulation."

"You bought stocks?"

"Nah. I don't really understand stocks." She smirked. When she sat in front of a computer screen, it was possible to see so many patterns in the data that she examined, to scrutinize code at an inhuman speed. "I did mine a ton of Bitcoin when it first came out. Hacked a bunch of university computers to do it when class wasn't in session. May have been slightly illegal. Tried to convince Dad we could afford to buy our own place wherever we wanted once the price went up, but he was against it. Apparently, money can buy everything but a magical barrier, and even those aren't a hundred percent foolproof. I even faked a human identity to cash out but don't want to pay taxes on it yet."

She picked up the drone and handed it to a rat. "Can you take this outside, please?"

The rat pondered the object in its paws and sniffed the edge before nibbling on the plastic.

"No, not food. Take it outside." She held up the piece of paper she had drawn on earlier. It was a cartoon rat holding the drone in the air outside the house. She had found some pens and paper in Murray's junk drawer and put them to good use.

The rat nodded and left, dragging the drone behind it.

Eulalie looked at the screen to her left. She had set the middle laptop up on top of a book to elevate it, and the other two were on the sides. She watched a rat's-eye view video feed on the screen and waited until it was outside to launch it. When its motors came to life, the rat nearly dropped it, then bolted back inside as the drone took off facing the wrong way.

On the middle screen, she logged in to her custom VPN and bounced the signal around the world a few dozen times before hacking into some local government accounts. She had been paid almost a decade back to do a threat analysis on a similar system, and apparently, these guys had never acted on the memo she'd sent about vulnerabilities.

On the third screen, she went through a similar process but also tried to dig up any cameras operating in the area. It took a bit longer, but she eventually used an old government contractor account that enabled her to download video logs from doorbell cameras around the neighborhood.

"I won't even pretend to understand what you're doing," Sofia muttered.

"I'm multitasking." Eulalie stared at the data as it came in on multiple screens. Her spider eyes allowed her to watch all three at once, and she sat back on her rear legs and used her front legs on the touchpads of the computers to help her navigate. "Looks like the drone is up."

On their screen, the house came into view. At first, it looked normal, but Eulalie realized that something was off. The yard was disproportionate to the house, and it seemed smaller somehow.

"Weren't there three levels?" she asked. "And the porch looks tiny. Wasn't there an extra room over here?"

"Shit." Sofia leaned in and squinted at the screen. "This is the version of the house that appears when the real house is asleep. That can only mean one thing."

"Which is?"

Sofia shook her head. "The Caretaker has died. Something has happened to Mike in Oregon. That's the only explanation." Tears shimmered in the corners of her eye.

"Oh." She felt her breath hitch in her chest. If Mike had died, what had happened to her sister? Or Bigfoot? Was Emery okay? It felt like the world was spinning around her, and her legs began to wobble. What had she gotten them into?

"Who's that?" The drone had been on a preprogrammed flight path, but she clicked it over to manual and had the drone fly lower. A pale figure was wandering along the edge of the property, scratching his head.

"That's Sulyvahn." Sofia frowned. "That doesn't make sense. If the house got locked up, it should have taken him too."

Eulalie lowered the drone until it was facing Sulyvahn. He gave it a suspicious look, his dark eyes menacing. The dullahan looked like he was ready to pounce. "If he's roaming around, then the house isn't under attack. It's getting dark. Please get his attention over the wall before he breaks my new toy."

"I'm on it." Sofia left the kitchen and went out the back door. Eulalie watched as Sulyvahn regarded the drone with anger, then turned in recognition. Satisfied that Sofia's job was done, she continued reconnaissance of the property.

Out behind the house, Amymone was sitting on the edge of the fountain. In her arms, Naia appeared to be weeping openly. "Interesting." So the house was asleep but hadn't taken anyone outside it. Why was that? Shouldn't the geas have kept them all together?

The back door of the house slammed shut, and Sofia appeared with Sulyvahn in tow.

"Yer a right sight," he declared. "Sofia tells me ye were stuck in the Library?"

"Indeed we were." Eulalie turned away from her computers. "Naia and Amymone are out back. Something is off."

Sulyvahn nodded. "The greenhouse is still open. I went to check on the centaurs, and when I came back, the house was locked up. I broke in through the back to find a dusty old home. It dinna make any sense!"

"Hmm." Eulalie steepled her fingers and pondered. There was plenty of data to be had, but she lacked the knowledge needed to consider the next step. "I take it this hasn't happened before?"

"It's like someone scooped up the house." Sofia's face was pale. "And that isn't all. The geas went with it. The neighbors saw me snooping around. Whatever happened there left everyone remaining vulnerable. If someone were to attempt something, the house is defenseless."

Eulalie looked at the small contingent of drones she had on the counter, waiting to be used. She looked back at the screen, her eyes focusing on Naia. She tapped the screen. "What did Naia say about all this?"

Sulyvahn shrugged. "She dinna say much, bein' a wee bit disheveled. Somethin' about a sleepin' home and bein' disconnected."

"Okay, so we've established that the house is there but only in facsimile. Assume it's like a virtual computer and could collapse at any time." Ideas were flitting through her head now at a rate she couldn't keep up with. "Establish a perimeter. We can monitor the situation from here. If the greenhouse was unaffected, it should be safe to use as a base of operations for the centaurs." She picked up the phone and handed it to Sulyvahn. "Your kind don't sleep, correct?"

"Nay, lass." He took the phone. "Seems like ye think yer in charge."

"That's because I am." She glowered at him. "I may be an apex predator with legs that just won't quit, but I'm also the only one here who understands how to live in the modern-day age of information. While I'm in here making certain that nobody makes a move on the house, I need you out there. You are the only one of us who can remotely pass as human, and I suspect you can handle yourself in a fight. You can use the phone to check in." She picked up an earpiece and gave it to him. "If I call, just press the button on the side.

Every eight hours, bring the earpiece and phone back for a fresh pair. I've programmed my number into them already. Just unlock it and find me in Contacts." She held up one of the spare phones and demonstrated.

Sulyvahn picked up the earpiece and shoved it in his ear. "I know a queen when I hear one," he muttered. "Ye never argue with a queen."

"I'll call if I catch any movement. Dana told me she was doing drone work for the centaurs. Take some rats and have them bring back whatever you can find in her workshop. I could use the spares."

"Aye." Sulyvahn gave her a salute and left out the back. Eulalie looked at her drone footage and saw him vault the fence into the front yard.

"What should I do?" Sofia asked.

Eulalie pondered it, her eyes sweeping to the cracks on her legs. If someone came to the house, she could fight if necessary, but it would be dangerous. There was also the possibility that Sulyvahn could get into trouble.

"You're backup." She let out a sigh. "You're stuck here with me, and you'll hate it. Will be very boring. But if something goes sideways, I need to know that I can depend on you to bail us out."

Sofia nodded. "You can count on me."

"Good." Eulalie turned her eyes back to the monitor. Sulyvahn was in the backyard now, talking to Naia and Amymone. Soon she would have more drones and would be better able to monitor things from the sky. Even though the house was vulnerable, the web she was setting would catch anyone who tried to enter it.

Speaking of webs, it wouldn't be a bad idea to set some literal ones of her own. She didn't want someone breaking into the house and disrupting her surveillance. With a groan, she pushed away from the desk and rose to her full height. The nearby rats didn't shy away from her but raised their beady gazes in curiosity.

It was going to be a long night.

WHAT HIDES IN THE SHADOWS

T he forest below Abella was a sea of white and green, interspersed by
rocky outcroppings and the occasional river. From her current altitude, she could actually see distortions in the land at the boundaries
along the barrier. It was like looking through a haze of rippling hot air as the
land attempted to fold and bend itself properly into shape before lining up
with the rest of the world.

Unfortunately, it also meant that she wasn't sure how far away the barrier
was. Sometimes it would look less than a mile but would then distort and reappear dozens of miles out.

"Does it always do that?" she asked. Emery, who had chased her down and
begged to tag along, was perched on her shoulder. He clung to her for dear
life, his tiny hands wrapped up in her hair.

"I've never been this high, big sister," he replied. While her interactions
with the imp had been few, he had come to the conclusion that because they
were both made of stone, they must be related. She had been hard-pressed to
correct him, and he really was adorable. "The winds are too strong for my
wings."

"Ah." She was disappointed. When she had taken Mike's phone, she had
flown in a random direction and was now wondering if she had picked the
worst direction to go. Still, it was interesting to be over such a large swath of
land without the immediate tug of guardianship pulling her back. For the first
time in over a century, she really felt like she could stretch her wings. It
occurred to her now that she could have probably accomplished such a thing

in the greenhouse. She had always been too nervous to leave the house unprotected.

And yet here she was, over a thousand miles away. It was no longer the house that she cared about but the man who served it. She couldn't wrap her head around her own feelings about him right now. He was family but also something more. Maybe there wasn't a word that existed for the relationship they had.

She definitely didn't know where she stood with Velvet. The sensation of cold metal pressed against the nape of her neck had made a lasting impression as she simmered with her face buried deep in the snow. Velvet had been far stronger and faster than Abella had expected. Even when the arachne had finally gotten the upper hand, she'd chosen to flee rather than take it.

Abella wasn't worried about the sword. She still had a trick up her sleeve that would have easily turned the tide on that particular fight. Instead, she was worried about why Velvet had been so quick to dismiss their fight, to flee into the woods.

No, *worried* was the wrong word for it. She had gone over the incident in her mind all night as she circled the cabin. Abella wanted to believe that this trip and Velvet's behavior were a ruse, an attempt to lure them all into a false sense of security. She had gone over a number of elaborate plots in her mind where the arachne would inevitably find a way to kill and eat the others and maybe even take over the house somehow.

Instead, her mental search for answers had revealed only one truth she couldn't deny: Abella's hate for the arachne had blinded her to other possibilities. When Velvet had spoken about wanting to be seen as something more than a monster, it was the exact same desire Abella had held in her own heart for decades. The two of them were more alike than Abella cared to admit, and their fight had really been her own fault.

At some point, she assumed Velvet would tell Mike what had happened. She wasn't sure she could handle the look of disappointment she would get from him. He was the single most important part of her world right now, and all she wanted was for him to be safe.

"Are you okay, big sister?" Emery's voice snapped her out of her funk.

"I'm fine." It was a lie, but what did the imp know?

"I think the boundary is coming up soon." He pointed ahead at what looked like a gap in the trees. The air rippled above it. "The Caretaker's phone should work soon."

"Great." She didn't bother conveying any enthusiasm. The main reason she had come out here was to build up some positive karma for the inevitable fallout to come over what had happened the previous night. She was sure things were fine at home, and—

Just short of the edge of the boundary, the air suddenly vanished from beneath her wings, and she dropped out of the sky. Bands of crimson light sprouted from the air behind her, wrapping around her ankles and yanking her back. Crying out in surprise, she tumbled over a hundred feet before the bands released her legs. Realizing she was on a collision course with the ground, she spread her wings wide and was able to generate enough lift that she pulled up at the last second, trimming off the tops of the pines below.

Emery tumbled from her shoulders and disappeared into the forest. She fared only slightly better as she crashed through the trees, splintering branches as she tumbled through them. Folding her wings in to protect her body, she slapped her tail into a thick pine to alter her trajectory at the last second and crashed into a shallow stream. The ice exploded as she came to a halt.

"What the fuck was that?" She stood up and shook the water off her wings. "Emery? Can you hear me?"

There was no answer from the imp. Grumbling, she splashed her way out of the stream. Broken branches littered the forest floor, and she contemplated them for a moment. She frowned, realizing she had forgotten something.

The phone! Gasping, she ran back to the stream and stumbled in. It took her almost a minute to find Mike's phone beneath the water. It was supposed to be waterproof, but the giant crack on the screen wasn't a good sign.

"Merde!" She tried to power it on, but it was no use. It had broken in the crash, and water was leaking from the case.

Abella stomped out of the stream toward the trees, determined to find Emery. As she walked, her path was blocked by the thick branches of the trees, so she was forced to walk around, calling Emery's name as she went.

"Big sister!" When Emery finally replied, it sounded like he was above her. Abella saw that he had gotten caught up in a thick cluster of branches. His wings were spread wide by forked limbs, and he was upside down.

The tree was thin, so she clobbered it with her tail. The trunk split, and she pushed on it until it crashed to the ground with Emery safely on top. The branches snapped beneath her feet as she made her way to his side and untangled him.

"Was that the barrier?" she asked, referring to the energy that had blocked her flight.

"It was not," Emery replied. "I've visited the barrier many times, but it has never prevented anyone from leaving."

She narrowed her eyes at the imp. "You sure?"

He nodded lamely. "I've never heard of such a thing."

Abella groaned. "I was afraid you would say that. Come, let us walk this time. It will be less traumatic."

They navigated the difficult foliage for almost half an hour before coming to a break in the tree line. It was a short field, maybe a hundred feet across. As she neared the edge, she could feel the distinct tingle caused by passing through the barrier. It wasn't until she was almost through that she felt the air harden and resist her forward movement.

"Interesting." She motioned for Emery to stay back and then shoved her way forward. At first, the air felt like it was stretching in an attempt to hold her in place. However, she made it far enough that the crimson bands of light manifested and wrapped themselves across her body. The magic stank of blood and copper, and she allowed it to push her back in place.

"This is troubling," Emery declared from his place on a rock.

Abella looked at him in exasperation. "You don't say?"

"I…just did say." The imp was fidgeting now. "Perhaps we shouldn't mess with it?"

She debated trying to push her way through, but if it had been able to resist her while flying, it was likely she would do no better down here. Using her feet as giant scoops, she dug through the snow until she found a rock the size of a basketball and hurled it forward. It passed through the boundary without an issue, and the crimson bands failed to appear.

"Targets living creatures, including me." Abella frowned. This was the sort of thing Yuki needed to see, for it was far outside of her own experience. Her kind was largely magic resistant because her body was made of living stone. The fact that the spell recognized her as alive spoke volumes of the caster's skill set.

Looking up at the sky, she wondered how high it went. She beckoned to Emery to follow her and then took off. Once she was above the tree line, she tried to fly out of the boundary at an angle, only to see the crimson bands reappear. Since she was skirting the edges, the pull wasn't as violent this time, allowing her to adjust course and stay aloft.

"Do you suppose it goes all the way around?" she asked Emery. The imp was close enough to land on her shoulder.

"That would be unlikely," he said. "I imagine it would take an incredibly powerful sorcerer to accomplish such a thing, and they would still need time to set it up."

Abella frowned, her thoughts immediately going to the society and Amir. How had they known they would be here? If they did, it could only mean that someone on the inside had informed them of their trip. If such a thing had taken so long to set up, then the arachne were the only option. But if that was the case, then why would Velvet let her go last night?

It had to be something else. She needed to stop clinging to the idea that the arachne were up to something, because now it was blinding her to other possibilities. As for the society's involvement, that didn't make a lick of sense either.

"Let's find out for sure," she said, then climbed even higher. The edge of her wing grazed the barrier, creating an eerie red smear in the air. The visual made it easy for Abella to track its path. The miles passed by beneath her, and a feeling of dread settled in her gut. The magical barrier had been placed just outside the boundaries of the land. It had clearly been built long before Eulalie had come for help. Had it even been intended for them, or were they just unlucky?

The sun reached its zenith and then began its descent toward the horizon. Abella had covered almost a hundred miles and failed to find any part of the barrier that would allow her through. The land wasn't perfectly circular, and the boundary had been tailored to fit. Should she keep going all the way around and confirm there was no exit, or would it be better to head back now and let everyone know?

Deciding to err on the side of caution, Abella performed a tight spiral and headed back toward the cabin. If she kept going like this, she wouldn't be home until tomorrow. If something was going to come for them, it would likely come tonight when everyone was sleeping.

"Big sister!" Emery leaned forward enough that she could just see his head and arms. He pointed down below at a clearing, and she saw a dark figure sitting on a rock in the shadow of a giant conifer.

She knew better than to land. If that creature was alone, it likely wouldn't be an issue, but what had happened to Pierre immediately came to mind.

A powerful force swatted her out of the air, causing her to tumble. She grabbed onto Emery and cradled him against her chest as they fell. As the tree line neared, she extended her wings once more and got another thirty feet before something grabbed her by the legs.

"Tell the others," she whispered to Emery as she hurled him over the tree line. The imp's wings opened just above the trees, and then she saw no more as she crashed into the ground.

Two hard falls in one day had left her body sore. She did a quick damage assessment and frowned when she realized her left wing had cracked. It wasn't as bad as the time rocks got dropped on her, but she would have to be careful. Wrapping her wings around her body, she rolled over and scowled at the dark, inky tendrils that had clutched her ankle. They were cool to the touch and lacked substance, as if made of shadows.

"I apologize for the rough greeting." The voice sounded like a man's, but it had a hollow timbre to it, as if he was speaking into a gourd. "But it seems that this was the only way to get your attention."

"Who are you?" she asked while scanning the trees. His voice seemed to come from multiple places at once, but there was no sign of him. She couldn't hear his movements or even his heartbeat.

"I've never seen one of your kind so close before." The voice sounded like it was right in her ear, but nobody was there.

"You can come closer if you want." She rolled over and contemplated the tendrils holding her feet. They weren't actually tendrils but a collection of shadows. She tried to cut them with her claws, but her fingers passed harmlessly over them. "Maybe quit being a pussy and show yourself."

"I doubt that you would like what you see." A dark shadow appeared next to a tree, but when she looked at it, it flickered and vanished. It reappeared to her left, leaning out from behind another tree. "I must say, you are the first of your kind I have had the pleasure of meeting. You…are a gargoyle, yes?"

Abella shook her head, refusing to answer. If he was just going to wander circles around her while asking questions, she had no interest in appeasing his curiosity.

"I find you strangely beautiful. You look just human enough that I can see the appeal." He was much closer now, and she caught sight of a clawed hand gripping the bark of a pine. "This man you travel with, does he accept you?"

She feigned looking away but was keeping watch from the corner of her eye. The shadow kept moving between the trees, but now she could hear the subtle shift of a branch or the crunching of snow. Her best guess was that he was teleporting between the trees.

"I saw what happened to you last night. With the arachne."

Abella turned her attention toward the shadow. "And? So what?"

"You are right to fear her." The shadow chuckled, then spoke from behind her. "But there are far scarier things in these woods."

"I'm not afraid of her." That much was true. Her only fear was for Mike's safety, and this asshole was rapidly climbing her list of potential threats.

"It was quite beautiful, seeing the two of you in your danse macabre. I held my breath, wondering which of you would win out in the end. I must admit, I was disappointed to see that she was in possession of that wretched blade." He spat his words out in anger, and the nearby trees quivered as if in fear. "But no matter."

"I was worried you were going to kill me," Abella told him. "And now I know you plan to do so by talking me to death."

"You are alive for two reasons. The first being that I am curious about you. A powerful creature in the thrall of such a simple man. The others are not as interesting to me as a creature made of stone.

"Which leads me to the second reason. I believe you are…unhappy with your current situation." The shadow's voice was now like honeyed smoke drifting through her mind. Hidden beneath his dulcet tones was a line of discord so subtle that she almost didn't hear it. It was the sound of untruths and treachery, of someone trying to get their way. She wondered if he was using a spell to sweeten his words like candy, unaware that she had no taste for sugar. "I bring this up because I feel a certain kinship with those who wish to better their situation. You see, the world is no longer the oasis it used to be for…beings of our disposition."

Abella tilted her head while pondering his words. "It was you who brought the Nirumbi, wasn't it?"

"Guilty." She could almost hear his smile. "They've been locked away underground for so long now, forced to feed on one another and whatever they could find. When I found them, they were quick to bargain with me."

"Bargain for what?"

His voice was now above her. When she looked up into the trees, all she could see were a pair of blazing eyes. He was backlit by the fading light of day, so little else was visible.

"I am building a new world, Abella. A place where creatures like us can be free to be ourselves. No hiding away from the men in white coats. No curious humans. This place could be our oasis, a land we can call our own."

"You are offering me…real estate? To betray my Caretaker?" She sighed in disgust. "I was honestly expecting something better. I decline."

He shook his head. "I offer far more than real estate. This is a legacy. This man of yours, how long is he truly expected to live? Whatever he offers you will be gone in a matter of decades, but this?" He gestured at the woods around them. "I wish to build a paradise that will be here long after humans cease to walk this world. Caretakers come and go, but this place will be my legacy. And perhaps yours too."

Abella frowned. "You don't even know me but wish to share centuries with me?"

"We have a lot in common." He crouched and steepled his hands together. His fingers were tipped with claws. "Shunned by mankind. Immortal, in our own way. How many years of blinding loneliness have you experienced? Nights spent with naught but the stars to keep you company? I once went over a decade without speaking to another living being, and I wonder if you've done the same."

Abella tightened her lips. In fact, she had. After being abandoned by the clan, she had spent years in absolute silence with only the birds to keep her company. On occasion, she'd hidden herself at street level in the city just so she could close her eyes and pretend to be part of the conversations of people as they walked past.

"How many men have tried to kill you?" he continued. "How many times have you heard the ominous cocking of a gun, or the ringing of steel being drawn, just because you looked different? Ever been hunted? I have."

She shook her head, trying to shut him out. There had been a few close calls with the Order, times she had flown until her wings ached from exertion. They had no way of knowing if she was a threat, and she found it hard to blame them. While her clan had been content to remain in the shadows, others of her kind had made sport of terrifying peasants in the countryside.

"You looked so peaceful when you were flying. Almost like an angel." He stood up and waved his arms around. "The sky above would be your paradise. I could even have the little people build you a home, a place for you alone. And while it may seem empty at first, I would dedicate myself to bringing others like you here. Creatures that are misunderstood, that have been vilified by history. This new world would be ours alone, and we could ride out the rest of eternity without a care in the world."

"I knew someone who tried something similar." Abella scowled, remembering Emily's efforts to populate the house. "Your intentions may be good, but I question your methods."

"On this, we agree. You cannot make an omelet without first cracking some eggs." He chuckled, and the trees trembled. "For example, the arachne is a problem that deserves to be cracked, don't you agree?"

"What would you have of me?" she asked, curious what he would say. The offer to deal with Velvet was obviously tailored for her, and she could detect an undercurrent of untruth to it.

"I couldn't ask you to turn on the others," he said. "It would be too hard; they are your friends. But maybe I could open the barrier and you could just… leave for a few days. Make it that much easier for me to finish what I started."

"And what of the Caretaker?" she asked.

"You still feel for him, and I understand." He reached down and touched her hair with a bony claw. His cowl shifted, and she thought she saw horns inside. "But does he feel the same about you? I had hoped to avoid the Caretaker's involvement, but now that he is here, he is another egg that needs cracking."

"So you would kill him?"

He sighed. "Humans are unpredictable. Perhaps he and I will speak and come to an arrangement. I would even lie on your behalf and explain that I trapped you outside. This place could be here waiting for you after he dies many years from now. He would never have to know."

Abella frowned. This guy was laying it on thick. Why did he need her to leave so bad? What was she missing?

"And if you can't come to an agreement?" she asked.

"I think you know the answer. I shouldn't have to say it." He almost sounded sad. "I can't make any guarantees. I have my own goals to pursue, and I won't be stopped."

"Why even attack the cabin in the first place? Why not just walk up and knock? This place was meant to be a refuge. Why not just ask to be included?"

"I have...bad blood with one of the occupants. It wouldn't have worked."

"Yet here you are, trying to get me to turn on my family?" She could feel a fire building inside her chest. "To get me to simply walk away? How could you ever trust someone willing to do that to the ones they love?"

"You love no one!" His voice was magnified, and the shadows all around her twisted about. "You think because he doesn't look at you with disgust that you are actually loved? Do you think he actually values you? Thinks of you as an equal? You fill a need, and nothing more."

She thought back to how Mike had held her hand in the forest. The times she had fought for him, and the times he had fought for them. He had bought her a tablet to watch movies on so she wouldn't get bored, had visited her on the roof just to say hi. Whenever he dropped by for a chat, he didn't see a monster or a guard dog. He saw her as a person.

It was the way Velvet wanted to be treated, and Abella already had it. She would be damned if she gave it up.

"Do you have an asshole?" she asked. "Because that's where you can stick your offer."

Those crimson eyes flashed, and the figure vanished. When he next spoke, his voice came from all around her.

"We could have made this work," he told her in a whisper. "I could have used a powerful ally such as you. In your final moments, I want you to know that I intend to rip your beloved human to shreds and feed him to the Nirumbi."

Before Abella could react, he snapped his fingers. The shadows tightened around her legs and yanked her through the forest. She crashed through the foliage with gradually increasing speed. The shadows were like giant elastic bands that somehow yanked harder the farther she traveled. She managed to sit up just as she crashed through a copse of trees and then skidded out onto the icy surface of a small lake.

The shadows were gone now. She coasted nearly sixty feet from the shore, her wings spread wide in an attempt to distribute her weight. Beneath her, the ice groaned in protest.

"Asshole," she muttered. Even if the ice broke, the cold was no danger to her, and she didn't need to breathe. It would take her some time, but she could make it back to shore. With her current energy levels, she could spend a few days at the bottom of the lake before she was in any real danger.

Beneath the ice, something moved. She looked down, then used her hand to rub away the snow, revealing a clear window into the murky depths. Instead of darkness, she was treated to the sight of scales shifting against the other side. The scales slid beneath the surface, their patterns shifting until an eye the size of her head opened. The pupil narrowed in the light of day, then focused on her.

"Merde."

When the ice shattered, she felt thick coils wrap around her body as she was dragged into the cold depths below.

The temperature in the house was dropping, and Beth wondered if it would get cold enough to need a fire in the fireplace. The house relied on hot water registers down by the floor, but without Naia or her spring, there would be no way to heat the whole house.

When Beth stepped into the kitchen, there was a noticeable chill in the air. The cupboards were all open as if someone had gone rummaging through them, and the basement door was closed. She closed all the cupboards, then rubbed at her arms. The hair on the back of her neck was standing up, and she didn't know why.

"Hey." Lily stepped into the kitchen from the dining room and hopped up to sit on the counter with her legs crossed.

"Well? Is she okay?" Beth had asked Lily to check on Tink, seeing as dreams were her domain.

Lily nodded. "It's a sleep spell. She's currently trapped in a dream but a far better one now that I've made a few tweaks. You would be absolutely astonished at the shit inside that goblin's head. It's like M. C. Escher got drunk with the Marquis de Sade! Anyway, it's not something I can easily break, which is worrisome. The process itself could hurt her."

Beth sighed. At least Tink would get better, whatever the problem was. She rubbed her arms again. "It wasn't even this cold outside," she grumbled. "How the fuck is it so cold in here?"

"I have one idea." Lily pointed at the door to the basement, which was now open. Beth inhaled sharply at the realization that the door had opened itself. "Maybe whatever got out of the Vault is sapping the energy out of here? Exorcist Barbie does a similar trick before she manifests, right?"

"I guess, but—Ticktock!" Beth ran over to the kitchen table and picked up the large backpack that was sitting in a chair. She was relieved that the mimic had made the transition with them.

"Hey there, little clock." Lily approached and playfully tugged at one of the zippers. When she let go, the zipper undid itself, making the flap look like a grinning mouth. "You still carrying precious cargo?"

"Let me check," Beth said, then stuck her hand into the bag. Her fingers closed on the edge of the grimoire, and she let out a sigh of relief. "Go ahead and keep it," she said, then zipped the bag shut. She slid the bag onto her shoulders, and the straps adjusted themselves.

"Looks like he's got a crush on you," Lily teased. "Maybe you can introduce him to that suitcase you've got. Do you think magic luggage likes to fuck? Instead of tops and bottoms, they could be ins and outs."

Beth ignored Lily, but her cheeks burned with embarrassment. Maybe it was time to store her collection somewhere else, since everyone seemed to know about it. Not that she had even really looked at it since moving in. Her monster infatuation was currently well fed.

At the top of the stairs, an icy gust of air blasted her hair away from her face. She covered her eyes and closed the door.

"Guess I'm getting my coat," she told Lily, then ran to her room to get it. When she came back, Lily was wearing a colander on her head and holding a spatula.

"What are you doing?" Beth asked.

"Isn't this what you wear to fight the monster in the basement?" Lily stuck out her tongue, and Beth laughed. It helped lighten her mood immensely, and she pulled out her phone to snap a picture. Maybe she would make a photo book of how fucked up her week had been and look at it fondly while being absolutely tanked on wine.

They opened the door and stared at the looming darkness. The bottom of the stairs wasn't visible, so Beth went to get a flashlight from the kitchen. When she returned, she clicked the light on and sighed.

"I don't remember this many steps," she said.

"Nope." Lily looked at Beth, then took the colander off her head and threw it down the stairs. They could hear the colander crashing against the concrete steps for quite some time before it finally went quiet.

"I hate this." Beth started down the stairs, but Lily grabbed her by the shoulder and stepped ahead.

"I can take a punch far better than you can." She winked at Beth. "And a bullet, a knife, a backhanded compliment…"

Beth playfully kicked at the succubus, and then the two of them started their descent. The house wall, which usually terminated only a couple of feet down, continued onward as if it had been stretched out to accommodate the new length of the stairs. After they had gone down for a minute, Beth turned to look back and frowned at how tiny the basement door looked.

"We're gonna have to climb back up these stairs," she mentioned. "At what point do we decide this is a bad idea?"

"When something tries to eat us."

"That's not very funny," Beth replied.

"And I'm not laughing." Lily looked over her shoulder. "Can you feel that shift in pressure? That's nothing friendly."

Beth shivered. Maybe she should have brought someone else with them, but who?

"Also keep in mind that Tink was down here unconscious. Kisa brought her back not that long ago, so this is new. If something is putting together a trap for us, it's probably tired."

"It almost sounds like you're trying to make me feel better."

"Is it working?"

Beth nodded. "A bit."

"Good." They kept going for a few more minutes before something shiny reflected the light from the flashlight. It was the colander, now covered in dents.

"Well, at least Sofia can make us pasta when she gets back," Beth quipped. "Maybe if you're good, I'll convince her to make you some devil's food cake."

"Now you're trying to make me feel better." Lily picked up the colander and studied it.

"Is it working?" Beth asked.

Lily shrugged. "I haven't decided yet." She threw the colander down into the darkness and then put her hands on her hips. After several seconds of metallic clattering, it stopped once more.

"How far do you think that was?" Beth asked.

"Too far." Lily started walking again, and Beth followed. After several more minutes, they eventually found the colander on the stairs again. This time, Beth picked it up.

"I'm starting to think that going any farther is a bad idea," she said, then turned her gaze toward the top of the stairs. The tiny square of light up at the kitchen was barely visible.

"What's eighty-two minus thirteen?" Lily asked, her face suddenly frantic. She grabbed onto Beth's arms. "Quick, it's important!"

"What? I—" Beth concentrated on trying to do the math in her head, then screamed when Lily pushed her backward. Terrified, she tried to catch herself against the wall but stumbled and fell.

Ticktock broke her fall, but the wind was knocked out of her lungs when she found herself lying on the cold, hard floor of the basement. Gasping for air, she rolled over and coughed a few times. Her breath turned into fog with each exhale.

"What the hell did you just do?" she asked, then turned toward the stairs. Lily had her arms crossed and stood on the bottom step.

"So if I did that correctly, you should be in the basement." A look of concern crossed Lily's face. "If not...I'm really sorry."

"Of course I'm in the basement." Beth shined the light in Lily's face. The beam also illuminated the stairwell, which now appeared normal. "How did you know that would work?"

"Beth?" Lily winced without recognition, then took a step forward. She vanished and reappeared at the top of the stairs. "Romeo is going to be so pissed at me if I accidentally killed you."

Puzzled, Beth waited for Lily to descend the stairs, then watched as she vanished and reappeared up top again. When Lily made it down to the last step this time, Beth reached out and grabbed her by the arm, then pulled.

There was a soft pop as Lily stepped onto the basement floor. She smiled when she saw Beth.

"Explain." Beth held the light in Lily's face, causing her to squint.

"Both times we threw the colander, we found it two hundred and fifty-six steps later. I started counting when we started. Demons are good at stuff like that." Lily gestured at the steps. "The odds that it would do that twice were exceedingly small. Why stop at all? I threw it way harder the second time. The house does weird shit, but an infinite stairwell? It's way easier to manipulate the space you're given, but even that has limits. Just some illusion magic coupled with reality warping."

"The math problem was to distract me?"

"Uses a different part of the brain, which weakens the illusion's hold. When I pushed you back, you were looking at me and the doorway. It couldn't teleport you up top, and it couldn't alter the doorway, so you fell out of the loop." A smoking jacket and a pipe appeared on Lily, and she took a deep puff and blew out a smoke ring. "Elementary magic theory."

"You didn't look too sure of yourself after I fell," Beth said in an angry tone.

Lily shrugged. "I would have kissed your boo-boos."

"I'm asking Sofia to make you angel food cake."

"Ooh, hurt me more." Lily's coat disappeared, but she kept the pipe. "Whatever will I do if I'm forced to eat a fucking cake?"

"We'll sing you 'Happy Birthday,'" Beth continued. "And add all those stupid fucking verses at the end."

"Ugh, fine, I'm sorry." Lily tossed the pipe into the shadows, where it disappeared in a puff of smoke. "Anything but listening to 'Happy Birthday' fan fiction."

Beth took a moment to survey the basement with her flashlight. There were dark stains on the walls and floors, and frost had formed around the doorway to the Vault. Along the opposite side of the room, the mysterious scarab room appeared empty.

It took her a moment to realize that the dark stains were actually moving. The one closest to her shifted toward her feet but then shrank away when Lily's tail took a stab at it.

"Probably shouldn't touch those," Lily said. "Give you an STD."

Beth mulled over the acronym. "Shadow transmitted disease?"

"And they say lawyers are dumb." Lily chased the shadows away with her tail, then stood before the door of the Vault. "So enlighten me. I've never come down here. This is supposed to close up?"

"Yeah. You draw a chalk outline to open the door, then it just vanishes when you close it."

"Looks like your magic door is out of power." Lily tried to pull it shut, but it didn't seal. She pushed the door back open and peered inside. "Okay, yeah, this place is terrible. It's like a clearance sale for cursed objects."

"You can sense them?"

Lily smirked. "More like I can feel them hiding from me. Most of what's in here knows better than to tangle with a soul-eating demon. Some stuff is just dangerous to have. For example, do you see that folding fan over there?"

Beth leaned in to the doorway and pointed her flashlight. It settled on a decorative fan with a picture of a Japanese man painting on a blank canvas.

"What's that do?" she asked.

"It steals faces." Lily summoned a fan of her own, then waved it over her face. Her head was now featureless, with only a pair of holes for breathing.

"Who the fuck invents a fan that does that?" Beth asked.

Lily snapped the fan shut and her face reappeared. "It wasn't meant to. You ever see those mask-changing acts? Was supposed to do that, but the enchantment broke. Now it only takes."

"You can tell all that from here? How?"

"I recognize it. When you are chained to the world's most knowledgeable bastard, you hear about these things. Even handling it could cause you to accidentally suck your own face right off. I bet a lot of stuff in here is like that. Too dangerous to let out but no safe way to dispose of it."

Beth frowned. If there was this much stuff down here, how would they keep the house safe until the Vault could be closed?

"So what do you think is missing?" Lily asked. "I'm guessing something escaped."

"The only person who might know is—" Beth groaned. "It's Tink. She came down here because I bet she suspected the Vault was open."

"And she's the only one who would know what got out. Clever." Lily looked around the room. "Do you think we could ask Jenny?"

"Good luck getting her to come down here. She hates this place." Beth raised the beam of light to Jenny's former prison and paused. "Ratu wanted me to keep that thing safe," she said, indicating the vial. "I should probably get it out."

"Allow me." Lily walked through the room, shrinking her body down to fit between the overstuffed shelves. Once on the other side of the room, she opened the glass case and pulled out the vial. "This your demon spunk?" she asked.

"If that's what we're calling it, then yes." Beth heard whispering in her ear. She looked over at the corner where the haunted painting was stored. It had been tilted toward the door, and the cloth covering had come partially undone. "Ugh, no thanks."

Lily chuckled and tucked the vial into her cleavage. "I think the locals are getting restless. Maybe we should—"

There was a ripping sound, and the air behind Lily turned black. Dozens of shadowy hands wrapped around her and pulled, causing her to vanish into the void.

"Lily!" Beth took a step into the Vault and stalled. The whispering was even louder now, and she froze in place as several objects in the room started moving. A creepy Elvis bobblehead doll rotated to look at her, and she jumped when a rocking chair slid toward her from across the room.

"Lily, where are you?" Beth shined the beam around. The whispering was grating at her nerves now, and she could hear Lily's voice echoing from different corners of the room. It sounded like she was fighting with something.

There was a rasping noise behind her of metal on metal, and Beth's gut filled with ice. She turned to see a fencing foil slide across the shelves and then hover in the air. It rotated in place, then shot across the room at her.

She threw herself back and out of the Vault. The foil shot through the air and bounced off the far wall of the basement. It clattered to the floor, then lifted itself again.

"Lily?!?" Beth looked at the stairs. If she ran up them, would she get caught in the loop again? If the sword chased her, her miserable last minutes would be spent running up an infinite number of stairs.

The sword came at her again, and she dodged to the side. This time, her foot landed in one of the shifting shadows, and she sank up to her shin.

"Oh, fucking hell!" She tried to pull her leg out, but a spectral hand came with it. The other shadows now moved toward her, and she saw the sword coming her way again.

Ticktock shifted violently, and then a pair of metallic arms swatted the sword out of the way. Beth said a silent prayer and tried again to free herself. The whispers from the painting were making her teeth itch. There was a loud thud, followed by the same tearing noise, and Lily's legs now dangled from the ceiling up above.

"Fuck you!" shouted Lily before her legs were slurped back up like spaghetti.

"Lily, I'm being eaten by the floor!" Beth saw that another shadow was coming close. Her leg was going numb below the knee.

There was a loud thud, and then Lily's head appeared from a nearby wall. Her eyes were bright yellow, and her horns were covered in black blood. "Then you should offer to pay for dinner," she hollered. Several hands grabbed her by the hair and horns and yanked her back into the wall.

There was a roar, and then the wall cracked. Beth was knocked down as Ticktock deflected another attack by the sword. When she pushed herself up, she saw that the painting was slowly scooting its way out of the Vault, the cloth now off it completely.

She let out a primal scream of rage and stuck her hand into the black void beneath her. The hand grabbing her leg shifted to her wrist, but she yanked it out until it was visible, then bit into it.

It felt like cotton candy beneath her teeth, but this somehow worked. The hand let go of her, and she was suddenly free. Scrambling to her feet, she moved away from the other shadows until she was near the freezer. She pulled it away from the wall and climbed on top.

A premonition of danger made her duck, and the sword sailed over her head. When it spun around to face her, she slid Ticktock off her shoulders.

"Shield!" she cried, then closed her eyes. The weight on her arms shifted, and she opened her eyes in time to see that Ticktock had become one. She also saw that Ticktock had dropped the grimoire by her knees.

"I don't understand," she said, then saw a pair of words written on the back of Ticktock's shiny new body.

USE BOOK

The sword careened off the mimic. Legs sprouted from the shield, and Ticktock shifted to intercept the next attack. Over by the door, the painting had flopped over, but it was still moving closer.

"Sure, fine, use a magic book with absolutely no experience." She opened the pages, only to discover that they were blank.

"Shit!" She flipped through the pages, surprised to see that there was nothing inside. "What do I do now?"

The whispering stopped. Beth looked up to see that the painting now faced her. Across its canvas surface, it had captured her terrified likeness perfectly as she sat atop the freezer.

"Ah, fuck bubbles."

The painting launched itself at her, and she slid off the freezer and opened the lid. The painting collided with the underside of the lid, and Beth shoved the freezer shut, trapping the painting inside with antique Otter Pops and ground beef that likely hadn't seen daylight in decades.

When she climbed back onto the freezer, Ticktock joined her. The painting tried to force the lid open, but the combined weight of Beth and Ticktock held it shut. The shadows were closing in, however, and the sword was still moving around.

"One crisis down." Beth looked at the Vault's doorway. She could hear things moving around inside. "Any ideas on how to close that?"

Ticktock shifted, revealing the same two words to her.

"It's blank, I—" She opened it again, and the book flipped itself open to a specific page. The symbols inside swirled about as the book rewrote itself in English, revealing a diagram of an opening being sealed by stone.

"Huh. Okay, then." She picked up the book, then moved behind Ticktock just as the foil bounced off it. The spell itself sounded like it allowed rock to melt. Was concrete a kind of rock?

The freezer shifted violently, and she almost fell off. One corner of it was now inside a floor shadow.

Oh, for crying out loud. Beth ran her finger along the text. Incantation? Check. Something about using her mind to shape intent? Okay. Did it require blood? Nope.

"Good enough for me." She held the book aloft and read the words. When it didn't work the first time, she grumbled and moved farther back along the lid as the freezer sank into the floor.

"C'mon, Beth," she whispered to herself, then glared at the Vault and said the incantation again. This time, she pictured the wall of concrete as if it was made of clay and wondered what it would feel like to smooth the whole thing over with her hand.

The freezer lurched and sank again. The edge of it caught on the ground.

Beth slammed the book shut, reached deep into her mind, then sang the words while stretching her hand toward the Vault door. For a moment, she felt her magic connect with the book and then the wall, so she swept her hand across the air. She pictured the palm of her hand moving across the concrete as if it was clay, smearing it out to cover the hole.

There was a grinding sound that filled the basement. She pointed her light at the Vault and saw that the wall had been smoothed over. There were still gaps in the stone, and she could hear things bouncing off the other side, but nothing else was coming out to get her.

"Yes!" She pumped the grimoire in the air, and the sword whipped by, slashing open her forearm from elbow to wrist.

Beth cried out in pain and tumbled off the freezer. She let go of the flash-light, choosing to hold the grimoire instead as she crashed into the floor. The flashlight spun in place, revealing that the sword was turning around to come at her again.

Ticktock, who was on the floor now, stumbled to get up, then vanished inside one of the shadows. There was a shriek of rage, and the shadow exploded, sending the mimic clattering across the room. For just a brief instant, Beth saw dozens of bladed legs and hands withdrawing into the shield, but they were gone once she blinked.

When the sword came at her again, Beth used the grimoire to deflect it into the wall. The invincible tome worked like a charm, though the impact knocked her back a little. When the sword pinged off the cold concrete, she grabbed it by the handle and felt an electric shock run through her body.

"I've lived with Quetzalli too long to give a shit," she mumbled, then stuck the blade into the closest shadow to her. A shadow hand grabbed it, then pulled it inside. The shadow quivered, then withdrew. The tip of the sword kept trying to emerge from the ground, but clearly, the shadows weren't picky about what they ate, aside from Ticktock.

"Lily, are you about done?" she shouted, then looked at her arm. She was bleeding quite a bit.

There was a loud thud, then Lily's ass appeared out of the ground, her tail whipping around. Beth grabbed onto Lily's tail and pulled, grunting with exertion. The grimoire nearly slipped out of her arms, so she pinned it against her chest with her bad arm.

Lily's tail whipped about, then pressed itself against Beth's mouth, forcing her lips open. Surprised, Beth froze in place as the glass vial was deposited in her mouth.

The succubus was pulled back into the floor, and Beth spat the vial into her bloody hand.

"Run!" Lily shouted through the wall. "I'll be fine, get that out of here!"

Beth knew better than to argue. She dashed across the basement and closed her eyes as she reached for Ticktock. The mimic shifted into a messenger bag, and she stuffed the grimoire and the vial inside as she stepped onto the stairs.

The infinite stairwell effect reappeared but only in the downward direction. The door to the kitchen wasn't far, and Beth tripped at the top of the stairs and fell down.

"Help!" she shouted, then kicked the basement door shut. In a matter of moments, Cecilia phased through the wall, concern on her face. Death appeared shortly after, a mug of tea in his hands. On the mug was a picture of a cat hanging from a rope with the words *Hang in there, Kitty!* underneath.

"Evil spirits in the basement!" she cried as the basement door rattled. She planted her feet against it to hold it shut. "They have Lily!"

Death frowned. "*Have* is a relative term, Princess Bethany, and I must ask for clarification—"

"Bad! It's all bad!" Beth braced her feet against the hallway as the door opened an inch and a dark hand tried to slide free. The air filled with ominous whispering, meaning the painting was free.

Cecilia passed through the door and shrieked. The door rattled, then stopped. Beth's ears were ringing, and she tried to stand but slipped in her own blood.

"Ah, jeez." She scooted away from her own mess and stood with Death's help.

"I should perhaps assist Lady Cecilia. Excuse me." Death, still holding his teacup, opened the door of the basement. The sound of banshee screams filled the kitchen as he casually descended the stairs.

Beth listened as the air filled with unholy shrieks and screams. The walls of the house creaked, and the floor vibrated beneath her feet. She used a towel to make a compress against her arm, hoping the sword wouldn't give her tetanus.

Kisa checked in with her just long enough to hear the cacophony from below. She closed the basement door, then ran off to find a first aid kit.

Beth moved to the table and sat with a groan. Her back hurt, and she was feeling dizzy. She lifted Ticktock onto the table and used the mimic as a makeshift pillow.

"You didn't get hurt, did you?" She patted the bag. "Thanks for saving my life down there. I owe you one."

Ticktock's zipper slid open, and the vial popped out.

Beth picked up the vial and held it up. In the dim light of the kitchen, the crystalline structure was filled with tiny rainbows. It occurred to her that Lily had been attacked after retrieving the vial from its cage. Had the spirits in the basement been trying to get their hands on it?

There was a hair on the vial, so she tried to pluck it off. After several attempts to grab it, she realized that the hair seemed to be on the inside. Wondering how a hair got inside, she used the light on her phone to get a better look.

It wasn't a hair but a thin crack. She watched in horror as a narrow bead of black pressed through, then ran up the side of the vial toward her fingers.

"No, no, no, no, no!" She stood and ran for one of Death's teacups. When she placed the vial inside, it leaked but was fully contained. Letting out a sigh of relief, she set the cup down. The vial continued to fill the cup, and when it was half full, she frowned.

The vial shouldn't have that much ooze in it.

She grabbed a bowl and poured the ooze into it. It stuck to itself, leaving the coffee cup clean behind it. The bowl was filling itself when she found a pitcher to transfer it to, the vial somehow releasing far more of the tar-like substance than it had contained.

"Fuck, fuck, fuck…," she muttered in horror as she ran out of the kitchen, holding the pitcher. Kisa was standing in the foyer when Beth ran past and up the stairs. The biggest vessel in the house was in Mike's bathroom, and Beth poured the pitcher into Naia's bath, hoping the nymph would forgive her.

As she watched the tub fill itself with goo, she shook her head in disbelief as it continued to fill. Leaning over the ever-rising tide of black, she realized just how sleepy she suddenly was. Blood was running down her arm again, dripping bits of crimson into the inky depths of the ooze.

That can't be good. She let out a giggle, then felt gravity lose its grip on her as she tilted forward into the tub. She heard Kisa calling her name but didn't have the strength to answer. The darkness was surprisingly warm, and all she wanted was to curl up and go to sleep in it.

In her semiconscious state, she felt her magic rise and surround her. Thousands of needles pierced her flesh, and then there was a bright green light.

"Beth!"

She felt the hard slap across her face and opened her eyes to see Kisa sitting over her. Beth squinted, trying to will the world into focus, but she had lost too much blood.

"Hey." Her voice was slurred, and she felt like she was drunk.

"What the hell is that?" Kisa muttered in horror, her eyes on the tub. From where she was lying, Beth couldn't see anything.

"Is it Naia?" she asked. Her brain was faring no better than her body. "Did we beat the Apocalypse?

"I can't move you. Hold on." Kisa dashed out of the bathroom, leaving Beth on the floor. It could have been seconds or hours; Beth had no way of knowing. She did, however, see a dark shape moving just below the edge of the tub.

A pair of hands appeared on the edge, and what looked like a head came next.

"Peek-a-boo." Beth laughed when the tub monster dropped back down. It shifted about, making sloshing sounds as it moved to the far end of the tub and repeated the process. This time when it appeared, it looked like it almost had a face.

"You remind me of that fan in the basement," Beth declared with a giggle. A little voice in her head warned her that she was bordering on delirium, but what did she care? "Are you here to steal my face?"

The dark mass contemplated her, then began to brighten. The darkness seemed to burn away as a bright green light formed inside of the thing in the tub. Beth immediately felt a strange sort of synergy with it.

"Stay back!" Kisa shouted as she ran into the bathroom. She was surrounded by rats, and they all closed in on Beth and tried to drag her away.

The thing in the tub spilled over, turning briefly into flowing liquid as it scattered the rats and coated Beth's body. There was a sensation of warmth, followed by a tingling in her arm. She opened her mouth to breathe, but there was no air.

"No!" Kisa was screaming now, her voice muffled by the ooze that covered Beth.

They say that drowning isn't a bad way to go, Beth thought. *But frankly, I prefer not to go at all.*

Air flooded her lungs, and she gasped for it, her throat suddenly raw. Kisa, the hair on her body sticking out, knelt by Beth.

"Are you okay?" she asked. "What just happened?"

"I don't know." Beth lifted her arm to look at it. The tingling sensation had passed, and the wound in her arm looked like it had scabbed over. When she touched the wound, she realized it wasn't a scab but some type of sticky residue. Most of the dizziness was gone now, but she still felt disoriented mentally.

The temperature in the room dropped, and Cecilia appeared, her hair floating wildly around her. Lily followed next, her face a mess of bloody scratches. Both of them stopped on the edge of the tile, disbelief on their faces.

"Lily!" Beth put her hand to her chest and sighed in relief. "You're okay!"

Lily opened her mouth as if to say something, then just shrugged. "I'm at a loss."

"What happened down there?"

Cecilia looked past Beth, then at her. "Um...it wasn't much I could help with. Kind of scary, actually. I didn't really know what was going on, so I just screamed a lot. My voice can disrupt spirits, so it weakened them."

Lily sneered. "Bogeymen in the shadows, by the way. Same guys that grab your feet from under the bed. No idea why there were so many. Some type of Babylonian demon in the painting. An actual nightmare of shadow people. Yes, that is what I'm calling a group of those bastards. Have only seen one or two at a time ever. There were almost twenty of them, transdimensional pricks!" Lily actually spat on the floor. "Those things were actually locked up somewhere in the Vault, and someone or something let them out. We need to talk to Romeo about the shit in that room when he gets back. There's no reason half of that stuff even needs to exist."

"What happened? How did you win?"

Cecilia looked at Lily, then laughed. "One of the shadow people broke Death's teacup. It was apparently one of his favorites."

"Shadow people aren't souls or spirits like you know them. His scythe didn't send them to the Underworld. It actually carved through them." Lily winced. "I'm fairly certain he sent them to the void. Utter oblivion."

"And they deserved it!" Death stormed in through the door, his eyes blazing. He still carried his scythe, which gleamed with its own supernatural aura.

"Sorry about your mug," Beth offered.

"Indeed." Death frowned. "I regret to inform you that the kitty from my mug is no longer hanging on. Though, it was an old mug; I doubt that cat is even alive anymore." He turned his attention to the tub and let out a gasp. "I was unaware we had company! Where are my manners? I must look a fright!"

He tapped the butt of his scythe on the ground, then folded it into his robes. Beth watched him as he walked past her and sat on the edge of the tub.

"I am the grim reaper," he said, extending a bony hand. "Though you may call me Death. You look familiar, but I don't think we've ever met."

A translucent hand the color of emeralds appeared and shook Death's hand. The figure in the tub sat up, revealing hair that literally flowed around a feminine body. At first, Beth thought she was looking at Naia in her water form, but there were too many differences.

For one, the being wasn't made of water. It was a viscous fluid that rippled with every movement and made a sloshing sound. It was also feminine, and when it turned to face Beth, she gasped.

The mysterious creature in the tub looked almost exactly like her.

"What…how…" Beth sputtered for a few more seconds, then grabbed her face to make sure it hadn't, in fact, been stolen. Why did this thing look like her? It clicked that she was looking at the ooze that she had dumped in the tub, but it was a different color now and had taken on a human form. Her form.

The ooze turned toward Beth and moved its hands. Beth immediately recognized the movements as American Sign Language.

"I'm just as surprised as you are," replied the ooze.

MIKE HAD PROMISED DANA TWENTY MINUTES, BUT IT WAS A COUPLE OF HOURS before he and Velvet climbed out of the hot springs. His legs were weak beneath him, but he eventually got his footing and dried off with some towels Velvet pulled from a nearby hut. She explained that her father had built it.

Once they were dry and properly attired, Velvet led him back up to the top of the ridge. They walked largely in silence. Velvet seemed to be deep in thought, and Mike's attempts to start a conversation yielded very little. The only talking he heard was the spiders around them that chattered incessantly to themselves.

Undeterred, he took Velvet by the hand. A thick bloom of red crossed her cheeks, and she smiled dreamily as they walked the rest of the way back.

What had happened to the two of them back there? Mike wondered. The intense feelings of longing had diminished, but it had almost felt like his magic had activated early. It wasn't something he could explain, as he was still writing the user manual on his own magic. Even now, the intense attraction he had originally felt for Velvet lingered.

Was it infatuation? A crush of sorts? It was unusual to contemplate feeling romantically inclined when he was surrounded by so many different women he had sex with. Somehow, Velvet was amplifying those feelings of attraction to the point he was already placing her above the others in his heart. He was already picturing those sweet moments of bliss with her in the spring, though the memories were so fresh.

It troubled him. He loved each of the women for different reasons, and the idea that he would suddenly like one above the others didn't sit well at all. What if Velvet wanted to be exclusive? Could he even say no?

These thoughts swirled through his head, and all he would ever remember from that walk would be the feel of her hand in his and the way the light bent through her auburn locks, giving her a halo.

Once the cabin was in sight, he knew something was wrong. Dana was lying outside the cabin in her underwear while Yuki and Quetzalli stood by in concern.

"Dana?" He let go of Velvet's hand and ran the rest of the way.

"Stay back!" Yuki cast a small wall of ice between them. Mike slid to a stop, his hands on top of the ice.

"What's wrong?" He looked down at Dana, who was groaning and holding her stomach.

"We're not sure," Yuki replied. "But she may bite you."

"Bite me?" Mike looked over at Dana. Quetzalli was using a shovel to cover the zombie's limbs in snow. "What happened?"

"Bad…reaction." Dana looked up at Mike and coughed. "After eating my meal, I briefly…" Her eyes widened, and she snarled, then lifted her hands. Shackles made of ice shattered but were grabbed by more.

"It's the poison in her system." Quetzalli used the shovel to pin Dana down. "She came to life, we made out a bit, but then she freaked out and went to the fridge…"

"She ate her entire supply." Yuki looked up at Mike. "Your sperm is triggering her cells to live, and the poison is killing them off, making her even hungrier than before. I'm hoping if I drop her body temperature, it will slow the poison down enough that she stabilizes. The poison doesn't seem to break down with time, which is a problem."

"So she's stuck like this?" Mike frowned.

"Well, you could fuck her." Yuki scowled. "But you would have to keep doing it until the poison was gone. I honestly don't know how that would work. One dose was enough to knock Bigfoot on his ass for several days. I estimate Dana got well over thirty. It may be something we need the centaurs to solve."

"Shit." He thought about the small supply of potions Zel had sent with him. Most of it was for injuries, though she had tossed in some stuff for water purification and some energy bars. He didn't think those were made with his spunk anymore, so they probably wouldn't work. She had also put in a couple of vials with warning labels on them, but he figured he wouldn't need them with the Nirumbi gone.

"Where's Bigfoot?" he asked. "It sounds like we may need to leave soon. How is he feeling?"

The front door slammed open, and Bigfoot limped out. He squatted down on the front porch with a groan, then sat on the steps.

"I was feeling better until I had to wrestle her outside." Bigfoot spat in the snow. "She trashed our kitchen before I could get my hands on her. Then she tried to bite me, but my fur is pretty thick. I've wrestled bears weaker than her. It's uncanny how strong she is."

Velvet left Mike's side and ran into the cabin. Puzzled, he watched her go.

"I'm sorry about that," he told Bigfoot while shaking his head. "Do you think you would be up to helping us get home? I think the Nirumbi are gone, so it should be safe to leave."

"And then what?" Bigfoot leaned back, a frown on his face. "Am I coming to live with you? Gonna be your big, hairy roommate?"

Mike shrugged. "That's your call. I assume you prefer the forest, but I'm sure we could buy a bed big enough for you. But what I want to do is bring a few rats back here. We can open a portal in your barn or wherever, and this place would be just like part of the house. You can come and go as you please; you'll just have a shortcut across the country."

Velvet opened the door and came out holding a couple of pans. "I really like that idea, Uncle Foot." She looked down at the pans in her hands. "Oh, right." The arachne went back inside, and Mike could hear pots clanging. From where he stood, he could see that she was trying to clean up Dana's mess. He hadn't realized she was so tidy. In fact, he didn't know much about her at all.

Bigfoot grunted. "I suppose tomorrow may work. I got winded dragging her out here and don't want to get stuck in the woods at night. If we leave first thing in the morning, it should be easy enough to get you all home by nightfall."

"Thank you." Mike walked next to Yuki. "Do you think you can keep our girl on ice for another day?"

"Oh God, he made that joke on purpose," Dana muttered, her teeth chattering. Her nipples stood up prominently against the thin fabric of her undershirt as she arched her back, causing one of her breasts to pop free. "Please just leave me out here if he's gonna do that."

"Let's get some real clothes on her." He took off his coat and draped it over Dana's torso. "Let her keep some dignity until we get this sorted."

Dana made eye contact with him and mouthed the words *thank you* just before baring her teeth and hissing.

Disturbed by the turn of events, Mike went inside to dig through Dana's stuff for clothes she could wear. He saw Velvet humming to herself in the kitchen, her whole back end swaying from side to side as she tidied up the room. The fridge had been emptied onto the floor, and there were a couple of broken glass bottles. Velvet stepped around them with delicate feet.

After picking out a sweater and some pants, he headed toward the front door but not before making a detour toward the kitchen and swatting Velvet playfully on the butt.

Velvet jumped, flipping over in the air and landing with her legs spread between the counter and the table. When she saw that it was Mike who had swatted her, she blushed.

"You startled me," she told him as she stepped back down. "I'm a bit distracted is all. Gotta clean this up."

"I'll be in to help." He went outside and had Yuki and Quetzalli assist him in getting Dana dressed. It took almost half an hour, and she had calmed down considerably by the time they were done. Still, she often bared her teeth while talking, so they put duct tape over her mouth. Mike was very apologetic during the whole thing until Dana told him it was fine and to please stop bringing it up.

Yuki stayed outside with Dana while Mike went inside to help Velvet and make sure they were ready to leave in the morning. He was sure Abella would be grateful to get home, and wondered if she was still sulking.

He and Quetzalli were in the middle of eating grilled cheese sandwiches for dinner when Yuki burst through the front door, carrying a tiny gray bundle in her arms.

"Mike!" She ran to the table and opened her arms. Emery rolled out of them and went limp on the table. He looked up at Mike and let out a sigh of relief.

"I didn't think I'd make it," he muttered. "Need to…tell you something."

"Emery, where's Abella?"

"Captured."

When Mike stood, his magic roared inside him. A blast of energy sent his chair skidding across the floor and into the pantry. Everybody jumped, but he was too worried about Abella to care much beyond that.

"Who has her?" he demanded.

"Don't know." Emery groaned and covered his head with his hands. "There was an ambush. She sent me to get help. I wanted to help, but there's nothing I could do!"

The floor of the cabin creaked as Bigfoot limped over to the table. "You tell me which direction and I can get us there," he said, then looked up at Mike. "It's likely a trap though."

"You're right, it is." Mike left his sandwich behind and ran to his bedroom. He picked up Darren's rifle and stuffed a box of ammo in his pocket. When he came back out, he saw that Quetzalli had finished off her own sandwich and was hastily devouring the rest of his.

When they stepped outside, Mike pondered Dana. They had moved her into a sitting position by the door, and Yuki had used one of her tarot cards to summon iron bands to shackle her to the floorboards.

"We can't just leave her here," he said.

"You won't have to." The voice came from everywhere at once. "You see, I've decided that the time has come to speak of many things. Of ships and shoes, and sealing—"

Yuki summoned a barrage of ice that shredded several nearby trees, coating the snow in branches and needles. The wind was picking up as she drew a handful of cards and threw them into the ground. Fountains of water appeared, and blue light emanated from her hands as she turned them into makeshift snow machines.

"I know this asshole!" she shouted, her eyes gleaming. "He can read your thoughts, be careful!"

"I'm touched that you remember me, little fox." The voice came from overhead, but when Mike looked up, all he saw was the sky. "I wasn't sure it was really you, but I knew you would recognize the quote. I see we have a new Caretaker. I take it Emily finally burned herself up?"

"Who is this?" Mike asked, looking at Yuki. She was scanning the woods, her glowing hands moving in slow circles. Large balls of snow were rolling around her, getting bigger with every second. "What does he want?"

Behind Mike, the front door of the cabin exploded off its hinges and Bigfoot stormed out. With each step, he seemed to become larger, and when he finally stood next to Mike, he was nearly twelve feet tall. Heat radiated from his body, and he bared his enormous teeth at the forest.

"*Leeds!*" Bigfoot howled in fury. "I should have known! How did you find me? I will fucking kill you for real this time!"

"Hello, old friend." This time, the voice came from its owner, a creature on the periphery of the woods with a cowl pulled over his face. "It's been far too many—"

An icicle the size of a car ripped through the air at Leeds. He stepped behind a small tree that was obliterated by the ice, only to reemerge somewhere else. He casually dusted ice off his shoulder with clawed hands.

"Well, I guess we're skipping formalities. As for killing me..." Leeds vanished again, and the woods around them came to life with the sounds of hooting and chirps. In the distance, something large let loose an ominous howl, and Leeds reappeared on the roof of the barn. From where Mike stood, he could see that Leeds had cloven hooves for feet and a forked tail that swished behind him.

"You're going to have a devil of a time," Leeds finished, his eyes blazing inside his cowl.

THE DEVIL OF THE FOREST

The Nirumbi emerged from the woods, their bows out and arrows nocked and ready. Mike walked backward toward the cabin, then jumped when the door banged open and Velvet emerged. She scowled at the Nirumbi, counting their numbers.

"There are way more than last time," she muttered.

"I see that." He raised the rifle and took a shot at Leeds. The moment he pulled the trigger, Leeds vanished as if he melted into the shadows. "You know this guy?"

"Nope. But I do know those arrows are bad news, and we're almost in range. If they can take down Uncle Foot, then we don't have a chance."

"Mike." Dana was nearby, and she raised her hands off the ground. "I'm willing to help, but I need to be let loose."

He looked at her, then at the others. Yuki's snowballs were forming on top of each other, and she was able to slow down the Nirumbi by casting defensive volleys of ice. Bigfoot crossed over to the barn and ripped the door off its hinges, using it as a shield against the few arrows that were landing nearby. Quetzalli had an intense look on her face, and her horn was glowing with energy. Dark clouds were forming overhead.

"Are you sure that's a good idea?" he asked the dead girl.

Dana bared her teeth. "I promise I won't bite. Well, anyone I know."

"Sounds good enough for me," Velvet decreed, then unfolded her sword and severed Dana's chains. Dana moved with astonishing speed, dragging her broken chains behind her in the snow. When she disappeared into the trees, there were cries of alarm from the Nirumbi.

I hope that wasn't a terrible idea, Mike thought, aiming his rifle at a Nirumbi that had broken free of the trees, sprinting toward Yuki. When he pulled the trigger, the Nirumbi spun around before collapsing into the snow. It reached a single arm to the heavens and let out a wail of agony.

Something about that anguished cry struck a chord deep inside him. When they had been ambushed, he had mostly run interference, scaring them away with his screams. While his friends did the heavy lifting, it had been easy to disconnect from the idea that they were living creatures, but now?

He shivered. It wasn't from the cold.

"Yuki! Bigfoot!" Mike raised the rifle again, watching for more movement. Pondering the ethics of the situation would have to wait for later. He pressed his back to the cabin and kept both eyes open. They couldn't get to him from behind but knew for damned sure he was vulnerable on his sides. "Tell me who we're dealing with!"

Bigfoot ignored him. He used his shield to make a dash into the nearest group of trees and then disappeared. Mike heard Bigfoot roar a few seconds later, but now he was on the other side of the clearing. The Nirumbi cried out in alarm, and he saw a few go flying through the air.

"I don't know," Yuki responded. She was holding her tarot cards as the snowballs finished assembling themselves into snowmen. As the featureless bodies hopped past her, she was jamming cards into their torsos and tossing others into the ground. Large stick arms emerged from the snowmen, and they paused only long enough to pick up the swords Yuki had summoned. "Ran across him once. Claimed to be the devil, but Emily told him he was full of shit. Did some sort of mumbo jumbo on us that got us locked in the Everglades for a week."

"How did you beat him?"

"We didn't." Yuki paused, looking away from her makeshift army. "He got bored and let us go."

"You'll find me far more entertaining today." Leeds's voice came from everywhere at once. "You have something I want, and I shall not rest until it is mine."

Velvet cocked her head, then pointed to the west. "He's over there," she said, then spun around just as a trio of Nirumbi appeared at the corner of the cabin. They raised their bows to fire, but their shots went wide when Dana tackled them from behind.

She hit them hard enough that they scattered like bowling pins. Dana let out a growl, sank her teeth into the throat of the one closest to her, and ripped. It was like watching a speed eater at a chicken-eating contest, except with far more blood and shrieking.

"Jesus Christ," Mike muttered. He could almost hear Lily chastising him for his language.

"Sword!" Dana whipped her head toward Velvet, her hand outstretched.

"What do you need it for?" asked Velvet as she tossed Dana the blade.

Dana snatched the sword out of the air and beheaded the Nirumbi she had just bitten.

"Zombie birth control." She tore into the other two before they could regain their footing and stabbed them in the heads to prevent them from turning. Dana bolted into the woods, leaving a trail of blood behind her footprints.

"I think I'm gonna be sick," Mike muttered, then placed a hand to his stomach. He was feeling woozy.

"It's us or them," Velvet told him, then ran back into the cabin. When she emerged, she was carrying her father's pistol. "We didn't start this. Remember that."

The steely glint in her eyes steadied his resolve, and he continued to watch the trees. The snowmen charged into the forest, filling the air with cries of alarm. With her army finished, Yuki returned to Mike's side and summoned tall walls of ice around them while leaving windows for him to shoot through.

Nirumbi charged at them, and he fired. Once they fell to the ground, he tried to ignore their cries while reloading, doing his best to focus on the task of protecting the others. Quetzalli summoned lightning blasts that struck her horn, allowing her to redirect them into small clusters of attackers that died on impact. The metallic smell of ozone filled the air.

"Something feels off about this," Yuki said, after almost ten minutes of killing Nirumbi. "It's clear the Nirumbi are outmatched, just like before."

"There are way more of them now," Velvet replied, then raised her gun to take down a Nirumbi that had scaled the wall. "Maybe it's a numbers game?"

"No, Yuki is right." Mike scanned the tree line. "What would be the point of sending them in just to die? Why would they do it?"

"Because they are less afraid of you than they are of me." The voice came from behind Mike, and when he spun in place, he saw Leeds standing on the roof of the cabin.

Both he and Velvet opened fire, but Leeds flickered as the bullets went through him.

"It's a projection," Yuki explained.

"What do you want?" Mike asked.

Leeds chuckled. "That's simple, dear Caretaker. I want this land."

"Why not just ask? Why not find a different way to reach out?" Mike felt his anger growing as his magic roared inside him. Tiny sparks formed on his fingertips, but he clenched his hands, willing them away. "I feel like you had options."

"Mike, don't." Yuki grabbed him by the shoulder. "Really, don't even talk to him. He's manipulative."

"Oh, I will only be honest with you, Mike Radley." Those crimson eyes glowed, as if burrowing into Mike's soul. "You see, I wanted to do this long before you took notice of this place. It would have been so easy to take this land, to become part of the great game before you even knew what was happening."

"So why didn't you?"

Leeds shook his head. Mike still couldn't see his features. "Because the spell I used to get everyone in required too much time. I couldn't accomplish it while that human was about, the father of the arachne. On more than one occasion, he disrupted my runes without even knowing it. When he died, I only had to wait for the spiders of the forest to slumber to complete my plans."

"My dad?" Velvet lowered his gun. "You were afraid of him?"

"*Afraid* is the wrong word, little spider. I respected him. He demonstrated true dedication to defending this place and an attention to detail that his progeny lack."

Yuki started to ask something, but Mike didn't hear what she said. Instead, he heard the distant hoots of the Nirumbi. They were excited again, which meant that something had changed, but what?

When he turned to look back toward the forest, he saw an immense figure moving just behind the trees. A pine was toppled as the being pushed its way into the light. Standing taller than even Bigfoot was a creature with stretched-out limbs and the head of a deer. It snatched up a Nirumbi that tried to run past and shoved the whole thing in its mouth. It chewed on its snack and let out a howl before charging at them.

Mike opened fire, but the thing kept coming. Velvet fired off a couple of rounds before Quetzalli summoned a lightning blast that knocked the creature off its feet. After only a couple of seconds, it leaped into a standing position, its whole body smoldering. Yuki summoned a wall of ice to protect them, but Mike knew it wouldn't last long when the creature dragged long fingernails against the other side and let out a howl of anger.

"Many men have met my wendigo, Mike Radley. None have lived to tell the tale." Leeds laughed, then vanished. The wendigo raised massive fists and slammed them into the ice, causing it to crack.

"Bastard distracted us." Mike chambered another round and raised the rifle. Did it have a weak spot? "What do we know about wendigo?"

"Eaters of flesh." Quetzalli snorted in disgust. "Not like Dana, not at all! They are once-men, driven by greed and power! Dark spirits walk these lands, and I will have none of it!"

Her eyes flashed a bright purple, and lightning from above blasted her horn. Instead of discharging, her whole body glowed as she stored it inside her body and repeated the process. Mike covered his ears and closed his eyes. He could feel the thunder rushing through his body, and the hair on his body stood on end as the dragon's electrical charge grew.

The wendigo shattered the ice and tried to force its way through when Quetzalli let loose a lightning blast that caught the wendigo in the chest and hurled it away from them. There was an explosion, and the air filled with the scent of blood and burned flesh.

"Gah!" Mike's ears were ringing, and he couldn't hear what Yuki was shouting. But he did see the wendigo stand up, its body smoldering. It picked up the nearby corpse of a Nirumbi and devoured it, walking toward them with purpose as it feasted with every step. A large hole had been blasted in its chest, revealing the wendigo's rib cage.

Someone yanked on Mike's arm. It was Velvet. She pointed at Quetzalli, who was lying down on the ground.

"Understood!" he said, his voice sounding muffled to his ringing ears. When he knelt to grab her, a jolt of energy ran through his body, numbing his legs. Cursing, he stumbled for a moment before scooping Quetzalli up in his arms.

The wendigo growled, then snatched up a Nirumbi that ran up and prostrated itself. After he'd consumed the little person, the wendigo's wound closed even further.

They're feeding themselves to it?! Mike stumbled into the cabin and laid Quetzalli on the ground. She was still breathing, but her horn was hot to the touch and she was out cold.

He made a quick detour to his room and dug through the potions Zel had sent with him. The healing ones had cute little handwritten labels that described their applications, but he didn't want those. Instead, he dug for the ones Zel had put warning labels on. He scooped up a bright-red one.

Dragon's Breath, the label declared. *Use with caution.*

Mike and Zel had become coated in Dragon's Breath shortly after they'd first met. He could still remember her stern warning to wash it off immediately and definitely to never scratch it or the burning would get worse.

He ran out of his room and then straight out the front door. The wendigo's legs had been frozen to the ground, and the Nirumbi were rushing within arm's reach.

"I can't stop them all," Yuki said as Velvet fired her gun at the wendigo, shattering part of an antler. "There are too many of them!"

"Where are your snowmen?" he asked.

"Fighting off the rest of the Nirumbi!" She chanced a look over her shoulder. "Mike, there are *hundreds* of them!"

His jaw dropped. Hundreds?! "Wh…why aren't they all attacking?"

She turned her attention back to the wendigo. The ice had encased its waist, but cracks had already formed. Was the wendigo getting bigger?

"They're luring the snowmen away from here. Leeds is out there too, taunting Bigfoot farther into the woods. This is intentional, he's spreading us too thin! I think he knows the Nirumbi don't pose a threat, but this…" She paused to hurl an icicle at the wendigo. It shattered on hard white flesh. "This thing is something else."

"Let's see if we can buy ourselves some breathing room." He held up the potion. "I don't think I can throw it from here without missing."

Velvet looked over at him and snatched the potion from his hand. "Seriously, Dragon's Breath?"

"Yep. Will do some damage, chase it off maybe."

"Roll to hit, add in that Dex modifier." Velvet smirked, then launched the potion. It soared through the air and shattered on the wendigo's chest, coating the creature in a thin film of red.

The wendigo immediately tried to remove the clinging slime but only succeeded in smearing it across its chest and stomach. Frustrated, it tried to wipe its hands in the snow, but whatever Zel had added to turn the fine powder into a liquid wasn't coming off.

Mike watched in satisfaction as it started scratching.

"That's right. Itches, doesn't it?" He grinned when the wendigo let out a growl, followed by a whimper. It had stopped grabbing Nirumbi and was now just scratching itself. A few Nirumbi had been exposed to the substance and were already rolling in the snow in an attempt to get it off.

"Magic itching powder?" Velvet cocked an eyebrow. "Seems a little—"

The wendigo roared, then broke free of its prison, scratching furiously at its chest. The red liquid had turned crimson, staining the wendigo's paper-white skin. It tumbled about in the snow, trying to rid itself of the Dragon's Breath.

Mike expected the wendigo to bolt. Instead, he was horrified when it crouched, dug large nails into its own flesh, and started peeling. Yuki gagged when the wendigo yanked a large strip of its own skin off and tossed it to the side, where it slapped loudly against a tree.

Yuki tried to encase it in ice once again while it proceeded to skin itself, but it was enraged now and easily broke free.

How the hell were they going to stop this thing? If they couldn't hurt it, then maybe they could trap it? But how? Yuki's ice wasn't slowing it down much, and the guns couldn't kill it. As long as the Nirumbi kept lining up to be snacks, there was no way they could continue to keep it away.

The wendigo tossed the rest of its ruined flesh to the ground and then regenerated by stuffing its face with more Nirumbi. It moved toward them, growling ominously.

"Retreat!" Yuki summoned another series of ice walls. "Into the cabin!"

Velvet went in first, followed by Mike and then Yuki. Once inside, they bolted the door shut and ran around to the nearest window. The wendigo had reached the porch, and it rammed its foot into the front door.

Mike expected it to explode, showering the room with shrapnel. Instead, the kick was little more than a muffled thud. The wendigo repeated the attack, then shifted over to a window and punched it. Instead of the glass breaking, the wendigo's knuckles split apart, revealing bone.

"That's not what I expected." Velvet put her hands against the glass. "You can't even feel the vibrations from the hit."

Mike shook his head in disbelief. "So you're telling me the exterior of the home is unbreakable?"

"Guess so." Velvet shrugged. "It's not like this has happened much. Even during the goblin attacks, their arrows would stick in the exterior. They never wielded anything bigger than a club, and dad would shoot them before they got close."

"Well okay, then." He would have to bring Ratu out here and figure out how to do something similar to the house defenses.

"We may be safe for now," Yuki said, her arms crossed. She was in the kitchen, her attention directed outward. "But we're trapped. Bigfoot and Dana are out in the forest, Abella is missing, and help isn't coming. I'm trying to bring the snowmen back, but they're outnumbered, and I don't think they'll do any good against the wendigo."

Mike groaned, then looked back outside. The Nirumbi had formed an outer perimeter, and the wendigo, whose flesh had regrown, was busy trying to rip the siding off the house. Every time those sharp claws dug into the side of the cabin, they seemed to slip right off. Would the magic that protected this place be enough? And if so, how long could they hole up here?

Up on the roof of the barn, Leeds reappeared. His laugh became a screeching sound, filling the air like thousands of angry cicadas. The Nirumbi were lighting torches, their angry little faces highlighted by the flames.

"Uh…" Velvet backed away from the windows. "I really hope this place is fireproof." She was wringing her hands , her unblinking eyes stuck on the torches that had surrounded her home.

The wendigo roared, then punched the front door again. This time, the wood groaned, and a split appeared in it.

"Yuki?" Mike's throat had gone dry. "Have any tricks up your sleeve?"

"Always." Dark lines had appeared on her face, and she was shuffling her tarot cards. "Is there a back door to this place? I'll hold them off while you run."

"You can't hold them on your own," he whispered.

"Probably not." When she looked over at him, there was a wild look in her eyes. "This is a bad situation, Mike. Very bad. That thing out there is possessed by some type of spirit that has an affinity for the ice. I can't hurt it."

His heart raced when he realized she was planning to buy them time with the cost of her own life.

"We need a plan," he replied. "A trap, maybe? What cards do you have?"

The door creaked again. The Nirumbi were chirping in delight, and Leeds was now speaking to them in a stilted language Mike didn't recognize.

"Velvet." Yuki looked at the arachne. "Drag him out of here if you have to."

"I…I…" Velvet's hands went to her throat and squeezed the dog tags she wore. She opened her mouth to say something, then paused, her eyes on the window.

Curious, Mike peered outside through the glass. The Nirumbi were still cheering, but the wendigo had gone still, its gaze toward the heavens.

With a sound like a car crash, Abella smashed into the wendigo from above. When she rose, the firelight from the torches revealed that her face was covered in purple blood. She grinned at the Nirumbi, revealing all her teeth, then looked up at Leeds. The wendigo had gone still beneath her feet.

"Rock beats slithers," she yelled. "Definitely not my first snake." With a grunt, she grabbed the wendigo by the antlers and ripped its head off.

ABELLA HAD BEEN TRAPPED BENEATH THE ICE WITH THAT GIANT SNAKE FOR over an hour as it tried to crush her in its coils.

They ended up on the murky bottom of the lake, the serpent incapable of crushing her and Abella unable to swim away. Her lucky break came when it tried to swallow her whole.

When the serpent opened its cavernous maw to devour her, she spread her

RADLEY'S APOCALYPSE FOR HORNY MONSTERS

wings and tail wide. During the struggle to swallow her, she grabbed its fangs and held on for dear life. The snake attempted to dislodge her, but once her grip was solid, she started pushing the snake's fangs apart.

The serpent tried to spit her out, but she refused to let go. After a short eternity in darkness, light appeared overhead as the snake moved into the shallows and tried bashing her into some rocks.

Undeterred, Abella continued to press, and one of the fangs shifted suddenly as it snapped at the root. She wiggled it back and forth, trying to pull it free.

Once they broke through the surface ice, the serpent let out a hiss like escaping steam, then smashed her into the shore. Abella sank her talons into the rocky ground, finding purchase on a huge boulder. The serpent cried out and coiled around her, trying to push her away from its head.

With a ripping sound, the fang came away in her hand. She flipped it over and jammed the giant tooth into the roof of the serpent's mouth. It let out a hiss of pain and then released her in a bid to get away.

Though she had an opportunity to escape, Abella wasn't about to let the serpent get away after trying to eat her. What if it came after the others? She dragged it farther onto the shore, her talons ripping holes in its iridescent scales. It tried to put up a fight, but now that she was on solid ground, it was easy enough to bludgeon it to death with her fists. Once it was dead, she noticed a beautiful gemstone embedded in its forehead. Curious, she plucked it out, spraying blood all over herself.

As she raced back, her whole body hurt. The cracks in her left wing were getting worse, and her legs felt stiff. She could hear the distant cries of the Nirumbi in the direction of the cabin and hoped she would make it in time.

The creature beating on the cabin was incapable of withstanding over a thousand pounds of angry stone coming at velocity.

Its head had come off with a satisfying rip that stunned the Nirumbi into silence.

However, the head she now held was hollow on the inside. It hadn't been obvious from the outside that it was simply the mummified head of a rather large deer. Stunned, she found herself staring down at the creature beneath her.

It growled and then tossed her away like a piece of trash.

She pulled her wings in and rolled, then smirked when several tiny arrows shattered on her hide. When the beast stood, she realized it was nothing more than a human that looked like it had been stretched out from the inside to fit on something over ten feet tall. It was emaciated and had milky white eyes that matched bloodless lips.

When it howled, she could see all its blood-stained teeth. It came at her so fast that she almost didn't react. Her instincts kicked in, and she slammed her fist into the creature's jaw so hard that there was an audible pop as the bone shattered. Dark blood spilled across her knuckles, but it kept moving.

"Wha—" Abella gasped as she was lifted into the air and tossed toward the barn. She smashed into the wall and fell down into the snow, her wings hanging limply around her. Up above, Leeds's burning-coal eyes regarded her with hatred.

"You never should have returned," he growled, then disappeared into the shadows. "Wendigo! Kill her!" Leeds reappeared in front of her and waved his hand.

Abella was yanked into the air by shadow hands and thrown toward the wendigo. The wendigo clamped powerful claws onto her legs and spun her in a circle before throwing her into a nearby tree.

"*Putain!*" she exclaimed upon impact. The trunk had snapped, and the pain in her wing was getting worse. How in the hell was this thing so strong?

The snow crunched under the wendigo's feet as it charged her. She looked up in time to get kicked through the trees. Branches snapped beneath her weight, and she crashed into a Nirumbi, killing it on impact.

"Ow." She picked herself up and dodged out of the way when the wendigo threw the tree she had felled at her.

A pair of shots rang out, and the wendigo turned its attention toward the sound in time to see Velvet leap onto its chest and shove a gun against its forehead.

Each bang was like a hammer on steel, and the wendigo went down in a heap. Velvet leaped free and rolled across the snow, landing in front of Abella.

Dumbfounded, Abella could only stare until the twang of a bowstring being plucked made her extend her wings forward to protect Velvet. A pair of arrows shattered against her wing, sending pain up into her shoulder.

"It's going to get back up," Velvet said, then turned back toward the wendigo. It was crawling toward them, both flesh and bone mending on top of its neck.

"How is it still alive?"

Before Velvet could answer, bands of darkness grabbed her around the body and hurled her away from the wendigo. Abella tried to follow, but the wendigo stood up in front of her, its skull re-formed now. Glowing blue light resided where its eyes should be as skin grew over muscle, and then its eyes reappeared.

It said something in a language she didn't recognize, then came at her. She jumped into the air and raked its face with her talons. The wendigo took the hit, grabbed her by the head with both hands, and squeezed.

The pressure was incredible. She grabbed at its hands, then its wrists. Her talons scraped off the skin on its chest as her heart thudded rapidly. Her core temperature was rising dramatically now, and her vision was going black.

"You should have stayed at the bottom of that lake." Leeds spoke to her from somewhere nearby. "I only hope you spared the offspring of the estakwv-nayv. A warrior like you would have been welcome in my new world but not if you are already harming the natives."

Abella groaned, then bit into the wendigo's palm. The flesh tasted like oversalted fish that had gone bad.

"I've worked hard to come this far," he continued. "And not only will I get what I want, but you will have lost your life for nothing! Nothing! You stupid gargoyle!"

Somewhere in the woods, Mike screamed in pain.

Abella took a deep breath through her nose, pulling in as much oxygen as she could. Her kind didn't need to breathe, not for survival. No, they had big lungs for something else entirely. All the while, she kept chewing, causing the wendigo to adjust its grip. Its blood was black, but it was also slippery.

The wendigo lost its grip and fell backward. Abella fell to the ground and saw the wendigo was now missing a hand.

Dana stood in the snow, her blade gleaming. The wendigo reached for her, but she slashed away, lacerating its other arm. Dark shadows wrapped around her waist and pulled her into the darkness.

"Your friends are fighting for you," Leeds told her as she rose. "And they will die for you as well."

"Do you ever wonder why humans cut off our heads and make us gargle rainwater?" Abella rose to her full height and took another deep breath. She didn't bother looking for Leeds, the Nirumbi, or anyone else. All her attention was on the wendigo as it came for her again, a skeletal hand emerging from its amputated limb.

Time distorted and slowed as she took one more breath. On the day she had hatched, she had been the smallest of her clutch. It had been suggested to her mother that she would be too weak to survive, too small to contribute meaningfully. But in those first moments of existing, she had let out a cry louder than any of her siblings, a cry that had commanded attention.

The name Abella meant "breath." Although she wasn't the strongest or the biggest of her clutch, it was neither of these things that mankind feared the most from her people.

Mike was hurt. Whether physically or emotionally, it didn't matter. Her friends had fought for her, even though she was stronger and immune to the arrows of the Nirumbi. Her rage ignited within, flooding her whole body with an immense heat that caused her stone skin to glow an eerie red.

When her own kind had turned their backs on her, she had lost her direction; there was no longer any purpose. Protecting the house had been her primary function, but she had come to know those who lived inside. Ever since Mike had moved in, she had also come to know them all better than ever. Her roof, once a lonely place, was shared with Kisa and occasionally Lily. The fairies would tease her until she gave chase, and there had even been a couple of nights where she had sat with Cecilia, the two of them watching romance shows on her tablet.

No, they weren't just her family. They were her clan. She would fight for them and they for her. And there was no doubt in her mind that they would die for her if needed.

She couldn't let that happen. Her heart pounded, each beat like thunder in her ears. Opening her mouth as wide as possible, Abella used the pressurized air in her lungs to expel the flames that had formed inside, releasing her heart fire in a high-pressure stream.

The icy-blue flame turned the wendigo's hand into ash on impact, and she quickly lost control of her heart fire as she always did. She had to kneel and sink her hands and talons into the ground beneath the snow to keep from blowing herself head over heels as she filled the air with a fire so hot that nearby trees ignited. The wendigo didn't even have time to turn and flee as its skin, then muscle flaked away into nothingness.

Leeds had been so determined to isolate her that she knew everyone was far enough away that they could run if necessary. The woods around her were filled with smoke and steam, and she could no longer see the cabin. Large swaths of snow contained Nirumbi that had been killed so quickly that they looked like smoldering statues.

Once ignited, her heart fire was difficult to stop. The air in her lungs was superheated, unable to simply cool on its own. The wendigo was a melted lump of flesh and stone now, so she turned her head toward the sky and bellowed fire into the night, chasing away the shadows. Several minutes passed before she could swallow it away, and her body cooled. She stood now in a patch of scorched earth, surrounded by slushy banks of snow. Her head pounded from the internal pressure of her breath attack, and she slumped down.

Groaning in pain, she turned to check on the wendigo. Small tendrils of flesh looked like they were trying to form into a network of veins, but one swat of her tail knocked it over, and it ceased to move. A dark mist formed above the corpse, then dissipated into the night.

The forest was burning all around her. She picked up the wendigo and tossed its body into the nearby flames before limping toward the cabin.

"ABELLA!" MIKE CRIED OUT AS HE RAN BACK OUTSIDE. THE WENDIGO HAD JUST knocked her away, so he opened fire on it, hoping to pull its attention back. His body flooded with a chill, and he threw himself to the ground as a spear shot through the air.

Right. The Nirumbi were still a threat. He tried to reload the rifle, but his fingers were wet from the snow. His vision filled with red fur as Yuki leaped in front of him and sent a swirling mass of snow toward their attackers.

"Get up!" she cried, then hurled even more ice outward.

"We have to help Abella," he commanded, then got to his feet. He turned toward the wendigo and saw that Velvet was already over there, attacking it with a gun.

"Go back inside!" Yuki yelled at him, but he didn't listen. He started running toward Abella but slid to a stop when he saw Velvet get tossed away. She crashed through the woods and disappeared.

"Shit." He could hear the Nirumbi hooting where Velvet had gone. Indecision flooded him, and when Abella collided with the wendigo, he realized there was very little he could do to help her. It was a clash between titans, and his one trick would disable her.

But Velvet could help, and right now, he could help her. He sprinted through the woods, dodging errant arrows as he went. Behind him, Yuki yelled his name as she followed, but all he could think about was Velvet. Was she hurt? Had the Nirumbi gotten her? His heartbeat roared in his ears as he leaped through the trees and landed in a small clearing, his rifle pointed toward the sky.

The Nirumbi were in a circle around Velvet, their spears held ready. The ground was littered with their bodies, and Velvet stood in the middle, her upper body covered in spiky brown armor. She turned her head at his arrival, and he slid to a stop, stunned by the sight.

Velvet pinwheeled through them, dodging blows and impaling them on the thick spikes protruding from her body. She moved like the wind, kicking out with her legs and smashing the Nirumbi through the trees.

A small cluster of Nirumbi readied their arrows. Mike charged them, using the rifle as a club. They were so intent on Velvet that they didn't see him coming.

The stock cracked when he slammed it into the head of the first Nirumbi. The creature's eyes went wide before it fell to the ground. Its compatriots dropped their bows and drew knives, and Mike held up what was left of his rifle.

There was a flash of metal, and now Dana was there. She growled, a feral sound that made him back away. She carved her way through the Nirumbi, taking hits from them that she didn't seem to notice.

"Abella needs help," he told her. "Back, by the cabin!"

Dana said nothing, just looked at him with red-rimmed eyes, then sprinted back the way he'd come, passing Yuki in the process. The kitsune threw a tarot card in the air that summoned a handful of razor-sharp blades that tore through the remaining Nirumbi.

"I'm almost out of cards," she yelled, then sent out a blast of frost that knocked nearby Nirumbi away. "We need to get back to the cabin!"

"We need to get to Abella!" He looked over at Velvet, who was in the middle of breaking a Nirumbi's spine.

His mind blanked from the carnage. Though his home had survived many attacks, it had never been this brutal or visceral. He could see the panic in the eyes of the Nirumbi as they were killed, watched them stare in disbelief and wonder as their brethren died. This was death, up close and personal. The last time he had seen such a thing was…

"Mike!" His mother reached toward him, the flames igniting her skin.

"Mike!" Yuki tackled him, an arrow whizzing through the air where he had stood. Velvet dodged a few arrows of her own, then used a couple of nearby Nirumbi as shields. "We need to go, they have reinforcements!"

"I…" He looked at his feet and saw the blank stare of a Nirumbi, its eyes focused on eternity. The flames were real again, his mother's screams for help filling his ears.

He stumbled around, suddenly lost. There was too much movement, and the forest was filled with noises that overwhelmed him. He fell, then got back up and staggered backward when he saw that he had blood on his hands.

"Move!" Yuki grabbed him and pulled. He blindly followed, his gaze sweeping across the woods. Velvet was behind them now, blocking the rear with one of the swords Yuki had summoned.

Disoriented, he stumbled over a log and fell to the ground. Yuki turned around to help him up, and between her splayed tails, he saw a Nirumbi step through the brush and aim its bow at her back.

The moment the bow twanged, he yanked Yuki toward himself and spun around. His gut was flooded with ice water, but he held strong as the arrow struck him in the back. He cried out in agony, and the world fell out from beneath him.

Yuki and Velvet both screamed his name, but everything was going dim. He felt hot, as if he was being cooked from the inside. Gasping through the pain, he pressed his face into the snow and let out a sigh that became a rattle.

VELVET SAW MIKE FALL TO THE GROUND, THE ARROW PROTRUDING FROM HIS back. Both her hearts stopped, the wind suddenly knocked from her body. Despite growing up in these woods, she suddenly felt lost and was unsure of how to proceed.

Yuki let out a shriek of rage, and her auburn hair developed several thick white streaks as the snow exploded all around them. Velvet became lost in the snow flurries, and she stumbled forward until she found Mike lying on the ground. His skin was pale, and he was barely breathing.

"Get him to the cabin!" Yuki screamed. Velvet couldn't see the kitsune but did catch a glimpse of something with bright white fur as it passed her by. "Give him the potions he brought!"

Velvet knelt and shed her armor. She was much faster without it, and time was of the essence. Scooping Mike up in her arms, she picked a direction and ran.

"Uncle Foot!" she cried out. "Please, I need you!"

She hadn't seen him since he'd stormed off after the Nirumbi. Where could he be? As she moved through the forest, she caught sight of the blazing light of a fire and headed toward it. She really hoped it wasn't the cabin.

"Just gotta..." Mike's hand reached away from her. "Need...pull me out...hot."

"It's not hot. Now be quiet," she whispered. If her uncle wasn't within earshot, she didn't want anyone else knowing their position.

"The fire is too hot!" he screamed, his eyes opening briefly. Around her, the forest came alive with hooting. At first, she thought they were coming for her, but was relieved when Dana stepped through the forest. She was covered in blood, and her left arm was broken in at least two places. There was a wild look in her eyes and a complete lack of recognition.

"Um...you good?" Velvet asked.

Dana scowled, her brow furrowing. After a couple of unintelligible grunts, she nodded.

"He's hurt," Velvet began. "We need to..."

"Leave me *alone*!" Mike's scream was magnified by his magic, and Velvet almost dropped him. "Let me out of the car, the fire is so hot! My world is burning! Oh God, my whole world is burning!"

Velvet headed toward the fire with Dana right behind her. Mike's shrieks were unintelligible again, and his breathing was unsteady. When they emerged from the woods, there was a clear line to the cabin.

The two of them ran and were over halfway there when Leeds landed in front of them.

Dana charged first, but Leeds grabbed her head with his forked tail and twisted her around. She slammed into the ground, her head now crooked on top of her neck. She let out an angry grunt, then fell silent.

"Leave us alone," Velvet whispered as she set Mike down.

"No." Leeds waved his hand, and bands of darkness grabbed Velvet by the legs, pulling them apart so that she fell to the ground. The sudden impact hurt her abdomen and made her painfully aware of the precious cargo developing within. Her eggs shifted, making her queasy.

"After I rip your legs off, I'm going to sit here and wait for your dear uncle to come back and find you." Leeds chuckled, then pointed at Mike. "And when this one dies, it all becomes mine."

"Why are you doing this?" she asked, then screamed when the bands pulled on her legs.

Leeds turned away from her. "It doesn't matter. You are already dead."

A bundle of white fur exploded from the trees and charged toward them. Shadow hands lifted free of the snow and reached for Yuki, but she slipped between their fingers and expanded upon impact with Leeds. The fur on her body was as white as the snow. Fox fire drifted free from her tails as she shoved her hands into Leeds's cowl and shrieked with rage.

Dozens of icicles manifested and pierced his body. Leeds let out a cry of pain, and then the shadows ripped Yuki off him and slammed her into the ground. Held in place by the icy spears, Leeds frantically tried to free himself by smacking his hands against them.

Velvet heard the heavy crunching of a pair of massive feet. Bigfoot stormed out of the forest, toppling a pair of small trees. His features twisted in rage as he smashed a fist into Leeds. The icicles shattered, and Leeds sailed through the air like crumpled paper.

"Why?" Bigfoot demanded, tears in his eyes. "Why have you brought this hell to my doorstep?"

Leeds groaned, then pulled himself up. His cowl had fallen free, revealing ram horns atop a horse's head. He blinked, his crimson eyes wincing in pain.

"Hello, old friend." Leeds struggled to stand. "I thought you were far away from here."

"Bah. Chasing one of your stupid doppelgängers when I ran into the Katshituashku. Really, Leeds? Turning the creatures of the land against me?" Bigfoot stomped closer. "I had to kill it, Leeds! To kill such a rare and beautiful thing! But you knew I would, didn't you? Because that's what you do. You force people to make choices that break them!"

Leeds chuckled. "The creatures of this continent are no friends of yours. You turned your back on the wilds, Sasquatch, and now the wilds have turned their back on you."

Bigfoot stomped toward Leeds. Once he was close enough, he lifted a massive foot in the air over Leeds.

"You will betray them," he stated. "Just as you betrayed me."

Leeds laughed, then winced. Bigfoot brought his foot down, and Leeds exploded into black smoke that drifted away into the air.

"Is he dead?" asked Velvet.

"No. But he is hurt very badly." He knelt and picked up Dana, who snarled at him. "I'll get her. You get Mike inside. I can come back for Yuki."

"I've got her." Abella limped from the darkness, her tail dragging behind her in the snow.

Velvet picked up Mike and rushed him toward the cabin. The Nirumbi had gone silent, and she assumed it was because they had seen their leader get dusted.

Once inside the cabin, she laid Mike down on his belly. The arrow sticking out of his back had gone through pretty far, and she suspected it may have hit a lung by the strange wheezing sound he made.

Bigfoot stepped into the cabin and roughly shoved Dana inside the closet. He held the door shut and shook his head at Velvet. "The poison they use will kill him. I'm sorry, fluffy girl."

She shook her head in denial, then knelt by Mike and lovingly stroked the hair away from his face. Black lines had formed along his veins and were getting wider.

"I'm sorry, I'm so sorry." Tears spilled freely, and she covered her eyes. The door opened again, and Abella came inside with Yuki. The kitsune stumbled over to Mike's bedroom and disappeared inside just long enough to come back out with a handful of potions.

"It isn't going to work," Bigfoot warned. When he saw the look Abella gave him, he shrugged. "I don't want you to get your hopes up. If it almost killed me, it will definitely kill a man."

"He isn't most men," declared Yuki. She grabbed the arrow and pulled it free, causing Mike to groan in agony. "And he isn't dead yet."

Bigfoot nodded. "He should be dead already. Perhaps there is hope after all."

Emery descended from the rafters, clutching his hands nervously. "What can I do?" he squeaked.

"Bandages. Any first aid supplies. Bring them to me right away." Yuki's eyelids fluttered, and her fur shimmered brightly and then faded back to its brown color. "And some coffee. Or tea. Anything caffeinated. I'm exhausted."

Emery flew away.

Velvet knelt by Mike's side and took his hand in hers.

"Please be okay," she whispered. A reassuring hand squeezed her shoulder. Assuming it was her uncle, she reached up to squeeze it back and was surprised to discover it was made of stone.

THE FLAMES OF HIS MOTHER'S STATION WAGON CURLED AROUND MIKE'S LEGS like slippery ropes, threatening to pull him farther into the blazing wreck. He could hear her screams of agony behind him like a record stuck on repeat. When Mike tried to close his eyes, he discovered that he couldn't—the flames had melted them away.

"I told you, Mike Radley!" The shadow sat in the back seat of the car, buckled in place so that he was hanging upside down. "Your world will burn!"

Mike cried out for help, but none came. Every time he tried to crawl out the window of the car, he was dragged back in again. Each attempt seemed to pull him closer to his mother, who was now trying to grab his ankles.

The inside of the car was distorted and huge, and the passenger window was nearly ten feet away. Was he shrinking? Or maybe just burning up?

It hurt to crawl. His shoulder was numb with pain, and he could no longer move his arm. Black lines ran up and down his skin, lines that smoldered with the flames.

"Hold him down!" someone yelled, and then he felt phantom hands on his body.

"Please!" he shrieked. "Somebody, anybody!"

"I can help," the shadow whispered. "But it will cost you!"

The flames were climbing Mike's legs now, threatening to consume him. When he reached for the window again, the world outside was dimmed by a large figure who blotted out the sun.

"Help me!" He crawled forward, his legs now numb as well. Was he dying, or had he found his own personal hell?

"How is he this strong?" someone wondered, and then he felt pressure on his shoulders, as if someone was holding him in place.

"Can anybody hear me?" He rolled on his back and tried to kick his mother's hands away.

"Mike Radley, of course we can hear you." Death now sat in the back seat next to the shadow. He was holding his cup of tea upside down to keep it from spilling. "You are making quite the commotion."

"I don't want to die!" He kicked at his mother again. "I'm not ready yet!"

"I'm afraid nobody is ever ready." Death sipped his upside-down tea. "Dying is quite like reading a book and having it close itself unexpectedly. Absolutely no one enjoys that."

Gasping for air, Mike sobbed as the flames crawled past his waist. His scars burned, the wounds suddenly fresh in his memory.

Powerful hands gripped him by the wrists, and he looked up to see Tink. She smirked at him, then looked over her shoulder.

"Tink has good grip! Pull!"

They slid across the car, the metal warping to extend the cab. His mother's arms stretched as well, but they eventually became too thin like putty and melted, leaving a trail behind him. Tink gritted her teeth as they were dragged into the sunlight. Once Mike's hands passed outside the car, he felt the body of the vehicle shrink around him.

"Pull!" someone yelled. More hands grabbed his, and the air was filled with the sound of wrenching metal after he was squeezed free of the wreckage. He looked back over his shoulder to see that the car was collapsing on itself until it resembled a bit of flaming tin foil no larger than a soda can.

"Well, that was close." Lily stepped forward and booted the foil off the sandy beach of the Dreamscape and into the ocean.

"You really shouldn't litter." Sofia scowled at the succubus.

Mike groaned, then rolled onto his side and puked. Instead of food, it was technicolor sand that stained the ground.

"Nasty." Tink forced him to sit. "Husband in bad shape, have big fever."

"Fever?" He looked around. "Why am I here?"

"You're dying." The voice was stern but sounded like several melodies blended together. With Tink's help, Mike sat up to look at the speaker.

"Hello, Titania." He did his best to greet her, but his head drooped at the last second.

"Hmmph." Titania, the Fairy Queen, crossed all four of her arms and frowned. "I truly didn't expect our agreement to be so short-lived, Caretaker."

Due to the soul-swapping nature of his magic during sex, his Dreamscape was occupied by many of the women he lived with. Whenever he slept, they were there for him in whatever way he desired.

Titania was the exception. Indivisible by nature, the queen of the fae had avoided swapping souls with him after their interlude. As she was allowed to use his mind as a private sanctuary, her presence meant she had come on purpose.

"Why are you here?" he asked. His vision dimmed, but Tink held him up. "Did you come to save me?"

"Hardly." She shook her head. "I am here on unrelated business. I've been waiting for you to fall asleep, but apparently, you are slipping in and out of consciousness as you die."

Again with the dying. His memories were fragmented, and all he could remember was snow and smoke. "What happened?"

"You tell me." She gestured over his shoulder.

When he turned to look, he saw that the island of his mind had shrunk down to roughly the size of a football field. The ocean had gone black, and the skies were gray. A replica of his house was in the middle of the island, but it was a miniature version, no taller than five feet. Rushing around the island were blurred figures that vaguely resembled the women of the house. These grim specters were using shovels to maintain the borders of the island, scooping sand into the waves. It was nonsensical, but so was the Dreamscape.

"I'm dying." He suddenly felt cold inside.

"All things die, Caretaker." She squatted down next to him, then grabbed his chin and inspected his face. "Hmm."

"Can you help me?"

"No. To interfere with mortal affairs would put me at odds with those who wish to usurp me." She sighed, then sat next to him. "However, your resident souls have contributed immensely to your survival. It seems that they are holding you together, metaphorically and literally."

Mike held up his hands. The dark lines were all along his skin, shifting back and forth like snakes. "I was poisoned. By an arrow. There are these little people called the Nirumbi. They attacked me."

Titania nodded. "Nirumbi poison is always fatal to humans within minutes at most, yet I suspect you have lasted far longer."

"But how?" He felt a small hand grab his own, and he looked over at Tink. The goblin grinned, showing all her teeth.

Goblins are immune to poison. In the Dreamscape, Mike could vividly hear Velvet's voice. Was that something he had gotten from Tink? It was an ability he never would have discovered otherwise.

"Not completely immune though." He looked at his fingers and then shook his hands. Some of the lines fell off like wet ink. "And not dead yet."

Titania held out her hand. "It would seem not. Come. Let's assess the damage."

He took her hand, marveling at how soft it felt. They walked the perimeter of the land, and he saw that most of the foliage had died.

"If I survive, this will all come back, yes?"

Titania nodded. "This place is as resilient as the human spirit. But you stand on death's door, Caretaker, and I fear that is not the worst news I have for you."

"What could be worse than dying?"

"I am here with grim tidings. Days in your world are only mere seconds of my own; otherwise, I would have been here sooner. Sulyvahn has sent word that your house is missing."

Mike paused, contemplating a stationary wave in the ocean. It looked as if it had been poorly painted in place. "Can you run that by me again?" he asked.

"Your house is missing. Its counterpart from the Underworld has taken its place. Sulyvahn's message implied that some sort of assault took place. I have been unable to contact Cecilia, who has vanished with the house."

"Someone stole…my whole house." He groaned. What was he even supposed to do with that information? Who could it have been? What was the name of the guy who controlled the Nirumbi? Leeds? Had Leeds done it? Who was Leeds, anyway? Was he a member of the society? "So what do you suggest I do?"

"Live." She turned to him, her golden eyes blazing. "Otherwise, I will be very upset with you."

"You…wouldn't be able to track me down in the afterlife, would you?"

"Is that something you really want to find out?" Titania chuckled. "Due to your current condition, your control on this place is minimal. I have interceded on your behalf. Moments in your world shall be minutes or even hours here. Your body is weak, but your spirit is strong. You may yet survive, but it will take everything in your power to do so."

Mike nodded, then looked back out at the ocean. Part of the sky had crumbled away, revealing a blank void behind it. There was simply nothing for his eyes to focus on.

"We are trapped in Oregon," he told her. "By someone named Leeds. He put together an army of Nirumbi and a…" He could picture the white monstrosity in his front yard, but the word wouldn't come. "A windy something. It kept eating the Nirumbi."

"A wendigo." Titania pursed her lips. "They are not known for following orders. And the Nirumbi were destroyed, but apparently, my information is bad."

"So no idea who Leeds is?"

"Without meeting him? No. But I have a suspicion that he is none other than the Devil of Jersey. By himself, he is dangerous. But leading an army? That sounds very unlike him."

"He wears a hood. Has hooves for feet."

"Then it must be him." Titania paused, her gaze on the water.

There was a large mass moving toward the beach that broke apart as it came close. It fractured into lumps, the shapes bobbing in the water until the waves carried them up onto the sand. Though covered in seaweed, it was easy to recognize the distorted features of the Nirumbi.

"Oh God." Mike fell to his knees, his hands pressed into the sand. "Why are they here?"

"It's called regret, Caretaker. Oftentimes, we find ourselves doing unpleasant things in the name of progress. Our actions can and do leave stains that cannot be scrubbed away."

It was suddenly hard to breathe. Mike choked, his hands clutching his throat. Not only had he killed some of them, but he had watched so many come to a brutal end that it was all he could picture.

The skies darkened, and the beach was now littered with their corpses, their eyes staring at him in blank accusation. The ocean hungrily gobbled up the sand, and he suddenly felt light-headed.

"Stop." Titania pulled him to his feet and embraced him. His face was forced between her breasts as she clutched him tight. "Now is not the time."

"But I just watched them die!" He thought back to arriving in Oregon, how he had practically skipped through the woods with Quetzalli as the others had fought them. What had he been thinking? "There had to be a better way! Maybe we could have reasoned with them, or something!"

"Altruism is considered a highly noble trait, and you wear it adorably. I believe your mortal saying is something about hindsight being perfect. The truth of the matter is that altruism can go fuck itself."

Mike twisted his face up toward the queen, suddenly wondering if she was actually Lily in disguise.

"There's this idea that it's possible to rise above your basic instincts, to pursue a greater good. The belief that everyone should have an equal chance is a wonderful one, but consider this. You should never assume that anyone is capable of meeting you halfway on anything. I know little of the Nirumbi today, but the Nirumbi of the past were a ruthless people. They hungered for the flesh of the living and never would have considered a compromise for it."

"But they aren't animals," Mike began.

"Please. You humans are still animals. Would you elevate the Nirumbi above your own kind?" She laughed. "I realize I speak so casually. Your life-times are like days to me. Up until recently, I found myself fairly uninterested in the inner workings of the mortal realm. And yes, while you may have done a fair amount of work to change my opinion, I still had to be willing to listen to reason."

He thought back to the battle he'd had with Titania inside his own head. It had taken quite some time to convince her to stand down and talk, and it had only worked because he was effectively immortal in his own Dreamscape.

"Would you allow them to come inside your head, one at a time?" Titania put her foot on one of the Nirumbi. "Bring them to your home? See if they are willing to chat?"

"I don't know," he admitted. "I don't know enough about them to judge."

"And what little you do know is this: if you die, it was their fault."

He shook his head. "Not really. Maybe Leeds tricked them, or——"

"No. Stop making excuses for others." Titania kicked the Nirumbi, and it shattered like glass. Motes of darkness rose into the air. "This place stinks of grief. If you were to die now, you would undoubtedly become a troubled spirit, much like that shadow of yours. Is that what you want?"

The idea that he could become a tormented soul chilled him to the core. Would he wander and slowly lose his sanity? What if Cecilia couldn't help him cross over? He might come back and make trouble for the others.

"No." He sat on the edge of the beach, pulled his knees up to his chin, and hugged them. "I don't want that at all."

"Then get your shit together." She picked up one of the Nirumbi and shook it at him. Its body flopped like a rag doll in her hands. "This thing chose to attack you. When you make the effort to take someone's life and then lose your own, that's on you, not them."

"But——"

"No!" Titania hurled the Nirumbi out into the dark waters of the ocean. It bounced off the water and came to rest beneath a wave. The wave came to life and grew several teeth before slamming down on the corpse. It made a loud sucking sound, the water swirling open to reveal a mouth that snapped shut on the Nirumbi.

"What the fuck was that?" Mike asked. Was that one of his nightmares? He turned back to Titania to see that her golden eyes had gone wide.

"I honestly don't know," she whispered. "That is no being you or I should encounter. I can only pray that it's a result of the poison, but you should definitely avoid it at all costs. But on this note, I must take my leave. On the chance you die, I do not wish to be inside your mind as it becomes swallowed by eternity."

"Titania, I...I don't want to be alone." He looked down at his feet. "Can you stay?"

The fairy queen smirked, then let out a laugh.

"Absolutely not," she told him. She knelt in front of him and leaned forward to place a kiss on his forehead, suffusing his body with warmth. "But, for the record, you should know I actually considered it. Make sure you stay alive in here until they can fix you out there."

There was a light pop, followed by the tinkling of bells. Ribbons of light hung in the air, shimmering like glitter as they fell into the sand.

The hungry waves moved closer to the shore, and Mike scooted away from them. There was a flurry of activity as the others, his soulmates, brought sand from inside the house and placed it on the shoreline. Though they were blurry and lacked defining details, he could tell them apart by shape alone. The little green smudge was Tink. The largest one was Sofia. Somehow, one of the blurs moved with an attitude problem. This was clearly Lily.

What did he look like to them? Was he a stationary mass? Did they wonder why he wasn't helping? He didn't have the first idea of what to do, and his legs felt weak beneath him.

Despite being surrounded by the others, he felt alone. Up above, a star emerged from the darkness and fell, crashing into the water and shattering like glass. The dark lines on his body were receding, but he estimated that the waves would claim the little island long before his skin was clear.

He buried his face in his knees. His friends were working hard to save him, but he felt like he couldn't even save himself. The bodies of the Nirumbi dotted the beach, and he couldn't help but feel like there was a better way.

"Penny for your thoughts?"

He flinched, then turned his head to see that Velvet sat next to him.

She reached out, took his hand, and gave it a squeeze.

"You're in here too."

She nodded. "Just woke up, actually. I've never been to the beach before. I've always wanted to go."

"Yeah, well..." He pointed to the mess on the sand. "It's usually even prettier."

"I bet." She squeezed herself in next to him and put her head on his shoulder. He put his arm around her and pulled her close. Somehow, she seemed to fit perfectly against him.

"Still waiting on those thoughts," she said.

"You never gave me a penny."

She laughed. "I don't even own a purse. Not sure where I could dig up a penny."

"I'm sorry for all this," he told her. He didn't know what else to say.

"Yeah, well, I'm not." She snuggled up against him. "This is the closest thing I've ever had to a date."

He snorted. "You set a very low bar. This place is just a mass grave that hasn't been covered yet."

"Then let's change that." She stood and pulled him with her. "This is your head, isn't it? Why look at such terrible things when you don't have to?"

"Because sometimes you need to face awful truths." He set his jaw. "It's all I can think about."

"My father used to feel the same way. He saw some things in Vietnam. Had terrible nightmares until he met my mother. It was her venom that brought them together. Isn't that strange? When she bit him, it helped him forget, move forward a bit. But it all came back after she died." Velvet leaned in close. Her hair smelled of hot springs and the forest. "But I don't think it was just her bite that helped him, not after a while."

"What do you mean?" he asked, curious.

"She gave him something to focus on. Raising us, protecting her. Fighting with Uncle Foot. There were plenty of happy times, but I know he always kept one foot in the past, no matter what. My whole life, I used to catch him talking to somebody who wasn't there. His brother died over there. So did the rest of his squad, for that matter. For the longest time, I thought maybe my dead uncle was an actual ghost. Dad always knew where I was hiding when we played hide-and-seek, and I can climb on the ceiling. When I got older, I started to think that maybe his mind had split and that something else had activated, like a sixth sense or something."

"So which was it?" he asked.

Velvet put her forehead against his. "It didn't matter. Either way, he was haunted just the same. I would never wish that on you. My father had to kill the enemy for survival, and it wasn't any different for you. You can mourn them. You can even respect them. But don't you dare place the burden of their choices on your own shoulders."

He had no argument. When he turned his head to look along the sand, he noticed that the beach was no longer receding. A bunch of the Nirumbi were now gone. A small pocket of warmth had found its way inside his chest, and he clung to it like a child with a night-light.

"Come on," she said, then took him by the hand. "I've always wanted to walk in the surf."

"I wouldn't," he said as she dragged him toward the water's edge. "It's dangerous, and—"

The dark waters sparkled with light and came to life as she walked through them. Laughing, she let out a cry of delight as the surf curled around her ankles and sprayed them with foam.

Stunned, he watched her as she ran away from a wave and then chased it back out to sea. The doom and gloom of the island avoided her like the plague.

Letting out a yell, Velvet picked up a turquoise crab.

"This one tried to pinch me!" She dropped it on the sand and chased the crab in circles, laughing as the frightened crustacean scurried away into the water. As she continued her dance, he realized that a beam of golden light surrounded her, sending the darkness away. He craved that light and everything it meant to him.

His arms felt wet. When he held them up, he saw that the dark lines had become even shorter now and vanished around his elbows. There were no more Nirumbi on the beach.

With a laugh of his own, he joined her. The two of them played together in the surf as a patch of darkness peeled away up above, revealing a blue sky behind it.

It was almost two in the morning when Eulalie felt movement in her web, and her eyes popped open.

She was hovering in a woven web over Murray's breakfast nook. Down below, a pair of rats were watching the monitors with strict instructions to wake her if they saw anything. Whoever had disturbed her web had somehow snuck past the rats monitoring the exterior of their current base.

"Sofia." Eulalie's voice was little more than a whisper, but the cyclops, who had stayed up to watch the house, heard her. Sofia leaned around the corner of the kitchen, concern on her face.

"Front door." Eulalie closed her eyes to concentrate on the near-invisible threads she had attached to the doors. "Someone is coming."

Sofia nodded and then disappeared. Eulalie frowned, wondering who it could be. Sulyvahn was busy watching Mike's house, so he wouldn't be of any immediate help.

There was a loud yell, followed by a flash of light. The rats below her took up weapons and created a protective ring beneath her as the sound of roaring fire filled the front entryway. Eulalie almost panicked but managed to keep her cool long enough to wait it out.

A minute later, Sofia appeared. Her sword was in her hand. "Got him," she said. "He's taking a nap right now, but he was expecting trouble. Tried to use this on me when he saw my sword."

Eulalie's eyes widened in surprise when Sofia tossed a magic wand onto her table. It rolled to a stop against a recharging drone.

"That thing real?" she asked.

Sofia held out a portion of her robes with a hole burned clean through it.

"Let's get him upstairs," Eulalie said. "See if he can answer some questions." Obviously this intruder had realized someone here was watching the house. The fact that he had a magic wand made it even more disturbing. Was he part of the society she had heard about? What was he up to?

"Okay, but…" Sofia frowned. "Is that a good idea?"

"Why wouldn't it be? As long as we take precautions, he should be rendered harmless. And if he's traveling with friends, we need to know. Maybe prep an escape route."

"It's not that, it's…" Sofia groaned. "I'll just be direct. He's a man. What if you see him and want to mate with him? Is that something you can even control?"

Eulalie snorted. "Even if I wasn't molting, which is super uncomfortable, by the way, the answer is no. I've just never had any interest in mating. Not even when I met Mike, who is definitely the hottest guy I've ever seen. I suspect that may be due to his magic."

"That's…unexpected." Sofia looked puzzled. "I thought all arachne had a high drive to eat and reproduce."

Eulalie shrugged. "You have to remember that my mother deliberately waited to have defective eggs. For the longest time, I assumed that just meant a lower than normal prey drive, but there's room for interpretation. I thought maybe it was something that wouldn't happen until I met the right person, but I've never actually had any of those thoughts. I've been curious about it, but it's been more like a spectator sport. No desire to participate. But my mom and sister? All the time. The only reason Velvet ever uses the computer is to watch porn and look up new modules for Dungeons and Dragons." She almost mentioned her own fascination with rope binding but figured it was something Sofia didn't need to know. The thought of tying someone up excited her, but sex itself? Meh.

"I literally have no words. But if you say it's fine, I believe you."

Sofia folded up her sword and left. She reappeared with a man slung over her shoulders. When she headed for the stairs, Eulalie followed. She cocked her head to get a better look at his face as it dangled over Sofia's back. His face was pockmarked with scars, and his wrinkled forehead and gray hair gave away his advanced age.

When they got him into Murray's bedroom, it was an easy feat to strip him to his boxers and tie him to the bed. Eulalie secured a pillowcase over his head and then unscrewed the only bulb in the room. The last thing she needed was for him to scream in terror upon seeing her.

Once they were finished, Eulalie attached her silken line to the man's toes, and then they headed back downstairs. She nestled back into her little hammock, making sure she was connected to their new guest.

Sofia just shook her head in amazement as she dug through the man's white coat. It was like watching a cartoon as the cyclops kept pulling objects from his pockets that were far too large to fit.

"Wake me if anything else comes up," Eulalie said with a yawn.

Sofia nodded in the affirmative as she tossed the coat into a nearby closet with the rest of the man's clothes.

Steepling her fingers together, Eulalie used a leg to swing her hammock, her mind racing as her body relaxed. This was a new development, a thread that demanded to be pulled. What secrets would she unravel when their new guest awoke? One way or another, she would get some answers.

If not, maybe she would eat him. Smirking at the silly thought, she drifted off to sleep but not before she noticed that some of the rats were using the butts of their spears to keep rocking her.

ON THE EDGE

When Beth opened her eyes, the first thing she saw was Lily sitting at the foot of Mike's bed. The succubus was staring at the opening to the bathroom. Lily was also unnaturally still, which was unnerving.

"Shit, what time is it?" Beth reached for her cell phone. When she turned it on, it revealed she had thirty-eight hours remaining until the angel came back with the other horsemen. "I didn't mean to sleep so long."

"You didn't mean to pass out is far more accurate." Lily leaned back and looked over her shoulder. "But I don't blame you, being a new mom and all."

"New mom?" Beth closed her eyes, the events of the previous night rushing through her head. Lily was obviously referring to the living ooze in Mike's bathtub. Shortly after greeting her clone, Beth had gotten light-headed and asked for some water. The details were fuzzy after that. "Did you carry me to bed?"

"I did. That thing out there sealed your wound, but you had already lost way too much blood to be considered healthy."

"I see." She tried to sit up, the effort making her head pound. "What did I miss?"

"Death and your demon semen had a little chat. Very adorable, by the way. She speaks using ooze noises, bubbles, and snot sounds. Apparently, Death understands her." Lily sat forward, her eyes still on the bathroom. "As far as answers, we don't have many. Your spawn—"

"Can we please call her something else?" She didn't like the constant reminder of her ordeal with Oliver. "Something nicer, maybe?"

"Princess Jellyfish in there doesn't know a whole lot about herself. She has some of your memories, but they're fragmented. Told Death all about your best friend in middle school and a bunch of stuff from your parents' house. Her first real memories seem to be waking up in the tub and seeing you leaning over her."

Beth felt her breath hitch in her throat. "So she's a copy of me?"

"No. Even she admits that much. Apparently, the logical part of you she inherited is smart enough to realize she isn't you. That, and she's made out of primordial ooze."

"So nobody knows what she is?"

"Gee, if only I could go to the Library and look it up." Lily rolled her eyes dramatically. "But no. She's an anomaly, which is saying something coming from me. I've seen a bunch of weird shit in my time with Amir and the society. The stuff in that vial was essentially pure, concentrated essence of demon."

"Demon?" Beth's mouth was suddenly dry.

"Sort of. That windmill motherfucker who showed up and I are both made of the same material. Hard to believe, right?" Lily put her hands under her breasts and jiggled them. "Not only are these tits perfect, but they're nigh indestructible."

Beth pointed at Lily's wounded arm. "I beg to differ."

"Ah. Let's clarify." Lily held up her damaged arm, still sealed beneath Eulalie's webs. "That magic goop of yours is kind of like human stem cells. It can be made into pretty much anything that can potentially exist. I'm a succubus, a lesser demon. I have to follow certain rules. Despite the fact that I am made of the same substance as the Annoyer of Worlds, I have a certain vulnerability to divinity. He outranks me in the hierarchy; ergo, he can hurt me."

"So you're only injured…because your cells are programmed that way?"

"Bingo. So when I say he can vaporize my ass into nothingness, I mean it." She shook her head. "Now, if I was Oliver, it would be a different story. He was a high-ranking angel back before the Fall. If not for being weakened and trapped inside of mirror land, I suspect he could have bitch-slapped Mecha-Hymen out there all the way back to Daddy's love hut in the sky. Would be quite the spectacle."

Beth giggled. "You're better at nicknames than Tink is."

"Oh, please, that girl is a fucking artist." Lily tapped her horns. "We only get to hear the scrambled shit that comes out of her mouth. After things go back to normal, I might hang around in her head and see if she can teach me a thing or two."

"You can't be serious."

Lily shrugged. "I've discovered that I'm more open to improvement these days. Anyway, back to Oliver. Your loogie love child—"

"No."

"Booger-skinned baby?"

"No."

"Goo girl?"

Beth sighed and waved her hand. She had a feeling Lily could do this all day if she chose. "Whatever. Please continue."

"Even though she's made of raw material, Oliver was the origin. I worry that somehow this is one of his tricks, and I have no way to tell." Lily crossed her arms. "Death seems to think she's great, but I can't exactly throw in with someone who tried to talk us out of the Apocalypse by discussing his tactics for finding Waldo. We also clearly have an internal affairs issue, and it's *so* convenient that she appeared when she did."

"Internal affairs?"

"Damn, apparently, some of your brain cells died off too." Lily moved toward Beth, her eyes still on the bathroom. "Remember that whole 'Tink is under a magic spell and something broke out of the Vault' thing we just went through? Something is loose in the house, and I have no idea what."

Beth had actually forgotten about that part. Nearly dying must have had that effect on her. "Where are the others?"

"Kisa is watching Tink. Ticktock is hiding under the bed as a backpack. Cecilia is watching the front yard with Death; apparently, they're becoming quite chummy. As for His Highness, I haven't seen him. Or Jenny for that matter." She paused for a second, as if lost in thought. "Or any of the fairies."

"Shit." Beth moved to get out of bed and groaned, barely managing to sit upright. Her joints hurt, but her head was a mess. It was as though a massive hangover had activated once she moved. "Aspirin first, Reggie and Jenny next."

"I'll get it." Lily walked into the bathroom, and Beth heard some cabinets bang. When Lily returned, she was holding pills in one hand and a cup of water in the other. "Your new friend would like to speak to you."

"She would?"

"I assume so. She's been a pool of motionless slime for a couple of hours now, so the fact that she's up must mean she heard you."

"Great." Disgruntled, Beth took the aspirin and swallowed them with the water. What the hell was she supposed to say to a slime version of herself?

When she walked into the bathroom, her clone was waiting. She felt a little relieved to see that the slime had changed her features slightly. She still had Beth's face, but the slime's hair now dangled in thick, fat drops that indeed made Beth think of a jellyfish.

"Hey. Lily said you wanted to talk to me?"

"Yes." The ooze moved her hands with purpose, but the words were tough to decipher. Beth didn't know how much of this was an inability to remember the right signs and how much was that pieces of the ooze fell off if she moved too quickly. "We need to prep for mediation."

"Mediation? Oh, right. With the horsemen."

The slime nodded. "This is weird for you, but it's also weird for me. I keep thinking I should be you and that you've somehow stolen my life from me."

Beth nodded. It made sense. If she had woken up in the bathtub as a sentient ooze, she would have assumed the same thing. "Is there anything I can do for you?"

The slime shook her head, casting sticky blue droplets onto the cold tile. "No. The horsemen are coming back soon, and you need to have an answer for them."

"I get that, but I have other problems to deal with as well. Someone put Tink under a spell and opened the Vault."

"I see. That sounds familiar, but my memory is blurry." Slime-Beth slumped over, and Beth half expected her to collapse back into the tub. "I'm afraid I can't help with any of that. I haven't figured out how to make legs yet."

"You're stuck in there?"

"Not unless you bring a really big bucket." A thin smile appeared on Slime-Beth's face. "I'm still new at this."

"Welcome to the story of my life here. Or our life—however you want to phrase it."

"I was going to suggest we put our heads together to figure out how to handle the horsemen. It's stressing me out so much that I've got a case of the ripples." As if to illustrate her point, ripples spread throughout Slime-Beth's body.

That is really convenient, Beth thought as she looked at the floor, pretending to consider her clone's idea. Was Slime-Beth part of some insidious plot? To what end? For all she knew, the slime had been sentient since Oliver had been filtered out of her soul.

And why was there so much of it? Did it replicate over time? There were too many questions, and the only person who might have answers was in a magical Labyrinth back on Earth. Or under it. Beth really had no idea how any of that worked.

"You think we should divide the work?"

Slime-Beth nodded. "The angel is highly likely to consider whatever the other horsemen bring to the table. We need to find a way to counter that isn't obvious."

"Agreed." If the slime was part of the plot, she wasn't really telling Beth anything she didn't already know. "I'll come up with some ideas and we can talk later?"

Slime-Beth nodded. "You know where to find me. Can I have a pen and paper?"

"You've got it." Beth walked out of the room and saw Lily waiting on the bed.

"And?" Lily asked.

"Apparently, she's going to brainstorm ideas to outwit the horsemen while we try to figure out what's up with the Vault."

"That's really—"

Beth put her hand over Lily's mouth. "Nice of her. C'mon, I need to get her something to write with." She didn't need the succubus voicing any more suspicions out loud and tipping off her slimy double.

Lily licked Beth's palm, then smirked when Beth yanked her hand away. "Lead the way."

Beth went to her room to retrieve a pen and paper. She also managed to find a couple of pencils, figuring that the pen might quit working if it got slimed. She gave everything to Slime-Beth, who thanked her and started making notes to herself.

Once out in the hallway, Lily closed the door.

"We assume she's just gonna stay in the tub and not go down the drain or anything." The succubus lifted an eyebrow. "What do you think?"

"I think I hate this. Hold on." She opened the front door and walked outside. Death and Cecilia were sitting on the porch swing, deep in conversation.

"Ahem." Beth cleared her throat to get their attention, then turned toward Cecilia. "A word, if I may?"

Cecilia nodded and floated from her seated position through the chains of the swing. "Do you need something?" she asked.

"I do. Can you be invisible for a bit and keep an eye on our bathtub buddy? I just want to make sure nothing happens to her." It wasn't that she distrusted Cecilia, but what if the ooze could read her mind? Or maybe she would be able to see the banshee and the two of them would hit it off?

"I can." Cecilia waved to Death, who waved back, then went inside. Beth followed her in, then watched Cecilia ascend the stairs, slowly vanishing with every step.

"Let's check on Kisa and Tink." Beth led the way to Kisa's bedroom on the second floor. The room itself was sparse of decoration. One of the walls was mirrored, with a ballet barre, and the floor consisted of polished hardwood. Kisa had a bed, a wardrobe, and a record player, and that was it.

Lying on Kisa's bed was Tink. At the foot of the bed was a large lump that opened brilliant emerald eyes. They reflected the dim light that came in from the nearby window, and Kisa's tail twitched nervously behind her. If Beth hadn't been looking specifically for her, she doubted she would have seen her there.

"How is she?" asked Beth.

"Still out." When Kisa sat up, it almost looked like a magic trick. She could become very small when she wanted. "She keeps grinning in her sleep, so I guess that's a good sign."

"That's my doing." Lily crossed the room and sat down on the edge of the bed. "Her dreams were a solid jumble. A bunch of dark corridors and angry voices. Shit ton of goblins. They sound like they're speaking German."

"Could you go in there and ask what she saw?"

Lily frowned. "I can try. Being in there isn't like other heads I've been in. It's both very abstract and intensely detailed, and she's…distracted. "

Tink giggled, then let out a gasp. She clutched the blankets tight against her body and groaned.

"Tink best wife," she muttered in her sleep, then sighed contentedly.

"Well, no time like the present." Lily sat next to Tink. "Maybe her postnut clarity will give me some answers. Take Kisa, see if she can help you sniff out your pet rat."

"I don't track by smell." Kisa slid out of bed and stretched. Her mouth opened wide, revealing all her teeth. "Also, I have to tell you something. I haven't been feeling the best since last night. My whole body aches like I have the flu."

"You're sick?"

"I think I had a fever for a bit but not anymore. Felt like the flu. Seems to be fading, but…" She yawned again. "I think Tink had something similar. May have just been a bug, or whatever. She kept wincing like she was in pain. Just thought you should know. Anyway, let's go."

The two of them did a quick search of the second floor. All the rooms the rats used were either empty or had a few of them about. Beth questioned them about Reggie's whereabouts, but none of them gave any indication that they understood what she was asking.

The study with large viewing windows that usually looked over an unexplored mountain range now looked directly into the insulated walls of the house. It was most likely another world like the greenhouse, but there hadn't been a safe way to explore it. Now it just looked like the symptoms of a mad architect.

The first floor was empty as well. The office and the parlor were empty, and both were so cold that Beth shivered. This led to her and Kisa stopping in Beth's room so that she could put on a sweater.

The other rooms on the third floor were also empty. The observatory no longer looked on eerie star fields but misty skies.

She and Kisa wandered out into the hallway. Beth leaned against the railing, her eyes on the first floor. From here, she could see part of the living room and the front door. Maybe even the door of the office if she leaned forward far enough.

"Where could they be?" asked Beth. She really hoped nothing had happened to Reggie or Jenny. It was starting to feel like everything going on was part of some overarching plot, but she also wondered how much of that was just her imagination.

"I'm out of ideas," Kisa admitted. "I can't think of anywhere else to look for them. They didn't go into the Vault, did they?"

Beth shivered. "If so, then they're stuck there until someone who actually knows how to use magic can go back in." She wondered if the grimoire would have a spell for locating someone.

"Beth?" Kisa was looking up at the ceiling.

When Beth looked up, she saw the small string dangling from the cord that released the spring-activated door to the attic. She had noticed it a handful of times but had never once considered what might be up there.

"Worth a look," she said. "But let me get reinforcements."

By reinforcements, she meant Ticktock. When she walked into Mike's room, she could hear sloshing sounds from the tub. Once at the bed, she lay on her belly and slid underneath to grab the mimic and pull him out. Hopefully she wouldn't need his assistance, but he also had the grimoire.

Back in the hall, she put her hands together over her knee to give Kisa a boost. The cat girl was very light and easily leaped into the air to grab the dangling cord. The door creaked and tilted, allowing a wooden ladder to slide free. Both Beth and Kisa jumped out of the way as it smacked into the floor, chipping the wood.

"Tink's gonna be pissed," Beth muttered.

"Then don't be around when she sees it." Kisa stared up into the darkness of the attic. "Guess you want me to go first?"

"Semi-invisible, phenomenal eyesight…I could go first, but if there are any surprises, I may fall on you."

"And squish me with your big ass…" Kisa immediately covered her mouth with both hands, her ears curling down. "Oh God, I'm sorry. That's how Tink has started referring to you."

"As big ass?" Beth frowned. She didn't think her ass was that big.

"Don't think of it as an insult. It isn't about weight. To her, everyone has a bigger ass. And it really is a step up from horny lawyer. You don't really practice law anymore, and…you know what? I'll just pop up and look around." Kisa went around Beth and scrambled up the ladder. She disappeared into the darkness without a sound.

A few moments later, Kisa reappeared and held a finger to her lips, then waved Beth up.

Strange. Beth climbed the ladder.

The attic was very dark, but there was a soft glow emanating from a corner of it. Kisa took Beth's hands and led her in a circuitous route around large objects Beth couldn't quite make out. She debated using the light on her phone, but the batteries were already running low.

As her vision acclimated, she realized the light seemed to be seeping in from below the edges of the walls. Kisa crouched in front of her and moved her fingers along the wall. Every few moments, she thought she heard a voice. It might have been Reggie's, but it was too faint for her to be sure.

"I don't see a door," Beth whispered. The two of them searched, though Beth wasn't very helpful. There was enough light to make out very large objects, but that was it.

The wooden slats of the wall were relatively smooth. She ran her hands along it carefully, worried about getting a nasty splinter. What was even up here? Dark shadows loomed over her, and they were all covered in protective blankets.

Nearly on the opposite side of the light source, she found an odd seam in the wood and felt around it. It was a square shape not much bigger than a dog door. When she pressed on the middle, she heard a soft click.

The wall sprang open, and she found herself looking into a dark tunnel. A similar light illuminated the opposite end.

"Good job," whispered Kisa, which nearly made Beth scream in fright. "I'll go first."

Kisa fit easily down the tunnel, but Beth did not. Her hips smacked against the edges of the tunnel, and she had to crawl on her belly to get through. She tried to get on her hands and knees, but it made her butt bump against the ceiling.

Big ass indeed. She scowled and continued forward. Her knees ached from contact on the hard floor, and she banged her knee more than once. The tunnel took a ninety-degree turn, and she found herself staring into what looked like a child's playroom.

This is how I die, she thought as she moved into the space.

Kisa was crouched nearby, and she was holding a finger to her lips again.

It was cold, and the dust made her want to sneeze. The walls had been decorated with stick figure drawings that she almost immediately recognized as people who lived in the house. Boxes had been stacked to make a maze, and Kisa led her through it. She heard someone speaking and immediately recognized Reggie's voice.

"I don't think that's how it's supposed to work," he said. There was a clacking sound, followed by something hitting the wall. "That isn't very ladylike."

What the fuck? Beth moved behind Kisa, who was peering around the corner. The room they were in was tall enough to stand in, but something about the attic had Beth fully paranoid about discovery.

A small tea table and chairs had been set up. Reggie sat across from Jenny. In the other seats were the dolls that had once filled the house. Beth remembered there had been plenty of them and had wondered where they'd all gone. It was eerie seeing them sitting there, almost as if the room was a small gladiator arena.

Along the opposite wall, Reggie's king's guard of rats had spread out. Half of them were napping, while the others watched. On the table, a board game had been set up. The room was lit with an electric lantern that hovered in the air over the table.

"Reggie?" Beth stood and moved around the corner. When the rat king turned to look at her, she noticed one of the pieces on the game board move while he wasn't looking. It was an old chess set, and the pieces looked like they were made of marble.

"Ah, Lady Beth, hello." He turned back around and gestured at the table. "We are just having a friendly game of chess." His nose and whiskers twitched, and he reached out and pushed the piece that had moved, a rook, back to where it had been.

The rook wiggled and then shot from the table. It bounced off a stuffed bear, which clapped its hands excitedly.

"Doesn't look friendly." Beth crouched next to them. Jenny was sitting on the other side of the table, her doll unmoving. "How are you supposed to win if she just removes the pieces?"

"Neither of us is playing to win." He let out a long sigh. "Jenny brought me up here when she discovered how down I was. Thought it might do me some good to get away for a bit. This room is where she used to hide back before she was welcome downstairs, so there are many toys and games to play with."

"It looks like a child lived here." As a rule, children's rooms hidden in attics were generally bad news, Beth thought. Especially in scary movies.

"Indeed." Reggie moved a pawn forward, putting Jenny's queen in jeopardy. Apparently, Jenny didn't like that move, because his pawn slid the rest of the way across the table and then fired through the air and bounced off the wall. "Jenny was once a child's toy, you know. She doesn't talk about it, and I know better than to ask."

"Your people should be safe," Beth told him. "We found out that the house has been locked away from the real world. It's what was happening when Murray was yelling out front."

Reggie watched as Jenny's knight moved five squares forward to take his bishop. He picked up the bishop and the knight and put them back where they had started, then turned back to Beth. "Do you really believe my people are safe?"

"I have every reason to think so."

Reggie let out a sigh that sounded more like a squeak. "This is good news indeed."

"There's more though." Beth filled him in on everything else that had happened. While he listened intently, he paused every few seconds to look at the board and undo Jenny's attempts to cheat. Once Beth was finished, he contemplated her for several moments.

"These are dangerous times," he said, then turned back toward Jenny. He tipped over his king and held out a paw toward the doll. "I yield. You have won this day."

Quitter. Jenny's voice was a whisper yet came from everywhere at once. The lantern flickered above them as if it would go out.

"Yes, I am. But I fear that the others need us. We all have a part to play in restoring the house to its former glory." He adjusted his glasses and hopped down from his seat.

The lantern dropped out of the air, but Beth grabbed it before it could hit the table. Jenny hopped down from her seat and held her arms up, waiting to be picked up.

"I've got you." Beth picked the doll up and cradled her in one arm. "Do you have any idea how worried I was? I thought something bad had happened to you." As she turned, she saw a stack of board games against the wall. Most of them were very old, and she couldn't help but notice that one of them was a burned copy of Clue. "Jenny, didn't we throw that away? You know that's a banned game."

"Sometimes we must be reminded of our past failures. Jenny kept it as a memento. Besides, there aren't enough pieces left to play a proper game." Reggie walked over to the box and placed a paw on it. "And to think I was so close to figuring out who the killer was."

"Your Majesty, might I remind you that we do not speak of the Clue incident?"

The walls around them groaned, and then Jenny's voice chuckled from the dark corners of the room.

I would have won, she added.

"You were cheating. That's not how we play family game night." Beth carried Jenny out of the room and was followed by Reggie and his rat guard. She started closing the secret door when Kisa bolted out, startling her. It was uncanny how she could forget that the cat girl was even there. Was it a similar spell to the geas? "Also, I think you should know that something escaped from the Vault."

What? The temperature dropped dramatically, and the dimly lit furniture in the room shook.

Beth gave Jenny and Reggie an abbreviated version of events as they exited the attic. Once on the floor, she set Jenny down next to Reggie and had Kisa help her push the attic door back up. Cecilia poked her head through the wall to check on them, gave Beth a thumbs-up, then went back to her surveillance.

The group headed to Kisa's bedroom, where Lily sat over Tink. Her face was flushed, and she kept licking her lips. She opened her eyes when they came in, and a bead of sweat rolled down her forehead.

"Everything okay?" Beth asked.

"Yeah." Lily removed her hands from Tink's head. "Just trying to mind meld with a brain-damaged genius who is currently dreaming about being gangbanged by Romeo."

"There's only one of him," Kisa said from behind Beth.

"Not in her mind. She's got an entire reverse harem in there. For example, she has one that lives in the bath and is made of water, one that's a ghost who sits on the porch…" Lily smirked. "I may have gotten distracted getting to know the one with wings and a tail."

"But what about the Vault?" Beth set Jenny down on the record player.

"Hmm." The succubus shook her head. "When Tink realized the house had been transported, she ran to check on the Vault. You know how all those portals closed? She was worried the Vault wouldn't be there anymore, which meant it was no longer properly sealed."

"I guess that makes sense. What happened?"

"She saw that it had been opened but was taken out before she could see anything else. The sleeping spell that put her down wasn't a minor enchantment by any means. We're talking Rip-van-Winkle-caliber shit. She's out at least a few more days. We'll have to figure out how to keep her hydrated."

"Fuck." Beth walked over to the window and looked outside. The mist shifted ominously around the perimeter of the home. She half expected dark shapes to flit around in it. "So it means someone else was in the house."

"And likely still is. There really isn't anywhere to go." Lily crossed her arms. "But let's address the real issue. Whoever did this was allowed in the house. Romeo hasn't invited anybody new in quite some time, other than Eulalie. And she was in the Library when it vanished."

The implications made Beth sick to her stomach. Whoever was causing trouble inside the house had been there for some time. She didn't think it was her doppelgänger upstairs; Slime-Beth couldn't even get out of her tub yet. That meant whoever was doing this was someone that had been in the house all this time.

"Ah, looks like my point is finally sinking in." Lily crossed her legs and leaned back on Tink's bed. "Whoever did this to Tink and opened the Vault…"

"Is still here with us," Beth finished. She looked around at the others. There wasn't a single reason she could think of for anybody in the room to betray them. Jenny was probably the only one who could have gotten away with doing something right under their noses. But despite the Clue incident, Beth trusted the little doll.

Was it Kisa? She could be essentially invisible. But why? It occurred to her that everybody was a potential suspect. Was that part of the intent? To tear them apart while they dealt with the horsemen?

"How do we figure out who did it?" she asked, then met Lily's gaze.

There was a loud splat from the hallway, like mud being dropped from a great distance. Puzzled, Beth walked out of Kisa's room, followed closely by Lily. At the end of the hallway, a large green mass had accumulated at the edge of the stairs and was moving their way.

"Is that…who I think it is?" Lily looked at Beth with concern on her face. Her question was answered when the slime pushed upward and formed into a naked torso. Slime-Beth's features were fixed in exaggerated horror as she pointed up the stairs with both hands.

"What's wrong?" Beth asked, but the slime continued to point.

"Let me check." Lily moved down the hall and had ascended a few of the stairs when her clicking heels came to a stop. "Motherfucker!" she swore.

Beth raced down the hall, nearly slipping in her doppelgänger. Lily moved her tail over to let Beth through, but she never finished climbing the stairs.

Hovering horizontally in the hallway was Cecilia. The banshee's hair floated around her as if she was sinking in a pool of invisible water, her hands crossed over her chest. Her eyes were closed, and her lips were pulled into a grimace.

"Cecilia?" Beth moved to the banshee's side and tried to touch her, but her hands passed through. "Cecilia!"

"She's...sleeping." Lily was by her side, her palm hovering over the banshee. "Dreaming, even. But how? Banshees don't sleep!"

"I just saw her not that long ago, right before we came to check on you and Tink." Her heart was pounding so loud that she could hear it. That meant that Cecilia had been attacked while she was in the room with everyone else. The only people not present were her doppelgänger and Death. Did this mean that the slime was the culprit?

But then why had Slime-Beth gone to the trouble to let them know? Was this a trick? She looked down the hallway at the other doors. They were all closed. If it wasn't the slime girl, then was the culprit still up here with them?

Lily was already moving down the hall. She opened up the bedroom doors and took a peek inside, then moved to the observatory. Beth held her breath, fearing the succubus would simply disappear. After a few minutes, Lily came back out, shaking her head.

"No sign of anyone." Her shoulders slumped. "This is almost as bad as the Clue incident."

Beth sighed. Things were bad all right, and the last thing she wanted was to be reminded of the Clue incident. "Let's figure out how to bring her with us. Maybe Jenny can do it? I want everyone gathered up somewhere downstairs where we can keep an eye on each other. Nobody goes anywhere alone starting now. Agreed?"

For just a moment, Lily looked like she was going to say something snarky. However, she glanced over at Cecilia and just nodded . "Agreed."

ABELLA STOOD ON THE ROOF OF THE BARN, HER WINGS SPREAD WIDE AS THE morning sun provided her with much-needed energy. The previous night's fight had been exhausting on its own, and her use of the heart fire had drained her reserves.

The large shadow she cast stretched behind her and touched the edge of the cabin. From where she stood, she could hear the quiet voices within. The night had been touch and go as Yuki fought to keep Mike alive using the potions Zel had sent with him.

Throughout the night, Abella had felt an odd tingling in her chest. It had come and gone, but now that the sun was up, it seemed to be gone for good. Though it had bothered her, the spiral fractures in her left wing concerned her even more.

She could heal from a wound over time, but if her wing shattered, there was no way to fix it. Though it was rarely spoken about, it wasn't uncommon for her kind to throw themselves from buildings if they broke a wing. Losing the sky was considered a fate far worse than death.

As she looked over at the cabin, she could think of something far worse than even that. The realization that she could have lost Mike had cemented a new reality for her. She would likely live for centuries, or even thousands of years. Her kind didn't age past maturity. The stone of her body would weather like any stone, and her time at the house protected her from the elements.

One day, she would be forced to live without him. It was a scary idea, a thought so powerful that it made the world tilt beneath her feet.

Mike moaned, and Yuki whispered words of comfort. The kitsune hadn't left his side, and Abella could hear the exhaustion in her voice. They were all battered and bruised, and if Leeds somehow returned in the near future, they wouldn't have the strength to hold him off.

Velvet bustled around the house, bringing food to Bigfoot and Yuki. The arachne kept humming little melodies to herself as she moved through the cabin, the hairs on her legs brushing against one another on occasion. It wasn't lost on Abella that Velvet had tried to rescue her from the wendigo. Had the arachne done it for her sake or Mike's?

It also wasn't lost on her that Mike had gotten hurt trying to save Yuki. She wanted to be angry at him for it, but how could she? It was no different from what she would have done for him. It gave her plenty to think about as she passed the hours up on the roof.

Her reverie was interrupted by the creaking of wood, and she turned around to see a large hand appear on the edge of the roof. Bigfoot pulled himself up without a sound and crouched in her shadow.

"I didn't hear you coming." She narrowed her eyes at him. If not for the roof, he could have gotten right behind her.

"It's my specialty." He grimaced and turned his body so he could lie down. "I couldn't stand to be inside any longer. The others think I'm out on patrol again, but it isn't necessary."

She noticed now that he was lying on the portion of the roof facing away from the cabin. "Why the deception?"

Bigfoot frowned, then sat forward. "Leeds may be a coward, but he's smart. We hurt him badly last night, and he'll need time to recover. The wendigo may come back someday, but it'll be a while. You killed its host, and it can't just possess the first poor bastard it comes upon. There are rules." He lifted a twelve-pack of beer. "You want one?"

"No, thank you."

"Good. More for me." These beers were in cans, and he didn't bother with the tab. He jammed his thumb into the lip and poked a hole for him to drink from.

"You seem to think you know Leeds pretty well."

Bigfoot sighed, then sucked down the contents of the can in just a few seconds. He smashed it into a thin disk and set it down on the roof, then opened another. "I do. Wish I didn't."

Abella waited for him to continue. Bigfoot slammed two more beers and then finally slowed his pace on the fourth.

"He and I were friends," he finally told her, his glistening eyes on the forest. "At least, I thought we were."

"How could you be friends with someone like that?"

He grimaced. "When we first met, we fought something fierce. I thought something evil had invaded the forests; that was kind of my thing for a few centuries. I had a much larger range then and heard rumors of some bat-winged bastard causing trouble for the new locals. Didn't care much for them, but the tribes in the area were seeing it too."

"So what happened?" she asked.

"Loneliness. Over the decades, my forests were chopped down, my tribes decimated. The white men were hungry to shoot anything they didn't understand with those guns of theirs. I once watched them shoot a herd of buffalo in cold blood, then leave the remains behind." He shuddered, then sucked down another can. "I actually came across him one night by accident. Little bastard was sittin' in the forest trying to read a book. If you can believe it, he was fuckin' crying to himself. I had already had a bad day and thought it was odd to see the Devil of Jersey himself all vulnerable, so I made one of the biggest mistakes in my life.

"I talked to him. Turned out he and I had quite a bit in common. Our beginnings couldn't have been any more different, but we shared that thread of loneliness. My kind had been disappearing over the years, and it was nice to speak with someone that was like me. Just another cryptid."

"I understand the loneliness all too well." She dipped her head in reverence. "Do not fault yourself for giving in."

"Well, I do. You see, we became thick as thieves for a while. Leeds has never had a family, not one that loved him anyway. His body was traded to a dark entity, a demon, and he is forced to live out his days in that taxidermic shitfest he calls a body. It's also why you can't kill him—his body is made mostly of shadows and magic. You can hurt him, you can make him go away, but he cannot be put in the ground."

Abella thought immediately of Lily. "Does that mean the demon is still around somewhere?"

Bigfoot nodded. "Somewhere out there is a demon wearing Leeds's skin suit and probably being a ripe cunt about it too. We spent over a century trying to find any clues that would help him. Thought maybe if we caught the demon, we could force them to change back. Never made any headway. Think it fucked Leeds up pretty bad, to be honest. His family didn't want him, nobody wants him. He can read minds, too. Knows what people think of him. Drives him absolutely nuts."

"So if you are friends, then why is he here trying to kill us?"

The Sasquatch sighed. "Honestly, I don't know. He's always had these ambitions that never really pan out, but I think that maybe he's here for revenge. You see, when we parted ways, it was under pretty severe terms. Late eighteen hundreds, the two of us got into it over humans. He had started killing them for sport, and I didn't take kindly to this. For one, it brought the men in white coats. Never been much of a fan. But two…he wasn't targeting humans that mattered. He was going after women and children, former slaves, people nobody would miss. His intent sounded noble, but his reality was as monstrous as he is."

"I understand this. My kind, we were often faced with fighting to survive or fleeing for our lives. It was not an easy choice to make."

Bigfoot rubbed his nose, then drew a finger across his eye. Dark stains had formed on his fur in the corners of his face. "We are peaceful. Or we used to be. Back before this land was colonized, I used to run wild with the deer, or wrestle bears for fun. The tribes, I looked out for those who revered me and avoided those who despised me. I was a danger to nobody, happy to be left on my own.

"But now? I can't even go anywhere without being afraid of being spotted.

I didn't used to care, but those assholes always find out, and they always come for me."

"The Order?"

"Do you know why they're called that?" Bigfoot shifted so he could see her better. "Because they want to help, to keep the peace. They are doing what I have been doing for centuries, only I got forced into early retirement. Chupacabra tried to wander up here one time, and I chased that little shit back down to the Southern border. It was never personal; it was about maintaining a balance. But that was before the balance included humans!"

He picked up a can and crushed it in his massive hands. It exploded, showering him with beer. "Now they show up with their wands and their swords! And they boss everyone around under the guise of maintaining peace between humans and cryptids? Well, what about me? What about my peace? Forced to live out here in hiding, just because people want to take selfies with me? And don't get me wrong, I loved living here, but my nieces? There's an entire world out there for them, but nobody is ever going to offer it to them!"

Abella winced. Bigfoot's voice was now loud enough that it hurt her ears. Down below, she saw Velvet open the door of the cabin and look around.

"Everything okay? Is Uncle Foot up there with you?" she asked.

"Shit, fuck…" Bigfoot lay flat on his back and slid farther down the roof. His left arm snagged on a shingle, causing one arm to hang comically above his body.

Abella looked down at Velvet. "How is Mike feeling?" she asked.

"Still the same. Yuki thinks he's turned a corner, but…" Velvet shrugged, seemingly unaware that Abella had changed the subject. "I wish I knew if he was going to be okay."

"And Dana?"

"Still have her locked in the closet. We think we have a way to fix her, but we need Mike to wake up first."

"I see." Abella turned her eyes back to the forest. "Then I shall continue to keep watch."

"Sounds good." Velvet turned to go inside, then paused in the door. "Don't let him drink that whole twelve-pack. It gives him the farts, and he can't sleep outside tonight." She went inside and closed the door.

"Damn it, fuzzy girl." Bigfoot rubbed at his eyes. "Knows me too well."

"You don't seem like the type to get weepy after just a few beers," Abella pointed out.

He chuckled, then sat up. "I have a stash out in the woods. I may have hit it a little hard this morning before coming up here. Probably should quit. I'm struggling with this whole thing, just so you know. Not just Leeds. The girls. I know at least one of them is leaving here. I can feel it in my bones."

Abella's lips pursed together. She didn't really want to discuss the arachne coming home with them. "Why does it upset you so if they leave?"

"It goes back to being lonely. In the last few decades, I've been happier than I can remember. I had a best friend, two of them, in fact. Ana and I were pretty close but nowhere near as close as I was with Darren. Thought of him like a brother. Gah! I see so much of him in my little fluffy girl that it hurts." He placed a hand against his chest and winced. "What we had out here now decays like a fallen tree. I can still see the shape of it everywhere I look, but it's fading into the forest and will eventually be gone. Majesty can be found even in the ends of things, but then Leeds shows up and spoils what's left of it, that rotten bastard! Puts my girl in danger, pisses all over my memories here!"

When Bigfoot went to grab another beer, Abella crossed the roof and slapped it out of his hand. Using her tail, she knocked the rest of the twelve-pack off the roof.

"I think you've had enough," she said.

"Has anyone ever told you that you shouldn't piss off Bigfoot?" he asked, his voice suddenly dangerous.

"Your fur looks tough. Is it fireproof?" She bared her teeth at him, then wrinkled her nose. "You stink."

"Yeah, I suppose I do." He sighed. "I guess you're right. I should probably go soak in the river, sober up a bit. It won't do us any good if I spend all day getting drunk. You all need me. My girls need me. I have better things to do than feel sorry for myself."

Abella had said none of these things but nodded in agreement.

"You're a good listener." He slid toward the edge of the roof and then turned to look at her. "Thanks for—"

Suddenly off-balance, he tipped over the edge and landed hard on the ground below. A couple seconds after landing, he let out a long fart that reached Abella's nostrils, making her flinch in disgust. Her eyes twitched as she held her breath and leaned over the edge to check on him.

"You okay?" she asked.

Down below, Bigfoot was sprawled on the hard ground, his brown eyes focused on the sky. With one hand, he toyed with the hair on his chin, wrapping it around his finger into a tight curl.

"Yeah. I've had worse." With a groan, he stood and walked toward the nearest tree. "Thanks again," he told her, then stepped behind it and vanished.

Shaking her head in disbelief, she took her post on the edge of the barn once more. The sun was out, and it was a beautiful day. She would do her best to soak it all in because even though Bigfoot thought they were safe for now, she had a sneaking suspicion that the worst was yet to come.

As the sun climbed higher, she decided to go do some reconnaissance. She jumped from the roof of the barn hard enough that the roof creaked in dismay. The cabin became a tiny dot below her as she ascended in a spiral. She could see where her heart fire had scorched thick lines through the forest. Bigfoot had dug a mass grave for the Nirumbi about a quarter of a mile from the cabin. It was meant to be a temporary measure, but Abella worried they would start to rot once the sun came up.

She thought back to when she had lost her brother to the arachne. It had been during one of the outbreaks of the plague. The sight of bodies on the street had become an everyday occurrence, and nobody had wanted to get too close to them for fear of catching the plague and joining the ranks of the dead. The difference between a plague-riddled corpse and one drained of its fluids wasn't readily visible, and the arachne had just been tossing their finished meals into the gutters where they were eventually found and collected.

They had preyed on the poor. If a starving family of five went missing overnight, nobody thought twice about it. All these details had come to light once the clan started their investigation, but there was little to be done.

Abella stayed higher than normal, half expecting to be snagged out of the sky by those shadowy tendrils. If she was going to get yanked down again, she wanted plenty of room to try to maneuver a safe landing. Her wing ached something fierce, and she had no doubt she might shatter it.

Her patrol revealed very little. The Nirumbi's tracks disappeared into rocky formations that likely led to tunnels. There were other tracks she didn't recognize, but none of them were remotely close to the cabin. Were there other creatures that weren't willing to participate in the fight?

Of Leeds, there was no trace. She wondered if he hid underground with the Nirumbi or if he used his magic to hide in plain sight. Each shadow was a potential threat, and it made her jumpy.

She reached the edge of the barrier and was disgruntled to discover that it was still in place. It wasn't worth investigating further; she would leave that to Yuki. On her way back to the cabin, the sun was already beginning its descent. Would the Nirumbi return with nightfall? Or had they bought themselves some time?

She landed next to the barn instead of on it, then folded her wings around her body and walked toward the cabin. It sounded like Bigfoot was inside; she could hear him talking to Quetzalli. There was a constant rattling sound, which she guessed was Dana.

She was almost at the door when she heard a different sound coming from the barn. It was that of someone crying.

Curious, she walked over to the barn, her tail dragging behind her in the snow. The heat of the day had thinned the snow out, and the bloody spots in the yard were now a pale pink as a result. When she walked inside the barn, she saw Velvet standing over by her father's jeep, her face in her hands.

Abella hesitated. Did she really feel like playing amateur counselor with Velvet? At best, they were temporary allies, and she knew she wouldn't feel like sharing her own problems with the arachne.

"Abella?" Velvet turned around, her cheeks stained with tears. "I heard you coming. You have no idea how glad I am to see you!"

"Hmm." That wasn't the reaction she had expected!

"I need your help." Velvet wiped her tears away, then turned back to the car. "Something happened while you were gone."

"Mike?" A feeling of dread settled in her gut.

"No, not that. But…almost as bad." Her shoulders tightened up, and Abella realized Velvet was holding her sword. "I need your help with something."

Wary, Abella moved toward the car but kept herself against the walls of the barn. The place was even more trashed than before, and dark streaks ran up the walls where fires had almost caught. "With what?" she asked.

"You hate my kind. That's okay, I get it. It's a good thing." Velvet turned to face the gargoyle and let out a heavy sigh. "I need you to do something for me that I can't do myself."

Abella frowned, but she was close enough now to see that something was sitting in the passenger seat of the car. She moved a bit closer and felt her entire body go numb when she realized what it was.

It was a clutch of eggs. Each one was like a giant, oblong pearl, and they were bundled together in a silken sack of webs.

"When?" Abella growled, her tail whipping behind her. With the others around, she couldn't believe the arachne had found a way to get him alone. And yet she now stared at the result in Velvet's hands.

"It doesn't matter." Velvet's features threatened to fracture, her eyes filled with anguish. "I need you to help me destroy them!"

Abella didn't have words for this, but her eyes flicked to the blade in Velvet's hand.

"Oh, sorry." Velvet put the sword away in her pocket. "I…this…about an hour ago, I felt them coming. So I snuck out here to lay them. Nobody else knows."

"They are dangerous!" Abella whispered angrily. "Why would you do such a thing?"

"Please understand. It was the urge to mate, it was overwhelming, but it's more than that." Velvet picked up one of the eggs. It was roughly the size of an eggplant. "When I'm around Mike, I can't help myself. It's like the world is ice-cold and he's a warm blanket I can bury myself under. I feel complete when I'm around him. It was all I could do just to wander off and do this! Danger speeds up the quickening process. It's a survival mechanism!"

She held the egg out toward Abella, who took a step away from it. "When I hold them, I can see their strengths. It's like staring into the night sky, each one of them a star sparkling with possibilities. They are absolutely flawless, probably the most dangerous arachne to walk the world in over a century."

"And you want me to destroy them? Why? If you know they are so dangerous, why don't you do it?"

Velvet's lower lip trembled. Her voice broke between words, as if there wasn't enough air to speak. "Because I can see what they look like," she whispered, then picked up one of the eggs. "This one has my father's eyes and Mike's nose. And this one over here has Mike's hair and my father's grin. I've only ever loved two humans in my entire life, and when I think about destroying them, I…" She bit her lip hard enough to draw blood, a single bead of it running down her chin before her tongue licked it away. Her hands went to the dog tags around her neck, and she squeezed them. "My father's legacy deserves better than this, but I can't help but feel like I'm losing him all over again. It's almost like a cruel prank played on me by Mother Nature."

"I think I understand." Abella moved closer, still wary of a trap. "I didn't think this would be a problem for an arachne. Your kind has always seemed so…methodical."

"It shouldn't be, but…" Velvet shook her head. "I have too much of my father's humanity in me. It's what makes me so flawed."

Abella thought about this for a moment. The barn was silent, save for the sound of the wind blowing through the slats, giving her plenty of time to think. She approached the jeep and moved a hand toward the eggs, curious how Velvet would react.

For a moment, it looked like the arachne would stop her, but Velvet held firm, her eyes welling up. Abella picked up an egg and was surprised at how warm it was. The future of the arachne was in her hands, and the only reason Velvet couldn't do it herself was because she wasn't the monster her kind needed her to be.

"Maybe…I think that maybe you've got it wrong," Abella told her. "Your father's humanity is precious. It is a gift that allows you to relate to the world in a whole different way. Instead of seeing it as a flaw, you should think of it as the thing that makes you…special."

Velvet opened her eyes and looked at Abella, those dark orbs of hers shimmering.

"Do you want to be here when it happens?" Abella asked.

Velvet whimpered. "Do I have to be?" she whispered.

"No." Abella picked up all the eggs. "Are these all of them?"

Velvet nodded.

"You can trust me. Go wait outside." Once the words crossed Abella's lips, Velvet bolted out of the barn. Not wanting to prolong the process, Abella set the eggs on the ground and lifted her foot.

Yet she hesitated. For just a moment, she could see them. She could never have children with Mike herself, nor did she want to. Yet the idea that she was destroying something he created pained her. It also made her appreciate Velvet's sacrifice far more.

Instead of slamming her foot down, she lowered it gently. The eggs were tough, but they cracked beneath her weight. The moment the yolks ran into the dirt, she heard Velvet let out a mournful wail outside the barn. The musty smell of the barn was briefly overpowered by the odor of ozone, but with another sniff, it was gone.

Determined to complete the job, she crushed them all until the shells were tiny fragments. As she ground them up beneath her feet, she couldn't help but think about how the arachne had dragged her brother to the top of that church and repeatedly slammed him into the ground. All she had seen was the ruthlessness in their eyes, their absolute lack of humanity.

Would these have been any different? Outside the barn, Velvet's wails diminished into hiccuping sobs. It was the sound of a mother's grief. Abella paused for a moment, the sound rocking her. It wasn't an emotion she had ever expected to see in an arachne, and she couldn't help but feel sadness at the mess beneath her feet. Determined to see the deed through, she used her talons to dig a hole and then pushed the remains of the eggs inside. The burial was easy, and she used her tail to smooth out the ground.

When she walked outside, she found Velvet huddled against the wall of the barn. The arachne was crying, her legs splayed on the ground. Abella helped her stand and then wrapped her arms around Velvet in a tight embrace and became a rock for her to lean on.

THE FRIDGE IN MURRAY'S KITCHEN RATTLED BRIEFLY BEFORE LETTING OUT A sigh and going silent. Eulalie threw a dirty glance at it, hoping it wouldn't decide to break down. Murray's interior aesthetic trended toward what the early eighties aspired to, and she was quite convinced the fridge was no different.

She turned her attention back to the computer and was about to change cameras when she felt the thread she had attached to their intruder shift. It was the tiniest of movements, but already she was across the room and climbing the stairs.

Sofia, who had been asleep on the couch, leaped to her feet and followed. She squinted against the bright light of morning and stumbled on one of the steps. The floor creaked beneath Sofia, and Eulalie frowned at the noise.

"Sorry," Sofia muttered. "Didn't sleep well. Felt like I had the flu or something for a bit."

"As long as you're okay now."

"I am." Sofia continued up, and Eulalie followed. They opened the door to Murray's room and walked inside. The intruder was holding perfectly still, and she wasn't even entirely certain he was breathing.

"Enough of that." Sofia pushed past Eulalie and extended her sword. Using the flat of her blade, she slapped it against the stranger's belly. The sound was loud, and his whole body jerked. A thin welt appeared across his sagging gut.

"Why did you do that?" asked Eulalie.

"He was attempting astral projection." She swatted his belly again. "Maybe remote viewing, or trying to contact someone, I don't know. But if he keeps it up, I'm going to start using the edge," she declared.

"Ow, enough, please." He turned his head back and forth. Eulalie figured he was trying to find a gap in the pillowcase to look through, but she had already checked. "Why are you doing this to me?"

"Why are you breaking into places with a magic wand?" Sofia dragged the tip of her sword along his foot, then up his calf. "Don't give me that innocent bullshit. Let's skip ahead to the part where you tell me something useful."

"I...uh..." He shifted. "I have to go to the bathroom."

"So go." Sofia now ran the blade up his thigh. "Nobody is stopping you."

The man sighed. "If you insist."

"Wait." Eulalie placed her hand on the man's belly and gave Sofia a dirty look. She really didn't want to deal with the mess and would be able to smell it throughout the house. "Perhaps we can come to an agreement."

"I'm listening." His voice was gravelly now.

"Why don't we start with just a few basic questions. Nothing invasive, just some basic manners. For instance, what is your name?"

He tilted his head in her direction. "Names are a powerful thing," he told them. "How do I know you aren't a witch who—"

WHAP! The flat of the blade smacked him on the bottom of his foot. Sofia grinned.

"Ow, fuck!" He jerked in his bonds. "You can call me Cyrus!"

"Okay, Cyrus. Nice to meet you." Eulalie moved her hands up to his neck. She could see the beating of his heart through his carotid artery. As she watched his pulse, she couldn't help but think she had heard that name before. "Why did you break into our house?"

"It isn't your house," Cyrus declared. "But I answered your question, so you owe me one."

Sofia slapped him again, but this time, he didn't utter a sound.

"Hmm. Looks like a protective aura is around him now." Sofia put her hand an inch above his skin. "Here, you can feel it. It's kind of like an electrical field."

Eulalie obeyed. Her fingertips felt like they were full of pins and needles.

"What happened to Murray?" Cyrus turned his head back and forth, as if trying to figure out where they were standing. "Did you hurt him?"

"Owner of this house? We're not sure." Eulalie looked at Sofia. There were so many lines to pluck at right now, but she didn't know where to proceed.

"Not sure isn't a great answer," Cyrus grumbled.

"Why does it matter?" Sofia asked.

"Because I want to know what kind of people I'm dealing with," he answered.

"We didn't hurt him. Is he a friend of yours?" Sofia asked, the tip of the blade now teasing his nipple. Her lips had parted slightly, and Eulalie wondered if she was getting off on this.

Cyrus paused, then shook his head. "I know everyone who lives on this street."

"Why?" Eulalie asked.

"Nope. My turn." He flinched when Sofia poked his nipple. "Why are you watching the Radley house?"

Eulalie and Sofia looked at each other.

"What makes you think we're—"

"Please, I have to pee. I'm an old man who got knocked out last night." He let out a disgruntled sigh. "I've been watching your drone. Not sure how you got the pet rats to do patrols, but I can also tell that something happened over at the house."

"What makes you such an expert?" Sofia asked. "On the house, I mean."

Cyrus groaned. "Please, I really have to pee."

Eulalie pursed her lips together, then looked at Sofia.

"I can take him," Sofia said. "If he tries anything, I'll just kill him."

Eulalie wasn't certain how serious Sofia was but nodded. They untied him, and Sofia marched him into the bathroom and pointed him toward the toilet. Once he was done, he was marched back to the bed and then held down while Eulalie retied her webs.

"What kind of rope is this?" he asked. "It feels like silk."

"I pulled it out of my ass. Now spill. Why are you watching the Radley house?"

"It wasn't just me. I was curious about the place for my own reasons, but there was someone else watching it too. That meant there must be something worth watching." He let out a sigh. "Or there was. It's been a couple of months since I've seen the others. I originally thought that maybe they came back and did something to the house."

"What makes you think something happened?" asked Sofia.

"I am…was considered an expert in extraplanar spellcraft. I can tell that something massive happened right at the edge of the property. Either a rift was opened, or something worse. I haven't been around much lately, the weather makes my joints hurt, but I assume it was recent. The only reason I even came last night was that I tracked a gargoyle who tossed a statue off a church back to the house. Wondered if something had happened, so I've been snooping around a bit more than usual."

Sofia rolled her eye and mouthed the word *Abella.*

"So a planar disturbance, huh?" Eulalie tapped her fingers on the frame of the bed. "How does one become an expert on such a thing?"

"I was a member of a secret society," he answered. "But I'm retired now."

"So why are you watching our house?" Sofia asked. "You still didn't answer that."

"You live there?" he asked. "Then you must know Lily."

"Lots of people know Lily," Sofia responded. "Bad people."

"What about Dana?"

"Same answer," Eulalie replied.

She could see him swallow hard. When he spoke, his voice croaked a little. "Ticktock?"

She looked at Sofia, who shrugged.

"We're at an impasse," Eulalie explained. "For all we know, you are pumping us for information about our friends. Give us something better to work with."

"I last saw them in Hawaii," he explained.

A light bulb went off in Eulalie's head. She remembered where she had heard the name. "Who did you fight there?"

"A dragon man named Tristan Edge. The fight went poorly for my people." Cyrus let out a sigh. "It's sort of the reason I'm in retirement."

Eulalie had heard this story from Lily and seen bits and pieces of it. Once she and Dana had left Oregon, Eulalie had tracked the two of them by hacking into cameras and then deleting the footage. Once they were in Hawaii, it had been quite tricky to track down footage from the Black Palace and delete it. She hadn't watched any of it, because it had been far more important to destroy all the footage so that nobody would know about Dana's existence. There had been an unexpected team-up with the Order to take down a man who had been eating virgins to become a dragon.

"You were a member of the Order." She took a step back, her eyes narrowing. The Order had tried to kill her parents before she was born.

He nodded.

"So then why are you here?"

"Truthfully? I'm not really sure. Things went very bad for us in Hawaii, and I was forced to confront some truths that were difficult to swallow. Lily, against her better judgment, I'm sure, spared me. I was able to track her here but wasn't sure what the next step was. I didn't know if Mike was a threat. It's kind of what I used to do."

Eulalie looked over at Sofia, who had gone red in the face. Her shoulders were tensed up, and when she saw Eulalie looking, she turned to face the wall.

"So you were here to hurt him?" Eulalie asked.

"No. Just to watch. After the things I saw in Hawaii, I don't know that I could do much against him or your friends. Hell, I didn't even know you had a gargoyle until I tracked it here. There are rumors out there about your house, stories that don't quite add up. You have some very powerful enemies."

She wanted him to elaborate but decided against it. "Does the Order know about us?"

He chuckled. "They didn't when I left. Whatever you are doing in that house hasn't violated the covenant, so you're well below their radar."

"Covenant?"

Sofia turned around with a sneer on her lips. "We haven't done anything to upset their precious Balance." She did finger quotes around this last word. "Namely, reveal that magic still exists."

"It's a bit more complicated, but yes." He sighed under the pillowcase.

"When I came inside and saw a cyclops, which are supposed to be extinct, wielding one of our swords, I must admit I panicked. Your kind's reputation for ferocity precedes you."

"My kind wouldn't be extinct if you assholes hadn't attacked us." She rotated the blade and pressed it against Cyrus's neck. "All because we had formed a sanctuary away from humans! We just wanted to be left alone!"

This was an interesting revelation, Eulalie thought. She desperately wanted to pluck at that thread and see it unwind, but now wasn't the best time for it.

"It was a knee-jerk reaction on my part," he admitted. "Ever since I was a child, I have been subjected to the Order's indoctrination. I've only recently come to understand that the world isn't as black and white as I thought it was. Lily and Dana helped me see that. When I saw that sword in your hands, all I could think of were the old stories, tales of one-eyed warriors capable of taking down a dozen men on their own. You should know I'm trying damn hard to be a better person, but decades of training are hard to overcome, especially when I think I'm about to get ripped in half."

Eulalie saw the edge of the sword tremble slightly. She stepped forward and put her hand on Sofia's, pushing the blade away from Cyrus's throat.

"Tell me more about extraplanar spellcraft. Do you know what happened to the house?"

He shook his head. "I was more interested in who else was watching the house, so no. I didn't have much time to look into it. Let me put on some clothes and I'll be happy to take a look for you."

She could use this. Precautions would be taken, but the man would make an invaluable ally. "I think we may be on the same side, but you should know we don't trust you. Don't take it personally."

He let out a sigh of relief. "I don't. I wouldn't trust me either. But I owe the succubus. How's that for irony? Tried to snuff her out on two separate occasions and she still saved my life."

"Hmm." Eulalie grabbed Sofia by the hand and led her from the room. Once out in the hall, she closed the door and turned to the cyclops. "So what do you think?" she whispered.

Sofia's face was scrunched up so hard that she looked like an angry Muppet. "I don't know that we can trust him, but…"

"But you think he could help us figure out the next step?"

She nodded. "I hate this, by the way."

"I know." Eulalie put her hand on the door, then looked down the stairs. "Take him outside. I'll get ahold of Suly and the two of you can escort him to the house. I don't know that our new friend's emotional metamorphosis is ready to handle all this." She sprawled her legs out for emphasis. "And I definitely don't want his people finding out."

"Done. I'll keep him bagged until he's outside." Sofia put her hand on the door and paused. "But are you sure?"

Eulalie nodded. "If Lily let him go, it was for a reason."

"The two of you must have really hit it off," Sofia remarked. "Guess I don't see it."

Eulalie thought back to when Lily had come out to the cabin. For most of the time she was there, her father's night terrors had gone away. For months after, her father had commented about the lovely dreams he had experienced involving their mother. Eulalie knew it hadn't been a coincidence.

"Let's just say I owe her as well." She pushed the door open, revealing that Cyrus was holding perfectly still. Staring at his helpless form, all she could think about was that her ropework could be so much better. "We're going to play nice for now," she told him. "But step out of line—"

"And you'll kill me?" She could almost hear him smiling.

"Please. We are women of sophistication." She walked over to the bed and tapped on his toe, making him flinch. "I will tie you to a chair and make you watch as I eat your fucking hands and feet. We'll make a game about how much of you is left when you finally kick the bucket."

"That doesn't sound very sophisticated," he said, the humor now gone from his voice.

"We'll be wearing fancy dresses with hats. You can wear a tie if you want. We have plenty of clip-ons lying around here." She moved to his ankles and started undoing her webs. "It will be fancy as fuck."

He went silent. It wasn't until she started undoing his wrists that he asked, "What are you?"

When she leaned toward him to respond, she didn't know what she was going to say. However, she noticed a small group of rats watching from the nearby dresser and decided to improvise.

"I'm the rat queen," she whispered in his ear. "So don't disappoint me."

THE SUN MELTED INTO THE HORIZON, SENDING STEAM UP INTO THE SKY THAT turned into colossal cloud butterflies that danced overhead. Mike was leaning back into Velvet's torso, her legs splayed around them in the sand.

He felt weak, as if he'd been running for days. Velvet stroked his hair, occasionally wrapping it around her fingers. There had been a period of time where the sun had set and darkness had fallen across the Dreamscape. Despite everyone's best efforts, darkness had eventually come for the island. During this time, he could see and hear nothing. If not for the feeling of Velvet's arms around him, he would have simply let go and accepted his fate.

When the sun had finally risen, the island had been reborn. Large swaths of it had been wiped clean, as if a massive wave had gobbled up the architecture of the land. Most of the trees were gone as well, and the only thing that remained the same was the presence of his tiny home.

Unable to move, he had let Velvet hold him up. She told him stories about her childhood, her hopes and her dreams. His only regret was that he had become too weak to speak back. He was completely drained.

The others checked in on him one at a time. No longer just blurs of energy, they all came by and sat with him as he recovered. Though they had done the bulk of the work rebuilding the beach and holding the dark waters at bay, it occurred to him that they were actually just extensions of his soul. Their drive had gotten the job done, but he was the one paying the price.

A golden glow settled over him, and he tilted his head enough to see Titania sit down on the beach next to him. Her body glowed as if she was bathed in moonlight, and her cloak swirled around her despite the lack of wind.

"I'm very impressed, Caretaker." She smiled wistfully, then looked at him. "There were many times during the night that I was certain you would fail."

"Ergh." It was all he could manage.

"I have news." She drew a circle in the sand. "After learning of your plight, I made a trip to your world. Specifically, to Oregon."

"Eh?" Curious, he was able to raise an eyebrow.

"I'm not at the cabin with you. On my way there, I discovered that a magical seal had been built around the land. It's one-way, so if anything walked in, they became trapped. The enchantment on your land couldn't turn them away, because they would simply be bounced back inside. Since they couldn't leave, it was only a matter of time before they were able to seep in and establish themselves.

"While breaking it myself would be seen as interference, I can tell you that the only way to get rid of it is to kill Leeds or force him to leave. As long as he is inside his own enchantment, you will be unable to leave. He could maybe let you go, but I don't know that he would be open to negotiation." She moved next to him and took his hand in hers. Warmth flooded his limbs, and he sighed in relief.

"You have quite the task ahead of you," she said, and then her features blurred. The world fizzled out like static and then sank into darkness. Velvet's body no longer felt warm and inviting but slightly damp and cool to the touch.

The sounds of the ocean had faded into nothingness, replaced by a distant rumble that sounded like snoring.

As he opened his eyes, the blurry figure over him shifted. He wasn't sure who it was until he saw large, furry ears rise up as he groaned.

"Mike?" Yuki's voice trembled.

"Ugh," he replied. His mouth was so dry that his lips had cracked. "Th…thirsty."

Yuki wrapped her arms around him and let out a sob of relief. Someone shifted in the corner, and now Velvet stood over him, lines of concern on her face.

"You're awake!" she declared. "Thank the gods!"

He smiled weakly, then tried to lift his arm to hug Yuki. His fingers wouldn't even curl.

"Don't move, not yet." Yuki sat up and wiped tears from her bloodshot eyes. She lifted his head with one hand and held up a cup of water. "Let's get some fluids into you, but I need you to promise me something."

"Okay?" He stuck his tongue out toward the cup, willing the liquid to flow across the air and into his mouth.

"Never again. Never ever do that again." Her face was stern. "If it ever comes down to a choice between you and me, you let me go, you hear me? You are far too important."

Unable to argue with her, he groaned in response. Satisfied, she held the cup to his lips and surprised him by lifting ice chips out of it. She stuck one in his mouth, and he let it sit under his tongue until it melted. They tasted better than anything he could remember drinking as the cold liquid ran down his throat.

Somewhere in the house, he heard a growl, followed by banging. He looked at Yuki and frowned.

"That's a problem for tomorrow," she told him. "You're in no shape to help yet."

He nodded.

"I've got this." Velvet took the cup from Yuki's hands. "Get some sleep. I'll wake you if I need you."

Yuki didn't bother leaving. She yawned and fell forward onto the bed, her body shrinking down until she was a normal-sized fox with three tails. Curling up next to his belly, she settled into the soft rhythm of sleep almost right away. With what little strength he had, he placed his hand gently on her head, right between her ears.

He didn't know what they had gone through or even how long it had been. The hopelessness he had experienced in the Dreamscape had seemed as if it would go on forever, but he had survived. Tender fingers touched his forehead, pausing just long enough to swirl his hair. When he looked up into Velvet's brown eyes as she fed him ice, all he could think about was her constant presence, both here and inside his head. She had kept him from slipping away, holding tight to him when the darkness threatened.

"What?" She paused, an uncertain look on her face. Her hair hung down, diffracting the light and making it seem as if her entire body glowed with an aura of warmth.

"Beautiful." He smiled, then let out a sigh. Despite being unconscious for so long, he was suddenly tired again. As she stroked his forehead, he slipped away into a dreamless sleep.

BACK FROM THE BRINK

Time was meaningless for Mike as he slipped back and forth into consciousness. Though he was no longer on the edge of death, his limbs were heavy with pain. He would sometimes close his eyes for a second only to open them and see that the occupants of the room had changed.

Yuki was a constant presence, either changing his bandages or fussing over him. He saw Quetzalli only briefly; the dragon looked like she had fallen ill. Abella sometimes watched through the window and actually came in a couple of times to sit with him. Of Dana and Bigfoot, there was no sign.

And then there was Velvet. She fed him soup when he was awake, encouraging him softly with her words. She was a constant presence, both when he was awake and in the Dreamscape. His weakness chased him even there, and she would hold him on the beach while he rested. Trapped in a state of perpetual exhaustion, he clung to her presence like moss to a rock.

Velvet was helping him eat some beef stew when he heard a loud crash, followed by banging. Yuki left the room with a worried look on her face.

"What is that?" he asked. It occurred to him now that he had heard the same noise numerous times during the day. His mind was finally clear enough to ask about it.

The arachne sighed and put down the can of soup. "That would be Dana," she explained. "She's going feral. Yuki has been using magic to freeze her in place so that she doesn't break out of the pantry."

There was a loud bang, followed by screams of panic. Something heavy thudded against the wall, and he heard Abella swearing.

"I should go help," he muttered, but even he didn't believe the words. His legs were like jelly. From the brief moments he had seen his own body when the blankets were lifted, he looked slightly emaciated. Much of it was from water loss; his fever had caused him to sweat so much that the sheets had been changed multiple times.

The rest was pure calorie loss. Yuki had stuffed him full of every curative potion Zel had sent with him. His body had fought to regenerate tissue damaged by the poison, and the process required energy. Though his bond with Tink had given him resistance to poison, it apparently wasn't strong enough to just brush aside the toxin the Nirumbi used. The wound from the arrow had also managed to nick a lung, which made breathing in deep more than a little painful.

"Abella has it under control," Velvet explained. "She's the only one that can't get scratched or bit."

At least we hope so, Mike thought. The idea of Abella turning into a zombie was a terrifying thought.

The cabin went quiet. Eventually, Yuki came back in, her face twisted into a mask of anguish. When she plopped down next to the bed, she let out a sigh and then leaned forward onto the bed.

"That bad?" he asked.

"Eating the Nirumbi triggered something in her," she stated. "Shortly after the battle, she was mostly herself, but the poison was still doing its thing. She's crazy strong right now. It's almost like feeding on living tissue caused her to bulk up. We think that if we can get her some of her usual food, she may revert, but..." Yuki gestured at him. "You're in absolutely no condition, and likely won't be for days."

He sighed. Maybe his magic could get him up, but he definitely couldn't participate while barely able to move. Sometimes staying awake was too much of a chore for him.

After a bit more soup, he shared what he had learned from Titania with the others. Yuki went pale and left for a while with Bigfoot to check out the perimeter of the barrier. Velvet and Quetzalli took turns giving him food and water as his strength returned. He could finally raise his arms a little, but the effort left him exhausted.

When Yuki and Bigfoot returned, they came and sat down next to Mike. The Sasquatch's face was serious, which was a rather frightening sight.

"How bad are we fucked?" Mike asked.

"We are trapped." Yuki had taken out her tarot cards and was flipping through them. "It's a powerful spell that took quite some time to set up. It could be disrupted from the outside, but we can't get word out."

"Can't we just use my phone?" he asked.

"No." Yuki frowned while fidgeting with her tarot cards. "It was broken when Leeds attacked Abella in the woods. We checked already. And Dana's is missing. We think it was in her pocket when she ran out into the woods."

"Shit." Mike closed his eyes. What options were left to them?

"I feel...," Bigfoot said, breaking the silence. "That I owe a massive apology to everyone here."

"How so?" Mike opened his eyes. "You didn't do anything wrong."

Bigfoot groaned and leaned against the wall, his arms folded across his massive torso. "I did, actually. I am fairly certain that I am the reason Leeds is here in the first place. He and I have a rather sordid history, and he holds a grudge better than anyone I've ever known."

"What happened?" Mike asked.

"We were very close friends for many, many years. His behavior toward humans was never friendly to begin with, but I was forced to act when I found out that he was tormenting and killing humans in secret. We fought for many days, and I finally crushed him under a large rock. I didn't know it at the time, but he can't be killed. Two days later, he ambushed me in the middle of the night. He almost killed me, but the forest came to my aid by sending a massive buck to tackle him and break his concentration. I snapped Leeds's neck, and he was mist once more."

"So he always comes back?"

Bigfoot nodded. "Always. He went missing for a while, and I discovered later that he was able to take over the Pine Barrens. The land and its creatures were no longer on my side, so I fled to the West Coast. We've avoided each other ever since, but I suspect I may be the main reason he came. I have no idea how he learned I was here."

Yuki groaned. "I do. Years back, when Emily and I first met him, she asked if he would be interested in moving somewhere safe for cryptids."

"And Emily told him about me?" Bigfoot pulled at some tangled strands of hair that hung from his face.

"She told him about the house first. When he didn't seem interested, she mentioned the cabin. Said that if it was good enough for Bigfoot, then he would be right at home."

"What did he do?" asked Mike.

"That's when he trapped us in the Everglades. Emily tried to jump us out using magic trees, but we learned later that he could read our thoughts. He stayed ahead of us and chopped down any of the trees we could use. There weren't many to begin with. Every time we got to the edge of the Everglades, the shadows would push us back in." Yuki looked at a card and then shook her head before tucking it back up her sleeve. "One day, we wandered out. It was like he had gotten bored or something."

"How do you defeat someone who can read your thoughts?" asked Mike.

"You either act without thinking or do something he can't avoid." Bigfoot mimed stomping on the floor. "He was distracted while fighting you, so I got the drop on him. What I can't understand is how he got the Nirumbi to team up with him. He is well known but not well liked."

Based on his brief experience with Leeds, Mike wasn't surprised to hear this at all. Leeds had mentioned taking the cabin and its land away from him. Maybe it was as simple as offering them a private sanctuary if they helped him take it by force. But more than just the Nirumbi had gotten involved. There was the wendigo and the snake thing Abella had encountered. If all these creatures were so powerful, why follow Leeds in the first place?

Thinking back on their fight, the devil had been fairly uninvolved for most of it. He was mainly content to disrupt and allow his troops to do the dirty work. Did he have low magic reserves? Was he just a big pussy? There was a missing piece to the puzzle, and Mike really wanted to discover it.

There was another loud bang, but this one was accompanied by the sound of things falling to the floor. Bigfoot jumped up and left, followed by Yuki. There was a lot of screaming shortly after, followed by the temperature of the cabin dropping dramatically.

Curious, Mike tried to slide his legs off the bed and take a peek, but he couldn't even lift his hips off the mattress using his arms. Frustrated, he had to sit and listen as everyone shouted at one another. Emery bolted into the room, a worried expression on his face.

"Is everything okay?" Mike asked.

"Dana has broken down the door of the cupboard," he explained. "They are chasing her through the cabin right now. It's my job to protect you in case she shows up."

Mike grimaced. The little imp looked like he would struggle to fight his way out of a mouse trap, but Mike had learned long ago that he shouldn't judge based on appearances.

Dana crashed through the doorway and landed on the floor, her features frozen in a snarl. She looked up at him and hissed.

"Eep," Mike whispered. He saw that she was missing her pants.

Emery dive-bombed Dana, and she swatted at him with frightening speed. Velvet's torso came through the door and grabbed the zombie by the ankles after tossing down a shredded pair of pants. Velvet yanked and threw Dana back into the living room. There were several more crashes before he heard Abella join the fight.

"She is quite strong," Emery muttered, fidgeting with his hands like an overgrown fly.

"Apparently." He hadn't realized Dana was capable of such a display.

"Hold her!" shouted Quetzalli, and there was a crackle of electricity, followed by Bigfoot howling in pain. The smell of burned hair flooded the cabin. "Sorry!"

After another crash, the house went quiet. Yuki walked through the door, her hair disheveled and her shirt torn.

"We need to talk about our zombie problem," she said and sat down on the bed with a sigh. "I thought it could wait, but that was really bad. I'm worried she is slipping away. For a bit, she was at least cognizant, but now? I really don't know."

He nodded. "I know what you want, but…" He waved his hand at his legs. How was he supposed to help feed her if he could barely move? "I'm not in any sort of condition to…produce."

"I've got some ideas, but they're unconventional." She made a face. "But I'm afraid unconventional is the story of my life."

"Whatever your idea is, let's try it. We need Dana on our side again."

Yuki stood and brushed herself off. "Let me talk to the others. We'll see you shortly."

When she left, he looked at the imp, who still hovered over the bed. "Are you as nervous about this as I am?"

Emery squeaked in response.

BETH AND THE OTHERS HAD TAKEN UP RESIDENCE IN THE OFFICE AND THE study next to it. Tink slept on one of the couches next to the window, her slumbering form watched over by Kisa and a statue of Anubis. Cecilia hovered in the office proper—they'd brought Death inside to bring the banshee down where they could keep an eye on her.

Beth sat in the only chair, her gaze constantly flicking to the large plastic tub they had dragged down from Yuki's room for the slime girl. It had been used to store paint and now acted as a container to keep the slime together. On her trip down the stairs to warn everyone, she had left a considerable amount of mass behind her and was apparently unable to reincorporate it.

They had let Death question her. The slime claimed that she had been busy brainstorming ideas for mediation when she heard a bizarre clicking sound from the bedroom. It had been followed by a flash of light, and she had watched as Cecilia's body floated by the tub and then through the wall. Death had pronounced the slime's innocence with a degree of finality that brooked no argument.

He'd also declared that he had decided to name her Opal.

"Why Opal?" Lily had asked.

"Because she is precious to me and she changes color," he answered. "Now if you'll excuse me, I have no way to heat my tea and must find a suitable cold brew."

He returned moments later to reveal the sleeping form of Carmina in one of his teacups. The fairy was moved to a small plate and now sat on the desk like a morbid snack. Beth had covered her up with a washrag. The house was colder than ever, causing her to wear a sweater and wrap herself in a blanket.

Opal was motionless in her tub. After her talk with Death, she had settled into her new home and flattened out, apparently exhausted. Her surface had turned a dark purple, highlighting her color-shifting abilities.

Beth's stomach growled. She had eaten a sandwich earlier, but it wasn't enough. The food in the fridge wasn't going to stay cold much longer, and without a means to cook it, it was eventually going to go bad. Death had somehow coaxed the last of the water out of the pipes for his tea, which meant Beth was left drinking milk to stay hydrated.

She hated milk.

"These ideas are good." Lily broke the silence, her hands on a small stack of papers. It was a bulleted list of Opal's ideas, and the white fibers were stained in different shades of blue. Beth had given it to her after reading it herself. "Mellow Jell-O over there has some solid predictions."

"Her name is Opal. And yes, she does. But I don't know how we're supposed to combat some of them." She could see the list in her mind. The horsemen wanted to raise havoc and have their full-blown Apocalypse. There wasn't a middle ground for something like that.

"I'm a personal fan of the rotating block." Lily pulled one of the sheets out. "Each incarnation gets to run around for four months, then swaps out. If Famine takes the harvesting season, you all are fucked."

"Don't you mean 'we'?"

Lily smirked. "Nah, I'll still have plenty to eat."

"You're being bitchy." Beth opened up her desk drawer and pulled out a candy bar. She threw it at Lily, who swatted it out of the air with her tail. "It's all that dick you suck."

"In all seriousness"—Lily picked up the candy bar and stuffed it into her cleavage—"she thought of what the horsemen would want. None of it is good. Anything we can remotely counteroffer isn't going to be enough to satisfy them. If even one of them gets to stay on Earth, everything goes to shit."

"So what do you suggest?"

Lily tilted her head forward. "We shouldn't be prepared for mediation. We should be ready to make war instead."

"How are we supposed to fight three horsemen and an angel?"

The succubus leaned back in thought. "You should see what the grimoire says. It's caused us enough trouble; maybe we should be the ones who dish it out for a change."

Beth frowned, but Lily was right. Even if the others hadn't been put to sleep, there wasn't anything they could do to battle the intruders out front. She had debated using it to find a counterspell to wake the others up, but Lily had cautioned her against it. Without knowing what kind of sorcery had put them under, any spell cast could have serious repercussions.

She stuck her hand in Ticktock's mouth. The mimic was stored under the desk, and she felt around in the extra-dimensional space for a few seconds before her hand touched the spine of the book.

"What do you think I should even look up?" Beth asked.

"Angels. If you can get rid of Big Brother, maybe the horsemen will be unsummoned."

Beth ran her fingers along the edge of the grimoire and focused hard on spells related to angels. Her fingertips tingled, and when she opened the book, silver letters appeared on the paper within.

"Well?" Lily asked.

Beth frowned. Instead of a spell, she found herself reading what looked like a diary entry.

"On the subject of angels," she read. "I have found considerable difficulty in my research. Such beings are rare to interact with and are protected by a divine aura. They are immune to all known forms of spellcraft, which leaves expulsion by force à la exorcism or Words of Creation. I have been unable to learn the correct sequence of these words to dismiss an angel."

"Great. Even the great grimoire can't help us now." Lily toyed with the pendant she wore around her neck. Beth had seen her wearing it more than once. It seemed to be the one mainstay of the succubus's many outfits.

"What's a Word of Creation?" Beth closed the book and got ready to open it again, but Lily leaped across the room to stop her.

"Don't. Not from the book." Her face was serious, and flames had sprouted in the corners of her eyes.

"Why not?" Beth let go of the book, and Lily set it on the table.

"Words of Creation are whispered about by demons of the highest order. You know that whole 'in the beginning' bullshit?"

"'Let there be light'?"

"A single Word of Creation was used to create everything. *Everything.* It's the magic of the true gods, shit that has existed since before our reality. The hard code of the universe, the thing that holds atoms together. You definitely aren't ready to look at them, much less contemplate their meaning."

Beth frowned. "That sounds more like science than magic."

"Any sufficiently advanced technology is indistinguishable from magic. I know you've heard that one before. Creation-level magic is terrifying, the last nongods I knew of who could command it were the upper djinn. You have to be painfully specific with them; otherwise, the results are catastrophic. One word created everything, but it took lots of words and billions of years to get everything in any sort of order that made sense."

"Kind of like a legal document? You know, I'm quite good at saying very little with a ton of words." If what Lily said was true, a few Words of Creation could easily solve all their problems. Besides, what was the harm in knowing a couple?

"*No.*" Lily put her hands on the table and stood, her horns appearing. "Do you know why they are called words? Because your simple mind can't handle what they actually are. They are concepts, raw and powerful. If you taught yourself the word for 'destroy,' you may utter it in an attempt to blow up an angel, only to destroy all of them, or maybe to disintegrate the air between you, or maybe even generate a giant, cosmic ripple that incinerates everything."

That didn't sound possible. "You're saying I could destroy everything with a random sound? That doesn't even make sense. This sounds like the magical equivalent of a conspiracy theory."

"Not sounds. *Words.* Shit, I forgot that you can't actually hear what I'm saying. This is *geas* level magic here, but I need you to understand that when I say Words of Creation, I am not saying words of creation." Lily snatched the book off the table and sat down. "You'd better fucking appreciate this."

Beth watched in fascination as Lily closed one eye and squinted the other, then cracked open the book. There was a flash of golden light, and Lily let out a roar. Golden light streamed from her mouth and eyes as she tilted her head back, scorching the ceiling of the room with the beams. She fell to the ground and twitched, the book falling out of her hands.

"Lily!" Beth knelt by the succubus, horrified. "What did you do?!"

The succubus moaned, revealing that her tongue had been burned out of her mouth. She held up a hand and mimed writing, then opened her eyes to reveal that they had been scorched out as well. Dark ash marks lined her temples, making her look like a cartoon that had smoked an exploding cigar.

Beth brought Lily a pen and paper. Smoke continued to pour out of Lily's face as she started writing.

Looked one up, she wrote in tiny letters. *Knew this was the only way to convince you.*

"You know one of these…words now?"

Nope. Looked at it from the corner of my eye. Forbidden knowledge. Protected.

"Wow." Beth shook her head in disbelief. If these words could kill, then how had the author learned them?

Be honest, Lily continued. *How do I look?*

"Like someone plugged a hot dog into an electrical outlet." She helped Lily rise, and the succubus scribbled a big word on her sheet of paper and held it up.

Cunt.

Death appeared in the doorway, his bony features scowling at an empty mug. When he looked up, he tilted his head to one side in curiosity.

"I am unfamiliar with this word," he informed them.

"And it will stay that way," Beth replied, snatching the paper out of Lily's hands. Dark ash flowed from around the room, filling in her sockets and allowing her eyes to regenerate. She sat down in Beth's chair and grunted throughout the process.

When Beth picked up the grimoire, it felt like holding a loaded gun, but she didn't know what direction to point it or how to pull the trigger. "So we can't use this against the angel," she said. "But what about the horsemen? Could we seal them off in their own dimension? Expel them?"

"That is a good question." Death sat in a chair by the wall and adjusted the hem of his robes to cover his bony knees. "It would be possible, but I do not think the angel would be very happy with you. He would likely just call them back. So about that word…"

Beth ignored the reaper. If she couldn't fight the horsemen, and she couldn't compromise with them, what did that leave? The running joke for a long time was that Mike either got lucky or fucked his way out of his problems, but she knew there was more to him than that.

What strategy would he apply? How would he approach the problem differently than she did? She sat in silence, the gears turning in her mind. He would probably do something unexpected, but what? She couldn't risk antagonizing either the angel or the horsemen, so whatever she did would have to catch them off guard while also being by the book.

"Aaaaaaagh." Lily stuck out her tongue, which was too large for her mouth. "Whath tha fackk?"

"Allow me." Death crossed the room and used bony fingers to try to shove Lily's tongue back into her head.

Distracted by the sight, Beth let out a laugh.

"Ith noth fanny," Lily protested, then tried to bite Death's fingers when they slid past her lips. She was now slapping her hands on Death's bony skull while he scowled at her.

"You should stop being a cunt and hold still," he told her. Her mouth dropped open in surprise, allowing him to successfully shove her tongue back inside.

"Death!" Beth just stared at the reaper.

"I already knew what that word meant," he explained. "If it's a four-letter word, I've heard it from Tinker Radley."

When the laughter came, Beth couldn't stop. Tears formed in the corners of her eyes, and she doubled over with her hands on her stomach. She leaned back on the desk and did her best to ignore the dirty look Lily was giving her.

"Impothible, both of hue." She stormed out of the office but clipped the frame of the door with her shoulder. "Fack!"

"So impolite," Death muttered. "Of everybody, she should appreciate a good stuffing the most."

"Death!" Surprised to hear Death's sass, Beth moved next to him. "Are you feeling okay?"

"No. No, I am not." He glared at the sitting room, his gaze locked on the window to the front yard. "I find myself in an impossible situation that could determine the fate of not only the world but my friends as well. I have very much come to appreciate all the mortal world has to offer. Your stories fascinate me, and I find our interactions delightful. My siblings would take all this away from me, and I see no solution. I cannot leave, and they refuse to."

"I'm sorry." Despite knowing it would feel like smashing her funny bone, she put her hand firmly on his shoulder and felt her entire arm zing. "I wish I could help more."

"It is not your fault, Viceroy Bethany. These are tough times, but the worst is yet to come."

"You mean when we have no plan and they win?" She shivered at the thought, then added, "And I don't like Viceroy."

"No. If they win, it will be awful, but that isn't the worst of it." He walked over to the desk and picked up an empty cup. "I am almost out of tea. By my best estimates, the end of the world will come shortly after I run out. I will be

ANNABELLE HAWTHORNE

forced to confront the horrors of the future with nary a drop to soothe my being."

Beth groaned and sat in a nearby chair. "Honestly, you're worried about tea? Everything else doesn't bother you?"

"I am the manifestation of an entity with but one purpose," he explained. "Please understand that it may make me one-dimensional at times, but I am growing. I like how it gives me warmth and comfort from within, for these are things I have never experienced on my own. Unlike my siblings, I have learned that there is value in the pursuit of experiences."

She thought about his words for a moment as he pondered the empty mug. "Do you think we could convince them of the same?" she asked.

He shook his head. "I differ from them. You see, they thrive on human misery. You cannot have war without misery, or famine without hunger. Pestilence is, at best, neutral in their feelings. I, however, am misunderstood.

"I am a bringer of peace. When I reap, it is to take away the pain and suffering. If I have any regret, it's that I often leave sadness in my wake. Consider my relationship with my siblings. What they create is awful, and I am the one left to take it all away once they're done. I think some people understand, but it isn't enough. The longer I'm here, the more I realize I have been lonely."

She nodded, then took her hand off his shoulder. Her entire arm was now numb.

"And do you know what's really weird? I miss my friend. Mike Radley is my best friend. Do you know what he said to me when we met? He invited me, Death, into his home. Gave me tea and maps to enjoy. Treated me with kindness." The molten flames inside his skull dimmed. "Can I tell you something?"

"Sure."

"While I was standing outside watching for my brothers, I got the feeling he was standing by my side. I know he wasn't, but it felt like I could reach out and touch him. Is that what it feels like for you? When someone is gone, I mean."

She nodded.

"When the feeling faded, I felt alone again. It shouldn't bother me, but it did. I have more feelings for one mortal than I do for my own siblings." Death sighed, a dry sound that was reminiscent of nails on a chalkboard. "I have unloaded many burdens on you. Thank you for helping me carry them."

"No problem."

He tapped the side of his cup. "I don't suppose you have any bottled water stashed away, do you? Even if I can't heat it up, I can pretend it's warm. Or maybe Lily can cook it with her magic."

Beth chuckled. "You really are obsessive, aren't you?"

Death nodded. "I prefer the term *goal-oriented*. It is the one thing I have in common with my siblings. Our desires are so singular that we become blind to other possibilities. I am grateful I have learned to think laterally; otherwise, I would still be stuck looking at maps."

She smiled. Death's map phase had definitely been her favorite. It had been a way for him to internalize all the places he had been while reaping souls, which was practically everywhere. The natural progression from there had been learning to read. If only she had a way to convince the other horsemen that fun could still be had without the Apocalypse.

Watching Death ponder his empty mug, something occurred to her. "Do you see mortals as beneath you?"

"Of course I do. They are mortals. I am the grim reaper." He spoke with no trace of malice. "However, I no longer view them with indifference."

"But if a mortal challenged you to a competition, would you believe they could beat you?"

He scoffed. "Haven't you heard the stories about me? I used to let mortals challenge me to competitions in order to stay my hand. I did this more out of curiosity and boredom, but"—he shrugged—"I'm not proud to admit this, but I can't actually stay my hand. I would often let them win and then reap them at the peak of happiness. It makes their souls shine so brightly before they cross over. I'm a force of nature, after all. Now, perhaps, maybe I could abstain, but I'm not sure."

Excited, Beth moved over to her desk. Could the horsemen be challenged to a competition? In their dealings, they had seemed pretty full of themselves, so they may see it as an easy win and accept. And if they did accept, how could she trick them? The terms would have to be something everyone agreed to.

Who was the weakest of the group? She thought back to their interaction. It had to be War. The way he had run his mouth, he would be the best one to challenge. The others seemed to follow his lead, and the angel would enforce their deal.

But what to challenge him at? It needed to be something War would want to do but that she could actually win. It wasn't like she could challenge him to target shooting or ripping peasants in half.

Frowning, she stared at the table. Seeing she was deep in thought, Death wandered away into the sitting room.

Think, damn it! She put her head in her hands and pulled at her hair. There was a kernel of an idea here, and she needed the damn thing to pop already!

A clattering of plastic on wood sounded out in the living room. Curious, she stood and walked to the door to see what was going on. Jenny and Reggie were at the table and at odds once more. This time they were playing The Game of Life. A few plastic cars were on the floor, and Jenny was holding her edge of the board.

"Necromancy is not a career path," Reggie told her, clutching a yellow car protectively in his paw. "You have to follow the rules. You can't just keep making things up."

Jenny scattered the board, and Reggie sighed. When he noticed Beth, he shook his head.

"I should have known better than to challenge a spirit to a game that *they failed in real life*!" He took his car and hurled it at Jenny. It bounced off her face, and Beth held her breath, expecting the doll to murder Reggie where he sat.

I would have won the real game of life if not for that fucking witch! Jenny replied, the walls shaking.

"That is because she cheated," Reggie told her. "She was playing by her own rules, and you got burned. That is how you make me feel when you insist on being such a child!"

"Wait!" Beth ran over to the table, her thoughts fluttering wildly like a trapped bird. "Stop fighting, I need silence!"

Reggie looked at Jenny and shrugged.

"Oh my God. Oh. My. God!" When the idea surfaced, it slammed into her like a gargoyle with a porn addiction. She reeled and sat down on the sofa, her eyes now on the ceiling.

"Lady Beth?" Reggie's voice was full of concern.

"I know how to beat them," she said, her voice barely a whisper. It was an idea so crazy, so absolutely insane, but the horsemen would never see it coming.

"The horsemen?" Reggie sat on the edge of the table, his beady eyes shimmering. "How?"

She looked up at both of them gravely. "When the horsemen return, they are going to make demands we can't give them. I'm going to challenge them to a game, one we can all play together. They won't know what hit them."

Game? Jenny cackled in delight. *What game?*

"Risk." Beth smiled, her lips curling upward. "It's the game of strategy, after all."

Reggie frowned, then adjusted his glasses. "I don't mean to disparage, but that game is rather difficult. Do you think it wise to challenge the horseman of war to a game based on, well, war?"

"I do, and I'm going to explain exactly how we do it. But to do it, we're going to have to break a huge fucking rule." She fixed both of them with a stare.

"You don't mean…" Reggie licked his lips nervously, then looked over at Jenny.

Beth nodded. "I do. It's time to talk about the Clue incident."

THERE WAS A LOT OF YELLING, FOLLOWED BY THE THUD OF STONE ON WOOD. The walls of the bedroom shook, showering dust down on Mike. After a few more thuds, the door swung open. Velvet backed in first, her hands tight on Dana's ankles. Abella was holding the zombie in a tight headlock, and they had used duct tape to cover her mouth and also to secure oven mitts to her hands. She was naked from the waist down, save for one sock on her left foot.

Dana saw Mike and growled through the tape. The whites of her eyes were now crimson, and her pupils narrowed to pinpricks.

He swallowed back anxiety as they got her to the corner of the room. Velvet moved out of the way, and Abella pinned Dana into the corner. Abella's talons dug into the floor, and she used her tail to keep them upright.

"Is she…" He wasn't even sure what to ask.

"She is still getting stronger." Abella's voice was tinged with concern. "I can hold her for now, but it is getting difficult."

"How? All this because she ate Nirumbi flesh?" Mike asked.

Yuki, who stood at the base of the bed, shrugged. "I don't pretend to understand zombie anatomy. This is why the undead pose such a threat. I know this may sound silly, but Emily once told me she thought zombie movies were meant to be educational primers, just in case an outbreak actually occurred. Regardless, we should hurry."

He nodded but couldn't take his eyes off Dana. Her rage was frightening, and he wasn't entirely certain he could do what needed to be done. He had some control of his arms, but he had almost no control over anything below his chest.

"Hey." Yuki put her hand on his foot and gave it a squeeze. "You're gonna be okay."

"This feels…" He let out a breath and just shook his head. "It's weird."

"You're good at weird." Yuki slid the blankets off him, revealing he was naked underneath. "Shall we get started?"

Quetzalli burst into the room wearing one of Velvet's flannel shirts and a pair of panties. "I heard somebody needed a hand in here." She winked at Mike, then flinched when Dana snarled at her.

"I can do the honors," Velvet said, then ran her arms along his thighs. Her touch was gentle, but her eyes were hungry.

"No, thanks." Yuki put herself between Mike and the arachne. "No judgment from me, but how are you going to react once we start?"

"I…" Velvet bit down on her lip and pouted. "Shit, you're right. I don't know."

"Don't take it personally. The last thing I want is to get in a fight with you over…" Yuki waved her hand at Mike's limp cock. "We've got enough on our plate dealing with Dana."

"Maybe…I think I'll go sit outside with Uncle Foot." She smiled and knelt to kiss Mike on the head. Bigfoot was watching the perimeter of the house, in case the Nirumbi returned. "Be a good boy for the doctor."

Mike stuck his tongue out at her, and then she left.

Yuki stepped back, allowing Quetzalli to take her place between Mike's legs. The dragon grinned mischievously, crawled onto the bed, and licked the tip of his penis.

"Uh…" He watched in amazement as she sucked him into her mouth. It wasn't the sight that shocked him but the realization that he could barely feel her. He wasn't worried about paralysis because he could still feel things below the waist.

Quetzalli noticed right away, allowing his cock to pop out of her mouth. "He isn't getting hard."

"So let's get creative. We're gonna need to get him off at least once." Yuki started digging through Mike's bag.

"What are you looking for?" he asked.

"Something I found earlier…aha!" She pulled a vial out of the bag. Inside was a shimmering fluid. "I spotted this tucked in with all the stuff Zel sent with you."

"Is that…fairy lube?" The fairies at home produced a lubricant that had no equal. It shimmered in the light as Yuki poured a little bit on Quetzalli's hands.

"Zel wanted to cover her bases, I'm sure." Yuki sighed. "I really wish she was here. This is absolutely her area of expertise."

Mike wished the same, but he wasn't going to say anything.

"So what now?" Quetzalli asked.

"I'm going to teach you how to stimulate a prostate." Yuki knelt by Quetzalli as Mike sat up.

"Excuse me?" he asked.

"We're going to get you off without a boner." Yuki raised an eyebrow. "Have you ever had your prostate massaged?"

"I have heard of this," Abella said with a grin. "And watched it. It is very interesting."

"Someone care to explain?" Mike asked.

"You're having trouble getting it up," Yuki explained. "But you can get a man off without an erection. It's all about the prostate."

Mike had a lot of questions but settled for the first one on his mind. "How do you know about this?"

"I've been around a long time and have enjoyed many lovers, both men and women. When you get to live for centuries, you try new things in the bedroom. It's no big deal. I would do it myself, but I need my hands free to freeze your cum once it's out so we can feed it to her without losing a hand." She tilted her head toward Dana, who was growling again.

Curious how it would work, he nodded. "Continue, I guess," he told them.

Yuki gave Quetzalli a rundown of how a prostate worked, and Mike noticed how the dragon's eyes lit up once she learned about where it was. It felt weird watching two women talk about how to do things to his butt. Then again, some people would pay good money to trade places with him, so he wasn't about to complain.

"It's all about relaxation," Yuki said, then adjusted her robes so her shoulders were exposed. The inner curvature of her breasts was now visible, and she adjusted her hair so that it tumbled down along her shoulders. "This isn't something you want to rush, so let's make sure he feels good first. Set the mood."

She leaned over him, pulling off his blankets to reveal his entire body. Her palms caught on fire, which she let burn for a minute. After blowing out the flames, she put some lube on her hands and started rubbing his neck and shoulders while sitting on his stomach. Her silken robes shifted against his skin, and he could feel the bare flesh of her thighs underneath.

Down below, Quetzalli started squeezing his thighs and legs. There was an enormous skill difference between the two women, and he barely felt the dragon's ministrations. Instead, he was focused on Yuki's slender form above him. Her tails were on the sides of the bed, two on his left, the last on his right. He had a strong urge to touch them to feel if they were as soft as they looked.

"Take some deep breaths," she commanded, and he obeyed. She leaned forward and rubbed his neck, her fingers eventually tracing circles around his temples. Yuki's breath smelled like wintergreen gum, and he could see that her hair turned into thin fuzz along the sides of her neck where it met her shoulder.

He was light-headed, and it almost felt like he was floating. Yuki did some work on his arms, and he was very aware of her weight on his body. He also noticed when her breasts brushed against his chest, which caused a contented sigh to escape his lips.

Down below, he felt Quetzalli grab the base of his cock and start stroking. He was disappointed that nothing was happening but figured he was doing pretty well for a man who had been dying only eighteen hours ago. He tried to tune out his feelings of inadequacy as well as the disturbing growls of the zombie trapped in the corner.

Yuki turned around to look at Quetzalli. One of her tails shifted so it brushed across his chest. He was able to lift his hand and run his fingers through it. The fur was impossibly soft, reminiscent of microfiber fabric.

"That's it, good." Yuki muttered instructions into Quetzalli's ear as she penetrated Mike with a finger. Between the numbness and the lube, he barely felt it. However, when she moved her hand around, he felt a sudden fullness in his body that surprised him. Pinned between Yuki's weight and the rising pressure of Quetzalli's finger, he felt a surge of warmth flow through him. He gasped in surprise.

"I think I found it!" Quetzalli declared in excitement.

"It looks like you did, but here." Yuki adjusted Quetzalli's arm, causing the pressure inside Mike to lessen. "There. Your wrist won't get tired nearly as fast."

Quetzalli's movements were foreign at first. He could feel her finger inside him but little else. However, at Yuki's coaxing, Quetzalli now used her other hand to massage his testicles and squeeze the base of his dick. The sensations were pleasant, and he let out a sigh while doing his best to relax. He couldn't remember the last time he had let someone else do all the work for him.

Yuki got off his belly and moved down to kneel behind Quetzalli. She started rubbing his calves and his feet, triggering pressure points that relaxed him even further. If not for Quetzalli rubbing his prostate, he would have fallen asleep already.

"Hey, check these out." Yuki's voice was playful, so he looked down at them to see that Quetzalli's flannel shirt had been undone and her breasts were on full display. The kitsune was squeezing them, causing Quetzalli's cheeks to darken. "What do you think? Wouldn't you just love to blow a huge load on these tits?"

"I…um…" The way Yuki pressed the breasts together was almost hypnotic, and he found his mind disappearing down that crease of flesh. In his pelvis, he felt a tiny flicker of energy. It was like a match had been lit and then immediately blown out. "Yes," he squeaked.

"That's embarrassing," Quetzalli complained, but her cheeks were now flushed with desire.

"C'mon, Mike. She wants to see that hot cum of yours. Spray it all over her tits." Yuki licked Quetzalli's ear, only to receive a nasty zap on the tongue. "Okay, maybe less of that. What about this?" She teased Quetzalli's nipples and then pinched one.

"Oh!" Quetzalli paused and then shuddered. "Those are really sensitive right now!"

"I know." Yuki grinned and lifted her fingertips to reveal that they shimmered in the light. She was using fairy lube. It hadn't even occurred to Mike that it had a use past being the ultimate lubricant. Had that enhanced the massage? What other properties did it have?

That fire in his belly caught once more, then managed a weak burn. He shivered in delight, causing a single spark to manifest on his belly and travel toward his groin. It disappeared back into his body but was followed by a couple more.

"Yeah, that's it, tell him how much you want his hot cum," Yuki whispered loud enough for Mike to hear.

"It's hard to say it out loud," Quetzalli replied. "Everyone is watching us!"

"No, they're just watching you." Yuki squeezed Quetzalli's breasts hard enough that the dragon groaned. "They want to see how shiny your tits are when you have cum all over them, but it isn't gonna happen. Do you know why? Because you won't tell him how bad you want it."

There was a loud thump. Mike turned his head to see that Abella had put Dana in a submission hold but was watching Quetzalli intently. The gargoyle's mouth was hanging open as she listened to every word. Despite the fact that she didn't need to breathe, she was panting.

"Don't forget to keep using that finger," Yuki growled, then pinched Quetzalli's nipple.

Quetzalli cried out in response, and Mike felt a surge of energy in his ass. His cock twitched and then felt heavy as he became semihard.

"Maybe..." Mike licked his lips. "Maybe two fingers would be better."

Abella's tail spasmed into the wall, knocking loose a chunk of wood. She hastily kicked the chunk underneath the nearby dresser as if trying to hide it.

"Yeah, you hear that, little dragon? He wants two of those strong, slender fingers inside him." Yuki stuck out her tongue to lick Quetzalli's neck but then thought better of it and blew on her ear instead. There was a quiet snap of static, but this time, Quetzalli let out a moan. "If a big, strong man can tell you he wants more in his ass, then why can't you tell him how much you want his cum?"

Quetzalli's face was beet red as she adjusted her hand to slide another finger inside him. This time, the sensation went from pressure to pleasure, and he groaned. More sparks crawled down his body, and then he jumped when he felt Yuki's hands on his thighs. She kneaded his muscles, and it felt like blood was being redirected through his groin.

"C'mon, he wants to hear you say it," Yuki muttered, her eyes on him now. She had a fierce look of determination that was almost frightening, and she extended her claws and dragged them down the sensitive flesh of his thighs.

His cock jumped, and a dribble of precum spilled free. It glistened under the light of the room, and then Yuki scooped it up with her nail and smeared it across Quetzalli's breasts. It shimmered like body glitter.

"You should tell him," she continued. "Tell him how you want to wear it like a badge of honor. To let everyone know these breasts belong to him."

Quetzalli looked confused and lowered her voice. "Should I keep acting embarrassed when I say it? I'm getting mixed signals."

Yuki rolled her eyes in exasperation. "Role-play means to roll with it. The brain is the best erogenous zone, so go stimulate it."

Dana stopped growling, as if listening.

"You know what? I'm so horny right now that I don't care if it's embarrassing." Quetzalli smirked at Mike. "Do you like seeing my boobs, Mike? They're pretty amazing, aren't they? But do you know what would make them better? If you could glaze them with your sperm. Bust your load all over them and pile it high like a big cumulonimbus—ow!"

Yuki cleared her throat and moved her hand away from where she had pinched Quetzalli's side.

"Sorry, I forgot." The dragon rolled her eyes. "It's just that all that *lightning* excites me."

At the word *lightning*, Mike felt a burst of energy inside his hips. He gasped, then groaned when a small surge of cum leaked from the head of his cock.

"What just happened?" Yuki asked, her hands moving fast. She scooped up the cum on her fingers and froze it immediately.

"Oh, Mike, I'm sorry, I shocked him...inside." Quetzalli looked horrified, but Mike couldn't concentrate. Purple tendrils of light manifested along his belly and then vanished back into his body. His left leg twitched, no longer feeling heavy.

"Do that again," he said, his limbs suddenly warm. "Please," he added.

Quetzalli looked at Yuki, who shrugged.

"It's his ass," she replied, then put Mike's frozen semen into a cup she had set aside. "If the man wants some sparks, give him some sparks."

Quetzalli stroked him some more, then the surging energy returned. Mike groaned as each zap made his whole groin tense up. In sporadic bursts, he pumped more cum into Yuki's hands, and all of it went into the cup.

"We may have enough," Yuki said. "But keep going, just in case." She moved to the floor where Abella had Dana pinned and pulled the tape away from her mouth. "It's time for your medicine."

Dana snapped at her, but Yuki tossed the first sperm shard into the zombie's mouth. It sparkled in the light before vanishing down her throat. One piece clearly wasn't enough, so Yuki kept at it. Each piece disappeared into Dana's mouth, and some semblance of sanity returned as her eyes focused on Yuki.

"More," she demanded, her voice a throaty growl.

Mike gasped, then blew another load. His magic was manifesting along his fingertips now, and his belly was covered in a thin layer of spooge. Quetzalli, clearly proud of herself, kept at it. With a grunt, Mike flexed his legs, and his cock expanded to its full, proud length.

"Well, would you look at that?" Yuki smirked at him from across the room. "Looks like we can get you what you need straight from the tap."

"Please don't," Mike said with a whimper. "She may bite me. Besides, I don't think she would want us taking advantage of her situation like this."

Yuki laughed. "Gods, no, we aren't putting anything near her mouth. While she was still coherent, Dana told us to do whatever was necessary to bring her back." Her face went serious. "Truly. She's afraid that going feral may become a one-way process. So let's help her the best way we can. Abella?"

The gargoyle nodded, then stood and pulled Dana off the floor. The zombie started struggling again, her mittened hands bouncing off stone as she was moved toward the bed. Dana took a deep sniff, and her gaze locked on Mike's cock. Her face was now gray with mottled pink patches that were already fading.

"She's dying faster than we can feed her." Yuki grabbed Dana's legs and pulled them over Mike's waist. "If we want to break the cycle, we're going to need you to—oh!"

With a growl, Dana mounted Mike, his cock sliding into her with little resistance. She leaned forward and snapped at his face, held back only by Abella, while her hips moved of their own volition.

"I've got it." Yuki leaned around the bed and came back with a roll of duct tape. She put it over Dana's mouth and made sure to flatten it along her cheeks. "Just to be safe."

Dana's body was cold, while his own felt like it was on fire. With another zap from Quetzalli, he cried out and shot a small load into Dana. The sparks along his body crawled onto her thighs and then vanished.

Dana's eyes went wide, and her growls turned into grunts as she tried to ride him. She flailed at him with her hands, but the oven mitts were adequate protection. Abella continued to hold the zombie away from his face. Yuki moved onto the floor because there was no longer enough room for her.

"Keep going. You're doing great," she told him from the side of the bed.

Between Quetzalli shocking his ass and Dana riding him, he didn't need any encouragement. His pelvis tightened as Quetzalli triggered another micro-orgasm, sending a cascade of sparks along his belly once more. A few of them lingered on Dana, then flowed back into him. Somehow, this only made his cock harder.

With a surge of strength, he grabbed Dana by the hips to guide her. All her movements were random, but now he could at least attempt to control her when she wasn't busy trying to eat his face.

The sparks were building up between them now, and Dana groaned through her tape. She shuddered, her skin briefly turning pink as blood flowed through her body. When she looked down at him, he caught a flicker of recognition, but it didn't last as her skin became gray again.

"Here." Yuki helped Mike sit up and gave him some water. He didn't realize how thirsty he was, and he sucked at it greedily. Naturally, it was ice-cold. Once finished, he shifted back down to allow Quetzalli access to his ass, and they resumed.

Dana's body temperature fluctuated wildly as he continued to blast small loads into her. With each orgasm, his magic flooded him with new strength, and he now had his hands on Dana's thighs. Her eyes were still bloodshot, but he caught glimpses of blue beneath her eyelids as she returned to them. She had placed her hands on his chest for balance, which allowed Abella to let go of her.

"Mmph," Dana muttered through the tape. She now alternated between grinding her clit on his pubic bone and lifting her body so he could slide most of the way out of her. When she did this, he could see Quetzalli down below, her eyes lit up in excitement. She was getting quite the show from her current spot but was still moving her fingers inside him. Her other hand was firmly planted between her legs, and the scale patterns on her face were shimmering in response.

Mike felt an immense pressure build inside his body. His magic suddenly uncurled, generating motes of light that hovered around them. Everyone stopped to watch except for Dana, who continued to fuck him hard enough that the bed was now groaning in protest. The lights swirled around Mike and Dana, and then a sizzling sound filled the air.

"Quetzalli?" Yuki moved away from the bed. "Your horn is sparking."

The motes of light turned into tiny stars, then suddenly connected to one another with dazzling streamers that flowed across the room. The lamps in the cabin flickered and went out as the motes spiraled around the room like a tornado of light, sucking electricity out of the cabin's outlets.

Mike's hair stood on end as the magic surrounded them. His consciousness expanded to fill the room, then the forest. For a moment, he was the soil beneath and the wind through the trees. Foreign thoughts shot through his mind like shooting stars, and then his mind snapped back into his body like a giant rubber band.

Dana collapsed on top of him as the energy brightened and then burned like thousands of tiny stars before rocketing across the room and into Quetzalli's horn. The dragon let out a gasp of surprise as her eyes lit up with power, and then she released all of it into Mike's ass.

The surge of energy through his prostate migrated through his entire body, and he felt time slow to a crawl. His own magic had been gathered up and focused back through his body. He could hear thunder inside his own head as the magic passed through his prostate and built up along his throbbing shaft. The pressure was immense, and his ears popped as he tensed up so hard that he couldn't even scream. Waves of pleasure ricocheted through his body as he blew a tremendous load.

Dana reacted immediately, her vagina clamping down on him as she sat upright, her arms going rigid. The magic swirled around her, and her eyes glowed with light as the magic went all the way through her body. Black lines formed along her skin and then burned away and vanished, her scream drastically muted by the duct tape.

A wave of light emanated from her, knocking Quetzalli into Yuki. The room was dark save for the waning light of day coming through the window.

"What in the gods was that?" Abella whispered.

Mike raised his arms, flexing his hands. He was able to move his legs again, and he shifted beneath Dana, grateful his strength had returned. Dana looked down at him, her eyes ablaze with their own inner light, and pointed at her mouth with one of her mittened hands.

He reached up and pulled off the strip of tape. Dana let out a loud, rumbling belch. She patted her belly and released a sigh of contentment.

"I'm finally full," she announced, pulling herself off Mike, her legs unsteady beneath her as she tried to get off the bed.

"Are you okay?" Mike asked.

"I think so." She rubbed her eyes. "Still wish you had tits, but that's a dead girl problem. Um…high five for the assist?"

He laughed and slapped the hand she held up. When he sat up, he saw that Yuki and Quetzalli were tangled up together but struggling to stand because the fairy lube had spilled all over both of them and coated the floor.

Abella moved to assist them while he took the tape off Dana's wrists. The weakness was gone, but he felt like he hadn't eaten in days. He really hoped there was some clam chowder in the soup box but would happily eat whatever came out of the can.

Dana stretched next to him, then frowned. "Where are my pants?"

"They were a casualty of your breakout," Yuki explained. "You're gonna have to wear something else."

Dana nodded, then looked at Mike. "Thank you. I know it's weird, but I appreciate it."

He nodded. It wasn't like it was a huge sacrifice on his part, but he had been happy to help. Taking a deep breath, he slid off the bed and went to find his own clothes. Once he got something to eat, it was time to figure out the next step. There were a massive number of problems he needed to address, and he would require every ounce of strength to make it happen.

Velvet found Uncle Foot up on the roof of the cabin. He stood next to the chimney, his face fixed in concentration as he surveyed the land. The sun was nearing the tree line, and his features were grim.

"You okay?" she asked him.

He shrugged, an expression that made his fur ripple. There was a scorch mark on his leg where Quetzalli had accidentally tased him. "There has been much change in the last few days," he told her. "And I fear the changes yet to come. Have I ever told you I can smell the future on the wind?"

"Only about a million times." She smiled. "But I don't ever get tired of hearing about it."

Bigfoot snorted. "I should have been able to sense them," he said. "The Nirumbi and Leeds. The forest should have told me, much in the same way it tells me where to find game, or if a hunter is lost."

"It is winter. The forest is asleep."

"Even asleep, the forest always watches." He frowned. "I wonder if what Leeds told me is true. Have I turned my back on the land? It would explain many things."

She snorted. "Please, he's so full of shit. He came storming in here with an army and every intent to kill us. You can't give him credit for that."

"Just because someone is your enemy does not automatically make them wrong." He fixed her with an intense gaze that made her look away. "I have long wondered if perhaps I have spent too much time in one place."

"What do you mean?"

He shook his head again. "I mean that I know about the eggs. And I know about your feelings for him."

She blushed and looked away from him. There was no use in denying any of it. Uncle Foot may play at being super laid-back, but he was still very perceptive. Maybe that was from centuries of wandering the forests of North America.

"You don't know everything," she told him.

"Of course not. But I do know that your place is by his side."

She groaned, then instinctively placed her hands on her belly. She could still feel the tightness of the clutch from before she had laid them. Her uncle wasn't wrong; she really wanted to go with Mike. His idea to open a portal and connect his home with the cabin's land had made her heart soar.

"You're planning to leave, aren't you?" Her voice was barely a whisper, but she knew he could hear it.

"Your father told me to take care of you. Mike seems like a good man. A very good man. He can give you many things that I cannot." He sighed and then sat down on the roof. "Can I tell you something I've never said out loud? I've always been scared of watching you girls grow old."

"What do you mean?"

"In all my life, I have wandered. I've had many friends, but I rarely stay in one place. You and Lala are the first mortals I have watched since the beginning. You were children, each of you fitting in my palm." He smiled wryly, then held up his giant hands.

"That isn't saying much," she pointed out.

"I watched you grow. Hell, I helped raise you. But I will also be here when you die. When Darren...when he got sick..." He turned his head away and took a moment before continuing. "I watched him grow old and waste away. It was one of the hardest things I've ever experienced. But I never thought of him as my own child. Time is a bastard. When you're young, you wish it would pass faster. When you're old, you wish you had more of it. But when you're like me, you take it for granted. The idea of watching you and your sister grow old terrifies me. And so I wonder. Have I stayed in one place too long?"

"Ah, Uncle Foot." She wrapped her arms around his and hugged his bicep. "We've still got maybe fifteen, twenty years left before that happens."

"It goes faster than you think." He wiped his eyes. "But it isn't just that. I—"

There was a rumble beneath them, and all the lights in the cabin went out.

"I wouldn't worry about it unless they come get us," she suggested. She could hear Mike's moans through the vibrations of the roof, which made her belly tighten up.

Bigfoot nodded in agreement. "What I was trying to tell you is that when the two of you are gone, that's it. Your family brought me so much damned joy, and it's hard knowing the end is coming."

"And so you want to leave?"

He shivered, even though she knew he never got cold. "I do, but I don't. I want to distance myself now, to spread the agony out over time. To reconnect with the land and scatter the grief to come over the years."

"I hate your plan." She let go of his arm and smacked him on the thigh. "It's a stupid fucking plan. Boo-hoo, I'm sad, so fuck you all?"

He snorted, then laughed. "Yeah, it does sound kind of stupid when you say it like that."

"If you want to wander the land, then go wander. Fuck the Order, fuck the internet. Lala can keep your travels scrubbed. She would probably see it as a personal challenge. Come back and visit, watch what happens next. You don't have to give up one thing to have another."

The two of them sat in silence for several minutes as Bigfoot contemplated her words. It was getting dark enough that a couple of the brightest stars had come out early to greet them, and he peered up at them.

"Shit." He turned to look at her. "When did you become so smart?"

She blushed again. Ordinarily, she would bask in his comment and maybe even gloat a little. However, his speech about her family had her mind whirling in circles. Uncle Foot had no way of knowing about what she had stashed in the glove box of her father's jeep moments before Abella had arrived. It was a single egg, very different from all the rest.

She wished she could talk to her sister about it. Out of the entire clutch, not only had this one felt different from all the rest, but when she'd touched it, she had seen her mysterious offspring again. How was it possible that she could have had a vision of someone before they were even conceived? Was she romanticizing the idea of reproducing with Mike? Or were her instincts on point?

It was a time-sensitive issue, though, and she desperately needed advice.

"Uncle Foot?" She unconsciously toyed with her father's dog tags. "I need to talk about something kind of important."

"Tell me what you need, fuzzy girl." When Bigfoot turned to look at her, the sun glinted off his eyes, making them glow. The grin on his face was safe and familiar, and she knew she was in good hands.

But that grin fell away as he rose and gripped the chimney so hard that a stone came loose.

"What is it?" she asked, but he had leaped free of the roof and onto the ground below. She followed him, suddenly aware she had left her father's pistol in the cabin.

Up on the roof of the barn, a massive snow owl watched them. It let out a hoot in greeting and then glided down to land roughly thirty feet away. Its wings were massive, and when it landed, it tumbled into a ball and unfolded itself into a woman who stood nearly eight feet tall. Her features were avian, as if she was more owl than human. She regarded them with wide, inscrutable eyes.

"Impossible," Bigfoot declared. "You are supposed to be dead."

"And yet here I stand." The woman bowed. "We wish to speak with the Caretaker."

"We who?" Velvet challenged the owl woman with a show of fangs.

"The children of the forest." She held a hand up and gave a wave. Nirumbi revealed themselves, though none were armed. Behind the trees, large creatures shifted about, revealing themselves through movement. They were completely surrounded. "We mean you no harm, but peace won't hold for long."

"Are you threatening us?" Bigfoot asked, his body expanding.

"While the Devil of Jersey is absent, we have an opportunity." Her voice clicked in places, and Velvet realized her lips were actually a flattened owl's beak. "If you wish for peace, then I suggest we hurry."

"Uncle Foot, who is this?"

Bigfoot balled up his fists, then looked at Velvet. "Her name has been forgotten by the forest. But I do know she's nothing but trouble, her and her troublesome sisters."

"It is just me now. And much like you, I have changed over these long years." She turned to gesture at the Nirumbi. "They won't wait long, and neither will Leeds. Please. The Caretaker. Only he can help us now."

Bigfoot growled, but Velvet put her hand on his arm.

"It's his decision," she told him. "We should let him make it."

He turned his head toward her and nodded. "Fine. But it'll probably be the wrong one."

Her uncle was likely right. But no matter Mike's choice, Velvet was prepared to stand by him when he made it.

TAKING RISKS

They walked through the forest. The owl woman had transformed back into her bird form and was leading them along a winding path. Around them, the Nirumbi chirped quietly as they watched the motley crew march through the snow, the crunching of the ice beneath their feet disturbed only by the sound of Mike eagerly slurping down yet another can of soup.

"Ugh, I hate split pea and ham," he declared, handing the empty can to Bigfoot, who crushed the can flat between his hands. Bigfoot stuck the flattened can in a small cloth bag he carried that was emblazoned with the words *Camp It In, Camp It Out.*

"Are you done yet?" Bigfoot asked, wiping his hands clean with snow.

"Hell, no. I saved the best for last." Mike swiveled his backpack around, reaching inside to grab a can of New England clam chowder. He popped the top and handed it over to Yuki, who heated it up with her fox fire. Steam rose from the can as the soup was heated to a level of perfection a microwave could only dream of.

"I don't know how you can stand to eat that garbage." Bigfoot shook his head in disgust. "It's like someone who's never eaten clam chowder tried to replicate it. And you're lucky if you get more than one bit of clam."

"You're lucky I couldn't carry more." Mike's stomach growled as if in agreement, and he took the can from Yuki and started drinking it. He had already handed her another can of clam chowder to heat up.

Upon the announcement that the Nirumbi had returned with a shapeshifting owl, Mike had gone outside to greet them. Though he had his doubts, the owl woman had seemed sincere, and he needed to get home as soon as possible. Some doubts had been voiced, but it was ultimately decided that the risk was worth taking.

After he'd loaded up his bag with as much soup as possible, the group set out. The Nirumbi had watched silently from the trees until Dana emerged from the cabin. Her eyes no longer glowed from within, but they were rimmed with crimson. She looked almost human again, but the Nirumbi gave her an exceptionally wide berth.

Bigfoot used portals to speed their journey as the owl flew ahead of them. The sensation of the forest shifting around them made Mike a little nauseous at first, but he was too hungry to give it much attention.

"So what can you tell me about the goblin king up there?" Mike nodded in the direction of the owl. "An old friend of yours?"

"Is that a *Labyrinth* reference?" A smile tugged at Bigfoot's mouth.

"Might be." Mike swallowed a good amount of his can, regretting that he didn't have any crackers.

Velvet appeared next to them, then wrapped an arm around Bigfoot's waist. "Do you remember that movie, Uncle Foot?"

"You two must have watched it a thousand times." Bigfoot's eyes crinkled in the corners. "The two of you would take turns being the girl from that movie. I was usually…was it Ludo?"

"It was." Velvet looked at Mike. "We would take him to the bog of eternal stench, which was just the hot spring, and take turns rescuing one another."

Bigfoot chuckled. "We had to stop watching it when Vee got older. She developed quite the crush on David Bowie."

Mike laughed. "Her and everyone else."

"I busted her kissing him on the TV when the movie was paused." Bigfoot immediately sidestepped through a portal just as Velvet tried to smack him. He reappeared twenty feet in front of them, only to vanish again when she tried to hit him with a snowball.

"Uncle Foot, you take that back!" She was remarkably quick, and her actions upset the Nirumbi watching them. They hooted before vanishing into the woods, leaving only the owl to watch their antics.

Bigfoot spent a couple of minutes making kissing sounds before Velvet nailed him with a snowball right in the face. Laughing, he waited for them to catch up, then scooped some snow out of his beard and rubbed it in Velvet's hair.

"So about this owl woman…," Mike muttered.

"Right, sorry." Bigfoot's grin turned to a frown. "She is not a friend of mine. Some years ago, she and her sisters were well known for terrorizing the tribes. They ate anything they could get their hands on, people included, so they were hunted until only two were left. Early last century, they stole a boy from one of the villages. The boy escaped and ran home to tell the elders where the sisters lived. I was under the impression they had all been killed, yet one survives."

"Definitely not a friend, then." He continued walking, then turned to look behind. Yuki was fine as she walked on top of the snow. Dana trudged forward without any problem. Quetzalli, however, struggled. She was sinking into the snow up to her shins and was obviously tired.

He slammed the rest of his soup and took the last can from Yuki. When Quetzalli caught up with him, he offered it to her and then slid a hand around her waist. "Here, let's walk together."

She smiled and took a sip of the can. "Oh, gods, this is just salt and cream," she exclaimed. "And was that a clam? What's wrong with it? It tastes like someone else ate it already!"

She handed the can back, and he took it.

"More for me, I guess." He bet Tink would have loved it. They had some differences in opinion when it came to cuisine, but he could easily imagine the goblin chugging a can of the stuff in between projects. He really hoped she was okay. As soon as thoughts about the house entered his head, he promptly shut them out. Worry and fear would paralyze him, and he needed his mind in the here and now to deal with whatever was coming.

As they crunched through the wilderness, he heard snippets of words nearby. They were solitary thoughts, barely audible in the cold dark of night. It was the spiders of the woods, just trying to survive until daybreak when they could warm back up and hunt for food.

But it wasn't just the spiders he sensed. Whenever he moved close to the trees, he was under the impression they were listening. On a few occasions, he would put his hand out to either steady himself on a trunk or move a branch, and he could have sworn he felt the tree shift beneath his touch.

"Are there dryads out here?" he asked, looking at Bigfoot.

"Nope," Velvet answered. "It's always just been us."

"But the trees…" He looked at a nearby pine. Though it looked like an ordinary tree, he could almost feel its presence in his mind. "It almost feels like they're watching me."

Bigfoot nodded. "The land watches you, Caretaker, as it watches us all. There are many spirits that reside in nature, many of which cannot be perceived. Each tree is alive in every sense of the word. They think and feel for themselves, much like children. Together, they make up the mind of the forest."

"Like a hive?" A chill went up his back.

"In a way. Everything out here is connected, Caretaker. This is an important thing for you to understand." Bigfoot put his hand on a fallen log. "I am very surprised you can feel it though."

Amymone. Sex with the dryad had apparently come with a perk of its own. Did the women he slept with gain something from him? Cecilia had that little red streak in her hair, but what about Lily? Or Naia for that matter? He looked at Quetzalli, Velvet, and then Dana. What part of his soul had he given to them? Peering up into the sky, it occurred to him that Abella seemed no different from when he had met her.

He should probably be keeping a little black book with this information in it, but he hated the idea of carrying around his own personal fantasy fuck list.

The more they walked, the more he could feel the forest. He no longer felt like the trees were watching him but that they were reaching toward him. When he first heard the whispers, he thought it was just more spiders suffering through their eight-legged anxieties, which were largely narrowed down to *eat*, *hide*, and *build*.

However, the longer he was steeped in these thoughts, the more he realized how much he missed the sun. He longed to feel its rays across his body and to soak in the cold, trickling water that would come from the melting ice. To feel thunder booming through him as the spring rains came, to feel the songs of the forest embrace him, and—

A heavy hand gripped him by the shoulder, snapping him out of his reverie. It was Bigfoot wearing a smile on his face.

"Perhaps, when this is over, I can teach you to listen to the trees without losing yourself." He gave Mike a firm squeeze. Mike looked around and realized they were somewhere new. How long had he been lost in thought?

"I would like that," he replied.

"It is an honor to speak with the forest," Bigfoot told him. "Never do anything to break that bond, for it is sacred and the forest will remember."

He nodded, and they all continued.

Guided by starlight and foxfire, they finally arrived at a small rock formation surrounded by snow-dusted bushes. The owl landed just ahead and transformed back into a humanoid, her dark eyes devoid of emotion. Before them, the night sky had been blotted out by a mountain.

"We are here," she announced. Mike couldn't help noticing that Bigfoot looked around with grim recognition.

The owl woman raised her arms and waved. Around them, the forest shifted as creatures slowly revealed themselves. Most of them were beast-like, but almost all were frightening to behold. A large bear with no fur and an oversize head regarded Mike with bared teeth. Above the rocks, a large eagle with a moose head landed, then stood to reveal the body of a man. More than a few serpents circled the area, but they all remained back.

"If this is an ambush…," Yuki growled, but the owl woman held up a hand for silence.

"This is not an ambush. We have brought you here so you can see our numbers. Other than the Nirumbi, none of us here were part of the assault on your home." The owl woman chirped softly, and a few Nirumbi came forward. "Time is short. We must descend into the earth."

"Why can't we talk out here?" Mike asked.

"There is much to discuss," replied the owl woman. "And you must see to understand."

Mike looked at the others. Uncertainty was written on their faces, but Bigfoot nodded.

"I know these caves well," Bigfoot explained. "If they hope to lose us, I can get us out. I believe I know what we have come here to see."

Mike nodded, then looked at the others. "At the first sign of trouble, you know what to do."

"There will be no trouble, Caretaker." The owl woman hopped down from the rocks and landed silently on the snowy ground. Her feathers swirled around her like a cloak. "You have survived the Nirumbi's arrows, and they now believe you to be one of the forest gods, like Bigfoot. Your companions are frightening, but the one who eats the dead frightens them the most."

Dana raised an eyebrow. "Technically, anyone who eats meat eats the dead."

"Do you know why the Nirumbi eat their own dead?" The owl woman stepped back toward one of the bushes, then grabbed a branch and pulled it to reveal a narrow opening. "By eating the flesh of their dead, they gain the strength of the fallen warriors. You consumed the flesh of many of their warriors while they lived, which is even more powerful but considered taboo. They fear the strength you have gained."

Dana smirked, then made a fist. Hidden in the trees, the Nirumbi chirped in fear, then went silent.

"Good. They should be afraid. Shall we?" Dana went first, ducking her head to go through the opening. Mike looked at the others, then up toward the sky. Abella hadn't bothered landing but now circled even higher than before. It was clear she intended to keep watch.

"Time is of the essence, Caretaker." The owl woman regarded him with mysterious eyes that reflected the starlight. "If you wish to beat the Devil of Jersey—"

"Yeah, yeah." He crouched and moved forward into the darkness. If it meant defeating Leeds and getting home, he would walk through fire if need be.

"WELL? WHAT DO YOU THINK?" BETH FROWNED NERVOUSLY AT OPAL, WHO was perusing a copy of Risk's instruction manual and the sheet of notebook paper where Beth had written her own ideas. The slime frowned as if in deep thought, then nodded her assent.

"I think it could work," she signed. "But you will have to be careful with the wording. The angel will take the agreement literally."

"Indeed." She stood and moved toward the window. They were sitting in the lounge with the Egyptian artifacts pushed aside to make room for everyone. The various books and pictures had been stacked on top of one another so they could cram the statues and assorted items onto the shelves where they would be out of the way.

With the deadline looming, she wanted to be able to see the horsemen in case they arrived early. After her lengthy discussion with Reggie and Jenny, she had chosen this room to sit down and draft out her plan in. Lily had read over it and pronounced the whole thing insane but believed it could work. Needing further assurance, Beth had brought it to Opal. Though she still had lingering doubts, she couldn't help but trust Death's instincts about the now sentient ooze.

Opal thumped on her tub to get Beth's attention. "I do foresee at least one problem. Can you trust Jenny to stick with the plan?"

Beth licked her lips, then nodded. "Jenny is a lot of things, but she loves this house in her own way."

"But you're basing this whole thing off the Clue incident." Opal frowned, and then ripples appeared along the surface of her body. "This is like playing Russian roulette with a nuclear weapon instead of a gun."

"I know. But unless you have a better idea, this is what we've got." She looked over at Tink, who was still grinning in her sleep. The blanket they had covered her with was slipping off, so Beth adjusted it. Noticing the goblin was still wearing her goggles, Beth slipped them off her head and sat down on the couch.

"Ticktock, keep these safe?" She held the goggles out, and the bag at her feet opened its mouth, allowing her to drop them into the unknown. She then looked at the grimoire. She had set it on the table, a large slab of black marble with no legs that had hieroglyphics carved into the edges. It had been covered in a bunch of magazines Death had borrowed from the Library, but Beth had put those away a bit ago. The grimoire was next to a glass of milk and a plate of mostly frozen Eggos. The chill in the house meant they would take forever to thaw, but she needed something to smear peanut butter on.

Sighing, she stared at the grimoire. The cover was embossed with an apple, and the thick binding made it feel heavy. She picked it up and opened it to a random page, which was blank.

"If you had the ability to use magic," she said, directing her question to Opal, "but could only learn one thing, what would it be?"

"I wouldn't mind being able to walk," Opal signed.

"That makes sense." This book held so many secrets, but it also held knowledge she could readily use. The words within would allow her to tap into the very universe, to master the elements or maybe even reality itself. Naia and the others had explained there were issues with taking shortcuts, but she had cast the spell in the basement without any problems. So why couldn't she just learn a few basic spells now that would speed along her growth?

Opal thumped her tub, then mimed fire coming out of her eyes once Beth was looking.

"Yeah, there was that." She closed the book again. "But I don't want to look up any Words of Creation. What about something simple, like a light spell? Or flight? Do you remember when the shadow used this book to cast that ball of light that blasted holes through everything?"

"That's not a memory I have," responded Opal.

"I keep hearing magic has a price, but I'm not really seeing it."

"Not all costs are things we can measure." Opal paused for a moment, as if deep in thought. "Look at Ratu, for example. Vast knowledge of enchantment. Powerful sorceress. But why is she living in the Labyrinth? Why not have her own castle somewhere?"

"Hmm." It wasn't something Beth had thought of. "You don't suppose it's just personal preference?"

"I doubt it." Opal paused, her face rippling violently. "In a way, I am the cost of magic. You have helped create a thinking being. Are you not responsible for my well-being? Think about the basic ethics of the situation."

Beth shook her head. "I didn't cast a spell with you as a by-product. You were the result of a very strange sequence of events."

"Again, you're thinking in terms of things we can measure. How do you explain Emily? Her obsession with magic led to her downfall."

"She got possessed, that's…" Beth paused. Emily had been attempting to gain magical knowledge, which had led to her being possessed by the shadow, who had then worn her body like a meat puppet. "Using magic doesn't always exact a price. Sometimes, it's the act of obtaining it that can lead to negative ramifications."

"I think you've got it." Opal relaxed and slid most of the way back into her tub. "Whatever you decide to learn from that book may change you. But you won't know until after it happens. Lily wasn't prepared to learn a Word of Creation, and look at what it did to her."

"You're right." Beth contemplated the book again. It was a decision that warranted some thinking. The spell she had cast in the basement had been easy enough, and she didn't doubt there were hundreds more. It was a book capable of opening right to the spell you needed, the ultimate shortcut. She could see why the society and the shadow had wanted it. Immense power waited for any who were ready to seek it out.

She bit into her frozen Eggo and blanched. Even with peanut butter, it didn't taste great. As she contemplated her meal, her gaze slid over to the grimoire. Would there be a spell that could cook her food? Surely a spell that low-key wouldn't exact too big a toll.

Five minutes later, Beth stood over the smoldering remains of a pair of burned Eggos and a smoking blanket. Luckily, the fire hadn't been magic in nature, allowing her to use the blanket to beat out the flames.

"That was stupid," Kisa told her, which made her jump.

"You saw that?" Beth realized it was a dumb question as soon as she asked it. Kisa hadn't left Tink's side, and the goblin snored quietly on the couch. The look on Kisa's face made it clear she thought it was a dumb question as well. She picked up the grimoire and ran her thumb along the edges.

"Every time I see you with this book, it makes me wonder. For instance, if there is a spell in here that could turn me back? Or maybe one to restore my memories." She opened it up to a random page, revealing a series of silvered letters that beckoned to them both. "And do you know what it reminds me of?"

"What's that?"

Kisa fixed Beth with a hard stare. "My memories are like a bad CD. They skip over songs and play things on repeat no matter how many times you push those buttons.

"But the memories I do have? They're vibrant. I get to live through them like I'm stuck in a bad dream. And every time I wonder about being human again, I remember how I got here."

Her hands touched her throat, and she let out a sigh. "It was an accident. I got hit by a car just when my life was gettin' good. Both of my legs were destroyed. I came from the streets, and dance was gonna be my ticket to a better future. Instead, my life was over. That's when we turned to magic. We tried to mend my legs with magic we didn't understand. I think you know what happened next."

She stretched out and gestured at her body. Her tail twitched behind her for emphasis. "This was my cost. A transformation I had no control over. I came here for help and found Emily instead. She forced me to continue my transformation until it suited her needs. It was a sequence of events we could have never predicted, but it all started with jumping in blind. The next time you think you know better, I think you should remember you don't. If it's something you really wanna dabble in, you should speak to someone who knows their shit, like Ratu. And you should keep in mind that she doesn't even want to touch this book until she's better. If a snake deity with hundreds of years of experience is wary of this fucking thing, then you should be too."

Kisa slammed the book shut, scattering the letters into the air where they melted into smoke. She handed the book back to Beth.

"Never rush into magic unless you have no choice." As Kisa spoke, her green eyes glowed. "You know why that thing has an apple on it? I think it's a warning. That book is full of forbidden knowledge, and you're about to get your ass thrown out of the garden for biting into it."

Beth sighed, then nodded. Kisa was right. The grimoire would wait until Ratu could properly examine it. Beth looked over at Opal, who nodded in agreement. Even the slime knew better than she did.

"Here," she said, holding the book out to Ticktock. The mimic opened its flaps, and she dropped the book inside, then sat down with a groan and examined the smoldering mess she had left on the table. She was still hungry, and now the room stank of smoke.

She used a rag from the kitchen to wipe down the table. Luckily, the dark marble was unmarred by her culinary experiment. In fact, the table seemed to absorb what little light there was in the room. Curious, she ran her fingers along the surface. It was smooth to the touch and felt like it was vibrating under her fingers.

Beneath the couch, she heard a clicking sound. She bent over to look but was interrupted by Lily, who knocked on the door.

"They're back," she announced, then pointed outside. Beth stood and watched as the mist swirled and billowed away, revealing the angel and his three riders. Death was already moving toward them, his pace casual.

"Guess I'd better go." She picked up Ticktock as she stood, pausing long enough to grab the instructions from Opal before moving into the living room.

Reggie and Jenny were already waiting by the front door, where the rat king held up the Risk box for her to grab.

"Let's go start an incident of our own, shall we?" Beth took the box and then picked Jenny up and cradled her like an infant. In the back of her mind, she could hear the doll's maniacal laughter.

THE CAVES WERE COLD AT FIRST BUT SOON BECAME WARMER THAN THE OUTSIDE air. Yuki had conjured a few balls of foxfire that floated along with the group, and Mike relied on them to see where he was going. He also had a flashlight but decided to save the batteries for the inevitable betrayal that would lead to the group being separated. They would be forced to escape the caves while being chased by spear-wielding boulder people who spat lava and farted fire.

The owl woman, who had never given her name, was waiting for them at the opening to a large chamber. Flickering lights beyond the entryway cast long, ominous shadows through stalactites and soda straws on the ceiling, which gave him an impression of a fearsome maw. He scowled in discomfort, half expecting to see a council of mythical creatures on the other side. They would all be sitting in a circle, ready to demand God only knew what from him.

He was wrong. The opening formed into a series of tunnels that contained glowing stones for illumination. Large columns vanished into the darkness above, revealing a massive chamber that was easily a hundred feet high in places. Holes in the bedrock revealed little hovels where Nirumbi families watched them from behind faded leather curtains.

"How can this be?" muttered Bigfoot. He was still hunched over, despite the tunnel's height. "I thought maybe a few had survived their war with the tribes, but this? This is unprecedented. "

The owl woman fixed Bigfoot with a stern gaze. "We are all capable of change. The Nirumbi, once fierce warriors who roamed the plains, learned long ago to live beneath the earth and have forsaken many of their warrior ways. They have done this for many generations along the mountain ranges of your country." She directed this comment to Mike.

"But surely someone would have seen them?" He looked over at a nearby hovel in time to see a pair of adults grab a child and pull them back inside. From what he could see, the males looked just like the females, so he had no way of knowing gender. Did they even have males and females? Or maybe it was asexual reproduction? The thought of watching one of the Nirumbi slowly split into two gave him the shivers.

The owl woman sighed. "Your people have but do not often live to tell the tale. You see, it is easy to make a human disappear when you eat it and toss its bones down a well inside a cave."

"Barbaric." Velvet snorted from behind Mike. "So, what, they just catch and kill whoever they wish?"

The owl woman dipped her head. "Some do. You see, the Nirumbi are at an important crossroads in their evolution. Many of them see the wisdom to keep to themselves and only feast on nonsentient beings. Others wish to return to their warrior ways. Leeds is the reason so many of them attacked you."

"Is he their leader?" Mike asked.

"In a way." The owl woman gestured for them to follow. The Nirumbi he spotted gave him determined looks, but he didn't see any of the ferocity that he had earlier.

They continued through the tunnels, revealing that hundreds of Nirumbi families lived there.

"Did they do all this?" Mike asked, gesturing to the stone-cut homes. He was surprised when Bigfoot answered.

"No," he said. "These caves were already here."

"They were," agreed the owl woman. "The Nirumbi are dying out. Despite having caves to live in, they still require the world above the ground to survive. After many close calls with the humans, the men with swords came and began an extermination."

"The Order?" asked Velvet.

"Yes." The owl woman was walking down the tunnel, but her head turned 180 degrees to face them. "Years ago, Leeds came to the Nirumbi and promised them a land where they could be free. In exchange, he needed their help to conquer it."

"That's a super dick move," Mike told her. "To just show up on my back porch and start shooting arrows at everyone."

"Your ancestors had no problem taming these lands with steel and gunpowder," she replied. "If you have a better suggestion for the Nirumbi, I would love to hear it."

"Why Leeds?" This came from Dana. "I saw all those creatures out there. Clearly, they didn't come help him fight. Why did the Nirumbi get to do all the dirty work while they just sat back? Except for the wendigo, of course."

"There were a few reasons for doing so." Her head swiveled around, and she took them down a narrow side passage. There were fewer Nirumbi living in this part of the cave. "The first is that he promised he could get everybody into this land. This was a feat that took him many years, and there were those who didn't believe he could do it."

"Opening a door doesn't make you a leader," Yuki said.

"Correct. What made him a leader was something he told us about called the great game."

Mike had been paying close attention to his surroundings, but now his interest was focused solely on the owl woman.

"What did he say?" he asked.

"Only a human soul could participate in the game, and despite his demonic appearance, his soul is that of a mortal. The plan was to take this land from the current Caretaker by any means. He claimed he could protect the vulnerable children of the forest but only if he was in charge."

"What else did he say? And where did he learn about the great game?"

The owl woman shook her head. "I do not know. Leeds is many things, but a reliable narrator is not one of them. I only heard this information thirdhand, and always after he had moved on. He has been preparing for many years now, and many thought he was a liar."

Mike nodded. "But then he actually brought them here."

"He sent out the call, and the children of the forest listened." The owl woman stopped and turned toward Bigfoot. "You of all people should know they have no leader. They were easily swayed by promises of a better world, much like you were."

Bigfoot held up his massive hands. "I'm not going to argue the point," he grumbled.

Mike looked at the owl woman, then Bigfoot. A thought occurred to him. "You don't want Leeds in charge," he said. "That's why you need me."

The owl woman twisted her head to look at him. "It is. You see, some of us have doubted Leeds's intentions all along, and his efforts to displace you have created a momentary breach of trust. The Nirumbi do not wish to continue feeding their warriors to your guardians, and many of the others fear retribution. The warriors of the Nirumbi are the next generation, and between you and the wendigo, they have already been halved. We now find ourselves at a tipping point where all that we want is finally within reach, but the cost has already been too high. We have seen the company you keep and wonder if there is a better way."

"They want my permission to stay, don't they?"

The owl woman sighed. "They do. We are tired of fleeing from your people, Caretaker. The Order has forced us to remain hidden from your world, which means we cannot retaliate in kind as our homes are bulldozed. This place is a sanctuary, an untouchable piece of paradise where they can live and be free."

"I doubt this." Bigfoot sneered at the owl woman. "Even if the Nirumbi are planning on playing nice from now on, I saw the creatures of the forest you had gathered out there. Some may be happy to piss away their days without bothering anyone, but you have a collective who's who of man-eating monsters up there."

"Really." Mike looked from Bigfoot to the owl woman. "I'm not keen on hosting creatures that will fight and potentially kill me or my friends."

The owl woman nodded. "And yet you did not see them attack you. But I do not expect that to be the proof you need to change your heart. There is more to see."

They followed her through a large cave with thick stalactites. The dripping water sounded almost like rain, and he could see thick tree roots up above. How far down beneath the ground were they?

"While Leeds is gone, it may be possible for you to win over the forest children by agreeing to let them stay, but I understand your hesitance. I would tell you my own story before we get to our destination. You see, I am one of these creatures Bigfoot would warn you about. My sisters and I—we used to hunt and devour humans."

"Tale as old as time. Please, continue." Mike waved his hand for her to go on.

The owl woman looked back at him as if judging his comment but continued. Her soft voice barely echoed in the cave. "You see, we didn't need to eat humans. Not only were they easy prey, but their parts made great materials for rituals. But we paid a price. There were once five of us. I lost three of my sisters to the tribes of this land. We only had ourselves to blame, if I'm being truthful. After their deaths, it occurred to us that maybe we were, in fact, wrong.

"My remaining sister and I decided that maybe it was time to understand the human world better, but we erred. We took a human child from his village and tried to raise him as our own."

"That didn't go well for you, did it?" Mike asked.

"It did not. Though we tried to offer the boy the secrets of our magic, thinking it would be enough, he betrayed us instead and returned to his people. When he led them back, we were caught off guard, and our home was destroyed. My sister died, but I was lucky and managed to escape." She stopped and put her hand on a rocky outcropping. Her clawed fingers ticked on the stone like an old clock.

"What happened then?" Velvet asked.

"I am the last of my kind. When I die, my legacy goes with me." The owl woman suddenly looked tired. "So I decided to try to become family with the others of the land, to pass on my knowledge. I encountered the Nirumbi decades back, and they revered me as an elder. Many of them came to realize the old ways are gone and it is time to adopt new methods of survival. That is part of the reason I am here; the others look to me for guidance as well. I know Leeds will outlive me. I would see the Nirumbi become something better than even I could be, but they will not do so with Leeds in charge. He hates humans and will spend his life forging the children of the forest into a terrible weapon to use against them."

She turned to Mike, her eyes suddenly wide. "But we cannot guide the children of the forest without you. Take away their reason for fighting, and Leeds loses his power over them. They are capable of learning, and I am not afraid to teach them the ways of peace."

Mike shook his head. "So you want me to, what? Forgive them for nearly killing me?"

"Yes." She bowed her head in supplication. "But do not speak your decision yet. For we have arrived."

Mike looked around but saw nothing out of the ordinary. Bigfoot, however, let out a grunt, then frowned.

"This way," he said, then crouched to crawl through an opening that had been hidden in the wall.

The darkness was difficult to navigate, but Mike found himself in a large chamber. Up above, large stony spikes glistened in the light of the foxfire. Multiple levels in the chamber made him realize that it had been carved out of the rock. The others came through and stood silently behind him.

"Where are we?" he asked, his voice gobbled up by the dark spaces above.

"The cave of the dead. The Nirumbi fear this place," replied the owl woman. She pointed out into the center of the chamber, and Velvet gasped.

It was covered in tiny skeletons, hundreds of them. They were curled up on the ground, their remains undisturbed. Mike moved into the middle of the chamber, his heart pounding. The tallest of the lot were perhaps four feet tall, and he could see the spiked protuberances at the fronts of their skulls. They were mostly mummified and still had their clothing and hair.

They were goblins.

"How did this happen?" Mike asked.

Bigfoot grunted, then wiped his nose. "Many years ago, the goblins emerged from the cave. They attacked our family, and we retaliated in kind."

"I heard, but this?" Mike ran up one of the nearby ramps. The hovels here were similar to what the Nirumbi lived in. He looked inside of one to see a goblin's remains lying across several smaller goblins. "You killed all of them?"

"There was no choice, Caretaker. We could not reason with them. They attacked us on a daily basis. It came down to them or us, and we won."

"Uncle Foot?" Velvet looked at her uncle with a mixture of awe and horror. "There are whole families here."

"I know." Bigfoot winced. "For your parents, your survival was far more important. This was not a choice made lightly."

"How did you do it?" Mike shook his head in shock. The goblin homes were everywhere. "I thought they were immune to poison."

Bigfoot grunted. "It wasn't easy. Ana and Darren spent weeks mapping out this cave system. Once it was done, they figured out the passageways where the air was coming in and then sealed them off. The goblins here had rituals that involved the phases of the moon. When we knew they would all be here worshipping their gods, we set up generators and flooded the tunnels with carbon monoxide. It was done in such a way that goblins sent to investigate the noise died first. Their bodies were immune to poison, but they still needed air to breathe."

Horrified, Mike sat down on one of the ledges. From where he sat, he could make out the central dais of the chamber. A figure in ceremonial garb lay nearby, the fabric now moldy from the dampness of the cave. Velvet's parents had slaughtered the goblins while they had essentially been attending church.

"There had to be a better way," he muttered. But was there? If the goblins kept attacking them, then there would have been no option. Still, to see that an entire tribe of goblins had been wiped out?

"Evil is in the eye of the beholder. The goblins didn't see themselves as evil; they were just doing what they have always done. This was the price they paid." The owl woman transformed and flew toward the top of the cave. "I have one last thing to show you," she said after transforming back.

He didn't want to see. The owl woman had already made her point. But he stood and followed. A cool hand found his, and he looked into Velvet's eyes.

"I had no idea," she told him. "I always thought they drove them off, or at least killed them in battle."

He nodded, then navigated his way up the path. The footing was treacherous, but Velvet had no problem with it. She supported him until they got to the top. The ceiling was low, and the passage led to a narrow chamber.

"Here." The owl woman pointed at the back of the cave. Mike clicked on his flashlight and almost dropped it.

The beam fell on a rudimentary bookshelf that had been carved into the wall. There were a few books still on the shelf, but they had long ago turned into little more than paper mush. On the nearby wall, he saw that someone had drawn symbols in dark paint. In crude letters, someone had practiced the alphabet over and over again, until the letters culminated in a declarative statement that sat away from the others.

I LYKE TO TINKR
TINKR IS ME NAME

Beneath the words there was a series of stick figures that were clearly meant to be goblins. They were drawn with angry faces and clubs standing around a tiny goblin with tears on her face and knees pulled up to her chest.

"Tink," he muttered. He had never thought to ask where she came from, and she had never brought it up. What little he did know was that the other goblins hadn't liked her. Was this where Emily had found her? How had the goblins come to be here in the first place?

"The goblins were ready to evolve. If one could learn to read and write, then why not more?" The owl woman hung her head. "Alas, we can never know. If they hadn't been exterminated, this one could have led them to a brighter tomorrow. I wanted you to see this, Caretaker, so that you would better understand why we can never predict the future of an entire species based on the truths of their past. Good men can become evil, and evil men can find redemption. Why not an entire people? My story alone may not be enough to sway you, but this should. The goblins have been seen as irredeemable for centuries, but this? This is proof they had the potential to change, to be better than what they were."

Mike reached out to touch the letters on the wall. How many decades had they been there?

"He can't lead the Nirumbi to a brighter tomorrow." Yuki's voice came from back in the cave. She stood at the edge of the goblin pit, her fists balled up at her side. Foxfire illuminated her from behind. "You can't just expect him to drop his life and come be a leader to people he doesn't even know. This isn't his burden to bear."

"You misunderstand. If the Caretaker agrees to let the forest children stay, then our only obstacle is Leeds. I will stay and guide the children of the forest. I have much to teach them and not enough years." She made a symbol with clawed hands that glowed an angry red color. "On the topic of Leeds, his is the magic of shadows. He learned it from a witch. Though I can't take down his barrier, it is in my strength to help you cast him out. Once he passes through the barrier, it will come down and you will be free to leave."

"What guarantee do we have that he won't come back and start this shit all over again?"

The owl woman shrugged, which sent a few loose feathers to the ground. "Even if he does, he won't be able to build his trap. I and the others will make sure of it."

Mike traced his fingers along the letters of the wall. Tink was in danger. Everyone at the house was. Maybe there was a catch in the owl woman's deal that he couldn't see, but he didn't have time to figure it out. The others could leave with him, and even if he were to lose the forest, he would still have his family and his home.

"I accept," he said, hoping this wasn't a huge mistake.

To his relief, Bigfoot grunted in approval. Even if they were both wrong, he at least felt better making a mistake with a friend by his side.

No, many friends. He took Velvet's hand and squeezed her fingers. He didn't have a word for their relationship yet, but he looked forward to figuring it out.

"Let's get out of here," he said, then turned to face the owl woman. "Do you think the children of the forest will help us with Leeds?"

She nodded. "Some will not. They abstain and wait for the victor. Please do not fault them, for it is their way. But you have my vow that I shall not rest until the Devil of Jersey has been captured."

Bigfoot held out his hand to the owl woman, like he was expecting her to slap him five. She timidly placed her claw over his.

"I misjudged you," he told her. "You see, I used to take my duties to the forest seriously but was blessed to become part of a family. Instead of wandering the land and fixing its ills, I indulged in matters of the heart and felt myself grow in ways I never imagined. Knowing now how that feels, I can understand why you did what you did."

"Thank you." The owl woman withdrew her hand, which disappeared into her feathers. "In that case, let's go meet with some of the others. I have an idea on how to capture Leeds, but we must move quickly. He will likely return in a day or so."

They walked away from the cave, but Mike hung back. He turned one last time to shine his light on Tink's words.

"I'm coming home, goblin wife. Just hang in there." Setting his jaw, he turned to join the others and descended to the bottom of the goblins' pit. When he got to the mouth of the cavern, he stopped and looked back. His goblin in-laws were in there somewhere.

He wished their spirits well, then hurried after the owl woman to catch up.

IT WAS NEARING THE MIDDLE OF THE NIGHT WHEN THE BACK DOOR OF THE house opened. Eulalie leaned away from her computer to see Sofia and Sulyvahn walk inside with Cyrus in tow. The man's head was back inside the pillowcase, and they directed him over to the couch.

The lights in the kitchen had been unscrewed. Even with his eyes unhindered, Cyrus would have trouble making out her form in the shadows.

"I hear you've had a productive day," she said. Other than sneaking a nap earlier, she had watched as Cyrus was led across the property. Naia and Amymone had hidden away once the man was out back with the idea that the less he knew about everyone else, the better.

"That's a matter of opinion." Cyrus scratched his head through the case. "I think I ended the day with more questions than answers though."

"Success isn't always a feature of productivity." She looked up at Sulyvahn, who handed her a diagram Cyrus had drawn. It was a map of the grounds around the house. There were several little dashed lines done in blue ink all over the property and inside the house. However, a thick red line had been drawn along the back where the gate was. "What am I looking at here?"

"That's a great question. Hard for me to tell you with this thing on." He gave the case a tug. "Don't suppose—"

"Nope. A girl's got her secrets."

"What is a rat queen, anyway? Other than the obvious, it's not a title I'm familiar with."

She smirked, then used the tips of her front legs to create a clicking sound that sounded very much like the grinding of teeth. It was a noise that had driven her parents and her sister nuts. "Oh, you definitely don't want to see what I've got going on. I'm all hair and teeth, and you will be driven mad at the sight of me."

"I've seen worse," he offered.

"No, I mean you will literally go mad. Part of my magical charm. It's a feature, not a bug."

Cyrus went quiet for a moment, then sighed. "Okay, whatever. Your rules. What are you asking about?"

"Let's start with the lines." She had heard some of his answers while spying with the drones. It had been child's play to attach a microphone to one and then land it around the yard while he did his work, but she had been unable to capture any good audio while flying. In retrospect, it should have been easy to write a Fourier Transform program to account for the changes in current to the rotors of the drone. Knowing the exact speed of the rotors could give her the frequency needed to generate the proper sound-canceling technology to clean up the signal.

However, the microphone wasn't that great to begin with, and if she had started such a project, she would already be arguing in a chat room full of like-minded programmers about why it should be technically feasible. Finding a way to blend engineering with programming was a special form of madness she didn't have the patience for.

"Okay, well, the small ones are remnants of extraplanar activity. A small, healed wound on the space-time continuum, or however you want to put it. There are a few on the grounds themselves, but even more inside. For instance, there was one on the closet inside the front door. Means that a portal was there at some point, for a long time. It's left a mark, but it's gone now."

"Go on." What he said made plenty of sense. The home had its quirks, after all. A parallel-universe greenhouse with a shortcut built into the front yard. An enormous Labyrinth in the basement. And what she assumed was access to the fabled Library of Alexandria.

And that was just the stuff she could remember off the top of her head.

While looking at the dotted lines, she saw the pattern emerge. Using a pencil, she connected some of the outermost lines together. It didn't take her long to realize that she was essentially sketching the borders of the house before it had changed. The lounge with all the Egyptian crap was clearly outlined on the map before her, and if she pretended the house was twenty feet longer, the back wall of the home now lined up with the dots.

These lines were proof that the real Radley house had been there but was now gone. She ran her fingers along the dotted lines, wondering just where it had gotten off to. All this extraplanar data must have been so confusing for Cyrus, but she wasn't about to fill him in on the truth of the house. It not only wasn't her place to do so, but she was still fuzzy on plenty of the details herself.

"But all these were trivial," Cyrus continued. "I could detect their essence, but it's something that will fade with time. I was lucky to spot them at all, a function of how recent the event was. Still confusing as hell, by the way, that you won't tell me what happened, but no matter. Now, the big red one in the backyard is far more interesting."

"How so?"

He tilted his head back and forth as if lost in thought. Or maybe there was a gap in the fibers and he was trying to get a good look at her. Just in case, she held perfectly still.

"Two scars, fairly large, one on top of the other. I imagine this place had magical connections to somewhere else, which I would love to discuss—"

"Nope." This came from Sofia. "We aren't talking about us right now. Answer the queen's question."

Cyrus groaned in annoyance. "Fine. The big iron gate you have out back was the boundary for somewhere big. That was no casual portal to somewhere else, I can tell you that much. These other marks I made were for little things, such as connecting one place to another. This, however, is like a giant scar on space-time that goes somewhere outside of, well, here. Like, this reality. What interests me the most about it is that I can see that someone stretched it open and used it very recently."

"How so?" Now this was interesting. If she remembered correctly, the gate went to the Underworld itself.

"Because of the overlap. When I was doing my experiments, I was detecting a portal inside of another portal, which is impossible for so many reasons. So I have a theory that—" Cyrus sneezed, then shook in his hood. "Oh, c'mon! This is just disgusting!"

Eulalie held back laughter as Cyrus shifted the hood around, clearly trying to wipe himself off. She didn't care if it was another attempt to remove the hood; it was pretty funny.

"Okay, I was going to give you an in-depth analysis of extra-dimensional folding, but I need to clean myself up. This is nasty!"

"Give me the TLDR."

"The what now?"

Eulalie rolled her human eyes. Her spider eyes stayed focused on the mage. "The Too Long, Didn't Read version."

"This must be a millennial thing," he muttered. "You're all too damn impatient. In short, I suspect someone folded another space inside the first one. A bubble in a bubble, if you will. The portal at the gate went somewhere large enough that it was far more convenient to stretch the portal itself out and just shove everything through, then let it snap back into place and gobble up whatever was taken. Kind of like how I'm using the inside of my hood to wipe snot off my face instead of a tissue or a rag." Cyrus leaned back in his chair and folded his arms over his chest.

Fascinating. So instead of the Radley house being moved, another dimension had been stretched over it and then closed off. Eulalie's fingers tapped a rhythm on the desk as she pondered the implications of what this meant. Whoever had done this would have to be insanely powerful. And if they were, then why not just attack the house? Why had it needed to be moved in the first place?

Sofia gasped at the revelation and grabbed Suly's arm hard enough that her knuckles popped. The dullahan winced, then yanked his arm away to rub the injured area.

"Ye damned giant women and yer man hands," he muttered as he shook his arm and took a step toward Cyrus. "Okay, I think we be done here. Let's take care of yer bogies."

"Thank you." Cyrus held up a hand and was led away by Sulyvahn, who would take him over to the Radley house. Though devoid of magic, it still had plumbing that worked, and Cyrus wouldn't accidentally see Eulalie.

"We need to get ahold of Ratu," Sofia said. "If Cyrus is right, then the others are trapped in the Underworld."

"Hmm." Eulalie pondered this with her chin in her hand. "If so, then why haven't they escaped?"

"You can't think of it as a local thing. The Underworld is infinitely large. They may be stuck somewhere millions of miles from here, or ten feet away behind a magical boundary. It isn't somewhere you can just casually escape. And even if they could escape, without a guide, you can't go more than a hundred feet without getting lost in the fog. There is also the problem of roaming demons."

Eulalie chewed her lip in contemplation. She couldn't worry about every possible iteration of the Underworld issue. "Let's just focus on solutions rather than potential problems. If they are trapped in the Underworld, how do we find them?"

"We could ask Cerberus, but…" Sofia frowned. "Last I checked, she only listens to Mike and Lily. And her gate is disabled."

"Yeah, well…" Eulalie looked at a nearby rat, who stared at her with eager eyes. "The rats can do it."

"They can't, actually. The rules for building portals have their limitations, and the Underworld is one of them." Sofia moved close by and knelt so that she was eye to eyes with Eulalie. "However, I bet Ratu will have some ideas. If we can somehow reconnect the gate, we can at least speak with Cerberus and figure out our options. Maybe she can sniff out the house?"

"Hmm." Eulalie tapped her fingers on the table, then turned her attention to her laptops. Despite the collective knowledge of mankind at her fingertips, this was a unique problem that required a solution that couldn't be dredged up from the internet. She had cast her net wide and succeeded in catching an interdimensional expert while also establishing a secure presence around the home. Now, though, it was time to change tactics.

"What are you thinking?" asked Sofia.

"My mom had a saying. Once a web has served its purpose, you build a new one." She leaned back with a grin. "It's a spider thing. She was actually full of spider-themed advice. They were kind of like dad jokes on steroids. A bug in the hand is worth two in the web, knock that shit off or I'll swat you with a newspaper…"

"Still waiting on your idea." Sofia didn't seem amused by spider jokes.

"We go back to the Library. The rats can watch this place, and Suly can keep tabs on Cyrus. He's sleeping in the main house, so we don't have to worry about him wandering over. We do some research of our own on extra-dimensional folding or whatever until we can speak to Ratu. Make good use of our time."

"Are we planning to sleep at all?" Sofia raised her eyebrow. "Some of us have been busy babysitting all day instead of playing on computers."

"Sleep is for bitches." Eulalie smirked. "But if you need your beauty rest, be my guest."

"Guess I'll brew some coffee." Sofia stood and walked into the kitchen. "If anyone knows how to properly pull an all-nighter, it's a librarian."

Eulalie smirked, then turned her attention back to the monitors. On the display, she could see that the rat guard had set up a perimeter around Murray's home. The longer she spent with the rats, the more self-sufficient they seemed.

She cleaned up the dining room, making sure to leave no webs behind. Once she was satisfied she had left no trace, she waited for Sofia to finish her coffee, and the two of them returned to the Library together.

BETH STOOD WITH HER ARMS CROSSED AS MEHKHKAHREL DESCENDED FROM the mists above, his whirling form somehow glistening with light that didn't exist. Beneath him, Murray pointed dramatically upward, surrounded by War, Pestilence, and Famine. It surprised her that the air outside the home was far warmer than inside. This caused tiny alarm bells to ring in her mind, but she turned her attention toward Murray as his floating body tilted in her direction.

"We shall act as the final arbiter in this mediation," Murray declared. Though his limbs stuck out in odd directions, his mouth now moved appropriately when he spoke. "Each party will now present what they wish to achieve by the end of this deliberation."

"We'll go first." War stepped forward and stabbed his sword into the ground. "When this is over, we wish to walk the earth. That is our bare minimum, and we will accept no other offers."

Famine and Pestilence nodded their agreement. Beth sighed and looked up at the angel. She had expected this.

"Our desire is to keep these three from being brought to Earth. Even if only one of them arrives, countless people will perish." Beth looked over at Death, who nodded in agreement. "Death will be allowed to remain."

"It would seem that your terms are at odds. We ask now that you attempt to come to an agreement." Murray turned his head and was able to look at both parties with his crooked eyes. "This mediation will continue until an agreement is made."

"I wish to clarify something." Beth looked up at the angel's true form. "It seems to me that neither party wishes to budge on their demands."

"You must come to an agreement," Murray declared.

"Right, about that. Hypothetically speaking, what would occur should we never agree?"

Murray's lips twisted into a sneer, then a frown. One eye rolled up into his head, and then it snapped back into place. "No party may leave this space until an agreement has been made."

"Good." Beth smirked at the horsemen, then directed her attention to War. "You see, as Death's legal counsel, I am mortal."

"We are aware of your failings." War grinned, revealing that his teeth were full of black stuff. "But please, continue."

"These people, who I am still unconvinced are *the* official horsemen, do not suffer from my mortal affliction. As time here progresses, I have nothing to eat or drink."

Famine chuckled, then pulled an apple out of his bag and proceeded to loudly consume it.

"That's not our problem." War tilted his head and licked his lips. "We figure, at some point, you'll be hungry enough to give us what we want."

"Or I won't." Beth crossed her arms, then looked up at Mehkhkahrel. "You see, if I were to become incapacitated, then I would be unable to complete this mediation. Is that correct?"

"You are stating the obvious," Murray replied.

"So let's just say, for the sake of argument, I can no longer continue to represent my client. He would be free to seek new counsel, yes?"

"This is true."

"Good. Death, if I succumb to dehydration, who shall represent you?"

Death stepped forward and crossed his arms. "I will represent myself."

War let out a laugh, followed by Famine. If Pestilence joined in, it was impossible to tell. Beth gave them plenty of time to yuck it up. The false sense of security that had just been established would give her an edge.

"Do you wish to give in to their demands?" Beth asked.

"No." Death's eyes filled with fire. "I shall sit here for an eternity before I allow these fools to walk the mortal realm. As I have walked this world since the beginning, so shall I sit until it meets its end. Even then, I shall maintain my vigil, purely out of spite for my brethren. They shall never again take part in the end of any world, and it shall put a smile on my face to crush their dreams."

The laughter stopped. War's mouth hung open for several moments before he looked over at Murray. "They can't do that!"

"You must come to an agreement." Murray turned his head, but his skin remained in place, allowing Beth to see his skull through what were now empty eye sockets. His jaw moved inside the flesh of his neck as he spoke. If she had actually eaten anything, she would have puked. "Nobody leaves until both sides agree."

"That isn't fair!" Famine pushed his way forward. "You can't hold us to an eternal stalemate!"

"You must come to an agreement." Murray was surrounded by an intense aura of light, which caused Famine to back away.

"You all fucked up. Probably should have picked a better leader." Beth examined her nails, pretending to be interested in imaginary dirt. "If you win, the world ends and I die anyway, along with everyone I've ever loved. If you really are the incarnation of war, you should know better than to pin a human in the corner and give them nothing to lose."

War let out a yell and picked up his sword. With a cry, he stepped forward as if to swing it. Several eyes on Mehkhkahrel's body appeared and blazed with golden light. The sword froze in midair, yanked out of War's hands.

"Physical aggression by either party will result in forfeiture," Murray declared in a booming voice. Pressure from above forced Beth and the horsemen to their knees, then released them. The sword slammed into the ground, cracking the dirt. "You will never again attempt to attack the other party."

"Then what do we do?" Thick veins in War's neck appeared as his face twisted up in frustration. He picked his sword back up, careful to do so in a nonmenacing way. "Would you have us quit? It isn't fair!"

"Brother." Famine put his hand on War's shoulder. "I have a better plan. We force mediation until this bitch dies, then let it go. That way, at least we don't stay trapped here forever, but she still gets to die for pissing us off."

"In that case..." Beth smiled and reached into Ticktock to pull out the grimoire. "What if I told you I had a way to become immortal using this book?" It was a deliberately vague statement. She didn't know if the grimoire could do such a thing, but Mehkhkahrel couldn't call her out for lying. "This is perhaps the most powerful magical tome in existence. It contains Words of Creation."

"That is forbidden knowledge," Murray declared, his face going slack as his skull repositioned itself correctly.

"Not by the laws of my people," Beth responded.

"Is she correct? Does that book contain Words of Creation?" War's voice actually squeaked.

"It does." Murray sounded angry when he said this.

"How many?" This came from Famine.

Murray's forehead wrinkled up, and a sneer formed on his face. "Enough to make me concerned."

The conversation was veering in an unexpected direction. Even though the grimoire had no information she had found regarding harming the angel, Mehkhkahrel was clearly concerned that Beth had such a thing. The last thing she wanted was for the angel to decide to take away the book, so Beth stuffed it back inside Ticktock. The horsemen were off-balance, so it was time for her next ploy.

"So it looks like we are at an impasse. We will never settle. If you had taken the time to make an actual list of demands, something like 'we want to be on Earth, only not as the horsemen of the Apocalypse,' we might have played ball with you."

"We are forces of nature," Famine hissed. "We do not 'play ball.'"

"What if I offered you a way around this impasse?" Beth tilted her head in a conspiratorial manner toward War.

War chewed his bottom lip so hard that it split and bled. His muscles tensed for several moments before he let out a disgusted sigh. "I'll hear your idea, but we won't back down on our demands."

"Perish the thought." Satisfied she had their attention, she grinned smugly. "I want to challenge you to a game of war. Winner takes all. If we win, you go back to wherever Mehkhkahrel summoned you from and will not return until the gods themselves decree that it's Apocalypse time. But if you win, you all get a one-way trip straight to Earth to do whatever the fuck you want."

"Heh. You assume you can challenge us to a game you can win?" War flexed his massive chest. "What game?"

Beth held up the Risk box.

"I'm not playing a fucking *board* game!" War tossed his sword onto the ground and groaned. "I demand a real challenge! I want my heart to race, to feel the blood of my enemies splash against my skin, to see the dying light fade from their eyes! You don't get that from a board game!"

She took a deep breath, then let it out. This had been an expected reaction, and she was properly prepared. "What if I told you that you could have all those things with this game?"

War rolled his eyes. "It's a cardboard box full of paper and plastic. Maybe, if things get really exciting, someone will choke to death on a piece."

Beth looked up at Mehkhkahrel. She hated looking at Murray. "As the mediator, it is your job to facilitate any sort of discussion or agreements we wish to pursue. Therefore, what I am about to suggest is dependent upon your abilities."

"I am listening," Murray replied.

"Some months back, I underwent an experience where myself and the people I live with were pulled into a board game much like this one." She shivered as a few memories immediately surfaced, but chased them away in case the angel was trying to read her mind. "From our perspective, the game was real. In fact, our memories had been wiped and we were stuck in the roles assigned by the game. After multiple days, we finally beat the game, only to discover that we had been sitting around and playing it for about an hour in the real world. It was very similar to the Dreamscape in this manner."

What she didn't say was that Jenny had taken over the game completely, filling the house with Eldritch horrors. While everyone had been trapped inside the game, Jenny had been able to move in and out of it at will while manipulating events from the outside. She had added pieces from other games and shifted characters around for her own amusement. It had been a flare-up of the magic Jenny had absorbed from Yuki's emerald months past, one final blast of Jenny/Jane insanity that had led to the destruction of the game and a vow to never discuss the events that had occurred while inside it.

She definitely didn't need to bring up the fact that their memories had also been messed up. For most of the game, she had been under the firm belief that she was, in fact, Professor Plum.

"Why would I even care?" asked War. "What makes this game so special?"

"It's a game of strategy. Here." Beth handed over the rules. "We each command our own army in hopes of achieving global domination—"

"Ah!" War snatched the rules and looked them over. "Global domination, you say!"

Famine looked uncertain. "You are challenging us, actual horsemen of the Apocalypse, to a game of global conquest?"

"Six people can play. Since the three of you would be playing, we would get to have three players as well. Of course, this really only works if Mehkhkahrel is willing to essentially construct a parallel universe for us to destroy. The key to making this work, though, is that the board's condition determines what happens inside. We roll dice out here but see soldiers slaughter each other in there."

Murray's eyelid twitched. "This could be arranged, if all parties agree to it. You would also have to agree to a set of rules."

Pestilence waved their hands around, and the air filled with buzzing.

"Good point. Who would your three players be?" asked Famine. "I assume our brother is one?"

Death narrowed his eyes. "I am no good with games. You know this."

"Who does that leave?"

Beth hid the smile from her face as she pointed to Reggie. "Our players will be me, the rat, and Jenny." She held up the doll for everyone to see. "These two have played more board games than anyone else and are quite good at it."

War laughed so hard that the others stepped away from him. Large tears formed in the corners of his eyes as he pointed at Beth.

"You challenge…us…with a rat and a child's toy?" He held his belly and crouched as if holding in his mirth. "Oh, this is rich!"

Reggie closed the distance between the two of them until he stood at War's feet. The horseman laughed again when the rat put his hands on his waist.

"I will have you know I am no mere rat," Reggie declared. "I am a king. You would be nothing without the greed of monarchs like myself. So if you think my diminutive stature is equivalent to my abilities, then you have already lost."

Play with me! Jenny's voice was distorted as if playing through an old speaker.

War wiped a tear from his cheek. "I'm sorry, this is too much. I can't wait to crush all of you! So how do we do this?"

"Simple. We agree on the rules first." Beth pulled them out. "What happens out here translates to in there. You get to choose what your troops look like and how they act. You are free to make alliances. Whoever wins the game decides the fate of the world. It will be just like a real war."

War rolled his eyes. "And that is why you will lose. While we are inside the game, it will feel real. The first time you see a man's skull explode, you'll forget how to play this game. You will freeze as we take everything from you, one by one. Your mind isn't strong enough, little girl. And once we are finished, we will do it on your planet, with everyone you've ever loved."

"All is fair in love and war. That's something we can all agree on, yes?"

War's smile faltered. It was almost as though he sensed the trap. He looked at his siblings, who both nodded their assent. With a shrug, he looked up at Mehkhkahrel.

"On behalf of my party, we agree to these terms."

Murray's eyes flashed, and a large table appeared. The board was already set up, and thick chairs made of stone appeared. Runes burned themselves into the stone, and fiery symbols now glowed.

"Here." Beth handed Ticktock to Death, who grabbed hold of the bag.

"Make sure nothing weird happens to us out here." She didn't want her body blindsided while her mind was inside the game.

"It's a little late for that," the grim reaper muttered. He held Ticktock as if the mimic were dirty. "This business is already weird enough. Also, one cannot wear a backpack properly in robes."

"You'll figure it out." Her palms were sweaty as she took her place at the table. Reggie sat on her left, and she set Jenny on her right. The mists swirled around Mehkhkahrel as if trying to consume the angel, and Murray's eyes drifted apart so he wasn't looking at anyone in particular.

"You guys ready for family game night?" she asked.

Reggie nodded, his eyes focused on the horsemen as they sat. Famine's big gut pressed against the table, so he had to sit farther away. War's massive torso looked out of place as well, and he had the appearance of a meat dreidel that was ready to topple forward any moment. Only Pestilence fit into their seat, their hazmat suit sagging noticeably when they sat forward.

"Let's see what you've got," War sneered.

"And so we begin," Murray declared, and a bright light enveloped the players. The world swirled violently around Beth, and she felt like she was falling as the light took her. Terror filled her body, and she bit her lip to hold back a scream.

She hoped she hadn't just fucked everything up.

RISKY BUSINESS

The walk back to the cabin took less than an hour, and Mike let out a sigh of relief when he saw it in the distance. Bigfoot had them utilizing tree portals to shorten their journey, with the owl always hopping through at the last second. The ominous creatures of the woods had watched them when they left the cave, and many followed them toward their destination, but a few were left behind with each jump. He assumed it was part of the treaty they had established with the owl, who had acted as both an interpreter and mediator.

It was a fairly simple agreement. If the Nirumbi and the other creatures agreed to peace with the occupants of the cabin, as well as each other, then they could stay. The owl would act as their leader instead of the current Caretaker, whoever that may be.

However, this agreement hinged largely on getting rid of Leeds. The owl had assured them that her magic was more than capable of trapping him and that it would be a simple matter of pushing him past his own boundary. Mike doubted it would be that easy. If history was any indicator, he was in for a rough night.

He took the morning to sleep. Between sex with Dana and his near-death experience, he had been fairly energized all night. Upon seeing the cabin, his feet had started to drag through the snow, and he'd stumbled. Quetzalli and Yuki had held his arms until they walked inside, and he had promptly gone to his room and fallen into a deep slumber.

At first, he dreamed in images. Instead of landing in the Dreamscape, he saw the events of the last few days as they flitted through his mind like photographs in a flip-book. Darkness came and then went, and when he finally awoke, he was alone.

Puzzled by the silence, he moved to get out of bed and nearly fell when his foot caught on something heavy under the covers.

"Ow!" The lump in his bed shifted, and Kisa appeared, rubbing at her face. "That really fucking hurt!"

"What are you doing here?" he asked, then looked around. He was still in the cabin. "Is this a dream?"

"Maybe." Kisa slapped her cheeks and winced. "I must have fallen asleep in the sitting room. This feels pretty real though. Hey, listen! You need to get home right away! Three horsemen of the Apocalypse trapped us in another dimension, and Beth is—"

"Wait, what? The Apocalypse?"

Kisa scowled at him and grabbed his face with her hands. The pads on her fingertips were soft, but her grip was borderline menacing. "Shut up for a second and just listen!"

She explained it all. An angel had spirited them away and locked them up in a world made of mist. Apparently, Beth was acting as Death's lawyer and now was playing board games in the front yard against War, Famine, and Pestilence for the fate of all mankind.

He wasn't certain yet that this wasn't a dream.

"Oh, and something in the house has been attacking us," she finished. "Knocking us out, one by one. Tink was put to sleep a couple days back, and she still hasn't woken up. Cecilia got knocked out, and so did one of the fairies. Oh, and Beth got cloned by primordial ooze, so now there's two of her, kind of. It's time you wrap up your vacation and come home!"

Mike took a deep breath through his nose, doing his best to lower his blood pressure. If everything Kisa had said was true, they were all in danger and there was nothing he could do. He wasn't even sure what to do with the knowledge that there were now two of Beth.

"It's hardly been a vacation, here. C'mon." He slid out of bed and noticed he was still fully dressed from last night. At least he wouldn't be walking through this dream in his underwear. Those were the worst! "Let's try to figure out what our current situation is while I tell you what's going on in Oregon."

He explained the situation with Leeds as he put on his shoes, and then they walked into the main room of the cabin. He had just finished telling her about the new truce when he noticed the building had changed.

The television and entertainment center were gone. Instead, a massive fireplace with a roaring fire greeted them, casting long shadows into the eaves of the cabin. When he looked in the kitchen, it was much bigger and had an assortment of drying meats hanging by the window.

Kisa whistled. "This place is impressive."

He frowned, then looked upstairs. The shadows parted, revealing that the walls of the cabin were covered in various animal trophies.

"This isn't what it looks like in the real world," he told her. "Stick close to me."

She pressed herself into him and sighed. "Damn, you feel good," she muttered. "Just having you close makes me feel better. And safe."

He put his arm around her and squeezed. His magic responded to her presence, filling him with warmth and calm.

There was a thump from upstairs. They looked at each other, and then Mike looked at the front door.

"Don't suppose it would make sense for us to run, do you?" he asked.

The thump repeated itself. Mike pushed Kisa behind him and moved toward the stairs, his palms suddenly sweaty. Kisa shoved past him before they got to the top of the stairs, and he tried to grab her and pull her back, but he was too slow.

"What the hell?" Kisa looked over her shoulder at him. "I don't get it."

He climbed the last three stairs and saw what she was looking at. Instead of the upper floor, they now stood in a thicket of pines. Between a pair of gnarled trees, a massive stag stopped to regard them.

Kisa moved toward the nearest wall and ran her hands along it. "It turns into this tree," she told him while peeking through its branches. "It's almost like the cabin—"

"Is the forest," he finished, then knelt to touch the soil. When he buried his finger in it deep enough, he could just scratch the wooden floor beneath it. "But that doesn't tell us where we are."

The trees around them rustled, but there was no wind. He tried to track the invisible breeze using his hands, then jumped when he watched a nearby tree pop out of existence, leaving behind a stump with a woman sitting on it.

"Greetings, Caretaker." She winked at him, a playful smile on her lips. Her dark hair was wavy and hung loosely around her ears in a bob cut. She wore a leather tunic with matching pants, and her boots looked to be made of deer-skin. "I see you brought your familiar with you. She's cute."

Mike tried hard to relax but was worried. He was already up shit creek without a paddle; he didn't need any further complications. Kisa growled a warning from the back of her throat.

"You seem to know who I am, but I have no idea who you are," he told her.

When she laughed, the sound triggered memories of a summer rain.

"That's intentional," she told him. "In fact, when I summoned you here, I was very surprised I could take this form at all. It's been a very long time since I've spoken to a mortal, and when I do, it's usually as a disembodied voice. Having a body is something I haven't done in a few centuries."

"That still doesn't tell us who you are." Kisa moved in front of Mike protectively. "So let's try again. Who the fuck are you?"

The woman answered. The moment the words left her mouth, Mike felt like his soul temporarily left his body, and the forest shook. Kisa actually lost her balance and fell. When he knelt to help her up, he realized he couldn't remember the woman's answer. His mind was full of static instead of sound, and even the movement of her lips had been blotted away like a stain on a rug.

"I imagine the experience was unpleasant, but I knew you wouldn't have believed me if I told you the truth. Suffice to say, sharing my name is against the rules." She stood and moved closer to them. "I must say I'm surprised to see our new champion is a man. That's quite out of character for my sister."

"Your sister?" Mike helped Kisa up. "Who is your sister?"

The woman smirked. "Not so much who anymore, but what. She's the house you live in."

"Which makes you the cabin, right?" Kisa pawed at her ears. "I feel fucking nauseous, what did you do to us?"

"I did nothing. That would be magic that was created for the sole purpose of protecting the sanctity of the game. If I had told you anything more, your head may have exploded." She moved next to Kisa, the scent of pine needles and campfire surrounding her like a cloak. She lifted her hands and touched Kisa's temples with glowing fingertips. "Better?" she asked.

"Much. Thank you." Kisa rubbed her eyes. "So where is this place?"

"That's a good question. Some of us think it's inside the champion's head, while others think it's inside ours." She turned to walk away, then looked over her shoulder at them. "You coming? Time is short."

Mike followed behind her. They walked into the forest, and it came alive with birdsong. The longer they were in the woods, the more surreal the environment became. It was as though they had stepped into a painting, and the colors were just a little too bright.

They came to a clearing with a table made of stone and two wooden chairs on one side woven from tree roots; he immediately recognized one of the game boards and the pieces that had been set on it. However, now there were a couple of boards. One looked like his house, while the other was clearly the cabin and surrounding forest. Mike and Kisa sat down.

"I assume you've seen this before," she said, then sat opposite of them. Roots sprang up from the ground and wove themselves into an intricately decorated seat that looked more throne than seat at a dinner party.

"I have," he admitted. "But it's never been properly explained to me."

"Nor could it be. That's part of the challenge." She picked up a piece that had been on the table between the game boards and scrutinized it. It was a tiny version of Kisa, which she handed to the cat girl. "The fact that you're here is very intriguing. Familiars are usually animals, or maybe a golem, but never an actual human."

Kisa's tail swished behind her. "Lucky me," she muttered, then handed the piece back. "Are those all of us?"

Mike looked at the board and frowned. He saw Bigfoot and the others, all carved in meticulous detail, inside the cabin. "I didn't think they were part of the geas," he said. "They were outside it."

"Oh, honey, the great game isn't location specific." She pushed the cabin board closer to him. "These pieces are on my board. The geas is for my sister's board only. As for you, Caretaker, I wouldn't have even noticed your presence if not for that sudden burst of magic inside my walls. Woke me right out of my slumber."

Kisa snorted. "Who did you fuck?" she asked.

"It's more like who hasn't he fucked?" The woman winked at him. "The forest has told me stories."

"Is Bigfoot a good kisser?" asked Kisa. "'Cause you know Beth is gonna ask."

Though he hadn't kissed Bigfoot himself, he did have Emily's memories of the time she had had sex with him. "I'm not the kind of guy to kiss and tell," he replied.

"Psshh. You never kiss and tell, but everyone in the house has seen your bare ass, usually plowing someone from behind." Kisa looked at the house's board. "Why is this piece so fuzzy?" she asked, pointing at one he didn't recognize. It was in the office.

"He can tell you." The woman moved next to Kisa and put an arm on the cat girl's shoulder. "I like you. If you ever tire of him, you can always come live with me. You're fun."

"It means someone hasn't been discovered yet," he explained, then frowned. The piece, though blurred, was also blackened as if it had been burned. He tried to touch it, but it was so hot that he yanked his hand away. "Why is this one so different?" he asked.

"Because it isn't your piece." The woman scowled as the piece shifted into the living room. "And you are definitely not the one moving it."

Mike felt the world around him go still. Was it Amir? Or had the shadow returned? His list of enemies was frustratingly long.

"Speaking of, you have a similar issue here." She waved her hand and revealed that another gnarled piece sat on the table. He immediately recognized Leeds. "This little shit stain wants to be king of the forest. Besides fucking up the flow of my woods, he is also the reason you cannot get home and fix your problem there. Even if he tries to bargain with you, you cannot let him have this place."

"Because he's an asshole?"

She nodded. "That too. He thinks he can become a Caretaker, but it's not that simple. He wasn't chosen, and he isn't part of the game. All he can do is disrupt it. Putting him in charge would be like swallowing poison. If you can push him beyond my boundaries, I will see to it that he never crosses again. I've tasted the blood he has spilled already on my land, and I am not impressed."

"Who chooses who becomes part of the game?" Mike felt his heart pounding in his chest. He had so many questions right now, and he didn't know which ones to ask. He also didn't want his head to explode.

"It's different for all of us. You see, I call you Caretaker because that is the role you have taken on. Others like me will call their champions something else, like Curator, Captain, and even Conqueror. Each of us, in the beginning, was bonded to an entity who helped us choose. In your case, it's a simple nymph. As the guardian of the home, she chooses."

"Who is your guardian?"

She frowned. "There used to be a dryad who lived by the cabin, but she was killed some time ago when the cabin was captured by a competitor. It was taken again by a former Caretaker from your home, which is also why my board is part of your game now. I can never again choose my own champion. It's a bit of a failsafe; it keeps people like me from backstabbing you."

"Why would you backstab me?"

She grinned. "All sorts of reasons. Maybe I don't like you. Or maybe I'm mad at my sister. However, my fate is now tied with hers, so if she dies, so do I. That reminds me." She held out her hand, and leaves swirled around it, forming into a tiny replica of Mike. He was screaming in agony, an arrow stuck in his back. "You almost died out there."

"I know," he said, suddenly solemn.

"No, I don't think you do. By all rights, you should have died. I actually felt you cross over hundreds of times during that night, like the ticking of a terrible metronome. But every time, you found your way back. It was almost like something kept you here."

He thought of the women of the Dreamscape, struggling to keep the island from being consumed. "I have some ideas," he began.

"Don't share them." She held a finger to her lips. "Even though this is a sacred place, we can never be sure that someone isn't listening in. It may even be someone sifting through your memories years from now, or your familiar's. You've found yourself on a dangerous path, Caretaker, and I suspect the others will take notice of you very soon, if they haven't already."

"The others?" he asked, his voice cracking. He wasn't in the mood to fight with a Conqueror.

"The other champions. But none quite like you." He didn't see her move, yet she was suddenly in front of him. She brushed a lock of hair away from his eyes, then traced his cheekbones with a finger. "My sister was never much of a fighter, and she doesn't attract them. I always thought a fighter would be best, but it turns out that succeeding at the hunt doesn't mean you can properly skin a deer."

"Uh…" He looked at Kisa, who just shrugged. The metaphor eluded him.

"It's your heart. The thing that makes you a good Caretaker." She tapped on his chest. "Your compassion and kindness have brought you some very powerful allies."

"And his dick." Kisa sniggered behind him.

"That too." The woman smiled. "I always thought a nymph was an odd choice for a guardian. My sister's methods are unique in that regard. The others choose their champions through trials of strength and wits. I, too, used to do the same, but no longer."

"So the others are fighters." He sighed. "Okay. Having my ass kicked is nothing new."

"Your greatest strength is also your weakness. A heart that lends itself so easily to others is easily broken." She reached her hand up, and a nearby tree bowed down until its branches touched her hand. With a sharp yank, she snapped off a long branch about an inch across. She turned it over in her hand and pulled a field knife from a belt on her waist. "Do you know how you make a spear, Caretaker? You first trim away the branches. Once they're all gone, you sharpen the tip. And sometimes, when the situation calls for it, you throw it and hope to hit what you're aiming for."

"I suspect this is a metaphor for something?" He watched as her knife blurred over the branch, turning it into a wicked-looking spike.

She nodded. "I speak of the previous Caretaker. She cut ties with everyone who ever loved her, sharpened her resolve, and then threw her life away, hoping it would stick. She was never meant to be a fighter, and the shade of a former champion caused her to throw her spear into the darkness and lose everything."

"Not bad for a metaphor," Kisa muttered. "Sums up what I remember, anyway."

"There are those who would see you become a spear, Mike Radley." She turned the spear over in her hands, then handed it to him. The wood was oddly smooth in his hands and felt heavier than steel. "They will try to prune your branches, to sharpen you into a weapon. I wonder what will become of you then?"

He didn't like the implication of what pruning branches meant. With a quick snap of his wrist, he pressed the butt of the spear into the ground and put his free hand on Kisa's shoulders.

"Think of it as a walking stick with attitude," he told her.

"If nothing else, you will be a fun one to watch." She was in his face again, her breath cool against his cheeks. "I shall share one more thing with you this night. I am not just a structure in the forest. I am also the ground beneath your feet and the trees around you. Your true power isn't something that grows from within; it is also your connection with me and with others. Throw not spears in a dark wood, Mike Radley."

She surprised him with a kiss on the lips, then gave him a hard shove backward. While falling, he grabbed onto Kisa, who let out a cry followed by a hiss. Instead of toppling onto the hard forest floor, he landed on something soft.

Opening his eyes, he saw that Quetzalli was clutching his right arm and Yuki was asleep by his feet in fox form. Puzzled at the strange dream, he rubbed at his eyes and felt something tickle his face. In the dim light of dawn, he saw that his fingers were full of black cat hair.

THERE WAS A LOUD CHIME, FOLLOWED BY A POP. BETH OPENED HER EYES AND saw that she was looking at Earth from high above as it spun in space. Other than the moon and the sun, there were no other objects to be seen in the infinite void. Twinkling lights appeared on the planet as it rotated from day to night, and she watched in awe as mankind did its best to chase away the darkness.

Tears formed in her eyes. At this moment, she was finally able to grasp what so many astronauts had tried to convey. From this high up, all of mankind was condensed onto a single rock, tiny and insignificant compared to the vastness of the universe. The human race had accomplished great things and could do even more if they could just learn to see beyond themselves, to look at the greater good. This planet wasn't just her home. It was a monument to life, a cradle of—

"I cannot wait to blow this fucker up!" War appeared next to her, astride his massive horse. Flames jetted from the horse's nostrils. "Just look at all that simmering hate! Can you feel it?"

"N…no."

"Oh, it's there. You just have to know where to look." He pointed at Earth with his sword. "Man-made borders, dark zones to prevent spying. Way too many coffee shops. This planet is just a bundle of rage waiting to be let loose."

Beth looked away from War, only to find herself looking at Famine on his horse.

"He isn't wrong," Famine informed her. "You see, those in power will spend vast amounts of money to not only hold on to their wealth but convince you that the other peasants are the ones to blame for your lot in life. Despite all you have in common, they will whip you into a frenzy over your differences in the hopes that you take it out on one another instead of them."

She looked away from Famine but now stared at Pestilence, also on a horse. Pestilence buzzed dramatically at her for almost a minute, but she didn't understand any of it. It was clear that the last horseman was getting heated, because condensation was forming on the inside of the hazmat suit's visor.

"Holy shit," muttered War once Pestilence was done. "You really laid into her."

Pestilence nodded, then gave Beth a rude gesture.

"Mankind is about to see its end." Famine slapped his hands together greedily. "And once we've simulated it here, you will see it again on your Earth!"

"That is where you are wrong." Reggie emerged from the darkness, a glittering crown of gold atop his head. Beth's jaw dropped when she saw he was piloting a mech suit that was nearly seven feet tall.

"Where the hell did you get that?" she asked.

"It is but a thought away, Lady Beth." He nodded encouragingly. "Almost like magic."

She looked down at herself and willed herself into a flowing silver gown adorned with armor. A staff made of ivory appeared in her hands, and a cloud formed beneath her feet. Energy swirled around her and crackled between the fingers of her outstretched hand. She looked over at the horsemen, wondering if she could summon a fireball and torch them into dust.

"It's all cosmetic," Famine explained. "So don't think you're gonna pull a fast one on us."

The void filled with the sound of creaking wood. They all turned to see a small figure emerge from the darkness, astride a rocking horse. It was Jenny, and her horse had a smile painted onto its features much like clown makeup. The paint wasn't dry, causing the red around its mouth to dribble down like drops of blood.

Jenny giggled but said nothing as she held on to the handlebars of her horse and rocked in place. Somehow, despite the fact that they were hovering in space, the horse continued to creak as if it was rocking on squeaky boards.

"Oh, this is going to be too fun," War declared, then poked at Jenny with the tip of his sword.

Ouch! That hurts my feelings! Jenny sounded very much like an upset four-year-old.

"I'm going to hurt a lot more than your feelings," War growled. "When this is all done, I'm going to rip the stuffing out of you and use you as a fuck toy."

Beth covered her mouth in horror, half expecting Jenny to fly into a blind rage. Instead, the rocking horse retreated to a safe distance from the others.

Stay away from me, mister. Jenny's voice was barely audible. *Or I'll tell a grown-up.*

War and Famine both chuckled at the doll. Pestilence may have done the same, as the buzzing sounds coming from them sounded slightly higher in pitch. They were underestimating Jenny, which was perhaps the dumbest thing they could do.

In a flash of light, Murray now stood before them.

"This is a game of strategy," he declared. "The rules of the game are still the same, and your corporeal forms are still sitting around the table. In here, I have created a simulacrum of the planet and everyone living on it. They are noncombatants and will provide no in-game benefit."

"Then why are they here at all?" Beth asked.

"You offered a game of conquest." Murray gestured at Earth. Golden lines made of light cut across its land, separating the planet into territories. "When you choose your territory, you may dispose of its occupants however you like. They are here purely for flavor and can provide no benefit."

"That's barbaric! Why can't we just have armies or whatever?" Beth hadn't expected Murray to replicate Earth's population.

"That's how conquest works, sweetheart." War let out a loud whoop. "You see, it isn't just about how we fight each other. It's also about collateral damage. When we fight, you'll get to watch people die. Even the act of occupying unclaimed territory lets us get our rocks off!"

"It is what you promised," Famine added. "The game inside here would present itself as we see fit. And it's what we want to see."

Appalled, Beth looked away from them toward Reggie.

"You must harden your heart, Lady Beth." His mech put a fist to its chest in a salute. "After all, it is family game night. And we take no prisoners."

Tensing her jaw, she turned back to Murray. "So how does this work exactly?"

"In the real world, you are all rolling to see who gets to go first." Murray waved his hand, and the space in front of him filled with light as it became a portal to the real world. Through it, Beth saw that she and the others were sitting at the table, their eyes glassy as they took turns rolling a single six-sided die. There must have been a tie for first, because Reggie and Famine both rolled again once everyone had a turn.

"Oh shit," she muttered when a golden light appeared over Famine's head. If she remembered right, play would proceed to the left, which meant War and Pestilence would get a turn before Jenny did. If the three of them were coordinating at all, it would give them an opening advantage.

"Ah, let's see!" Famine slapped his hands together and looked at Earth. It rotated once every few seconds, allowing them to see every available territory. The world stopped moving, and they descended almost instantly to hover over South America.

Of course. Australia and South America only had four territories apiece, making them the easiest to conquer. Owning a continent gave a player extra troops at the start of their turn. The word *Peru* appeared in golden letters across the western side of the continent.

"It's go time!" Famine declared, and they were now on the ground. Beth looked around, curious about their destination. They were in a large city teeming with people.

"Lima," War informed her. People were milling about a city filled with both old and modern structures, some taking in the distant mountain views while others went about their day with nary a care.

Dark shadows swirled along the ground before bursting forth from the soil beneath. Horrific beings made of teeth and claws tore into the local populace, spraying the streets with blood.

"What the hell are those things?" Beth recoiled as one came near her.

"The Hunger." Famine grinned. "Made them myself."

Aghast, Beth watched as Famine's shadow troops formed after devouring the people of Lima. As their screams quieted, the group shifted back into space so suddenly that Beth felt her head spin.

"My turn!" War cackled and pointed his sword at Earth. Their viewpoint shifted slightly, and the words *Central America* appeared across Mexico. When they zoomed in, they were standing on the beaches of Cozumel.

Tourists on the beach began screaming when men emerged from the sea, wearing high-tech ballistic gear and firing guns. War's soldiers could easily be men from any continent, and their liberal use of bullets and explosives turned the beach into a bloody mess. War himself joined in, cleaving people in half as he ran them down.

Beth turned away and held her ears, doing her best to fight back tears. In her head, she knew none of this was real, but she could easily distinguish the anguished cries of men, women, and children as their beach vacation was turned into a bloodbath. War's turn seemed extraordinarily long, and by the time it was over, she found that her ears were ringing from the sounds of violence.

Back above the planet, she watched Pestilence pick North Africa. Down on the surface, Pestilence unzipped their hazmat suit, releasing ominous yellow pollen. People dusted with it grabbed at their heads in agony until large fungal colonies burst from their eyes. Instead of wiping out the locals, Pestilence made them into an army of zombies that groaned in agony as they were controlled by their new hosts.

It was Reggie's turn next. He looked over at her, his whiskers twitching in anticipation.

"Where should I pick?" he asked.

She didn't know and wasn't sure she could even formulate an answer. The number of atrocities she had seen in the last few hours was more than any human could endure, and she now saw the trap the horsemen had laid out for her. How could she distance herself from the macabre scene below?

"Lady Beth?" Reggie moved close and made his mech kneel so that he could reach out and touch her face. "These horrid visions will be the truth of tomorrow if we do not act today."

Shivering, she looked at the map again. The horsemen had deliberately picked countries that would block them from taking South America. If Reggie chose Brazil or Venezuela, he would be vulnerable on two fronts. It was clear the horsemen wanted Famine to take South America and gain a troop advantage.

Could they do something similar with Australia? She looked at the map and frowned. Or was that what the horsemen wanted of her? The troop advantage would help, but it would put her in a bad spot.

"The clock is ticking!" Famine shouted. "I want my turn!"

"There is no time limit during this period," Murray explained. "This is, after all, a game of strategy."

Beth looked at Reggie, then back at the board. When she looked at Jenny, she saw that the doll was still on her horse, but now she was floating upside down and staring at the moon.

"There also isn't a rule about sportsmanship!" War moved close to Beth and got in her face. "C'mon, you stupid cunt! Tell your pet what he's doing so we can get around to killing you!"

The world closed in on her until all she could see was War's smug face. Heat filled her cheeks as she gritted her teeth and pressed her forehead against War's.

"Reggie. Southeast Asia. We're taking Australia." She sneered at War, then pushed him away with her staff.

"As you wish." They teleported to the ground in time to watch as bright lights appeared in the sky. Rats wearing mech assault suits jumped out of transport ships and crashed to the ground. Though they didn't attack anyone, the local population panicked and ran for cover.

"Boring," War muttered to himself. He yawned dramatically as they moved back into outer space.

"Eastern Australia," Beth said. When they landed, she thought long and hard about what her troops should look like. The others had been ready right away, but it wasn't something she had thought very long about.

Turning around, she studied the Sydney Opera House. It was somewhere she had always wanted to go in person. The native Australians paid no mind to her or the other players as they moved around them.

Pestilence buzzed impatiently behind her. She bit her lip and closed her eyes.

What would her army be? It came to her so suddenly that she couldn't help but grin.

The people closest to her transformed. There was no pain or fear, just sparkling light and smiles. When the transformation was done, she found herself standing among a small army reminiscent of modern fantasy literature. Dwarves, elves, and humans were all equipped in medieval armor and weaponry.

A big grin broke across her face as the army turned to face her and saluted.

"This is so boring!" War rolled his eyes so hard he almost fell off his horse. "Men with swords? Really?"

"And women." Beth gestured to an elven maiden nearby. "The fights are determined by rolling the dice. Which means I'll get to watch them destroy your soldiers without firing a single bullet."

"Blah, blah, blah." War shook his head as the world receded, and they were in orbit again. The group turned their attention to Jenny, who was surrounded by golden light. She was still busy staring at the moon.

"It's the toy's turn." Famine leaned forward on his stallion. "What sort of asinine shit will we get from her?"

Jenny didn't respond. Instead, they were all yanked straight down to Japan.

"Jenny!" Beth looked around. She recognized the Tokyo Tower, which was very similar to the Eiffel Tower. "Why did you bring us here?"

Toys! Jenny waved her hand, and a nearby building exploded with gift boxes. Little parachutes deployed, and the Japanese people watched in wonderment as the presents drifted down into their hands. Nearby, a little boy snatched a gift out of the air and opened it. Inside was a stuffed kitty that looked very similar to Kisa.

The boy hugged it. People who collected gifts smiled and laughed in delight. Those who didn't simply vanished. Instead of an army, Jenny was surrounded by people holding toys.

"Jenny." Beth's voice was quiet. "You were supposed to help us capture Australia."

I wanted to go to Japan. Jenny watched a young girl stroke the silken hair of a doll in a kimono that looked very much like Ratu. *You never take me anywhere.*

"Jenny, please!" The world was ripped away, and they were in space once more.

"Looks like your toy needs new batteries. And a brain." Famine grinned. "I'm up."

The process felt like it took days, but it was probably only minutes. The territories were brutally conquered by the horsemen, and Beth ended up closing her eyes for most of the process. The screams still made it through her hands, slashing against her psyche like a flail made of barbed wire.

Reggie took Argentina to prevent Famine from getting his continent bonus on the first turn. Famine took Indonesia in retaliation. When all was said and done, Reggie and Beth managed to keep anyone from getting a continent bonus, but it also meant their defenses weren't great.

Jenny put zero effort into any sort of strategy. Instead, she whimsically picked places based on who she thought wanted to play toys with her. Beth assumed the people who took her toys would be her army, but it was impossible to tell what the doll was thinking. Was Jenny still able to move in and out of the game?

If not, they were royally fucked. Despite having never played, the horsemen had a definable strategy. She assumed it was because they were physical manifestations of concepts that transcended understanding, but also worried that maybe they had some tricks up their sleeve as well.

The Earth spun lazily beneath them as a tone sounded, signaling that all territories were occupied. The zones glowed different colors based on who owned them. War's zones were red. Famine had black. Pestilence's were green. Reggie's were blue. Beth's glowed yellow, while Jenny's were all the bright pink of a highlighter.

Famine cackled in delight as he was assigned troops at the beginning of his turn for the number of territories he had. He distributed a few to Peru, then turned to Reggie.

"It's time to catch some mice." They were pulled down to Argentina, where Reggie's rat troops stood anxiously around a set of enormous waterfalls. The mist from the falls blew upward, casting rainbows into the sky.

Reggie cast a dirty look in Famine's direction, then looked over at Beth. "The numbers are not in my favor," he informed her.

"No, they are not." Famine laughed and disappeared. He reappeared upstream of the falls just as an enormous horde of his Hunger appeared. "Slay them!" he cried, his voice rending the sky like thunder.

Reggie's troops opened fire with blaster rifles that ionized the air around them. When the Hunger came, it tore through the ranks of the rats, ripping them out of their suits and casting the mechs aside to get caught up in the flow of the falls.

Famine howled in delight as the Hunger made quick work of the rats. Reggie narrowed his eyes at the horsemen but was caught off guard when the Hunger suddenly descended on him as well.

"Reggie!" Beth tried to reach his side, but it was as if she was a ghost. Unable to touch Reggie or the Hunger, she watched helplessly as he fired his weapons and was toppled over. The Hunger pulled him free of his mech and ripped him apart.

Beth screamed, her own ears ringing as the Hunger swirled around her. When they ascended into the sky, Argentina was now black with Famine's troops.

"This doesn't make any sense!" She turned to Murray. "How is this a game if we can be killed in it?"

"There is no true death here," Murray explained as golden light swirled around the space next to him. When it was gone, Reggie reappeared, visibly shaken inside his suit. "On your turn, you are part of the battle. It was what you agreed on."

War laughed heartily and slapped Beth on the back hard enough that she winced.

"Now you see!" he declared. "You offered us everything we could have ever wanted, and we took it!"

"But…that means…" She turned on him, her voice filled with venom. "It means you will be killed too!"

"Meh." War shrugged, then shifted his sword. "Wouldn't be the first time, won't be the last. I'm War, darling. Wherever people fight, I'm there. It's not about who wins or loses; it's about chaos, blood, and righteous fury! When a man dies in battle, I ride that last bit of light in his eyes into the dark, then watch as my brother claims him. I don't favor victor or loser, for I experience the fight from both sides. It's the fight itself that thrills me."

"You're a psychopath," she replied.

"If this is too hard for you, you can quit." He sneered, revealing crimson gums. "What was all that talk about backing a human into a corner if you're gonna be a huge pussy about it?"

Beth growled. "I'll have you know that a pussy is built to take a beating. Not that you'd know anything about that. I assume the sword is compensating for something, and you're definitely not used to swinging it more than once, if you know what I mean."

War laughed for a few seconds, then went completely still.

"I can't wait until it's my turn," he told her through gritted teeth.

"But it's still my turn," Famine said. "I'm attacking Japan."

No! Jenny's cry echoed around them as they were taken down to Japan. She had failed to put more than one troop in Japan and paid the price as the Hunger devoured screaming grown-ups and children who clung to their toys. *My friends!*

Beth stared in horror as Famine commanded the Hunger to capture the doll and rip her apart. Jenny was jerked free of her rocking horse, the Hunger yanking at her limbs until they ripped and she was dragged away by the shadowy horde.

Once they were back in space, Jenny reappeared. She had a teardrop drawn on her cheek, and she cowered beneath Famine's withering stare.

You're mean, the doll declared, then turned her back on the group.

"Ooh, ooh, me next!" War was practically hopping up and down on his horse's back.

"Fine." Famine waved a hand dismissively.

"This bitch is mine." He leveled his sword at Beth, then pointed it at Earth. "Congo, now!"

Beth frowned as she was pulled to her defensive position in the Congo. She could see the other players, but War was missing. Standing around her were three infantries' worth of soldiers who eyed the surrounding forests in trepidation. Bird calls echoed across the hills as the minutes passed.

He's toying with me. She looked into the woods and raised her staff. Golden light formed a tight beam that incinerated the nearby woods, casting smoke into the sky. She clutched the staff tightly, focusing her wrath into a tight beam of energy that sliced cleanly through wood and caused it to ignite.

The beam also carved its way through War's first battalion. The men screamed in agony as they went up in flames, and cavalries made of men and elves charged forward on their horses. Gunfire mowed them down but not before they closed the gap and tore into War's forces.

Back and forth the battle surged, Beth's nerves fraying at the edges. Her battle was far longer than the others had been, and it was hard to tell who had the advantage until almost an hour later when War stumbled out of the woods, his body pincushioned with dozens of arrows.

"Fuckin' bitch," he muttered as a dwarf buried her ax into War's skull.

Beth let out the breath she had been holding as she was pulled into the sky once more. She caught a brief glimpse of the board and saw that she and War had both lost forces, but she had come out ahead in the fight. It was still hard to think that this was a physical manifestation of a dice roll.

On each turn, the attacker could commit their forces to an assault but had to leave one unit behind in their territory. Both the attacker and defender rolled, with the higher value winning. This meant both sides could lose forces, and ties would always go to the defender. Luck was a fickle mistress, so it turned into a numbers game. With enough troops, an attacker could overwhelm even the toughest defense eventually. But should they overextend themselves, then their own forces became vulnerable.

War had attacked from South Africa, and Reggie currently held Madagascar. It was likely the rat king would come down on War's lone infantry and destroy them. This brought a grin to her face that was quickly wiped away when War pointed at her.

"Again!" he shouted, then attacked another one of her territories.

This time, she wasn't so lucky. She was in Egypt and spent almost two hours trying to hide among the pyramids before War found her. The massive horseman cackled in delight as he brought his sword down on her head and ended their battle with blinding pain followed by darkness.

THE CABIN WAS QUIET. AFTER WAKING UP FROM HIS DREAM, MIKE HAD somehow been able to fall asleep for a few more hours. After a dreamless sleep, he woke to discover that he was alone in his room, which was a bit of a surprise. However, he welcomed the moment of solitude as he tried to gather his thoughts.

Emery had greeted him the moment Mike left his room, the imp wringing his hands in anticipation. He had prepared Mike a massive breakfast burrito smothered in green chili sauce along with a cup of coffee. Although puzzled by the absence of the others, he spent the next fifteen minutes greedily devouring the chorizo-laden meal in silence.

As he approached the end of his meal, Emery gave him a rundown of where everyone had gone. Yuki and Quetzalli were having a meeting with the owl out in the woods. It bothered him that he didn't know her name, but it brought to mind the idea that names were powerful tools for magic users.

Velvet was out getting food. With their temporary truce in effect, the Nirumbi had divulged where they had driven the prey animals to, and she was famished. Bigfoot had gone with her, which made him feel marginally better.

Dana was out in the barn. Emery had no idea what she was doing out there. On the roof, Abella stood with her wings opened wide, as if defiant in the face of the sun.

Glad he hadn't been totally abandoned, he had Emery start him a new pot of coffee and then wandered upstairs while the imp stayed behind to clean. Despite the events of the last couple of days, Emery hummed a delightful melody as he cleaned the kitchen.

At the top of the stairs, Mike tapped the wood with his shoes. It didn't look anything like it had in his dream, and he stopped just short of going into Velvet's room. The door was closed, so he turned and walked down the hall to the other door. The letter *E* had been carved into the wood, so he left that one alone too.

There was a small room at the end of the hall that overlooked the first floor. A few bookshelves were set up, populated mostly with books for running Dungeons and Dragons. campaigns. Curious, he looked through a couple of them, thinking back to the few times he had dabbled in role-playing games in college.

In the process of putting away a book, he caught a flash of color out the corner of his eye. Walking over toward the railing, he saw that someone had drawn a picture in crayon on the wall just behind one of the supports. Using a nearby chair as a footstool, he stepped up onto the balcony, which let him reach the beam and pull himself up.

He was more than a little surprised at how easy it was to climb up into the rafters. Usually, such a maneuver would take a bit of huffing and puffing, but he slid into the space effortlessly. He was greeted by dozens of drawings done in crayon, tucked away from watchful eyes below.

They were mostly stick figures. He recognized Eulalie and Velvet right away, as well as Bigfoot. There was a man who must have been Darren, and then there was their mother, Ana. She was often drawn with an apron around her waist.

Had Velvet done these? Or had it been Eulalie? Looking around, he saw that the pictures were squirreled away in a few other locations, but these would be harder to get to. Climbing through the rafters of the house sounded like a dumb way to get injured, so he stayed where he was and just looked around.

What had living here for an entire lifetime been like? He wondered if Velvet and Eulalie had played tag up here, or maybe even an epic game of hide-and-seek with their father. As he listened to Emery humming, he didn't doubt that this was a place that had once been filled with love and laughter. It had seen so much violence in the last few days; it must have been jarring.

Down below, he saw Emery sneak a peek over his shoulder, then pull a silver coin out of a hiding spot and start polishing it.

The cabin was alive, just like the house. What kind of people had lived in these walls? What sort of deeds had the cabin witnessed over the years? Mike slid off the beam and casually hopped down from the railing to the floor. When he was halfway down the stairs, he saw the coin in Emery's hand disappear as if by magic.

"You don't have to hide your treasure," he told the imp. "I'm not going to take it."

Emery bit his lip in frustration and then looked down at his feet, his wings drooping. "It's my job to take care of this place," he explained, "not polish my collection."

"Does polishing your collection make you happy?" Mike asked.

The imp nodded tentatively.

"Do you do a better job when you're happy?" Mike asked.

Emery scrunched up his face, as if afraid to answer. When he spoke, his voice was a hopeful squeak. "I think so."

"From now on, I want you to take some time for yourself. Every single day." Mike pulled the now full carafe of coffee off the counter. "Polish your collection. Go for a walk, er, fly. Whatever. Consider it an order if that's what it takes."

A look of sheer joy bloomed across the imp's face, and the coin reappeared in his hands.

"This one is a silver dollar from 1901," Emery declared, then set it on the table between them. Mike noticed that the coin looked clean as if it had recently come from the mint. "The woman on it is very pretty."

"She is."

"I like the ones with faces on them the best. During the lonely times, it felt like they were my friends." Emery picked up the coin and smiled at it as a mother would a child.

"Speaking of being lonely, do you ever feel..." Mike looked around conspiratorially and lowered his voice. "Do you ever feel like this place is *alive?*"

Emery's eyes widened even further, and then he nodded.

"Every home is alive in its own way, Caretaker. If you stand in the door, you can feel it breathing around you. Stand on its floors and you can feel its heartbeat." The imp grabbed Mike's finger in his tiny hands. "When you fill a good house with love, it loves you back. It will shelter you in a storm and warm you when you are cold. I think you know by now that this place is very special."

The conversation was taking an unexpected turn.

"Special how, Emery?"

The imp grinned, and then his eyes flicked to the woman on the coin. "Special in ways I can't say. In the same ways the trees speak to Master Foot, this place can speak through you."

"You mean to me?"

Emery smiled, his brow furrowing up and making him look like an old man.

"I said what I said." He let go of Mike's hand and picked up the coin. "My magic helps me keep the coins clean. I'm an earth elemental. Anything that comes out of the ground, I can manipulate, even restore it to its previous luster. I suspect you have a similar ability when it comes to Velvet. I haven't seen her this happy in months. When you take her from this place, I ask that you take very good care of her."

Mike laughed, then held out a finger for the imp to shake. "You've got yourself a deal," he said.

They sat and chatted until the coffee was gone. Emery told stories about the girls growing up and how much he'd enjoyed playing with them as children. Once his mug was empty, Mike excused himself and went outside for some fresh air.

It was warmer today than it had been all week. The snow was like slush near the grove of trees that had burned down the other night. What few trees still stood were ashen specters with skeletal limbs that reached for the sky. Mike wondered how long it would take for them to grow back.

He found Dana out in the barn with the hood of the jeep up. She had found an old radio and was blasting some hits from the eighties while giving the car a tune-up (at least, that was his assumption). As she was wearing a white tank top that barely covered her midriff, it rode up and revealed the tattoo of gears at the base of her spine every time she leaned into the car.

"What's going on?" he asked.

Dana backed out of the car and regarded him with red-tinged eyes. He couldn't help but notice that her biceps looked more defined than before.

"Needed something to do." She set a ratchet on the edge of the car, then used a rag to wipe some grease off her fingers. "Wondered if this thing still ran. Might need it for tonight."

Mike nodded. He sincerely doubted that the jeep would be of any use in capturing the Jersey Devil, but he wasn't about to argue with her.

"Everything okay? Your eyes don't look so great."

Dana smirked, then leaned against the jeep with her arms crossed. "Funny that you ask. I'm okay, I think. Ever since the other day, I've felt more energized than I usually do. Like I've downed a bunch of caffeine or something. Senses are heightened even more than usual. I feel kind of like I do right after feedings, only it isn't fading like it usually does."

Uh-oh. He thought about the weird electrical storm he had summoned and then subsequently poured into Dana. Had he changed her? He could only hope it was for the better.

He offered his help, but she declined. They both knew there was little he could do to contribute, but he wanted to be polite.

Outside the barn, he found some good handholds and climbed up to the roof, where Abella waited.

Her eyes were closed, a thin smile on her lips as she soaked up the sunlight.

"What brings you to my neck of the woods?" She grinned at her own joke.

"I came to check on you, actually." He walked across the roof, wondering how it was even strong enough to hold her. Looking down, he noticed that she had left several gouges in the roof with her talons, most likely from walking across it.

She opened her eyes and looked at her wing with a frown.

"I'm fine," she said, but he just shook his head.

"You aren't." He stopped in front of her and ran his hands along her cracked wing. The dark lines were flecked with stone that glistened in the light.

"It doesn't hurt," she reassured him. "It will heal. Eventually."

He frowned. "Even your body can only take so much punishment," he said.

"And since it is my body, it is my choice." She folded her wings around her. "I do not wish to talk about it. One of my greatest fears is to lose the sky."

"Then let's do everything in our power to avoid that." He examined her face, then brushed a lock of hair away from her brow. "So you can breathe fire…"

She shrugged. "Not that it's a big deal, but yes. It is called heart fire. By my former clan, anyway. I'm not very good at it and lost control."

"Is that why you've never used it before?" He had seen her in more than a couple of fights where it would have come in handy.

"Heart fire is different for every one of my kind. I have a powerful flame but a tiny body, so it's difficult to control." She put her hands on her hips. "It also uses a tremendous amount of energy. If I use too much, I can fall into hibernation until the sun's light awakens me once again."

"Like when we first met?" She had been tucked in a shadowed alcove and covered with Mandragora vines, the plant siphoning away her energy. "You were asleep."

"My people get our energy from many places." Her dark eyes sparkled, and she glanced down at his crotch. "But you know this already."

He laughed, then looked out into the forest. It felt as though he was being watched but in a nonthreatening way. Was it the trees?

"I was thinking about taking a walk. Would you like to come with me?"

She nodded. "I will follow you from above."

"Nah, not like that. Come see the forest with me."

Her cheeks darkened, and she licked her lips. "I would like this."

"C'mon, let's go." He walked to the edge of the barn and was grabbed from behind. The roof disappeared from beneath his feet as Abella glided through the air and then landed roughly near the tree line. He stumbled a few feet before regaining his balance.

"That hurt more than I thought it would," she explained, rubbing at her wing joint. "Sorry, I thought I could carry you."

"As long as you're okay." He held out a hand, and she took it with a smile.

The trails around the cabin were covered in thin snow that did little to slow Mike down. Every step Abella took made a crunching sound, her toes spreading apart to leave wide tracks. Her tail swished in a serpentine pattern, which left a smooth furrow behind them. If they somehow got lost, someone would easily be able to find them.

He didn't worry about losing his way. Even with the cabin still close by, he could feel it. His magic shifted inside him, like a magical compass that always pointed the direction home.

Abella told him stories from centuries past, and he shared a few tales from when he was younger, mostly camping while in the Boy Scouts and college. She hung on every word, and he noticed that her wings would make a rippling noise when she laughed, like a tarp in the wind.

ANNABELLE HAWTHORNE

They skirted the area of the forest that had burned. He couldn't help but notice that the subconscious hum that hovered around him all the time dimmed when they passed through the scorched areas. It was as if he had been disconnected from the woods, a sensation that left him feeling hollow inside.

Abella noticed this, her eyes dropping to the ground.

"I couldn't control myself," she explained, but he stopped her by putting his arm around her shoulders.

"I always knew you were hot," he joked. "Guess we now have proof, eh?"

She elbowed him in jest, a casual act on her part that knocked the wind from his lungs. He coughed and took a moment to compose himself.

"It's just that I had no idea you could breathe fire," he told her with a wheeze. "Is it difficult?"

"It depends. Some of my kind couldn't even light a candle, but their strengths lay elsewhere. I could boil away a small pond if I could control it."

"Why not practice, then?" He put his hand on hers and squeezed to reassure her he was just curious.

"Heart fire doesn't just burn things. It also changes you." She explored her forehead with her free hand, then let out a sigh. "If I were to practice, my outer appearance would eventually change. Perhaps I would grow horns, or my face would deform. I like my body the way it is, much more human than monster."

"Is that why your kind can look so different from one another? Do you all look the same when you're born, and then change, or…?"

She chuckled. "When we hatch, we vary wildly in appearance. However, the use of heart fire always results in a more fearsome visage. My flames are so strong that I fear what I could become."

"I see. Fire breath that could change the appearance of the user. Interesting." Mike stroked his chin thoughtfully.

They moved away from the scorched clearing and toward one of the nearby hills. Eventually, they found themselves in the rocks that surrounded the hot springs. All around him, he could hear the mutterings of the forest, with the occasional chatter of the spiders.

"Something on your mind?" Abella asked. "You're distracted."

He didn't even know where to begin. Sensing the forest was likely related to his interlude with Amymone before coming here, and he definitely didn't want to bring up the spiders. Struggling to come up with an answer for her, he thought about his discussion with Emery.

"You've been at the house a long time. Did you ever sense that it was alive?" he asked.

"Hmm. Interesting question." She paused, her tail crunching against some rocks through the thin layer of snow. "I guess it depends on what you mean. Ever since you came, I would argue that it feels more alive than ever."

"I don't mean in a metaphorical sense. I mean that it's sentient." He explained how he sometimes spoke with the house while wearing its body, and then went ahead and told her about the dream from the previous night. When he finished, Abella regarded him with glittering eyes.

"You know, my kind used to talk about the Earth Mother," she said. "This planet is a giant rock that hurtles through space with a molten core. In this way, she is not so different from our kind. I wouldn't say we were a religious people, but my mother was fond of saying 'if the Earth Mother wills it' when making important decisions."

"Do you think the planet is alive?" Suddenly curious, he found a nearby rock and sat down.

"Life isn't something we can so casually define," she answered. "I would argue that she lives, in her own way. But could you talk to her? Perhaps not."

"The forest is alive. I can hear it, right on the edge of my thoughts." Even now, it was like voices being carried across the wind.

"Is it the noise that bothers you?" Abella laughed. "I hear everything. It can be very obnoxious."

Mike nodded. "It's like hearing pieces of a conversation. I want to know more, but the words just aren't there. And I don't like the idea that the cabin and the house are alive but won't just talk to me like this. It's always on their terms, and often in riddles."

"Maybe it's no different from listening to the forest. Maybe when you speak, they don't always hear you." She looked around at the trees. "I bet you can't understand the woods because they aren't fully awake yet."

Realization blossomed through him. Was that the key to finding out more about the house and the great game? As the house expanded, so had his interactions with it. Did he need to do more for the house to notice him?

Then again, that was the same line of thinking that had led Emily astray. Her need to fill the home with cryptids had segued into protecting its occupants at all costs. As she was led astray by the shadow, her desire for power had ultimately led to her tragic demise.

"Damn," he muttered in frustration. The last thing he wanted was to see his own desire to understand the great game be twisted into a journey toward madness.

"Come." Abella took him by the hand. "Let's see if we can find someplace where the woods have woken up already. Maybe then you can put your mind to rest."

She had misunderstood him, but he didn't feel the need to correct her. Abella led him through the forest, taking him through heavy brush where no trails existed. She would often turn around and walk backward, her wings unfolding just enough to push aside the foliage and allow them to pass unhindered.

"I saw this spot the other day," she explained as she guided him. "It's not too far from the hot springs, and it gets plenty of sunlight."

"What do you mean?" he asked, but she only grinned in response.

The hum inside his head grew louder, and they moved into a clearing with a river running through it. Steam hovered above the water in places, fed by small bubbling pools on the shore. The snow here was melted along the banks of the stream, and the nearby trees rustled in the wind.

The humming had been replaced by the sound of music. As it was ethereal in nature, he couldn't identify a single instrument being played. It was hundreds of voices all at once, singing a song of waking.

"Well?" Abella asked. "Is it different here?"

He nodded, then wiped a tear from his eye. It was a song of hope, one that immediately reminded him of Amymone. Among the trees, he could hear the steady chittering of the spiders as well, raising their voices to join in the harmony. While the woods sang of waking and sunlight, the spiders sang of the hunt to come. They were hungry yet hopeful.

"There's so much to hear," he told her. "It's actually quite pleasant. This spot is beautiful. Thank you for bringing me here."

She nodded in approval, then knelt by the stream. "I don't hear what you do, but it's the same. The rustling of the leaves. The sound of snow dripping, animals scurrying everywhere. But in a way, we are both hearing the heartbeat of the Earth Mother. At least, that is what my mother would say."

Content to listen for a while, he closed his eyes and let the music flow through him. The tune had been nonsensical at first, but now he could pick out some of its nuances. The trees whispered to one another in singsong voices, and the clusters of grass that had pushed through the snow made a sound like tinkling bells.

Behind the music, he picked up on a background melody consisting of deep bass tones. Doing his best to tune out the others, he focused on those deep beats and was surprised when his magic responded. It spiraled around inside him, unwinding in slow motion.

In the darkness of his own mind, he suddenly saw the clearing around him in intricate detail. Every blade of grass, rock, and tree was there for his perusal. Waves of light pulsed through them from below the ground, diffracting and changing colors as it passed through the foliage. The grass glowed a cheerful blue, while the trees were yellow and green. The rocks soaked up the noise, appearing black to his mind's eye.

He was humming now. It was like being a child again and trying to hum along with the vacuum cleaner. The vibrations filled his body and resonated outward, causing the colors around him to shift and glow even brighter. By altering the pitch of his voice, he could cause different elements of the clearing to ignite like tiny stars.

"Are you doing this?" Abella's awe-filled voice sounded far away.

He opened his eyes to see that the clearing was no longer bound in snow. The grass and bushes had shoved their way free of winter's icy embrace, and the trees rustled as if caught in a heavy wind. All around them, flowers were blooming and turning to face the sun.

It wasn't just the flora that was reacting either. Woodland creatures were appearing along the edge of the clearing. Squirrels and raccoons sat in trees, and a pair of bucks circled the outside. Mice sat on their haunches by the river's edge, their eyes shining with curiosity.

The river sparkled in the sun's light as bubbles broke free of its surface and floated in the air, bouncing around like tiny beach balls. The air shimmered with motes of light that swirled around him like fireflies, his magic manifesting in a new way altogether.

This was like Amymone's magic, he thought. Stunned by this develop-ment, he turned to face Abella. The gargoyle's eyes were bright with wonder as she held up a hand and a finch landed on it and sang to her.

"It's almost like a fairy tale," she whispered.

Afraid he would break the spell, he said nothing. Animals approached them both, bowed as if paying their respects, then disappeared into the woods. Mike picked some golden flowers that sprouted by his feet and walked toward Abella.

"These are for you," he told her but was surprised to see that the flowers had woven themselves into a crown. There was no beginning or end; it was almost like the stalks had melted into one another.

Smiling, Abella took the crown from him and placed it on her head.

"Thank you." She put her hands against his chest, then slid them down his sides and around his waist. "I didn't know a walk with you could be so exciting."

"Abella, I…" He was cut off when she pressed her firm lips against his. Her hands slid up to his shoulders but then down to his butt. She squeezed him, then pulled him against her.

The music around them intensified, but Abella showed no reaction to it.

Assuming only he could hear it, he was suddenly distracted by the feeling of Abella's flat stomach rubbing against his groin.

He moved his hands up her back until he found her wing joints. She moaned into his mouth as he rubbed them, then moved a hand down to the base of her tail. She crouched and pulled him with her until she was on her back. The thick reeds of grass leaned away from them, silhouetting Abella's body on the ground.

Mike broke the kiss and straddled her, his fingers moving along her chest. She pressed her breasts together and grinned.

"I saw something in one of my shows that I kind of want to try with you," she said with a blush. "It's called a boob fuck."

He didn't have the heart to correct her online terminology, so he pulled off his pants to oblige.

Though the air was cold, he barely felt it. Abella's body was radiating heat that he now had a better understanding of, and he shifted his hips forward until his pelvis was just below her breasts.

"Like this?" he asked, then pressed his cock between her breasts.

"Almost." She leaned forward enough to lick his cock and then smear her spit along the length of his shaft. "That should work."

When she lay back down, he pushed forward. As firm as they were, they didn't yield at all. The sensation was nice, and she stuck out her tongue to tease the head of his cock whenever it poked above her breasts.

"This feels good, but what do you get out of it?" he asked.

"Are you kidding? I can feel how warm and soft it is. Well, relatively speaking." She squeezed her breasts together, which increased the pressure on his shaft. "And I'll admit I love how fragile you feel."

"Fragile?"

She smirked. "I can easily crush a rock between my breasts. It's…one of those weird things you do a few times for fun when you're young and tired of looking at birds on the cathedral roof."

It was an oddly specific statement, but Mike let it go. He could see Abella's cheeks darkening in passion as he fucked her breasts, and knew that she was getting far more out of it than he was. He didn't mind. After all, sex wasn't about keeping score, and if this was something that excited her, he was happy to oblige.

She grunted, and her hips lifted off the ground. When he looked back, he saw that she was teasing her pussy with the pliable tip of her tail. It was a bit difficult, but he was able to reach back to help penetrate her with her own tail.

Abella licked her lips, then licked the head of his cock. Precum created a sticky strand that temporarily connected them until she broke it with her finger and then shoved it in her mouth.

"Yummy," she commented, then gasped. Her eyes flashed with an inner light, and a breeze blew through the clearing, ruffling his hair.

"Everything okay?" he asked.

"Yeah, it's fine." She grabbed the shaft of his cock and gave him a couple of tight strokes. He groaned as she managed to extract some more cum and then ate it. The same phenomenon manifested, and she closed her eyes and groaned.

"What's happening?" he asked.

"You've changed," she told him. "Since the last time we did this, anyway. Your essence, it has become far more...potent." She arched an eyebrow at him.

He didn't bother trying to come up with an explanation. Ever since his threesome with Dana and Quetzalli, and the previous night's dream, he had felt different. His magic was no longer confined to crawling sparks, or sex lightning, as he called it. Something bigger was happening to him, and he was really only along for the ride.

He moved down her body, and she groaned in disappointment when his cock was no longer between her breasts. Her legs moved apart, and he maneuvered himself between them to get a clear view of her tail. He took it from her hands and spent a few minutes fucking her with it. The stone of her tail was even smoother than her breasts, as if it had been polished.

"You have something I want far more than my tail," she finally muttered.

He was about to pull her tail out but paused. After watching all three of her labia expand and contract to accommodate the girth of her tail, it occurred to him that she could probably be stretched even farther.

He lowered his bare ass onto her tail, using it to support his weight. Once his cock was just outside her pussy, he pulled her tail out until it tapered to a blunt point. Satisfied that what was about to happen was possible, he rubbed his cock along her tail and then held them together before pushing them back against her labia.

"Why not both?" he asked, then pushed his way forward.

Abella gasped and slammed her hands into the ground hard enough to tear gouges in the turf. Mike groaned with effort as he attempted to handle his own cock and her tail, eventually stretching out her lips. Double penetrating her vaginally was difficult due to her stony exterior, but her interior was hot and inviting. Her tail looked smooth from a distance but actually had ridges that rubbed against the bottom of his shaft as he pressed into her.

The gargoyle had slipped into French, her eyes closed as she released a monologue of words "Oh *mon Dieu*, merde! *Putain oui!*"

Around them, the clearing blazed with color as the stream erupted. Bubbles circled them, each one looking like a tiny plasma ball as the sparks that formed along his body jumped into them. He watched in astonishment as his magic spread out and dominated the clearing.

Flowers bloomed in fast-forward until they exploded, and the trees shook so hard that he thought a storm was blowing in. All the while, Abella cried out as her hands and feet tore grooves in the dirt and stone beneath them.

He was shaking now, unable to control his muscles as his magic raced free. One moment, it felt like electricity. The next, it became music. It was wild and uncontrollable, and he had no idea how to make it stop or otherwise control it.

Abella grabbed him by the thighs, her fingers pressing into his flesh hard enough that he gritted his teeth in pain. Letting go of her tail, he pumped himself into her tight, pulsing sex as tiny spurts of cum left his body. The water was circling them now, hissing with magic.

Abella's wings unfurled, crushing the nearby flowers as she let out a cry. Mike leaned forward to kiss her breasts, but she put up a hand and held him back. Steam rose from her sternum as bubbles popped against her skin, and when she came, a tiny burst of heart fire shot into the sky from her mouth and vanished in the breeze.

"Don't...not inside...," she managed to gasp out between balls of fire.

"Holy shit!" It occurred to him now that whatever was happening to him was now being directly channeled into her body as fuel. He moved his hips until his cock popped free, causing her tail to unfold beneath him with a thud.

The cold air on his cock sent chills up his spine, and he let out a grunt and grabbed the base of his shaft. Uncertain where to spill his seed, he groaned and blasted thick ropes of cum all across Abella's stomach and torso.

There was a thunderclap overhead as the clearing came to a standstill. Bubbles turned into mist that fell from the sky like a light rain, and he fell forward onto Abella, fully aware that he was also lying in his own bodily fluids.

The gargoyle sighed and played with his hair.

"Are you okay?" he asked.

She nodded. "I will be," she said. "I could feel your magic deep inside, traveling through my body. When it reached my heart, I...couldn't hold it in any longer. I was afraid if you came inside me, I might explode."

"That's...not a thing, is it?"

She laughed. "No, not literally. I eat energy, and I haven't felt so full in a long time." She patted her belly for emphasis.

He looked up at her, rolling his head along her breast so he could see her better. "It didn't happen to heal your wing, did it?"

"Hmm?" She flexed her wing, and he saw the cracks were still there. "Should it have?"

"I suppose not." It would have been damn convenient though.

"Mike?" Abella moved her hand into his hair and held him close. "Are you glad I came?"

He ran his hand along her belly, then squeezed her hip. "Of course I am."

"Am I…are we enough for you? Me and the others?"

He could feel the insecurity in her voice, the sudden shift in her tone. Where was this coming from? He had a pretty good idea but didn't want to discuss his relationship with Velvet. Even he didn't entirely know what was going on there.

"Each one of you is more than I can handle," he told her. "But I manage, somehow. I spend every day hoping I'm still enough. I'll admit there are times I worry I'm neglecting one of you, or that I haven't given you enough attention. I promise it's purely a numbers game; there's only one of me after all."

"I see."

"I'm sorry if I've ever made you feel forgotten." He gave her another squeeze. "But I promise, I'm trying my best."

She squeezed him tight, which made his back pop.

They lay there for quite some time. When he decided to help her up, he discovered the crown of flowers on her head had rooted itself into the ground. All around them, the clearing was now filled with wildflowers growing several feet high, many having burst through the snow. Abella marveled at the sudden change in scenery, but Mike was filled with an uneasy chill.

What was happening to him?

FAMILY GAME NIGHT

Pain rippled through Beth's entire body as she re-formed in a golden blaze of light next to Murray. Already, the sensation of being hung from a tree was fading from her memory as if it was nothing more than a bad dream.

"Ah, there's our princess now!" War announced with a laugh. "How did you like the gallows?"

She said nothing. Instead, she closed her eyes and took several deep, cleansing breaths.

After being killed the first time, she'd cried hysterically while huddled in a ball. Murray had appeared to her in a place full of white light and informed her that her reconstruction would be on a mental, emotional, and spiritual level. The angel explained that the purpose of doing so was to prevent a complete mental breakdown as a result of being killed repeatedly.

That, and it would disrupt the game.

While the memory of being cut in half remained, it now felt like little more than a distant memory or a bad dream. Every death afterward was brutal and terrifying to experience, but the angel made sure that all she retained from them was the memory rather than the trauma.

In a way, she was grateful to the angel for ensuring her mental safety. Given half a chance, she would pluck the fucker and cast him into the void with Oliver. But seeing as how she was just a mere mortal, she would have to settle for dreaming about revenge rather than exacting it.

"And there goes Alaska," War declared. The territory Beth had held turned red. "North America is officially mine!"

Again, she said nothing. But she did look over at where Jenny was sitting. The doll had been unusually quiet, and it was taking everything in Beth's power not to scream at the ghost.

The original plan had been for Jenny to manipulate her own die rolls using telekinesis. With three on three, even a slight manipulation in the odds would be beneficial and allow their deception to go unnoticed.

Instead, Jenny was sullen. She had lost a few territories without so much as a fight and had yet to win a single round. When a round started, neither side knew who won until the battle was over, and it didn't seem to occur to the horsemen that Jenny seemed to be exempt. On her turn, all the doll did was add troops and move them away from harm. Reggie would often move troops and try to bolster defenses for Beth, or at least discuss strategies between rounds.

It had effectively become three versus two, with Jenny barely spectating. The doll often wandered off during turns and would look on in disinterest as the loser was shot, set on fire, or executed in whatever gory manner the winner preferred.

Beth particularly enjoyed her winning rounds. The horsemen didn't seem all that creative with how they chose to kill her so would often pick something quick and messy. She tried to rattle them with creative means of dismemberment and was particularly proud of the time her elves had tossed Famine into a live volcano.

Reggie's unique brand of torture usually involved rats. He strapped a cage full of rats to War's belly and then put burning coals on the top so that the rats would chew their way through the horseman to get away from the heat. There was also the time Reggie dragged Pestilence into the subway tunnels of New York and creamed him with a subway train. It had revealed that the horseman was, in fact, composed of glowing insects.

None of this deterred the horsemen. They shifted troops around and would leave a single troop behind to be taken by their teammates so they could gain continent bonuses. It had pissed her off when the last battle between War and Pestilence had been a simple game of pinball. War had given his sibling a high five upon losing, which allowed Pestilence to gain control of Africa.

"Three territories left," War told her. "And then you're out of the game."

Still, she said nothing. Once she was knocked out, Reggie and Jenny would be on their own. Reggie almost had control of Europe, while Jenny had crammed almost all her troops into East Asia.

It all came down to trust. She wanted to believe that Jenny had some sort of a plan, but she just couldn't see it. The doll's infamous outbursts hadn't shown up even once. They were ignoring her entirely, so it was likely that Reggie would be the next to go. The horsemen would come for Jenny only when she was the last one remaining.

The horsemen had learned some time ago how to stretch out their turns. Since the results were determined by unseen die rolls, time didn't actually affect the battle. What had started as hour-long skirmishes had become days, depending on the size of the defending armies. Losing Australia had taken almost a month from her perspective, but Murray had assured her that only minutes had passed in the real world.

The men and women of Middle Earth put up a brave fight over the next few rounds. Beth, fully on the defensive now, didn't make any attacks of her own and chose to bolster her defenses. Her brain compressed the last week of her battles into moments as her territories dwindled down to one final location.

She had taken Iceland on a lark and found it a fitting location for her last stand. Her troops managed to buy her another week of in-game time as War attacked her from Greenland with ships that fired missiles into the Icelandic countryside. While the city of Reykjavik burned, Beth's army was forced to retreat inland.

Her final stand was at Eyjafjallajökull. She rode her horse up and down the line, doing her best to give a speech about how they were the last line of defense and that she was so proud. The words didn't come easy and were heavily plagiarized from different movies. Her people cheered as they turned as one to face the oncoming army, ready to take down as many of War's troops as they could.

Instead, War bombed the volcano, which caused it to erupt violently. It exploded, the pyroclastic flow incinerating Beth and her troops where they stood. There were no last moments of honor or glory, just the howl of angry winds followed by fire, dirt, and pain.

Hovering above Earth afterward, Beth couldn't help but break into tears. She didn't have enough energy to acknowledge War, who taunted her failures. Nor could she yell at Jenny for abandoning them. She wanted to believe in the plan, but her faith had finally been broken.

"Since you are no longer a player, you may wait here between rounds." Murray spoke matter-of-factly, as if Beth hadn't just lost the fate of the world in a board game gone wrong. "It is your choice."

"I'll keep watching," she announced, then looked over at Reggie. "To provide moral support."

Reggie nodded in thanks.

Several weeks passed as Reggie's position in Europe was gobbled away. The horsemen started a blazing wall of fire that gobbled up the land as they conquered his territories. Reggie was able to hold them off for a bit, but it was purely a numbers game at this point. The horsemen had surrounded Reggie, pressing him from multiple directions. His numbers dwindled faster than theirs, and his remaining troops clung to the Eiffel Tower as Famine detonated a nuke right on top of them.

The mushroom cloud could still be seen from space as Reggie re-formed. His mech suit was gone, and he wore neither his glasses nor his crown.

"I have failed you," he told her morosely.

"You did your best," she said, kneeling to pick him up. "We did our best." She gave him a hug, his whiskers tickling her ear.

"The best is yet to come," he whispered in her ear, his voice barely audible. She wasn't even sure he had said anything.

"Do you wish to continue your turn?" Murray asked Famine.

"Huh?" Famine looked up at Earth, then over at Jenny. She was looking away from the horsemen, her horse squeaking ominously. "Oh, right. Forgot about her. I need to move some troops first, but then I'll pass." He looked to War. "Thought you might have more fun with her."

War grinned, his teeth glinting in the unfiltered light of the sun.

"I'm going to grind you into paste, little girl." He licked his lips in anticipation.

Jenny stopped rocking on her horse. Her head rotated around until she was looking backward at the horsemen.

I look forward to ripping your eyes from your head and shoving them up your ass. Her voice was composed of multiple wavelengths—as if several men and women spoke through her body. With a click, it became a little girl's voice again. *That way, you can watch me kick your butt, mister.*

War was clearly taken aback. He looked over at Pestilence, who just shrugged. It was the first aggressive thing she had said this whole time, and it was clear that it had caught them off guard.

It was Jenny's turn next. Her territories were massed together, but she shifted the bulk of her troops to the outer ring. Being left alone each turn, she had amassed a rather large force that now formed a barrier around East Asia.

Pestilence didn't have any troops nearby so moved them around. When War's turn came, he pointed at Kamchatka.

"I attack from Alaska," he declared. He had been building a small army there, and everyone teleported down to the ground and watched as War's military presence came from the sea. Large boats dumped troops and equipment on the shore, but there was no sign of Jenny's army anywhere.

"What the fuck is this?" War stood on the beach, his sword slung over a shoulder. "I don't see anybody here."

That's 'cause we're playing hide-and-seek, silly! Jenny's voice came from the distant hills. *Can you find all of us?*

"I'm not here to play games. I'm here to kill you!" War's voice magnified and bounced off the hills like distant thunder.

That's too bad! I'm here to play games with you! The clouds up above formed into a rocking horse with a figure on top. A demonic face formed by opening holes in the cloud, revealing blue sky behind. *And you can't kill me until you find me.*

War almost dropped his sword. "That's not how this works! You have to face me!"

It's a game of war, silly! If you don't like it…quit!

"She is correct." Murray hovered in the sky behind them like a marionette. "For the turn to end, one of you must kill the other."

"Fucking hell." War stormed off with his troops. Beth wanted to laugh, wanted to have hope, but was afraid to voice it out loud.

Down by her side, Reggie was wringing his hands in anticipation, a giddy gleam in his eyes.

War's troops scoured the countryside for hours. As spectators, Beth and the others were able to hover above the scene and move about, unrestricted by physics. War and Jenny were the only ones confined to the playing field, and Jenny was using it to her advantage.

Night was falling before anything happened. The movement was so subtle that Beth thought she had made a mistake. One of War's soldiers had walked behind a boulder and had simply vanished in the shadow of the rocks. Not a sound was uttered, and the nearby troops didn't see what happened either.

An apple a day keeps the doctor away, Jenny announced. *You suck at this game.*

War said nothing, but Beth saw that the veins in his neck bulged dramatically. He tapped his sword on the ground, then growled in frustration.

"What are you playing at, Raggedy Ann?" He looked up and around. "You mad that nobody ever loved you?"

My little girl grew up to be a complete whore. Jenny giggled. *She was your mom.*

This actually made Famine burst into laughter. It quickly became a belly laugh, and Famine wiped some tears from his eyes.

"Oh, she's trying to go so hard on you," he cried. "Stupid girl doesn't even know that we don't have a mother."

That's what the angels told you so you wouldn't feel sad. Jenny's voice was behind them now. *Just you wait, fat ass. I have something special planned for you.*

"Whatever you say." He sat on a couch that appeared behind him and pulled popcorn out of the air. Beth recalled a particularly bloody confrontation Reggie had had with War where Famine had pulled out a charcuterie board and feasted on cheese and apple slices as the two of them leveled a city.

Pestilence buzzed something at Jenny.

Nobody cares what you have to say, she replied in a sweet voice. *You're just a bag of farts.*

The sun set on Kamchatka, and all hell broke loose. As the shadows grew longer, War's troops disappeared at an exponential rate. Once the disappearances had been noticed, gunfire erupted as they tried to fight an enemy they couldn't see. War had his soldiers set up a base at the foot of a hill and trained spotlights on the surrounding area. Instead of chasing away whatever hid in the shadows, it just revealed a landscape soaked in blood.

"What the fuck is this?" War, just as baffled as his troops, ordered them to form up on the perimeter wall of their base. Shadows flitted about, but the soldiers were unable to catch one properly in the light.

As I lay me down to sleep, Jenny began.

"Fuck off!" War replied.

I pray the Lord my soul to keep. The shadows moved so abruptly now that they left large dust trails behind them that blew across the base like fog. *And when you die because you suck...*

"Shut up!" War was so angry he hopped over the walls of the base and charged at the shadows. He swung his sword at them, creating a commotion that drew everyone's attention. In the span of an instant, the lights at the base went out and the soldiers left behind screamed in agony. An explosion rocked the structure, and Beth caught a brief glimpse of twisted beings that disappeared into the darkness, beings made of teeth and knives.

I'll find your mom and then we'll fuck.

War was the only one left. He yelled at the sky, but the shadows avoided him. Despite his shouting, the shadows left him to seethe.

"What is she playing at?" Famine leaned forward on his couch.

Now quit being a bitch and find me! Jenny giggled. *When you do, I'll put you out of your misery.*

"This has to be against the rules!" War turned to Murray. "She can't make me find her. This territory is huge, and she's just a doll!"

All is fair in love and war, Jenny replied. *And I love playing games with you!*

Murray stared at the scene below, then nodded.

"These are the terms you agreed to," he stated. "You would play a game of conquest where you were able to fully participate. At any point, you may choose to stop playing, but that would be equivalent to forfeit on the part of the player."

"But this isn't conquest. It's fucking hide-and-seek!"

Aw, are you gonna cry? Jenny giggled. *You can quit if you want.*

"And if she's hiding, why can I hear her?" War swung around, squinting in the darkness. "Does that mean she's nearby?"

"Her ability to speak doesn't affect gameplay," Murray said. "She doesn't have lips, so I allowed her to use her psychic abilities for communication purposes."

War hollered illegibly and threw his sword before storming off. A couple of hours passed before Jenny started singing nursery rhymes in a discordant manner that set Beth on edge.

"I can't believe we have to sit through this shit," muttered Famine. "Hey, angel! Since it's obvious already that she won this round, would it be okay if we helped find her? It doesn't technically affect gameplay, right?"

Murray went walleyed for a moment, then nodded.

"It would be permitted," he informed them.

"C'mon." Famine rose from his couch and looked at Pestilence. "Let's find the little bitch so we can move on."

Beth looked at Reggie and let out a sigh. "Should we go find somewhere quiet to sit? It could be a while."

The rat king looked at her with quivering whiskers, then let out a hearty laugh.

"Why would I stay?" he asked. "I'm not technically playing anymore, remember?"

With a flash of light, Reggie was gone. Beth's jaw dropped open at the ramifications of his statement, then looked across the dark hills of Kamchatka. How long would Jenny make the horsemen look for her? Had this been her plan the whole time? Already, Beth could hear War absolutely losing his shit in frustration. The horsemen were capable of many things, but apparently, patience wasn't one of them.

With a grin, Beth willed herself back into space.

"I WOULD HAVE EXPECTED THE ENTRANCE TO HELL TO BE BIGGER," EULALIE said, staring at the wrought-iron gate behind the house.

"It goes to the Underworld, not Hell." Amymone had her face in one of the books from the Library. It was a primer on dimensional folding. "And I'm not seeing a damn thing in here about reconnecting it."

"Not without Mike." Naia pouted on top of her fountain.

It was late at night. Suly had escorted Cyrus back to his apartment to get a change of clothes and spend the night there. While the mage was gone, Eulalie had come over to the house to speak with the others. The rats had set up a perimeter around the house with instructions to chase off anyone who came snooping.

Eulalie was rather proud of how far her relationship had come with the rats. They were much smarter than they had originally seemed, and a couple of them seemed to understand some sophisticated commands. She noticed that a self-appointed group of rats now followed her around while carrying spears.

She knelt to drink some of the deer the centaurs had brought her. Hunger had gotten the best of her earlier that day, and she had sent out an emergency request for food before she snacked on a rat. The deer was trussed up nicely in a cocoon she could easily move around, and neither Naia nor Amymone seemed to be bothered by it.

"How does it taste?" Amymone asked. "I'm curious."

"Imagine a smoothie made of butter and meat that has little chunks in it," Eulalie replied. "And when you drink it, you can feel warmth diffuse throughout your entire body."

Amymone nodded. "I figured you were a good person to ask, since you can eat that and human food."

"We don't technically eat," Naia said. "Amymone absorbs nutrients from the sun and earth. She also likes it when I do this."

The nymph sprayed the dryad with water from her hands, which caused Amymone's dress to cling to her body, revealing her nipples. Amymone licked her lips and absorbed the liquid into her skin, which made her dress stop sticking to her. The gesture was blatantly sexual, but Eulalie ignored it.

"So we don't have a way to connect to the Underworld through this gate?" she asked.

"Mike might be able to." Naia stood up straight, the runes on her torso glowing through the fabric of her dress. "The geas is supposed to regulate everything that happens here. When I choose the new Caretaker, I am able to bring the true house into this world. Whoever took the house will be strong, but Mike's bond will be stronger. With his help, I might be able to reconnect the gate, and then we can try to find the house in the Underworld."

"That sounds like a pretty big assumption." Eulalie wiped some blood away from her mouth, then looked at the runes on Naia's body. Her human eyes found them difficult to look at and comprehend, but her spider eyes saw how they actually floated in and out of Naia's body on the surface of her skin. For some strange reason, Eulalie got the impression that the runes were multi-dimensional and were doing their best to fit along the curves of Naia's body.

"It's more like magical instinct," Naia replied. The runes on her body shimmered as if in agreement, but it was only visible on the ultraviolet wavelength of light. "With my magic, I sometimes get hunches whether something will work."

"Are you referring to your own magic or the magic the house gave you?" Eulalie picked at her teeth with a fingernail. A piece of fur had gotten stuck there.

"What do you mean?" Naia asked.

Eulalie's eyes flicked to Amymone and back. If this was supposed to be a secret, it was Naia's fault for requesting clarification. "Oh, it's clear you aren't an ordinary nymph. You exhibit traits and qualities that fall well outside the standard deviation for your mythos. My theory is that you started as a nymph but were changed in some way. That being said, your nymph magic is separate from your house magic unless there was some type of convergent evolution upon your ascension."

Naia blinked in shock. "You…figured that out pretty fast."

"I've been ass deep in books about magic all week. I'm a quick learner, and I have a big ass."

"Clearly." Naia smiled. "Both types of magic work that way. House magic isn't really something I can control. It has a will of its own, but I can help direct its attention. When I say I think I can use Mike to restore the gate, it's almost like I can tell that the house agrees with me. It doesn't feel that way all the time, so I'm confident that we're at least on the right track. As for my own magic, I can usually just tell if it would work. It's instinctual."

Eulalie nodded. "I would know something about that. So out of curiosity…would your magic work on me?"

Amymone nearly dropped her book. "Why wouldn't it?"

Naia tilted her head. "That depends. I can do all sorts of things with my magic, so I need you to be more specific."

"Could you turn me on?" Eulalie set down her deer. "Seduce me. Make me horny. Do you require more euphemisms?" Many hours of research had been spent on this topic, and she was happy to provide more.

Amymone laughed. "Naia could turn on a broken light bulb."

Naia held up her hand for silence. "Is there a reason you want me to try?" she asked.

Eulalie opened her mouth and hesitated. At her core, she knew sex wasn't written into her code. Her desire to mate was nonexistent, and even her self-explorations had been minimally enjoyable. It was like a yawning void inside that had only been put there by the realization that she was different.

In truth, she was almost afraid that Naia could do it.

"You answered my question with a question," she replied. "That makes me think you can't."

Naia tilted her head. "That's not quite true. My magic doesn't seduce anyone. I can only amplify desires that are already there. If I were to use it on you, I know it wouldn't result in sex."

"Hmm." Eulalie pondered this for a moment. How could there be desire without sex? That sounded so self-defeating. "Would you be willing to enlighten me?"

"Just a touch." Naia's eyes sparkled.

Eulalie felt nothing at first. She looked at her own body, then over to Amymone. The dryad watched them with great interest.

When Eulalie looked back at Naia, her mouth was suddenly dry. The nymph stood before her with one hip cocked out, and Eulalie had a sudden desire to spin some web and use it to tie her legs together. Or perhaps bind her so that her chest was pushed out, or maybe...

"Oh!" Eulalie felt her spinnerets moving, and she realized that her body was producing webs. Knots, hundreds of them, flitted through her mind, each one perfect for a different situation. Some were good to prevent strain on the rope, others to prevent strain on the participant. Different weaves could produce ropes so smooth that they wouldn't leave a mark or thick ones that prevented muscles from flexing. If she wanted, she could easily get Naia's hands behind her back, perhaps bind her forearms together. Would she look better on her knees, or—

"I think that's enough," Naia replied.

Eulalie realized she was on the edge of the fountain, her mouth open in anticipation and a piece of webbing in her hand. Her deft fingers had already braided it into a simple rope nearly six feet long.

"But this...this isn't sexual." She looked around, trying to find somewhere to stash her rope. It was too big of a piece to eat. "I'm not...horny. Why does it feel like this?"

"Desire isn't always about sex, little spider." Naia leaned forward and booped Eulalie on the nose. "But once my house is back, you can tie me up anytime."

Those last six words sent a rush of excitement through Eulalie. Not only would Naia look beautiful all tied up, but her aqueous body meant that Eulalie didn't have to worry about hurting her. She could just phase through the bindings and escape, giving Eulalie plenty of feedback to pursue her passions.

"Okay, right, the house." She coiled the rope around her waist like a belt. "So we can't open the portal; we need to wait for Mike. So what can we do

347

now to prepare him for when he gets home? My assumption is that he's going into a trap."

"A trap set by someone powerful," Amymone agreed. "That could be problematic."

"So let's make sure he's ready for anything." Eulalie turned and looked at the dummy house. "I don't suppose you keep a stash of magical items in that version of the house for emergencies, do you?"

"Anything of interest would be in the Vault," Naia replied. "Ratu may have something, but that stuff is extremely dangerous. And I don't think she has any weapons if that's what you're getting at."

"Well, shit." Eulalie stomped a foot in frustration. "I was really hoping we could find a magic sword or something."

"Magic swords?" Amymone's face lit up in excitement. "What would you say if I told you I know about a magic tower full of them?"

Eulalie smiled so hard that her fangs extended.

BETH HAD BEEN IN SPACE FOR LESS THAN A MINUTE BEFORE THE OTHERS appeared in a blaze of golden light. Pestilence and Famine looked livid, but Jenny sat calmly on her rocking horse.

When War appeared, his features were tightly pinched. Every vein in his body bulged dramatically as he clenched his fists and shrieked.

"Sixty! Fucking! Years!" War turned toward Murray. "This has to be a violation of the rules!"

"I assure you that only a couple of minutes have passed in the real world," replied Murray.

"She made me dig holes to find her!" War grabbed at his face in frustration. "That has to be against the rules!"

"The winner of each round has been able to kill the loser in the manner of their choice," Murray said. "She wanted you to dig a hole to find her and then have it cave in on you and crush your skull. That does not violate the terms of your agreement."

"The fuck it doesn't!" War took a swing at Jenny, but his sword passed harmlessly through her.

Fucking crybaby, she replied. War continued to attack her, his movements harmless.

Beth put her hands over her mouth. To an observer, she probably looked shocked. In reality, she was trying to hide the biggest smile ever. Jenny had not only won the round but had trapped the horsemen for sixty years just for the fun of it.

And she would bet good money that Jenny hadn't experienced all sixty of those years. All the doll had to do was withdraw her consciousness so she was at the table. Those years would have taken mere moments.

"Would you like to attack again?" Murray asked.

War's eyes bulged out of his head, and he looked at his siblings. The three of them huddled up and muttered to one another. Beth wondered what they were even talking about.

You could always quit, Jenny offered.

War broke the huddle and started to say something, but Pestilence yanked him back in.

"What happened in there?" asked Reggie. "Did you really make them dig you up?"

I got bored. Jenny let out a giggle, then rocked her horse over to where Beth stood. *So I gave them hints. War had to use his sword to dig me up like a bitch.*

"I attack again!" War declared.

I wouldn't, Jenny warned. *I'm the hide-and-seek champion!*

"Fuck you," he replied.

They found themselves on the ground in Kamchatka again. This time, War's army arrived with several aircraft carriers full of planes and drones. His troops never set foot on land. Instead, they launched an aerial assault.

War, who stood with them, sneered in anger. Jenny was nowhere to be seen.

"Let's see your shadow people take something out of the sky," he muttered. "Each of these planes is equipped with the best surveillance technology known to man, so even if you pull your bullshit, I won't have to spend nearly as much time—"

A plane exploded overhead, the wreckage crashing into the side of a nearby mountain.

Beth could no longer contain her laughter, which drew dirty looks from the horsemen.

"But I thought she was using shadow people for her troops!" Famine's face paled. "It had to be. The toys were acting as gateways, right?"

Guess again! Jenny then blew a raspberry at them and made airplane noises as War's air force was destroyed one plane at a time. Beth clapped her hands in glee while Reggie did a series of dance moves next to her.

"Knock that shit off," Famine told them, but they ignored him.

In a desperate attempt to accomplish something, the planes dropped their bombs. The bombs fell only halfway to the ground before they rocketed back into the sky and exploded. It was like a Fourth of July show on steroids, and Beth cheered when it came to an end.

If you count to a million and say, "Ready or not, here I come," I'll give you a hint. Jenny's laughter was distorted. *You can get as many hints as you want!*

"You know what? Fuck you. I'm not even going to look." War sat down with his legs crossed. "I'm the personification of *War.* I'm immortal. You will go mad long before I do."

Quitter, Jenny replied. *Quitter-quitter. Quitterquitterquitterquitter...*

"Lady Beth?" Reggie took her by the hand as Jenny's voice steadily grew louder. "I think it's time we take our leave."

"I agree."

The two of them waited in space for a minute before the others returned. The horsemen looked defeated, and War appeared in a golden nimbus of light. He looked at Murray with a scowl.

"I end my turn." He moved away from the group and contemplated Earth.

Quitter, whispered Jenny. *You needed a lot of hints.*

"Saying hot and cold didn't accomplish anything," Famine muttered.

"I would like to reassure everyone that only a couple of minutes passed during the last round," Murray added. "It is Pestilence's turn."

Pestilence attacked Irkutsk from Siberia. They won the first two rounds, but Jenny's mysterious troops didn't make a single appearance. Instead, the doll just appeared in Pestilence's hands both times.

The horseman, clearly lacking creativity or patience, had promptly torn her apart.

On the third round, the shadows gobbled up Pestilence's troops without a sound. Jenny didn't bother taunting Pestilence like she had War. Instead, a group of people arrived holding bug nets and glass jars.

Puzzled by this development, everyone watched in silence as Pestilence was stabbed with a knife and the bugs were rounded up and caught. Beth wondered if Pestilence's consciousness was contained in just one specific bug or all of them.

The glowing bugs were then separated into individual glass jars. The humans laughed maliciously as they shook them, jostling the bugs inside.

Whoever keeps their bug alive wins a prize! Jenny announced. The humans let out a cheer as they separated. *And don't forget, they love to listen to music and need to eat shit to survive!*

"This is inhumane!" Famine declared, then looked at Murray. "You can't allow this!"

"Sounds like you're just mad you didn't think of something equally insidious," Beth responded. Through the months of torture fighting these guys, it occurred to her that they could have put her in a POW camp and starved her to death, or something similar. Instead, they had focused on the brutality of her death rather than breaking her spirit.

Jenny had been infinitely more calculating in her strategy and had zero qualms about torture of any kind.

Murray said nothing. Beth and Reggie stepped out of the round and waited. When Pestilence re-formed, their shoulders were slumped forward as if under a heavy strain. The horseman buzzed something at their brothers, and War's face turned bright red.

"If you back out, I will kill you myself!" he declared.

War's statement was very curious. She had been under the impression that a horseman couldn't be killed. Was War just angry, or did he mean it?

Pestilence buzzed some more but then shrugged.

It was Jenny's turn. She cackled maniacally and added troops to territories that needed them, then ended her turn.

Famine looked uncertain. The horsemen had been cocky the entire game but now were avoiding eye contact with one another. Their morale had taken a heavy hit.

When Famine attacked, he stood on top of a building while commanding the Hunger. The dark beings tore through the city, looking for any sign of Jenny or her army. The search went on for quite some time before the Hunger began to disappear.

"How is she doing this?" War asked, his voice unusually quiet.

Famine looked over at his brother. Sweat had beaded upon his brow as it became clear that Jenny had won the die rolls.

"Pop Goes the Weasel" began to play, and the group turned to see a jack-in-the-box on the ground, its mechanical arm moving by itself.

"I'm not going near that," Famine declared.

Jenny appeared on the roof of the building, her body as large as a small child. She flickered in and out of existence as she picked up the jack-in-the-box and walked toward Famine.

Don't be a baby, she told him. *After all, it's just a child's toy.*

Famine backed away from her until his back was against the edge of the roof. He looked over the side, nodded to himself, and jumped.

There was a loud clang of metal, and Famine was tossed back onto the roof by a metal ladder with legs like a centipede. Beth gasped when she saw it, suddenly realizing exactly what kind of troops Jenny had picked.

Ticktock, motherfucker. Jenny played the final note, and the lid of the Jack-and-the-Box lifted away to reveal a tube-like creature made of fangs that expanded and swallowed Famine whole. Everyone on the roof save for Murray cried out in alarm as the mimic shrank down and pulled itself back into the Jack-in-a-Box.

Moments passed, and Jenny looked around at everyone.

This will take a while, she announced. *They digest things really slowly. And it hurts the whole time that you're dying.* Her laughter ricocheted around them.

"There's no way he fits inside there," War pointed out.

They're bigger on the inside, Jenny replied, then looked at Pestilence. *I should have done this with the jars.*

Pestilence made an alarmed buzzing sound.

"You can quit after this turn," Murray said. "But not during."

War turned to argue with Pestilence just as a tiny drop of black blood squeezed out of the jack-in-the-box. Beth and Reggie disappeared, leaving the horsemen to their torment.

It had taken the better part of the afternoon to get home, but Mike didn't mind. Abella was content to walk in silence while clinging to his arm. It threw off his gait a bit, but he had more important things to think about.

Ever since the incident in the clearing, the sounds and feelings he experienced had gotten more intense. It was as though he had opened the window into a different world and then forgotten to close it all the way. Each tree they walked past whispered to him in greeting, and on more than one occasion, a tree branch would pat his shoulder as if they were old friends.

Though the paths were buried in snow, he could sense them. The thin trails were lacking in foliage, so they were the quiet parts of the forest. It was almost like having a song stuck in his head, except now it was several radio stations running at the same time.

He thought of Bigfoot's offer to help him speak with the forest. It was something he would need to look into right away.

It also felt like he was being watched. It wasn't a malicious gaze, by any means. In fact, it felt almost playful, and he had a suspicion that it was the cabin herself, keeping an eye on him.

No, not quite the cabin. She was also the land; she had told him as much. He thought back to the times he had conversed with the house. This was far different, with the cabin less secretive and much chattier than her sister.

And were they actual siblings? Or was it more of an honorific? Had some guy gone around knocking women up with baby buildings? Was that where the term laying wood came from?

"Oh!" Abella squeezed his arm, causing him to stop. A large white rabbit stood in front of them, its nose twitching as it sniffed the air. "It's not scared of us!"

"You know, I've always been told that wild animals who let you come near are dange—okay, yeah, go ahead." He watched as Abella scooped the rabbit in her arms. It looked like a snowshoe hare with its massive back legs, but he wasn't an expert by any means.

"It's so fluffy!" Abella rubbed her cheek against it, and he half expected it to go full Monty Python and take off her head. The creature was content to accept Abella's love for a few more moments, then kicked its feet to let them know it was done. Abella set it on the ground, and it hopped off into the woods.

"So like I was saying, you shouldn't handle wild animals," he told her. "It can mean they're sick, injured, or any number of bad things."

"You shoot lightning out of your dick, and I breathe fire." She cocked her head at him and arched an eyebrow. "I think I can handle petting wild bunnies."

He rolled his eyes but didn't argue, though he did want to clarify the dick comment. His magic had been related to sexual intimacy, but clearly, it was attempting to do something new.

Did magic evolve over time? Or was it a result of the abilities he had gained from the others creating something new? As he thought on this idea, he realized the weird stuff had started happening after sex with Quetzalli. Was it because her affinity was storms, or was it related to her draconic nature?

He was probably the only man alive to stick his dick in a dragon. Not exactly something you could find a support group for.

When the cabin came into view, Abella unfolded her wings.

"I need to go back to my duties," she told him. "But count me down for a walk anytime."

With a wink, she took to the sky and started her ascent. He watched her climb until she looked like a distant bird. Now flight would have been a fun ability to gain, but if Abella had stone wings, would his just be skin? On top of having to alter all his shirts, he didn't want wings that looked like a stretched scrotum.

"You have returned." The owl stepped out of her hiding place beneath a large pine tree. "I wondered if you would return."

"This is the safest place to be," he replied.

"Humans aren't necessarily known for being trustworthy," she countered. "I suspected you to hide somewhere else and leave the work to the others. You cannot fault me for having doubts."

ANNABELLE HAWTHORNE

"When you ate humans, did you barf up their remains in large pellets?" He held out an imaginary football. "Like, if I dissected it, would I find finger bones and shit?"

Her brow furrowed, giving her a frightening countenance. "Are you trying to insult me?"

He took a step toward her, never breaking her gaze. "No. Just reminding you that respect runs both ways. You came to me, remember?"

The owl clacked her beak, then slumped her shoulders. "My apologies. I am nervous about our encounter with Leeds and may not have chosen my words wisely. My path with humans has been difficult, and I lean on old habits when stressed."

He nodded. "I'm nervous too, but this isn't my first near-death situation. Your plan sounds like it will work."

"And it should. However…" She held up a clawed hand. Crimson light danced along her talons. "I feel as if I have overlooked something."

"Well, I hope you remember it." He backed away to give her some space. "When I went camping as a kid, I always felt like I was forgetting something. It seemed like the more convinced I was that I'd left it behind, the less likely I had actually screwed up."

"So if you weren't worried, it was because you forgot it entirely?"

He nodded. "You got it. Right now, I spend almost every day waiting for the other shoe to drop. Maybe I forgot whatever or didn't think everything through, and it will come back to bite me in a bad way. I'm the kind of person who is quick to adapt, 'cause I'm used to my plans going wrong."

The owl's feathers rippled, sending a couple onto the ground. They were larger than her bird form's, and he wondered if her current size dictated how large they were when they fell off.

"I am poor at adaptation," she replied. "When it comes to the hunt itself, I am fine. But that is instinct and planning. My spells take time to weave, for that is the cost of my magic." She shuddered again, sending more feathers to the ground. It seemed to be the equivalent of losing hair when stressed. "I suspect yours is your unpredictability."

"How do you figure?" he asked.

"When last we spoke, you did not carry such an earthen aura. You smelled of storms and lust but now carry a certain heaviness. It is very much like the fae but also the magic of the forest. Magic was never meant to be mixed in such a manner, for it generates chaos."

"Story of my life," he muttered. "So that's what I have? Chaos magic?"

"Caretaker." She clicked her beak for a few moments as if deep in thought. "The name itself isn't important but appropriate. You should know

354

that magic like yours can be quite powerful but only if it can be controlled. Be warned that it has a life of its own, very much like a roaring fire. If you aren't careful, it will consume you."

"Metaphorically?" he asked, thinking of Emily.

"No. Literally. In its haste to help you, your magic could tear your body apart. And when you die, the magic doesn't simply vanish. It will be let loose in the world in ways we cannot predict. Never start a fire you cannot put out." She flapped her wings a couple of times and transformed back into bird form. With a cautionary hoot, she flew away.

"Thanks for the advice, Hedwig," he muttered. He watched until she disappeared into the trees and then continued toward the cabin, his hands in his pocket. Finding out that he was potentially a magic bomb had dulled his enthusiasm, so he took his time walking.

As he was passing the barn, he saw movement within. Dana was still there, and she had taken apart most of the jeep. She stood in the middle of a mess as if contemplating her next move.

"What the hell are you doing?" he asked.

"Hmm?" She regarded him coolly, then stared at the disassembled jeep. "What time is it?"

"Don't know. My phone was my watch." He knelt to examine what might have been a carburetor. His knowledge was hardly extensive, so this was mostly a guess.

"I must have lost track of time." She wiped some grease off her face, only to smear some more from her hands onto her cheek. "I do that when I'm working on stuff."

"But why dismantle the whole thing?" He moved over to the body of the jeep and realized she had pulled out most of the engine.

"It started as an oil change, and I got carried away." She pulled a spark plug out of her pocket. "Found a box of these and wanted to put some new ones in. Figured I would change the air filter, and it kind of snowballed."

Mike kicked a tire. They had been stacked in the corner. "You don't say."

"Figured I would rotate them. Don't move those, I need to put them back on in a certain order."

"If you say so." He sat down in the passenger seat, which was on the floor next to the body. "Velvet is going to freak when she sees her dad's car like this."

Dana's face darkened. "Shit, you're right." She looked around her feet. "Don't suppose you want to help me?"

"Reassemble a car? Not really." He picked up a ratchet. "I don't know where most of this stuff goes. Didn't have a garage growing up or anyone willing to teach me about it."

Dana snorted. "It's not that different from your usual approach to things. Tab A in slot B, you know what I mean."

Mike looked up at Dana. Even though she was looking away from him, he could see the small grin on her face. It had been hours since she had fed, so he was surprised to see her so…lively.

"My dad restored an old car when I was seven," she told him as she started putting stuff back under the hood of the jeep. He couldn't see what she was doing because she was moving too fast. Between her memory and the fact that she didn't tire, it was like watching a one-woman pit crew. "It seems dumb, but I don't remember much about it now. He would only work on it on the weekends, and my mom let me stay up late to spend time with him. He was always working long hours, so weekends were our only time together. There was one Sunday night that my mom went to bed early, so he let me stay up until almost three on a school night. Mom gave him hell for that."

Mike chuckled but said nothing. He didn't have a story of his own to add and was too busy watching Dana's facial expressions. He had spent so many months seeing Dana devoid of almost all emotion, and he was now seeing tiny bursts of it. It was almost like watching an actor in a play break character. Was Dana even aware she was doing it?

"So what has your panties in a bunch?" she asked him.

"Who told you I'm wearing panties?" he asked.

Dana snorted. "Are they mine or Quetzalli's? I don't think you'd fit in mine, and if you stretch them out, I'll eat your hands. Don't dodge the question."

"I had an experience with Abella in the woods," he replied. "My magic did something weird, and now the owl has me all paranoid I'm going to explode."

She stopped what she was doing and stared at him. "I'm going to need you to run all that by me again. More details this time."

Except for the sexual details of his interlude with Abella, he told her everything. How the magic had connected him to the land, how Abella had started breathing fire. She listened without a single word until he had finished.

"So what do you think?" he asked. "And before you answer, we both know you're acting differently than you usually do. Something has changed, and you were affected too."

Dana bowed her head in contemplation, then nodded. "This rush of mine should have worn off some time ago. I think it's why I lost track of time. I'm used to falling out of the rush. It's like having the perfect amount of caffeine;

you feel all inspired and energized, but you know it's going to wear off eventually so you try to get as much done as you can."

"You're smiling," he told her.

"Why, so I am." She grinned at him. "And before you ask, I'm not fixed or anything. Slashed open my forearm earlier, didn't even hurt. Being dead has made me a little careless at times, I will admit. Has its perks though." With that statement, she rolled a tire over to the jeep and lifted the chassis off a group of cinder blocks with one hand.

"I knew you were strong, but this?" He watched in amazement as she casually stuck the wheel back on and then tightened the nuts down with an old-style bar-type lug wrench.

"That's about my limit," she explained. "I can actually feel the strain in my bones from it. If I lifted it too quick, I would probably snap my spine or rip a muscle. The human body is an interesting place when you don't feel pain anymore. It really reminds you that you're just a bowl of pudding piloting around a robot made of meat."

He frowned at the visual, but she wasn't wrong.

"Sometimes, if I'm not too involved with whatever I'm working on, I can actually feel how my joints work," she continued. "Or how my muscles contract and extend. It's almost like I'm able to shut out the noise and really feel all the things my body can do."

"You mean kind of like when you're falling asleep and can hear your own heartbeat if it's quiet enough?"

She feigned shock. "Discrimination! Check your privilege, beating heart."

It had been a while since he had seen Dana and Lily hanging out, and he now worried just how much the succubus had rubbed off on the zombie.

"But yeah, close enough." She put another tire on the opposite side of the first. "You wear your body your whole life without really understanding how it moves. There's a process in there that we take for granted. Have you ever tried to program a robot to walk? It's super hard, but toddlers can nail it pretty quick. I had a professor once who was obsessed with biometric design."

He nodded, now lost in thought. It was easy to see her point, but now he could apply it to his immediate problem. Instead of his own body, it was his magic that had him flummoxed. He used to have good control of it, but those were just baby steps.

"What's the fine line between understanding how something works versus just figuring it out?" he asked. "When do I know if I'm overthinking it?"

She shrugged. "Ask a baby, I guess."

Frowning, he turned his attention to the dirt floor of the barn. Thinking about how a baby learned to walk, he could easily picture how they would use something to stand up first, then move. Was there a way he could learn to stand first instead of having to hit the ground running?

The clearing Abella had taken him to was teeming with life, which had overwhelmed him. Looking at the dirty floor of the barn, he could see the occasional sprout of dead grass along the boundaries of the building. This was a place that was connected to the earth but minimal on nature. Could he connect with it as he had in the glade?

When he closed his eyes, he could sense that thick bass note from before. It was dim, as if very far away. He tried to focus on it and shifted in his chair to get comfortable. His hand slipped off the side, causing him to brush his fingertips in the dirt. The volume in his head jumped several levels on contact.

Okay. That's interesting. He put the palm of his hand on the ground and waited. The musical tones pressed against his flesh, and a sense of peace permeated his body. His magic matched the rhythm and pulsed outward from him, scattering loose dirt away from his hand.

Even with his eyes closed, he could sense where Dana stood. His senses expanded, and now he could feel the family of mice that lived in the corner behind boxes of motor oil.

The sensations were there, but they were quiet compared to the cacophony from before. Little by little, he expanded outward from the barn. The land around them was largely short brush, so he met plenty of burrowing critters waiting on warmer days to emerge from their homes. He felt the corners of the cabin, then immediately withdrew when he discovered an intense presence. Unsure if it was the entity that he sensed, he decided to expand his senses somewhere else.

The land around the barn was covered in snow, yet teemed with life that hungered for warmth. The fleeting thoughts of small mammals and insects touched his consciousness like whispers. As he explored the land, he felt it try to cling to his magic. It was easy to imagine that his magic was similar to sunlight and that it could nourish the surrounding property. If he wanted, could he wake up the vegetation as he had in the clearing?

He took in a sharp breath as he realized that the sexual nature of his magic still applied here. While he hadn't dug a hole in the ground and fucked it physically, his magic was currently mixing with the earth in a very intimate manner. It was inside him just as much as he was inside it.

For just a second, he thought he heard a woman's laugh. Whether illusory or not, it definitely belonged to the cabin.

What could he even do with this knowledge? Was it just this land, or could he connect with the house too? Maybe it would be a means to speak directly to the house, or even his other properties. If they were alive, then surely they had desires he could assist them with. Maybe the house wanted a new coat of paint or the cabin wanted to cut some trees for a better view of the mountains.

In turn, maybe they would be more forthcoming about what was expected of him. It would be nice for a change to simply be told what to do next.

Sparks flowed down his arm and into the ground, and he gasped when he felt the trees touch on his consciousness. Even with his eyes closed, he could see the tiny flames at their center, each one connected to its neighbor by gossamer strands of light. More and more flames appeared of all shapes and sizes, and it wasn't until he saw one swoop through the air like a bird that he realized that he was looking at souls.

In awe, he tilted his head in Dana's direction. Hers was like a tiny star strapped in chains of darkness, bound tightly to her body. Fascinated by the sight, he didn't notice the chill in his gut until it bloomed violently throughout his entire body.

Distant flames were being snuffed out at an incredible rate. As they vanished, he realized that whatever was happening was headed right for him.

"Dana!" He opened his eyes and pointed at the wall of the barn. "Something is coming!"

There was the loud snapping of wood, followed by a high-pitched shriek. The wall of the barn exploded inward as a massive figure crashed through it. Mike held up his hands, only catching a brief glimpse of the beast through his outstretched hands.

Dana, already in motion, had picked up the tire closest to her and whipped her body around to throw it like a discus. The tire slammed into the intruder hard enough that it was knocked off course, crashing into the ground next to Mike.

"What the fuck is that?" he cried, jumping to his feet. The thing on the floor was a tangle of long black hair that was filled with branches. Expecting the creature to stand, he flinched when it levitated off the ground and turned to face them.

"Holy fucking hell," Dana muttered.

It was a giant head, almost six feet tall. Fearsome eyes that blazed with malevolent intent sat over daggerlike teeth. With a cry, it flew toward them, its hair spreading out like a pair of black wings.

Dana shoulder checked Mike out of the way. He crashed hard into the ground and felt something in his knee pop. The sharp pain of impact vanished in the rush of adrenaline as he leaped to his feet and looked for a weapon.

The head had Dana in its teeth and was growling as it tried to bite through her. In the corner of its mouth was a lug wrench that Dana held, using it as a wedge to keep it from closing.

It floated around the barn, slamming itself into the walls in an attempt to dislodge her. Up above, the barn creaked dangerously as if it was going to topple any moment.

"Abella! I need you!" he shouted, then ran to the back of the head. The long hair was matted and smelled swampy, but he jumped on and tried to climb up the scalp. The odor made his eyes water, but once he was on top, he tried to punch the head in the eye.

It slammed its eyelid closed, pinning his hand in place.

The head spiraled around, scattering the pieces of the jeep before colliding with the chassis. The jeep toppled over with a large screech, the undercarriage sliding violently over the cinder blocks.

"Shit!" Dana cried, then disappeared from sight as she moved farther into the head's mouth.

The smell of gasoline filled the air, and Mike realized that the tank must have been ripped open. He really hoped the giant head hadn't brought along a giant cigarette to light up.

"Mike!" Abella's cry came from outside, and he saw her from a distance through the broken wall. She was still far away, her face set in determination.

A metal blade popped through the head's eye, and it emitted a terrible shriek as Dana stabbed it from within. It spun violently, throwing Mike to the ground, followed shortly by Dana. Both of her arms were bent the wrong way, and her clothes had been slashed up.

"What the hell is that thing?" he asked her as the head fell over, its mouth gasping like a fish out of water. He had so many questions, like how it breathed and if it needed to eat.

Up above, he heard a chuckle. When he looked up, he watched in horror as the shadows coalesced into a dark figure with bat-like wings and a horse's head.

"That was my insurance policy," Leeds told them as the head shuddered one last time, its remaining eye going slack and its mouth hanging open. "What is that phrase that always bounces through your head? Be prepared?"

Mike was going to say something witty but held his breath instead when Leeds held up an old Zippo lighter.

"Burn in Hell, Caretaker." Leeds tossed the lighter toward the spreading pool of gasoline. It clanged against the jeep and promptly put itself out when it landed upside down in the dirt.

"Dumbass," Dana muttered as she tried to stand up. One of her legs was crooked. "By the way, you give terrible head."

Leeds snorted and dropped from the rafters onto the ground near the jeep. Mike tried to tackle Leeds away but was grabbed from behind by a shadow that yanked him off his feet. The pain in his knee blossomed, and he almost blacked out.

"Let's try this again," Leeds muttered, then picked up the lighter and lit it. He knelt and held the flame against a line of gas until it ignited and the fire rolled toward the gas tank. With a laugh, Leeds stepped into a shadow and vanished.

Mike closed his eyes, thinking the jeep would explode. When it didn't, he opened his eyes and saw that the shadow holding him was gone. He crawled over to Dana.

"There wasn't much gas in the tank," she explained, using her one good limb to scoot toward the exit. "Darren never bothered refilling it before he died. Most of it has probably leaked out already."

"So it won't explode?" he asked.

"Not a lot, but—" There was a loud boom, followed by a roar as the fire expanded, filling the air with smoke and fumes. The barn shifted around them, the structure groaning. "We need to go."

They crawled toward the door as the flames surrounded them. The barn was old and full of plenty of things for the fire to consume. His leg dragged across the uneven ground, each bump causing him to grit his teeth in agony. He didn't bother looking back over his shoulder at the burning vehicle nor contemplate how this was exactly the kind of situation that would put him back in therapy.

He could feel the flames licking at his back when Abella arrived. Saying nothing to Dana, she picked up the zombie and threw her out the door. Dana bounced and then slid across the snow, safe from the flames almost thirty feet away.

"Didn't take you long to get in trouble," she muttered, kneeling to pick him up. With her body between him and the flames, he felt the temperature drop several degrees. Abella looked over at the giant head, which had caught on fire, and gaped. "What the fuck is that thing?"

"I call him Todd." Mike tried to laugh at his weak attempt at a joke but started coughing instead. "Nine out of ten dentists hate him."

She cradled him against her body and leaned forward, hot embers bouncing off her back. Once they were outside, she set him in the snow and turned her gaze toward the roof of the barn.

Leeds stood up there, his coal-red eyes blazing in the fading light of day.

Abella tried to leap toward him, but the shadows at her feet wrapped around her ankles and held tight. She stomped her talons but couldn't get free.

"I don't think so, gargoyle." He sneered in their direction. "With that busted wing of yours, you'll never be strong enough."

Mike looked toward the forest. Leeds had come far earlier than predicted, but the owl should still be watching. Where the fuck was she?

"Maybe she's dead," Leeds replied, likely reading Mike's thoughts. "Or maybe she betrayed you. Wouldn't that just be delicious? Or maybe I'll kill you and you'll spend the rest of your life wondering which it was?"

"Are you going to talk me to de——" Something wrapped around his neck and squeezed. He turned his head to see that his own shadow had reached up to strangle him.

His magic raced through him as he let out a scream of rage. Streamers of white light leaped from his hands and twisted around his shadow, causing it to burst and reappear back where it should be.

"Maybe you should come down here and finish the job," Mike said, his voice raspy. His magic was crackling through his body, just below the surface of his skin.

Leeds sniffed the air, then stomped his hooves on the roof.

"A temporary setback, Caretaker. I have all the time in the world, and you? I am well aware you are operating under a time limit."

Mike's nostrils flared, and the air around him sizzled, his magic hungry for blood. Behind him, he heard Abella grunting as she fought to free herself.

"I have no intention of leaving this land or letting you capture me. Kill me a hundred times and I shall only return to torment you again." Leeds laughed, the smoke of the fire billowing up around his body. "And you certainly can't kill me. One way or another, I will win."

The farm groaned beneath Leeds, who took a couple of cautionary steps, then fixed Mike with his blazing eyes.

I will take everyone from you that you love. Leeds's voice was like nails on a chalkboard inside Mike's head. *It is no longer enough to have your land. I would have your absolute misery, to see you wallow in grief as I crush your family into blood and bones.*

The smoke billowed upward, obscuring Leeds from sight.

Who should I take first, Caretaker?

"Ah, there you are." Bigfoot stepped from between a pair of trees, his colossal shoulders knocking free a bunch of snow. Velvet watched him approach from atop a young buck. It flailed its legs, unable to gain any purchase in the snow. "I've been looking for you."

"Sorry, Uncle Foot." She didn't have the heart to tell him she had been trying to lose him all day. Not only did she feel his attention would be best used elsewhere, but she also wanted to go check on her egg. The glove box had been a safe place to store it, but with Abella always atop the barn, she hadn't been able to relocate it somewhere better, like her own room.

What would the gargoyle think if she knew one of the eggs survived? Velvet felt guilty about the deception but had no regrets. Of all the clutch, that one had been the most important to her, and she still needed some time to contemplate whether she should even let it hatch.

"Don't play with your food," he chastised.

The buck let out a pathetic bleat. She had bitten it a few minutes ago, the frantic beating of the deer's heart speeding the digestive enzyme through its body. It had grown considerably weaker, and she gave its haunch an exploratory squeeze.

Satisfied the buck would make a good meal, she snapped its neck. A final gasp escaped the beast along with some steam from its nostrils. Her dad used to tell her that it was the animal's soul escaping the body, but he also used to tell her that there was a monster on the roof that ate little spider girls if they snuck out of the house.

Still, it was a poetic thought. She took an exploratory bite and almost moaned in relief when liquefied protein filled her mouth.

"C'mon, it's getting dark," he said. "We should get back home soon. I don't know if Leeds is coming tonight, but I don't want to be caught in the woods if we can help it."

"Why? It's just Leeds now, right?"

Bigfoot shook his head. "You remember those documentaries about sharks? They have those fish that follow them around and eat their leftovers. Well, some of the creatures in the woods are like those fish. They didn't follow him here for altruistic reasons. Even the owl believes a bunch of the Nirumbi still seek his favor."

"Dumbasses." She contemplated the buck. "I don't feel like taking this to-go. If you want to head back now, I'll follow when I'm done."

He crossed his arms. "Not gonna happen. If I didn't know any better, I'd wonder if you were trying to get rid of me."

"Why would I want to do that?" She bit the deer again. "I just know you hate watching this."

"I've had decades to get used to it." He sat down on the ground. "I've gotten used to lots of things I never thought I would."

"Mm-hmm." Velvet tried to come up with a different excuse to go home without him. With any luck, maybe Abella would be on patrol. She already had a great spot for the egg picked out in her room.

Bigfoot chatted with her as she consumed her meal. He was feeling nostalgic, but all Velvet could think about was her egg. It had been smaller than the rest with a very faint blue sheen to it and could easily fit inside a pocket. She was hoping to stash it away until she could talk to Eulalie about what to do next.

It wasn't just the issue of the survival of her species. She recalled plenty of conversations with her mother about what the Arachne were and how it would probably be best that they never return. It had been a moot point for the most part because her desire to breed hadn't kicked in until she'd met Mike. But now she felt as though her mother had been a massive hypocrite in expecting her own children not to pursue the life she'd had.

If her parents had made raising a child work; perhaps she could make it work with Mike? Sure, it would be difficult at times. Arachne children were their own kind of trouble, and it had taken both her parents and Bigfoot to keep them in line. A child living in a magic house would probably sneak away every chance she got.

Would the others help too? Abella probably wouldn't. Thinking of her made Velvet's stomach clench into knots. The tenuous understanding they seemed to have now would likely be over. And what would happen if her daughter tried to eat someone? It wasn't like they could just move out.

The cabin would likely be the safest place for her daughter. Even with the newest immigrants, it would probably be okay. But what about Mike? He had his own responsibilities and probably wouldn't live with her full-time if she stayed in Oregon.

"You okay, fluff ball?" Bigfoot stared at her. "You aren't eating."

"Yeah, I'm fine." She resumed her meal but only out of habit. There was no telling when she would find something else to eat.

Once she was done, she tossed aside the shriveled husk and used her legs to dig a hole. The remains were buried beneath the earth, and she made sure to say a small prayer of thanks to the forest. It was something her mother had taught her, a way to remember and appreciate that an Arachne's life could only continue at the cost of another's.

Maybe that would be something she taught her daughter. A bunch of things would come instinctually, but morality? That was something she would have to make sure was instilled early on. She had a good feeling about her daughter, but there was no telling what her actual strengths and weaknesses would be. Eulalie could probably help in areas where Velvet was weak.

She fought back a sigh. Eulalie would probably be mad that she had done this. It wasn't as though she had any control over it. Being horny from time to time was a far cry from becoming obsessed with procreating, and now that the deed was done, she was experiencing what the internet called "postnut clarity."

Sex with Mike had been fantastic, but now that she had an egg to worry about, all she felt was some intense feelings for him. If they were to fuck, she probably wouldn't lay any more eggs for a bit. Her body needed time to produce more, and she simply wasn't ready for it. In fact, she was now worried she wasn't ready for motherhood in general.

A small grin crossed her lips. The fear of being a bad parent was the human part of her talking. She remembered snooping on many conversations between her parents where her father had expressed those same concerns. Her mother had always been supportive, but she had been largely a creature of instinct and hadn't had the same concerns he had. Or if she had, she hadn't expressed them.

Done with the buck, Velvet allowed Bigfoot to lead her home. All around her, she could hear the spiders chattering anxiously. Spring was on its way, and they were eager to wake up and go about their simple little lives. None of them had to worry about devils, or falling in love, or angry stone women who would want to cave in their skulls.

Abella. There was a thousand-pound problem she had no answer to. Having her destroy the clutch had been hard but necessary. She had been too caught up in the emotions of the moment to do the deed herself, and she was ashamed.

She would have to tell her, and soon. Though the gargoyle was made of stone, Velvet sensed she had a good heart. If she explained that the egg was good, maybe she could get the gargoyle to forgive her. The longer she waited, the heavier her betrayal would become.

"I hate human problems," she muttered. If she were a regular Arachne, she would just say nothing and hide the egg away until it hatched, then disappear. If she really wanted to, maybe that could be an option.

But where would they hide?

"You've got an awful lot on your mind," Bigfoot said, interrupting her thoughts. "And don't bother lying to me about it. I can tell something's up."

"It's about Mike," she replied, realizing that if there was someone who would see things her way, it would be her uncle. Instead of spending all day trying to dodge him, she could have told him what was going on, and maybe he could have offered help or advice. It was something Eulalie would have told her to do, or even her father.

God, she missed them both.

"I always dreaded the day you discovered boys." Bigfoot chuckled at his joke. "Tell me."

She opened her mouth to say something, but the harsh stench of fire flitted across her nostrils. Frozen in place, she looked around in fright, trying to determine where it was coming from.

"Fire," she whispered as if afraid nearby trees would ignite at the word.

Bigfoot sniffed the air deeply, then growled. "Shit!"

He took off in a sprint, and she chased him as they leaped through several tree portals. The smell of flames continued growing until they burst through the trees and into a thick cloud of smoke.

Velvet choked on the ashes in the air, her eyes watering. The sun was little more than a dim orb through the smoke-laden air, and Bigfoot gasped in horror.

The wind changed direction, revealing that the source was the barn. Thick flames reached for the sky like hungry hands, each one curling around a dark figure who moved along the roof, his body barely visible against the smoke. The setting sun gleamed off of Leeds's horns.

My egg! No sooner had the thought crossed her mind did Leeds turn his snarling visage in her direction. His horse lips twisted up into a sadistic grin, revealing thick buck teeth.

No. My egg. His voice penetrated her mind, freezing her in place. Unfurling his wings, he took to the sky with maniacal laughter that boomed across the landscape.

Bigfoot yelled her name, but she barely heard him as she gave chase.

TEMPTATION

The flames fully engulfed the barn, sending the structure crumbling to the ground. Mike had pulled himself farther from the fire, the throbbing in his knee blooming into full-blown agony. Abella walked behind him with her wings outstretched to protect him from the heat and burning embers while carrying Dana. After being thrown out of the barn, she had injured her last remaining limb and had been trying to roll away from the fire.

Bigfoot came charging around the barn so fast that he slid sideways across the snow. "Velvet is gone!" he cried as he came to a stop. "Leeds did something to her, she went after him!"

Mike tried to stand but fell down with a groan. "Why didn't you go after her?"

"She's way faster than I am and can jump along the treetops. Without knowing where she's going, I can't exactly cut her off." He turned his eyes on Abella. "But you. You could track her, right?"

Abella frowned, then looked down at Mike.

"You realize Leeds is trying to separate us, yes?" she asked.

Mike let out a grunt, then nodded. There was no doubt this was all according to Leeds's plan, but they couldn't just leave Velvet to whatever fate he had in store for her.

"And you still want me to go?" Abella looked uncertain.

"We need to regroup. If you can catch her now, you can bring her back. We need to find Quetzalli, Yuki, and that damn owl. Something went wrong, and until we know what, we're going to be stuck here while he picks us off." He fixed Abella with a hard stare, trying his best to hold back tears of pain. "He's planning to kill us one at a time. I think Velvet is his first target."

Bigfoot roared, his body expanding as he slammed a fist into a nearby tree. The trunk cracked, the impact causing the branches to shed their snow.

"I will make him suffer," he declared. "Even if it takes me the rest of my days!"

"I'll be safe with this guy," Mike continued. "We're stronger together than apart. Please." His eyes now shimmered with tears as he tried to shift his leg. "Bring her back for me."

She responded by spreading her wings and taking to the sky. He watched her go with a tight feeling in his chest, followed by a chill. Leeds had outplayed them again, and he wouldn't feel good until they were all together.

"We need to find the others." He laid both of his legs out and frowned. His injured knee was swollen, but he was able to bend it a little. It was probably just a sprain, which was preferable to pretty much anything else knee related.

Dana grunted. She had finally gotten one of her arms twisted back into place and was flexing her fingers.

"Fucker couldn't bite me so used his tongue to crush me against the roof of his mouth." She grabbed onto her other arm and twisted it. There was a loud crunch, and a bone popped through the skin. "Can someone help me with this?"

Mike gagged, then turned away.

"I can help." Bigfoot knelt and, with directions from Dana, helped get her bones realigned so that her rapid healing could take over. The luster faded from her hair, and her skin paled until she nearly matched the snow, but she was back on her feet. Her eyes were still rimmed with red as she pulled out her sword.

"The good vibes are officially gone," she growled. "Gonna have to straddle the line between apathy and rage, I guess."

A gray figure descended from above. It was Emery, his hands fidgeting as he darted around.

"Emery. We need you." Mike let Dana help him up. The pure agony in his knee had faded to tolerable levels, allowing him to put a bit of weight on it. "With Abella gone, you're our eyes in the sky. We need to find Yuki, Quetzalli, and the owl." He looked over his shoulder at the forest, then pointed. "Last I saw the owl, she was headed that way."

Emery nodded, then shot into the air.

"Then we shall head that way as well." Bigfoot moved ahead of him. "I will ask the trees if they've seen them."

"Good thing the others are memorable," Mike muttered with a wince. He wasn't entirely certain how a tree's memories worked, but imagined the magical trio would be fairly distinct. He took a step that became a hop. "Do we have anything I can use as a crutch?"

Bigfoot looked over his shoulder. "We've never had a shortage of legs around here, but I'll see if I can find you something." He disappeared into the trees, leaving Mike with Dana.

"Glad to see he still has a sense of humor," Mike said.

"It's either that or scream." Dana helped him walk toward the trees where Bigfoot had disappeared. Once they were there, Bigfoot appeared with a large branch with a scoop that would fit beneath Mike's armpit. Dana used her sword to cut it to the right size.

His knee was already feeling better, but the crutch helped immensely. Bigfoot moved ahead of them and would come back every few minutes to check in. Emery would dive down to hear the report, then take to the sky once more.

Moving through the dense woods, Mike felt the familiar humming return. If he tried to focus on it, he could hear individual whispers in a language he couldn't quite grasp. Every now and then, he would get the impression that someone had passed by recently or hear two trees speaking with each other. If he closed his eyes, he could almost see the words translated to images in his head, like a waking dream.

It was nearly an hour later when Emery dropped down and flitted about like a hummingbird. At the same time, Mike detected a dead spot in the ramblings of the woods, as though a part of it had gone silent.

"There's something over there!" Emery pointed off to the left. "There was a fight!"

Mike limped ahead as fast as he could but was grabbed from behind by Bigfoot, who pulled him through a portal with Dana. For just a moment, he could hear the forest as it shouted in his ears, and then it went quiet when they came out of the portal and into a small clearing. At its center was a spiked dome made of ice, the ugly love child of an igloo and a morning star. All around the dome, dead Nirumbi with bloody handprints on their foreheads lay on the ground. A small group of Nirumbi who were attacking the dome froze when they saw Dana.

Dana let out a shriek before diving into their ranks, causing panic among the Nirumbi. The sword whipped through the air, removing limbs as the zombie carved up the remaining attackers.

"What the hell?" Mike knelt to check one of the dead Nirumbi. The handprint was distorted, a definitive match for Leeds's claws. The body was riddled with bloody wounds, some still packed with shards of ice.

"Quetzalli?" Dana moved up to the dome and knocked on it with the butt of her sword. "You in there?"

"We're all in here!" The muffled voice that answered was Yuki's. The ice crumbled and turned to slush, revealing the kitsune standing over Quetzalli. The dragon was kneeling over a bloody figure on the ground.

It was the owl. Her body was broken, and her wide eyes darted back and forth from Mike to Bigfoot as they came near.

"It was an ambush," she whispered, her cracked beak clacking. "These Nirumbi were loyal to Leeds, please do not punish..."

"Easy." Mike knelt by her side and tried to maintain a neutral expression when he realized there was no way she was going to survive her injuries. He was fairly certain there were bones protruding beneath her thick feathers and wasn't about to ask. "We won't punish the others for the crimes of the few."

The owl relaxed, letting out a sigh mixed with a gurgle.

"I don't understand." Bigfoot knelt by the owl. "Leeds shouldn't have been back until nightfall at the earliest."

The owl coughed, then tilted her head toward Mike.

"I underestimated him," she said. "These Nirumbi weren't just looking for...a leader, they... wanted a god. We stumbled on...shrine..."

"Shhh." Yuki knelt and put her hand on the owl's forehead, then looked at Mike. "The Nirumbi built an altar in the woods. When we found it, they ambushed us. They were using ritual sacrifices to summon him."

"How does that even work?" Mike asked.

"A life for a life. They were able to shorten his revival at the cost of many of their own. He is technically a demon, and they can be summoned for a price." She looked sadly at the owl. "We thought we had him. The Nirumbi were only armed with spears, but then Leeds summoned this giant floating head from deep in the woods. It bit down on her and then spit her out when Quetzalli zapped it. That's when I summoned my barrier, but we thought it was still out here waiting."

"I killed the head," Dana added. "It's just Leeds now."

"Don't...assume..." The owl looked at Mike. "Caretaker. I am unable to hold up my end of the bargain."

Mike gritted his teeth. He couldn't exactly hold it against her. The plan had been to lure Leeds into a set of runes powered by the owl's magic. The runes had been carved into a large log that could be carried as a mobile prison. Bigfoot was going to carry it out of the woods, thereby breaking Leeds's barrier.

"We'll figure something ou—holy shit, no, stop!"

The owl, using her clawed finger, had jammed the talon into the soft flesh of her orbital socket. With a yank, she pulled her eye free as light burst from her socket. She handed it over to Yuki.

"All my knowledge," she explained. "In exchange, someone must care for the forest children. Please…," she begged, blood now leaking from her beak.

Bigfoot put her hands together and placed them on her belly, his massive hand covering both of them.

"I will guide them, sister owl." He stroked the feathers on her head. "I regret that I couldn't know you better. Now sleep and be one with the woods."

Yuki took the bloody orb from the owl. Upon touching her fingers, it solidified into a crystalline sphere, which she tucked into her robes.

The owl gasped for air, then fell silent. Her chest fell one last time, and an ominous wind swept through the clearing. The feathers blew off her body and filled the air, blinding Mike temporarily.

When the wind was gone, so was the owl.

"Shit," he muttered to himself, then looked at Yuki. "She ripped out her own eye and just…handed it over. How does that even work?"

"It's an old-school thing you should be familiar with. Far preferable to having someone else rip it out for you." She stood and looked at everyone else. "Where are the others?"

"Chasing Leeds." Mike looked at Bigfoot. "We're good here if you want to try to track them down."

Bigfoot nodded, then stood.

"I'll try to bring him to you in one piece," he said. "But no promises. You can survive without a limb, right?"

With that, Bigfoot took off, vanishing into the woods. Mike sighed and looked down at the remaining feathers still on the ground. Everything had gone sideways fast, but he felt as though he should be used to it.

"Hey." Yuki put a calming hand on his shoulder. "We can still do this."

He put his hand on hers and sighed. "I sure hope you're right."

THOUGH THE BATTLE FOR THE FATE OF THE WORLD CONTINUED FOR COUNTLESS millennia, Beth experienced it as a matter of hours.

Jenny's turns had become so long that Earth rotated in fast-forward from Beth's perspective. It was little more than a whirling blue-and-green mass, the landscape often changing drastically as a result of whatever hell the doll unleashed.

Pestilence, despite hours of pleading that sounded like a hive of caffeinated wasps, had been forced to continue playing. Every round they had lost always ended up with their body being separated into individual bugs and then spread apart. Beth got the impression that Pestilence, as a hive mind, was forced to endure everything each insect experienced. Between rounds, Pestilence sat on the ground and rocked, hugging their legs close to their chest.

Famine lasted a bit longer, but Jenny's troops had developed a real taste for him. Jenny cackled in glee, forcing Famine to endure being consumed at the end of each of his rounds and then slowly digested for an amount of time Famine was unable to describe to his siblings. Her real masterstroke had begun when she had the mimics become microscopic and eat him from the inside. This method of torment soon evolved into a single mimic eating Famine's brain cells while War and Pestilence were forced to care for him as he wasted away into madness.

War, true to his name, put up a much tougher fight. While Jenny found new and interesting ways to make him spend years with nothing to do, he attempted to fight back by doing the same. As the two of them tried to one-up each other, it was clear that Jenny was completely unfazed.

Eventually, Famine and Pestilence lost the game. They were disheartened between rounds and made terrible decisions. Beth noticed that both of them started going all in, wagering the maximum number of troops regardless of strategy. Once beaten, neither of them spoke or even seemed to be paying attention to the game anymore; rather, they looked absolutely exhausted. Their former bluster was gone, as they seemed to know they had been thoroughly beaten.

Beth thought back to how Murray had made sure to rebuild her mind each time to prevent her from going mad. For the horsemen, the sheer dread of starting each round seemed to have broken them.

As angry and bitter as War had become, it was clear that Jenny refused to give him what he wanted. In rounds she lost, she always showed up wherever he was. In rounds she won, she stole his troops away as silently as possible and then made War come looking for her.

The end came for War when he had the bright idea of encasing Jenny in a giant metal cube and then using a drill to bury her deep beneath the ground in Yellowstone National Park. He seemed extremely proud of the fact that Jenny would have to sit around for hundreds of thousands of years in quiet contemplation until the supervolcano beneath finally erupted.

Beth actually got to watch the blast from her viewing position and had been terrified that something had happened to the game itself. Murray had appeared to reassure everybody that all was well and then reminded them that only a couple of minutes had passed in the real world.

Beth had no idea what War had done while stuck on Earth for so long, and his shit-eating grin of victory turned sour when Jenny appeared in a blaze of golden light.

Boring! Jenny had exclaimed, then mimed a yawn. Beth was a hundred percent convinced Jenny was bouncing her consciousness out of the game but didn't want to risk confirming it. *But since you want to play dirty, let's do it.*

On her next victory, she blinded War at the beginning of the round and then hid deep in the mountains. Next round, she blinded him again, then had him captured and took his legs. She made him squirm, crawl, and roll across entire countries, looking for her while she taunted him with nursery rhymes when he got close. Earth was now spinning so fast during each turn that Murray declared he was having to reset geological events just to prevent game issues due to continental drift.

"How long has it been?" Beth finally asked Murray before the next round could start. He opened his mouth to reply, and she quickly added, "Inside the game, down on the virtual Earth."

"Eons," he replied as War reappeared.

The horseman only lasted a couple more rounds before he finally broke apart. Heavy muscles sagged as he dropped his sword to the ground and wept.

"I can't go on any longer," he cried. "I don't even remember what killing feels like. I'm just so numb, that I...that I..."

Aw, c'mon, mister. Jenny rocked her horse violently, making it scoot closer to War. *This is the most fun I've had in years!*

"Stay away from me!" He backed away from Jenny and hid behind Murray. "She's done things to me! You've seen it, you even told me it was getting hard to rebuild me!"

"Rest assured that each round is only—"

"I don't care!" War yanked on Murray's robes, causing the man's head to snap back and forth. "I quit! I quit! Please, send me back!"

Quitterquitterquitterquitter...

Beth felt light-headed, as if she was falling, and then the world beneath them was flattened like a giant ball of clay, turning into a map. A golden fire rolled across it, destroying all War's remaining troops. The scene dramatically transitioned again, and now she was staring at the game board proper.

"We're back," she whispered.

"Agh!" War looked over at Jenny and fell backward out of his chair.

Screaming, he ran away from them and out into the surrounding mists, leaving his massive sword behind.

"And with this, I conclude our mediation." Murray clapped his hands together. The pieces of the board game floated neatly back into the box, and then the box slid toward Beth.

"Good game," she told Famine and Pestilence.

"Fuck you," Famine replied, then stood and stormed off. Pestilence stayed behind only to slump forward with their face in their hands.

Beth's initial reaction was to feel bad. Despite how they had treated her, she knew well the effect of Jenny's in-game wrath. They had received it on a scale she couldn't possibly fathom.

"Fuck those guys," she muttered. With a deep breath to steady herself, she turned away from the table.

"It was very boring to watch." Death held out Ticktock. "You all just sat around staring at the board and rolling dice. Though you did make my brother cry during one of the last rounds. That was amusing."

"It was far more interesting from our point of view, I assure you. Especially when we were winning." She took Ticktock, then stuffed the Risk game inside. Reggie hopped down from his seat as Beth took Jenny in her arms. The doll's laughter filled her head, and she chuckled.

"You did good," she told Jenny. "We couldn't have won without you."

That's because I'm the house champion, Jenny declared. *They didn't know what hit them.*

"Let's talk about it later," she muttered, then looked up at Murray. The angel was trying to smile in her direction but had opened his mouth into a comically wide grimace.

"So you're taking them back?" she asked. "We're done, everything goes back to the way it was?"

"Almost." Murray stared at Death for a moment. "I will have to dismiss the horsemen first before returning you to your realm. Since they have wandered off, it may take me some time to find them. But I must warn you that there will be consequences to your actions."

Beth narrowed her eyes. "Why the fuck should we have to suffer consequences?"

Murray held up his hands. "Peace, child. These are natural consequences, and this one cannot be avoided. I fear that the horsemen have been permanently damaged by your actions here."

"We're not paying for their therapy," Reggie declared.

"The horsemen of the Apocalypse are physical manifestations of an idea or construct. They aren't people like you or..." Murray looked at Reggie, then

Jenny, then back to Beth. "Or other humans," he finished. "Death is the exception, for he is merely the cessation of life. The others have been intricately woven into your society. Upon our return, the ideas of Pestilence, War, and Famine will have shifted. I cannot promise that it will be for better or for worse."

"Then I demand compensation," Beth declared. "For all mankind."

"Denied." Murray licked his teeth, then his lips. "Though you were the victors of your game, your actions while playing were based solidly on free will. My job here was never to fix your mistakes but to investigate a complaint."

"Who complained? In a court of law, you are entitled to face your accuser."

"The complaint wasn't filed in a court of law. Rather, I chose to indulge you before for the sake of the Father and His divine will."

His divine will can suck a...

Beth covered Jenny's mouth, knowing it would do no good. Luckily, Jenny took the hint.

"Are you going to do that hideous screaming thing again?" she asked.

Murray nodded.

"If you need us, we'll be inside." She turned away from the angel and walked toward the house. The mist swirled around her ankles until she made it onto the steps. Death rushed ahead of her to open the door, and they all walked inside.

Death closed the door behind them and locked it.

"Oh my God, we fucking did it!" Beth let out a whoop of delight, then knelt to high-five Reggie. The rat king did a little dance on the floor, then tossed his crown into the air before catching it.

Tears of joy and relief sprang to her eyes, and she wiped them away before turning around and giving Death a big hug. This, of course, was a huge mistake. It felt like the air had been sucked out of her body upon contact, and he patted her delicately on the back like she might break. Each touch of his hand felt like a jolt to her nervous system.

"We beat them, we won," she muttered into his robes, then shivered. Her teeth were chattering now, and she stepped away from Death. "Shit, I'm freezing."

No sooner had the words left her mouth did she see the cloud of condensation form in front of her and then disperse. Death always left her with a bit of a chill, but this was more than that.

"Um, Lady Beth?" Reggie looked around the living room. "Doesn't it seem far too quiet in here?"

She looked around the front of the house and frowned. Someone should have come to congratulate them already…right?

"Lily? Kisa?" She walked toward the office and frowned at the sight of a rat lying in the boundary of the door. It was on its back and breathing slowly. Farther into the office, there were even more of them. It looked like they had all grouped together in a defensive phalanx, but their weapons lay on the floor as if discarded.

"Are they…" Reggie's question went unasked. He stood away from them, as if afraid to know the truth.

"They're asleep, not dead." Beth looked at the door to the parlor with a frown. It was coated in a light-green substance that she recognized immediately as chunks of Opal. She took a tentative step forward, and something crunched beneath her foot. Startled, she stepped back to reveal the corpse of a scarab beetle, its metallic wings damaged.

"Motherfucker," she muttered, then turned the corner into the lounge.

The room had been destroyed. The statues of Anubis were missing, and most of the artifacts were strewn around the room and broken. Opal's plastic tub was cracked and lying on its side with traces of green, blue, and red slime everywhere. Of Tink, Kisa, and Lily, there was no sign.

Beth's attention was drawn to the middle of the room where the thick marble table was. The top had been moved away from the base, revealing the empty void within. Decorated in glowing hieroglyphics, it held a few loose pieces of rotting fabric that definitely resembled gauze.

The table had been a sarcophagus, and its occupant was on the loose.

WITH DARKNESS COMING, ABELLA HAD TO RELY LARGELY ON HER EARS TO track Velvet. The Arachne was making a horrid sound as she ran, something between a growl and a wheeze. If she didn't know better, she would assume it was a wild animal she tracked and not Velvet.

She could also hear Leeds. The bastard was laughing, but Abella got the impression he was being deliberately loud about it. He wasn't traveling in a straight line either, and the terrain made it impossible for Abella to land. She could try to outpace the Arachne and crash down in front of her, but that would only work if Velvet decided to stop. If she didn't, it would take too long to get back into the sky and she might lose them both.

A band of shadows burst from the canopy below, but Abella had been watching for just such an event. She rolled to the left, which cost her altitude but caused the shadows to miss. Spreading her wings once more, she used the sudden burst in downward speed to power her new ascent into the sky. The dark bands trailed her upward, but eventually could reach no farther. Hands formed on the end reaching for her before the long tendrils retracted into the forest below.

At her new altitude, she could barely hear Velvet over the wind. However, there were a few low-lying clouds she was able to fly through and hide herself from sight. She lost track of Velvet a couple of times but eventually caught her voice on the wind as she shouted at Leeds.

"Give it back!" she cried, her voice distant.

Give what back? Abella tilted her wings and dropped out of the clouds, mist clinging to her wings and tail. Had Leeds taken something from Velvet? When would he have had the chance to do that? Velvet had been nowhere near the barn when...

"No." Abella was hit by the horrifying possibility that one of the eggs had survived. Had Velvet hidden it from her? Or had she missed one when she broke them?

Distracted, she lost track of Leeds and Velvet. Cursing inwardly, she looked around, hoping to figure out where the two of them could have gone. The sun was officially over the horizon, leaving inky pools of blackness beneath her. Some of the stars had already come out, but they were nowhere near bright enough for her to navigate by.

Scowling, she realized the tree line wasn't as far away as she'd thought it was. There was a mountain beneath her, and the topography was immediately familiar. It was the mountain where the Nirumbi lived. Velvet and Leeds hadn't moved out of her range. Rather, they must have gone underground.

She found the clearing from the previous night and landed. There were dead Nirumbi scattered around the entrance. She knelt by one of the corpses and frowned. It had been dead for long enough that it had become cold like the stone beneath.

"*Fils de pute.*" From the entrance, she could hear Leeds's raucous laughter. She hadn't been inside a cave in centuries, the last time being with her clan. It had been after her brother's death, right before her banishment.

"I don't understand why we have to find a new cave." Abella groaned, her hands full of stone. She placed the loose rock into the basket her mother had brought. The opening to this cavern wasn't big enough for some of the elders to pass through, so it had fallen on the smaller members of the clan to widen it.

"Because the old one was discovered by smugglers. You know this," her mother responded. She carved a chunk of granite away with her talons, then crushed it beneath her feet. Abella knelt to pick up the rubble, then handed the basket to another child, who carried it up the tunnel.

"I still think we should have just chased them off." Abella examined one of the stones that had broken off. It was some kind of gemstone, and she imagined it would sparkle if she could carry it back up to the surface. What little light there was down here didn't do it any justice.

"That is not our way." She could hear the smile in her mother's voice but decided to say it anyway.

"Instead of chasing them off, maybe we could make friends with them?" It was an old argument but one she was willing to make every day. She loved watching them, seeing their clothing swish behind them as they walked, hearing their hair rustle in a stiff breeze. What would life be like if she could just befriend one?

"That is also not our way." Her mother put her hand against the stone and frowned. "No more digging on this side. We need to shift."

"Or it will collapse?" Abella asked.

Her mother nodded. "The stone here is strong and stable. We can widen the other side without any issues, but tampering with this would be a gamble."

Abella put her hand against the wall. "How can you tell?"

Her mother smiled. "It's always easiest to hear the Earth Mother's heartbeat through the sturdiest stone. Can you hear it?"

Abella put her ears against the rock and frowned. "I don't hear anything."

"It isn't something you hear with your ears, my gem." Her mother knelt and took the stone from Abella's hands. "It's something you can only hear with your heart."

The cavern walls were narrow, and she crouched to crawl inside. So many centuries ago, she had finally learned to hear the beating heart of the Earth Mother. It wasn't a heart at all but the flow of natural magic through the stone. The magic traveled best through the strongest rock, and she was unnerved by how quiet the tunnel itself was.

Without the open sky above her, she fought off a case of the shivers. Her clan had rarely gone more than a hundred feet into the mountain, and she always preferred to be outside if possible.

Up ahead, she could hear Velvet shouting obscenities, but the echoing of the cave made her words unintelligible. Leeds would laugh on occasion, but there was nothing else to be heard.

This troubled Abella because she knew there should be a whole tribe of Nirumbi beneath the earth. It wasn't long before she crawled over a couple of bodies in the darkness and then moved into a large chamber with a massive column in the middle. The chamber was decorated with glowing stones that had been tossed about the chamber yet still provided enough illumination to see by.

The column resonated heavily in the silent chamber and was likely the primary support. All around, she saw the empty abodes of the Nirumbi, along with their dead scattered. The moisture-laden air was heavy with the smell of blood.

It had been a slaughter. She nudged a Nirumbi with her foot and scowled at the claw marks on its body. How long ago had this been done? There were arrows everywhere but no sign of who or what had killed them.

"Give it back!" Velvet's shrill cry echoed from up above. "Please, I'll do anything!"

Leeds laughed in response.

Abella gritted her teeth. It had to be an egg; nothing else made sense. Instead of scaling the ramp, she started climbing the rock. Her nails sank easily into the stone surface, allowing her to scale it quickly. The whole time, all she could think about was Velvet's deception.

When she had destroyed Velvet's clutch, the Arachne had been an emotional mess. If it had been a charade, it was a good one. But why fake such a thing when she could have just hidden them in the woods?

Maybe it was bad timing, Abella thought. She had arrived at the barn shortly after they had been laid, and Velvet had only been able to hide one. That didn't make much sense either because they weren't very large. Velvet could easily have stuffed a few into her pockets.

Velvet's cries right now were that of a terrified mother, filled with rage and worry. She begged and pleaded between shouts of fury, and Abella winced at the sound of gunfire. Hearing the pain in Velvet's voice, Abella continued onward, swearing to kick the Arachne's ass after she saved it.

Beth moved to the sarcophagus and knelt, her hands on the side. There were chunks of slime smeared all along its edges, which she scooped into her hands. Frowning, she realized she had no idea what to do with it so promptly wiped her hands on the couch.

"I don't understand." Reggie hopped onto the sarcophagus and sniffed the air. "There was someone here all this time?"

"Are we really surprised?" Beth gestured at the room.

"I guess not." Reggie jumped into the sarcophagus, then slipped on a piece of Opal and landed on his face, causing his crown to fall off. Jenny laughed, but the rat king ignored her.

"What are you doing?" Beth leaned in to help him stand.

"I wanted a closer look at the glyphs. They're heavily enchanted."

She would ask how he could tell, but considering that all the symbols were glowing, it would be a dumb thing to ask. With a groan, she stood and turned to face Death. "What do you make of all…"

Her voice trailed off. Death was holding a large chunk of slime in his hands, his jaw hanging down as the fire deep in his sockets swirled like miniature tornados. He lifted his gaze to meet hers, and she felt her soul freeze in place as anger washed over her.

"Whoever did this shall pay." Though he whispered, Death's voice penetrated her entire body like a maelstrom of nails. "THEY! SHALL! PAY!"

His scythe slid from his sleeves and opened by itself before he snatched it out of the air. With agony in his eyes, Death tucked the chunk of slime into his robes and hefted his weapon. With a yell, he swung it into the sarcophagus, spearing one of the larger runes and sending a wave of hot magic through the room. Beth and Reggie fled as Death destroyed the vessel, the room awash in stray magic that made her feel sick to her stomach.

"Death, stop!" Beth tried to get close to him but was scared of getting hit by accident. "This doesn't help!"

"Ah, but it does, General Bethany." With a final slash, he cut the coffin in two. "For I am angry not only for Opal's sake but for my own. You see, these runes were designed to hide the occupant from my sight and forestall their inevitable demise. Whoever was inside has perverted the laws of nature itself. For this, I shall reap them with prejudice."

Beth looked at the rubble. "So a creature that avoided death in a sarcophagus. My assumption is that we're dealing with a mummy of some sort."

"I don't think so, Lady Beth." Reggie picked up one of the chunks of stone and contemplated it. "From what I know of mummies, their intent was never to return to life but to honor their place in the afterlife."

"Where did you learn that?" she asked.

Reggie gestured at the room they stood in. "There were plenty of books here. Jenny read many of them to me. She found them fascinating, and I found it preferable to playing Sorry!. And even if our perpetrator was a mummy, this knowledge doesn't help us."

"Damn." Beth turned to face Death. "I guess we search the house?"

Death nodded. "And I know where we should search first." He scooped up another piece of Opal and stuck it in his pocket. "The room in the basement, across from the Vault. The perpetrator used our absence during the game to secure their freedom, and that room is our only lead."

"That's very astute, Death."

"Thank you." He turned away from her. "I've been enjoying Encyclopedia Brown lately. I like how you can turn to the back of the books to see if you have solved the mystery."

Stunned, she followed the grim reaper as he led them all to the basement. Nobody was surprised to see the door to the basement open, and Beth waited at the top for Death to declare the area as safe. Reggie and Jenny hid inside Ticktock as Beth descended the steps. Whatever enchantment had been there before hadn't been reset, and she stepped onto the cold concrete of the basement and clicked on the flashlight she had grabbed from the kitchen.

She swept the beam over the entrance to the Vault and was happy to see it was still sealed. Despite this, Beth could hear the troublesome whispers from the other side, so she tuned them out and turned toward Death.

"I sense something in there." He pointed at the room opposite. Beth directed her light and saw that Tink and Kisa had been placed on the table inside. Cecilia hovered in the background, but there was no sign of Lily or Opal.

"Should we take them upstairs?" Beth asked.

"Not yet." Death walked into the room and looked around. "I fear a tra—"

A dark figure stepped between her and Death. It was one of the Anubis statues, and it pushed Death farther into the room. The wall slammed shut, trapping them inside. Beth ran to the wall and pounded on the concrete with the palms of her hands.

"Death! Hey, Death!" Inside the wall, she could hear Death howling in anger, followed by the sound of metal on concrete. Realizing he was trying to battle the statue and free himself, she stepped away from the wall.

Behind her, something clicked. Turning around, she saw that a few scarabs watched her from the floor, their mandibles moving excitedly. The stairs creaked as someone walked down them, and Beth raised her light to reveal a figure in an advanced state of decay and wrapped in bandages being helped down the stairs by another statue.

"I told you it was a mummy," she muttered. The scarabs took off and flew around the room but not before their eyes glowed an ominous green color matched by the mummy itself.

You will make a perfect vessel. A voice filled her head as a wave of drowsiness struck.

"Who are you?" Beth asked, her voice slurring. Her eyelids fluttered as she felt the presence invade her mind.

I am the one who takes, the voice replied, stronger this time. It was a woman's voice, and Beth now stood in a palace. Her bare feet were on a stone floor that had been polished and inlaid with beautiful gems. She was in a white gown with a blue belt that hung to her ankles.

You are a strong one. The pressure increased, but Beth pushed back. Her mind had been invaded too many times to topple so easily, and she felt the presence ease off a bit.

"I've had a shit day," Beth replied. "I'm not about to let you be the cherry on top of it."

Oh, I differ. The air shimmered in front of her, and a woman stepped out. She had golden skin with dark ringlets of hair that draped over her naked shoulders. Linen fabric hung from her body, just barely covering her breasts. Armlets depicting a monstrous serpent decorated both her biceps. "Tell me, child. What is your name?"

"My name is Fuck Off." Beth raised her fists and sneered. "I'm known for punching bitches who come in my head."

The woman scowled, then toyed with a leather bag she wore around her neck. The instant she touched the bag, Beth felt a wave of energy pass through her, and her hands went numb and fell by her side.

"Your name is Beth." The figure sat down, a golden chair appearing underneath her. "Well, Beth. My name is Neferisfet, and I am the last priestess of Apophis, the Great Serpent."

"Never heard of him."

Neferisfet nodded. "I don't expect you would. As his last follower, I have spent thousands of years entombed, waiting to be discovered and resurrected so I may return him to glory. My spirit has hovered between life and death, sanity and madness, just to bring me to this moment."

Beth bit her lip and grunted, then managed to take a step toward Neferisfet.

"Your spirit impresses me." Neferisfet steepled her fingers together. "Tell me more about yourself, Beth."

Beth took another step forward but fell to her knees when Neferisfet touched the bag around her neck once more. This time, warmth flooded her chest, and it was suddenly hard to breathe.

"Hmm. You have an aura of magic. This will make things easier." Neferisfet stood from her throne and walked around Beth, inspecting her. "I was once a powerful sorceress, dedicated to assisting my master in his fight against the sun god. Together we sought eternal darkness, to return the universe to its original state."

"You must be great at parties." Beth's limbs surged with power, and she swung her fist at Neferisfet. The woman vanished and reappeared next to her.

"Oh, we had quite the parties. Feasts that would last for days." Neferisfet licked her lips. "If not for that wretched Caretaker, I would be well on my way to restoring the glory of Apophis. Alas, she not only turned me down but trapped me in that room."

"Do you mean Emily?"

Neferisfet nodded. "That woman double-crossed me before I could double-cross her. Milked me for magical knowledge and then sealed me away before I could make my move. But her loss is your gain. Observe."

She raised her hands in the air and clapped. Tables covered in luxurious meats and cheeses appeared, and the air filled with the sounds of music and people chatting.

"Oh, so I give you my body and you get to live it up. No thanks, hard pass."

"It's more than that." Neferisfet circled Beth now. "I don't take over your body. Rather, we merge and become one entity. Since I cannot dominate you, I must take a different approach. You will require finesse, some kind of bargain."

"I'm not in the mood for bargains. I've had a shit week."

"If you had just given up the reaper, it wouldn't have been a problem." Neferisfet frowned. "Why didn't you give him up when the others came?"

"You seem to know an awful lot about the situation, considering you've been living in a box…" Realization dawned on her. "It was you, wasn't it? That reported Death to the angel?"

Neferisfet nodded. "I fear very few things in this world. The personification of death could easily undo me. I am in no state to fight."

Beth fought the paralysis and managed to take another step. "This whole time, that was you? Do you have any idea what I've been through?" Her voice was loud enough that the invisible party went silent.

"Please. I have spent centuries hovering on the edge of life and death. Each breath was like drowning. I care very little for the discomfort of but a few days." Neferisfet sneered. "Why bother hanging on to the reaper in the first place?"

"Because he's family. It's something you wouldn't understand."

Neferisfet bit back a retort, then tilted her head. Her bright-green eyes were flecked with gold, and her face softened.

"This is true," she muttered. "Yet another reason a merger makes more sense. We need each other. I have lost touch with life itself, and you could be my guide."

"Again, hard pass."

The sorceress sighed and turned away. "I have so much to offer you. How can I make you see this?" She waved her hand and summoned a staff with a serpent's head. "I could instruct you in magic, teach you to become a power unto yourself. You could protect this house for eternity if you wished, for that is in my power."

"After what you did to my friends, I don't think they would just let you hang around."

Neferisfet groaned. "That was...regrettable. The beetles were supposed to find me a human host. How was I to know that so many humanoids live in this home and none of them are true humans? The bugs can't tell the difference." She spat the words with much venom. "I spent hours inside that goblin's head, feeling like my world would cave in on me. I can free them from their dreams. It is an easy task if you know how to do it."

"If you couldn't find a host, then how did you get out?"

"Desperation. I knew I wouldn't be able to get you alone. You are always with someone. So I spent the last couple of days absorbing energy from the house that I could open the sarcophagus myself and activate my guardians. The cat would have made a wonderful host, but she is someone's familiar. Her bond with her master was far too great. So I had the scarabs put her down, as well as anyone else who might stand in my way."

Beth took a deep breath. Out in the real world, Death would eventually fight his way free. She needed to stall in the hopes that he would end the sorceress, so she decided to use the oldest trick in the book: keep them talking about their evil plan. "And what about Opal?"

"The slime girl? When I tried to press myself into her, she exploded. I thought maybe she was made of sterner stuff, but alas..." Neferisfet waved dismissively. "I didn't see where the succubus went, but she is no threat to me. The cat and the reaper were all I feared, but I have plenty of time in here with you now."

"It won't work."

Neferisfet grinned and touched the pouch at her neck. "Please. I know your weakness." She stepped behind a pillar and disappeared in a flowing of robes. Asterion and Suly stepped out in her place, both of them grinning maniacally.

"They aren't real," Beth said. "Not even here."

"Of course they aren't real." Neferisfet's voice came from the ceiling. "This is just a taste of the greatness you could achieve with me at your side." The music started back up, but this time, it was a heavy, pulsing beat. Beth shivered as the two of them came close. She knew they were just images, but the sight of the two of them only brought her happiness.

"It's been a long stretch, lass." Suly stepped behind her and started rubbing her shoulders. "Why not let us work some kinks out for ye?"

Asterion crouched and picked up one of her feet, then placed it on his knee. He rubbed her ankle with strong hands that caused her belly to fill with fire.

"You're not going to fool me so easily," she muttered, yet allowed the illusions to pamper her.

"Come now, surely there's something I could offer you?" Neferisfet's hands appeared around Beth's stomach. Somehow, the sorceress was standing where Suly was. "I can feel the want inside your aching body. After a hard day at the office, there's nothing better than coming home and opening up that briefcase of yours, is there?"

"Ha! That thing has been gathering dust ever since...since..." Her thoughts trailed off as Neferisfet tugged upward on the fabric of Beth's gown. The air was cold against her revealed thighs, and Asterion took this as an invitation to run his hands up them.

"They're so smooth," the Minotaur noted, then leaned in to lick her skin. His rough tongue sent shivers up her spine.

"You realize I could have this without you?" Beth swatted away Neferisfet's hands when they tried to dip beneath the band of her panties. "Once the horsemen leave, I could invite my boys out for a walk, let them take turns leaving me a dripping mess. I could probably convince Suly to eat Asterion's cream pies. They're very salty and—"

"Shh." The masculine hand around her waist belonged to neither Neferisfet nor Suly. Suly's hands slid up her gown and caressed her breast from beneath as the figure moved into view.

"Oh. Hey, Mike." Her confidence fled as she faced him. He was radiating an energy that made her light-headed as he stroked her jaw. His fingers were gentle yet strong, and tiny sparks danced along her skin.

"You could have me," he told her. "The dance would finally end, and you could find out whether you truly desire the man or the magic."

"Not real, not real, not real." She whispered the words like a mantra, trying her best to concentrate. With all these hands on her body, it was getting harder to do so, and she was becoming wet.

"It's real enough." Mike put his hands around her waist, turning sideways so that Asterion could continue touching her thighs. Suly pushed Beth's bra aside and was playing with her nipples as Asterion's hand found its way up to her crotch and was teasing her through the fabric of her panties.

"Not fair, not fair." The mantra had changed, and Beth tried to distance herself. Death wasn't the only one outside her head right now, and maybe one of the others would bail her out.

"You just need to let me in," Mike told her. "You can have it all."

Suly pinched one of her nipples just as Asterion moved her panties to the side and pressed a thick finger against her wet labia. It slid in with little resistance, and she moaned.

"I don't know," she told Mike with a gasp. "Looks like I'm going to be rather full in a minute, might not have any room for you."

Suly was kissing her neck now, occasionally nibbling the sensitive spot beneath her ear while he squeezed her breasts. Asterion had shifted to her side and was fingering her with one hand while squeezing her butt with the other. Mike moved forward, effectively pinning her between everyone, and her resolve melted.

"Every day could be like this." Mike took her hand and moved it down to the bulge in his pants. It was warm, even through the fabric, and his magic sparks spiraled up her arm and settled into her chest. "Living out every fantasy inside your brilliant mind."

She tried to respond, but a moan broke free of her lips. Leaning backward into Suly, she raised her leg even higher to give Asterion better access, which allowed her to place her foot on the minotaur's shoulder. When she looked down, she could see Asterion's cock hanging out of his loincloth. It looked even bigger than usual, and she closed her eyes and tried to block the scene out.

Mike ran his hands over her hips while the others continued to tease her. She tried to shut them out, but the temptation kept drawing her in. Mike kept asking to be let in, and she made sure to stay quiet.

Suly's cock was pressing into her ass now, and she couldn't help but grind against it. Neferisfet had been right about her preferred method of stress release, and she was desperately in need of it.

Asterion used his horn to hold Beth's leg up so he could start licking around her labia, his rough tongue teasing her clitoris. The sensation made her whole body buzz, and it was now just as hard to breathe as it was to think. Suly was getting rough with her, and when she opened her eyes, she saw Mike reach past her to undo the buckles on Suly's pants.

"Feel their desire for you," Mike told her as Suly slid his cock between her butt cheeks, his glans touching the small of her back.

"Still not real," she whispered, holding in a gasp when Asterion's finger teased her G-spot.

"These feelings you have are very real." Mike leaned forward, his breath hot against her lips. "And why fight them?"

He kissed her, and she felt a surge of magic flow through her body. It traveled down her throat and radiated outward from her heart, warming her limbs. At that moment, she could tell it was Neferisfet's best estimate of what Mike's magic actually did. Though she had never experienced it firsthand, she had both seen it in action and heard talk of it later.

This wasn't magic that connected her to him. Rather, it was heightening her senses and filling her to the brim with sexual energy and a strong desire for release. It was nothing like Mike's magic, a mere imitation created as a best-guess effort. In pushing the issue, Neferisfet had overplayed her hand.

Beth felt the magic spin through her body as her belly muscles fluttered. Asterion lifted Beth off the ground to help Suly penetrate her from behind, the cold radiating from his body mixing with the heat of her own. She expected the dullahan to fuck her mercilessly, but all he did was get his cock nice and wet before pulling it back out and pressing it against her ass.

Oh, fuck yeah, she thought as Suly pressed himself into her. There was no pain, only pleasure and pressure as he slowly moved into her. Was this how her body would feel if she tried it in the real world?

Black straps of leather wrapped around her wrists as Suly used his buckles to bind her arms behind her. Asterion lay down and pushed his loincloth aside, revealing his massive member. She licked her lips in anticipation as Mike assisted Suly in lowering her onto it.

Her labia spread wide as a tingling sensation flooded through her loins. She stretched to accommodate him, letting out a strangled cry at being penetrated so completely. The bony ridges of Suly's cock pressed through the thin membrane that separated her ass from her vagina, making her dizzy.

"Every possible combination you could ever imagine," Mike told her as he stood over Asterion and unbuckled his pants. His cock was now level with her face, shining magnificently in the torchlight of the palace. She had accidentally seen it so many times but never this close. "With me at your side, you could have your fill every day, just like the nymph. And the power, Beth, so glorious! I have centuries of spellcraft to share with you."

He grabbed her jaw and pinched, causing her mouth to open. When he slid himself into her mouth, her eyes rolled up into her head as an orgasm exploded through her body, turning her brain to mush. She couldn't even focus on any one sensation, it was simply too much to comprehend, so she rode it like the waves in the ocean.

A ripple of energy formed inside her chest, but the others took no notice. She was pounded violently from all three sides, but her mind hung onto that stray sensation as she felt something inside her body expand.

There was very little she understood about her own magic, but she recognized it immediately. Able to separate her mind from her body, she pulled deep within herself and pictured her magic as a glowing pool of water. She only had a single finger inside it, sending out ripples into the darkness of her mind.

Laughing, she realized that if there was one thing that would empower magic given to you by a nymph, it would definitely be sex.

Mike was now practically shouting, telling her all the things he was going to do with her body, but she ignored him. The three of them were having their way with her as she charged herself up, building her own power until it was no longer a pond beneath her but a full-blown lake.

"Just let her in, lass," Suly whispered in her ear. "I bet she'll feel good inside ye much as I do."

"Mmph," Asterion grunted as his balls smacked into her. "Let her in, friend."

"Just let me in," Mike whispered. "It can all be yours."

Beth filled herself with power, then wrapped it around her like a cocoon. She tilted her head back, allowing Mike's cock to pop free of her mouth. This wasn't the real world, there was no need for breathing here, but she still took in a huge breath before speaking.

"I…," she began, feeling the men stop as they waited for her to speak. The tension was suddenly high, and with two cocks twitching inside her, she held on to that beautiful moment for as long as possible.

"Yes?" Mike finally asked in a whisper.

The magical pressure inside her had built to critical mass, and she giggled.

"I want you out of my head, you undying bitch." She released it all at once and watched as a wave of light tore through the palace and turned it all to dust. Mike screamed and took a step back as the magic blew him away and revealed the decaying body of Neferisfet, holding up her arms as if to ward away a blow.

Her Anubis guardian moved toward Beth, but Ticktock rustled on her back, and both Jenny and Reggie leaped from their hiding place and held on to the statue's face. The guardian stumbled around, trying frantically to rip them both off, but they were tiny and motivated.

Neferisfet hissed and moved toward Beth, but several bladed arms popped out of Ticktock, making Beth look like a cybernetic spider. The mummy clutched the bag hanging around her neck and made a run for the stairs while casting dark-green fire behind her.

"That's right, get the fuck out of my basement!" Beth yelled, then turned her attention to the guardian. It had grabbed Reggie by the scruff of his neck and tried to throw him, but its arm seemed to be caught on something.

Jenny's laughter filled the room as the arm trembled, then cracked. Beth unfolded the fingers as Ticktock slashed away at the statue, pushing it back until she could free the rat king.

"We have to free Death," she yelled, then moved toward the wall. "Jenny, try to get this thing over here. Maybe we can trick it into breaking down this section of the wall."

Jenny cackled, and the temperature of the room dropped so hard that it took Beth's breath away. An eerie glow surrounded the guardian moments before it rocketed across the room, just missing Beth, to crash into the wall. The concrete cracked—but held.

Beth ran up behind the statue and tackled it into the wall. One of its ears snapped off, and it spun around and cocked its fist. She felt a chill in her belly and ducked in time to avoid the blow. It came for her again, but that eerie glow surrounded it once more and spun it around. The statue's fist connected solidly with the wall. Small cracks formed along its knuckles, but the cracks in the wall widened.

Ticktock yanked himself free of Beth's shoulders and leaped over her head. Sharp talons embedded themselves in the wall and ceiling as the mimic wedged itself in place. With a pair of bladed arms, it smashed the statue into the wall over and over until Anubis cracked and fell apart.

A hole formed in the wall, and a skeletal finger poked through it.

"Death!" Beth knelt and looked inside, but she could only see darkness.

"I have been bamboozled," the reaper responded. "It will take me some time to get out of here. There are runes in here meant to trap me."

"Don't worry. He isn't alone." The voice was Lily's. A glowing red eye appeared in the hole and winked.

"How? I didn't see you in there!"

"You did, actually. When that cunt blew out of her sarcophagus, I could tell things were going sideways, so I took Kisa's place. Bitch had no clue, but she did knock me out for a bit."

Beth frowned. She wasn't aware Lily could even sleep.

"Where's Kisa?" she asked.

"No idea. I told her to hide, and she took Opal with her. What was left of her, anyway. But listen, that's not what's important. That bag around her neck is what is keeping her alive. You get that away from her and she's toast."

"What is it?"

"It's a divine object, but that's all I know. But there's something else. Romeo is stuck in Oregon. He's trying to come back, but we're probably on our own on this."

"How do you—"

"Fucking hell, would you go snatch that mummy's magic coin purse already? Shit!" Lily moved away from the wall and mumbled something to Death. Death's fiery orb appeared in the hole.

"You must make haste, Director Bethany. That woman is more powerful than we realized."

"Why? She needs a human body to inhabit, and the only one within a million miles just booted her out."

"Wrong." Death's flames intensified. "There is one other human nearby."

Beth frowned. "You mean Murray? He's that angel's bitch already."

Death was shoved aside, and Lily was back. "All she has to do is hide from you until we're back on Earth. Then it's open season on the first person she sees. You cannot let her get away."

"Got it. You can count on us." Beth looked over at Jenny. "You up for one more round of hide-and-seek?"

The doll clapped her hands in glee.

"Good luck," Lily yelled through the wall as they all ran up the stairs.

VELVET'S HEARTS WERE POUNDING AS SHE SCRAMBLED ACROSS THE CEILING OF the cave. Leeds had led her through the woods, his magic flooding her mind with images of shattering her egg, consuming it, or even letting it hatch and tormenting her child.

He had brought her to the goblin caves. Down below, in the darkness, she could hear him scrambling among the bones. The bastard was up to something; she just couldn't tell what.

"Please," she begged. "Just give it—"

A shadow tried to grab her leg, but she released her hold on the ceiling and fell about fifteen feet before grabbing the edge of a stalactite and swinging over to stick to the wall.

What could I do with the child of a cursed union? he wondered in her head. *Perhaps it would be best to turn her loose in the city, where there is plenty of prey.*

"Not going to happen!" She aimed her pistol at a moving shadow and fired. The brief muzzle flash illuminated the cave and revealed he was actually hiding far to her left, just beneath a ridge of stone. With a powerful leap, she crossed the space in a moment, her fingers briefly closing on his cloak.

I will be such a good father to her, Leeds told her.

"She already has a father!" She scanned the darkness, the sensitive hairs on her body allowing her to sense his movements. When she felt him, she jumped again and crashed face-first into another stalactite. With a grunt, she fell and landed clumsily on the ground.

I can teach her to be a monster like her grandparents.

"Fuck you!" She fired the gun again—but didn't see him in the flash this time. By a quick mental count, she was nearly out of bullets.

This place is a shrine to their transgressions, little spider. There is no hiding where you came from.

"What matters more is where you're going, you sick fuck!"

How old will she need to be before she can mate? Leeds actually laughed out loud, his voice echoing from every direction. *I would be such a good grandpa to—*

Leeds made a choking sound, which was followed by the impact of flesh on stone. For several moments, all Velvet heard was dripping water from somewhere in the darkness.

The silence was broken by the sound of rustling fabric.

"If he took something from you, it isn't here." It was Abella's voice, and she didn't sound very happy.

"It's not what you think," Velvet whispered.

"Enlighten me." There was another meaty thunk, followed by a groan from Leeds.

"Do you have him?" Velvet asked.

"For now. Have to be careful not to kill him is all."

There was a small rush of movement, and Velvet could almost picture Abella smashing Leeds's face into a nearby wall. The devil was being repeatedly stunned.

"Abella, I—"

"Had you smash my eggs but hid one from you?"

In the silence that followed, Leeds groaned.

Velvet wasn't sure how to respond. She moved toward Abella's voice and got her hands on Leeds. He tried to fight her off as she searched him again, then grabbed his throat.

"Where is it?" she asked. A shadow grabbed her by the leg but vanished when she squeezed his throat hard enough that something popped.

"So I was right." Anger and disappointment laced Abella's words.

"Listen. There's a lot I need to say about—"

She's going to attack you, Leeds whispered in her mind. *Your betrayal has enraged her!*

Velvet stepped back and put up her hands. "Please, just hear me out before you do something you regret."

"Huh?" There was genuine confusion now. "I'm not going to risk letting this piece of shit go, even if I'm pissed at you."

She lies. There was just a hint of desperation in Leeds's tone.

"Leeds says you want to hurt me," Velvet admitted. "I can hear him in my head. He keeps taunting me."

There was a loud snap, followed by a scream from Leeds. She felt him withdraw his presence and let out a sigh of relief.

"You only have one wrist left," Abella growled once he quieted down. "You go in her head again, I'll break the other one. Or the first one again, whichever hurts worse."

Velvet let out a sigh. "It's true, I did hide one of my eggs from you. But it wasn't like the others, I promise. When Mike and I…when I held those eggs, they really were bad. Each one of them was a killing spree waiting to happen, but the one I hid was different." The other eggs in the clutch had all been a mottled gray, but the one she had kept had been the most beautiful blue she had ever seen in her life. Upon touching it, she had received a static shock that had set her hair on end. Whereas the other eggs had radiated hunger and intensity, this one had an aura of curiosity to it.

She didn't know how to convey all these things to Abella, not in the dark where they couldn't even see each other. She needed the gargoyle to see how genuine she was, to know these weren't just lies spoken in the dark.

"Look," she began, her hearts pounding loudly in her throat. "You know it exists now. This bastard said he had it, and since he was on the roof of the barn, I figured he stole it out of the jeep. It was in the glove compartment. After we take care of this, you and I and Mike can sit down and discuss what happens next. I need you to trust me, to trust that my kind can be different. Despite our differences, you should know I trust you. Maybe it's just because Mike does, and I'm in love with him, or maybe it's something more. I just…I need you to give me some time. "

There was a long moment of silence, broken only by a groan of agony from Leeds.

"Velvet." Abella's tone had shifted drastically. "The jeep was the first thing to burn. If he didn't take it, then…"

The beating of her hearts was like a pair of hammers now, and Velvet's limited vision blurred in anger. She lunged toward Leeds and grabbed him by the shoulders.

"Did you take it? DID. YOU. TAKE. IT?" She was shouting now, her veins filled with ice water as her human heart dropped through the floor and spiraled toward Hell itself. She was hyperventilating, waiting desperately for his response. When he said nothing, she shook him violently, his head flopping back and forth.

Leeds let out a cough-filled chuckle.

"Never even went inside," he declared. "I was too busy here, slaughtering the Nirumbi with the help of their own. You see, we're all monsters here, inside and out. And to be honest, even if I had stolen your egg, I would have smashed it on my own because we all know your kind are little more than—"

Velvet let out a roar and ripped Leeds free from Abella's grip. She smashed the demon into the stone walls of the cave, her fingers digging into the horse-flesh of his head. Leeds let out a strangled cry, and the air grew thick around them.

The hairs on Velvet's body stood on end as a wave of darkness picked her up and smashed her into a nearby wall. Abella was shouting something, but Velvet couldn't make out a single word of it. She fought to stand, her legs weak beneath her as Leeds ran back out into the main cavern, his cape flapping noisily behind him.

"Grab him!" Abella cried as she moved toward the exit. The ceiling was too low for the gargoyle to fly, and her running speed was very slow. Velvet could feel the impact of her massive steps as tremors that reverberated throughout her body.

Cursing, Velvet bolted past Abella in time to see Leeds gliding down to the bottom of the Nirumbi's main chamber. He cackled maniacally as the shadows thickened and broke free from the ceiling, each one a massive tentacle that reached for her. She dodged a few and took aim with her pistol, but Leeds had moved around the massive pillar in the middle of the cave.

"Shit!" She sprinted along the nearest wall, her feet slipping on the wet surface of the cave. When she fell, she scraped up her arms as she tumbled to a stop near the bottom of the cavern. Her head was spinning now, and she stumbled sideways and tripped over a pile of bodies.

Up above, the shadows were no longer reaching for her. Instead, they were wrapping around the main pillar of the cavern like a nest of anacondas. Each coiled shadow squeezed, making the rock beneath them groan.

"Velvet!" Abella shrieked in panic from up above. "Run!"

"Abella, I…" She was simply too dizzy. The dim light of the cave plus the odd echoes of laughter and breaking rock had thoroughly disoriented her. Stumbling forward, she heard a loud groan from the stone above, followed by a sharp crack.

Up above, the ceiling broke apart. The shadows continued to squeeze as large fragments rained down. Stunned, Velvet looked up in time to see Abella swoop down through the chaos and grab her by the shoulders with her talons. Pain bloomed through her upper arms as the talons dug in so deep that she bled through her shirt, and the world fell apart as the main pillar shattered.

The opening to the chamber was close, but Abella had to tuck in her wings for them both to fit. Unable to fly, the two of them crashed into the tunnel and then slid to a stop. It was becoming impossible to breathe. Up ahead, Abella let out a cry of agony, which helped Velvet find her.

"Come on," she whispered as her fingers settled on stony flesh. She hooked her hands around Abella's waist and pulled. It was hard to maneuver in the narrow passageway, and the gargoyle had gone completely limp. Stumbling forward, she realized her gait was off. She had lost one of her legs in the crash.

The ground rumbled again, and something else collapsed behind them. The passageway was so choked with dust she could hardly breathe.

Leeds had planned this all along, she realized. To lure her away from the others. Had he known Abella would follow? Or maybe he'd thought it would be someone else.

She was disoriented, and it occurred to her that she might be moving deeper into the tunnels. The air was so clogged she couldn't sense where it was flowing to or from.

The ground shook, and a chunk of rock fell in their path. Velvet let go of Abella and tried to push it out of the way.

"Leave…me…" Abella's voice was muffled.

"No man left behind," Velvet rasped. "Family motto."

"Not a man," Abella replied. "Just a rock with…wings."

Velvet shoved the rock around a corner and grabbed Abella by the wrist. "You're family as far as I'm concerned, damn it!"

She pulled, tears flowing down her cheeks. The world was closing in, and she couldn't see. Her hands had gotten wet somehow, and Abella kept slipping free, so she wedged herself beneath the gargoyle's body and crawled forward on her belly, hoping they were headed toward freedom.

"This is my fault." Velvet was on her abdomen now, using her legs like poles to push them both forward. "I shouldn't have let him trick me."

"Not your fault," Abella replied. "Leeds. Huge…bastard."

Velvet wanted to laugh but couldn't. It was too painful. She moved down the tunnel, her fingers searching for purchase. A rock fell from the ceiling and clipped her in the head, and it felt like the world was sideways.

"Must get out," she mumbled to herself.

The tunnel widened, and she lost her way. Sliding free of Abella, she moved around in an attempt to explore her options. There were three directions she could go, but which one was right? Crawling deeper into the earth would do them no good.

Sobbing, she wrapped her hands around her father's dog tags. What would he do if he were here?

Velvet. Her father's voice startled her, and she turned her head to hear it better. It had come from the tunnel to her left.

"Daddy?" She waited, not sure what she would do if she heard him again. There was only silence now, and she pondered waiting longer, but the ground rumbled beneath her again. The main cavern's collapse was triggering more activity in the tunnel, and she didn't have time to indulge her hallucinations.

Picking up Abella, she moved toward a bigger opening to her right.

Velvet. This time, his voice was stronger and from the same place.

Gasping for air, she crawled toward his voice. She had been in the dark for so long that she was seeing lights where there weren't any. Abella had gone silent, which concerned her even more. Was she just unconscious? Had the gargoyle died? Abella definitely wasn't breathing, but did she even need to?

"No man left behind," Velvet growled, crawling forward a few more feet. She could feel him now, always just around the corner. If she could just make it a little bit farther, she would get to see him again. The minutes stretched into hours, and the flashes of light were becoming images. She saw her daughter first, a young woman with intense eyes that sparkled with magic. Mike came next, his smile warm as he laughed. They were connected in a way she couldn't explain, and a strange sense of peace overcame her.

She saw her sister, then Uncle Foot, then Mike again. The images flickered rapidly now, and she realized she had fallen asleep. Groaning, she grabbed onto some rocks and pulled herself forward. The tunnel behind her collapsed, jettisoning another blast of dirt and gravel.

If she put Abella down, maybe she would make it. In a moment of weakness, she tried to shrug herself free of the burden. Maybe the gargoyle would be fine and the others would come rescue her later.

Velvet. His voice was disapproving, and she felt a chill on the back of her neck.

"I'm sorry, I…Abella, I'm sorry." She grabbed onto the gargoyle's wrist and pulled but was too tired. "I want to, I really do, but I can't. I can't!"

We can. She felt him now, standing right behind her. The sound of boots on stone filled the narrow passageway, and she felt their hands on her body. She couldn't tell how many of them, numbers had become a foreign concept, but they pulled on her, helping her drag Abella farther into the tunnel.

"No man left…behind. No man…left…" She was light-headed, the air insufficient for breathing. Her thoughts were like balloons, each one floating away until she only had one thought left.

No man left behind. It had been her father's mantra, one he'd even said in his sleep. The words repeated in her head as the others helped pull Abella to safety.

The cavern widened, and she felt a cool breeze over her shoulder. She thought she could make out the twinkle of a star or two over the distant pines, but her vision was too blurry to see much.

She needed to rest. There was a good spot not far from the entrance, a smooth one that looked borderline comfortable. The others guided her as she slumped over, her eyes on Abella. The gargoyle wasn't moving, but the two of them had made it.

The earth rumbled once more, and the cavern belched out stone and dirt from where they had come. Gasping, Velvet turned her attention to the shades who had guided her.

"Daddy?" She let out a chuckle. "There are two of you."

My Velvet. Her father put his hand against her cheek. She was surprised at how warm it felt. *I'm so proud of you.*

"I'm tired," she mumbled, her eyes closing.

I know, he replied. *Rest now. You're in good hands.*

With a sigh, she let the strength leave her body as the darkness swooped in to claim her. Her father took her by the hand and gave it a squeeze.

"I missed you," she whispered to the darkness.

Nobody is ever truly gone, fluffy girl.

She wanted to say more but couldn't. Somewhere in the darkness, she heard singing and knew it was just for her.

LOVE AND LOSS

Reggie took the lead at the top of the steps, ducking low just in case Neferisfet was waiting to strike at the top. Beth held her breath, half convinced the rat king would get punted back down the stairs. The mummy had seemed to be in rough shape, but the fact that she had sprinted up the stairs meant appearances were deceiving.

"Clear!" Reggie reappeared in the doorway. "The kitchen is empty, but I think she is armed."

"What makes you think...oh." Beth stepped into the kitchen and saw that several drawers had been opened, their contents on the floor. The knife block next to the sink had been tipped over, and several blades were missing from it.

Stabby stabby, Jenny commented.

Hide-and-go-seek was far more appealing without the possibility of being stabbed. Nervous, Beth looked around the kitchen for something to protect herself with and settled on a cast-iron skillet.

"You could use the book," Reggie offered. "Both to find her and to defend yourself."

Smacking herself on the forehead, she pulled the grimoire out of Ticktock, then set the mimic on the counter.

"If you see that bitch, feel free to eat her." She set the book on the counter and took a deep breath. "I need a spell to track someone," she stated clearly. "One that doesn't alert them that I'm watching."

She opened the book and watched the page fill with information. As she read it, she frowned.

"Okay, same spell but one that doesn't require a piece of their hair," she repeated, then turned to the next page. "Or body heat. I suspect she's room temperature."

It took a few tries, but she narrowed down her options to a spoken spell. Picturing the priestess in her mind, she carefully recited the words while summoning her magic.

Glowing footprints appeared on the floor.

"That's step one," she declared, then paused. Was there a spell in the book she could cast to just kill the priestess? Maybe something that would force her to cross over, or...

Jenny kicked the book shut, then put her hands on her hips.

"Yeah, yeah, I get it." She picked up the book and held it tight against her chest. If Jenny of all people thought she was about to cross a line, then she knew to listen. Still, the book itself was practically indestructible and far easier to wield than a skillet.

They followed the footprints through the house. Unfortunately, the prints only manifested a few steps out, meaning Beth followed them into the office, the lounge, then back out to the living room. The prints took her up the stairs, and she slowed down as she neared the top.

The attic was open, the steps pulled down. Footprints glowed on each of the rungs.

Reggie and Jenny led the way, the rat king stopping on the last step to toss Jenny into the darkness above before following her. Beth was two rungs up when she heard the door to Mike's bedroom open.

Whirling around, she was surprised when Neferisfet came at her, not with a knife, but with a floor lamp. The priestess whipped it around like a staff, catching Beth in the shoulder and knocking her free of the ladder. With a wave of her hand, the priestess sent a ball of blue energy at the ladder, causing it to retract and close.

Bladed hands popped free of Ticktock, but Neferisfet used the lamp to swat them away. Beth struggled to get to her feet, but Ticktock's shifting weight kept throwing off her balance. Through the ceiling, Beth heard Reggie shouting.

Neferisfet whispered something under her breath as she attacked, coating her hands in an eerie green glow. She dropped the lamp and put her back against the wall.

Beth stood just as the glow coalesced around Neferisfet's palms and flared outward.

"Shit!" She raised the grimoire in time to block the magical bolt, but the force of it knocked her backward and through the railing. Screaming, she fell a couple of feet before Ticktock's blades slammed into the wooden floor, halting her descent. The magical tome tumbled to the floor below.

Up above, Neferisfet was summoning green light into her hands again. Her decaying face twisted into a grin as she pointed her fingers at Beth.

Kisa appeared in the corner of the hall and leaped onto Neferisfet, causing the spell to fire into the wall and send green flames along the wallpaper. Neferisfet cried out in alarm as Kisa scratched her face, causing the flesh to hiss as if being burned.

The priestess pulled a knife out of her belt and tried to stab the cat girl, but Kisa dropped to the floor, scrambled forward, and picked up the lamp. Beth grunted as she and Ticktock pulled her back onto the third floor.

"Give up," Beth declared. "There's nowhere to run, and nowhere to hide."

Neferisfet drew a second knife and sneered at both of them as she backed down the hall. "I haven't survived this long to just—"

The attic door opened hard, the ladder swinging down and catching Neferisfet in the back of the head. The priestess stumbled forward, and Kisa rammed her in the gut with the floor lamp, sending her over what was left of the railing. Beth swung to one side to get out of the way and then watched Neferisfet as she fell to the floor below with a scream.

"C'mon, get up here." Kisa grabbed onto Beth's wrist and pulled. Jenny and Reggie came down the ladder. "I've been hiding from her ever since she attacked everyone. Was just waiting for the perfect moment."

"Where's Opal?" Beth asked once she was safely on the floor.

Kisa pulled the cracked vial out of her pocket and handed it to Beth. "Still in here. When that bitch attacked us, she sucked what was left of herself back inside and I brought her with me."

"Thanks." Beth pocketed Opal's vial and looked over the railing. Down below, Neferisfet was getting to her feet. The priestess looked over at the grimoire, then stumbled toward it.

Beth pulled off Ticktock and threw the mimic down. Ticktock sprouted mechanical legs and landed in a crouch on top of the grimoire, pausing long enough to gobble it up.

Neferisfet let out a shriek and blasted the mimic with more of her green fire, which sent it out of view. Beth and Kisa were already running down the stairs but came to a stop when Neferisfet looked up at them.

Her leathery features were oozing pus from the wounds Kisa had inflicted. Neferisfet hissed at them like a cornered animal and ran toward the front door.

"Oh, no you don't." Kisa vaulted the railing and ran after her. Neferisfet opened the front door, and the house was filled with the sound of Murray's eerie cry. Kisa tipped over and crashed into the closet as Neferisfet limped out the front door.

"Kisa!" Beth stumbled toward the door and kicked it shut, closing out the angel's call.

"Damn, I didn't expect that." Kisa winced and put her hands on her ears. "Feel sick already."

"We cannot let her escape," Reggie called from above. "She will make it back to Earth and possess someone there."

Beth groaned and looked down at Kisa. "Close the door behind me."

Kisa nodded, then put her hands over her ears. Beth yanked open the door, jammed her fingers into her ears, and ran outside.

The swirling mists were bubbling along the edges of the property. Murray was hovering in place, shrieking in that dissonant tone. Above him, the angel's wings were spinning, as if it were a giant engine powering the process.

What concerned Beth was the fact that Neferisfet was moving toward Murray, holding that weird bag aloft. She was shouting something in an ancient language, causing the bag and her entire arm to pulsate with magical energy.

"She tried to kill me," Beth shouted at the angel. "Do something!"

Mehkhkahrel's many eyes focused on Neferisfet, and Beth saw that the whites of those eyes were starting to flash. The lights were sporadic at first but began to synchronize.

"Hey!" She stumbled forward, trying her best to keep her balance. "This is the bad guy. Aren't you gonna do something?"

"YE HAVE BEEN JUDGED." The voice came from Mehkhkahrel itself, a sound so powerful that Beth's hair blew backward and she fell to her knees. Every eye on the angel flashed simultaneously, and then a massive eye opened in the middle of its body. The spinning wings looked very much like a turbine, glittering with silver light.

Neferisfet straightened her back just a moment before a blinding light fired out of the center of Mehkhkahrel and into the priestess. Beth blinked away the spots in her vision as dry ash blew across her face. Neferisfet was gone, and in her spot, there was a small pile of dusty remains.

"Thank God," Beth muttered, then leaned forward and put her hands on the ground. It was over.

Murray closed his mouth and descended until his feet were on the ground. He walked over toward the pile of ash and squatted down to examine it. Above him, Mehkhkahrel's powerful wings had stopped spinning in place.

"There you are." Murray pulled the pouch out of the ashes and grinned. "Wasn't sure it would survive."

"Do you know what that thing is?" Beth asked. She was surprised it hadn't been destroyed by the angel. What the hell kind of magic had that been?

"Of course I do." Murray winked at her. It was such a simple expression but one that had been beyond him since being possessed. She couldn't help but notice that Murray had left glowing footprints behind him.

In horror, Beth watched Murray hold up the bag. Streamers of light bled off the angel and into the fleshy sack, causing it to expand. It elongated first, revealing fleshy veins and a thick head that bloomed from beneath the fore-skin. It radiated with power, filling the air with a low hum. "I haven't held on to the phallus of Osiris for thousands of years without knowing what it is."

Golden light sparkled along its length as he pointed the stiff member at the angel, and a blue aura surrounded Murray's entire body. Up above, Mehkhkahrel's wings started spinning in reverse as the angel's eyes blinked out of existence, then returned. The mostly human pupils were gone, now trans-formed into the narrow slits of a snake.

"But how? How?" Beth backed away from the angel, her eyes wide.

"The soul in this body agreed to merge with me, and I am not so weak as to be dominated by the angel's will." Murray spun around with a grin, clutching the dick of a dead god in his hands. "As the mouthpiece of Mehkhkahrel, the angel is sworn to protect me from harm. And I've decided that means you!"

The man burst into maniacal laughter as Beth ran back toward the house. She didn't understand how or why, but Neferisfet was now some sort of super priest. She was nearly at the door when Death burst out, his cloak flapping dramatically behind him.

"Marchioness Bethany!" The grim reaper threw himself through the air and passed through her, freezing the blood in her veins. There was a blast of golden light, followed by the smell of dust.

"Oh God, Death!" She spun around and saw that Death stood naked behind her, his robes obliterated by the angel's beam. His stark white bones were marred with scorch marks.

"I see you're still going to be a problem." Murray sneered as his body levi-tated into the air. "I honestly thought the angel would be strong enough."

"Unlike my siblings, I am not just an idea." Death twirled his scythe dramatically, and the floating ashes in the air formed around him and trans-formed into his cloak. "I am the fate that awaits all beings. Mice, men, gods, the stars, the universe. I shall bear witness to their final moments, shall watch this realm collapse into darkness long before my own time is up. For I am Death! And I am inevitable!"

A second golden beam hit the grim reaper and slammed him into the ground. His cloak exploded, and he dropped his scythe on the ground.

"Stop smiting me!" He looked up at Beth. "Get in the house! It can protect—"

The beam returned, pinning him in place. The ashes of his cloak swirled like a small tornado as it tried to reform around him. Mehkhkahrel moved to hover directly over Death, trapping him beneath the golden light.

"I believe that will hold you. Once I return to Earth, there will be no stopping me." Murray grabbed at his shirt and ripped it away, revealing a fancy body stocking underneath. "I shall usher in a new age of darkness with the return of my god!"

"I...can...stop her...if I can just...get free!" Death shouted between blasts, his eyes on Beth.

"Not so fast." Murray pointed the dick at Beth. "I haven't forgotten about you. And neither have they."

"They who...oh. Shit." Beth watched as three shadowy figures appeared in the mists, each one on horseback.

"That's right. Behold the three horsemen of Apophis!" Murray waved a hand and dispersed the mist. The horsemen were back, and both War and Famine grinned at Beth. Their features were now serpentine, and War flicked his long tongue between sharp teeth.

"Looks like we're going to have our fun after all," he told her. "So you just sit there and look pretty for us."

The horsemen surrounded Murray as he opened his mouth wide and unleashed an eerie howl. It was similar to the one from before, but there was an extra tone behind it, one that promised blood and violence. The world tilted sideways, and Beth dry-heaved from the sudden shift.

Realizing there was nothing she could do for Death, she stumbled toward the house and pushed her way inside. Kisa sat near the bottom of the stairs, her arms wrapped around Ticktock. Lily was in the living room, her face pressed against the glass.

Beth's heart pounded in her chest as she gasped for air. Sobbing, she slid down the door and hugged her legs to her chest.

"Bad?" asked Kisa.

"The worst." Lily looked at Kisa, then at Beth. "I don't think we're gonna win this one with a board game. I'm not even entirely sure what's going on out there, but it looks like the boy band has a new manager. Stupid bitch, if the angel had gotten her just a second sooner..."

Rattled, Beth hugged her knees even tighter. They had failed. Everything they had accomplished up until this point had been for nothing.

Mike. Tears burned in her eyes. She was hungry, had barely slept in days, and had finally met a crisis she couldn't figure out. *I'm sorry.*

"So I know things are kind of hopeless right now, but I have some news." Kisa slid Ticktock next to Beth. "Right before everything happened with dead girl out there, I had a really interesting dream. In fact, I think it's because I was asleep that she didn't know I was there."

Beth looked up at Kisa. "I hope you have something better than being naked in school," she stated.

"I talked to Mike. We actually saw each other. I told him everything about what's going on here, and—"

Beth spun in place and put her hands on Kisa's. She looked the cat girl in the eyes and took a deep breath. If they could speak with Mike, then they were no longer alone. Even if minor, any amount of hope would have to be enough to sustain her. Otherwise, she was lost.

"Tell me everything," she demanded. "But first things first. Do you think you could do it again?"

EULALIE STEPPED THROUGH THE PORTAL, FEELING THE FLOOR OF THE STONE tower cool against her feet. A small retinue of rats waited for her, their weapons held ready. Most of them carried spears, but she was fairly certain one of them was carrying a crossbow.

"Looks like you have your own royal guard," Zel told her. The centaur had agreed to bring them to the tower, arriving earlier to warn the guards that Eulalie was coming. Ever since being abandoned by Yuki, the tower had been occupied by a small force of centaurs from Zel's tribe. Their main job was to act as liaisons for the herd in the valley, but they were also in charge of keeping everyone else out. The tower was also being used to grow plants that thrived at cooler temperatures than what could be found in the greenhouse.

"I may have told someone I was the rat queen, and they've accepted it." As she walked past the rats, she used some of her feet to pat them on either the head or shoulder. They seemed to enjoy the acknowledgment, then fell in line behind her. "So this is Yuki's tower."

"Indeed." Sofia's voice was distorted as she knelt to walk through the portal. "We'll find what we're looking for upstairs."

Eulalie looked over toward the spiral staircase along the wall. "That thing doesn't have a railing," she noted. "Clear OSHA violation."

"The last occupant used to turn things to stone because they pissed her off," Zel replied. "And I would also point out that this was a home, not a place of employment."

"Fair." Eulalie grinned. "So a whole stash of magic weapons upstairs?"

Zel nodded. "I would show you myself, but I'm in no condition to climb the stairs."

"Because you're pregnant?" Eulalie's eyes flicked to Zel's stomach. She didn't know enough about horse anatomy to tell if Zel was showing yet. "I'm fairly certain pregnant women are capable of climbing stairs."

Zel started to say something, but Sofia interrupted.

"She's just pulling your tail," she said. "I think it's because she's settling in. Now we get to see the spider behind the mask."

"I would like to point out that I'm a centaur, not a woman." Zel scrunched up her face. "If you have any questions about the difference, I'd be happy to enlighten you."

"Actually, I find centaur reproduction extremely fascinating, because the dichotomy between human babies and foals——" Eulalie was interrupted by Sofia's hand over her mouth.

"Magic weapons," Sofia reiterated. "Stay on task."

Eulalie nodded and moved toward the stairs. She spread her legs wide and ascended with half her legs on the steps and the other half on the wall. The feel of stone and grout beneath her feet tickled.

"So is there a good reason you're trying to antagonize Zel?" Sofia asked once they were up a floor.

Eulalie frowned. "Habit, I suppose. Like me, she's essentially human from the waist up. I guess maybe I felt a connection like I do with my sister, an extra level of familiarity."

"You have to earn that familiarity," Sofia scolded. "You barely know her. And don't talk about her pregnancy. From what I've heard, she's really shy about it."

"What do you mean?"

"She doesn't like talking about it. Anytime someone brings up her pregnancy, she changes the subject right away."

"Why wouldn't she want to talk about it?" Eulalie asked. "I was under the impression that some women love the attention."

"Based on what, may I ask?"

Eulalie shrugged. "The internet, which I admit isn't always accurate. Certainly it doesn't help that my only exposure to it is how it's portrayed in movies and magazines. Pregnancy has always fascinated me. Can you imagine having a living thing inside your body? Moving around, displacing your guts.

My mother said she felt something similar, but those were eggs developing, not a baby, so I imagine it's different."

Sofia paused for a moment, her hand on the wall as if leaning on it for support.

"I'm not certain how, but did I say something wrong?" Reading body language had always been difficult for Eulalie. Her father had been largely unreadable, a man who preferred to stew quietly on things. Her mother and sister were easier but only because they shared morphology. Sofia's larger-than-normal size was easy to relate to Bigfoot, and right now she stood like her uncle would when coming across a dead animal with a hunter's arrow in it. Uncle Foot wasn't opposed to hunting by any means, but the idea that someone had shot the animal and allowed it to wander off and suffer was something that hurt him deeply.

"It's tough to talk about, but if I've learned anything about you, it's that you won't just let it go." Sofia turned around, her cheeks red and her jaw set. "When I first came to the Library, I wasn't a librarian. Not a full-fledged one, anyway. More of a volunteer."

Eulalie nodded, urging the cyclops to continue.

"My job was to read books to the children. There were so many of them, from all kinds of races." Sofia turned to the nearest window and looked outside with her hands on the sill. "I loved children, wanted to have some of my own one day."

Eulalie almost interrupted, wanting to point out that Sofia didn't seem like the maternal type. In the silence between words, it dawned on her that this would be the worst thing she could say. Data was easy, but people were hard. She liked Sofia because the cyclops reminded her a bit of her mother and was generally easy to read. Only having one eye seemed to limit her facial expressions, which was also something Eulalie preferred.

"When the Order came to the island of my people, nobody was spared. Founded by the more peaceful members of my species, it had become a cultural center for man and monster alike. This was a line they could not tolerate us to cross." She wiped a tear from her eye, then gritted her teeth as if in pain. "They killed everyone they could find, regardless of age. The Order can hide under the pretense of keeping the peace, but I've suspected for many centuries that their real target was the Library. They didn't expect it to be so well defended, nor for the nearby community to be ready to fight back."

"That's horrible." The thought of any thinking creature deliberately targeting children made Eulalie's blood boil. She had been online long enough to encounter all kinds of child predation and had even strongly debated traveling a hundred miles to rip the head off one in Bend, Oregon. After an argument with her father, she had settled on outing him to the authorities, which was far less satisfying than pulling his spine through his asshole would have been.

Sofia shook her head. "I was in the village during the initial attack but ran to the Library to defend it. The Order was attacking my village, and I knew that many of my people would be there to protect it. When I arrived, the first place I ran to was the reading room. There was a man there, a Knight of the Order, standing over the bodies of children. I was so surprised to see him there, to see their bodies, that I barely reacted to the vision warning me of injury. He tried to run me through the belly, but I was able to jump out of the way. What was supposed to be a fatal stomach wound became..." She sighed. "I took his sword, then his life. When I left that room, I thought I was dying. I was a woman possessed and killed over thirty of the bastards before they fled. When all was said and done, I and a few others locked the building down, breaking its link with the island so they could no longer attack it. My wound was treatable, but the scar tissue, it..."

Eulalie put her hand on Sofia's. "I'm sorry," she told her.

The cyclops nodded, then wiped another tear from her eye. "I gave up on having a family long ago, much less children. The house, though, it has given me purpose outside of being the Librarian. I enjoy every minute of it, even though my job suffers."

"You can't just hire more people to help you? I mean, you are in charge."

Sofia chuckled dryly. "I haven't really had the opportunity to do so. When only a handful of people even know you exist, it's kind of hard to get the word out. People don't age in the Library, and humans are prone to seeking immortality that way. Once they learn they will age if they leave, they slowly go mad, counting each precious second outside the Library's walls. Apparently books aren't enough to keep most people happy, so they inevitably stay away too long or go insane and must be removed."

"My mom loved books. I bet she would have been very happy there. She even used to be a librarian but never talked about it much." She smiled, thinking about her mother. *If you could only see me now, Mom. I'm making so many friends!*

"Do you love books?" Sofia asked. "Maybe you want a job?"

Eulalie shrugged. "I don't know. The whole reason I became an internet nerd was books couldn't be published fast enough to sate my curiosity. I wanted to experience the world through others, for all the typical reasons." She scurried up the wall as if to illustrate her point. "I'm afraid I've always been more into audio and visual media. Movies, music, that kind of thing."

"Maybe the Library needs a modern touch." Sofia smirked, then looked at the stairs to the next level. "But perhaps we should get back to why we are here."

"Magic weapons!" Eulalie rubbed her hands together in anticipation as they continued up the stairs.

When Amymone had informed them that there were magic weapons stored in an otherworldly tower, Eulalie had actually gotten down on all her knees and begged to be told more. Decades of fantasy books, games, and Dungeons and Dragons campaigns had instilled in her an absolute love for magic. She had seen her uncle do small things with it, like commune with trees or portal hop. In reality, he was more of a druid than a sorcerer or wizard.

Her mother had often told them about the magic she had seen members of the Order use. It was both terrifying and exciting to know that magic not only existed but was apparently some huge secret. It was the main reason she had gone to work for the government. There was always the hope of discovering that the US government was stashing magical books in the Library of Congress, or maybe even a wizarding school at Area 51.

"I'm hoping for a flaming sword," Eulalie declared when they found themselves outside the armory. "One that ignites when you say its name or something fancy in Elvish. It's way cooler than a sword that can fold itself up, no offense. Grew up with one, but we used it mostly for chopping wood."

"Elves are dicks." Sofia gazed cautiously at the entrance. "Ratu warned us that this stuff is bad news, so please don't just grab the first thing you see. We have a purpose here."

"I know, I know." Eulalie rubbed her hands together. "Find weapons we can potentially use once Mike returns. Categorize them based on strengths and weaknesses so we can form a...wait, elves are real? Are they like the ones from Lord of the Rings?"

"It's a rather generic term that can refer to lots of different creatures. But yes, they're all dicks." Sofia frowned. "Wait, I take that back. There is one curious exception to the rule."

"Who are they?"

"Let's just say they're the epitome of nice." Sofia inspected the door. "Yuki and Ratu had a magical lock installed here. Give me a second." She pulled out a crystal ball from one of her pockets and held it up. "Ratu?"

The naga's face appeared. She was soaking in a hot bath.

"Move me a little higher," Ratu said. Sofia lifted the ball, and a thin beam of blue light came from the crystal ball and struck a hidden rune just to the left of the doorway. The rune sent out a ripple of energy that caused another set of hidden runes to appear and then vanish.

Eulalie skittered about with anticipation as Sofia opened the door.

"Velvet's never gonna believe this," she said as she shot through the door and looked around.

It was an armory, lit from above by skylights. The dark corners of the room were illuminated with torches that burned brightly without generating any smoke. Much of the room looked damaged, but a few items were locked up in display cases that were up against the wall.

There was a loud thud as a mace lifted off the ground and slammed into the glass of its display case. Eulalie ran up to the case and danced around it with her hands over her mouth.

Several thick chains held the mace down, but it was able to thud against the edges of the case. She put her hands against the thick glass out of curiosity and was surprised when the mace moved away from her.

"Check this one out." Sofia gestured at a glass case full of water. When she walked close to it, it transformed into a replica of her sword, then shifted into a staff eerily reminiscent of the one she carried in the Library.

"Made of water, changes shapes…" Eulalie bit her lip. The data was there; she just couldn't put it together fast enough. It didn't help that her knowledge base was polluted with video game references.

"The legendary weapon Varunastra. It can be anything you want it to be."

"Should we take it?"

Sofia grimaced. "Well, about that. It certainly seems accommodating, but if you aren't deemed worthy enough to wield it, it's supposed to kill the wielder. Maybe."

"How does it 'maybe' kill you?"

"Legends say it destroys you. Not technically the same as killing, so there's room for interpretation."

"Maybe it'll log into my social media and spout a bunch of racist shit." Eulalie wandered over toward the case and pressed her hands against it. The water bubbled and then turned into a net. "You'll never guess my password," she whispered dramatically.

The mace continued its incessant banging as they examined the rest of the room. There were other weapons of unknown origin, but the one that caught her eye was a sword with a hooked blade built into it.

"Any ideas on this one?" she asked.

"Hmm." Sofia frowned at it. "Shape rings a bell."

"Looks really sharp." Eulalie inspected the edges of the case. "There's no actual lock on these. How are we supposed to get in?"

The thudding behind them became even louder, and she turned around to see that the mace had gotten itself twisted up in the chains. The heavy links were crashing against the glass as the mace tried to rotate and free itself.

"That one really seems like it wants some attention." She looked over at Sofia. "Thoughts?"

"Weapons that have their own desires are almost always bad news." Sofia looked back at the hooked blade. "I'm starting to think we might not be able to use anything here."

"It's all a matter of perspective." Eulalie looked at the sword, then ran her fingers along the case. She tapped her fingers on the glass, then wrapped her fist in spider silk.

"What are you doing?" asked Sofia.

"Just a little percussive maintenance." Satisfied that her hand and forearm were protected, she slammed her fist into the glass. It cracked after the first blow, then shattered on the second. Smiling in delight, Eulalie pulled the blade free and gave it a test swing.

"Please be careful with that," Sofia cautioned.

Eulalie inspected the sword. "It's insanely light. Feels like I'm swinging a dowel rod." She moved toward a broken case and swung the sword.

It was almost a casual gesture, but the blade passed through the case with ease. Stunned, she took a step back and examined the sword once again.

"Oh, wow, I think I know what this is." Sofia took the sword from Eulalie and turned it over in her hands. "I'm actually surprised to see it still exists. Gaia forged it so that one of her sons could overthrow Uranus. The sword was lost for some time, and it's been rumored that Perseus used it to behead Medusa. That's the last anyone heard of it, to my knowledge."

"Well, great! If it's sharp enough to cut a god, then it's probably perfect for what we need." She took it back from Sofia, then looked around. "You don't happen to see a scabbard for it, do you? Feel kind of dumb just walking around with it."

Sofia shook her head. "This room's a mess. If there's a scabbard here, it's long gone."

Eulalie held the sword up and grinned. "It doesn't have a name, does it?"

"That's arguable, actually. Scholars call it the Harpe." Sofia walked over toward the door. "We should have Ratu examine it to make certain there aren't any surprises though."

"Solid plan." Grinning, she swung the Harpe a couple more times and followed Sofia. She was about to step through the door when she felt a touch at the back of her neck.

Lala. The voice was barely a whisper, and she wasn't entirely certain she had heard it. It sounded like Velvet, and she was suddenly taken back to hours around the game table, her sorcerer and Velvet's ranger traveling the realm and defeating monsters. How many times had their characters found themselves in a magical tower? Whether fighting monsters, defeating an evil wizard, or just rescuing a prince, there was always a theme, a method to the madness.

Unsure why the memories were coming to her, she looked around the room. It had been ransacked, many of the items destroyed or left behind. What was the theme of this place? What secret had it held?

"Everything okay?" Sofia watched her from the hallway.

Eulalie looked around the room, expecting to see someone moving among the shadows. The room was quiet, save for the frantic rattling of the chained-up mace.

"Tell me again about this tower." She walked over toward the display case with the mace. "It was that shadow guy who owned it, right?"

"That's the theory. This tower was part of his property. The rest of it is trapped in the Underworld. We think this was his private stash of weapons."

"He was a magic user, right?" When she placed her hand against the glass, the mace went still once more, as if watching her. An evil wizard with a stash of magical weapons. This room had a secret; she just knew it.

"On top of being a manipulative bastard, yes." Sofia moved to the center of the room and crossed her arms. "Without knowing his name, we couldn't do any research into him. Why do you ask?"

"It just strikes me as odd. On the one hand, you have this powerful sorcerer who is hoarding magical weapons, right? But I don't think he ever planned to use them. Take Varunastra over there. Supremely powerful, so why not use it? Paranoia. Can't risk destroying yourself for a fancy poking stick. Now, the sword, it's nice and all but useless in the hands of someone who doesn't know how to use it."

"I guess. Where are you going with this?"

Eulalie held up a hand for silence as the web spread out in her mind. The shadow had collected all these magical weapons but had no intention of using them. Why? Because he couldn't. No, this wasn't a collection of weapons to be loaned out to his lackeys or even used by him. Maybe these items held value, but what was money to a powerful sorcerer? Perhaps he meant to study them, to unlock their secrets? Or maybe…

"I think these weapons weren't for him to use," she said. "I think he kept them because he was afraid they would be used against him. Master manipulator, right? The shape-shifter is powerful, but it would kill him. The sword was just a sword, but sharp enough for a god is sharp enough for a wizard."

"Good points, but I'm not sure where you're going with this."

Eulalie pressed her hand against the glass and stared at the mace. The head had a looping design that was weathered with age, and the patina had been worn off in spots that could reach the glass. The links of the chain were thicker than her fingers and looked to be made of a black metal she didn't recognize.

"Are you alive?" she asked while tapping on the glass. "Tap twice if you understand me."

The mace hovered in place for a moment, then tilted toward her hand and tapped twice.

Eulalie grinned, then whispered, "Secret's out, you shadowy fuck."

"I have serious doubts about the wisdom of—" Sofia gasped midsentence as Eulalie swung the Harpe of Perseus into the case, slicing cleanly through the wood and glass. The chain links parted easily, and the mace lifted into the air, toppling the display as it hovered in the middle of the room, bogged down by the remaining chains.

The mace spun about, causing the chains to rattle, then flew through the skylight, causing the glass to explode outward.

"Oh." Eulalie grimaced. "Well…shit."

"Shit? All you have to say is shit?" Sofia was yelling now as she pointed at the skylight. "You just released a potentially bloodthirsty magical weapon on an unsuspecting populace, and that's all you have to say for yourself?"

"Look, I thought maybe it would be grateful. Why lock up a sentient weapon unless it disagreed with the shit you were doing?" In hindsight, her enthusiasm had gotten the best of her.

"Because maybe it's chaotic and just wants to smash everything!" Sofia stormed off toward the door. "We need to fix this, and quickly!"

Eulalie followed behind the cyclops, careful to hold the sword up. She didn't dare to hold it at waist height; she feared cutting one of her legs.

They ran down the stairs, followed by a retinue of rats. Once outside, they saw the centaurs pointing at the sky as the mace did whirling loops around the apex of the tower. Zel was shouting commands, urging the others to get to safety.

"What the hell is that thing doing?" Sofia shaded her eye with one hand.

The mace slammed into the tower a few times, knocking loose the chains attached to it. One of the chains dropped onto a large planter and shattered it.

Centaurs cried out in alarm as the mace swooped down on them. Eulalie stuck her sword into the soft dirt of a nearby planter and sprinted up the stone wall of the exterior, her eyes locked on the mace. The mace swung by several centaurs but always pulled up at the last moment.

When it came near the tower, she leaped for it, both hands clasping the handle. In response, the mace shot upward.

I didn't think this through. Swallowing the lump in her throat, she held on for dear life as the mace carried her into the clouds. Mist formed on her hands and body, and she used her spinnerets to put together some sticky webs that she looped over the head of the mace to give her a better grip.

The weapon swooped down, and she twisted her body to cling to it with her feet. In the valley below, she could see distant centaurs pausing to watch, but her main concern was on the horizon. A vast ocean greeted them, and she watched in horror as the coastline receded behind them.

"This is a terrible way to say thank you," she shouted at the mace, then smacked the palm of her hand on its head. "Take me back right now or I'll have you recycled into a prison toilet!"

Laughter bloomed in her mind as the mace did a sharp turn in the air. She twisted herself around so she could see where they were going. By her estimates, the magic weapon had a top speed of maybe fifty miles an hour.

Centaurs along the shoreline watched in horror as the mace descended toward them, hovering almost forty feet overhead. Their horror-filled faces made Eulalie frown, and more than a couple reached for their bows as she shot past.

An arrow pinged off the head of the mace, and the weapon ascended out of range.

"Fuck you too!" She flipped off the centaurs, then grabbed back onto the mace as it climbed back into the mountains and toward the tower. Sofia stood on the outer walls, waving frantically at Eulalie.

"I need you to drop me off," she told the mace. "Nicely."

The mace slowed and then stopped above the garden. It moved down at elevator speed until her legs were back on the ground, then fell to the ground with a clunk. Sofia came running up, followed by a bunch of very upset rats.

"Are you okay?" the cyclops asked.

"Just went for a joyride is all." Eulalie picked up the mace and held it out. "I asked it to return me, and it did."

"Maybe we should lock it back up," Sofia suggested.

The mace tried to fly away, but Eulalie gripped the cobblestones beneath her with all eight of her legs.

"Nobody is locking it away," she hollered, then tugged the mace down to eye level. "Nobody is locking you away," she repeated, then patted the head of the mace as if it were a cat. "As long as you behave, that is."

The restless weapon went still in her hands, and gratitude filled her mind.

Sofia looked at the weapon with distrust, then back at Eulalie. "You had better know what you're doing."

The Arachne chuckled. She had no idea what she was doing but had just taken a magic weapon for a joyride across the surrounding countryside.

It was officially the best day ever. The only thing that would have made it better was if her sister could have been there.

THE EVENING HOURS HAD CRAWLED, EVERY MINUTE STRETCHING ITSELF impossibly thin in an attempt to smother the room. Mike had chewed his fingernails down to the quick as he paced in the front room of the cabin. At the kitchen table, Dana sat perfectly still with her collapsed sword right in front of her. It was unlike the zombie to be so unproductive, and if not for the occasional twitching of her eyelids, she may have been a statue.

The others had gone to bed long ago, but Mike doubted they were asleep. Any moment now, Abella would return with Velvet and all of them would discuss the next step. He stuck his hand in his pocket and closed his fingers around the crystalline orb the owl had given them.

Yuki had assured them that the spell to trap Leeds could be cast by the artifact in his hands, but he wasn't so sure. Was the owl's spirit still inside such a thing? For perhaps the hundredth time, he pulled it from his pocket and contemplated the thing. It was a yellow sphere with a dilated pupil in the middle. No matter how he twisted it in his hand, the eye was always looking right at him.

"That thing stinks," Dana told him.

He held it to his nose and sniffed it. "What does it smell like to you?" he asked. It didn't have an odor he could detect.

"I don't think I'm smelling the eye itself," she replied. "It must be the magic. Have you ever smelled rotting meat? It's like that."

Mike had a sudden urge to put the eye down but settled on sticking it back in his pocket. "So you can smell magic?"

"A bit," she explained. "On people, mostly. You. Naia. Sometimes Quetzalli. Definitely that thing. You all have a very distinct odor."

"Why does it smell so bad to you?" he asked. "My magic doesn't stink, right?"

She shook her head. "Yours doesn't. I think maybe it's where the magic came from. Bigfoot mentioned that the owl used to eat people, so maybe that's the reason. I get the feeling that she was trying to turn over a new leaf, but even a few decades of good behavior versus centuries of bad stuff doesn't make you smell like roses."

"Guess that makes sense." Mike sat across from her.

"Your magic smells different now," Dana added. "Though I suspect you're already aware. It's changed."

He nodded. "I haven't had a chance to talk about it with anyone. Maybe Yuki can help me, or Naia when I get back. It's…" Words failed him. How could he even begin to describe something he'd never fully understood to begin with? He examined his hand, thinking about the magic just beneath the surface. With just a little concentration, he found he could summon a handful of sparks that danced back and forth between his fingers. He wiggled his fingers as if playing an imaginary piano. It could have been his imagination, but it sounded like the pitch of the buzzing streamers shifted.

"Neat trick," Dana told him, curiosity in her eyes.

"Thanks. I do birthday parties." He put his hands on the table and watched the sparks crawl across the wood toward Dana. She shifted away from him and held up her hands.

"No offense," she told him. "I'm trying to cut back is all."

He laughed, then watched as the sparks poofed out of existence. Was magic like energy? Had it been conserved? Would it sink down through the table and travel through the earth until it found someone to affect? Would someone in Australia have a random orgasm because of it?

"What on earth are you thinking about?" Dana frowned at him. "You look like you're trying to solve a math problem, but then you get this goofy grin."

In a way, maybe he was.

"I was just wondering about magic in general," he explained. "Sometimes I think there are rules, but I can't for the life of me figure out what they are."

"'All magic has a price' tends to be the first rule," Dana replied. "Maybe even the only one. Don't think I've gotten any other pearls of wisdom since I died."

"Nah, the second one is intent. There's a price to pay, and magic is all about intent." He nodded to himself. That was one he had proven time and again. Intent often fueled what happened next. That made two rules. He would bet good money that there was a third because it seemed to be a good number for pretty much everything else.

"Do you think magic is hereditary?" Dana asked.

Her question surprised him. "Why wouldn't it be? I don't think it would be any different than hair color or whatever. Then again, that would mean there was some spiritual component similar to genetics." The image of a transdimensional double helix with glowing lights filled his head. It was a fun thought.

"I guess I mean types of magic. For example, would Yuki's children have ice magic that smelled like hers does?"

It was often hard to read Dana, but there was something behind her expression that made him pause and consider. She seemed to be deliberately ignoring his gaze.

"Maybe?" He shrugged. "Couldn't say, but that's specifically suspicious. Why are you asking?"

She screwed up her face, then sighed. "I think that I should tell you—"

He didn't hear what she said next. Instead, the room was yanked out from underneath him, and he was falling through darkness, his limbs flailing wildly. Gasping, he slammed his hand into a palm tree and steadied himself.

"What the hell?" He let go of the tree and stumbled backward onto the beach. The dark waters of the Dreamscape swirled menacingly around the island, and some of the others stood along its shore.

"Hey. Hey!" He ran to the others, but they weren't looking at him. Their gazes were fixed on a figure who stood in the water, several yards out from where the waves kissed the sand.

"Velvet?" He started to walk into the water, but a hand grabbed onto his and held on tightly.

"Mike." Lily's voice had an edge to it he hadn't heard before. "This…I…"

"What?" When he looked at the others, he saw nothing but sadness reflected in their eyes. "What's going on?"

"My love?" Velvet's voice was soft like feathered down, and there was a tightness to it that shook him to the core. "I'm sorry, but I have to go."

"Go? Go where?"

She grimaced, then looked at the others. "I think you know."

"I don't understand. You can't leave here, nobody can leave." He looked to Lily for support. "Aren't you all knitted into my soul or something?"

Lily lowered her gaze to the ground. "There's always been one way for someone to leave, Romeo."

The sky darkened up above, revealing a clear night sky. The stars all twinkled, but one of them sparkled more brightly than the others. Velvet looked at it with longing, and suddenly he understood.

Fiery pain passed through his chest, and he clutched at his ribs in agony.

"NO!" Mike's voice came from everywhere as he shot across the Dreamscape, his feet hovering over the water, to grab onto Velvet's hand. "I don't know what's happened, but I can hold you here like you did me! You held me here so I wouldn't die, maybe I can do the same!"

"It isn't the same, and we both know it." She smiled weakly at the women behind him. "Because of you, I've loved more deeply in the last three days than I ever could have imagined. Thank you."

"Don't talk like that, I—" He sputtered, the words tangling into letters that spilled from his lips and floated away in the dark sea. The star above had become a ball of blazing light, overwhelming the others until they were no longer visible.

How could he tell her how he felt? Did he even know? He had experienced love before and often with the others, but their connection had been so intense. They barely knew each other, but they fit together so perfectly.

The Dreamscape shook as an earthquake hit the island, the result of his grief. He let out a cry of agony as the sea swelled beneath him and slammed into the beach.

"Velvet, no." His voice was little more than a whisper. "Please don't go."

"I don't have a choice." When she smiled, the skin around her eyes crinkled. She put her hand against his cheek and held it there. "Please tell my sister I'm sorry. I didn't mean to leave her alone in this world."

She looked up at the star and took a deep breath.

"I'm afraid," she told him. "For all the magic and beauty in this world, I'm afraid of what comes next."

He was gasping for air now, and rings of light had formed around his feet beneath the water. His magic bubbled up from the depths and filled the air with ominous whispers.

The words made no sense to him, but he could tell it was a question. When he closed his eyes, he could hear what his magic asked of him, and he inhaled sharply.

Do you want her to stay? There was no malevolence behind the voice, if it could be called such a thing. The power inside him had felt his pain and was reacting, to grant him what he wanted. If he willed it, his magic would cling to this tiny part of her soul, and a piece of her would be with him always.

But then what would happen to the rest of her soul? He thought of Emily, trapped as a tormented specter in the Underworld. No, he didn't want that at all.

He just wanted her.

A cold hand slid into his. He opened his eyes to see Cecilia hovering next to him.

"It is time, *mo shíorghrá*." She wiped the tears from his cheeks, then used her free hand to take Velvet's from his own. "I am sorry."

Velvet was watching him, her spirit fading into the churning mists of the ocean. It was like she was being diluted into nothingness.

"No." He took her by the hand once more, then looked at Cecilia. "She can't stay, but...maybe we can help her go?"

The banshee nodded, a sad smile on her face.

Cecilia's lips parted, and the song of mourning filled the air. The seas calmed, and the air went still as her powerful voice filled the cosmos and bent it to her will. The three of them stood in a triangle as a golden light formed around Velvet's silhouette, and her spirit snapped back into focus. Wonderment filled her eyes as she looked into that night sky and saw something he couldn't.

"Mike?" Velvet smiled. "Thank you for loving me."

There was a lot he wanted to say in that moment, but words would never be enough. Instead, he joined in with Cecilia's song. Though the words were in a language he didn't know, they spilled from his lips as easily as secrets that no longer mattered. The air thrummed with power, and he pulled Velvet in for one last embrace.

Other voices joined in behind him. He recognized the husky lilt of Lily's voice and could tell Zel's soprano from Sofia's alto. Tink's singing voice was devoid of words—she just sang the notes, her voice rising and falling with the waves around them.

Naia, Ratu, and all the others sang out his grief as the star in the sky descended upon them. A beam of light connected Velvet to the sky, and she looked up in wonder.

"Daddy?" A smile crossed Velvet's face, and she no longer seemed afraid.

There was a flash of light, and she was gone. The star in the sky pulsed three times and then disappeared, leaving the night sky as it was.

Cecilia put her arms around him and held him close, but he wasn't interested in the comfort they provided. With great effort, he willed the Dreamscape to crumble away from him, leaving him on the wooden floor of the kitchen.

"Hey, are you okay?" Dana knelt over his chest and was slapping lightly at his cheeks. Emery hovered nervously overhead, wringing his hands. The bedroom door creaked as Yuki stepped into the living room, concern on her face.

"No." Mike stared blankly at the ceiling for a moment, his thoughts waiting to crash down on him like heavy weights. The song lingered in his head, the eerie melody causing tears to slide down his temples and onto the floor.

"Mike." Yuki knelt by him, her eyes wide. "Did something happen? You're so pale."

His breath hitched in his chest, and he felt his whole body tense up. He scrunched up his face as his anger boiled over the surface, causing the magic to churn within him.

"Leeds happened." He stood up, his hands trembling. "I need everyone to stay back."

Nobody said a word as Mike stood there, his magic filling the air with a steady hum. The others didn't seem to hear it, but that didn't matter to him. It was like a giant beating heart, just waiting to take on some semblance of life.

"He took something from me," Mike told everyone. "Something I can never get back." He wanted to say more but was afraid that nobody would believe him. The truth threatened to overwhelm him, and if he spoke the words aloud, it would break him.

Yuki shook her head. "You're not making any sense."

"Doesn't matter." Mike's eyes flicked toward the door, and his magic reached across the room and yanked it open. Everyone turned to face the door as he walked outside, stopping just long enough to grab his coat. "Come with me if you want a piece of him."

"Where are you going?" Yuki called from behind him.

He turned to look at her, and she took a step back.

"Hunting," he replied. He stepped out into the cold, his feet crunching in the snow. It was still dark and would be for a couple more hours, but that didn't matter. He could feel the forest around him, hear the whisper of its creatures as they watched him approach.

He could hear the others scrambling to follow him, but he was moving at a jog now, his magic radiating out into the forest. When he got to the tree line, he looked up at them and bared his teeth.

"Where is he?" he asked.

The trees rustled as if caught in the wind. He could hear the sound spread away from him, like an arboreal radar. Perhaps a minute passed, and he heard both Dana and Yuki come up behind him.

"Mike, you're scaring me." Yuki's voice was drowned out by the sounds of the forest. Off to his left, he heard the trees creak in an attempt to get his attention.

"This way," he yelled, then bolted forward. They hollered for him to wait up, but the anger had consumed his thoughts. His magic buzzed alongside him, sending out tendrils of light that connected briefly with trees and plants as he passed, ready to assist him with whatever he desired. The sky rumbled above him, and a wicked smile broke across his face as the forest parted to allow him to run freely.

It was time to kill the devil.

"ABELLA? COME FORWARD, CHILD."

She walked deeper into the cave, her chin held high in defiance. The elders of the clan, all three of them, sat in a squat, their eyes level with hers. Scattered along the walls of the cave were the heads of the different families, including her own mother. It wasn't her first time before the elders, but this time was different. Getting in trouble was a rite of passage for the young, but even she knew she had overstepped her boundaries.

"Are you aware why you are here?" This came from the elder on her left, Gaia. She was thousands of years old with fearsome horns that curled menacingly around high cheekbones.

"It is about the man from the village."

Gaia nodded. "The blind one who frequents the fishing bridge, yes."

The central figure cleared his throat. Torma was the most human in appearance, but he had long fangs that extended down past his chin. Despite his angry visage, he was considered the kindest of the elders.

"It is forbidden to speak with them, young one. Are you aware why?"

She nodded. "I am aware, elder. But I don't understand why I cannot speak with this one. He cannot see me and is content to catch his fish and then go. He believes I am a young woman from the village, and—"

"Therein lies the problem." Gaia shook her head. "What if he goes looking for this young woman? Should he decide to pursue your identity, suddenly the humans will hear about a strange voice that can be heard down at the bridge."

"Let them talk, then." Abella waved her hand at the others. "Those who are made of stone do not fear words."

The third elder, Lave, growled. Long ago, he had used so much heart fire that his mouth had stretched and distorted until he was no longer capable of proper speech. Through some means, the other elders understood him.

"Elder Lave informs you that words are rarely harmless," Torma said. "You are only thinking about what is right before you and not what lies ahead."

"They are one and the same," Abella replied.

Gaia shifted, which caused her wings to briefly unfurl. "Consider this, child. Should this man try to learn who you are from the village, the other humans will learn there is a young woman unaccounted for, should they choose to believe him."

"I don't see the problem."

"That is because you are young." Gaia crossed her arms. "Should the others see fit to help this man, then one of two things happens. The first is that they decide this woman is real and hiding. As they look for her and discover nothing, they eventually determine you must be a spirit, or some other entity trying to lure him to his doom. Humans are notoriously suspicious of what they do not understand and will often go to extremes. Suddenly, we have a mob of humans looking everywhere and chasing rumors until they end up here. The clan has to move, which is no simple feat."

Abella shrugged. "We are moving next spring. By the time the humans can get organized, we will be long gone."

"And what of this man you are so fascinated with?" Torma shook his head. "What if they decide he is simply hearing voices? What will the humans do with him?"

Abella opened her mouth, then sighed. If history was any indicator, he would likely become an outcast. The village tolerated him only because he was self-sufficient and lived with his mother. Did she really want him to end up alone simply because she wanted to get to know him better?

Or worse, he could be labeled a witch. He would likely be drowned in the very river that was his livelihood.

Lave grunted, then pointed at Abella with one of his many hands.

Gaia frowned at Lave. "That punishment is not fit for this crime."

Lave snapped his teeth and continued speaking. Abella had rarely heard such continuous sound from the elder and could almost make out a rumbling voice beneath the noise.

Torma held up a hand and waited for silence from his fellow elder. Lave shook his head in disgust.

"Elder Lave wishes to subject you to a punishment known as the Earth Mother's Embrace."

This caused the members of the clan to mutter to themselves, but they were silenced by a dirty glare from Gaia.

"I have not heard of this punishment," Abella replied, her voice shaking.

Torma looked around the room. "As we come from the earth, we must someday return to it. It is a punishment we have not done since before your time due to its cruelty. It is a punishment by which you are buried alive beneath the stone of the earth. There, in the Earth Mother's Embrace, you will slip in and out of consciousness as your body gathers just enough energy to keep you alive but not enough to escape."

Abella's jaw dropped open in astonishment.

"It used to be done as a punishment to enforce the will of the clan," Gaia continued. "We were created by the Earth Mother to be her eyes and ears, to soar among the clouds, and to be confined to the rocky depths is to deprive us of our purpose. Those who have suffered the Embrace have explained that they are aware the whole time of their misery. There are those who have been buried and forgotten, or the earth has moved and crushed them into dust. It is dangerous and reserved for crimes only against our own kind."

Lave growled again.

"And while I agree, Elder, that the young one has made a mistake that risks our safety, it was not deliberate. She did not make her choice with disregard for the clan. Rather, she is selfish, as most of the young ones tend to be." Torma bared his teeth. "As one who has been punished with the Embrace, I would vote against it."

"As would I," Gaia added. "But be warned, child. Should your continued love of humans risk our safety, we would rather exile you than bury you beneath the ground and away from the sky. Do you understand?"

Abella swallowed the lump in her throat. "Yes, I do, Elder."

Elder Torma opened his mouth, and an eerie ringing sound made Abella's teeth buzz in harmony. The other elders opened their mouths to make the same noise, and her eyes fluttered open, revealing darkness. Though the memory had burst like a grape beneath her feet, that infernal sound remained.

Her ears were ringing, and she groaned. Where was she? Her whole body ached, and she lifted her head to look around. There was a tiny sliver of light that illuminated the rock above her. She was in the mouth of a cave.

Cave. Velvet. Leeds. She had tried to rescue Velvet, swooping down to grab her before the cave could collapse. But then what?

There was a sharp pain in her left wing, and her eyes popped open the rest of the way. A rock had fallen and hit her in the wing, and they had crashed. As the ground had rumbled around them, she had faded in and out of consciousness from the pain. Was her wing even still there, or had it been shattered? She flexed it and felt tremendous pain along its length. She bit back a groan but was grateful to feel anything at all.

"No man left behind," she muttered. It was something Velvet had muttered, over and over again. Where was the Arachne?

Abella tried to move forward, but her feet and tail were pinned down by heavy rocks. She had a moment of panic but reassured herself she could probably get free. The sliver of light above was expanding and would eventually illuminate the rubble and allow her to figure out how to best extricate her feet.

The ringing in her ears faded over the long minutes until it was finally gone. The cave was silent, save for the occasional drip of water and the breeze that flowed over the entrance.

"Velvet? Are you there?" She turned her head painfully and was able to make out a pair of legs sticking out from beneath an overhang in the corner of the cave. The air was unnaturally cold.

"I am," Velvet replied, her voice weak and airy.

Sighing with relief, Abella lay back down and relaxed. "You saved me, didn't you?"

"I did."

Abella sighed. If not for Velvet, she would have been crushed beneath the ground. Or worse, trapped for all eternity in the Earth Mother's Embrace. A chill ran up her spine at the thought of it.

When Mike had first discovered her, it was after the Mandragora had leached away her life force, putting her in a similar state. Her mind had come and gone, but in those waking moments, she had experienced a dull pain throughout her entire body. Maybe it was analogous to hunger in humans or not having enough air to breathe. Either way, it was something she hoped to never experience again.

"Thank you." She tapped on the cold stone of the ground, feeling the grit beneath her fingertips. All sorts of emotions rolled through her, but the biggest one was regret.

"And also…I am sorry." Abella paused, half expecting Velvet to say something.

The Arachne remained silent.

"I am sorry we fought. I didn't give you the benefit of the doubt. You are the first of your kind to embrace their humanity, and I refused to believe it possible. And so I tried to kill you and am ashamed.

"I came for you because I love him." Abella squeezed her eyes shut, the warmth in her chest threatening to overwhelm her. "I wanted to protect you for his sake, but I know now that I should have come for your own. You could have left me behind. I am aware of this. And maybe you saved me for the same reason I tried to save you. For Mike."

"No man left behind," Velvet whispered.

Abella chuckled. "No man or monster, maybe. I doubted you, and I shouldn't have. We are different, but maybe we have more in common than I was willing to acknowledge. If nothing else, we have him in common, and that should have been enough."

The ground behind her rumbled as distant stones settled. Abella waited for the cave to become quiet before continuing.

"And maybe that is my way of saying I see things your way. You shared an experience with him that resulted in something beautiful and lasting. I can't understand what it means to be a mother, to hold a child or egg of my own. It isn't even something I want. But if I had found myself in your shoes, or legs as it were, I think I would have made the same choice. I wouldn't have considered anyone else's feelings in the matter."

The light was brighter now, and Abella looked back at her feet. Her legs and tail were pinched between two rocks. She shifted her tail around, which caused the troublesome boulders to move.

With a groan, she pulled herself forward and collapsed on her belly.

"I'm sorry about your egg," she continued. "When we return, I will help you look through the ashes until we find it."

Velvet sighed.

"If you say this child is different, then I trust you," Abella continued. "Because I know *he* will trust you. And if any of the others try to give you problems, they will have to go through me first."

She moved toward a nearby wall and used it to stand. Her knees hurt, but once she was upright, it was easy to stand. The mouth of the cave was nearby, and she limped her way toward it in a crouch to avoid smashing her head on the ceiling.

The sun was coming up, and she squinted into its light.

"We need to get back," she said. "The others are waiting for us. He is waiting for you."

The breeze stopped, allowing silence to descend on the cave. Abella half expected to hear the rustle of hairy legs or even Velvet snoring. She hadn't exactly held up her end of the conversation.

However, the silence that ensued was absolute. Other than the occasional drip of water, nothing could be heard.

"Velvet?" She turned around, the light shining in over her shoulders. The beam was just low enough to illuminate the top of the huddled form in the back of the cave.

Abella crouched and moved to where Velvet sat. Her eyes adjusted to the darkness, and she let out a gasp of surprise.

"*Non!*" She reached into the gap beneath the rock to pull Velvet free, convinced she had just stopped breathing. But the rigidity of the Arachne's body indicated it had been some time since Velvet had passed.

Stunned, Abella sat back on her haunches. How could this have happened? They had just been talking…right? Velvet's lower half was sprawled out, her damaged legs forming a spiral beneath her. She was hunched forward as if asleep, her dog tags clutched in a single hand and tearstains down her cheeks. The blue blood of the Arachne had formed a pool underneath her body, and Abella watched as a drop of it fell from Velvet's free hand and splashed into the puddle below.

It hadn't been water dripping after all.

"*Mon Dieu…*," she muttered, then backed away and out of the cave.

Velvet was dead. In the light of the rising sun, Abella stumbled until she found somewhere to sit, the world spinning around her. She was no stranger to death, but this felt different. It was like someone had twisted up her insides with a hot knife.

"But how?" she asked. Velvet had been talking to her just minutes ago, right? Looking down at her feet, she realized she was covered in bloody blue handprints.

It wasn't just that Velvet had died. The Arachne had given the rest of her life to save Abella's.

The heart fire erupted from Abella, and she tilted her head back to fire her rage into the sky. Birds in nearby trees took flight and scattered as the hot flame caused nearby snow to melt.

"NO!" Abella bit off the flame and put her face in her hands. Not only had Velvet died, but Abella had failed to protect her. It had been the one job Mike had given her, and she had screwed up.

What would she tell Mike? How could she even face him? She cried out in agony, raking her hands and feet against the ground.

"Leeds!" she screamed. No matter how much she hated herself right now, she hated him a thousand times more.

She walked back into the cave and knelt in front of Velvet.

"I am supposed to be the strong one," she told the Arachne. "And in my weakest moment, you were my protector. That makes you and your kin clan, and I shall never forget."

Abella took Velvet's hand and pried the dog tags free. Though they weighed next to nothing in her hands, it felt as though she moved the earth itself just to lift the chain over Velvet's head.

"May the Earth Mother watch over you," she said, her voice wavering. "I will make sure your sister receives these."

Back outside, she spent a few minutes using loose stones to block off the entrance. She didn't want Velvet's rest to be disturbed by scavengers.

Once the entrance was sealed, Abella took a deep breath and spread out her wings. Her right wing was fine, but her left wing was in bad shape. The membrane had been shattered out in several places, but the structural parts were still intact.

It could be much worse, she thought to herself. Maybe Ratu or Zel would have something to patch the holes. If so, she would be able to fly again, which meant Velvet hadn't just saved her life but perhaps her very soul.

"Every time I fly, I shall think of you." She turned to face the blocked entrance and bowed her head. "Thank you, Velvet."

Nobody is ever truly gone, Velvet replied, her voice vanishing on the wind.

Blinking in surprise, Abella nodded in agreement. Whether she had actually heard the Arachne didn't matter because she had a promise to keep. With a heavy heart, she turned toward the cabin and wrapped her wings around herself like a cloak, carefully tucking the damaged one inside.

The sunlight glistened off the dog tags around her neck.

A PRUNED BRANCH

The world was quiet, save for the occasional thump of melting snow. Abella trudged along what may have been a trail. She had some sense of where Mike was but dreaded meeting up with him. The dog tags around her neck were far heavier than anything she had ever carried, and she would often pause and touch them for strength. How would she break the news to him?

She wished she could fly, but that was out of the question. Her wing throbbed painfully as she pushed her way through the deeper drifts, and there was no way it would support her weight.

A few of the forest children were scattered through the woods. They were animals and hybrids she was unfamiliar with, but some Nirumbi children came out of hiding to greet her. She was surprised when they hooted to get her attention but even more so when they took her by the hand and led her away from the trail.

Minutes later, she found herself looking at a small camp of Nirumbi. They were huddled around a couple of fires for warmth. The children led her through the refugee camp to a large makeshift tent made of animal hides.

Abella pushed the flaps aside and walked in. Blankets had been placed on the ground, and each one was occupied by a Nirumbi. Upon closer inspection, she realized they were all injured.

"Why have you brought me here?" she asked, only to realize the children were gone.

"Because I told them to." Bigfoot rose from the corner, his eyes tired. The dim light of the tent made him look like a hairy shadow, and he stepped toward her. "I tracked Vee to the mountain but lost the trail. The mountain imploded sometime last night. This whole area is a mess. The Nirumbi needed my help, so…" He let out a heavy sigh. "Leeds had formed a cult, using the young warriors of the tribe. They slaughtered the others in the caves, and these were the ones who were lucky enough to get away. I told everyone to keep an eye out for anyone from the cabin and to bring them here."

"Where is the owl woman? Shouldn't she be here?"

"Gone. Leeds had her killed." Bigfoot knelt to help one of the Nirumbi sip water from a ceramic bowl. "Did you ever catch up to Velvet?"

Abella didn't know what to say. The moment of indecision was not missed by Bigfoot, who stood slowly with his fists at his side.

"Well?" he asked, an edge to his voice that she didn't like.

"I'm so sorry," she whispered, then let go of the dog tags she had unconsciously been holding. They jingled against her chest and then went still. "Leeds destroyed the cave while we were inside. Velvet saved my life but lost hers in the process."

Bigfoot let out a groan as if struck, then stomped past her and outside of the tent. She followed. The forest children gave him plenty of room as he stormed out of the camp, his breaths accompanied by a growl. Once safely away from the camp, he let out a roar and kicked down a tree.

"NO!" He grabbed onto his hair and pulled, ripping out giant clumps of fur before letting out a howl that scared the birds out of nearby trees. With a strangled cry, he fell to his knees and sobbed.

"I'm sorry, Darren, I'm so sorry." As he wept, Abella moved to his side and put a hand on his shoulder. His fur was surprisingly soft in her hands, and she wrapped her arms around his mighty neck and hugged him.

"I need you to help me get to Mike," she told him. "When he finds out… He's going to need us."

Bigfoot snarled, his body expanding with every breath he took until he was enormous. He cracked his knuckles and let out a growl.

"You point, I'll get us there."

Abella obeyed, and Bigfoot walked to a nearby clump of trees, opening a portal between them. Abella felt the distance between her and Mike shrink considerably through the portal and let out a sigh of relief.

Soon, they would be together again.

THE AIR WAS SO COLD THAT EVERY BREATH INWARD FELT LIKE DAGGERS, tearing away at Mike's lungs as he ran through the forest. He had been hunting Leeds for a few hours now, the Jersey Devil bouncing around the woods seemingly at random. Leeds would often stop for a bit, which made him think the demon was meeting with his followers.

The chill of the night had long ago permeated his boots and his coat, but his magic sustained him, warming him from within. With every step he took, he was that much closer to catching Leeds, to ripping the demon apart with his bare hands.

A tiny voice inside fought to gain his attention, but he was so consumed with rage that he ignored it. Behind him, Yuki and Dana struggled to keep up, the kitsune's labored breaths filling the silence of the woods. They had given up trying to speak with him, for he was a man possessed and could not be reached.

His magic had formed a tiny storm around him as he ran, sending ice and snow billowing outward as tendrils of light connected with the surrounding trees and animals. He could sense the forest waking up as it eased his passage and guided him to wherever Leeds had gone next.

In those brief moments of clarity, thoughts of Velvet bubbled to the surface. They were brief yet intense, and he was fairly certain frozen tears clung to his cheeks.

He caught movement in his peripheral vision, and a white stag bounded ahead of him and then vanished. It had been doing this for the last hour and would be waiting up ahead just to watch him. Sure enough, the stag stood on a rock Mike was forced to go around, but he couldn't help but notice that the beast stared him directly in the eyes.

Succeeding at a hunt doesn't mean you can skin a deer. The voice was faint but very persistent.

He ignored it and kept running. The stag outpaced him again and waited for him on top of a fallen tree.

A heart that lends itself so easily to others is easily broken. The stag grunted, sending a cloud of vapor into the air. *You've only had one branch pruned, Caretaker. Do you think you're ready to be a spear?*

He bared his teeth and hissed. Yelling would only alert Leeds that he was coming, and he didn't want the demon to have any time to prepare. Leeds was always one step ahead of them, and Mike needed every advantage he could get.

Throw not spears in a dark wood, Mike Radley! The stag stepped off the log and vanished.

"Fuck your metaphors," he spat between breaths in a low tone. He didn't need a lecture, an explanation, or even advice. What he needed was revenge, plain and simple. To hear Leeds beg, to squeeze whatever color blood could be spilled from his body.

The trees rustled around him, and he could see it in his mind. Up ahead there was a clearing where several creatures stood in a circle. At its center was a darkness that felt like poison, a stain on the landscape yearning for removal.

A guttural growl snuck free of his lips, and flickering motes of blue light formed in the air around him. They crackled in the crisp air, shifting colors until they turned red. Now transformed, they flew toward him and disappeared, hidden just below the surface of his skin.

His fingers trembled, but he couldn't tell if it was from anger or the cold. Yuki, in fox form, jumped onto a nearby rock and did a quick turn, her tails twirling widely as she shifted into human form. She opened her mouth to scold him, but he held a finger to his lips.

"Leeds is nearby." He pointed off toward where he sensed the darkness. "There are others. Nirumbi, I assume. Won't be easy."

"And then what? An ambush?" He could hear the anger in her whispering voice. "What the fuck do you think you're doing?"

"Revenge." Dana had caught up to them, her blade still folded up in her right hand. "Don't tell me you can't sense it. Something happened back at the cabin, and now we're out here to fuck up his day, right?"

Mike nodded.

"What happened, Mike?" Yuki crossed her arms. "We have a few seconds. Tell us."

"Velvet's dead." There were no tears to be shed, not right now. The words only served to fuel the fire that raged inside him.

Yuki gasped. "How?" she asked.

"Don't know. Felt her being ripped away in the Dreamscape." He looked over at Dana and was surprised to see that her bloodshot eyes were now brimming with tears. "Dana?"

"What?" She looked at the two of them in puzzlement, then wiped a tear from her face and examined it. "That's weird. It's like I feel it, but I don't."

"We can worry about it later. I'm going in. Anyone with Leeds is fair game." He turned to go, but a wall of snow blocked his departure.

"Not good enough." Yuki hopped over him and stood on the snow pile with her arms out. "You're mad, and that's fine. But you're also being stupid about this."

The red lights briefly appeared, swirling around Yuki like angry bees, but he pulled them back inside his body.

"You don't understand, Yuki. He has to pay." The trees around him groaned in agreement, and he could feel the ground rumble in anticipation. The forest was silent as a tomb and had been for most of his hunt. The wildlife had recognized that he was the top predator and was doing its best to stay out of his way.

"And he will, but we have a plan. Capture him, yes, but tear him apart? He can't be killed. If you go in there looking for murder, all you are doing is costing us time."

Mike growled. "And so what if I am? Let's tear him apart, devote every day to a unique brand of torture! Drown him, stab him, set him on fire, rip off—"

Sharp icicles appeared in a circle around him, trapping him in the center. Their sharpened points were at neck level, and even the act of turning his head pressed one into the soft flesh beneath his ear.

"We made each other a promise, do you remember?" Her ears twitched as she glared at him. "I would be your weapon, remember? And in return, if you should ever lose yourself like Emily did…"

"You would stop me." He glowered at her through the ice. "But this isn't about learning dark magic or trying to gain power. This is about justice, Yuki!" The swirling lights shifted around him, passing through the ice and melting it.

"Don't." Dana got in between them. "Take it from someone who gets it. You aren't being logical, Mike. Not only are your emotions out of control, but so is your magic."

"Why are you stopping me?" He pushed forward against the nearest icicle, his magic circling the conical shape and turning it to ice crystals. "You both understand how this feels!"

"And that's exactly why we're stopping you." Yuki shook her head. "We came to help you, but you need to do this the right way."

He took a deep breath, focusing on her words. Of all people, Yuki would know best how this had felt. Emily had been the love of her life, and that same woman would abandon her on another world and steal her eye.

The eye. Mike put his hand in his pocket and caressed the glassy orb. The owl had hastened her own death just to hand over a way to contain Leeds. Was he really willing to risk everything just to feed his own desires?

Yes, you are. A band of darkness stole through the forest, seizing Yuki and Dana around the waist. They both cried out in surprise as they were ripped away from him. Dana dropped her sword, the blade pinging off a nearby rock. *Come for me, Caretaker! Show me how strong you are without your allies!*

Mike's magic ignited, destroying his icy prison and scattering the snow around his feet. He paused just long enough to pick up Dana's sword and then sprinted through the woods.

Hesitation had cost him. He had decided to hear out his friends rather than act, and he was about to lose someone else; he could feel it. One by one, the branches would be pruned until all that was left of him was a weapon.

Yes, that's right. Come for me, mortal. Take your revenge.

The red motes were now spreading out into the forest, each one hissing with sinister energy as it disappeared into the woods. His footfalls were so fast that he hardly felt the ground. It was almost like flying.

You're worthless, you little pervert. His mother's voice was harsh, grating against his very soul. *You only care about them because you can stick your dick in them.*

"No!" he screamed in response, desperate to stay focused on Leeds's location.

They represent power. Amir's voice was smug. *You fear losing access to the power they provide. And you will fail.*

"Not true!" Trees were now bending out of his way, their branches moving up to allow him safe passage. "They're important to me because of who they are, not what they can give!"

You'll make a mistake. Sarah laughed in his mind. *It won't be the first time or the last. So who's gonna die this time?*

They were all laughing now, his mind filled with their echoes.

When he burst into the clearing, he saw that in the middle Leeds had constructed an altar out of wood and stone. At its center was an upside down cross, and a group of Nirumbi were frantically trying to strap Yuki onto it. The kitsune was fighting them, but the shadow bands kept grabbing at her hands and feet. Standing above the altar, Leeds was doing a little dance as the Nirumbi worshipping him from below turned to face Mike. There were maybe a hundred of them, each one with a fanatical glint in their eyes.

Behind the altar, a bonfire had been lit. Dana was being dragged toward it, a panicked look on her face.

Your world is going to burn, Mike Radley! The shadow cackled with glee. *Your world is going to—*

Mike let out a horrifying screech, forcing his magic free of his lips, willing death on his enemies. The banshee's scream was accompanied by a wave of force and light that scattered the Nirumbi lurking nearby and blasted Leeds from his perch. The demon fell backward into his own bonfire, and the shadows pinning Yuki in place vanished.

"Mike!" She screamed his name, her fur turning white as she grabbed the Nirumbi nearest to her and flash froze him. Spinning around, she used the Nirumbi as a projectile and sent it flying toward Dana's captors. "He's in your head, don't listen to him!"

Clenching his hands, Mike sprinted toward Dana, his own magic forming bands of light that scattered his enemies. His whole body tingled as he casually dodged arrows, clubs, and even rocks that were thrown at him. Some of the Nirumbi, each marked with a bloody handprint, panicked and ran, but his magic grabbed them and pulled them back into the fray.

"Mike, stop!" Yuki's words were lost when he howled again. Those closest to him were blown away, their bodies smashing into trees and rocks. The clearing was already red with blood, and he licked his lips in anticipation.

Dana was wrestling with one of the Nirumbi, so he tossed her the sword. She snatched it out of the air and killed her foe with a bloody thrust.

"LEEDS!" Mike sent his magic into the fire, tearing it apart and scattering ashes to the sky. "I CAN FEEL YOU IN THERE!"

The Jersey Devil burst into the sky, his wings pumping as he tried to get away. Desperate, Mike reached into his pocket and pulled out the orb. Pointing the pupil at the devil, he willed it to work.

Intent. It may not be the first rule of magic, but it was going to be his. "No escape, you shadowy fuck!" Magic crackled along his forearm and sank into the orb before turning into a crimson beam of energy that roped itself around Leeds's legs. The devil, now caught, looked back at Mike in dismay.

He waved the orb toward the ground, causing Leeds to slam into the ice and snow. Satisfied, he swung it from side to side, smashing the Jersey Devil against the trees as he crossed the distance between them. His precognition filled his chest with ice, and he threw himself backward to avoid a cluster of arrows that littered the ground around him.

Yuki pincushioned his attackers, then raised clawed hands and created a barrier of ice around the clearing. She collapsed to one knee, panting from the exertion.

"You may have won the battle, Caretaker, but this is a war of attrition!" Leeds tried to crawl, his hands digging in the snow. Mike leaped on his back and fought to roll him over. The crimson light disappeared as the orb fell to the side, forgotten.

"You killed her!" He smashed a fist into Leeds's face. The devil brayed like a donkey in pain as red light flashed from Mike's knuckles. "You killed her, you killed her!"

I did, Leeds replied in his mind. *And I killed the gargoyle too!*

Mike screamed in the devil's face, his magic shredding the flesh from along his muzzle. Leeds flinched, then tried to kick Mike off of him.

"Not going to happen!" He smashed his fists into Leeds over and over. Leeds retaliated by pushing images of Velvet begging into his mind.

Something popped in Mike's hand, and he could no longer hold his fist shut. Howling in desperation, Mike picked up the owl's eye and used it to bash Leeds's skull in.

After the third hit, his magic flowed into the orb and sent a shock wave through his body. His muscles tensed as images flitted through his mind, thousands of them.

Memories flooded his mind, centuries worth of magical lore, of exploring the limits of enchantment and spellcasting. He could see them now, the owl and her sisters, feel the possibilities that had been open to them. They had hunted, they had killed. They had survived on knowledge and power alone, and he craved that for himself.

His magic curled around him, forming into crimson bands of light that hovered over his body like a spider trapping its prey. Panic crossed Leeds's features as those limbs descended and sank into his flesh. Black blood flowed from open wounds that no longer healed. Shadows tried to rip Mike free, but his magic would not allow it.

He could see it now, the intricate process that had put Leeds together. A human soul bonded to demonic flesh, incapable of transformation. That was his weakness, his inability to be anything other than the monster he was. The magic was like lines of code now, and code was something Mike understood.

It was suddenly simple. He could see the flow of magic, understood what it would take to disrupt it. Leeds was now bared before him as a being before a god, and Mike was ready to pass judgment.

Around him, Yuki and Dana were screaming his name as the magic swirled overhead, forming into a crimson tempest of energy. Chunks of the Jersey Devil were being ripped free and sucked up into the maelstrom. If he wanted to, he could destroy Leeds. Not just his body but his soul as well. There would be no resurrections, no coming back to taunt him.

Energy flowed through his limbs as he cackled madly, then raised the hand holding the orb to the sky. The energy coalesced around it, forming into a vibrating blade.

My sister was never much of a fighter, and she doesn't attract them.

He hesitated, unsure if the voice was just a memory or something else. The world around him was moving slowly, almost as if reality itself was holding its breath.

More images came. This time, he was seeing the forest from the owl's point of view, watching as she met the Nirumbi for the first time. They had been afraid of her, but she had gained their trust.

A maternal feeling overwhelmed him as more images came. The Nirumbi hunting deer in the woods. Sitting around the owl as she told them stories. Letting her play with their children.

She spoke to the mystical creatures of the woods, pleaded with them to band together and find someplace safe, somewhere away from humans. He watched as many of them died, from forest fires, deforestation, and even men in white coats with swords. So many painful memories surfaced, and the pain filled him up until he threatened to burst.

And then it would shift. Long walks with Nirumbi elders, speaking about philosophy to a giant bear that walked on stilted legs, flying through the sky with an emerald serpent. There were peaceful times amid the chaos, and almost none of them involved power or magic of any kind. She had formed bonds with the other creatures, bonds that had eventually cost her life.

His own face appeared. There was an upswell of hope that was almost scary to experience, and then she was speaking to him with her clacking beak. The world was still now, save for the sound of his own heart beating deep within.

You should know that magic like yours can be quite powerful but only if it can be controlled. Be warned that it has a life of its own, very much like a roaring fire. If you aren't careful, it will consume you.

The words resonated with him, and he contemplated the blade of magic in his right hand. He could drive it into Leeds right now, sever the bond between spirit and body and banish him from the world.

There's always a cost. They were his own words now, and they gave him pause. For the first time in hours, he truly saw the brutality of the magic he had summoned. It had indeed become a wildfire, one that threatened to escape him. If he destroyed Leeds, it wasn't just on a physical level but a spiritual one. Immortality required a high price to achieve, but what was the cost of destroying a soul?

There were suddenly too many questions, and he could feel the pressure building in his head. He had summoned this magic, and it demanded an outlet, craved the change that would come once it was released.

I am not just a structure in the forest. The stag was watching him from the edge of the clearing, its dark eyes brimming with power. *I am also the ground beneath your feet and the trees around you.*

Mike screamed, desperately trying to regain control of his hand. The blade was swinging down in slow motion, aimed for the center of Leeds's chest. The magic had been born of rage, and it hungered for the demon's blood.

Your true power isn't something that grows from within. The stag walked toward the trees, immune to the slowing of time. It flicked its tail once and then looked back at him. *It is also your connection with me and with others.*

"Aagh!" Fiery pain lanced through his shoulder as he tried to force the blade to stop. Leeds's eyes had widened in terror as the blade moved closer to the demon, now less than a foot away.

When last we spoke, you did not carry such an earthen aura. He saw himself through the owl woman's eyes once more, but now he saw the magical aura that surrounded him. It was a cloud of colors that sank deep into the ground and spread out like tree roots. *It is very much like the fae but also the magic of the forest.*

The fae. The forest. His mind flashed to Titania, then back to the incident in the clearing with Abella. The queen of the fae was triggering a memory of his own.

This little shit stain wants to be king of the forest. Besides fucking up the flow of my woods, he is also the reason you cannot get home. He couldn't tell if he was remembering the cabin's words or hearing them live in his head. *Your compassion and kindness have brought you some very powerful allies.*

Allies. From the corner of his eye, he saw Yuki summoning a barrage of ice and skewering the Nirumbi. Dana was frozen midkick, sending another one of their warriors across the clearing.

Someone must care for the forest children. He was the owl woman now, holding out her eye to Mike. He could see the concern in his own face, the lines of despair that were already forming. This was the Mike he had been, the one who didn't know he would never see Velvet alive again.

Yuki took the eye from the owl woman's hands, and then Bigfoot leaned in, his body smelling of cloves. Below Mike, the steady humming of the forest was beating in time with his own heart as the owl woman's final memory came to a close.

Now sleep and be one with the woods, Bigfoot told her as everything went dark.

The blade was inches away, and Mike's eyes locked on his hand. He had become so lost in his rage that he had forgotten who he was, what he was meant to be. His magic had been summoned in a fit of rage, and he could now feel it simmering beneath his skin, spreading through his body like a poison.

Driving that blade into Leeds would kill him, but it would change Mike forever. Over the last nine months, his actions had not only shaped his magic but had changed him. Acts of love, lust, and kindness had changed him for the better. Would participating in this act of rage do the same?

He tried to withdraw the magic, but it burned deep inside him, like inhaling hot smoke. Time was going back to normal, and the next few moments of his life would change everything. He had come into this fight with the attitude that nothing else mattered, but he knew now that it wasn't true.

No matter what was going on in his life, there were still plenty of people who mattered to him.

And right now, they needed him to come back alive.

"No," he muttered through gritted teeth, feeling his magic try to feed his rage back into him. It was trying to establish a feedback loop, and he fought back. The anger needed to go somewhere else, but where?

The magic couldn't be stopped; the spell had already begun. He thought back to sitting at the table with Dana, wondering if magic was like energy. The sparks had sunk into the wood of the table and vanished. He couldn't let it back into his own body, nor could he use it to kill Leeds. It would have to go somewhere else, but where could he put it without causing destruction?

Be one with the woods. It wasn't Bigfoot's voice he heard but the owl woman's. He could almost feel her gaze on him, see those intense eyes peering through his very soul.

Screaming in fury, he stopped fighting the magic and fought to adjust his aim. The blade twisted and missed Leeds's chest, piercing the demon's wing and sinking deep into the ground. Blue-and-red flames ate away at the membrane of the wing, searing the flesh as Leeds howled in agony.

Crimson bands of light swirled around the two of them as Mike forced his mind into the ground, seeking out every strand of life he could find. He could feel the land beneath him, his magic touching every tree, bush, and animal. Their minds were briefly part of him, and he was them, and then he was everywhere. For a split second, he and the land were one, and it felt like his head would explode from the pressure.

He channeled his anger, grief, and rage into the spell, willing it to depart from him, to feed the land and make it grow. In that moment, he felt how everything was connected, saw how he could turn tragedy and death into beauty and life.

"Velvet." He whispered her name like a prayer, letting her go.

The swirling maelstrom of magic channeled itself through his elbow and down into the bowels of the earth itself, spreading far and wide. His rage was sucked along with it as the magic spread out like a blanket and warmed the tired soil beneath. Stubborn foliage pushed its way through the snow, and the trees shook off their snow and held their branches high in pride.

There was a loud snap, and pain flared up Mike's arm as the last of the magic passed through it. Gasping in agony, he was unable to stop Leeds from kicking him hard in the chest, which sent him sprawling across the snow.

"Fool!" Leeds leaped to his feet and laughed. "You were so close, closer than anyone's ever gotten!" He flapped his wings and jumped into the air, only to tumble about before coming to rest in the low branches of a tree. Puzzled, the Jersey Devil extended the wing Mike had pierced to reveal a large hole.

"Looks like your flying days are over," Mike told him between gritted teeth.

"This? This will heal." Leeds summoned the shadows around him. "But your friends? They will be dead fore—"

The tree swung one of its upper branches into Leeds, cracking him in the back of the skull and knocking him down to the ground. He landed with a thud, then cried out in pain when flowers burst out of the snow and wrapped around his neck.

What few Nirumbi were left froze as the trees around them came to life. Tree roots ripped free from beneath the snow and grabbed Leeds by the ankles to drag him away. He let out a cry of terror as the beasts of the woods descended on him, scratching and biting as he passed. The roots transported him from trunk to trunk as nearby bushes scoured his flesh with thorns and sharp branches.

Mike stood, wincing as he tucked his arm into his belly. Nearby trees smashed the altar as he followed after Leeds.

"What happened?" Dana sniffed the air, then looked at him. "It's your magic. I can smell it everywhere."

"I woke up the forest," he told them as he followed Leeds's cries. "It might not be alive in a way we can understand , but it knows a shit stain when it sees one."

The trees were unable to move Leeds quickly, but between his damaged wing and the consecutive animal attacks, he was unable to escape. Occasionally a portal would open between the trees, and the devil would be tossed through and carried away. Mike was surprised at first when the portals remained open for him and the others, but the trees that touched him conveyed feelings of mutual grief and respect. When he touched their branches, it felt like greeting an old friend.

A song played in his mind, one only he could hear. The forest shared more memories with him, memories of Darren and his daughters as they played in the woods. There was an older Arachne who looked startlingly like Eulalie, and he caught brief glimpses of their lives in no particular order. The girls as children, chasing their mother through the trees. Darren trying to give Eulalie a piggyback ride. Velvet trying to sneak up on Bigfoot while he was reading a Harlequin romance novel with Fabio on the cover. They had been the keepers of this land for decades, and the forest had not forgotten.

The forest would never forget.

Leeds shouted in agony. Wolves had emerged from the woods to tear chunks out of him as he went past. Mike had worried he might end up dying, but the animals seemed to know and understand the limit of what the demon could survive. The land was pissed, and it was letting him know.

"Mike, you're bleeding."

"Huh?" He held up his injured arm and winced. The owl's orb had shattered in his hand, the shards of glass slicing up his flesh. His arm was numb from the bicep down, which probably wasn't a good sign.

"Gods." Yuki reached into her coat and pulled out a piece of fabric. "Your hand is a mess."

"We can deal with that later." He nodded toward Leeds, who was being pulled up a stream. "I need to see this through."

"Mike, what happened back there, I…" Yuki grabbed his good hand and squeezed it. "I thought we were going to lose you. Your eyes, they were—"

"Don't." He leaned onto her and was surprised at how warm she felt. "I don't want to talk about it. I know how close I came. And you would have been right to stop me. You need to hear me say that."

She nodded, and he suddenly felt so tired. Dana got on his other side, and they helped him through the woods as they neared the boundary. They had come down in elevation, enough that the snow was actually gone from several places, and the forest was making sure to drag Leeds through all the muddy parts.

They were at the boundary when a roar came through the forest. It was a howl of pain, and Mike saw a portal between the trees. Bigfoot stepped through it, his features borderline feral. Behind him was Abella, her eyes widening at the sight of Mike.

His eyes flicked to the dog tags on her chest.

"LEEDS!" Bigfoot stomped over toward the devil, his huge body making the ground tremble. He swatted away the branches as they tried to form a barrier, then roared to chase away the animals. Relief shined in the devil's eyes as Bigfoot raised a giant fist to strike him.

"What do you think you're doing, you damned Yeti?" Mike wasn't even sure why he said those particular words, but they caused Bigfoot to spin around, anger in his eyes.

"He killed Vee! He killed my fluffy girl!" He grabbed Leeds by the ankle and picked him up, ripping the roots that held him down. "He has to pay!"

"And he will. But right now, stomping his ugly ass is what he wants." Mike approached Bigfoot and stared into the Sasquatch's eyes. "He wants you to take a piece out of him. Don't give him what he wants."

Bigfoot huffed for a couple of seconds, then roared in Mike's face, spraying him with spit. "You don't understand, he—"

"I know." He put his good hand on Bigfoot's arm and squeezed. "This piece of shit owes you a pound of flesh. But you have to understand, he's banking on it. He's been playing us since we got here, and your only response so far is to go storming off in a rage. If you do that here, if you crush his skull just to feel a little bit better, she will have died for nothing."

Bigfoot hesitated, his hot breath filling the air with vapor. His fur was ruffled like a cornered animal's, and his lips kept pulling back to reveal his teeth.

"There are better ways to make him pay." Mike stared at Leeds. "I have a whole house full of people who would love to sit down and discuss how to punish him. You and Eulalie *will* be part of that discussion. She deserves a say as well. But right now I need you to stand down."

"Pathetic." Leeds spat on the ground as he dangled upside down, his tail whipping uselessly against Bigfoot's chest. "It's because you don't have the guts to kill me. Go ahead, *Yeti.* Break the barrier first and then crush me, snap my neck, torture me until I beg for death! You've gotten soft, listening to filthy fucking humans!"

Bigfoot looked at Leeds, then Mike. Doubt, grief, and anger all played about behind his furry visage before he let out a pained groan as if injured. With a grunt, he threw Leeds through the air. The Jersey Devil's body passed through the red barrier at the edge of the property. With a quiet pop, the spell dissipated, and Leeds bounced off a tree and fell to the ground.

"You're the big hero now, aren't you, Caretaker?" Leeds chuckled and stood. "Gonna run home to your *family* and try to save them. Don't look so surprised. I can hear your thoughts. I know all about the angel, the horsemen. I'm willing to bet that—"

"Shut this fucker up," Mike snapped, and a massive pine outside the boundary bent itself over and smashed Leeds into the ground with a pair of long branches. The demon was flattened beneath heavy boughs, then roots ripped free of the earth to wrap him up tight into a bundle.

"How?" Leeds asked, his fiery coal eyes blazing. "These trees aren't part of your land!"

Mike approached Leeds, then crouched and smirked. "The forest doesn't belong to anyone," he told the Jersey Devil. "The land doesn't belong to me either. I had the choice to destroy you, and we both know it. I think maybe you even welcomed it, you poor, tormented soul. But that's not who I am." He stood and walked over to the nearest tree, then placed his hand on it. "And it isn't who I plan to become. All I did was let the land know how I felt about you. And it agreed."

He sensed a presence over his shoulder, then turned and saw the stag watching him from between the trees.

"I know you said you would keep him out," he told the beast. "But would you consider letting him back in? I need somewhere to keep him for a little bit."

"Who are you talking to?" Bigfoot asked, craning his neck to look around.

Mike shrugged. "I'm not entirely sure, to be honest," he replied.

The stag bowed its head, and the trees outside the boundary passed Leeds back over. Animals appeared from the trees and bit into Leeds's flesh, then dragged him through the woods.

"The forest is going to hold him for us." He put a hand on Bigfoot's forearm. "Follow him and figure out where that is, make sure he can't escape. Meet us at the cabin after so we can plan our next steps."

The Sasquatch deflated, his eyes brimming with tears. "You speak for the forest," he muttered beneath his breath. "You're just full of surprises." He wandered off with Leeds, his shoulders drooping. It was clear the Sasquatch had mixed feelings but even clearer to Mike that this was the correct choice. Allowing Leeds to wander off again would just create a problem in the future that he might not have a solution for.

Even worse, someone else could die because of it. He winced, feeling the pain of Velvet's death anew. Though his anger was gone, his sorrow had been planted deep.

"Abella." He walked over to the gargoyle and put his hands on her shoulders. "Are you okay?"

She looked at him for several moments, then shrugged. "I've had better days," she told him.

With a sigh, he touched the dog tags around her neck. The soft jingle reminded him of Velvet, her head tilted to one side with a smile on her face.

"Here." Abella started to lift the tags off her neck, but he stopped her.

"Hold on to them for me," he said. "I'm about to be neck deep in shit soon, and I know you'll take care of them."

She looked away from him, her tail thumping on the ground. "I can barely take care of myself, much less anyone else." Her voice was harsh and laced with venom.

"You are nothing short of amazing," he said, then placed his forehead against hers, his voice wavering. "I'm broken inside, and it feels like the world is spinning, but if I had lost you too, I want you to know it would have killed me."

Firm hands gripped his back as she held him close.

"She lost her life saving me," she whispered. "How can I live with that?"

He tried to answer her, but the spinning sensation intensified. He mumbled something, the words dripping from his mouth like molasses as he lost consciousness.

It would have taken Abella and Mike far longer to return to the cabin if not for the fact that the forest seemed to sense their urgency to return. Abella cradled Mike's unconscious form as they were led by deer through a series of glittering portals that returned them to the cabin.

Smoke rose from the chimney, and Quetzalli burst out of the front door, her cheeks and eyes red from crying.

"You left me here!" she shouted, then paused when she saw Mike. "Is he okay?"

"Exhausted," Dana replied, then took Quetzalli by the hand. "Sorry we ran off. It was everything we could do to even keep up with him."

Yuki put her hand on Quetzalli's shoulder. "We need to get him inside. He's freezing."

"Yeah, okay." She walked back toward the cabin and opened the door. Emery shot out through the gap and hovered overhead.

"Big sister!" he cried, then zoomed down to hover in front of her face. "You've been injured!"

"I'll be fine," she replied, a little surprised the imp could tell she had been hurt.

"Where is Miss Velvet?" he asked. "Did you catch up to her?"

"She didn't make it."

The little imp let out a pained cry and simply fell out of the sky, clutching his chest and landing on the ground with his wings outstretched. Dana picked him up and held him to her chest as they went into the cabin.

Despite the warmth of the fire, the space felt lonely, as if the building itself knew something had changed. Abella took Mike to his room and placed him on the bed. Yuki helped cover him up with blankets as Quetzalli pulled his shoes off.

"What happened to his arm?" Quetzalli asked, staring at the purple mass.

"I'm not sure." They had walked back in silence, so Abella hadn't bothered asking. However, she had noticed that everything from his right elbow down to his fingers had turned a mottled purple color, like one giant bruise.

"He channeled a massive spell through it," Yuki replied softly. "Essentially used living tissue as a magic wand. His fingers are all cut up. We may need to stitch the wounds."

"On it." Dana walked in carrying the suture kit Eulalie had made for her last year.

Mike groaned in his sleep as Dana and Yuki started working on his arm. The kitsune was fairly certain there were broken bones, and Dana stitched up the worst wounds on his hands, licking her fingers off when she was done. Yuki created some ice compresses to help mitigate swelling in his arms, then used a tarot card and a kitchen knife to fashion him a makeshift brace.

Abella watched them in silence. When they were done, they tucked him in. Yuki transformed into a fox and took her place at the foot of the bed. Dana and Quetzalli left, leaving Abella to watch over him.

Almost an hour passed before she took off the dog tags and set them on the bedside table. Trying to move silently, she walked out of the room and shut the door behind her.

Emery sat on the kitchen table across from Dana. The little imp was staring forlornly at nothing. Quetzalli was scrounging up food for a proper meal, which consisted solely of soup cans that hadn't gotten consumed earlier.

Despite Abella's phenomenal hearing, the house was eerily quiet.

Unable to do anything of use, she went outside. The air was crisp, and the forest around the cabin was actively shaking off snow. It was surreal to see trees moving their own branches, and the animals of the forest seemed to pay their movement no attention.

Abella walked over to the remains of the barn. The fire had burned hot, and there wasn't much of anything to go through. Still, she picked her way through the scorched timbers until she found the melted remains of the jeep.

"Merde," she muttered, then spent several minutes clearing debris off the top of it. Once the cabin was revealed, she dug her talons into the dashboard and ripped it away to reveal the contents of the glovebox. Inside there were chunks of melted plastic and what looked like melted wax from a box of crayons. She dug through the mess, grumbling to herself as she paused every couple of minutes to wipe her fingers off on a nearby piece of metal.

"Big sister?"

Abella turned around and saw Emery sitting on the burned remains of a stud. He was hugging his knees to his chest.

"Hey." She wiped her fingers off again, then turned to face the little imp. "How are you feeling?"

"Miserable." He hunched forward, looking almost like he would disappear into his wings. "It feels like there's a pressure inside my body, like I'm going to explode if I can't let it out. I don't know what to do with myself."

"That is called grief." She moved closer to him and crouched so they were at eye level. "Have you never experienced it before?"

He shrugged. "I don't think so," he informed her. "When I was created, my job was to take care of this place and any who were welcome here. I'm an elemental. I'm only happy when I'm doing my job. It's really the only thing I've ever known for sure. I learned about sadness when Darren and Ana died, but it never felt anything like this."

She nodded, then touched his foot with a finger. "You have lived more in the last few decades than you have in all the rest of your life, haven't you?"

He pondered this for a moment, his eyes widening at the revelation.

"It is something I have come to realize myself," she added. "Creatures like us can live for centuries, not realizing the joy and warmth that can come from a loving home. Darren and Ana, they got a chance to live full lives here. I think maybe you understand that an entire lifetime was stolen from Velvet, a life that should have been full of laughter and happiness. Now that we know how much joy can be crammed into such a short time, we recognize the true tragedy of a life cut short. My own heart feels broken, and I was not as close to her as you were."

The imp let out a sigh, then shook out his wings.

"I feel like I can't fly anymore," he told her. "I feel too heavy now. Like I'm carrying a giant weight in my chest."

She patted him on the head. "It may take some time, but you will know the joy of the sky once again."

"But is that okay?" He tilted his head to one side, considering her words. "I feel guilty wanting to feel better. It feels so wrong."

"Wanting to feel better doesn't betray those we have lost. After all, our time here is still limited." She looked up at the sun, squinting into its harsh rays. Knowing now that it was a sight she might not have seen if not for Velvet, she closed her eyes and cherished the warmth. "No matter how long you think you have, death has a way of sneaking up on you."

"My kind don't have souls," he told her. "When I die, I just become rocks and sand once again."

"Perhaps that is true," she told him. "But I am starting to learn that nothing is as simple as we believe it to be."

"You are hurt." He cleared his throat and stood. "I can tell by the way you hold your wing. I almost lost a wing myself, one time. Velvet…" Emery choked on her name. "She got into an argument with her mom and slammed the front door as I was coming in."

Abella winced. "I am indeed damaged," she told him. What she didn't tell him was that she was afraid to look closer at the damage. She was still in shock from discovering Velvet's body and may have lied to herself about how bad her wing actually was.

"I may be able to help," he told her, standing to his full height.

"I'm not sure you can." She smiled at him. "But thank you for offering."

"You misunderstand." He stomped his foot in indignation. "I am an earth elemental. In the same way they are stitching together the master's wounds, I may be able to assist you with yours."

"You can do that?" she asked, incredulous.

Emery nodded. "I can. It would give me something to do," he told her with confidence. "I could use something to do right now."

Shrugging, she unfurled her wings. The look of shock on Emery's face when he saw what was left of her damaged wing almost made her walk away, but he demanded that she hold still while he inspected her joints. The little imp's wings fluttered as he checked her body, pausing every now and then to mutter under his breath.

"The structure is good," he declared after landing on her shoulder. "The joint here is the most important, and it remains undamaged." He kicked at the base of her wing where it met her shoulder blade for emphasis. "These holes that you have will not close on their own. They are too ragged, and the wound will become like a human scar. Useless for flying."

"So you can't help me."

"I never said that." He leaped off her shoulder and flew toward the house. When he was about twenty feet away, he turned around. "Come, I have just the thing."

Figuring she had nothing to lose, she followed him. He took her back inside the cabin, where Quetzalli greeted them with a ladle in her hand. The cabin was still quiet but felt less like a tomb.

"Can you keep a secret?" he asked.

Abella nodded.

Emery looked over her shoulder. She turned around and saw that Quetzalli was busy in the kitchen while Dana sat on the couch with a pair of earbuds in. The imp held a finger to his lips and led her beneath the stairs and into a small storage area.

"Down here," he whispered, then put his hands on the wall. Green light surrounded his fingers, and a section of wood paneling slid to one side. Inside, she could see light glittering off a stash of silver coins.

"I don't understand," she said as he pulled several out and handed them over to her. "What are we doing?"

"We need this," he informed her. "You need to have silver for powerful earth magic. It's why my kind love it so much. It's a powerful catalyst. Same applies to dragons, especially of the earth variety. With enough of it, I can help you fix your wing."

"You really think so?" She looked at the coins in her hand, afraid to let herself hope.

"I know so," he stated matter-of-factly. "My leg got broken off once by a hunter who shot me. I used a silver dollar from the late eighteen hundreds, and...oh no!"

Emery's wings flapped frantically as he dug deeper into his stash. The little imp was making choking sounds as he tossed coins onto the ground. Abella picked one up and saw that the silver on it was tarnished badly. The profile on the coin was almost nonexistent, as if it had been rubbed away.

"What's wrong?" she asked, but he threw a few more coins out. These ones weren't just tarnished but looked as if acid had etched away their features, leaving behind dark pits.

"It's all gone bad!" he declared, then crawled into the hole and grunted. When he scooted back out, he threw a blackened stone on the ground. Abella picked it up and recognized it immediately. She had pulled it out of the head of the serpent from the lake.

"Silver tarnishes, but it doesn't go bad," she said, then held the stone up to the light. It felt like weeks ago that she had pulled it from the serpent's head. She could have sworn the stone had been a ruby.

"Something happened, it's..." Emery went quiet, his gaze locked on something in the hole. "Oh. Oh my."

Curious what had his attention, Abella flattened her body to the floor to see what he was looking at. The inside panel of the wall went farther back than she realized, revealing the size of Emery's secret stash. The coins inside looked as if the silver had been stripped from them, and she could see where it had gone.

In the middle of the stash, as if sitting in a nest, was a metallic blue egg with silver swirls running along its outside edges.

"Where did you find this?" she asked.

Emery folded his hands between his legs and sat down. "After you destroyed the others," he whispered. "I was there when Velvet was laying them, in case she needed help. Sometimes her mom needed help. She hid this one in the glove box, and I snuck it out when Dana started working on the car."

"I see." She reached toward the egg, but Emery blocked her hand.

"Please." He shook his head fervently. "Don't break it. I was only going to grab enough coins to help you. You weren't supposed to see it. It's all that I have left of her, I—"

"Emery." She touched him calmly on the head, her eyes on the egg. It looked vastly different from the clutch she had shattered. "I owe Velvet my life. The least I can do is ensure that her legacy lives on."

He bit his lip, then let out a sigh and stepped aside.

Abella reached into the stash, picked the egg up, and held it gently in both hands. Pain blossomed in her chest as she held the egg against her chest and mourned once more for the dead.

MIKE SAT ON THE SHORE OF THE DREAMSCAPE, HIS EYES OUT ON THE HORIZON. Spectral arms clutched him from behind as Tink sat on his lap. He had wrapped his arms around the goblin and was using her as a headrest while Cecilia hugged him tight.

The others sat on the beach with him, but nobody spoke. A gloom had settled over the island, one that pressed down so hard that it threatened to squeeze out any remaining joy. The Technicolor was all gray now and moved about sluggishly where the ocean gripped the sand.

His right arm was smoky. The few times he had contemplated it, it kept blurring itself out as if being censored on a show.

Dark shadows watched him with angry eyes from beneath the waves. He wasn't entirely certain what they were, but he could feel their anger whenever they breached the surface and hissed. Were they a manifestation of his wrath? Or perhaps something far more sinister that had been waiting to catch him if he fell from grace?

"That's a good way to think of them."

The voice startled him, and he looked over his shoulder to see the woman from the cabin standing a few yards away. She was barefoot in the sand, but he noticed she wasn't leaving any footprints.

"What are you doing here?" he asked.

"Mourning, like you." She smiled sadly, and he noticed she was wearing black. Her hair flowed behind her, blowing by a nonexistent breeze. "The forest grieves for its fallen child."

"So you're the forest."

"Nope." She winked. "It's far more complicated than that."

"Dare I ask?"

"You really shouldn't." She squinted at the creatures below the water. "If you hadn't heeded my advice when you did, you would probably be dead. Or worse, with them."

"What are they?"

"Trouble." She summoned a bow from the air and pulled back on its string. A golden arrow appeared moments before she fired. It streaked through the air and pierced one of the creatures the moment it surfaced. It let out a screech of pain, causing the water around it to turn black and then freeze. "There isn't a word for them. They're scavengers, hovering at the boundaries of reality while patiently waiting for their next meal. Most of the time they feed on fear, sustaining themselves on sheer terror alone. But you? You're not just a meal, not anymore. You may be a means for them to cross over into this realm, which is something you must never allow to happen."

He frowned. "That sounds very much like the kind of warning you gave me earlier. Did you know Velvet was going to die?" He tried to muster some anger to go along with his words, but he had given it all to the forest.

"I didn't, but I've been part of the game for a very long time, Caretaker. There are certain patterns that repeat themselves, and all I did was warn you about a potential threat." She nocked another arrow and let it fly, piercing another creature. When this one shrieked, the water exploded and sent a geyser of steam into the air.

"Is that even hurting them?" he asked.

"It breaks their connection, albeit temporarily. They shouldn't even be here, but your misery has allowed them in. As long as you don't hand yourself over to them, they can't hurt you. They are a natural consequence of becoming a bigger player in the game."

"I don't want to play the game," he said, then lowered his gaze. "Not if it means losing people I love."

"We're always playing someone's game, Caretaker." She dismissed the bow and sat down next to him. "Order and chaos. Life or death. Some games can't ever be won; you're simply playing until you lose."

"Sounds grim." He sighed, squeezing Tink so tight that she let out a squeak. "I know you can't tell me your name, but what do I call you, anyway? Cabin? Forest? Autumn? Meadow?"

When she didn't respond, he turned to see she had vanished.

"Figures," he muttered. Out in the water, something briefly surfaced and then disappeared. It was roughly between the two creatures that had been shot, a black mass that moved toward the shore.

Worried, Mike stood up as the black creature rode a sudden wave up onto the shore and then crawled its way through the surf until it stood on its back legs. it regarded him from beneath a thick layer of seaweed before yanking it off.

"Kisa?" He turned around and saw that Kisa still stood behind him on the beach. There were two of them.

"That was *way* harder than I thought it would be," she said, then coughed up a bunch of water. "I feel so loopy. It's from all that swimming."

"What are you doing here?" he moved toward the water and then hesitated. Was this a trap of some kind?

"Being a messenger girl, apparently." She tilted her head to one side and smacked it. Water *sploosh*ed free of her ears, followed by a small fish. "You've got to be fucking kidding me," she mumbled. "This place is weirder than I thought."

Mike remained silent, waiting for an answer.

"Things have gone from bad to worse," Kisa explained. "Lily knocked me out with her venom and is doing some sort of trick to try to bridge the gap between us because I need to talk to you. No questions until the end. I don't know how long I'll be in here."

She then told him all about how an ancient priestess had taken over Murray's body and that the horsemen were back and hitching a ride to Earth. As heartbreaking as his own situation was, the one at the house had become dire.

Once Kisa finished, she let out her breath in a rush. "We need you to figure out how to help us. It's just Beth and me, and we're out of food and water. Beth thinks she can cause a diversion using the grimoire, but it's risky."

Mike groaned and then flopped over on the sand. He was exhausted, both physically and spiritually, but the house needed him. Even here, in the Dreamscape, he could feel the dull ache in his shattered arm. He needed a plan, and he needed it yesterday. The stress of the situation had him staring blankly at the sky as his mind struggled to function.

"Oh, and one more thing." Kisa knelt and pinched Mike's nipple through his shirt, giving it a twist.

"Ouch, what the hell?" He rubbed at it with his left hand, wincing.

"That's from Lily. She says to tell you that—" Kisa's mouth kept moving, but it was like someone had muted her. She scrunched up her face in concentration, then tried to speak again and failed. Mike was fairly certain she was trying to tell him to quit being a little bitch and come help them.

"Tell the others I'm on my way," he said. "The barrier is down, so I'll be there soon."

Kisa nodded, relief spreading across her face in a wave that turned into a smile. She blew him a kiss and then evaporated into smoke that drifted away into the Dreamscape.

He opened his eyes and sat up in bed. Yuki lifted her head and yawned, revealing all her teeth.

"We need to go home," he said, then turned to slide out of bed. The splint on his arm caught the blankets, sending a painful twinge up his shoulder.

Yuki transformed, her hands on her hips. "Hold it right there. The last time you tried to bolt, you almost tore yourself apart with magic."

Mike knelt, looking for his shoes. "This is different. Things at the house have gotten worse. If we don't figure out how to stop them, it might be the end of the world."

"Shit." Yuki reached under the bed and pulled his shoes out. She coaxed him back onto the bed and then helped him tie the laces while he told her what Kisa had said. As he spoke, he saw Velvet's dog tags sitting on the nightstand. Doing his best to maintain his composure, he stuck them in his pocket.

Minutes later, they were outside the bedroom. Quetzalli was ready with a bowl of hot soup she had been keeping warm on the stove while Dana stood at the window, her gaze locked on something he couldn't see.

"Where's Abella?" he asked. "We need to head home."

"She's been outside with Emery," Dana replied. "He thinks he can fix her wing, but they need plenty of room to do it."

Yuki explained the severity of the situation as Mike devoured the soup Quetzalli had made. Abella appeared a few minutes later, her wings wrapped tight around her body as Mike got his things together.

"Has Bigfoot checked in?" he asked.

"No," Abella replied. "But I can explain to him what is happening when he returns."

"You aren't coming with us?"

She shook her head sadly. "What Emery has promised me will take many days. I do not move quickly and will not be able to fight for you. Not this time."

"Besides that, we have a problem. Even with the barrier down, we've somehow managed to end up with no way to contact the others to have the rats chew us a portal." Dana pulled out her broken cell phone. "I could call Eulalie if we get our hands on a new phone, but that means heading into town. Then we'll have to find a phone place and hope she answers calls from unlisted numbers. Find somewhere good for the rats to chew a portal…shit, can they even do that if Reggie is trapped? Don't they need his permission?"

Quetzalli sighed and sat down at the table. "If you are planning on running off again, then I will just slow you down as well. This body is far too jiggly to run for long, and I hate all the sweat that comes along with it. Time is of the essence, and this is a wise decision."

Mike looked at Abella, then Quetzalli. "Thank you for coming here with me," he told them. "The selfish part of me wishes you could come with us, but there are important things to do here as well. As for getting home, we'll figure something out, but it won't be by standing around here."

It was agreed that Quetzalli and Abella would assist Bigfoot in keeping Leeds locked away until Mike could return. Dana and Yuki got their stuff together and were waiting for him outside as he told the others goodbye. Emery seemed particularly choked up at his departure, but he promised the imp he would return.

When he hugged Abella, she surprised him with a small envelope. It was sealed shut and had Eulalie's name written on the outside.

"This is for her," she told him. "It's about her sister. Once I knew I wouldn't be coming with you, I needed a way to get Eulalie a message. These are words that cannot wait for my return."

He put a hand on her shoulder and squeezed. "It must have been hard to write," he said.

She nodded. "It was. Now go. I have plenty to protect here without worrying about you." She wrapped an arm around his waist and pulled him in for a hard kiss, then hugged him vigorously enough that his back popped.

"Come back to me," she whispered. "Or I will make you regret it."

"I have no doubt," he replied with a smile.

Once outside, they ran toward the nearest clump of trees and came to a stop as Mike put his hand on the nearest one.

We need to go home, he thought toward the forest. *Will you help me?*

A portal appeared off to their left. He pulled the straps on his bag tight, and they ran through it together. Animals on the other side led them through the woods for half an hour until they approached the next portal. The miles became easier as the snow disappeared, and Dana carried Yuki in her arms as they ran. Even in fox form, the kitsune had finally hit the wall for physical exhaustion and needed some help.

Several portals later, he stood on the edge of his property. He could feel the land beneath his feet, vibrating with energy and magic as he stepped off of it. They took a break while he drank some water and ate another can of soup. His arm throbbed with pain, but he did his best to ignore it.

"So where to from here?" Dana asked.

"I suppose we could hitch a ride to the nearest airport," he replied. "Maybe charter something private, I don't know." He looked back at the boundary and wiped some tears from his eyes. Only a few days ago, he had walked into that place a completely different person. In such a brief span of time, he had loved, lost, and walked the boundary of death itself. It had been a crucible of sorts, and he could only hope he had come out strong enough for the trials yet ahead.

An owl hooted from a nearby tree. He turned his attention upward and was surprised to see a familiar face up in the branches. The spectral owl clicked her beak at him several times, then Bigfoot emerged from the shadows beneath.

"The forest told me you were leaving." Bigfoot spoke softly as he approached Mike. "I would not see you leave without saying goodbye."

Mike nodded. "I would have waited for you, but the situation at home has taken a turn for the worse."

"You're a busy man, Caretaker." Bigfoot put his hand on Mike's shoulder. "Tell Eulalie I'm sorry."

"The blame falls squarely on Leeds," Mike replied, his hand slipping into his pocket to squeeze the dog tags reassuringly. "His actions are not your failures."

Bigfoot licked his lips and nodded. "Then if nothing else, tell her I'm sorry I could not be the one to tell her about her sister. The forest has done its best to imprison Leeds, but he still has allies among the forest children. I would not see him escape."

"Nor would I. Abella and Quetzalli have agreed to help. They're back at the cabin. When I'm done fixing things at home, I'll have the rats open a portal and come right back to help you figure out what to do with him." Mike narrowed his eyes. "I promise you the punishment will be fitting."

"I would like that." Bigfoot stepped toward Dana and pulled her in for a big hug. "Make sure you give that to Eulalie," he told her.

"I think you broke a rib," Dana muttered from beneath his fur.

"That's why I gave it to you and not him. He looks too soft." Bigfoot winked at Mike, then put Dana down.

"I'm not that fragile," Mike muttered, then yelled in surprise as Bigfoot lifted him into the air and squeezed him tight.

"You sound like a squeaky toy!" Bigfoot declared loudly as Dana and Yuki laughed. He put his lips against Mike's ear and dropped his voice to a whisper. "You ever call me a Yeti again and I'll rip your arm off and fist your asshole with it."

"Don't threaten…me with…a good time," Mike gasped in response.

The Sasquatch laughed and set him down. He offered Yuki a fist bump and headed toward the trees behind him. "As for how you're getting home, just ask the trees. Looks like you've learned their language without my help." With that, he vanished into the woods without a sound.

Mike contemplated Bigfoot's words with a smile, then looked up at the owl. She hooted her agreement and flapped her wings.

"What are you looking at?" Dana asked as she scanned the trees.

"Just a spirit of the woods," he replied with a grin. Though he was leaving this place behind, he knew it would be in good hands.

The owl flapped her wings and flew back into the woods, disappearing through a tree. Mike took one more swig of water and thought about home. A portal opened to his right, about thirty feet away.

"Looks like we're taking some shortcuts," he said, then looked at the others. "Who's up for a run? Should just be a couple thousand miles."

Yuki groaned and turned back into a fox. Dana ran ahead of Mike, her ponytail bouncing on her shoulders.

"Try to keep up," she hollered as she sprinted ahead.

Beth looked up from the grimoire in time to see Kisa snap awake dramatically. The cat girl clutched her head and dry-heaved over the side of the couch as Lily's tail twitched back and forth. They were sitting in the front room so they could keep an eye on what was happening outside.

"Well?" she asked, afraid to hear the answer.

"Success." Lily smirked as she stroked Kisa's back. "We made contact with Romeo."

"Finally some good news." She closed the grimoire and turned to look out the window. Murray was hovering in the air, his mouth stretched wide as the mist swirled around him. He and the others now stood between Death and the house, ensuring nobody could go to the grim reaper's aid. "Any idea how long it will be?"

"No," Kisa groaned. "But he's coming right now."

Sighing, Beth looked back at the grimoire and focused on the spell she had chosen. The words weren't complicated, and she felt a rush of energy move through her body as a ball of water formed over the table and then fell. It made quite a mess but did fill up all the coffee mugs they had set out to catch the moisture.

Reggie picked one up and slurped greedily, his tail twitching as he did so. When he got toward the end of his mug, Jenny (who was sitting next to him) tipped it up far enough that water ran down his face.

"I don't even care," he declared as water beaded up on his whiskers. He wiped his face off and flicked the water at Jenny.

Smiling, Beth picked up a couple of mugs and drank it down. The house was much warmer without the priestess, so they had that going for them. Summoning water made a mess, but she didn't dare move away from the front windows. The horsemen occasionally wandered, and she wanted to know where they were at all times.

"Any chance you're gonna make snacks later?" asked Kisa as she picked up a mug.

"Spontaneous generation is trickier than expected," Beth replied. "This was just a way to condense the moisture already in the air. If I do it enough times, the spell won't work anymore because of the lack of humidity."

"Think we'll live long enough to run out of water?" Kisa asked. "Once we're back on Earth, I don't see these guys being content to just chill on our front yard."

Beth frowned, then looked back outside. Unless she was mistaken, the swirling mists circling the house had thickened.

"Doubt it," she replied, then turned her attention to Opal. The slime girl was only a foot tall right now and had crawled under the table to absorb the moisture from the carpet. As Opal sucked the water out with a wide mouth, Beth watched the slime's body expand a little.

The ooze had emerged from her crystalline core a couple of hours ago and had signed some seriously foul language in regard to the priestess. Apparently her consciousness resided inside the crystalline vial. Whatever spell had latched onto the vessel had caused it to create a little bit of primordial ooze every day. Any type of moisture could be absorbed and used to create more slime, allowing Opal to be far larger than the contents of a magic jar.

This little fact had actually inspired Beth to attempt the spell in the first place. She was already getting dehydration headaches and had seen the bags under her eyes while looking in a mirror.

She looked at the others, then back out the window. The mood was grim, and she didn't like it.

"We're going to need a plan," she declared. "For when Mike arrives, or maybe even before. I have no idea what he's going to do when he gets here, but I want to have something ready in case we need to buy him time or create a distraction. Any ideas?"

"You're not gonna get a lot of opportunities," Lily declared with her arms crossed. "As soon as you step out there, I bet you get blasted. Or stabbed. Or both."

Beth looked down at Opal, who paused to return her gaze.

"Maybe…that's something we can use?" she asked the slime.

Opal gave her a thumbs-up, then signed the word for "thirsty." Without delay, Beth summoned another sphere of water. The inkling of a plan had formed in her head, and she was fairly certain she and Opal were in agreement.

"You've got something, don't you?" Lily grinned and leaned forward. "Let's hear it."

"Oh, it's a good one. Like everything else we do, it'll be dangerous, borderline stupid, and cause a lot of chaos."

"I'm in." Lily put her hands together and leaned forward. "I'm not sure what I can do, but I'm itching for action."

"Same." Kisa looked out the window. "Wouldn't mind a second crack at that bitch."

Beth looked at Jenny and Reggie. The rat king gave her a thumbs-up while sipping some more water. Jenny nodded, then tried to slap the mug out of Reggie's hand.

"Excellent!" Beth said, clapping her hands together. "First thing's first—it's time to teach the new girl how to walk!"

THE COMING APOCALYPSE

Eulalie threw a rock in the air and watched in delight as the enchanted mace zoomed through the sky to swat the stone into the forest behind the house. The rock ricocheted off a tree and vanished into the weeds, startling a pair of birds and a rabbit out into the open.

"Twenty points," she declared, then threw another rock in a different direction. The mace spiraled through the air and hit it hard enough that the rock broke in two. One piece bounced off the house while another passed through Naia's watery body and splashed into the fountain.

"Maybe it's time we tone it down a little." Naia held out her hand, and the rock reappeared in her palm. She tossed the offending stone out of the fountain. "For so many reasons."

"Yeah, sorry." Eulalie whistled, and the mace flew down by her side. "We'll play later," she told it while wiping some dust off its head.

It was late afternoon. Eulalie had left Murray's home shortly after the police had come by to perform a wellness check. She had hidden away from the windows as they circled the house, then put away everything she could before they entered. Lucky for her, she had been keeping the place clean, and their cursory sweep was for Murray or his body, not for the magical portal she had hidden by pulling the couch against the wall as she backed through it.

Once the police were gone, she and the rats moved everything back into the Library. The mace had become restless indoors, so she had brought it over to the house to let it fly around the backyard. The sky was overcast with the potential for storms, so she figured the mace was unlikely to be spotted.

The back door banged open, and Suly came walking into the backyard with Cyrus in tow. "Company," he declared while leading the mage over to the fountain. Cyrus had a much nicer bag on his head, one Zel had brought yesterday from her village.

"This is a surprise." Eulalie frowned at Sofia, who was soaking her feet in the fountain. "I didn't expect you until tonight."

Cyrus shrugged. "I found out the local police stopped by your neighbor's house and came to see if I could be of any help."

"Ah." As helpful as Cyrus had been the last few days, it didn't surprise her. On the one hand, she wanted to be suspicious of his motives. On the other hand, maybe he really was just trying to help, do some good for others with his golden years. "We should have that sorted, but thank you."

"Not quite," Cyrus replied, then turned his head vaguely toward Suly.

"This one just spent the last hour scrubbin' yer prints out o' yer rental." Suly winked at Eulalie. "Had me come with 'cause I think he wants a trophy for it."

Eulalie slapped her forehead. She hadn't even considered potential forensic investigations of Murray's home. If he never returned to his job, they would definitely do more than just drop by and knock. It wasn't like her actual prints were on file, but the last thing they needed was a police investigation right next door.

"I don't want a trophy," Cyrus declared from inside his hood. "However, I do think I've demonstrated I am an ally and can be trusted."

Eulalie narrowed her eyes. "You want us to take the hood off, don't you?"

Cyrus nodded. "I've already seen plenty. To be honest, I've noticed the only one I have to wear it around is you, and I want to know why."

Eulalie looked at Naia, who just shrugged. Amymone was no help. She had her nose buried in a book.

Cyrus had proven himself several times over, but it was still a big gamble. Other than tossing a fireball at Sofia, he hadn't reacted poorly to any of the others. Maybe now that he knew everyone better, it would be okay.

Sofia looked dubious but said nothing as Eulalie reached out to undo the drawstrings holding the bag shut at the bottom.

Deciding to just rip off the Band-Aid, she tensed her arm to yank the bag free but was stopped at the last moment by Sofia. The cyclops had grabbed Eulalie's wrist with both her hands, her purple iris ablaze with magic. Eulalie had questioned the cyclops at length about her unique precognitive ability and was under the impression that seeing such a thing meant personal injury was in Sofia's immediate future.

Eulalie arched an eyebrow and looked at Sofia.

"Seriously?" she mouthed.

Sofia nodded. "Very bad idea," she mouthed back.

Eulalie made a mental note to ask Sofia later what she had seen. It was concerning to know that Cyrus, despite all his talk, would freak out bad enough to harm the others.

"Um, is everything okay?" Cyrus reached for the rim of his bag, but Eulalie deftly retied it before he could even touch the hem.

"I had a change of heart," she declared. "Queen's prerogative. I'm like an internet troll. Prefer to remain anonymous."

Cyrus groaned, then took a step back. "Can someone at least help me sit, then?" he asked. "My knees hurt from scrubbing rat prints off the baseboards."

Suly guided the mage over to the fountain, where Naia helped him sit, then started massaging his shoulders. Cyrus let out a sigh but sat like a scorned child.

"So what now?" he asked. "I'm already here, may as well stay. I'm happy to assist with keeping the police away for another couple of days, or maybe you need a night watchman?"

"Yer too eager," Suly said.

"I'll do whatever if it means I don't have to wear this hood," Cyrus replied.

"I can find other stuff to do so the others can let you out to play," Eulalie offered. If nothing else, she could look at some of the research in the Library and see if she could learn more about the magical mace she had found. Or maybe even try to find more info on dimensional rifts. She already had dozens of books set aside for when the current crisis was over; the Library was an absolute treasure trove of information.

Naia froze in place, her hands squeezing Cyrus's shoulders. Her blue eyes flashed brightly as she turned her head toward the house. Amymone nearly dropped her book in a similar reaction, and Sofia gasped, her hand going to her belly.

"Is that him?" asked the cyclops.

Naia smiled and nodded.

Moments later, they heard the sound of a car shrieking to a halt out in front of the house. Eulalie desperately wanted to climb on the roof and see what was happening, but that was a great way to scare the shit out of anyone who might be looking.

"Hello?" Mike's voice carried over the house.

"We're back here!" Amymone tucked her book into a nook in her tree and stood, her hands clasped to her chest. "Do you feel that?" she asked her sister.

"I do." Naia frowned. "But there's something else."

Moments later, Mike appeared through the back door. His hair was wild and somehow noticeably longer than when he had left. Stubble had formed along his chin, and he tossed his bag on the ground as he ran across the yard and nearly knocked Cyrus into the water as he stepped into the fountain and threw himself into Naia's arms.

Naia squeezed him, tears filling her eyes. Eulalie noticed one of Mike's arms was in a splint, his fingers discolored like they had been bruised.

"Oh, Mike, I'm so sorry," she said as she squeezed him.

"What's happening?" asked Cyrus, turning his head uselessly. "Is it him? The Caretaker guy?"

"Cyrus?" Dana stood on the back porch, a look of disbelief on her face. "Is that you? Why are you wearing that bag on your head?"

"Dana!" Relief filled Cyrus's voice. "I honestly don't know!"

Dana looked at Eulalie, then back at Cyrus. Understanding crossed her features, and she stepped off the porch as Yuki followed her.

"Damn, this is weird," Yuki said as she turned to look back at the house. "This is the one from the Underworld, isn't it?"

"We have so much to tell you," Sofia added, but Mike held up his good hand and just sobbed into Naia's shoulders for a minute longer.

Sheesh, what happened to this guy? Eulalie paced while Mike had his breakdown. Impatient, she pulled out a piece of webbing and twisted it around in her hands like a piece of string.

"Sorry, sorry, everyone." Mike took a deep breath and surveyed the scene. "A lot has happened, and there's still plenty to do. I've been in contact with the house and...who the fuck are you?" He was looking at Cyrus.

Mike's body language shifted dramatically, and Eulalie felt the wind move around her. Naia put a calming hand on his shoulder, and the wind died down.

"That's Cyrus," Dana replied. "He's the guy Lily and I met when we were in Hawaii."

"Yes, pleasure to make your acquaintance." Cyrus stood and offered his right hand for Mike to shake. "I've been looking forward to this meeting for some time."

"Not to be rude, but I can't shake hands right now. I have an injury." Mike looked from the hood to Eulalie, then nodded knowingly. "Are you aware of our situation?"

"That the house behind us isn't your actual house and members of your family are trapped there, including Lily? Yes, I am." Cyrus lowered his hand. "I came to investigate and kind of fell in with this crowd."

"Then we're glad to have you." Mike pulled away from Naia. "There's a lot we have to discuss, but there's something that can't wait." He reached into his pocket and pulled something out. "Eulalie, I…um…"

When he spoke, the words became so much buzzing in her ears as he handed over her father's dog tags. Each word was like a drop of rain on hot steel, sizzling loudly before evaporating into the air to be forgotten. The world dropped out from beneath Eulalie, and she stood in silence for several moments, contemplating the cold metal in her hands.

Without a word, she turned from the group and fled into the house.

MIKE WATCHED EULALIE AS SHE DISAPPEARED, THEN LET OUT A SIGH. He had spent the last several hours trying to figure out what to say, how to break the news to someone that a loved one had died.

In the end, he'd stumbled over his words, eventually spitting out that Velvet was gone. He wasn't even entirely sure what all he had said as his brain had rushed to fill the silence with words that had garnered no reaction. It could have gone way better, and he hoped Eulalie wouldn't hate him for it. As bad as he felt about Velvet's death, it paled in comparison to what she must be feeling.

Both Sofia and Dana went into the house together, presumably to find Eulalie.

"I'm sorry, someone died?" Cyrus shifted back and forth on the fountain as if uncomfortable. "I would excuse myself, but…"

"One of our own crossed over." Suly put a hand on Mike's shoulder. "I'm not as sensitive as this lot, but I can feel yer grief. Ye have my condolences."

"Thank you." Mike sighed again. "I wish I had time for condolences, but we simply don't."

He spent several minutes explaining what had happened to the house, only to be interrupted by the surprise arrival of Asterion carrying Ratu. The naga greeted him with a kiss on the cheek and declared she had sensed his arrival and wanted him to tell her everything. He helped her sit on the edge of the fountain as he started over from the beginning. He told them about the horsemen, the angel, and then Nesferisfet.

When he finished, he looked over at Ratu. "So I need to know what we can do to find the house and take out this priestess and the angel. And potentially the horsemen, if that's even possible."

The naga laughed. "To think I've spent the last few days lounging when the end times have been upon us. I would have worn something prettier." She waved her hand and summoned a silver goblet. "The answer to your question is that we've been busy here, trying to account for all possibilities. Our guest here has been a big help."

"Even with this damned bag on my head," Cyrus grumbled. "Your rat queen has insisted I wear it to protect sensitive information, but I know she's just doing it to hide her identity."

"Sorry." Mike looked at Naia, who gave him a nod. He reached over, undid the straps, and removed the hood.

The old man beneath had a scarred face, his mouth falling open upon seeing Mike.

"Better?" Mike asked.

Cyrus looked like a fish out of water, his mouth opening and closing rapidly. He cleared his throat and sat up straight.

"I apologize for asking, but…you are a human, right?"

Mike nodded. "I'm supposed to be, but it's very complicated."

"What happened to your arm? That looks bad."

"Got into a fight with the Jersey Devil." Mike frowned. Dana claimed Cyrus was okay, but he wasn't about to go into more detail about Oregon with a stranger.

"Leeds, huh?" Cyrus shook his head. "That one is a real bastard. Hope you gave him hell, he's slippery. We've been trying to pin that one down for a bit, but he's been far too quiet lately so fell to the bottom of our list."

Mike set his jaw. "Chances are good you'll never hear from him again. Ratu says you can help us?"

Cyrus waggled his hand. "I'm afraid I am of limited use in what you need to accomplish. I determined some time ago that your home was taken by stretching a dimensional gateway over it." He turned and pointed at the back gate. "Wherever that goes is where you will find your house and your people."

"That's easy enough. Naia? Gonna need that key in a minute." He turned his attention back to Ratu. "That's one problem down. What else do you have for me?"

The naga grinned. "I've got a magic sword that will cut through almost anything. That will be of some use."

Mike held up his broken arm. "I'm right-handed," he said. "Afraid someone else will have to use it."

"Oh." The smile on Ratu's face faded. "I'm sure someone else can use it."

"Probably. Speaking of, I need to know who's going with me. If this fails…" Mike sighed. It wasn't just about the house anymore. The whole world was at stake and all because some crusty bitch in a sarcophagus had tattled on Death.

"We also have this." Ratu pointed to the spot near where Eulalie had been sitting. A large mace lifted off the ground and came to hover in front of them.

"Wait, I recognize this." Mike moved closer and held out his hand to touch it. The mace moved away from his fingers. "This was in the tower, right?"

"It was. The story about how and why it's here doesn't matter, but it is sentient and, I think, wishes to help." She tried to touch it, but it dodged away from her fingertips. "Hey, look, I'm sorry I didn't set you free last year. I didn't know."

"Ah, shit, that's right. I'm sorry too." Mike held his palm out as if waiting for a dog to sniff it. "Do you wanna come with me and smash up some bad guys? Maybe save the world, rescue the princess? Princesses?" He just hoped there would be somebody to save once they got there.

The mace tilted forward and pressed its head into his hands, like a cat rubbing against its owner. He liked how the metal felt in his hands, and he gave it a squeeze.

"I think it likes you," Suly said. "I'm with ye, by the by. Can't have my favorite girl wonderin' why ye've come alone."

"I wish to come as well." Asterion's rumbling voice surprised Mike. Despite the minotaur's imposing size, it was easy to forget he was there.

"I would assist as well but am far from mobile." Ratu shook her head. "And if you are all passing through the Underworld, small and fast will be better. Those demons are likely to still be hanging around."

"Excuse me, demons? Underworld?" Cyrus looked gobsmacked. "What the hell have you gotten yourselves into?"

"You coming?" Mike asked. "Sounds like you know some things. You could be the Merlin to my Arthur."

Cyrus shook his head vehemently. "I lack the proper preparations to simply tag along where you plan to go. And if you must travel some distance, my stamina is not what it used to be and I may become a burden."

"Oh." Mike shrugged. "No big deal. It's just the end of the world is all."

"If I could do anything to help, I would," Cyrus protested. "But a large-scale battle against an angel is beyond me."

"How about dealing with a stolen car?" Mike pulled some keys out of his pocket and tossed them to Cyrus. "Won't bore you with the details, but our shortcut ran out of juice about twenty miles from here. Nobody plants the right trees in this neighborhood."

"Trees?" Cyrus looked confused, but Yuki stood behind him now, her hand on his shoulder.

"It would be immensely helpful if you could drop that car off somewhere else," she told him as she walked him toward the back door. "You do know how to drive, right?"

"I do," he replied. "But I'm sure that—"

"Oh, and you know how to remove fingerprints," Amymone added. "That means you can remove the evidence!"

"Yes, but—"

"Cyrus." Mike stared at the man. "Do this for me and I'll be happy to sit down with you sometime and we can just talk. I'm sure you have questions, and maybe I have answers to give."

Cyrus paused, conflict in his eyes. Finally, he nodded and held up the keys.

"It's a deal," he said. He turned to Yuki and gave her a small bow. "I know my way out, thank you."

With that, he disappeared into the house. Mike waited until he heard the car being started before letting out a sigh of relief. He half expected screams of fright followed by lightning or fire. Even in grieving, Eulalie had made sure to hide herself away.

"Didn't want him around?" asked Ratu. "He seems friendly enough."

"He's not family." Mike looked at the others. "He's an ally, but he's not one of us. I know it sounds strange to say it like that, but I feel it in my gut."

His feelings about Cyrus were severely mixed, as if his own senses were ambivalent on what he should do. The last thing he needed right now was another complication, so he had erred on the side of caution.

They spoke at length, comparing notes on what they knew. Naia seemed to think Mike would be able to use his connection with the house to open the gate to the Underworld. Sofia eventually returned, then sat and listened as Mike detailed what they would be facing if they could get back to the house.

"Apophis, really?" Sofia shook her head in disgust at the mention of the priestess. "Doomsday cults are a dime a dozen, but this one was backed by an actual deity."

Ratu nodded. "The Great Serpent was infamous among my people, for obvious reasons. His fights with Ra were the stuff of legend, but his followers were the absolute worst. Their desire for chaos was largely what led to their own demise as a religion. Pretty much self-destructed right after Apophis was killed, but it sounds like one of them actually had long-term plans."

"And a magic cock, apparently." Mike shifted his arm and winced. It was throbbing now.

"Ah, yes. The phallus of Osiris. I won't bore you with the details, but it was lost a long time ago. If Isis was still around, she would probably grant you a huge boon if you could return it to her."

Mike lifted an eyebrow. "Why would Isis care?"

"Osiris was her husband. He was the god of fertility, agriculture, the Underworld..." Ratu waved her hand dismissively. "So not just any magic cock. Divine magical cock. And right now, with them being in the Underworld, that thing has what you would call the home court advantage. It would also explain how this priestess was able to subjugate an angel. When she combined her soul with Murray, it allowed her a direct connection to the angel. The cock of Osiris would give her the strength to control it. However, if you take away the artifact, you may weaken or break that connection."

As they continued to discuss options, the skies up above darkened. Looking up at the sky, he was filled with an inexplicable dread.

"Naia? Can I get that key?" He held out his hand, and Naia gave it over. Everyone stopped talking as he walked over to the wrought-iron gate at the back of the property.

When he slipped the key in and turned it, the gate opened, only revealing the forest behind his house. There was no sign of Cerberus or the Underworld.

"Figured it wouldn't be so easy," he muttered, then closed the gate again. He took a deep breath and closed his eyes, summoning the magic. It manifested weakly at first, as if reluctant.

He put his hand on the gate and closed his eyes. The world around him went quiet as he spread his consciousness wide, hoping to grab onto a thread of magic. There were whispers of it shifting around beneath the soil, and it took a few tries before he was able to latch onto one.

A jolt of power raced through him, and he opened his eyes to gaze upon a beautiful garden. His hand was wrapped around an iron pole with an unlit lamp up above.

"This...is not what I expected." He looked down at his feet and realized he was in his own body. A quick survey of the place revealed this was definitely the magical gardens where he often met the house. He had only ever been there in her body, and he was all alone.

"Hello?" He walked around, curious if his body was still in the real world. If he had teleported here, it had probably scared the shit out of everyone. The most likely idea was that it was just his consciousness that had made the trip.

I see you've met my sister. The voice was coy and carried by the breeze. *You carry her scent.*

"I have," he replied, recognizing the house's voice. "I'm trying to open up the Underworld so I can come find you. Well, your Earth body. My house. Any advice on that?"

The voice laughed, and he felt a soft breeze caress his body.

I'm never more than a thought away, Caretaker. The presence tickled the back of his neck and tousled his hair. *They say home is where your heart is. So come find me.*

"That's very cryptic, thanks for your…" He was suddenly back in his yard. "Help," he finished.

It was frustrating never being given a direct answer, but he knew the house, in her own way, had somehow given him the answer without violating whatever rules had been set forth. Now he just needed to dissect the words and figure out how much was metaphor and how much was literal.

"Mike? Is everything okay?" Naia's voice was filled with concern. "It looked like you passed out for a second there."

"Might have," he replied, then turned to look at her.

Naia. She smiled at him, her thick locks being tugged by the stormy weather that had formed overhead. Though he had loved Velvet fiercely, Naia had been the first love of his new life, the woman who had captured his heart and bound him to this place. He had missed her, but those emotions had been set aside by his short, passionate affair with Velvet.

Why was that? The attraction had been intense but mutual. Had his magic reacted to Velvet's own desires? Or had it been something else?

Velvet. He touched the envelope in his pocket and let out a groan. Eulalie had run off so fast that he had forgotten about Abella's letter!

"Excuse me, I have to take care of something important." He looked up at the sky and grimaced. "Will just take me a few minutes, then we can try to figure out what to do next."

Naia shrugged, her whole body rippling. It was a familiar gesture that brought a small smile to his face.

When he walked inside the house, he paused. When he had first come home, he had practically run through here without a second glance. Now that he had a moment, he could tell this was definitely the version of the house that usually resided in the Underworld. Meant to be a placeholder for when the true house rested, this building was much smaller.

That made it easier to find Eulalie and Dana sitting in what was normally his room. The Arachne was sitting on the bed, her legs sprawled out around her. Her cheeks were flushed, and she stared helplessly at the floor.

"She isn't saying anything," Dana told him. Her face was shining with tears, but her features were placid, as if she was watching a boring video. He wondered if she was even aware of the tears. "I don't know that she wants to talk to anyone right now."

"None of us have the luxury of time, but I'm the one who will be doing all the talking anyway." He walked over to the bed and sat next to Dana. "Also, I wanted to tell you that when I go into the Underworld, you have to stay here. If something happens to Beth and me…"

"I become the new Caretaker and inherit Lily." Dana's lip twitched, then she smiled. "Well, and everything else. But mostly Lily."

"Not if I can't find them."

"Oh. Right." Dana frowned.

"Do you mind if I speak with her alone for a minute?" Mike glanced at the door. "It won't be long, I promise."

"Call if you need me." Dana put a hand on one of Eulalie's glossy legs. The Arachne didn't react. With a nod to Mike, Dana left.

Mike sat next to Eulalie and let out a weary sigh. "I'm not good at this," he began. "I wish I had words of comfort or something other than the fact that I'm sorry. Did Dana tell you what happened?"

Eulalie stared intently at the wall for several seconds before she nodded.

"She did." She looked at Mike. "I…only remember parts of what she said. All I could think about was how I'm all alone now. My mother was the last of her kind until she had us, and now I am the last of my kind. It feels like the whole world is pressing against me and I can't breathe."

Mike swallowed the lump in his throat. "I guess I can't speak to all that. Your sister and I had something special. It was brief but devastating. I almost lost myself in my own grief, and I want to make sure you don't do the same." He pulled the envelope from his pocket and handed it over. "Abella wrote this. She was with Velvet at the end and said it couldn't wait. I wanted to make sure you had it before I go after the others."

Eulalie took the envelope but didn't open it. "I was planning to come with you, but now I don't know. This will sound dumb, but up until you came back, this whole thing felt like a giant game. Now I realize it isn't."

I wouldn't go that far, Mike thought but kept that to himself. "You should know I loved your sister very much. Well, I think I did. I'm still not entirely sure how to define my feelings for her other than that. It's not something I've ever felt so intensely before. I know you feel like you're all alone, but…" He reached over and took her by the hand. "As long as you have us, you will only be as alone as you want to be."

Tears shimmered in Eulalie's eyes, and she wiped them away. She squeezed Mike's hand, then held up the envelope. "Do you mind staying while I read this? I'm not very good with strong emotions and wouldn't mind a friend."

"I can take a few minutes. I'm sorry I can't do more."

"Appreciated." Eulalie opened the envelope and scanned the letter. Her face was unreadable, and when she was finished, she folded the letter up and stuck it in her skirt pocket.

"Are you okay?" he asked.

"There's a lot to think about." She gestured to his arm. "Can I see that?"

"I guess, but I'm not sure—" He froze in place as she opened her mouth and sank her fangs into his forearm. His body hadn't warned him of an assault, so this had to be something else.

The pressure faded first, followed by the pain. The swelling in his fingers decreased as Eulalie drank his blood, and he sighed in relief as he flexed his fingers.

"Did you just heal me?" he asked when she pulled her mouth away.

"Hardly. I drained some of the excess blood and then gave you something for the pain. Your blood didn't taste very good. You should definitely see a doctor about that arm. My bite also has an anticoagulant, so that helped get your blood flowing again, and you won't have to worry about clots. I thought I was going to help with whatever came next, but this is the best I can do for now." Her front legs spread wide, and she reached under her skirt and pulled out a long silken thread. "Take off that brace. I can make you something better. I'm not a doctor, but you definitely shouldn't be using that arm for anything."

"Yes, ma'am."

He waited while she dismantled the makeshift brace and then wrapped his arm in spider silk. She applied it to his arm like a compression bandage, and he could actually make a fist now with that hand. It was fascinating to watch her weave the accompanying sling, and he thanked her as she placed the final loop over his neck.

"I have to go home," she replied. "There are some things I need to see to right away. Try to make sure you're still alive when I return."

"I'll do my best." He stood and walked toward the door. "And again…I'm really sorry."

"I know." She stood and gestured to the door. "The others are waiting for you."

"They are. Now if only I knew what to do next." He chuckled. "I wanted to speak with you before I left, but I'm not certain how to go about leaving."

"I thought you just needed to go to the Underworld? Through the gate?"

Mike sighed. "It's disconnected. This place is a copy of the real one, which gets locked away until a new Caretaker inherits the place and summons it. I thought I could open it by using magic, but it didn't work."

"How did you summon the house the first time? Can't you just do that?"

"I…" His jaw flexed as his thoughts turned to Naia. She had appeared in his bathtub and fucked him, using her magic to bond him to the house. She was the guardian of the house, linked to the entity that controlled it, and the first woman to capture his heart. "I suppose I can."

"Then go do it." She reached into her pocket, pulled out the dog tags, and threw them to him. "And take these."

He caught the dog tags. "I don't understand. I thought you would want them."

"Oh, I do." She smiled sadly, a single tear sliding down her face. "Consider them on loan, for luck. I want them back."

"Thank you." He slid them around his neck, the cool metal resting against his skin. "If you'll excuse me, I need to do one of the two things I'm well known for."

Eulalie nodded. "Sounds like you're getting lucky either way."

Outside the room, he ran past a small group of rats that were waiting out in the hallway, then slid down the railing of the stairs. Now on the landing, he hopped down, feeling a distant ache in his arm on impact.

Out back, everyone was just standing around talking. Despite the stormy weather overhead, which he assumed was related to the horsemen, they seemed calm. It may as well have been a regular day with a storm blowing in, rather than the end of the world.

Maybe it was optimism, or just a delusion, but he wondered if they were calm because they believed in him. No matter what trouble blew their way, he could be relied on to handle it. And if he couldn't do it alone, they were there to help.

Power hummed through the core of his body, and his magic came alive and spread out, sending sparks along his legs and into the ground. Gone was the destructive force that had powered it in Oregon. Instead, his magic briefly touched everyone as if making sure they were there, and his senses expanded to take in the scene. Different magic flowed through everyone, creating a kaleidoscope of colors in his backyard. Suly's was a ghastly hue of green that looked like mist, while Ratu's was red and black like lava. Amymone's magic flowed into the ground and spread out like roots, touching all the plants in the yard.

And then there was Naia. Her magic flowed into the ground, deep beneath where her spring lay. In the center of her body was a core made of blinding light that spun like a tiny star.

Naia smiled at him and stuck her chest out as he vaulted the edge of the fountain and grabbed her around the waist with his good arm.

"Hello, lover." Her voice was a purr as his magic danced along the water in the fountain. "This is a surprise."

"I need you to connect me with the house, like you did before." His magic unfurled around him, and he heard Ratu scrambling away with Asterion's help. "Like on that first day. But mainly with the back yard. I need the gate to properly reappear so I can open it."

She cocked her head and laughed. "I guess we can try. I'm not certain what will happen though." She moved in close, her breath cool against his neck. "We also have quite the audience," she whispered.

"It's fine. Apparently everyone has seen my butthole already." He pressed his lips to her, his magic causing the fountain to swell and overflow. The wind shifted upward, sending a spray of water toward the storm clouds up above. As her tongue wrestled with his, her magic seeped up his legs and into his groin. His cock was rock-hard now, and she teased it through his pants.

"Anyone who isn't interested in getting seriously horny should head inside right now." Ratu spoke from the back door, a quirky grin on her face. "It's about to get really wet out here."

Everyone else ran for the door, except for Amymone, who couldn't.

"Eh. Trees like rain anyway." She licked her lips hungrily. "I just hope you're ready to share."

Naia broke the kiss and smirked at her sister. "I suppose I can make room for my sister. We're gonna need some serious—OH!" The water beneath her rushed up and swirled around her body, obeying Mike's whims. He mentally commanded the water to move up her legs and tease her nymph's pearl, causing her to gasp in pleasure.

"Looks like lover boy has learned some new tricks. But just to play devil's advocate, is now the time for this?" The dryad put her hands on her hips and cocked them outward. "I thought you were going to the Underworld?"

Mike turned his attention to Amymone and beckoned her toward them with a crooked finger. "Yes," he replied, answering both her questions.

"Hey, say no more." She hopped into the fountain, the leaves of her skirt floating on the surface of the water. "I'm sure I'll figure it out later."

Amymone pressed her hips into Mike from behind, as if steadying him. Strong hands moved around his body and settled on his crotch, stroking him through the fabric of his pants.

There was a temporary pang of guilt as he thought of Velvet. Though her loss was still fresh in his mind, he was about to have sex with at least one of the women here, if not both.

He closed his eyes and let Naia and Amymone attend to him, the sensations of their hands and mouths on his body flowing through his very soul. Naia kissed him on the mouth as Amymone sucked on his neck, her hands pushing aside his clothes. If not for the fact that he had planted his grief in the forests of Oregon, there was no way he would even be able to function right now.

"Lover, are you okay?" Naia's voice was full of concern. She and Amymone stopped what they were doing, and he let out a sigh.

"No." When he opened his eyes, he was staring into the beautiful azure depths of Naia's eyes. There was nothing but love and light for him in the windows to her soul, and he gratefully submerged himself in their calming waters. "But I will be."

She kissed him again, her lips aggressive against his. Amymone had pushed his shirt up, and he could feel her long fingers sliding beneath the waistband of his pants and teasing the delicate skin of his cock.

He hardened at her touch, and the air around them became thick with magic.

"Holy shit," Amymone muttered, sounding breathless. "This feels way different from last time. Is it…bigger?"

"Might be." Naia caressed Mike's cheek as her dress melted away, revealing her bare breasts. "He's a different man now. But he's still very much our Caretaker."

He and Naia continued kissing, his hands exploring her body as Amymone pulled down his pants and started sucking on his cock. The fountain sprayed water into the air that hovered in place in the shape of a dome around them. Above, the stormy weather rolled in and threatened them with thunder that sounded like distant explosions.

"I don't think we have much time," he told the women after breaking his kiss with Naia. "I need to get that gate open."

Naia nodded, then knelt by her sister. The two of them tag-teamed his cock, and the hovering drops of water sizzled as his magic leaped between them. Through one of the windows of the house, he noticed Suly's face pressed against the glass.

The dullahan gave him a smile and a double thumbs-up. Mike looked away, afraid to see who else was watching him.

Amymone got on her hands and knees as Naia sat on her back, her legs wrapping around Mike's waist to pull him in. When the head of his cock brushed against her labia, a jolt passed between them that had both of them gasping for air.

"Even I felt that." Amymone's dress split apart, revealing her bare behind. She was fingering herself as the sparks from their bodies fell into the fountain and gathered around her legs. "Oh gods, it feels like I'm wired directly to a ley line or something."

"We'll teach you how to control the intensity of your magic later," Naia told him. "But for now, I just want you to fuck—*me!*"

Mike slid into her before she was done speaking. Her vaginal walls were swirling around his shaft, but his magic encountered her own, and it spiraled outward in a devastating combination. The overflowing water in the fountain consolidated into giant spheres that hovered around them, scattering purple energy that turned into streamers of light.

Naia howled in pleasure, her eyes glowing from within as Mike fucked her with abandon. Beneath them, Amymone cried out her own pleasure as the magic in the water attempted to move through her to get up to her sister. Tiny flowers blossomed along her skin, making her look like a living wreath.

Oh, lover. Naia's voice was in the water now. *What am I going to do with you?*

He couldn't respond. Her magic was now beating inside his chest, and whenever he pressed his throbbing shaft to its maximum length inside her, it almost felt like they were merging. Her magic and his own weren't so different, and the feedback loop had already soaked the backyard in water and magic. The grass and flowers around the fountain leaned toward them as if bowing in reverence, and even Amymone's tree creaked as it tried to move closer by bending.

Mike babbled incoherently as the magic filled him with light. That burning desire to come and fill Naia with his seed had consumed his thoughts, placing him in a mindless state of bliss. Here there was no pain, no fear, no grief.

Only Naia.

That's right, lover, it's just me. Always me.

He saw glimpses of her now, moments they had shared in the tub and the fountain. Memories of kissing with their limbs tangled as they fought to discover pleasurable new positions. The times he had bathed with her and Tink, that time he had tried to start a water fight with her and gotten blasted out of the fountain, all the moments when he had stared into her eyes as she came for him over, and over, and over…

The memories broke, and Mike was floating in a field of stars. Glittering light flowed like water, and he saw Naia across from him, his hands in hers. The runes on her torso blazed with an intensity that was painful to look at as they shifted around beneath his gaze.

"Your magic is all over the place, lover." She grabbed his face with her hands and pulled him close. Nebulous clouds of red and purple floated ominously in the distance as if watching them. "Let's see if we can't set you right again."

And when she pressed herself into him, he felt their souls mix and spin. It was new yet familiar, and the distant clouds broke apart into stars that doubled in number the ones he could already see. Each one sparkled as if polished anew, and his soul filled with light.

Mike arched his back as he groaned, then came hard inside Naia. A magical wave of light radiated outward, scattering the levitating water droplets. The resulting spray soaked everything around them as it was carried along by both his magic and Naia's. The swirling core in the center of Naia's body unleashed a beam of light in the direction of the wrought-iron gate. It glowed briefly, then faded back to normal.

The ground around the fountain vibrated as he caught his breath, his limp body being squeezed between Naia's legs as she held him close against her skin. Below them, Amymone was gasping for air, her arms shaking.

"That was hot and all," Amymone said, breaking the silence. "But after that orgasm, I'm tired of being your furniture."

"You have the personality for it." Naia laughed as she slapped her sister on the ass, causing Amymone to squawk. "Maybe I'll have Mike polish you later."

"Holy shit," Mike muttered, gasping for air. His heart pounded as he slid out of Naia and fell into the remaining water of the fountain. Amymone stood, causing Naia to tumble over and transform back into water on impact with the ground.

"Here, let me help." The dryad pulled Mike to his feet and helped him to the edge of the fountain. He thanked her and got out, his legs shaking beneath him. "Do you think it worked?" she asked as Naia re-formed behind her.

"I really hope so."

He walked toward the edge of his yard as the others came out of the house behind him. Up above, the clouds were building up into a massive thunderhead, one that Quetzalli would have been proud to spend hours detailing to him.

Once at the gate, he touched the bars again and stared through them, willing the land beyond to change.

His senses expanded once again, but this time, he felt the magic wrap itself around the stone fence as the forest beyond filled with fog. A shape moved among the trees, and the three-headed human form of Cerberus emerged.

"You are back," she said, each head looking hesitantly out into the fog. "Things are wrong in here."

"How so?" he asked as he pulled open the door.

"The gate was gone," she told him as she walked forward and pressed against his body. He could hear her inhaling his scent, and then a triple sigh of contentment followed. "The demons were chased away. It has been too quiet."

As he held her, he felt a presence deep in the fog of the Underworld. It was a sensation similar to waking up to an imaginary sound, or thinking someone had called his name. When he concentrated on it, he had no doubts that it was the house he was feeling. His magic practically sang now, his whole body vibrating in anticipation.

Even though it was some distance away, he could feel the house approaching. Up above, the gloomy skies of the Underworld had become stormy like the clouds over his house. The horsemen were coming, and it was time to stop them. If they managed to make it back to Earth, it was game over.

"Well?" Yuki stood behind him now, her face serious.

"I can feel it," he replied, then pointed. Asterion and Sulyvahn appeared, the latter astride his dark horse. The dullahan's spinal-column whip was coiled up in his hands, and Asterion's ax was strapped to his back. They all looked at one another, and Mike nodded. "It's time to go."

Cerberus transformed back into her animal form, and both Mike and Yuki mounted her. Mike used his fingers to blow a piercing whistle. He wasn't certain where the mace had been hiding, but it shot toward him from over the roof and landed in his outstretched hand.

"We need to stick together," he told the others. "This place is dangerous."

"I've got this one's back," Sulyvahn replied, then patted Asterion's shoulder. "Ye just need to lead the way to our girl. Don't wait on us."

"Will do." He stared into the mists and scowled at the dark shapes that flitted within them. Anything that tried to stop them was about to have a very bad day.

"Wait!" Ratu stood at the gate with a scowl. "Don't forget this!"

She held up Harpe, which had been wrapped in a thick blanket. Mike took it from her, then contemplated the blade. He couldn't use it, and nobody else seemed that interested in it.

"Suly? Can you carry that?" he asked.

"Don't know that I'm much for the sword," Suly grumbled in reply.

"I'm out of hands is all. Maybe someone at the house can use it?"

Suly laughed so hard that the seam in his neck spilled black smoke. "Oh, I like that plan, I do!" He grabbed the blade with his free hand and tucked it under his arm. "I'll try not to fall on it."

Mike nodded, then looked over at Yuki. She was clutching Cerberus's fur tightly in her fists.

"Ready to be my weapon?" he asked her.

"Fuck yeah," she responded with a grin that showed all her teeth. Her features became feral, her face elongating slightly as Cerberus dashed forward into the fog.

Together, the group disappeared into the mist.

"Well?" Beth stepped back from Opal, a roll of duct tape in one hand and a pair of scissors in the other.

"That still doesn't look right." Reggie stroked his chin as he contemplated Opal's jiggling body. The slime stood in the living room, wearing a pair of leggings and boots. The boots had been duct-taped to the leggings to keep them from sliding free when Opal took a step.

"I'm doing my best here." Beth frowned at Opal's legs. They'd unwound a bunch of metal hangers and bundled them together to make a skeletal structure for Opal's body to adhere to. However, her feet kept popping out of the boots whenever she walked, so Beth had improvised.

"C'mon, like this." Lily was leaning off the back of the couch, her face inches from Opal's. She wore Beth's face, only patches of it were translucent like Opal's. "You need to set that bottom layer. Otherwise, you look like a porcelain doll."

Opal's face rippled as one layer turned pink while the other turned white. Lily had been using Opal's color shifting to replicate Beth's skin tone.

"Good, now harden that outer layer." Lily held up Beth's makeup palette. "Now are we thinking some fall colors or full-blown whore?"

Opal gave Lily the finger.

"They're being weird again." Kisa was keeping watch through the front window.

Lily groaned in exasperation and held the palette against her chest. "Is it a circle jerk?" she asked.

Kisa snorted. "Nah, they're spreading out and looking into the fog."

"I really could have used five more minutes." Lily pulled a pair of sunglasses out of her cleavage and stuck them to Opal's face. "You're the kind of girl who is hot but only from a distance."

"That's still my face," Beth protested.

"I've always liked you better from behind." Lily winked. "You pack ass like a goddess. A couple hundred years ago, your butt would have had its own religion."

Beth's cheeks felt hot as she took a step away from Opal. The slime's butt looked fantastic in leggings, though she was wearing three pairs. One pair by themselves had been too porous, causing Opal to ooze outward. Luckily, Opal's control of her upper body was much better, meaning she was able to wear a shirt and sweater combo.

"Uh…" Kisa pressed her face against the window and turned it sideways.

"Those fuckers are up to something. They're at the sides of the house now. The fog out there looks like it may be thinning."

"Then we might be out of time." Beth pulled Opal's sweater down. On close inspection, it was clear Opal was not human at all. However, Beth was betting on the fact that the horsemen would be out for blood and would kill first, ask questions later.

"So run this by me again?" Lily turned into Beth, only her butt was unusually large. "Because I'm still not sure how I don't get blasted into dust."

"They don't know Opal is still with us." Beth picked up a book they had drastically altered to look like the grimoire and handed it to Lily. "Her shapeshifting capabilities are an unknown quantity. So when they see two of me, they will assume one of them is you."

"But one of them *is* me." Lily pouted.

"Right. They know you can't hurt Murray or the angel, so you aren't a threat. So one of you two must be me, and therefore both of you will be taken out with extreme prejudice. But Mehkhkahrel's busy holding Death down with those blasts. If Murray, or Neferisfet, or whatever the fuck they're calling themselves doesn't want an ass beating, they can't call off the angel to disintegrate you."

"I hate this plan."

"You don't have to like it." Beth slapped Lily's ass, causing it to pop into her normal shape. She handed another fake grimoire to Opal. "You can handle a stabbing or two, but I can't."

Lily rolled her eyes. "Size queen here is worried about being stabbed," she muttered under her breath.

"Look, you two will be a diversion, and I will blast the fucker with the grimoire." She had dug through so many spells until she had found one that was intended to disrupt dimensional shifts. It took almost twenty seconds to cast, and that was if she didn't screw up the pronunciations. "If the book is right, this place will become dimensionally locked for at least a few hours, which should buy Mike more time."

"Romeo better come through," Lily said, licking her lips. "If he does, I'm gonna blow him until he can't see straight."

"You and me both," Kisa added, then flushed. "I...didn't mean to say that out loud."

"Ah, it's okay, kitten." Lily moved next to Kisa and stroked her cheek with the back of a finger. "We could make it a team effort. Do that thing where our tongues run across each other, it'll be hot."

Beth cleared her throat. "If you are done distracting everyone, we should get to it. Opal, you ready?"

The slime held up a thumb, then stumbled forward. Beth caught her and held her up.

"Kisa, grab Ticktock."

"On it." She picked up the mimic and slung it over her shoulders. Beth walked behind her and stuffed the duct tape and scissors into the bag. She doubted she would need them, but if she was walking into the end of the world, she wanted access to duct tape.

Besides, it wasn't the only weird thing she had tossed into Ticktock for their fight. She didn't know if the mimic minded the eclectic mix of objects she had fed it, but it was hard to know what they might end up needing.

"Reggie, you're our backup for when everything goes wrong."

"I know my role." The rat king bowed his head. "I genuinely hope that my services are not needed."

"I know." She patted Reggie on the head, then picked up Jenny, who stood nearby. "And you've got my back?"

Jenny giggled. *Your packed ass is protected.*

Beth frowned but knew better than to state how much she disliked that term. "All right, so let's do this. Plugs and places!"

As one, everyone but Opal stuffed cotton plugs into their ears. Kisa stood by the door, her hand on the latch. Reggie moved to the window and picked up a pair of binoculars. Lily stood at the door, followed by Opal.

"I would like to go on record—" Lily began.

"Noted." Beth nodded at Kisa, who opened the door.

The hideous shrieking was diminished by the cotton, and Lily burst out of the house first, holding up the grimoire. She pointed at Murray dramatically and started shouting.

"There once was a man from Nantuck—" Lily was cut off when War threw his sword, spearing her though the side and sending her sprawling across the ground.

Opal got farther into the yard, her whole body wobbling dramatically. Pestilence flew through the air in an attempt to keep up.

Beth crouched and walked along the deck until she had a good view of Murray. Opening the grimoire, she began reading the incantation, feeling her entire body knot up in pain. The foreign magic she summoned coated her like glue, then spread outward along the ground. Unseen by Murray, it homed in on him and latched onto whatever magic he was using to move them back to Earth. Her magic sniffed out the boundaries of Murray's spell and sank into place.

"Aargh!" Lily squirted blood dramatically while holding her stomach. War strolled casually over, a shit-eating grin on his serpentine face.

"That was stupid," he told her once he was close. Over his shoulder, Pestilence had gotten ahold of Opal and carried her up into the air. Opal's body stretched dramatically, but the slime held it together as they disappeared into the mist.

Doing her best to ignore the others, Beth continued the recitation. The hair on her arms stood on end as she summoned primal forces that would lock the house in one location.

"Dumb bitch." War pulled his sword out of Lily, then picked her up. "I've been looking forward to this."

"Me too." Lily's eyes lit up, and her tail appeared. It darted forward and buried itself in War's eye.

The horseman let out a scream as he tried to push Lily away from him. She held on tight, her tail withdrawing and stabbing again. War turned his face away, sparing his remaining eye, then slammed Lily into the ground. The succubus let out a grunt of pain, then cried out when War smashed her into the ground.

"Shit!" He gave her a kick, which sent her sliding across the ground. She tumbled dramatically, transforming back into her usual form. When she tried to stand, Famine stepped from the gloom and smashed her in the face with his heavy scales. Moments later, Opal fell out of the sky and exploded on impact with the ground. The sound was akin to a bag of soup striking concrete.

Beth finished the chant, and the ground lurched beneath her. The whole house creaked and groaned overhead, and everyone but Murray fell to the ground. Death slid out of the angel's golden beam and was almost to his feet before the light came crashing down on him again.

Murray's face twisted into a mask of anger as he dropped his attention to the house. Spotting Beth, he lifted a hand and pointed at her.

"She's there!"

Beth slammed the grimoire shut and tossed it to the side where Kisa waited. The cat girl slid the book into Ticktock as Beth went running sideways along the front porch. She felt powerful magic swirling in her hands as she chanted a series of words that condensed the air around her into a hot ball of energy.

Pestilence appeared from above, their body surrounded by black insects that swirled around them.

"Fireball, motherfucker!" Beth hurled the energy, willing it to ignite. The ball of fire caught Pestilence by surprise, and they fell onto the ground and rolled back and forth to smother the flames.

War smashed through the lattice of the porch, his sword left behind. He was almost upon her when Beth pulled Jenny out of her hiding place inside her sweater and threw her.

PLAY WITH ME!

Jenny smacked War in the face, causing him to backpedal in terror. He swatted the doll away, but she hovered in midair, a sickly aura surrounding her body as wooden planks and siding ripped free of the ground and smashed into the horseman.

Distracted, War didn't notice Kisa come from behind and unleash Ticktock. Bladed arms slashed into War's legs, toppling him.

A void formed in Beth's gut, and she clutched her belly in agony. A thick hand grabbed her by the hair and pulled her over the edge of the railing and onto the ground.

"You like that?" Famine asked. "That's what true hunger feels like. It isn't when you just miss a snack or a meal. We're talking days on end, a sensation that consumes your every thought."

Kisa came running up behind Famine, the scissors in her hand. Famine stepped aside at the last second and brought his hand down on the back of her head. Kisa let out a yowl as she hit the ground and went still.

Ticktock sprouted metal legs, causing Famine to step away from Kisa. The mimic carried her away as Famine grabbed Beth by the collar and tossed her toward Murray.

"You have only delayed the inevitable." Murray shook his head. "I'm not sure what is sadder. The fact that you could have been my vessel, or the fact that mankind will never know you bought them an additional two hours of peace."

"I liked it better when you were a table," Beth said, then summoned another fireball and threw it.

The blast caught Murray in the face, scorching skin and hair. He cried out in pain, and Mehkhkahrel stopped blasting Death and turned its attention toward Beth.

"YE HAVE BEEN JUDGED," it declared, then lit up with golden fire.

"No!" Murray stepped between Beth and the angel. "Keep him down!"

Death was already on his feet, his dark cloak forming around him as he dashed toward Murray. Less than ten feet away, the grim reaper was blasted into the ground.

"That was close," Famine declared. Behind him, Pestilence rose from the ground, their hazmat suit covered in soot.

"Die! Die! Die!" War had grabbed onto Jenny and was busy smashing her into the ground with his foot. He stuck his hand out, and his sword flew through the air and into his palm with a meaty thwack. Raising the blade high, tip pointed down, he laughed in glee.

Reggie bolted out of the door and climbed up the horseman's leg from behind. He disappeared under the loincloth, and War dropped the sword, barely missing Jenny, then clutched his groin.

As War yelled in agony, Reggie fell to the ground and scrambled to retrieve Jenny. He disappeared between the splintered boards of the porch, dragging the doll to safety.

"I am so tired of this fucking house!" War declared, then lifted his sword and slammed it into the siding. His blade splintered the siding but did little damage otherwise.

"Soon, brother." Famine grabbed Beth from behind and pulled the cotton from her ears before pushing her to the ground. That gnawing pain filled her again as the strength was leached from her body. "Time to die, little girl."

"Wait!" Murray put out a hand and landed on the ground. "Don't kill her yet."

"Why?" War had stepped off the porch, dragging his sword behind him. "We don't need her. And don't you dare tell me you want her to watch as the end of the world comes. That's fucking amateur-hour bullshit."

"It isn't that." Murray's eyes gleamed as he knelt to scoop up some soil. He licked it with an abnormally long tongue. "Oh, you are a clever one."

Beth groaned. She had figured out long ago that they were in a pocket dimension, and the spell she had chosen didn't just anchor the house in place. It anchored the house and the land around them to her very soul. If she died, there was a good chance the horsemen would be cast into the Underworld, or wherever she was destined to go. The grimoire hadn't been clear on what would happen, but the spell had explicitly warned about the dangers of tethering a location to a living being and then slaying it.

"If you kill her, it will be days before we return, if not weeks." Murray's eyes narrowed until they became angry slits. "It can be undone in hours while she lives, so don't harm her."

"Can we kill the others?" War glared at Lily with his remaining eye. "The human is off-limits, but what about that demonic bitch?"

Lily spread her wings and took to the sky, only to be tackled by Pestilence. She fought back, slashing with daggerlike nails, but Pestilence didn't seem to care.

"The human lives until I say otherwise. The others belong to you." Murray's jaw unhinged, and he lifted into the air to sing his song of damnation once more.

Pain racked Beth's body as she felt the spell she had cast being undone.

The scream seemed to worm its way through her bones, vibrating her whole body.

The horsemen held a debate she couldn't hear, and then War started shouting at Mehkhkahrel.

"Stop smiting him!" he yelled, holding his hands to his mouth. "Hey! Stop for a moment! We need you to do something else!"

Mehkhkahrel ignored them as Murray continued to scream. War waved his hands in frustration, but Beth couldn't follow what was being said. Between Murray's spell and Famine's magical hunger, she couldn't concentrate on anything other than breathing. Pestilence and Lily were trapped in a wrestling match where neither had the upper hand.

Every minute that passed felt like an hour. Beth felt the breath ripped from her as Murray finally undid her spell. The ground rumbled violently, and Famine released her, tossing her to the ground.

"Hey, we need to borrow your angel for a second," Famine yelled at Murray. "To smite the demon over there."

Murray's eyes barely registered recognition as his scream took on a different pitch. However, Mehkhkahrel stopped blasting Death, allowing War to lift his sword and shove it down through his brother's rib cage. This pinned him to the ground, and the fire in Death's eyes blazed hot.

"I have decided I am adopted," he declared loudly.

"Nobody cares, you skinny little shit," War replied.

Beth struggled to her feet, but Murray's eerie shriek had her so dizzy now that she was dry heaving. She raised her hand and tried to summon another ball of fire to assist Lily but was pushed from behind by Famine.

"You bit off more than you could chew," Famine told her. "Made a pretty big show at the end. But now you're going to pay for it. When we get back, I'm going to hunt down anyone you've ever loved and personally devour them."

"You're free to smite the others now," War said, his missing eye swollen shut. He pointed at Lily. "Start with that bitch."

Lily fought even harder, but Pestilence was unaffected by her efforts. The angel's eyes blinked out of order, as if malfunctioning.

"Fucker is all messed up now," War muttered. "Hey! Mehkhkahrel! That's a succubus right over there! She's a demon! Angels smite demons!"

The angel didn't move. Instead, it shifted, as if reality warped around it. It's baleful center eye was now looking at Lily, who crumpled under its golden gaze.

"DEMON SPAWN," it declared, and the air around it shifted. "YE HAVE BEEN JUDGED."

"Suck my dick!" Lily cried, smoke rising from her body. She cried out in agony as sparkling lights danced around her, like sadistic fireflies.

When the beam of light burst from Mehkhkahrel, Beth closed her eyes and screamed. Hot liquid sprayed across her body, and she fell to the ground in shock. When she opened her eyes, she saw she was covered in Opal's blue slime.

Opal, or what was left of her, lay melted on top of Lily. The crystalline decanter lay on its side, slowly dripping ooze onto the ground.

Murray stopped screaming and looked down at himself in shock. Not only was he coated in Opal's remains, but it had been sprayed everywhere. Bits of the slime girl had sprayed across the three horsemen, as well as Mehkhkahrel.

"YE HAVE BEEN...YE HAVE BEEN..." Golden light sparked across the Mehkhkahrel's wings, and then it fired a beam of light into Pestilence. The whirling mass twisted aimlessly, the eyes blinking rapidly and out of sync. A sound like static filled the air as the angel spoke over itself.

Pestilence raised their hands in defense and then exploded into a cloud of angry insects that dispersed into the gloom. Ashes drifted across the ground.

"What the hell?" War covered his head and managed to narrowly avoid a random blast of light.

"He attacked the wrong person!" Murray held up the dick of Osiris and summoned a magical shield just in time to block an attack. "That girl didn't attack me or him, so it violated its own protocols! My control is slipping!"

Mehkhkahrel let out a scream that caused Murray and the horsemen to stumble and fall. The mists around the house curled inward like fingers and scratched at the exterior, taking away paint and wood. Beth was lying flat on the ground now, terrified of what the mist would do if it touched her.

Murray sent a green beam of light into Mehkhkahrel's core, sweat beading up on his brow. Mehkhkahrel's wings stopped spinning as it let out a groan that sounded like fatigued metal.

There was a flash of light, and then everyone standing was knocked off their feet. Up above, the angel's wings started to char around the edges and turn black.

"No, no, no!" Murray held up his hands and tried to bind Mehkhkahrel once again.

"ENOUGH!" Mehkhkahrel's voice felt like a bomb inside Beth's gut, and she curled into the fetal position. The air filled with an ominous ticking noise she realized was coming from the angel above. It stared down with angry eyes, and she saw that several of them were looking right at her. One by one, their gaze turned toward Lily, who lay smoldering on the ground.

"Fuck you," Lily whispered, then grabbed Opal's vessel and flung it far away from her own body to protect it from the coming blast.

"HELLSPAWN." Energy crackled around Mehkhkahrel's wings as it prepared to smite the succubus. "I SMITE THEE IN HIS GLORIOUS NAME."

Lily shrieked defiantly at the angel but then stopped, her jaw dropping in surprise.

When the beam of light burst forth from Mehkhkahrel, Lily vanished in a cloud of smoke just before it reached her. The beam scoured the ground, sending molten rock through the air as it tried to find her.

The mists swirled around the house, then coiled upward as if being pushed from below. A dark figure approached through the gloom, blue eyes glowing with an intensity that made Beth squint.

The mists parted, revealing a male figure with his arm in a sling. It was Mike, and he glared angrily at the angel above. An aura of blue-and-green light surrounded him, pushing the mists away from where he stood and radiating outward through the ground. Where he walked, grass and tiny blue flowers burst through the sterile soil, and she could feel the ground beneath her beating like a drum.

"Are you the one who took my house?" He sounded calm, but there was a dangerous edge to his voice that made Beth think of a sheathed blade. "The one who hurt my family? The one who just tried to kill my Lily?"

"BE NOT AFRAID." Mehkhkahrel's voice flattened Beth into the ground so hard that she couldn't breathe. Her hair whipped around her head as if she was caught in a storm. Nearby, she heard Murray cry out in rage as he, too, was flattened. Whatever malfunction the angel was experiencing had either scrambled its circuits completely or pissed it off.

The wave of force that burst forth from the angel traveled across the ground and washed over Mike. He barely flinched, his face twisting into an angry mask as he lifted his good arm and pointed at Mehkhkahrel.

"Cerberus." Mike's voice thrummed with power, and Beth watched in awe as three pairs of blazing red lights formed just above and behind him as the hellhound stepped out of the mists. Her teeth were bared and hackles raised as each head growled in a different tone, filling the air with a malevolent melody.

Mike twisted his hand around to make a gun out of it with two fingers for the barrel. When he parted his lips to speak, his teeth were pressed tightly together in barely suppressed rage. "Fetch."

With a triple howl, Cerberus bounded forward and tackled Mehkhkahrel out of the sky. Feathers scattered everywhere as the powerful force crushing Beth suddenly vanished and she was able to rise. Mehkhkahrel and Cerberus tumbled out of sight into the mist, but the air filled with blasts of light and fire as the two battled in the fog.

"Caretaker!" Murray hissed in surprise as he held up his magical dick like a protective talisman. "How are you here?"

Mike didn't answer. Instead, Lily stepped from behind him, her tail wrapping coyly around Mike's torso, the stinger resting gently against his neck.

"Daddy's home," she announced with glee. "And he is pissed." She planted a kiss on his cheek and then disappeared in a puff of smoke.

A CARETAKER'S RESOLVE

M ike sniffed involuntarily at the sulfur cloud that surrounded him
with Lily's disappearance. Her malevolent glee was so palpable
he could almost taste it.

It had taken almost two hours at a blistering pace in the Underworld
before Mike and the others had reached the edge of the dome-shaped pocket
dimension his home had been tucked away in. It had formed an impenetrable
barrier to the demonic denizens of the blighted landscape who were circling it
hungrily. At the sight of the hellhound, they'd dispersed with harsh cries.

Mike had hopped off Cerberus to place his hands on the solidified light. It
had denied his efforts, but he could feel the geas just on the other side. It had
reached out for him, as if to welcome him home, but the barrier had opposed
his efforts.

The geas had built in power, concentrating magic just beneath his hands
until it tunneled through the barrier, connecting to Mike's magic. Like he'd
turned a key in a lock, the protective shield had burst apart to allow him entry.
The thick mist had resisted his passage by curling around him and solidifying,
but he had pushed through with the others behind him. He had arrived just in
time to see the angel Mehkhkahrel try to scour Lily from existence.

Cold fury had filled him as he commanded Cerberus to take down
Mehkhkahrel. If anyone was a match for the angel, it would be her. Cerberus
had tackled the angel into the mist, but hellfire had torn through the fog and
revealed Mehkhkahrel on the ground.

Its feathers smoldered as it tried to move back into the air. Every now and then, the shadows shifted, and it looked as though the winged entity had unfolded terrifying limbs consisting of blades and spikes.

"*Yes!*" A bulky figure with red skin reached into the air and pulled out a large battle-ax. Mike assumed this was War but didn't care what he was called. "Let's do this!" War cried as he charged toward Mike.

"Yuki." Mike knew the kitsune was right behind him. "Freeze this turd."

A gale of icy wind blew past him, slowing War's progress. The warrior howled, the veins in his neck bulging as he muscled forward, ice forming on his face and chest.

"Do you think I'm afraid of a little cold?" He barked a laugh as the distance between them narrowed.

"You'll be afraid of this." Yuki's voice was full of contempt as a giant icicle, nearly fifteen feet long, ripped through the air. It shattered just before impact with War when a yellow beam of light intercepted it.

"You will not stop me," Murray yelled, his voice crackling. "I have spent too many centuries waiting for this moment!"

"I'm putting you back on ice." Yuki dashed past Mike, her tails swishing behind her as she held up both hands, each filled with tarot cards. She cast them into the air where they transformed into giant silver goblets that poured water onto the ground. She summoned large icicles from the now moist soil, then launched them at Murray with a wave of her clawed hands.

War, no longer impeded by Yuki, ran at Mike with his ax held high.

With a bellow, Asterion emerged from the fog and slammed into War headfirst from the side. His horns penetrated War's thick skin as he lifted the horseman into the air.

A horrible gnawing feeling took Mike to his knees, and he narrowed his eyes at the dark figure by the house who was pointing at him.

"You must be Famine," he muttered, then whistled and held up his hand. The mace, which had been circling them for the entire trip, appeared from above and landed in his hand. "Beat this fucker's teeth in," he told the mace, then threw it.

Even though the throw was clumsy, the mace took care of the dirty work and covered the distance between Famine and Mike in moments. It smashed into Famine's face, knocking the horseman onto the ground.

Mike's precognition triggered, and he leaped out of the way as a colony of insects formed into a humanoid and took a swipe at him.

"Mike Radley!" Death had turned his head around with his hands to watch the battle, War's massive sword pinning him to the ground. "You have come for me!"

Mike didn't respond, his attention on the figure before him. Every fiber of his being screamed *Danger!* as Pestilence tried to get ahold of him. He imagined a single touch would infect him with every disease known to man, plus a few extra.

Lily emerged from above and flapped her wings, scattering the cloud of insects. When she landed, her tail curled protectively around Mike's waist.

"You make quite an entrance," she told him. "What's with the arm?"

"Got into a fight with a demon." He noticed that one of her arms was similarly wrapped. "And you? Trying to match my outfit?"

"Fight with an angel." She looked over her shoulder and smirked. "We can compare scars later."

"Agreed." He grabbed Lily by the shoulders and pulled her back as a beam of golden light came from the gloom and passed less than a foot away. "How do we end this?"

She pointed to Death, who was still pinned in place. "The bitch is afraid of him."

"Then let's give her something to be afraid of." He sprinted toward Death and slid to a stop just inches away. Grabbing the hilt of the sword with both hands, he let out a yell and pulled it upward. Pain flooded his busted arm, causing his hand to slip free.

The sword hadn't moved an inch.

"Only War can lift his own talisman," Death informed him. "You must find another way to free me, Mike Radley."

"Fuck!" Mike kicked the flat of the blade in frustration, then turned his attention to the others in time to see Murray summoning a ball of green light in his hands, his shining eyes locked on Beth.

Beth scrambled to her feet and ran to Kisa's aid. The cat girl was still unconscious, her body limp as Beth dragged her back into the house while the fight continued to unfold outside.

Satisfied Kisa was at least out of harm's reach, she pulled Ticktock off Kisa's back and slung him over her own.

"It's time to do our part," she said, then ran back outside. Asterion and War were pounding the shit out of each other in a bare-knuckle brawl, their weapons forgotten. She was almost off the porch when a thick hand grabbed her by the shoulder.

"Noth tho fath!" It was Famine, his face bloodied and several teeth missing. Behind him, his damaged scales had been wrapped around a mace that clattered to get free.

A bony whip wrapped around Famine's wrist, drawing blood. He cried out in agony as Suly yanked on the other end, freeing Beth.

"Hands off the lady," the dullahan shouted from atop his horse. He took a bundle from beneath his arm and tossed it to Beth. "Special delivery."

Famine ripped the whip free from his arm, taking chunks of skin with it. Suly rode past Famine and scooped up Beth just as she picked up the bundle.

"I'm so glad to see you," she said, but Suly's response was lost as a blast of green light caved in his horse. The nightmare crumpled inward, making a screeching sound before it vanished with a loud pop. Suly wrapped his arms protectively around Beth as his horse vanished and they crashed, but his head was ripped free and rolled into the fog.

"*Shite!*" screamed the dullahan before his head disappeared completely.

"You're going nowhere!" Murray's face was covered in blood, but there were no visible wounds. He raised the magic cock and pointed it at Beth.

Mike tackled Murray from the side, knocking him to the ground. Beth noticed that Yuki was now fighting Pestilence with freezing clouds. Lily was helping Asterion, the two of them struggling against a frenzied War.

"Use the sword," Mike called out. Beth looked at the bundle she had dropped, then pushed away Suly's arms as she crawled over to retrieve it. Unwrapping the blade, she marveled at the glistening edge.

Without wasting another moment, she charged toward Murray and swung the blade, cleaving neatly through his neck.

Bands of golden light emerged from the wound as Murray's head fell, the bands connecting his head to his body. His head was yanked back into place, the wound vanishing before her eyes.

"This body is powered by the divine and controlled by chaos," he cackled, then punched Mike in the face, knocking him to the ground. Blood flowed freely from Murray's wound until it closed completely. "A mere sword cannot hurt me."

A cloud of acrid smoke emerged from Murray's hands, but he paused when a loud roar was followed by Mehkhkahrel flying backward out of the fog. Its spiraling wings generated winds that knocked everyone down as it fired golden light into the fog. Cerberus appeared, golden blood in her mouths as she dashed around the smiting attacks. A blast scorched a bloody trail along Cerberus's left leg, but the hellhound ignored it, leaping through the air and clamping teeth into the angel's body once again.

Everyone had been scattered. Beth was near Mike, who was groaning and holding his head.

There was a bellow of alarm behind her, and she turned to see that War had Asterion in a headlock. He had pinned the minotaur from behind and was grabbing his horns in an attempt to break his neck.

Panicked, Beth looked around for the sword, but it was lying almost twenty feet away. Knowing she wouldn't have enough time, she ran toward War and Asterion, pulling the backpack off her arms and unzipping it.

War was much taller than she was. When she jumped, she lifted Ticktock as high as possible and swung the bag over the top of War's head.

"Snack attack!" she cried. They had come up with several silly code phrases, but this had been one of her favorites.

War's whole body tensed up as Ticktock tried to devour his head, causing an immense amount of blood to gush from its open flaps. The mimic shuddered as War let go of Asterion and frantically tried to pull Ticktock off his head before it was bitten off.

Famine came to his brother's aid, ripping Ticktock free. Ticktock sprouted a dozen blades that stabbed Famine repeatedly.

War groaned, his features covered in blood. He wiped his good eye clean as Beth ran for the sword. Pestilence manifested before her, but a violent gust of wind blew them away as Yuki ran up, holding a glowing Seven of Swords card in her outstretched hand.

"Should have brought a bug zapper," she declared, then hurled a ray of frost. Several hundred bugs were caught, falling to the ground in blocks of ice.

Beth yelled her thanks and made it to the sword just as extreme hunger filled her body. She groaned and fell to her knees, suddenly too weak to stand.

"Oh, you are gon pah," Famine growled as he stomped toward her. Ticktock had been bunched up and pinned beneath the bulk of his arm. One mechanical arm with a tiny blade stabbed him repeatedly in the belly, but Famine paid it no mind.

Metal clanged nearby, and Beth saw that the mace was fighting to get free from the scales. Hoping it could help her, she crawled toward the mace, grabbed onto the scales with both hands, and pulled.

Despite their relatively small size, the scales were impossibly heavy. Touching them filled her with dread, and she felt the strength in her limbs sapped away.

"Thtupid girl." Famine was almost on top of her. "Only a hortheman cah lif their own talithman."

The mace was practically spinning in place, but the scales had it pinned. Frantic, Beth tried to stand, holding the sword in front of her. She moved behind the scales and paused, her eyes on the gleaming edge of the blade. There was a weird little hook on the end, which seemed more cosmetic than useful.

Just how sharp was this thing? Famine had bent the top bar of the scale around the mace, which meant the metal itself couldn't be invincible. She placed the hook over the bent metal rod and gave the sword a good yank.

Nothing happened at first. She pulled a couple more times as Famine loomed over her, his fingertips glowing with a dark energy that had her gasping for air.

She wasn't sure if the fall came before or after, but the sword yanked free as the hook severed the metal loop holding the mace. It rocketed forward, smashing into Famine and making him drop Ticktock. The mimic sprouted legs that slashed into Famine's tendons, sending the horseman to the ground.

The mace and the mimic reduced Famine to a bloody mess, the horseman thrashing about. War came running over but was tripped by Lily's tail as she appeared next to him.

"Did you know there is no *i* in war?" she asked, then gouged out his other eye with her tail. War cried out in pain and pushed himself to his feet, then ran out into the mist.

A dark energy crushed Beth from above, and Murray descended from the sky. His body was covered in golden light as he came between them, the dick of Osiris pointed at her chest. In the fog, Cerberus yelped in pain, and a heavy pressure filled the air as Mehkhkahrel hovered ominously overhead.

"Enough!" Murray opened his mouth to say something else but choked when Suly's thorny whip wrapped around his throat and yanked him backward. The golden light traveled down the bone whip and burned along Suly's skin.

"I ain't one o' yers," Suly growled as his skin sizzled. "Yer magic means little to the fae!"

"You…all…are…dead!" Murray's eyes were triumphant as a chorus of voices cried out from above. Mehkhkahrel's wings were spinning as the air filled with golden light. "You just…don't…"

Mike screamed, his body tense with rage as he directed his wrath at the angel. When his voice left him, it transformed into shards of blue light that ripped through the air and tore chunks out of Mehkhkahrel's wings. The angel's spell was disrupted, and it turned its attention toward Mike. Golden light built up behind Mehkhkahrel, and it unleashed its magic.

Mike's voice tunneled into the light, and a protective barrier made of floating motes of light whirled around him. Bits of Mehkhkahrel's magic struck the barrier and pushed Mike back, but the blue light surrounding him coalesced into six spectral legs that spread wide behind him to prevent him from succumbing to the blast.

A feminine figure clutched him from behind, both her hands resting directly over his heart and her legs around his waist. Mike paused to take a breath, then let out a cry that surpassed any frequency Beth could hear. The air rippled as the phantom woman held Mike in place, her legs bracing him against the onslaught of magic. He put his hands over hers, clutching tightly at something just under the fabric of his shirt.

Murray was stunned by the sight developing before him. Beth took advantage of the distraction and brought the sword up and into Murray's wand hand.

She had been hoping to cut the magic dick in half. Somehow, she had managed to slice through his fingers. The golden light appeared and caught his digits before they hit the ground but not before the dick of Osiris was smacked into the air.

"No!" Murray backhanded Beth, knocking her down. He flew beneath the magic dick, his dark eyes following its trajectory.

"Ticktock!" Beth stuck out her hand, and the backpack leaped to her side, the empty nylon loop now in reach. She grabbed onto the mimic and said a little prayer. "Sausage party!"

When she threw Ticktock at Murray, the mimic's flaps opened and launched several objects into the air. There were plates and knives and even a few books. Those were just meant to be a visual distraction, because Ticktock also spat out every single rubber dildo Beth owned.

It had been a stupid idea, one Lily had teased her about, but Beth had wondered more than once if they could swap something from her collection for Murray's pride and joy. At a glance, she recognized each and every one of them. They had been part of her most intimate moments. She had agonized over which ones to buy on the internet for hours. If she had to, she could identify them with her eyes closed.

And right now, the one she wanted was headed her way.

Murray looked confused as he was pelted by several dicks at once. He snatched one out of the air and flew up out of reach. As he spun around, he leveled the cock at her.

The words he spoke tore through the air, and the tip of the cock emitted a bright yellow light as it powered up. When he finished his incantation, he pointed the cock at Beth and then flinched when it exploded in a mass of sticky goo.

"What?" He held up the remains of the dark-blue cock and squinted at it. "What is this?"

"It was the Delightful Dragon," Beth told him as she held up Osiris's cock. She had grabbed it out of the air. "You've got to start small and work your way up."

Murray let out a scream of rage and held his hands out. Malevolent energy crackled along his fingertips.

"Fireball, motherfucker!" Beth channeled the energy through Osiris's cock and was blasted backward as a ten-foot-wide fireball erupted from its head. It crashed into Murray and knocked him out of the sky.

"Beth!" Lily pulled Beth to her feet. "Romeo isn't going to last!"

Mike was on his knees now, energy crackling around him as the angel won out. Yuki had joined the fray, summoning a stream of magic that absorbed some of the impact, but she was gasping for air as her arms trembled.

"What do you want me to do?" Beth asked.

"Point your dick at that windmill motherfucker!"

Beth held up the dick of Osiris like a wand, but nothing happened. She wondered if she should cast a spell out of it when Cerberus appeared from the mists. All three heads roared and sent hellfire into Mehkhkahrel, scorching his already blackened wings and diverting its attention. Over by the house, Murray was staggering to his feet, his clothing similarly scorched.

"Shit!" Beth stuck the "wand" in her pocket and looked around. The sword was nearby, but she wouldn't be able to reach the angel with it. What was she supposed to do?

"No!" Death's sudden cry shocked her, and she turned to see that he was staring directly at Mike, one bony hand outstretched toward the Caretaker. "Please, stop! He's my friend! *He's my friend!*"

Beth picked up the sword and ran to the grim reaper's aid. She knew nobody could lift War's sword, but Famine's scales had fared poorly against the sharp edge of her blade. Was her blade sharp enough to break apart War's weapon?

She swung the sword hard, driving it deep into War's blade and showering the ground with sparks. The first swing didn't do the trick, but it sank in a few inches. She hacked away at War's weapon, less than a foot over Death's torso. The tip of her sword snapped off, but she kept hitting, sweat pouring down her face and into her eyes.

Asterion appeared, hefting his battle-ax. Seeing what she was up to, he struck the blade from the other side. His ax cracked, so he grabbed onto the hilt of the blade and pulled sideways in an attempt to widen the gap.

"*C'mon!*" Beth screamed as she used what was left of her magic sword to sever the base of War's blade. Lily and Suly helped Asterion, pulling the sword sideways to make a notch for Beth to focus her efforts on. An eerie light formed over the surface of War's weapon that seemed to weaken in intensity every time she struck a blow.

Screaming in rage, she swung one more time. A blast of light knocked her onto her butt and the others away as War's blade toppled to the ground and sent a cloud of dust into the air.

Death rose from the ground, the blade snapping open on his scythe as fury manifested in his eyes. He swung his blade, emitting a black wave of force that severed several of Mehkhkahrel's wings. The angel fell from the sky, landing hard on the ground while its eyes all looked around in panic.

Cerberus pounced on the angel, all three heads ripping flesh free and filling the air with scorched angel feathers.

"Can that thing even die?" Beth asked.

"All things die," Death replied, then turned his attention to Murray. "Especially you."

Murray's eyes went wide in shock, but he turned his attention toward Mike. Mike was on the ground, his free hand clutching his chest as if in agony. Murray grinned and closed his eyes.

"Stop him!" Beth cried. "He's trying to possess Mike!"

Murray let out a cry of agony and clutched at his face.

"Didn't expect to meet that many people inside my head, did you, asshole?" Mike stood, tears in his eyes. The ferocity there was terrifying to behold as he walked over, his magic gathering behind him. "That beating they gave you was just the beginning. Where I am weak, they are strong. Where you are alone, we are many."

Mike's magic unfolded behind him like a pair of wings, and Murray stared in wonderment. The shimmering wings burst into tiny motes of light, revealing the looming specter of Death himself with fire in his eyes and grim determination on his jaw.

Death dashed past Mike and stabbed his bony fingers into Murray's eyes, causing him to scream. Light emerged from Murray's open mouth as Death stretched a diaphanous substance out of Murray, then ripped it free. Murray collapsed on the ground without a mark on his body as the filmy substance took form.

It was a woman with golden skin and a crown on her head. She stumbled around, staring at her translucent hands in disbelief.

"No," she whispered, then looked at the others. Her face distorted, revealing Murray's twisted features beneath the surface as his soul fought to break free. Sickly clouds of light swirled around her as she regained her composure and pointed a gnarled finger at Mike. "NO!"

When she raised her hands, dark clouds formed at their feet. Beth watched in awe as the spell fizzled, due to the thorned, bony whip that had encircled Nesferisfet and now pinned her arms in place.

"Hurts, doesn't it?" Suly yanked Nesferisfet off her feet, causing her to fall to the ground. "Sorry I lost my head for a bit. I'm ready to contribute now."

Beth smiled. "You contributed plenty," she told him, then planted a kiss on his cheek.

"Are the others inside?" Mike asked with a raspy voice, his features pale. It looked like he had run a marathon, his cheeks sunken in. "Nobody died?"

"Yeah, we're all here. Except..." Beth turned her attention out into the fog. It took her a few minutes of looking, but she found Opal's core where Lily had thrown it. The vial vibrated lightly in her hands as if saying hello, and she sighed in relief. "Now we're all here."

Mike nodded, then sank to the ground. "That's great news," he told her, then looked up at the house. "Hey, the roof is intact. Not bad for your second time house sitting."

"Kids got rowdy," she replied, then sat down next to him. "Threw an unexpected party. You okay?"

"Nope." He pulled a pair of dog tags out of his shirt and gazed at them in awe. "But I will be."

"I hate to interrupt your circle jerk," Lily interjected, her face stuck in a frown. "But how the hell are we getting the house home?"

Mike flopped onto his back and groaned. "I just need a nap," he replied. "I can barely think straight, and everything hurts. But I do have a plan." He turned his attention over to Cerberus. Beth watched as the hellhound happily ripped off one of the angel's wings, causing two of the heads to fight over it.

"Speaking of plans, what about this one?" Suly gave Nesferisfet a kick. She hissed at him and tried to roll away, so he yanked on his whip, causing the bone thorns to bite into her soul.

"Is Murray still in there?" he asked.

"No." Death stroked his chin. "The being known as Murray was consumed by this foul creature when they mixed together. She is a parasite."

"Fuck you," Nesferisfet cried.

"Can we feed her to Cerberus?" Beth asked, scowling at Nesferisfet.

"Probably shouldn't," Lily replied. "Despite what it looks like, the dog doesn't technically eat. I would hate to learn that this bitch will reappear someday and cause even more problems. And I can't do anything with her either."

"So what do we do?" asked Beth.

Mike stared at the ground as if lost in thought, then nodded solemnly. "No more loose ends," he declared, then turned his gaze on Nesferisfet. His eyes flashed dangerously as he rose from the ground. "I know exactly what to do with you."

His raspy voice became a growl, which sent shivers down Beth's spine. He gestured for Lily and Death to join him, then whistled for Cerberus. The hellhound padded over and lay down where Mike could put his hand on the center head's nose. Yuki stood back, her eyes on the mist around the house. It was already starting to thin, revealing dark shapes that shifted without.

"Here's what's going to happen. Cerberus?"

The hellhound responded with a whine.

"You're my good girls, aren't you?" He wrapped his arm around the center head's muzzle and squeezed while the side heads licked his arms and face. "I need you to track down a gate to Hell."

Nesferisfet panicked and tried to fight her way free but was properly secured by Suly's whip. She ended up falling down on her face instead.

"Lily and Death, please go with her in case the horsemen are planning something. The barrier is down, so they're out in the Underworld now." Mike sighed and rubbed his temples. "Not much help for that, I guess."

"Do this, do that." Lily grumbled as she walked over to Cerberus and started to climb up. "When do I get told I'm a good girl? Never. No head pats, no thank-yous…"

"Once you find a gate, come back. We'll form a proper escort and shove this bitch in there." Mike jerked his thumb at Nesferisfet. "She won't go easy, but I know you can handle it."

Nesferisfet howled at him, but Suly grabbed her from behind and clamped his hand over her mouth.

"The master is speakin'," he whispered. "Shut yer damn mouth."

She struggled, but Suly held her tight. Mike held his hand out to Beth, and she moved to join him.

"What do you need from me?" she asked, her body suddenly sore. She had been knocked around so much during the fight that the adrenaline was already wearing off. Her back and sides hurt the most, and she wondered if she had bruised some ribs.

He moved close to her side until his lips were almost on her ear. "I need you to help me inside," he whispered. "Before I collapse."

She looped her arm around his waist and guided him toward the house. Nesferisfet was pulled toward the porch and strapped to one of the pillars while Suly and Yuki kept watch. The mace joined them, laying itself next to the front door as Asterion appeared from out of the mists. Beth hadn't even realized he had left.

"The blind one got away," Asterion grumbled, then sat down on the steps with a grunt. "His footsteps disappear not far from here. I am sorry."

"You have nothing to be sorry for," she replied as she pushed open the door. Mike stumbled a couple of feet as she helped him fall face down onto the nearest couch. Behind them, Ticktock shut the door and withdrew his bladed limbs, once more a nondescript backpack.

"Are the others still alive?" he asked, slurring his words. "Did I make it in time?"

She looked around the room. Reggie sat on top of the nearest table, clutching Jenny like a talisman against evil. Kisa was where Beth had left her but was still breathing.

"I think so," she answered. "Banged up but all here."

Mike mumbled something in reply, but she didn't understand it. As he slumbered, she sat next to him on the love seat and pulled her legs up to her chest and let out a deep breath.

Within seconds, she was asleep too.

IT WAS A BEAUTIFUL SPRING MORNING. THE BIRDS IN THE GARDEN CHIRPED greetings to one another, their songs transforming into terrified squawks as the fairies chased them from their perches with childlike laughter. Mike was lying on the front porch bench, his eyes closed and his head in Cecilia's lap. Her thighs were soft to begin with, but she had figured out some trick with her spectral body that made her legs cooler and more comfortable then any pillow he had ever used.

She was playing with his hair, her cool fingers sending prickles across his scalp. He was lying down so his right arm lay across his belly. His broken arm was wrapped in a fresh layer of spider silk.

It had been nearly a month since his return from the Underworld. After a four-hour nap in his house, he had gone back to Naia and used her connection with the house to properly return it. Even though he was exhausted, Naia had been able to coax a strong orgasm out of him that had yanked the home back through the Underworld and placed it where it belonged. He couldn't be sure, but he had a suspicion the house had been put back slightly crooked and several feet to the left.

While he had been putting back the house, Suly, Lily, and Death had escorted Nesferisfet to the nearest Hell gate. Mike had wondered if he should ask her how to undo the sleeping curse but strongly suspected that any help she provided would have ulterior motives. She had almost ended the world in a mad bid for power, and he fully expected to be double-crossed. Lily told him later that, at the end, she had begged for mercy as they pushed her between the one-way blades meant to ensnare souls.

Death had responded by using the butt of his scythe to shove her the rest of the way in. The demons on the other side, smelling a powerful soul, had dragged her away screaming.

Fortunately, once he'd returned the house to its proper location, Ratu had been able to undo the curse. His unique bond with Tink and Cecilia had allowed him to pull them out through the Dreamscape with Lily's help. Without such a connection, several of the slumbering rats had died of dehydration in the process. Reggie had taken the loss hard but understood that Ratu had tried her hardest to save them.

Of Eulalie and Sofia, he had seen very little. The Arachne was already gone upon his return to the house. A decent population of rats had decided Eulalie was their new leader during his absence, and she had convinced them to chew a portal to her home in Oregon. He had been surprised to discover that Sofia had gone with her. He hadn't wanted to pry into Eulalie's affairs out of respect for her sister but had to admit he was curious.

He had wondered if she would stay there now that Velvet was gone, but she had come back to the house for a couple of days before announcing that she and Sofia had an important project to work on. For the last couple of weeks, she and Sofia had been holed up in the Library, and he had no idea why. The couple of times Eulalie had stopped by to visit him, she had stayed long enough to rewrap his arm while saying very little. His primary worry was that she blamed him or the others for Velvet's death, but Sofia reassured him that Eulalie had hyperfocused on some new task that would be revealed in time.

To say Zel had been upset about his injury was an understatement. She had yelled at him until she was red in the face, all while having Ratu reset some of his bones. The spell he had cast on the forest had created a spiral fracture in his radius and ulna, and his attempt to lift War's sword free had only made it worse. A series of long metal pins now held everything in place until his bones could fuse. Sometimes, when he was lying in bed, he thought he could actually feel his break mending.

The front door swung open, breaking his reverie. Mike heard soft footsteps approaching and smiled.

"Morning, Kisa." He could sense her by proximity now, their connection stronger than ever. He bent his legs, making room on the bench. "Plenty of room for my favorite familiar."

Kisa snorted, then sat on the bench. After shifting around, she pushed his legs apart so she could lay her head down on his stomach.

"I see how it is," the cat girl grumbled. "Turn my back for one second and find you in the arms of another woman."

"You certainly didn't mind sharing me last night," he replied with a smile. When he had crawled into bed, Lily and Kisa had been waiting for him. The two of them had grinned in amusement at each other the whole time they were blowing him, as if parties to a secret. He didn't bother asking; he had been too distracted by the semirough texture of Kisa's tongue on the head of his cock while Lily had forked her own tongue to squeeze the base of his shaft. When he'd come in Kisa's mouth, Lily had pinned him down while the two of them kept sucking until he blew his load in her mouth again.

"Your head still feeling okay?" he asked Kisa as he ran his fingers along the base of her ears.

"Mm-hmm," she replied with a purr. She had suffered a pretty bad concussion during the fight with the horsemen. It had affected her balance, and Tink had been mothering her all month. "Wasn't last night proof enough?"

He smiled, feeling the heat rise to his cheeks.

The three of them cuddled this way for nearly an hour when the front door opened again. It was Death, and he was holding a small tray with a pot of tea and biscuits.

"It is nearly time, Mike Radley." Death stared down at them for several moments as if waiting for a reply. "For our appointment."

Mike groaned. He was comfortable and fairly certain Kisa had fallen asleep with her legs wrapped around one of his. It took him a minute to untangle himself, then he walked out into the garden with Death at his back.

The hedge maze was even larger than before. Luckily, it was no more than belly height, but Kisa and Tink could officially get lost in it. Fae creatures could be spotted moving through the underbrush, and there was a particularly grumpy gnome at one end, who decorated his home with bottle caps that the fairies brought him from neighboring yards. The Jabberwock, happy to have its bigger yard back, guarded the opening closest to the front entrance. Anyone not paying attention would think it was some sort of concrete/topiary hybrid.

Mike allowed Death to lead him into the maze. They navigated the outer rim until they found a shortcut toward the center. A table and chairs had been set in a quiet location not too far from the sundial specifically for teatime. The metal table was held in place by thick roots that had sprouted from beneath. Mike took a seat just as Beth appeared several hedges over. Her hair was mussed, and there were a couple of sticks caught in it.

"Shit, is it that time already?" She adjusted her outfit and cleared her throat as Suly stood up next to her. The dullahan grinned and waved at Mike.

"We'll be out o' yer hair soon," he said, then leaned down to pull Asterion to his feet. The minotaur appeared to be in a daze, but he locked eyes with Mike and nodded.

"We are all friends now," Asterion said, then guided Beth and Suly through the maze and toward the house.

"How the hell did I not see them?" Mike wondered aloud.

"Because you did not have their consent to watch them," Death replied. "Sorceress Bethany cast a concealment spell. It is one of the spells she has been working on all week with Ratu. She is becoming quite good."

"I see." He had been so busy this last week that he hadn't had a chance to talk with her. Most of their interactions had concerned the slime girl currently living in his bathtub. Ever since getting blasted by the angel, Opal was having trouble holding a human form. "I'm probably overdue for my own tutelage."

"It would serve you well." Death arranged the crockery on the table. "You should learn a spell to reheat my tea for me. It would be most convenient."

In front of the house, a car door slammed. Cyrus appeared between the lions, his eyes darting back and forth as he carried a briefcase past the Jabberwock and into the hedge maze. It took him a couple minutes to wind his way toward them, but he came to a stop on the other side of a thick bush.

"I swear I had the route figured out this time," he mumbled while scratching his chin. A rough beard was coming in, but the scars on his face meant it would never be uniform.

"It changes," Mike replied. He touched a nearby leaf and made his will known to the hedges. The foliage parted, allowing a wide-eyed Cyrus to come through and sit with them.

"Was that you?" he asked.

"Not quite," Mike replied. The roses around his house stubbornly refused his commands, so he was always siccing Suly on them. Some of the plants were manifesting personalities, and he could only wonder what he would have learned from the Mandragora if he could have spoken to it before it left so long ago. It wasn't so much that he made the bushes part—he had asked nicely and let them decide. "Have a seat."

"I have made us chamomile," Death declared, causing Cyrus to flinch. "It is a friendly tea."

"Thank you." Cyrus took his seat and accepted a cup from Death. "I'm sorry I keep reacting that way. It's something about your voice."

"You and I have met on many occasions. It has never been friendly." Death winked at Mike, an action that caused one of his flames to temporarily go out. "Until now."

"So what do you have for me today?" Mike leaned forward, ignoring the cup of tea Death put in front of him.

Cyrus pulled some papers out of his briefcase and slid them across. It was a coroner's report for Murray. They had brought his body back and slumped him over the toilet in his bedroom. The police had found him a couple days later after Eulalie sent an anonymous email complaining about the smell.

"Positional asphyxia?" Mike looked up at Cyrus from the document.

"They think he passed out on the toilet and suffocated while slumped over." Cyrus sipped his tea. "This is really good, by the way."

"You are too kind." Death sat down and drank from his own cup. Cyrus watched with interest as the liquid disappeared in Death's mouth.

"Don't bother asking where it goes," Mike told him as he set the papers down. "Did you find out that other thing I wanted to know?"

"Angelic retribution?" Cyrus frowned. "For obvious reasons, there aren't any records on killing an angel and if God Himself will come after you."

"Damn." Mike picked up his cup and held it without drinking. After Cerberus had killed Mehkhkahrel, it had slowly expanded in size. The damn thing was nearly the size of a mountain now in the Underworld, and scavengers were slowly picking it apart.

"Based on my experience, you can't keep thinking of the Great Almighty as some old guy who knows all and sees all." Cyrus set down his cup and crossed his legs. "We know that other gods existed. Some still might."

"I just don't want one descending on my house." Mike looked at the edge of his property. The geas had been weakened by the angel's search for Death, and it seemed to be stuck that way. A couple of joggers had stopped to watch centaurs in the yard just yesterday. Lily had followed one home and discovered that the geas made them see a child's birthday party where they chased each other on ponies.

Mike was having a privacy gate put up once the materials arrived.

The conversation steered away from the Apocalypse and toward more mundane things. Cyrus asked plenty of questions about the Underworld itself and provided Mike with anecdotal tales from his time in the Order. It was hard not to like the man, but Mike could tell theirs wasn't just a casual relationship.

It was part of the reason he had Death with him. The grim reaper not only interjected at odd moments and provided a distraction, but Mike knew if the Order were to ever assemble a dossier on him, it would likely include the fact that the physical manifestation of Death itself was one of his best friends.

Anyone who chose to fuck with him or his family while knowing that information deserved whatever fate they got, which brought him back to Leeds. The bastard was still locked down in Oregon, but the opportunity to escape would come eventually. That was a problem that required a unique solution.

"Mike Radley." Death loomed over him now, his eyes shining brightly despite it being midday. "Your tea has gone cold."

"You're right. It has." He held up his cup. "Top me off, would you? I promise I'll finish it this time."

"You seem distracted. Maybe it's something I could help with?" Cyrus leaned forward, his eyes wide with excitement. "I bet I can help. Please let me help."

Mike chuckled, then held his freshly filled cup to his lips.

"I could tell you the details, but then I'd have to kill you." He winked, causing Cyrus to groan. The man knew all about the incident with the horsemen, but it would be a cold day in Hell before Mike shared anything about Oregon.

That, after all, was strictly a family matter. By the time he bade Cyrus farewell, it was early evening and his stomach rumbled with hunger. Anticipating a large meal, he walked into the house and noticed immediately that the air lacked the familiar scent of dinner. Puzzled, he walked into the dining hall to find Beth and Reggie eating plain sandwiches and chips while going over some documents.

"Where's Sofia?" he asked.

Beth shrugged, then held up her sandwich. "No idea. Looks like we're fending for ourselves tonight."

Without fail, the cyclops had prepared meals like clockwork for the entire time he had known her. Worried something had happened to her, he grabbed a handful of chips from the bag on the table and then ran to his office to move the red book to its proper location. The world blurred around him as he was transported to the Library.

What had once been a lonely space was now bustling with activity. Hundreds of rats scurried about in organized chaos, several of them pulling carts full of books across the lobby. A few stopped when they saw Mike, and a couple even waved.

"What the hell is going on here?" He walked up to the front desk and saw that a golden bell had been placed on the counter. Curious, he hit the plunger. A ringing sound echoed along the colossal stacks for several seconds before disappearing.

A platform loomed overhead, then sank down to the floor. Standing on it was Sofia, looking regal in her Head Librarian's gown.

"I must have lost track of time," she muttered, then stepped off the platform.

"Is everything okay?" he asked. "You never showed up for dinner."

"You know, it was never my job to cook meals for you." She narrowed her eye at him and frowned.

"That's not what I meant, and you know it. I don't care that you didn't cook for us, but when someone breaks from their routine, I go check on them." He took a step forward and slipped his hands around her waist. "So what are you up to? Anything I can help with?"

Sofia kept a stern look about her, but her cheeks reddened. "As a matter of fact, there is plenty of work to do around here. After the incident with the horsemen, it was discovered that we did in fact have some texts that pertained to our situation. The Library, first and foremost, is a repository of knowledge. It is time that I work to restore its function, which includes better cataloging and access to materials."

"That's great," he said. "But it doesn't have to be something you do alone."

"And it isn't." Sofia sauntered away, her large ass swaying as she did so. She stood on the platform and tapped her staff. "I have something to show you. Are you coming?"

Not yet, he thought with a grin. He stood next to her and grabbed onto the railing. "Let's see what you've got going on."

Sofia stood stoic as the platform rose, her hair rustling around her as they lifted into the air. From up above, Mike could see the rats were surprisingly coordinated in their efforts. It seemed they were gathering up books from distant stacks and moving them to an empty section of the Library.

"There's quite a backlog of incoming books," Sofia explained. "The rats haven't learned to read yet, but the Library has a translation feature. While they don't completely understand the wording, they have been taught the difference between genres."

"That's great, but does Reggie know about this?"

"It was his idea. Ever since the last incursion, he decided his people would be safer in a more neutral territory. To that end, we put them to work for room and board."

The platform was moving fast enough now that the breeze was pushing Mike's hair back. "So what do you need from me?"

Sofia looked over his shoulder with a grin. "You'll see."

They traveled for a few more minutes before landing on a giant stack that had been hollowed out. Most of the books had been removed, leaving behind what looked like a bundle of networking cables that looped around the structure.

"Is that..." He stepped off the platform in disbelief. "Did you guys build a giant server room?"

"The biggest on Earth." Eulalie descended from above, her hands and front legs clinging to a braided web. She dropped the last ten feet and tumbled, landing in a crouch, the dog tags jingling around her neck. "Well, not Earth, technically. These cables are connected to secret locations across the planet. Do you know what's better than using a VPN? Actually using routers on different parts of the planet." The Arachne was smug as she dropped a bundle of cables from her arms. "The rats can nibble these really tiny holes, just big enough for a cable. Even if the router is discovered, all they will ever find is a mysterious hole in the wall. Any attempt to widen it will disrupt the portal, and then poof!" She clapped her hands together. "All evidence is erased."

Mike nodded appreciatively. "I admit, that's pretty cool. But what is it for?"

"This place is a sanctuary for information. We are pulling information from some of the most protected areas of Earth." She patted the floor beneath her. "We're not just connected to routers, you know. If you ever want to use a supercomputer or experimental AI for anything, you just let me know."

"To what end though?"

Eulalie smiled. "You let me worry about that."

"I have to admit, this is really cool. How are you powering it?"

"We got Zel to agree to some solar panels in the greenhouse. She and I actually had a very enlightening discussion about many things. I think we may actually be friends now. Also may have tapped into the electrical grid in places." Eulalie wiggled her eyebrows, which made it look like her lower spider eyes were blinking. "If you hear about rolling brownouts, it might be us."

"So this is what you need help with?" Mike gestured at the array of cables. "I mean, I can help with some stuff, but I kind of feel like it would take you longer to explain to me than to just do it yourself."

"Never have you spoken truer words. You're actually here to see me." Eulalie walked onto the platform, followed by Sofia and then Mike. It sank down through the Library, then veered down a narrow corridor full of stacks of books.

It was another ten minutes before they got to their destination. They arrived at a large stone column with a solitary arch nearly a hundred feet off the ground. A trio of rats stood guard, standing at attention the moment Eulalie stepped off the platform.

"Good job, guys." She made sure to pat each one on the head, then walked inside.

"So what is this place?" he asked.

"It was used to store dangerous texts," Sofia replied. "But for now, it's Eulalie's home."

"Home?" He hadn't spoken to Eulalie about living arrangements but had figured she would move into the house.

"I'm going to live here," Eulalie said, moving into a cavernous space. A small bank of monitors was still being assembled along the walls, and small pockets of webbing had been scattered around the ceiling. A hammock dangled in one corner with a pillow inside it. "Since I am going to be the Assistant Librarian, it only makes sense."

"Assistant?" He looked at Sofia. "You've got help now?"

"Yes. We are planning to get this place back up and running." Sofia smiled. "It'll take some time, but we'll get there eventually."

"Which brings me to why you're here." Eulalie moved to the back wall of the room and stuck her hands through a thick band of webs. She removed something and walked back over to him, the object concealed by her arms. "I think you should see this."

"What is it?" Mike held out his hands as Eulalie handed him the object.

There was a faint pop as the object shocked him. The odor of the woods filled his nostrils, followed by the smell of hot springs. Jumbled thoughts were tossed through his mind, most of them just sounds. Eventually a single image burned bright in his mind. It was Velvet, standing on a cliff with the wind in her hair. She turned around to smile at him as the memory faded.

The object warmed in his hands, sending a pleasurable buzz throughout his body. It was a thick ovoid with red-and-blue swirls across its surface. It looked like a gemstone but radiated a life force he immediately recognized.

"Velvet?" He ran his fingers across the pebbled surface of the egg, then clutched it to his chest. It hummed in time with the beating of his own heart. The ramifications of what he held raced through him, and he chose to immerse himself in the moment. A small part of her still existed, and he didn't care how or why. During the fight with Mehkhkahrel, he had felt her presence, but he couldn't be sure if it had been her or just his magic trying to meet his desires. It was almost like she had been holding him up as he unleashed every ounce of energy.

Later, he had asked Cecilia if it could have been her. The banshee had shrugged and explained that the Underworld could be a strange place in terms of spirits and what they could accomplish.

"My dad had a saying." Eulalie placed her hand on his shoulder. "Nobody is ever truly gone. When she died, I wasn't sure what to do when I found out she had laid an egg. I don't have her instincts, and I'm not cut out to be a mother. I debated having it smashed and just ending the Arachne once and for all, but the moment I touched it..." She shrugged. "It was almost like seeing her one last time. If she spared it, she had good reasons to do so."

"We're going to raise it here," Sofia announced. "The house is no place for a child. This place is safe from outside threats. It's possible her upbringing could be difficult, but we are up to the task. And someday, when she is old enough to leave the nest..."

"Then we will let her decide what comes next." Eulalie squeezed his shoulder. "The egg will have to leave the Library on occasion, because time doesn't pass in here. That will be one of your jobs, to help us grow and hatch it by taking it for walks outside these halls. Bring her with you when you aren't busy hunting demons or arguing with magical royalty."

"And once she's here, I'll help raise her. Or try to, anyway." Mike ran his fingers over the surface of the egg in awe. So many feelings begged for his attention, and he couldn't focus on any of them. This wasn't just about Velvet's legacy but his own.

He was about to become a father, but he was also reminded that Velvet was gone. These thoughts and ideas would take some time to absorb, and he promised to focus on the positives. The others would help because that was what family did.

At the very least, he would be a better parent than his own mother had been. "Does she have a name?" he asked.

Eulalie and Sofia smiled at each other.

"That depends on you," Eulalie replied. "What do you want to call her?"

Cyrus turned onto the unmarked road off Highway 104, the tires on his rental kicking up giant clouds of dust behind him. It had been almost an hour since he had seen another car, which included the fact that he had been forced to turn around after missing his exit.

Though he had not seen anyone, he had no doubt he was being watched. For almost half an hour, he slalomed along the road through the sagebrush-covered plains, making sure to keep his windows rolled up to keep out the heat and dust. The air conditioning was doing its best, but the car was emitting a high-pitched whine that threatened to test the limits of the engine.

Anyone following would have been surprised to see him gun the engine and drive straight into a large boulder. It was a security precaution, a spell that would only allow someone to pass if they were going faster than twenty-five miles per hour. White light sizzled along the exterior of his black Nissan, and then a dull building the size of a garage popped into existence on the other side of the boulder. The sky was cast in gray, as if filtering out any color from the outside world.

By the time he came to a stop, there was a small group of men and women assembled outside the entrance of the building.

Upon exiting the car, he sensed the barrage of spells meant to verify his identity. He leaned against the car and stretched while they scanned him. It had been a long drive, and his legs were stiff.

"Master Cyrus." A woman broke away from the pack and handed him a visitor's badge. "If you would wear this please."

"A badge? Really?" He put it over his head. "Seems kind of redundant now that you know who I am." Though he had never visited this facility, protocols were fairly standard across the world. The badge felt oddly heavy, but he assumed it was spell related.

"Let's just say the badge is a necessary precaution." The woman handed him a small stone. It had a groove in it, and he recognized it as a worry stone. "Also, keep this in your pocket while inside the building. Don't lose it or you may be subjected to termination with prejudice."

He frowned at the rock, then looked at the woman. "What the hell is going on with the Order?" he asked.

She shook her head. "I'm not permitted to give you that information, sorry."

He waved his hand dismissively. "I understand. I suppose I have people I could ask."

Relief crossed her face, and she nodded. "Shall we?" She gestured behind them, and the others opened the door to the building. He noticed they all watched the surrounding land as he walked inside, then backed into the space one at a time. Whatever was going on had them spooked bad.

The garage-like building housed a single elevator. Once everyone was inside, two of the men grabbed onto a pair of silver rods along opposite walls. Their magic flowed into the motor, allowing the elevator to descend. The trip was long, but Cyrus was simply grateful not to be sitting anymore.

At the bottom of the shaft, the group disembarked, then took their positions in a room overlooking the opening to the elevator. There was a good chance it was the only entrance to this place.

"Right this way." The woman turned away from him, and he realized he didn't know her name. Typically, members of the Order would identify themselves upon meeting to avoid confusion. Whether this was an oversight on her part due to the new security precautions or something else entirely, he had no way of knowing.

Still, the woman's identity didn't matter. He had come to see someone else.

At the end of a long corridor, they came to a circular door embedded into the stone. She placed her hand on a scanner, and the door slid open.

"He's been expecting you," she said, stepping aside. "For a couple of months now. Demanded we keep his calendar clear for today."

Cyrus nodded. It wasn't a surprise that he had been expected. After all, the Oracle often saw things long before they happened.

When he walked into the room, a red light turned on above the door once it shut behind him. It was like being inside of an extra-large darkroom for developing photographs, only the center of the room was occupied by a giant glass cylinder filled with mist. The cylinder itself was nearly a hundred feet across and five stories high.

"Master Cyrus." The voice spoke to him from a mechanical grill at the bottom of the tube. Somewhere inside the glass, the Oracle was speaking into a microphone.

"I like the new housing unit." He had been with the Order when they had first captured the Oracle. Originally, the creature had been contained in a metal box not much larger than a coffin with a vent at the bottom. Good behavior over the years had allowed it substantially more freedom. Attracted to tragedy like a moth to a flame, the creature had a flair for prophecy that had resulted in its imprisonment rather than destruction. There was still significant doubt that the Oracle hadn't caused the Silver Bridge collapse of '67, so it remained somewhere it could be safely studied.

"Prison," the Oracle corrected as if reading Cyrus's mind. "You may use fancy words for it, but it is still a prison." A dark shape moved behind the mist as the Oracle came near the glass. "It has been many years since we last spoke in person."

"It has." Cyrus licked his lips, which had suddenly gone dry. "I have a question of a delicate nature."

"Indeed." The Oracle shifted in his enclosure, his glowing eyes visible through the mist. "Just think of the journey it has been to bring you to this point."

"So you know the question I want to ask?"

The Oracle chuckled. "Perhaps. But I am not ready to answer it yet. Indulge me. I would hear about your reasons for asking it."

Cyrus frowned. "You can't see what brings me here?"

"There are many places on this planet that obscure my vision." The swirling mists parted, briefly revealing a pair of damaged wings. "You have recently steeped yourself in such a place, like a fine tea. I would hear of it that I may taste such a place for myself."

"I have taken an oath not to share the details," Cyrus replied.

"Ah, still a man of your word." The Oracle made a clicking sound, then disappeared into the mists. "Instead of details, maybe you can summarize? It'll be like old times."

Cyrus nodded, understanding at once what the Oracle meant by old times. The Oracle and anyone who spoke with him used to be under heavy surveillance shortly after his capture. This extra attention had waned over the years once the Order was confident the Oracle wasn't going to possess some-one's body or manipulate them. Cyrus had developed these gestures to gain the Oracle's trust and had never once abused it.

However, things had obviously changed for the Order. They were being listened to, and what he had to say was for the Oracle alone. To anyone listen-ing, it sounded like he was rambling, talking about a man who had discovered a treasure trove of magic. However, the Oracle watched him closely as he made innocuous hand gestures that conveyed additional meaning. Certain signals meant he was lying; others implied he was selling it short.

For example, when the Oracle interrupted to ask about how powerful the inherited magic was, Cyrus had shrugged while scratching his chin. "No more than anyone else who comes into magic," he said, but his actions told the Oracle the opposite. There were no monitors in the Oracle's chamber—any cameras that watched him only captured static.

The Oracle listened quietly, occasionally moving back into the mysterious mists of its prison. Some of the top minds of the Order had tried to study the mist's composition, but anytime they managed to capture a sample, it would somehow disappear. When asked about it, the Oracle tended to dodge the question. It liked to talk but refused to elaborate on what it was or where it had come from. The mist didn't come from the Oracle but somehow manifested whenever the creature was confined.

Finished with his tale, Cyrus moved to sit on a seat that had been carved into the wall. He had been grateful to stand after such a long time driving, but now his legs hurt and he needed to sit. Furniture of any kind wasn't allowed in the Oracle's chamber. For the longest time, it was feared the Oracle was tele-kinetic and could free itself with a heavy enough object. Ever since the day of its capture, however, it had shown no talent for telekinesis.

Still, Cyrus was not alone in the idea that the Oracle was simply playing a long game where each move was decades in the making. Since it was impos-sible to know how long the Oracle would live, it was simply better to take extra precautions.

"You weave a good tale, Master Cyrus." The Oracle turned around, his large wings brushing against the glass. "But for the life of me, I am uncertain what this has to do with your question."

Cyrus felt a yawning pit in his belly, and he swallowed the lump in his throat. "While I was…a guest of this household, there was a woman there."

"Maybe I don't know your question after all." The Oracle snorted, causing the mists to swirl. "Could it be love after so many years?"

"Do you remember when you would answer all my questions with stupid poems? I far prefer that to your sense of humor." Cyrus tightened his lips. "The woman who held me captive…her voice was familiar. And she wouldn't let me view her, never directly. I suspect she isn't what she said she was."

"Surely it couldn't be the woman who gave you those scars."

Cyrus touched his face and shivered. Hundreds, if not thousands, of spiders had attacked him at the command of an Arachne he had hunted back in the early seventies. He had lost his partner in the fight, but the creature had been destroyed.

Or at least, so he thought. While wiping down Murray's house, he had discovered odd footprints that had raised all the hairs on his neck. If the Arachne had survived, she would be well over eighty years old, which was far older than one should live.

Which meant she had reproduced.

"It couldn't be her," he replied. "But what if she had offspring?" If Eulalie really was an Arachne, that also meant her sister who had died was probably an Arachne herself. Was Mike Radley hiding a nest of them?

The Oracle tsked at him while tapping a long digit against the glass.

"I can only see what is or what will be," it replied. "If you want answers about the past, then open a history book."

Cyrus stood and smoothed out his shirt. "Fine, then. I'll be direct. Are the Arachne gone or do they still walk the earth?"

"And what would you do with this information? Would you gather a holy crusade and set forth to stomp them out? Or perhaps your new perspective would give you pause?"

"It shouldn't matter to you what I do," Cyrus retorted angrily. "What we do with the answers to our questions is none of your damned business."

Crimson eyes glowed brightly in the fog as if studying him. "Maybe what you do with yourself matters more than you could ever know, Master Cyrus. Perhaps your new…enlightened state gave me a false sense of familiarity."

"You're stalling." Ultimately, it didn't matter. If the Oracle chose not to answer, he wouldn't. During those rare occasions, he would either go quiet or simply refuse. As long as the Oracle kept talking, it meant an answer was coming.

"Then here is your answer." The mists thickened and pressed against the glass as if trying to pass through it. Some of it squeezed out of the mechanical speaker. Cyrus made a mental note to mention it to maintenance once he was done. "You fear the past, but your time is better spent looking to the future. But you will never fulfill your destiny as long as you continue looking over your shoulder."

Destiny? Cyrus snorted but said nothing.

"On the fate of the Arachne, know that not a single Arachne walks this earth."

Cyrus frowned. "That's only a half answer. That could mean that several Arachne are alive and well, and you know it."

The Oracle sighed. "I tire of this topic, but fine, I shall humor you. At this very moment in time, no Arachne nor its eggs exist on Earth. Does this please you?"

Cyrus could hear the sneer in the Oracle's voice. It would bother him more, but he was so flooded with relief that he didn't really care how he was spoken to. More mist drifted from the speaker, curling in on itself like a snake.

"This is good news," he replied, then turned to walk away. "I'll let them know you behaved."

"Like the animal I am, right?" There was a coldness to the Oracle that Cyrus hadn't heard in a while. "Tell them I want more mystery novels this time. I'm tired of action books. They're too predictable."

"I don't know how you read with all that shit in there." Cyrus put his hands on the door.

"And you assume we only see the best things in life with our eyes." The Oracle slapped a hand against the glass. "Master Cyrus?"

Cyrus paused, then looked back at the Oracle. "What?"

"I have a question for you." The anger was gone, and the mists had thinned out. "If this Caretaker you spoke of were to find such a wretch as myself, do you think he would have locked me away?"

Cyrus shook his head in frustration and moved to leave.

"Please, answer me!" The Oracle slapped on the glass again, desperation in its voice. "Does such a human exist that could see past all that I am? Would he sit with me as you do, yet without these walls to confine me?"

Cyrus paused, then let out a sigh. When he turned around, he was surprised to see the Oracle had pressed itself against the glass, as if to see him better. It was a hideous sight, seeing all of the creature at once. It looked to be in poor shape, but Cyrus knew better.

The damned thing seemed to shape-shift at times but never in a measurable way. It was always a humanoid with a pair of large wings and glowing eyes, but that was where the similarities ended. Sometimes the antennae would be much longer and thin, or short and furry. Its wings would droop and drag behind it on the ground, but now they stuck out and fluttered as it moved. Decades of researchers had studied this demonstrable evidence of the Mandela effect, but progress was greatly hindered by the fact that files and pictures would alter themselves to match the current variant they could see. Any sort of research based solely on shifting memories and opinions would inevitably lead nowhere, but the Order was determined to keep trying.

"I don't know," he replied. "Not because I think less of you or him. But if I were to guess...I think he's a good man. Better than you or I deserve, that's for certain."

"I see." The Oracle sounded relieved as it moved back from the glass. "If given the opportunity, I would so love to meet him."

"Fat chance," Cyrus muttered as he let himself out. His escort waited for him outside, and they led him to a room where he could spend the night before setting out in the morning. As sleep came for him, he kept going over his conversation with the Oracle.

No matter how many times he replayed the words, he knew the Oracle had gotten the better of him. He just couldn't figure out how. As he tried to tease out what he had missed, a random thought surfaced.

He had forgotten to mention the broken speaker to maintenance. Shaking his head, he reached for the nearby landline to let someone know.

THE FOREST WAS ALIVE IN A MANNER ABELLA HAD NEVER EXPERIENCED IN HER centuries of life. The trees rustled their branches at her in greeting as Nirumbi children circled their base, playing a game that involved two sticks and a stone. Up above, a tiny cluster of sprites watched with great interest.

Ever since Mike had awakened the forest, fae creatures had returned to the land. Some of them had been in a state of hibernation, surviving deep within the soil. Others had migrated over from the fae realm with the blessing of the queen. It was part of a treaty he had signed with the queen, allowing her people a place to stay outside her realm as long as she devoted defenders to the border. A tribe of rock trolls now patrolled the edges of his property and reported directly to Bigfoot.

Walking past the fairy glade, she approached the large spider's web in the middle of a clearing. Ensnarled twenty feet above, Leeds glared down at her with a malice that nearly radiated heat.

"You look comfortable," she told him.

Leeds spat at her, only to be zapped by one of the many sprites supervising him. The sprites were humanoid in shape and carried little rods that fired bursts of magic that caused a terrible burning sensation. Leeds flinched, his lips curling up in pain.

"So is today the day?" he asked. "After so many weeks, has the Caretaker decided what is to become of me?"

Abella shook her head. "I'm just here to move you," she told him, then nodded to a group of nearby gnomes. They gave her a salute and scrambled up the trees that supported the web. Using sharp blades, they cut the ropes in a manner that had Leeds sink to the ground as if in slow motion. Once he was within reach, Abella slapped a silver collar around his neck.

"What is this?" he asked.

"You tell me," she replied. Ratu had made it to keep him from ducking into the shadows and escaping. Suspending him in the air had prevented this, but keeping the area well lit every night had been a time-intensive endeavor.

Leeds regarded her with anger, then grunted. "You know I can't read your mind, don't you?"

Abella nodded. She had wondered for a long time why he had taken special care to remove her before the fight. Originally, she'd thought it had been her strength he feared. But after much discussion with the others, she'd concluded it was the fact that she had figured out he couldn't read her thoughts. Without knowing what was going on in her head, he couldn't predict her actions nor use them against her.

It was also the reason she had been sent to move him.

"This way." She grabbed him by the scruff of the neck and pulled him to his feet. The webbing Eulalie had wrapped him in lasted for a few days at a time. These strands had another day of use at most, and a couple ripped free. Grabbing hold of a loose (but strong) strand, she pulled him forward.

It didn't surprise her when Leeds fell onto the ground and went limp.

"If you expect me to behave, you are wrong," he explained.

"Suit yourself." She grabbed him by the tail and dragged him through the woods. Just beyond the clearing was a tiny shed without any windows, and she stopped just short of the door.

"Is this to be my new home?" he asked sarcastically. "You are locking me in a porta-potty?"

When she opened the door, a blast of cold air blew across her skin. Leeds recoiled at first, then tilted his head for a better look.

"I don't understand," he said.

"You will." Abella grabbed him by the wings and threw him through the portal on the far wall. When she followed, she found him biting at his bonds in a last-minute bid for freedom. They now stood in a small yurt with no windows and a flap for a door.

"Where have you brought me?" he demanded.

"I'll let the Caretaker explain." With a smirk, she wrestled Leeds onto a nearby gurney made of steel. Ratu had enchanted the cuffs to clamp down on his limbs, and Abella was soon pushing him through the leather flap and outside. They were on a rocky trail, surrounded by steep cliffs.

"Where is he?" Leeds snorted, and fog billowed from his lips. "I would have him see me like this! Come see your own cruelty, damn it!"

"Oh, he's busy. Sorry, I almost forgot." She knelt below the gurney and turned on the speaker that sat on the bottom. It was plugged into an old MP3 player that had been duct-taped to the back of it.

"Hello, Leeds." Mike's voice crackled to life through the speaker. "I'm sorry I couldn't be there in person to see just how wretched you are, but I have been busy with important things."

"He lies!" Leeds laughed hysterically. "He is afraid of me and cannot bear to watch my execution! Not that it will work," he hastily added.

"I will try to keep this brief," Mike continued. "You see, you took something from me that can never be replaced. You were inside my head, saw how much she meant to me, maybe even how much we meant to each other."

"Kiss my ass, Caretaker. Wait, where are we?" Leeds craned his head to look at the rocky overhang that blotted out the sun. The overhang became a cave, eight feet tall and cut in a perfect circle. It descended at a gentle angle, and Abella clicked the button on the side of the gurney that turned on the headlights that Tink had made for her.

"You are a complicated man, Leeds. Brought into this world and cursed with a human soul while wearing the body of a hideous beast. If I had been cursed as you, would I have done the same? Would I have gone out of my way to cause pain and suffering? It's not something I can answer, but I will say this: if I had, then I deserved whatever I had coming."

Leeds struggled against his bonds as Abella knelt to pause the audio.

"Why don't you just dip me in holy water and get it over with? Oh, that's right, I'll be back in a couple of days," Leeds yelled. "You had a chance to destroy me, do you know that? *You could have ended me!* I felt all that dark, beautiful power, and you *wasted it!*"

Abella winced once the shouting was too loud. She slapped Leeds hard enough that the gurney teetered.

"You are too noisy," she told him. "Now it's my turn to speak, and you're going to listen. Understand?"

"What the fuck are you on about?" Leeds asked, one wing popping free. Abella paused long enough to clamp it down to the gurney, then continued her descent. "I don't give a shit what you have to say."

Abella raised a hand in warning, and Leeds became quiet.

"When you trapped us in that cave, I thought my life was over. In the process of trying to save someone, I nearly died," she said.

"I wish you ha—AAAH!" Leeds cried out when Abella hooked her fingers into his nostrils and pulled.

"My wing was busted. I could barely move. I slipped in and out of consciousness from the pain." Abella relaxed her fingers a bit. Satisfied Leeds would be quiet, she continued.

"Velvet and I had a brief but complicated relationship."

"I'm aware," Leeds replied softly. "I could see inside her head."

"That's right, you could." The house had discussed Leeds's ability to read minds. In their discussions about what to do with him, they knew he would try to manipulate them using their own thoughts. However, it had been brought up that Leeds needed to feel superior to whoever he was dealing with. At best, he was a narcissist, and they would use that to break him.

"If she had left me behind, maybe she would have made it out and lived. It's not really my place to say." Abella kept her gaze on the stone walls of the corridor. She was afraid that if she looked at Leeds, she would be unable to continue speaking. "I know I wouldn't have survived. My kind aren't invincible."

"Does this discussion have a point?" he asked.

"She spent the rest of her life dragging me free of that mountain. I owe her my life, and that's not a debt that's easily repaid. Maybe it's a kind of poetry that I am pushing her killer down into a mountain."

Leeds groaned. "Please don't tell me you're about to get weepy."

"I am not." In fact, she wanted to say more on the subject, to tell him her path to salvation was about to become his path to damnation.

But she knew better than to ruin the surprise. He would have plenty of time soon to contemplate this conversation. The subject of Leeds had been hotly debated, and Mike's plan had been complicated.

"I don't understand," Eulalie had argued early on. "Why can't you just force him through a Hell gate, like you did with that priestess lady? He could suffer for all eternity in there. Why go through all this extra effort?"

"Because Leeds is a demon," Lily replied. "His soul will suffer while he's there, but he could be summoned back someday. It could be never, or it could be next week. Is that a risk we want to take?"

After some more back-and-forth, Eulalie had finally realized the brilliance of Mike's plan and agreed. Since she was constantly securing him in her webs, Ratu had used an amnesia spell utilizing a glass jar and some marbles to steal those memories away. They didn't want Leeds extracting the information from her.

Abella arrived at the end of the corridor. Leaning against the wall was Ratu, a glowing light hovering overhead as she paged through the grimoire.

"What do we have here?" Ratu kept her face solemn with the greeting, her scales shifting over her skin. "Is this that little troublemaker I've heard so much about?"

"Please." Leeds started laughing. "You can act tough, but someday, I'll come for you too. I'll come for all of you! Maybe it'll be when you're asleep, or maybe I'll wait until that little egg of yours hatches! That's right, I know the sister has it!"

Abella jammed her thumb into one of Leeds's eyes. While he screamed in pain, she knelt to hit play on the MP3 player as she stopped squeezing his eye.

"Leeds. I want you to understand something about me. All my life, I've been told that forgiveness is the answer. I should forgive my mother, I should forgive my ex-girlfriend, I should forgive that friend in college who stole my credit cards. You should be aware by now that humans make entire movies about the power of forgiveness."

"Oh, please forgive me, Caretaker. I need it so bad!" Leeds jerked his head away and tried to spit on Abella. "Did he forgive you for failing?"

"There was nothing to forgive," she replied, then held up the player and pressed play again. The next part of the message was too important not to be heard.

"They say that you should forgive but not forget," Mike continued. "That there's a lesson to be learned from all this by the people on both sides. But you know what? I'm so fucking tired of being the better person. I'm tired of living with the pain of your deeds and being expected to measure up to a higher standard.

"So here's what I'm going to do. Since I can never forgive you, I'm going to forget you. We all are. Once this message is done, I am meeting with a man from the Order and he is going to wipe away our memories of you."

"Wait, what? The Order?" Leeds looked from Ratu to Abella. "There's no way you have contacts inside the Order; those guys are assholes. If they knew you existed, they would come down on you and..."

"A deal was made," Abella replied. "It doesn't matter if you believe it or not. Once we're done here, we will forget you as well."

In fact, there was no such deal. Mike had no intention of cheapening Velvet's death by erasing his memories of her killer, but that wasn't the point. They needed Leeds to believe he had been forgotten, because it would make what came next a thousand times worse.

"You can't forget about me!" Leeds puffed up his chest on the gurney. "I'm the Jersey Fucking Devil! So that's it, you all are going to lock me away? In a cave? You're all insane if you think this will stop me."

Abella noticed Leeds's collar had flashed a couple times and now glowed as if heated. She hit play on the MP3 player and then helped Ratu remove Leeds from the gurney.

"There are so many things I want to say to you," Mike continued. "But why bother? In just a few minutes, you will mean nothing to me. You'll be reduced to little more than a Wikipedia page and shitty truck stop merch, so nobody will ever give a fuck about you ever again."

The speaker went silent as Ratu and Abella shoved Leeds up against the wall.

"You can't do this to me! You can't...what's your story?" Leeds asked, looking at Ratu. His eyes glowed, but his face faltered. "You're...different. It's like you're hollow inside."

"My mind is a mirror," Ratu replied. "So all you will see is a reflection of your true self." As a demigod, she was easily capable of thwarting a simple mind read.

"I am not hollow!" Leeds struggled against his bonds. "I am not just a footnote in history!"

"Maybe not today. But soon." Ratu shoved Leeds into the smooth alcove behind them with surprising strength. The Jersey Devil fought and screamed as they pushed him in and forced him into the fetal position as Ratu shrank the stone walls around him.

Leeds shrieked at them from his stone prison as the walls closed in.

"He needs to come see me!" he screamed, his voice echoing down the tunnel. "I deserve better than this! I will come for him, and I will come for his daughter! You haven't seen the last of me!"

"Do you know what I think?" Abella moved her face closer to the shrinking hole in the wall. Leeds shifted his face around so he could see her. "I think you're about to get the one thing your mother never gave you."

Leeds's eyes went wide in fury.

"A really long hug," Abella told him, then backed away. His response was drowned out as the stone closed around him, but she could already hear his screams. The silver collar would keep him from escaping for now, but he would have plenty of time to remove it. Lack of food, air, or water would make him extremely uncomfortable but definitely wouldn't kill him.

"Let's roll." Ratu sat down on the gurney, her legs splayed to either side as she held the grimoire in her hands. Abella pulled the naga up the tunnel as Ratu performed a complex spell that generated tons of granite behind them.

The plan had been devious. Mike and Ratu had located a mountain in the tower world that the centaurs would never have a use for. The area wasn't suited for agriculture of any kind, and the cliffs were unclimbable. The terrain was treacherous enough that no path even existed within miles of the area.

For two weeks, Ratu had used the grimoire to scour the entire mountain free of its cave network and replace its composition with granite. This pocket dimension had no plate tectonics, and they had placed Leeds deep beneath the world. In the eons to come, even if the winds scoured the world free of mountains, he would remain beneath its lifeless surface, screaming for all eternity.

Or the world would collapse and destroy him. Abella didn't care which came first. But the most important thing was to make him believe he had been forgotten, that nothing he had done had even mattered to Mike.

It was slow work as Ratu filled in miles of tunnel with more granite, pausing occasionally to drink a tea she had brought to replenish her magic.

"Why do you need the book to keep using that spell?" Abella asked during one of the breaks. "I figured you would have it memorized by now."

"The spells in this book are very special," Ratu replied. "And their cost is forgetfulness. Once the book is closed, the forgetting begins. A simple mistake on my part could spell the end of us or give Leeds a way out."

Abella nodded. Even if Leeds regained his ability to move through the shadows, there was over a mile of solid stone in every direction. With no hollow spaces, he would be forced to teleport or even resurrect in his own personal hell.

It was the Mother's Embrace taken to the next level. Death would never come for Leeds, and Ratu had embedded sigils made of metal all over the mountain to ensure he could never be summoned away. It was an eternal prison of their own making, and it was the perfect place for him to be alone with all his thoughts—forever.

When they left the cave, Mike stood there with Eulalie and Bigfoot. It was clear that tears had been shed, and the Arachne held hands with her uncle as Abella and Ratu emerged into the light.

"It is done?" Bigfoot asked.

"It is." Ratu turned around and erased the cave opening from existence.

There was no sign they had ever been there, save for the structure built to establish a portal.

"With his misery, my healing shall finally begin." Bigfoot turned to Mike and put a hand on his shoulder. "And let us never speak of this place."

Mike nodded, then let Bigfoot pull him in for a hug. Eulalie said nothing as she fingered the dog tags around her neck, then hugged Mike as well. Ratu led the others through the portal, leaving just Mike and Abella behind.

"Thank you," he told her. "I couldn't have done this without you."

"Nor I you." When she hugged him, she buried her face in his shoulder and inhaled his scent. She had worried for the longest time that he would hold Velvet's death against her, but it never came up. He was too good for that, maybe even too good for her.

Still, being able to be the instrument of Leeds's burial was cathartic. Burying Leeds alive had been her idea, and the others had been all for it. "He was panicking as we left," she told him. "Freaking out that we weren't taking him seriously anymore. I could still hear him screaming through the rock for a bit after we left him there. He was more upset that you didn't come than anything else."

He nodded. "That was Jenny's idea. I'm debating therapy for her but think she would break the therapist."

"Maybe she's fine the way she is. We all have our quirks, after all." Abella ran her fingers through his hair. "I like it now that it's getting long," she told him.

"Been too busy fucking for a haircut," he told her, then turned toward the portal. "Did you still want to do the honors?"

"Absolutely."

"See you soon." He gave her a kiss on the forehead and then left through the portal.

She watched him exit the shed on the other side, then walked back out of the hut. Staring at the wall of the cliff, she thought of the wretched being entombed inside for all eternity and found herself smiling.

With that, she summoned her heart fire and burned down the hut. It didn't take very long, and she was careful to spread the ashes with her tail, grinding them into the shattered rocks beneath her feet. Satisfied the evidence was removed, she stretched her wings wide, stopping briefly to admire the glittering silver veins that ran throughout her left wing. Emery had done a phenomenal job patching her up.

With a powerful burst, she launched herself into the air, circling higher and higher until the cliffs were far below her. In the distance, she could make out the valley where the centaurs roamed and the vast ocean that surrounded the island. Up on one of the highest mountain peaks, a single tower glistened in the sun, watching over the land. She could sense him already, her Caretaker, like a shining beacon guiding her home.

Knowing Mike was waiting for her, she soared through the clouds, leaving the darkness of the Jersey Devil behind.

MIKE STOOD ON THE BLUFFS OVERLOOKING THE GREENHOUSE'S JUNGLE. DOWN below, the centaurs had finally cleared enough land to establish the beginnings of full-blown agriculture. In the distance, he could see the thunderbird as it soared toward the horizon, creating a fresh storm behind it.

Across his chest, he wore a special bag Tink had designed for him. Inside, the egg thrummed against his chest. It had been nearly a month since Leeds had been entombed, and his world had finally reached a state of calm.

Most of his time recently had been spent clearing out the Vault. After Beth had sealed it away, the entities inside had made a mess of the place in their attempts to escape. Ratu had helped them with identifying, relocating, and sometimes destroying dangerous objects that might have caused trouble in the future. Now that the naga was feeling better, she had taken custody of both the grimoire and Osiris's magic cock for further study.

"There you are." Quetzalli came through the greenhouse door, her skirt catching briefly on the latch. Grumbling, she fixed her outfit and closed the door. "Naia said you would be here."

"I sensed him." He waved his hand at the thunderbird. "I was out in the garden with Amymone when I felt the thunderbird's presence."

"Your senses are getting stronger." Without warning, she flicked a stone at him, boosting it with a powerful shock from her fingertips.

His precognition activated, and Mike willed the stone away from him. His magic reacted, swatting the stone back with a burst of static when it was inches away.

With so many powerful magic users, it had been a difficult choice picking someone to train him. His magic relied heavily on instinct, which made early lessons with Ratu and Yuki difficult to follow. Naia and Amymone had been able to show him some basics, but it was nowhere near the level of control Beth already showed. It didn't surprise him how quickly she took to her new abilities.

In fact, during her tutelage, she had discovered the cabin was actually a better place for her to learn elemental magic. The hot springs in particular gave her insight into earth, fire, and water, but that was above Mike's head.

Oregon was still a difficult place for him to visit, so when Beth asked if he would mind if she stayed there for a while to develop her magic, he agreed on the condition that she try to help Bigfoot organize the forest children. While the forest children respected him, the Sasquatch lacked leadership skills and planning that Beth could provide.

That, and if the gossip he heard from the fairies was true, Beth was indeed discovering just how good of a kisser Bigfoot really was. It made him smile to know she was living her own dreams, though he did miss having her in the room next door. The two of them had been bonding over their newfound magical abilities, but Beth had soon eclipsed him.

After weeks of frustration, a chance encounter with the fairy queen had given him the solution to his magic problem. Titania had explained that his magic was simply too wild. Whereas Beth was learning how to manipulate the elements using spoken words and gestures, his magic acted on will alone, both conscious and subconscious. He was a force of nature and needed someone with experience handling vast amounts of destructive power.

Quetzalli the storm dragon had been an unexpected, perfect fit. Mike's magic was very much like a storm cloud, building in power before releasing all at once.

"Reactions are getting better." She walked up by his side and leaned her head onto his arm. "I checked in with Bigfoot this morning. He's been teaching English to the Nirumbi. It's mostly the children for now; they're the easiest. He's been reading them books the girls grew up with."

"That's wonderful." He debated asking if Bigfoot would save those books for him but decided not to. Eulalie had warned him that his daughter might be a danger to him in the first couple of years. Eulalie had bitten her father a couple of times by accident, and Velvet had broken Darren's wrist. It wouldn't be simple being a father to a child with eight legs and fangs, and things would never remotely resemble normal ever again. By the time it was safe to cuddle up with his daughter and read her tales about the Poky Little Puppy, she would probably be past those storybooks.

Besides, Ratu was already working on an artifact that would allow his daughter to age naturally in the Library. He would have every book at his disposal if he wanted to try reading to her. If he broke a few limbs along the way, it wouldn't be the end of the world…right?

He put his hand on the egg and let out a sigh. While he couldn't wait to meet her, he knew things were going to change. He was a target, and there would be times when the best thing to do would be to keep his child at arm's length. While the others understood, how would he tell his daughter that he was too busy not being murdered to play with her?

He held out his hand and concentrated his magic. Lights danced along his fingertips as it formed into the shape of a spider. It was a great spell to work on when he needed to take his mind off his worries.

"That's neat." Quetzalli contemplated his design. "What are you planning to do with that?"

"It helps me talk to them." He had the little lightning spider wave. Despite Velvet's death, he had discovered he could still communicate with spiders. Many of them feared humans, but the illusory spider seemed to break the ice. It was another thing Velvet had left behind, something that was just for him. He dismissed the magic, then sighed. "Some days are easier than others."

"Agreed." She rubbed his back through the fabric of his shirt. "Speaking of easy...what would you say to finding somewhere private for a bit? Dana has been having more issues with her emotions, and time for us has been...sparse."

Quetzalli was likely understating it. Ever since the fight in Oregon, Dana's emotions had been all over the place. It was like the emotional side of her brain had been restored but never properly synced to the rest of her body. She would laugh at inappropriate times or sob uncontrollably while she went about her business. Ratu's theory was that it had to do with all the magic Mike had poured into her, along with the Nirumbi flesh she had devoured. The naga was working hard on figuring out a possible fix for the issue. Despite the potential meaning of Dana's new behavior, her soul was still very much locked to her body.

"We could make some time," he told her with a smile. "I know of a pretty waterfall nearby if you want to go for a swim."

"Can that wait for a little while?" Zel walked up on the path from the valley below with a small retinue behind her. "I saw you up here and have some important things to discuss."

"Sounds serious." He saw a weird look on Zel's face. "Everything okay?"

"To start with, we have some news." She reached into a pouch around her waist and pulled something out. "What does this look like?"

She tossed it over, and Mike snatched it out of the air, then nearly dropped it in surprise. It was a thick vine with wilted leaves, but he recognized them immediately. They were the same vines that had once dragged him through the jungle to what was almost a very messy end.

"I thought the Mandragora left," he said.

"So did I." She made a face. "Some of our livestock went missing, and we think this is the culprit. Maybe it came back or was just dormant for a while. We found this stuck under a fence that collapsed."

"Well, we know who we can ask." He stuck the vine in his pocket, planning a conversation with Amymone once he returned. "Just make sure it doesn't snatch anyone up."

"Nobody has disappeared yet." She looked over her shoulder at the centaurs with her. At some unseen signal, they turned around and went back down into the valley. "I wanted to have a word with you in private."

"Say no more," said Quetzalli as she sat on a nearby rock. When Zel stared at her, the dragon laughed. "I'm just fucking with you. I'll be in Oregon when you need me. I prefer the skies there." She stood and went through the door of the greenhouse. The path to Oregon was through a small cabin, somewhat like a playhouse, that Tink had built by the wrought-iron gate. The portal inside went to a room in the new barn that had been built in Oregon.

"What's up?" he asked once Quetzalli was gone.

"I have a confession to make." Zel made a face as she paced by the side of the cliff. "You see, I had a choice a while back, and I don't know that I made the right one."

"Life is full of choices, and hindsight is twenty-twenty." He walked up behind her and put his hand on the small of her human back. "I'm willing to bet you thought long and hard before making it."

"I did. But a conversation with a friend has been playing itself over and over in my head." She looked at the egg pouch and smiled. "How long until it hatches?"

"No idea. I take her for walks, talk to her, that kind of thing. As for keeping track of time…" He shrugged. "I'm trying to enjoy the moment is all."

"You and I once enjoyed a moment here. Do you remember?"

He smiled. "How could I forget? It was quite the moment."

Zel looked at the ground while pawing at the dirt with a hoof. "About that. I need you to know that what occurred that night was probably one of the most important things that has ever happened to me. It validated me as a person. You made me feel special, accepted in a way I never thought I could be."

He pulled Zel toward him, then wrapped his arms around her waist. "Believe it or not, it's one of my favorite memories. I've been thinking a lot lately about not just how my magic works but my heart. I have so many cherished memories with all of you it's hard to pick a favorite. But that one? No argument." He could still hear the music from that night, see Zel smiling in the moonlight as they made love beneath an alien sky. It was a nice change of pace to lose himself in a happy memory.

"Uh, Mike?" Zel stiffened in his arms.

"Shit, sorry." He let go of her and stepped back. "I got nostalgic is all. I wasn't trying to put moves on you, I promise. I definitely don't need to start a fight with the centaur in your life, and we certainly don't need a repeat of the Orion incident."

Zel made a sound like a balloon deflating as her shoulders drooped. "It's not that. I enjoy your touch, but I don't deserve it, not when you hear what I have to say." Her face scrunched up as she took a calming breath. "Mike. There is no centaur in my life. I made him up. There's only ever been you."

"But I don't get it. What about…" He gestured toward her equine belly, his lips suddenly numb.

The look on her face spoke volumes. She turned away from him, and her arms crossed her stomach. "I lied. That was the choice I made, and I regret it."

So many questions raced through his head he couldn't figure out which to ask first. "How?" was the best he could manage.

"Humans and centaurs can't interbreed. But I was using a potion to make myself human, remember?" She shook her head, the feathers in her hair fluttering wildly in the breeze. "My best guess is that we crossed whatever line that separated us biologically. The child won't be human or centaur but something in between."

"But why keep it from me?"

She shrugged. "Fear. Not for you but for our child. I had become a leader to my people, which comes with responsibilities. You are the Caretaker. How many times have you almost died? How many times has the house been attacked?"

"You spoke with Eulalie about this, didn't you?" He thought back to what the arachne had told him. Zel was saying a lot of the same.

"She figured it out on her own. Snuck into my home in the middle of the night and confronted me where nobody else could hear us. Scared the crap out of me when she dropped out of the shadows." Zel shivered. "It was a heated conversation at first because I tried to deny it. She had plenty of evidence, then told me about the egg, so I finally caved and admitted it. All my thoughts and fears came spilling out that night. It was the first time I had told anyone the whole truth of the matter."

"So why wait until now? Why not tell me sooner?"

She sighed. "I wanted to see how you reacted to the news about Velvet's egg first."

"Why, to see if I would be a good parent?" He felt his anger rising as he cradled the egg protectively. "I mean, yeah, I'm essentially doing the egg-baby project from middle school, but I think it's real shitty that you were trying to vet me before informing me we're having a child together."

"That's where you're wrong." She moved toward him and put her hand on his chest. "I wanted to see if you would force traditional human customs on Eulalie. Make her give the egg to you, demand that your daughter live in the house full-time instead of taking her advice. I can't blame you for holding to human norms for child-rearing, but our foal will require their connection to the herd. The herd raises all offspring together; it's the centaur way. Yes, we have parents, but this child will have hundreds of parents watching out for them, all day long. If you made them live with you in your house, they wouldn't have that direct connection to their own tribe and would never be more than a visitor." She paused for a second and smiled wistfully. "It would also be hell on your wooden floors."

Mike contemplated her logic, his anger at her deception fading. The real-ization that Zel's choice had been more about the child than him tempered his feelings. His own damaged childhood had been the result of destructive self-ishness, and he had vowed long ago to be different.

"I still don't like that you lied to me," he muttered. "You make good points, but I really wish you had more faith in me as a person. I don't know the first thing about being a parent, especially one of a child that isn't fully human. I would have deferred."

"And for that, I'm truly sorry." She moved her hand to his cheek. "And I want you to be there for our foal, but we both know you can't be around full-time. You're the Caretaker; your role is so much bigger than either of us real-ize. After what happened with the horsemen, I can't help but feel you have a bigger destiny waiting for you."

"I certainly hope not." He patted the egg. "I've got enough excitement in the near future as it is."

"In just a few more months, actually." Her lips were now next to his. "That is, if you can forgive me."

When Zel moved close, he felt the egg vibrate against his chest. Waves of heat traveled through his chest to his hands.

"Oh!" Zel's flanks rippled, and her eyes widened in surprise. "It just kicked! Want to feel?"

He paused, taking in the excitement in her eyes. Nothing about his life was ordinary, and it never would be again. As waves of heat pressed into his finger-tips, he shifted to the side so that he could place his hand on Zel's horse stom-ach. A sharp poke hit the palm of his hand, like a high five.

A feeling of recognition radiated from the egg in response.

"We're going to be parents." He took Zel's hand in his and squeezed. "I'll try not to fuck it up."

"So you forgive me?" Her eyes were full of shimmering hope.

"We're both going to make a lot of mistakes." He placed his hand on the egg and smiled. "Maybe forgiveness is a great thing to have in common."

"Thank you." She kissed him lightly on the cheek.

"Do you want to hear something funny?" A small grin broke through his lips.

"I would love to." She hugged his arm and laid her head on his shoulder.

"I'm going to have two kids with a total of twelve legs yet will never have to spend money on socks, shoes, or pants." He waved his hand dramatically at the sky. "Just think of the savings."

She rolled her eyes. "I thought dads were supposed to be funny," she said.

"I've still got a lot to learn about being a dad," he replied with a grin. "But I'm looking forward to the challenge." It was going to be hard but worth it. He stood there with Zel, their gazes on the horizon as the egg pulsed in its carrier, filling him with love and light.

THE STEADY THUMP OF RAIN ON THE ROOF WAS PUNCTUATED BY DISTANT thunder that made the old plantation house's bones creak. Moonlight reflected in the dozens of puddles that had formed in the front yard, making it look as if hidden creatures watched the home in anticipation.

A cry of agony fluttered down the hall, making Elizabeth shiver. She ran her hands down the long braid of her hair and turned her attention away from the window toward the small figure who sat across from her, reading a book. It was a young man with bleach-blond hair and a tattoo on his wrist. The skin around his hairline was peeling away to reveal gray patches underneath.

"You're going to need a new body soon," Elizabeth said. "That one doesn't have much time left."

"Tell me something I don't know." Sarah's voice was husky, a result of male vocal cords. She adjusted the glittering stone that hung around her neck. "With this weather being so shitty, my options have been limited, Mother."

There was another cry of pain, but Elizabeth put it out of her mind. There was nothing that could be done for Amir in his current state, but now that he had a mouth, his regeneration was quite unnerving. It was why they were using a property that had been abandoned long ago. While they could afford to stay somewhere nicer, the screams would be hard to explain.

Amir shrieked, causing the lights above them to turn on spontaneously and then flicker.

"Shit." Elizabeth walked over to the nearest lamp to unscrew the bulb, but it continued to glow in her hand.

"At least we know he's still as powerful as ever," muttered Sarah. "Would hate to go through all this and—"

Elizabeth summoned a spectral hand and slapped her daughter with it.

"He may not have ears yet, but he has ways of hearing us," she warned. "Unless you want him to make a pig wear that necklace, I suggest you shut the fuck up."

Sarah rolled her eyes. "Fine," she muttered, setting down her book. "I just hate what we've been reduced to. We were once the most powerful men and women in the world, and now we're...this." She gestured at herself in disgust. "And let me tell you something else. I've been—"

Someone knocked on the door, cutting Sarah off midsentence.

Elizabeth scowled, then walked toward the front door. There was absolutely no good reason for anyone to be on the property in the middle of a rainy night, so she summoned shadowy tendrils around her body as she walked. Once at the door, she started weaving a spell that would allow her to see through it when the knock came again.

"You can forget about using your magic," a voice warned her through the thick wood. "At best, you will need a new door. It has been a long journey, and I am tired."

Cautious, Elizabeth opened the door, wondering if someone else from the society had survived. As far as she knew, it was just her, Amir, and Sarah, but stranger things had happened.

The dark figure on the porch was pale with a cruel, bloodless smile on his lips. He took off the hat he wore and placed it over his stomach as if getting ready to enter church.

"The hour is late," he informed her. "I have words I would discuss with your master."

Elizabeth frowned, then opened her mouth to ask who he was, but no sound emerged. She clawed at her throat, gasping for air.

"I don't speak with underlings," he declared. "Unless you were going to invite me in?"

She gasped and nodded, beckoning the man inside.

"Thank you." He stepped across the boundary and handed Elizabeth his hat. "Show me where he is."

Stunned, she obeyed without a second thought. The stranger followed her through the house, pausing long enough to hold his hand out at Sarah.

"You can sit there and be quiet," he commanded.

Sarah obeyed, panic filling her eyes.

Elizabeth led him farther into the home, then down into the basement. In a dimly lit room, what was left of Amir had been strapped to an old wooden chair. Large parts of his body were simply missing, though his hands and feet were connected to his torso by thick tendrils of darkness. His head had only formed up to his upper lip, and Elizabeth winced as he cried out in pain.

A patch of darkness stained the air over Amir, and bits of ash drifted down across his body. If she stayed and watched, she might see one or two of them ignite and stick to his body.

It had been months since Amir had been pulled into the mirror world and destroyed. As he was immune to harm, his magic had been forcing his body through gaps in time and space to return here to Earth. Not only was the process long, but it was apparently very painful as he was reassembled on a molecular level. From where she stood, she could see veins and arteries, as well as some of his internal organs. She imagined the pain came from having severed nerves exposed to the air, but it was a guess at best.

"Now, now, this simply won't do." The stranger pulled a small black doctor's bag from nowhere and opened it. "By my estimates, it will be a better part of a decade before he comes all the way back."

"A decade?" Elizabeth looked at Amir. "By the looks of it, maybe a couple of years?"

"The process starts fast, ends very slow." He pulled a pair of syringes from his bag and jammed one into Amir's neck. A blue fluid disappeared, and Amir relaxed.

"You stopped the pain?" Elizabeth moved closer to see what the man was doing.

"No. I paralyzed his vocal cords. He still suffers, but now I don't." He grinned and used the other syringe to draw blood. "I believe I can speed up the process, maybe have him back together in a few years. But it will take time and resources."

"Who are you?" she asked. When the man looked at her, she felt her whole body tense up as he appraised her.

"You can think of me as a collector of sorts." He reached into his bag and pulled something out. "I'm here regarding this."

He tossed something to her, and she caught it. It was a figurine holding a staff, but its features had been charred away.

"I don't understand." She looked at the man as he rose from a crouch.

"And I don't expect you to." He held out his hand, and the figurine shot toward his outstretched palm. "You see, this piece in particular was very precious to me. It took me a lot of years to get it exactly where I wanted it, and now?" He squeezed the figurine into ash. "Now it's useless."

"What do you want from us?" Elizabeth didn't know why, but she was suddenly afraid.

The man grinned, then took the syringe and squirted Amir's blood on his tongue. He licked his lips and made a sour face.

"I want your master back in one piece. We have much to discuss, after all. Until then, I suppose we shall have to find other things to talk about." He walked closer to Elizabeth, his eyes shining with malice.

"Tell me everything you know about Mike Radley," he whispered, his voice like broken glass. He placed his long fingers around her neck and squeezed hard enough that she knew it would bruise. "And leave nothing out. After all, we've got plenty of time."

END

AFTERWORD

This story started out as a dare. A silly tale about a nymph in a bathtub has become its own literary universe!

First, I need to thank my Patrons. Their support was mandatory for this endeavor, and they really are an amazing group of people. You can find some of my donors at https://annabellehawthorne.com/hall-of-caretakers/

Second, I firmly believe in the idea that an author is only as good as their readers. There's a Velvet support group for those who need it, come meet the monster family over on my Discord channel at https://discord.gg/gWjTY8D

A special thanks to my beta team who give up their free time to spend hours finding my goofs and point them out to me. Special thanks to Tj Skywind, all the Mikes, Edward, Pastor of Muppets, Artvr and Zing. They're the ones who call me out on my bullshit.

A huge special thanks to my editor, Lyss Em. She is absolutely amazing and I couldn't do this without her!

And now I thank you, the reader. I hope you've enjoyed this tale and that you are eager to tell all your friends and family about it! (Or, at the least, leave it a review here!

"No one is actually dead until the ripples they cause in the world die away." - *Terry Pratchett*

"Hello?" Holly stepped away from the giant fireplace, the magical flames crackling behind her in passing. It was Christmas Eve, and the Workshop should have been bustling with frantic activity. Every year, the lobby would be packed with hundreds of elves trying to complete last minute tasks in order for Santa to leave on time.

Now, though? There wasn't a single soul in sight. She turned around, triple checking that she had actually come home to the North Pole and not some poorly made facsimile. While such a thing shouldn't have been possible, magic had a way of doing the impossible sometimes.

The stockings on the massive hearth were all names she recognized. She spotted her own stocking in its usual spot. Someone had even put a candy cane in it.

Walking quietly into the building, her heart thudded loudly in her chest. Even the music in the Hot Cocoa lounge had been turned off. The North Pole felt abandoned.

She had been out on a special assignment and had no idea what sort of event could have shut everything down. Snow swirled outside the large windows of the Workshop, and so she pressed her face to the glass to see if she spotted anyone. Even the large cobblestone streets were empty.

A heavy feeling settled over her, like someone was watching. Scowling, she turned her attention to the room and tried to ponder the strange silence that called to her. It took her almost a minute to realize why the silence was so striking: the furnace was off.

With a gasp, Holly ran to the nearest heat vent and crouched down to look inside. Despite the constant chill of the north, the only thing keeping Santa's Workshop from freezing had indeed been turned off.

Stunned, Holly wandered in silence, hoping to find someone who could explain what had happened. Lost in her thoughts, she meandered through the different rooms of the Workshop until she remembered that there was a place she might find some answers.

Down in the loading docks, she found Santa's sleigh. The exterior doors were still locked tight, but the massive bags of gifts had been loaded up. That meant that Santa himself had been here not too long ago, for he was the only one who could lift the bag.

"Santa?" Her voice came out as a squeak. Holly climbed into the sleigh and sat for a bit, waiting to see if Santa would come back. If there was one thing Santa wouldn't do, it was disappoint the children of the world.

Holly was nodding off by the time the alarm sounded at the North Pole. With a start, she looked up and saw the red light over the exterior doors flashing. It was a warning for the time lock, a powerful magic that would halt the flow of time and enable Santa to deliver all of his presents in a single night.

Now panicking, Holly realized that there were only twenty minutes left before Christmas started. Santa hadn't come. Nobody had.

That could only mean one thing: something had happened to the big man himself. Holly jumped off the sleigh and contemplated it.

"What do I do?" No, that was the wrong question to ask. She was only one person. Even if she could pilot the sleigh and somehow deliver the presents herself, that still wouldn't solve what had happened to Santa and the other elves. She needed help from someone else, but who?

A chill had already settled into the loading bay, giving her an idea. Holly pressed her hands against the back of the sleigh and pushed, moving it back into the lobby. The recently polished runners slid across the smooth, wooden floor. It was hard work, but Holly managed to get the sleigh back into the Lobby. Another alarm chimed, there was only ten minutes left before the lock engaged.

Nervously humming *Jingle Bells*, Holly pushed the sleigh ever closer to the massive fireplace. She was already exhausted, but that didn't matter. If the toys were never delivered, children would stop believing. To solve this mysterious, she needed to turn to someone clever, someone with the brains to figure it all out.

The final warning chimed. She only had sixty seconds and the runners had caught on the rough stones of the massive fireplace. With a yell, she got a running start and slammed her entire body into the sleigh. It popped forward, the magical flames curling around it. With moments to spare, Holly jumped into the sleigh and closed her eyes, demanding the flames take her to the smartest person she knew. An alarm sounded as the time lock activated.

"Take me to the home of Tinker the goblin."

ABOUT THE AUTHOR

Annabelle Hawthorne lives in a top secret location somewhere in the Rocky Mountains with a loving family and potentially a dog or two. The mysterious Hawthorne can usually be found with coffee and a good horror novel.

Find Annabelle on Twitter @authorannabelle

Support Annabelle's Patreon to get exclusive access to art and more! www.Patreon.com/sexyannabelle

Official website at https://www.annabellehawthorne.com

Chat with other readers at https://discord.gg/gWjTY8D

Thanks for reading!

ABOUT THE PUBLISHER

Wet Leaf Press is a small press dedicated to providing high-quality erotica to discerning readers.

You deserve smart.
You deserve sexy.
You deserve quality erotica.

ALSO BY ANNABELLE HAWTHORNE

Stories in the Horny Monsters Series (Chronological)

The Last of Her Kind

Radley's Home for Horny Monsters

Radley's Labyrinth for Horny Monsters

Radley's Wardrobe for Horny Monsters

Dead and Horny

Other Series

Master Class: A Slice of Life LitRPG Harem (w/ Virgil Knightley)

Succubus Summoner (w/ Virgil Knightley)